# WHAT WOULD SCOTLAND YARD DO WITHOUT DEAR MRS. JEFFRIES?

*Even Inspector Witherspoon himself doesn't know—because his secret weapon is as ladylike as she is clever. She's Mrs. Jeffries—the charming detective who stars in this unique Victorian mystery series. Enjoy them all . . .*

### The Inspector and Mrs. Jeffries
A doctor is found dead in his own office—and Mrs. Jeffries must scour the premises to find the prescription for murder.

### Mrs. Jeffries Dusts for Clues
One case is solved and another is opened when the Inspector finds a missing brooch—pinned to a dead woman's gown. But Mrs. Jeffries never cleans a room without dusting under the bed—and never gives up on a case before every loose end is tightly tied . . .

### The Ghost and Mrs. Jeffries
Death is unpredictable . . . but the murder of Mrs. Hodges was foreseen at a spooky séance. The practical-minded housekeeper may not be able to see the future—but she can look into the past and put things in order to solve this haunting crime.

### Mrs. Jeffries Takes Stock
A businessman has been murdered—and it could be because he cheated his stockholders. The housekeeper's interest is piqued . . . and when it comes to catching killers, the smart money's on Mrs. Jeffries.

*continued . . .*

### Mrs. Jeffries Takes the Cake

The evidence was all there: a dead body, two dessert plates, and a gun. As if Mr. Ashbury had been sharing cake with his own killer. Now Mrs. Jeffries will have to do some snooping around to dish up clues . . .

### Mrs. Jeffries Rocks the Boat

Mirabelle had traveled by boat all the way from Australia to visit her sister—only to wind up murdered. Now Mrs. Jeffries must solve the case—and it's sink or swim . . .

### Mrs. Jeffries Weeds the Plot

Three attempts have been made on Annabeth Gentry's life. Is it due to her recent inheritance, or was it because her bloodhound dug up the body of a murdered thief? Mrs. Jeffries will have to sniff out some clues before the plot thickens . . .

### Mrs. Jeffries Pinches the Post

Harrison Nye may have had some dubious business dealings, but no one expected him to be murdered. Now Mrs. Jeffries and her staff must root through the sins of his past to discover which one caught up with him . . .

### Mrs. Jeffries Pleads Her Case

Harlan Westover's death was deemed a suicide by the magistrate. But Inspector Witherspoon is willing to risk his career to prove otherwise. Mrs. Jeffries must ensure the good inspector remains afloat . . .

### Mrs. Jeffries Sweeps the Chimney

A dead vicar has been found, propped against a church wall. And Inspector Witherspoon's only prayer is to seek the divinations of Mrs. Jeffries . . .

### Mrs. Jeffries Stalks the Hunter

Puppy love turns to obsession which leads to murder. Who better to get to the heart of the matter than Inspector Witherspoon's indomitable companion, Mrs. Jeffries . . .

*continued . . .*

### Mrs. Jeffries and the Silent Knight
The yuletide murder of an elderly man is complicated by several suspects—
none of whom were in the Christmas spirit . . .

### Mrs. Jeffries Appeals the Verdict
Mrs. Jeffries and her belowstairs cohorts have their work cut out for them
if they want to save an innocent man from the gallows . . .

### Mrs. Jeffries and the Best Laid Plans
Banker Lawrence Boyd didn't waste his time making friends, which is why
hardly anyone mourns his death. With a list of enemies including just about
everyone the miser's ever met, it will take Mrs. Jeffries' shrewd eye to find
the killer . . .

### Mrs. Jeffries and the Feast of St. Stephen
'Tis the season for sleuthing when wealthy Stephen Whitfield is murdered
during his holiday dinner party. It's up to Mrs. Jeffries to solve the case in
time for Christmas . . .

### Mrs. Jeffries Holds the Trump
A very well-liked but very dead magnate is found floating down the river.
Now Mrs. Jeffries and company will have to dive into a mystery that only
grows more complex . . .

### Mrs. Jeffries in the Nick of Time
Mrs. Jeffries lends her downstairs common sense to this upstairs murder
mystery—and hopes that she and the Inspector don't get derailed in the
case of a rich uncle-cum-model-train-enthusiast . . .

### Mrs. Jeffries and the Yuletide Weddings
Wedding bells will make this season all the more jolly. Until one humbug
sings a carol of murder . . .

### Mrs. Jeffries Speaks Her Mind

Someone is trying to kill the eccentric Olive Kettering, but no one believes her—until she's proven right. Without witnesses and plenty of suspects, Mrs. Jeffries will see justice served . . .

### Mrs. Jeffries Forges Ahead

The marriageable daughters of the upper crust are outraged when the rich and handsome Lewis Banfield marries an artist's model. But when someone poisons the new bride's champagne, Mrs. Jeffries must discover if envy led to murder . . .

### Mrs. Jeffries and the Mistletoe Mix-Up

When art collector Daniel McCourt is found murdered under the mistletoe, it's up to Mrs. Jeffries to find out who gave him the kiss of death . . .

### Mrs. Jeffries Defends Her Own

When the general office manager of Sutcliffe Manufacturing is murdered, Mrs. Jeffries must figure out who hated him enough to put a bullet between his eyes . . .

Visit Emily Brightwell's website at
www.emilybrightwell.com

**Also available from Berkley Prime Crime:**
**The first six Mrs. Jeffries Mysteries in two volumes**
*Mrs. Jeffries Learns the Trade* and *Mrs. Jeffries Takes a Second Look*

# MRS. JEFFRIES
# TAKES TEA AT THREE

## EMILY BRIGHTWELL

BERKLEY PRIME CRIME, NEW YORK

**THE BERKLEY PUBLISHING GROUP**
Published by the Penguin Group
Penguin Group (USA) Inc.
375 Hudson Street, New York, New York 10014, USA

USA / Canada / UK / Ireland / Australia / New Zealand / India / South Africa / China

Penguin Books Ltd., Registered Offices: 80 Strand, London WC2R 0RL, England
For more information about the Penguin Group, visit penguin.com.

MRS. JEFFRIES TAKES TEA AT THREE

Berkley Prime Crime Books are published by The Berkley Publishing Group.
BERKLEY® PRIME CRIME and the PRIME CRIME logo are
trademarks of Penguin Group (USA) Inc.

Berkley Prime Crime trade paperback ISBN: 978-0-425-26359-4

An application to register this book for cataloging has been submitted to the Library of Congress.

PUBLISHING HISTORY
Berkley Prime Crime trade paperback edition / April 2013

PRINTED IN THE UNITED STATES OF AMERICA

10   9   8   7   6   5   4   3

Cover illustration by Jeff Walker.

# CONTENTS

# MRS. JEFFRIES PLAYS THE COOK

With love and gratitude to Beryl and Gladys Lanham—two very special people who truly make the world a better place

# CHAPTER 1

"Before I say another word," Lady Cannonberry said earnestly, "I do have one request. You must keep everything I tell you very, very confidential. You can't breathe a word to anyone, especially the inspector."

Everyone at the kitchen table stared at her. The household of Upper Edmonton Gardens, home of Inspector Gerald Witherspoon, was used to unusual requests. But this was startling, even by their rather relaxed standards of behaviour.

Lady Cannonberry, their neighbour on the Gardens, had popped in only a few moments ago while the household and their trusted friends, Luty Belle Crookshank and her butler Hatchet, were celebrating the successful conclusion of one of the inspector's more baffling murder cases.

Betsy, the lovely, blond-haired maid, looked inquiringly at the housekeeper, Mrs. Jeffries. The eyes of the cook, Mrs. Goodge, bulged behind her spectacles. Smythe, the coachman, raised one dark eyebrow, and Luty Belle Crookshank, an elderly American with a love of six-shooters and a mind sharp as a barber's razor, looked positively enthralled. Hatchet, as usual, was unperturbed. But the footman Wiggins's mouth gaped so wide that if it had been June and not November, he would have been in danger of catching flies.

"Lady Cannonberry," Mrs. Jeffries said hesitantly.

"Ruth, please," their guest said quickly, flashing a charming smile that took years off her middle-aged face. "I think we all know each other well enough to dispense with the formalities."

Mrs. Goodge gasped in shock. Calling the widow of a peer of the realm by her first name was as unthinkable as shopping on the high street with her petticoat showing.

But Lady Cannonberry appeared not to notice the cook's reaction. "It doesn't seem fair that because one is a servant one is forced to use these ridiculous modes of address," she continued blithely. "I always thought Lady Cannonberry was such a ridiculous way to address someone. Ruth sounds ever so much nicer. Friendlier too, and as I've come to you as a friend and not a Lady, then I do think we ought to dispense with the title."

"Er, Ruth, of course, we'll use any mode of address you prefer." Mrs. Jeffries didn't quite know what to say. Naturally, she wanted to help her. But on the other hand, she didn't want any more people than absolutely necessary knowing their secret. The fact that Ruth had come to them seemed to indicate that she knew they were more than a housekeeper and servants to a Scotland Yard police inspector. "But I've no idea what we could possibly do for you."

"You can hear me out!" she cried. "You can help someone who's in a great deal of trouble."

Mrs. Jeffries frowned slightly as her conscience did battle with their need for caution. Her conscience won. "Of course we'll hear what you've got to say. Actually, we're quite flattered you've come to us. But honestly, I've no idea why you think—"

"I promise I'll not say anything to Gerald," Ruth interrupted, shaking her head earnestly. A lock of blond hair slipped down from her topknot and dangled over her ear. "I know you've been helping him solve his cases. . . ."

Smythe, who'd just taken a swig of tea, choked.

Betsy dropped a spoon.

Wiggins gasped.

Mrs. Goodge's eyes bulged again, and Luty Belle started to snicker.

Hatchet, as always, remained perfectly calm.

"Where on earth would you get an idea like that?" Mrs. Jeffries said faintly. But the game was up and she knew it.

A half-wit could see by the guilty way they'd all reacted that Ruth was right on the mark. They did help the inspector with his cases, and of course, he didn't know it. That would never do.

"Oh, give it up, Hepzibah," Luty said, slapping her knee and cackling. "Ruth found out the same way I did, by watchin' and listenin'." She grinned at their guest. "I figured out what they was doin' back when that neighbour of mine got himself poisoned."

"Really? Which case was that?"

"Quack by the name of Slocum got poisoned a couple of years back. I spotted Hepzibah and the others snoopin' around and askin' questions. Mind ya, they was right good at what they was doin'. But I figured it out. How'd you?"

"I've suspected for quite some time now," she said with an apologetic smile. "But I didn't know for certain until I overheard Mrs. Jeffries talking to that nice young doctor at the tea shop."

Mrs. Jeffries sighed inwardly and wished she'd been a bit more discreet in her inquiries on their last case. No doubt Lady Cannonberry had got an earful when she overheard her conversation with Dr. Bosworth that day. But they'd solved the case successfully and that was what counted. Now, though, she had to think of a way to deal with this. "How very resourceful of you," she murmured.

Ruth blushed slightly. "I'm sorry, I'm not usually so bold. But I do have a friend and she's in a great deal of trouble. I didn't know where else to turn. But I promise, my lips are sealed. I'll not breathe a word to anyone about your activities."

Mrs. Jeffries hesitated before answering. She'd no idea what to do or whether or not they could trust their neighbour.

Luty apparently had no such reservations. "If'n she says she'll not say anything to the inspector," she said slowly, "I reckon we can trust her."

"Well, really, madam," Hatchet said pompously. "I hardly think it's our place to speak for everyone."

"It's quite all right, Hatchet," the housekeeper replied, smiling at Lady Cannonberry. She trusted Luty's judgement. "Luty's right. I'm sure we can trust Lady Cannonberry to keep her word."

"Indeed you can," Ruth said quickly. "I've never betrayed a confidence in my life."

Wiggins cleared his throat. "We 'elps the inspector some," he said, an earnest expression on his innocent boyish face, "but 'e does most of it 'imself. 'E's a smart man, our inspector."

"We only does a little bit of snoopin'," Betsy put in. "The inspector does all the rest."

Mrs. Jeffries was touched by their efforts to bolster their employer's status. They were all intensely loyal. Of course they had good reason to be devoted to Gerald Witherspoon, she thought.

Betsy, now a healthy young woman of twenty with rosy cheeks and clear blue eyes, had been a half-starved waif when he'd taken her in and given her employment. Smythe and Wiggins had both worked for the inspector's late Aunt Euphemia. Upon her death, he'd kept them employed even though he rarely used the carriage and he needed an untrained footman about as much as he needed a hole in his head. But jobs were hard to come by, and when the inspector had inherited a modest fortune and this big, beautiful home, he'd decided to keep the two men employed rather than toss them out onto the streets. Mrs. Goodge, having lost her last position because of her age, had also been in need of a place to call home. Gerald Witherspoon had given her one.

Naturally, Mrs. Jeffries was loyal as well. She genuinely admired her employer. Inspector Witherspoon was one of nature's real gentlemen, and of course, being in his employ meant she could use her own rather unique detective skills. All in all, it was a most satisfactory arrangement for all concerned. But she was becoming alarmed by the number of people who'd figured out what she and the staff were up to. They really must be more careful in the future. Perhaps after Lady Cannonberry told them her troubles, she'd call a meeting and they could discuss the problem.

"Betsy is absolutely correct," she said with a calm smile. "Inspector Witherspoon is a wonderful detective. Positively brilliant."

"But of course he is," Ruth agreed.

Mrs. Jeffries thought it best to determine exactly how Lady Cannonberry had caught on to what they were doing. One overheard conversation at a tea shop wasn't quite enough evidence. "I know you overheard me talking with Dr. Bosworth that day," she began. "But is that all? I mean, was there anything else you saw or heard us do that gave us away?"

"Oh, it's been obvious ever since that nasty murder of that woman in my literary circle," Ruth replied honestly. "If you'll remember I was somewhat involved in that myself, only as a witness of course. But I couldn't help but notice that you in particular, Mrs. Jeffries, were always asking questions. Why, every time I took Bodaceia for a walk, there you were."

Mrs. Jeffries wished a hole would open up in the floor. *She* was the one who gave them away. Gracious, how could she have been so careless!

"I've so admired all of you," Ruth continued. "I think what you're doing is ever so interesting. Far more exciting than boring old tea parties and shopping on Regent Street. I've so longed to participate."

"Was that all that gave us away?" Wiggins asked.

"Well," Ruth said thoughtfully. "I did notice that all of you were out and about so much. You never were here doing the normal things that servants do. Frankly, you all do far more dashing about than any household I've ever seen. But only when the inspector is on a case. The rest of the time, you behave just as every other household. But once I realized that you help him, I thought perhaps you could help me with my friend's problem."

"A problem you don't want us sharin' with the police?" Smythe reminded her softly. He was a big, muscular man with harsh features, black hair, heavy eyebrows and the kindest brown eyes on the face of the earth.

"That's right." Ruth nodded. "I really must have your promise you won't say a word to anyone outside this room."

Everyone at the table looked at the housekeeper. Mrs. Jeffries was in a quandary. She didn't wish to turn Lady Cannonberry away, but on the other hand, if the woman confessed to a heinous crime, they could hardly keep silent. "You've placed us in a rather awkward position."

"Don't worry, I haven't done anything criminal," Ruth said earnestly. "As I said, it's my friend who's in trouble. And, well, what she's done is wrong, but it's not criminal. . . . Well, not *too* criminal, that is. You see, poor Minerva can't help herself. Besides, she always puts everything back, so it isn't really stealing. But you really mustn't say anything to the inspector. He is, after all, a policeman. I don't think he'd view Minerva's problem quite the way I do."

"All right," Mrs. Jeffries said cautiously, "we'll not say anything to Inspector Witherspoon." However, if what she heard was too dastardly, she wouldn't hesitate to say something to Constable Barnes, the inspector's right-hand man. "Please, do tell us what's on your mind. If we can help, we certainly will."

Ruth took a deep breath. "I have a very dear friend, Minerva Kenny. She's a very nice woman, a spinster about my age. She lives over on Markham Place. Minerva's a very gentle person, really, rather unworldy, if you know what I mean."

"Keeps herself to herself, does she?" Mrs. Goodge asked.

"Not at all. Minerva's a very social person. She delights in the company of her friends," she explained. "By unworldly I meant that she's not really aware of how cruel and hard the world can be sometimes."

"Bit of an innocent, then?" Smythe commented.

Ruth nodded. "That's it exactly. She's very innocent."

"If she's so innocent," he continued, "then why is she in trouble?"

"Unfortunately"—Ruth paused and cleared her throat—"Minerva has a rather strange affliction. It's not really her fault, though. She can't help herself."

"Can't help what?" Mrs. Goodge prompted. The cook wasn't the most patient of women.

"Stealing," Ruth replied. "But it's not *really* stealing, because she always puts them back."

"She's got sticky fingers, then?" Wiggins said.

"No, she just sees things, usually just pretty knickknacks and shiny objects in other peoples homes," Ruth explained hurriedly, "and she can't help herself. She puts them in her pocket, takes them home for a day or two to, well . . . play with them, and then manages to put them back. Most of the time people aren't even aware the object is gone. Certainly the Astleys' have no idea their little painted bluebird is gone. Goodness, their drawing room is so full of things, I don't think they'd notice if half of it disappeared."

"So what's the problem this time?" Smythe asked, leaning forward. "Someone catch her filchin' the bird?"

"Oh, no, that dreadful man didn't catch her taking it; he caught her when she tried to put it back."

"Matilda," Adrian Spears said to the parlour maid, "have you seen King?" The middle-aged man frowned slightly as he bent down and peered behind the settee. Sometimes King wedged himself behind the settee when he wanted a good, solid sleep. But there was no bundle of black-and-white fur curled up there. "I've not seen him since lunch."

"I've not seen him, sir," the parlour maid answered. She glanced at the rug by the big walnut desk. Usually the dog lay next to Mr. Spears as he worked in his study. His fat body would be rolled tight in front of the fire and he'd be snoring. But the rug was bare.

Matilda sat the silver tea tray down on a rosewood table next to the settee. On the tray was a pot of tea, milk, sugar, a cup and spoon and a plate with four biscuits. Two for Mr. Spears and two for King. The King

Charles spaniel loved his afternoon treat. "That's odd, sir, I've not seen him all afternoon."

"Perhaps Cook let him out in the gardens for some fresh air," Spears suggested. "I'd best go see. I don't want that awful man harassing my poor dog."

"Cook wouldn't do that, sir," Matilda said quickly. "Not after what happened yesterday. Pembroke said we're only to let King out with one of us. One of the footmen took him out at lunchtime, but I saw him bring the dog back inside."

"Has anyone gone in or out?" Spears asked. "Could King have gotten out on his own?"

Matilda swallowed. She didn't want to tell her employer that Janie, the tweeny, had left the back door open. Janie was her friend, and if something had happened to King, Janie'd be out on her ear.

"No, sir," she lied. Someone else might tell, but Mr. Spears wasn't going to hear nothing from her. He was a good employer, God knows she'd worked in worse houses, but he was daft about that dog. "I don't think so. We've all been careful after what happened yesterday. We make sure the doors are closed."

Spears's lips pursed in disgust. "I should hope so. With neighbors like Barrett, we ought to make sure the doors are locked as well. Odious creature. Imagine, throwing stones at an innocent animal."

"He's not a nice man, sir," Matilda said. She began edging toward the door of the study. She wanted to warn Janie that she'd best get out in the gardens and look for that ruddy dog.

"He's a callous brute," Spears said harshly. He was frightened for his pet but loathe to let it show. "But brute or not, I'll not have him bullying my dog." He walked briskly toward the hall. "I won't have him harassing anyone from my household, including King. We've as much right to use these gardens as Barrett, and if he's thrown any more stones at King, he'll answer to me."

But King didn't come when Adrian Spears called for him.

Alarmed, he called the servants, and together, they searched the huge communal gardens.

Spears peered down the side of Barrett's house, straining his eyes to see in the failing light. He thought he'd heard sounds coming from the passageway. "King," he called. "King, where are you, boy?"

Suddenly a footman shouted, "Over here, sir!"

Spears swiveled on his heel and saw the footman standing in the heavy foliage in the small plot behind Barrett's terrace.

"What is it?" he cried. "Is it King? Is he hurt?" He ran toward the footman, ducking branches and charging through the high bushes. He skidded to a stop at the footman's pale face and then looked down. At the sight of the twisted black-and-white body, his heart broke. King was curled in a semicircle, one paw resting on his snout. There was blood everywhere.

"Oh, my God," Spears moaned. Dropping to his knees, he tenderly lifted King's head. But the dog's big brown eyes were closed forever. Tears of grief—and rage—swam in Spears's eyes. King was dead. His head had been smashed in.

"Look at this." The footman pointed to a spot a few feet away. A bloodstained hammer lay atop a mound of leaves.

The other servants had gathered around. Matilda shot a warning glance at Janie, who was biting her lip and twisting her hands together. God, if Spears found out Janie had left that door open and that she, Matilda had covered for her, they'd both be sacked.

Spears climbed to his feet, turned toward the Barrett house, and bellowed his rage at the open back door. "Barrett, you bastard, come out and face me like a man."

"Sir," Pembroke, Spears's butler, said hesitantly. But Adrian Spears paid him no mind.

"You brute!" he bellowed again. "I demand that you come out here and face me."

By this time servants were coming to the window and the open back door. Spears continued to shout at the top of his lungs. More and more people came out of the house. Even the painters and carpenters who'd been working on the third floor were now out and standing on the small terrace facing the garden.

"What's going on here?" William Barrett demanded. He pushed past a maid. "What are you people doing? That plot you're standing on is private. Get off—get off at once! You'll ruin those plants."

Spears, his voice shaking with rage, pointed to the brush where his pet lay dead. "To hell with your plants, you disgusting brute. You've killed my dog!"

"I'll thank you not to talk to me like that," Barrett replied. He started toward Spears. "And I've no idea what you're talking about. Get all these people out of here."

"I'm not letting you get away with murdering my dog."

"I've nothing to do with your wretched dog," Barrett sneered. "But whatever's happened, make sure you keep the stupid animal out of my plot."

With a scream of rage, Spears leapt for the man's throat.

Across the gardens from the distraught Mr. Spears, Mr. Thornton Astley paced his study. He kicked a footstool out of the way and glared at the young man sitting at the small desk by the door. "Why on earth should I drop the suit against the devil?" he snapped. "He's guilty of theft!"

"But you may find that difficult to prove," Neville Sharpe, Astley's private secretary, said reasonably. "He covered his tracks quite well. You've no real evidence against the man."

"How much more evidence do I need?" Astley yelled. He picked up a handful of papers from his desk and shook them in the air. "These prove nothing. For all we know, every one of them could have been forged by Barrett himself."

"But they could be genuine too," Sharpe pointed out. "And according to those notices, the overpayments were clerical errors and the overpaid invoices were the result of a mistake. Elliot says the clerk responsible has been sacked."

"But I know Barrett put him up to saying that!" Astley cried. "I know the man's a thief. I've asked a number of questions about Mr. William Barrett, and this isn't the first time he's done this. I'm disgusted that I was ever stupid enough to go into business with him. I must have been blind not to see the kind of man he is."

Sharpe glanced at his watch. "Mr. Astley, I really must get going. This tooth is causing me great pain." He held his hand up to his cheek. "If I don't get there before five, the dentist mightn't be able to see me until tomorrow."

"Go on and go," Astley said. "There's no need for you to suffer. What time is it exactly?"

"Four-thirty, sir."

"Maud's late," he muttered irritably. "All right, then," he said as his secretary put his papers away. "Perhaps I'll think about dropping the lawsuit."

"I think that's wise, sir." Sharpe put the pen back in the drawer and snapped the ledger shut.

"But by God, I'm angry." Astley began pacing again. "Angrier than I've been in years. I'll see to it that that man can't show his face in any respectable house in London. Just see if I don't. No one robs me and gets away with it. One way or the other, William Barrett is going to pay."

"He'll claim that it was Elliott who inflated the invoices," Sharpe pointed out. "And then it would be Mr. Elliott's word against Barrett's if we took him to court."

"I've said I'll think about dropping the damned lawsuit. You needn't keep harping about it, Neville. But I'm not letting that man get away with it. He almost forced me into bankruptcy when he was my partner, and now I've evidence he's been stealing me blind now. I'll not have it, do you hear, I'll not have it."

The woman pulled her coat tighter against the wind. She wondered if anyone had seen her leave and then decided it didn't matter. If she'd been seen, she'd claim she only went for a walk. There was no harm in that.

She smiled mirthlessly as she went toward the big redbrick house. It was time to take matters into her own hands.

Barrett was a savage.

There was only one way to deal with savages.

And she meant to deal with him before tonight. Before the dinner party. She couldn't stand the thought of sitting across from him, watching the ugly, knowing smirk on his face as he worked his way through soup and fish and meat. No, it was too much. No woman could be expected to endure such torment.

And she didn't intend to endure it a moment more. He'd sit there as if he were the Prince of Wales when he was the one who should be ashamed.

He was a brute. A cold unfeeling cad. But she was the one who would have to endure the pain, the humiliation, the awful agony of wondering when and if he would speak up.

For speak he surely would.

She knew that as well as she knew her own name. Men like William Barrett couldn't be trusted with anyone's secret.

She clenched her hands into fists and drug a deep, heavy breath into her lungs. Her teeth chattered lightly, but it had nothing to do with the cold, damp November air. Nerves, she told herself as she clamped her mouth tightly shut. It's just nerves. But it will be over soon.

It was almost dark now, even if it was only a half past four.

She heard the *clip-clop* of a hansom coming from down the street, so she ducked behind a hedge until it went past.

It wouldn't do to be seen here. She didn't want to have to explain her presence to anyone. Not until after she'd seen Barrett.

She kept her hands balled into fists to keep them from shaking. Fear turned her knees to jelly and made her insides shake. But she had no choice. She stepped out from behind the hedge and started up the walkway.

The front door was wide open. It was almost as if he were expecting her.

"'E caught her puttin' it back?" Wiggins muttered. "That's a bita' bad luck."

"Indeed it was," Ruth agreed. "And even worse, the awful man snatched the bird right out of Minerva's hand and put it in his pocket."

"You mean he's a thief, too?" Mrs. Goodge queried.

"No, no. I mean he took it to torment poor Minerva. He grabbed it and told her he'd hang on to it until he can decide what to do about the situation." She shook her head sadly. "Poor Minerva is in a state. If that awful man says anything to the Astleys, she'll be ruined. Absolutely ruined."

Mrs. Jeffries realized they'd better learn a few more facts. "First of all, why don't you tell us who this man is and when all of this took place."

"Oh, I'm sorry. I suppose that might be useful. The man's name is William Barrett. He's some sort of business associate of Thornton Astley's. Everything happened yesterday afternoon at the Astley house. That's over on Kildare Gardens."

"I take it that Miss Kenny had . . . uh . . . appropriated this bird from the Astleys' drawing room sometime prior to her attempt to return it?" Mrs. Jeffries was always of the opinion that one couldn't have too much information.

"Oh, yes." Ruth smiled sadly. "Minerva and Maud Astley are great friends, despite the fact that Minerva's years older than Maud. She goes

there frequently for tea and dinner parties, that sort of thing. She'd seen
this ridiculous china bird and she took a fancy to it. Unfortunately, Mr.
Barrett was sitting in the drawing room when Miss Kenny was trying to
get in and put the bird back where it belonged. The Astleys kept it up on
a high shelf. Minerva was dragging a chair over to put it back when Barrett suddenly popped up. She didn't see him right away; she claimed she
was too busy watching the door for servants. Barrett came sneaking up
behind her and snatched it right out of her hand."

"Were the Astleys at home?" Smythe asked.

Ruth shook her head. "Oh, no, that's why Minerva tried to put it back.
She was certain she'd be able to do it without getting caught. She knew
Maud and Thornton were out."

"Why did the servants let her in?" Betsy asked curiously. "I mean,
when the Inspector's not at home, we don't let people in to go wanderin'
about the drawin' room."

"She had a story ready," Ruth replied. "She told the parlour maid she
thought a pearl button had fallen off her sleeve the day before—that's
when she took the bird in the first place. The girl was busy, so she let
Minerva go into the room to search for her button."

"Sounds like it'd work," Smythe said thoughtfully. "But why was Barrett there?"

"He'd come to see Astley's secretary." Ruth shrugged. "At least that's
what he told poor Minerva. She was so shaken by being discovered, she
didn't think to question Barrett further."

"Perhaps the Astleys were due back soon," Mrs. Jeffries mused. The
man being in the house was unusual but perhaps explainable.

"Oh, no," Ruth said quickly. "Minerva wouldn't have dared go near
the place if any of the family were there. They'd told her they were going
to be out for the day."

"I see."

Ruth glanced uneasily around the table. "I know this is a very peculiar
story, but Minerva Kenny is one of the nicest people in the world. Please,
you must help her. She's nowhere else to turn and time is running out
for her."

Mrs. Jeffries smiled weakly at Lady Cannonberry. Gracious, this was
a problem. She didn't approve of stealing—if what Miss Minerva Kenny
did could be called stealing. But on the other hand, she did think that Mr.
Barrett's behaviour was rather odious. Imagine torturing a poor woman

that way. Surely if this Mr. Barrett were dreadfully opposed to theft, he'd have informed the Astleys immediately about Miss Kenny's behaviour. No, it sounded to Mrs. Jeffries as if this man had something else in mind. Blackmail, perhaps?

"Well, I'm not really sure what to say," she began weakly.

"Oh, please, you must help my friend," Ruth pleaded. "You don't understand. She's at her wit's end. If Barrett tells what she's done, she'll be ruined. For a woman like Minerva, death would be preferable."

"But she's a thief," Mrs. Goodge said quietly.

"But that's just it, she's not. She always puts what she takes back."

"That doesn't make takin' it in the first place right," the cook said stoutly.

"But she can't help herself," Ruth persisted. "Please, listen to me. Do any of you think a man ought to be hanged for stealing a loaf of bread because he's hungry?"

There was a general murmur of "no" and "course not" around the table.

"So in some cases, you'd say that stealing was right," Ruth said doggedly.

"Now, we never said that," Luty Belle corrected.

"But that's really the point, isn't it? Sometimes the law is wrong. I know what Minerva does isn't right, but I honestly believe she can't help herself. She's not a criminal, she's ill. Only instead of the infection being in her arm or her chest, it's in her head!" Ruth cried passionately. "Minerva Kenny is a wonderful woman. If you knew her, you'd understand."

"Are you saying, Lady Cannonberry," said Hatchet, who wouldn't call a titled lady by her christian name if someone put a knife to his throat, "that you think we ought to help this person because she's ill?"

"Yes, that's exactly what I'm saying." Ruth slowly gazed around the table, taking a moment to meet the eyes of each and every one of them, "This is a matter of justice. It isn't right that a woman like her could be utterly ruined by a horrible man like Barrett. He isn't concerned in the least about the morality of what she did, but only in keeping her within his power. William Barrett couldn't care less about whether she's a thief, but only in how he can use this information to make her life miserable. That's absolutely wrong. No human being should ever have that kind of power over another."

Mrs. Jeffries rather agreed. "What does everyone think?" she asked, gazing around the table. "Should we help?"

Betsy spoke first. "I'm for helpin' the woman. Lord knows, I've been in a tight spot a time or two in my life."

"Me too," Wiggins agreed. "This Mr. Barrett sounds like a right old prig."

"Count me in!" Luty exclaimed. "Can't stand people who bully others."

"As Madam has agreed," Hatchet said slowly, "I suppose I've no recourse but to agree as well."

"Fiddlesticks!" Luty glared accusingly at her butler. "You're just as eager to have something else to stick yer nose in as the rest of us."

"I do not, as you so quaintly put it, 'stick my nose' in matters that do not concern me," Hatchet responded. "Unless, of course, a greater purpose—such as justice—is being served. In this case, it certainly sounds as if the poor woman is being treated most unjustly. Lady Cannonberry"—he bowed regally—"I am at your disposal."

Luty snorted.

"Smythe?" Mrs. Jeffries queried.

The coachman nodded slowly. "I'll have a go. Men like this Barrett fellow stick in my craw."

"Mrs. Goodge?"

"Well," the cook said doubtfully, "I'm not sure about this. Where I come from, stealin' is stealin'. But I don't rightly think that's what Miss Kenny's doin'. Oh, bother, of course I'll help."

"Good." Mrs. Jeffries smiled brightly at Lady Cannonberry. "We're all agreed."

"What did ya mean when you said time was runnin' out for Miss Kenny?" Smythe asked.

"Minerva's been invited to dinner at the Astley house tonight. Barrett's going to be there too. She's terrified he'll bring the bird with him and tell them what she's done. A number of other people have been invited as well. Her greatest fear is that he'll wait till everyone's seated at the dinner table and then accuse her of being a thief."

They all looked at one another. "She's left gettin' 'elp a bit late, 'asn't she?" Wiggins said what they all were thinking. "Cor, there inn't much we can do in the next few hours."

"Oh, dear," Mrs. Jeffries murmured.

"I'm sorry." Ruth looked down at the table. "I don't know what I expected you to do on such short notice, but you see, I only got the whole story out of Minerva today at lunch. It's hopeless, isn't it?"

"I don't know," Mrs. Jeffries replied honestly. "Why don't you give us more information." She cast a quick glance at the clock. "We may be able to do something. First of all, where does this Barrett live? Do you know?"

"Kildare Gardens." Ruth replied.

"Is Barrett married?" Smythe asked. "I mean, does 'e live alone or with family?"

"He's unwed," she answered. "And I've taken the liberty of making a few inquiries of my own. He lives alone except for his servants. But the staffing in his house is sparse. I believe he has a difficult time keeping servants."

"Where does 'e work?" Wiggins asked. "Is 'e gone durin' the day?"

They all began asking questions at once. Lady Cannonberry tried her best to answer them. But it was clear that she hadn't much more information to share.

"All right, so now we knows where 'e lives and that 'e spends part of the time at 'is office," Wiggins complained. "I don't see 'ow that's gonna do us much good. 'E's still got Miss Kenny's bird."

"You mean he's got the Astley bird," Betsy corrected. She thought Wiggins was right. She didn't see that they were going to be of much use to Minerva Kenny. Not if William Barrett talked tonight at that dinner party. By tomorrow morning Miss Kenny might be the most-gossiped-about woman in London.

"This is a most difficult problem," Mrs. Jeffries murmured.

"No, it's not," Smythe announced. Everyone looked at him. He gave them a wide cocky smile.

Betsy's eyes narrowed dangerously. "You've got a solution, then?"

"Course I have," he replied. "Barrett's got the bird, right? And that's all the evidence he's got against Miss Kenny. Without the bird he's got nothin'. It'd be 'is word against 'ers if he goes to the Astley family tellin' tales tonight. The solution's as plain as the 'eadlines in the mornin' papers." He leaned back in his chair, crossed his arms over his chest, and said, "We'll steal the bird right out from under his bloomin' nose."

# CHAPTER 2

"I don't think this is goin' to work," Betsy said. She held up the heavy black wool coat and squinted at the seam she'd just mended. "The plan's daft. It'll be too easy to get caught."

"Don't worry so, lass," Smythe said easily. He frowned at the garment Betsy held up. He'd not put on that old coat for years. He hoped it still fit. But whether it was tight across the shoulders or not, he needed it. "I know what I'm doin'."

"It's not like we've got any other ideas," Wiggins pointed out.

"I'm afraid I agree with Betsy," Mrs. Jeffries said. Her normally placid face was creased with worry. She stared at the coachman. "Are you absolutely certain your information is correct?"

After Lady Cannonberry had left, Smythe and Wiggins had made a fast trip out to learn more about Barrett.

"Sure as I can be," he replied, "Barrett's had workmen in his house today, and he's supposed to be goin' to a fancy dinner party at Thornton Astley's tonight. It'll be no trouble to get in an' out. All I have to do is convince one of the maids that I'm gettin' some tools that one of me mates left upstairs."

"Servants aren't stupid, you know. They'll know good and well you're not one of the labourers that's been workin' there," Mrs. Goodge snapped. "And even if you manage to sweet-talk your way past some maid, someone's bound to want to go upstairs with you to keep an eye on you."

"Let me worry about that part," he said.

"But I still don't see how you're goin' to do it. Barrett's goin' to that dinner party tonight. What if he's already left and taken the bird with him?" Betsy said worriedly.

Smythe was touched by her concern. "Stop frettin' so. The man only has to walk to the other end of the Gardens, 'e'll not be gettin' there early. Even if 'e is plannin' on takin' the bird, I should be able to nip in and pinch it before 'e leaves for the Astley 'ouse."

Mrs. Jeffries had a very bad feeling about all this. She wished they hadn't gotten involved. "How do you plan on getting it out of the house while Barrett's still there?" she asked.

Smythe grinned confidently. "Barrett won't be gettin' dressed for a fancy evenin' out in 'is study, now, will 'e? I'll wait till 'e's changin'." The plan was bold as brass and he wasn't sure it would work. But it was worth a try.

"I still don't like it," Betsy mumbled.

"I'll be dressed like a workman," Smythe replied. "In that old coat no one will think I'm anything but one of the bloomin' painters' mates, come back to pick up a tool. This time of night the servant's'll be tired. None of 'em will be wantin' to climb up to the third floor and keep their eye on me."

"But what if someone does come with you?" Betsy persisted. "And how do you know where to look for the wretched bird once you're in there?"

"Betsy's got a point," Mrs. Jeffries said hastily. "Barrett could have put the figurine anywhere. You won't have time to search the whole house."

"I won't have to," Smythe said. "Lay you odds that he's got that bird tucked away in his desk. Isn't that where the Inspector puts important things he don't want to lose?"

"Well, yes," the housekeeper said doubtfully. "But that doesn't mean that that's what Barrett did. For all we know, he could have put it under his mattress or in a drawer in his dining room."

Smythe shook his head. "Nah, he put it in his desk. Now stop yer worryin'. I'll nip up the back stairs, find the man's study, snatch the figurine and be out before you can snap yer fingers. I'll be in and out so fast the only thing anyone'll remember is the back of me coat."

"I still don't like it," Betsy said. "If you get caught, they'll call the police."

Smythe hated to see the fear in Betsy's pretty blue eyes. He wouldn't have her frettin' over him and wringin' her hands if he could help it. But he didn't see they had much choice. If they was goin' to help Minerva Kenny, they had to take a few chances. Far better to try and talk his way past a maid on the excuse that he needed some tools than waitin' about and tryin' to sneak in in the dead of night. "I'll be fine, Betsy."

"I think I ought to go with you," Wiggins said. "I can wait outside with the carriage. Keep everything ready in case we have to make a fast getaway."

"Now Wiggins—" Mrs. Goodge began.

"That's a splendid idea," Mrs. Jeffries interrupted. "I'd rather there were two of you there than just Smythe on his own."

"Humph," the cook snorted delicately. "I don't know why we're mixed up in this. We don't even know this woman. And I'm not sure that she isn't deserving of getting caught."

"No one deserves being tortured," Betsy said. "And we're mixed up in this because we're all scared that if we don't help Lady Cannonberry's friend, she'll 'accidentally' let it slip to the inspector that we've been helpin' on his cases."

"Why, Lady Cannonberry would never do that," Wiggins said indignantly. "She give us her word."

"Of course she wouldn't," the cook put in.

Mrs. Jeffries wanted to believe that Ruth would hold her tongue. But she wasn't willing to bet her next quarter's wages on it. She didn't like to think that their motives for helping someone in trouble were so self-serving, but she had considered the fact that refusing to help could influence how Lady Cannonberry felt about them.


Barrett's house in Kildare Gardens was built much like the Inspector's home at Upper Edmonton Gardens, so Smythe had little trouble determining the layout of the rooms. He drove past the tall redbrick structure, circled the houses and drove out again through Kildare Terrace. He pulled the carriage up in front of St. Stephen's Church.

Tossing the reins to Wiggins, Smythe jumped down. "It's just gone on six-fifteen. Barrett should be gettin' ready about now. Let's 'ope the old boy is as vain as 'e is mean and needs plenty of time to tart 'imself up."

"Blimey, I hope so." Wiggins nervously clutched the reins. Bow and Arrow, the inspector's carriage horses, snorted softly and tossed their heads.

"If I'm not back in half an hour," Smythe said as he stroked Bow's nose, "you take the carriage and get out of 'ere."

"Drive the carriage! Me?" Wiggins screeched. "But I've only driven it once before. We're a long ways from 'ome. I don't think I can do it."

"Don't be daft, boy," Smythe hissed. "If I'm not back, then you've got no choice. We're less than fifteen minutes away. If you have any trouble, just head for the Uxbridge Road. Bow and Arrow knows their way back from there and the road's wide enough, even for yer drivin'."

"Cor, please come back," Wiggins pleaded. The thought of driving the inspector's great carriage through the London streets filled him with dread.

"I intend to," Smythe snapped, worried now at the thought of Bow and Arrow, his personal pride and joy, being in the hands of a nervous Nellie like Wiggins. He gave the horses one last pat and turned toward Kildare Terrace. Moving quietly, he kept to the shadows as he made his way to the Gardens.

The street in front of the house was as silent as a church. The lamplights were lit but their glow was dimmed by a heavy mist drifting in from the river.

Smythe headed for the side of the house. He paused in the silent passage, his gaze fixed on a brilliant shaft of light coming from a window. Moving stealthily, he crept down the passage and peeked through the glass.

Several scullery maids, a serving maid and a uniformed footman bustled back and forth in the brightly lighted kitchen. On the opposite side of the long trestle table he could see the remains of the evening meal. One of the maids slowly stacked plates while another one emptied scraps into a bucket on the floor.

Smythe tiptoed toward the passage, around the corner and to the back door.

He reached for the handle, praying it wasn't locked. The door opened quietly. He peeked inside and realized this door opened into a long, dark hallway. Holding his breath, he eased inside and shut the door behind him. From the kitchen at the front of the house, he could hear voices.

"What time was he supposed to go out, then?" a woman's voice asked.

"What's it to do with you?" another voice replied. "What he does is 'is business."

Smythe tiptoed past a half-closed door, the cooling pantry probably, he thought. He hoped no one would take it into their heads to go for a walk just now. He reached the end of the hall and wanted to laugh in triumph. Instead of having to cross into the kitchen and try talking his way upstairs, he found another doorway right in front of him. It led directly to the back stairs.

"Watch what yer doin' there!" a maid yelled. There was the sound of laughter and a clatter as something metal hit the floor. Smythe waited a moment, listening for footsteps and then he stepped onto the first stair.

Squeak. It creaked louder than an old granny's bones. He took another step. Squeak. He paused, waiting to see if someone from the kitchen would come and check. Nothing. Holding his breath, he hurried up the stairs. As he neared the top, he heard footsteps coming down the hall.

Smythe took the last two stairs in one leap, glanced to his left, saw that the coast was clear and then dashed forwards towards the second set of stairs leading to the upper floors. He made it into the darkened corridor just as the footsteps rounded the corner and the butler appeared. Smythe waited until the man had disappeared down the stairs before continuing. He made it to the next floor without incident. It took only a moment to locate Barrett's study.

Smythe edged the door open and saw a fire burning in the grate. There was a balloon-backed chair set at an angle in front of the fireplace and beside that was a desk. Bookcases and tables edged the walls. He squinted, trying to adjust to the sudden dimness. From the corner of his eye, he caught a glint of silver. He glanced to the side and saw a sword and scabbard hanging on the wall above a long, low table.

But the room was empty. Breathing a heartfelt sigh of relief, Smythe gently closed the door and walked softly toward the desk. Keeping one eye on the door, he rounded the desk and pulled open the top drawer. Nothing but papers. He tried the second drawer. More papers. He stuck his hand inside and felt around at the back. Nothing.

He tried the next drawer, wincing as it creaked in protest when he yanked it open. More papers, but he'd heard something rattle at the back. As he reached inside, his fingers brushed against china. Smiling in triumph, he pulled the object out.

In the dim light he couldn't quite see what it was, so he leaned forward, closer to the fire. It was the bluebird. He grinned at the china beastie.

As he straightened, he caught sight of another glint of silver. He cocked his head so that he could see the back of the huge, overstuffed chair near the fireplace. Something was sticking out of the upholstery. Curious, he moved closer.

Startled, he blinked to make sure the dim light wasn't playing tricks on his eyes. Cor blimey, he thought as his gaze focused on the curved handle, that looks like the hilt to one of them fancy swords. He glanced at the wall by the door and realized the sword hanging above the desk was only an empty scabbard.

Smythe swallowed, inched closer and peeked over the top of the huge chair. At the sight that met his eyes, he thought he'd lose his dinner.

A man was sitting there, pinned like a bug on a board. His eyes were open, staring straight ahead. The sharp edge of a sword stuck out of the center of his chest.

Smythe knew the man was dead. His chest weren't movin' and with them eyes popped wider than fried eggs, he couldn't be still breathin'. Just to make sure, he reached for the man's wrist and felt for a pulse. Nothing. "Blimey," he muttered, "this is a fine fix I've got into."

He was pretty sure he knew who the feller was too. William Barrett. Someone had skewered the ruddy bastard.

For a moment he didn't know what to do. Then he caught himself, tucked the china bird in the pocket of his jacket and tiptoed toward the door. Easing it open, he checked to see that no one was coming. He had to get out of there. Fast.

Smythe retraced his steps. When he got to the bottom of the steps going into the kitchen, he stopped and listened.

"The master said he wasn't to be disturbed," the butler was saying to someone. "So we'll not. It's hardly our place to remind him that he has a dinner engagement. But as he'll probably be hungry, I'd suggest you get some of that joint out of the cooling pantry and do up a plate. Just in case he decides not to go out. *Some* people consider it the height of rudeness to be late to dinner engagements."

Suddenly a heavy set of footsteps sounded in the downstairs hallway, blocking his escape through the back door.

Damn. He couldn't get out that way. Sounded like there was a bleedin' army in that kitchen now, not to mention the cook rootin' around in the pantry.

Smythe tiptoed back down the hallway. There was a door at the far end. He opened the door, saw a small sitting room and went inside, He hurried toward the window. The ground was a goodly drop, but he'd take his chances. Opening the window, he took a deep breath, swung his legs out and jumped. It was only as he hit the ground that he realized what he'd done. With the window left open, the police would assume that the killer had gotten in or out that way.

Smythe ran to where he'd left Wiggins and the carriage, taking care not to be seen.

"Everythin' go all right, then?" Wiggins asked, clearly relieved to see the coachman.

"I got the bird," Smythe said, climbing up and grabbing the reins. "But we've got us another problem."

"Someone saw you?"

"No one saw me." He made a clicking sound through his teeth and the horses took off with a great lurch. Smythe never used a whip. "But there's a dead body in William Barrett's study."

"Are you sure he was dead?" Mrs. Jeffries asked.

"'E was dead, all right," Smythe replied, "He 'ad the sword coming out of his 'eart, no pulse and his eyes open wide like 'e was starin' into the bowels of 'ell. I hope I did right, comin' back 'ere. But considerin' the circumstances, I didn't think it'd look good me bein' found there."

"You did the right thing, Smythe." Mrs. Jeffries pursed her lips.

"We goin' to tell the inspector?" Wiggins asked.

She shook her head. "Not directly. No."

"We can't just let a dead man sit there all night." Mrs. Goodge looked utterly scandalized by that thought.

"Why not?" Wiggins muttered. "It's not like it makes any difference to 'im."

"Of course we're going to tell the police," Mrs. Jeffries said quickly. "We're just going to have to think of a way to do it without bringing our involvement into it."

"Oh, dear," Lady Cannonberry said. "This is all my fault. . . ."

"Nonsense," the cook said briskly. "You was just tryin' to help your friend."

"Thank God Smythe wasn't caught!" Betsy exclaimed. She was sitting at the kitchen table, her face pale and her hands clenched together in her lap.

Suddenly Mrs. Jeffries looked at Lady Cannonberry and asked, "Does the inspector know what your handwriting looks like?"

"Why, no."

"Good. Wait here, all of you. I'll be right back."

She came back a few minutes later carrying a plain white paper, a pen and an envelope. Handing them to Lady Cannonberry, she said, "Would you please write what I dictate? We must let the police know about the murder, but we don't want to implicate ourselves."

She told Lady Cannonberry exactly what to write. Then she turned to Wiggins and said, "Go round to the front door and bang on it hard, hard enough for the inspector to hear. Leave the envelope on the doormat. When you hear my footsteps, make sure you're gone by the time I get to the door."

Wiggins grabbed the envelope and dashed for the back door. Everyone else stood around Mrs. Jeffries looking anxious and worried. "Let's hope this little trick works," she murmured. "Now, everyone go sit down and pretend to be going about your business."

Along with everyone else, Lady Cannonberry started toward the table.

"No, no, Ruth," Mrs. Jeffries said. "Please don't think me rude, but I do believe our plan has more of a chance of succeeding if you're not here."

"Oh, yes." She blushed slightly. "Of course. I'll be off, then. Do keep me informed and I'm so very grateful for your help." She smiled quickly at the other servants and held up the china bird. "Whether you know it or not, you've probably saved Minerva's life. I do believe that if that dreadful man had accused poor Minerva of being a thief, she'd have jumped off a bridge."

No one mentioned that the "dreadful man" was now dead and that Minerva would have to be considered a suspect. Lady Cannonberry waved a goodbye and left. A few moments later there was a loud banging on the front door.

Mrs. Jeffries waited for a moment before heading for the stairs. She paused on the step, waited till the banging came again and then started up. She stomped her feet as loudly as she dared. As she reached the end of the hallway, Inspector Witherspoon was coming down the front staircase.

"Gracious, who on earth could be making such a racket?" he murmured. Behind the rim of his spectacles, his blue-grey eyes were narrowed and his long, bony face creased in worry. His thinning dark hair stood straight up in spots, as though he'd been lying down, and he'd taken off his vest. Though it was only eight, the inspector had obviously been planning on having an early night.

"I've no idea, sir," she replied, stomping across the entryway. She reached for the door handle.

"Mrs. Jeffries, don't answer that," he ordered. "Let me get it. Please. I'm always a bit suspicious of people banging on my door this time of night. Especially when they're pounding loud enough to wake the dead."

"Of course, sir," she replied, stepping back.

Witherspoon pulled open the door, and a blast of chilly damp air blew inside. "Drat. There's no one here." He started to close the door.

Mrs. Jeffries dashed forward. "Look, sir, there's an envelope." She pointed to the stoop.

Witherspoon bent down and scooped it up. "It's addressed to me."

She quickly shut the door, keeping her eye on the inspector as he tore open the envelope. His expression turned puzzled as he read the paper. "Goodness," he murmured. "This is most odd." He reached for the handle, jerked the door open and dashed out onto the stairs. Turning left and right, he squinted into the dark night. "No one there. I wonder who brought this?"

"May I ask what it is, sir?" Mrs. Jeffries queried softly.

"Oh, yes, of course. It's quite strange really." He cleared his throat and started to read. "'Inspector Witherspoon. There is a dead man in the study of Number fifteen Kildare Gardens off the Talbot Road. He has a sword through his heart. Come at once.' It's signed, 'A Concerned Citizen.'"

Perplexed, he stared at the note for a moment longer, then looked at Mrs. Jeffries. "Do you think this is someone's idea of a joke?"

"Well"—she had to be very careful here—"it could be, sir. A note is rather an unusual way to summon the police to a murder. But honestly, you don't have any friends or acquaintances who would do such a thing. Perhaps you'd better go."

"But it's so odd," he protested. He'd just solved one murder, and he really wasn't all that keen to have a go at another. "I mean, if someone's been murdered, why not call a constable? Why bring a note all the way round here?"

Mrs. Jeffries decided to fire every bit of ammunition at her disposal. "Now don't be so modest, sir. It's quite obvious why someone brought the note here instead of taking it to a police station or calling a police constable."

He stared at her blankly.

"Your reputation, sir. You must admit, you've become rather well known for solving the most heinous and complex of crimes."

He smiled and his narrow chest swelled slightly. Dear Mrs. Jeffries, she always knew just the right thing to say. "You're right of course." He sighed theatrically. "I suppose I'd better nip along and see if there's anything to this." He started for the stairs, stopped and turned back. "Send Wiggins over to fetch Constable Barnes, Mrs. Jeffries. Have him ask the constable to meet me at Kildare Gardens. If this isn't someone's idea of a silly prank, I may need Barnes's assistance."

"Should we go right to the front door?" Constable Barnes asked. He was a tall man with a head full of thick, iron-grey hair beneath his police helmet, a lined craggy face and a pragmatic, kind disposition.

"Yes, we've no other choice," Witherspoon replied as he started up the short flight of steps. Dash it all, he thought, this is most awkward. If there wasn't a body in here, he would have a lot of explaining to do. He banged the brass doorknocker. "Skulking about trying to determine whether or not this is a hoax wouldn't be right."

The door opened and a tall, bald man in a butler's uniform stuck his head out. "Good evening," he said slowly, his eyes widening slightly at the sight of Barnes.

"Good evening," the inspector began. "Could you please tell us who owns this house?" He thought it best to learn who the owner might be. That way, if he had to apologize, he could at least use the correct name.

"This is Mr. Barrett's residence, sir," the butler replied, looking even more puzzled.

"Is Mr. Barrett at home?"

"Yes. Who may I say is asking for him?"

Witherspoon identified himself and Barnes. "This is rather awkward, I'm afraid," he explained, "but we really must speak to Mr. Barrett. We've had a communication that claims there is a dead man in the study of this house."

"That is absurd. You're making a dreadful mistake. Mr. Barrett's in the study." The butler sniffed. "And I'm quite sure he'd have noticed if there was a corpse there as well." He started to close the door.

Barnes flattened his palm against the panel and pushed hard. "Then would you mind showin' us in so we can see for ourselves?"

The butler's stiff face looked as if it were going to crack, but he jerked his chin, inviting them inside. Turning on his heel, he called, "It's this way. But Mr. Barrett's going to be very angry about this. He doesn't like to be disturbed when he's working."

The door opened into a wide entryway paved with black-and-white tiles. There was a huge ornate mirror with a gold gilt frame on one side of the hall and an elegant gaslamp, its flame flaring brightly, on the other side. The walls were papered in white-and-gold empire stripes and decorated with pictures of hunting scenes with red-coated aristocrats riding to the hounds. A mahogany table with a large potted plant stood beside the staircase. Beyond the staircase was a long hallway with doors on each side.

The butler, muttering about chief inspectors just loudly enough for Witherspoon to hear, tromped up the stairs. He led them down a long thickly carpeted hallway to a closed door. Knocking once, he called out, "Mr. Barrett, sorry for disturbing you, sir. But the police are here." He shot them a sour look. "They insist on seeing you."

There was no answer.

The butler frowned. He knocked again. "Mr. Barrett, sir."

Still no answer.

Witherspoon and Barnes exchanged a glance and stepped closer to the door.

"Mr. Barrett," the butler tried again, and this time his voice was high-pitched and frightened. "Please, sir. Is everything all right?"

"Go in," Witherspoon instructed.

The butler nodded, grabbed the brass knob and opened the door. The three men stepped inside.

The room was dim, the dying fire in the hearth being the only source of illumination. The butler stared at the empty desk and moved closer into the room. "Mr. Barrett," he said softly.

"I say," Witherspoon called out. "So sorry to disturb you, but we've had a most unusual note."

"Who're you talkin' to?" Barnes asked. He glanced around the darkened room wondering if the inspector could see someone he couldn't. "I don't see anyone here."

"Perhaps he's in the chair," Witherspoon replied.

The servant hurried forward, angled his head to see into the chair and made a funny, strangling noise. Barnes and Witherspoon sprang across the room.

Barnes was the first to speak. "Looks like that note wasn't a joke," he said softly. "Poor fellow's been poked clean through."

He grabbed the man's wrist and felt for a pulse. Then he looked into the man's open, glassy-eyed gaze. "He's dead, sir. And as the blood's starting to clump around the wound, I'd reckon it was at least an hour or two ago that he got done in."

Witherspoon forced himself to look. He hated looking at bodies. But weak stomach or not, he knew his duty. Drat. Why did these things always happen to him? And so soon after supper, too. "Er, yes," he gulped and wiped his face as his gaze fastened on the end of the sword sticking out of the man's chest. "He does look . . . Well . . . dead. Obviously not self-inflicted."

"It's Mr. Barrett!" the butler cried. "Good God, and skewered clean through like one of the cook's roast chickens."

Witherspoon looked at Barnes. "You'd best get some help."

Barnes nodded. "I'll go up to the end of the Gardens and blow the whistle. There's constables walkin' the beat near the train station."

Barnes left and Witherspoon turned to the wide-eyed servant. Even in the dim light, he could see the man had gone as white as chalk. "Perhaps we'd best step outside into the hall," the inspector suggested.

"We can't just leave him alone," the man mumbled.

"Well, he isn't going anywhere. I'd rather no one touch anything until after the police surgeon arrives."

The butler nodded and shuffled toward the door. As soon as they were in the hallway, Witherspoon asked, "Is there somewhere up here where we can sit down?"

"There's a small sitting room on the next floor." The butler nodded, turned and went down the stairs. He carried himself rigidly, as though he were bracing for a heavy blow.

Feeling sorry for the poor man, Witherspoon silently followed him. But the servant had recovered somewhat by the time they reached the sitting room. He ushered the inspector inside and then started to shut the door. Witherspoon stopped him. "Leave it open. We don't want any of the other staff going upstairs."

"Yes, sir."

"Why don't you sit down." Witherspoon gestured toward a settee. He also noticed how cold the room was.

The man sat. Some of his color was returning. "This is the worst thing that's ever happened here," he murmured. "Never worked in a house where someone's been murdered before."

"What's your name?" The inspector thought the butler must have gone into another state of nerves. He was starting to mumble to himself now. Naturally, it must be quite a shock to find one's employer with a sword sticking out of his chest, so he could understand how the servant felt. But the best thing for shock was to direct the poor fellow's attention elsewhere. Questions, that's right. Lots of questions.

"Hadley, sir." He shivered. "Reginald Hadley."

"Right. Hadley. Tell me, how many servants are there in the house?"

"Not a full staff, sir." Hadley swallowed heavily. "Myself, of course, two scullery maids, a serving maid, a parlour maid, a footman and a cook."

"No housekeeper?"

"No, sir. Not since Mrs. Pretman passed away. Mr. Barrett was trying to find one, sir, but he never found one he liked. Particular he was. Real particular."

"Is there anyone else in the house? Any guests or relatives?"

Hadley shook his head. "Mr. Barrett doesn't have any relatives and he rarely invited houseguests to stay. The only people here tonight are the staff."

"Was the entire staff here all evening?"

"Yes, sir. But this time of the night, most of them have finished their duties and gone to their rooms." He wiped a trembling hand across his face. "But none of us would have done a thing like this."

"I'm not accusing anyone," the inspector assured him. "I'm merely asking a few, very ordinary questions. When was the last time you saw Mr. Barrett?"

"About five o'clock, sir. He told me he was going to be working in his study. He didn't wish to be disturbed. That was the last time any of us saw him."

"He had no plans to eat supper?"

"Oh, yes, sir. He was going out this evening."

"I see," Witherspoon replied. "What time was he supposed to go out?"

"He was due at the Astley residence at seven for a dinner party, sir."

"Didn't anyone go and knock on his door when it got late and he still hadn't come down?" Witherspoon asked. "It's past eight. Surely you realized he'd be late for his appointment."

"We realized it, sir. But it wasn't worth my position to be telling him what to do. When he went into that office and said he didn't want to be disturbed, then he didn't want to be disturbed. If you understand my meaning, sir."

Witherspoon did. The late Mr. Barrett did not sound like the kindest of employers. "Was Mr. Barrett expecting any visitors tonight?"

"No, sir."

"Has anyone unexpected been to the house tonight? Have you seen any strangers lurking about?"

"Strangers, sir? No, not really. We had workmen in and out all day. Mr. Barrett's having the third floor redone."

"Were the doors unlocked?"

"Yes, sir, and open most of the day too. Mr. Barrett wanted the air to circulate. As you can feel, sir." The butler shivered slightly. "It's made the house cold. November isn't really the best time for painting, but once Mr. Barrett made up his mind, that was that."

"Did any of the staff have reason to go into Mr. Barrett's study?"

"No, sir. The staff had their supper at six, finished their chores and then went off to their rooms. As Mr. Barrett was going out, there was no reason for anyone to stay on duty except for myself."

"I'll need to question the other servants," Witherspoon said. "Could you please gather them together?"

"In here, sir?"

Witherspoon started to say yes, caught himself and realized he'd probably get a lot more out of them if they were warm and comfortable. This room was wretchedly miserable. His feet were freezing.

"How about the kitchen," he suggested. "Perhaps, if you wouldn't mind, we can have the cook brew up a pot of tea. This has been a terrible shock. I'm sure the rest of the household will need some sustenance."

"It certainly has, sir," Hadley said with feeling as he got to his feet. Suddenly the curtains on the other side of the room billowed as a gust of air blew in.

Hadley stared at them for a moment, a frown on his face. "That's not right," he mumbled. He crossed the room and drew the curtains back. "Look here, sir. This window shouldn't be open."

"Are you sure? You said you'd left doors open for the air to circulate. Perhaps someone opened this window as well."

"It was open, sir, but I remember closing it myself. Right after the painters left at six o'clock."

# CHAPTER 3

—◆◆◆—

"How long do you think the inspector'll be?" Wiggins asked.

"Several hours, I expect," Mrs. Jeffries replied. She saw that everyone at the table already had a cup of tea in front of him before pouring her own. "He'll have to take statements from the servants and then wait for the police surgeon to arrive."

"Let's hope it's old Dr. Potter, then," Smythe added. "He takes hours before he'll even decide if someone's dead or not."

Everyone laughed. Dr. Potter had been involved in several of their other cases, and he was not held in high esteem by either the household or Inspector Witherspoon.

"Mrs. Jeffries," Betsy said, "they'll let the inspector have this one, won't they?"

"Why wouldn't they give it to the inspector?" Mrs. Goodge interjected impatiently. "He's the best man they've got."

"Yes, but what about that Inspector Nivens?" Betsy explained. "Remember how he carried on the last time? He's been itching to get himself a murder. You don't think the chief inspector will let *him* have it?"

Mrs. Jeffries shuddered delicately. Inspector Nigel Nivens was a thorn in her side. Not only did he bitterly resent Inspector Witherspoon's startling success, he'd let it be known on more than one occasion that he was certain their dear inspector had help. But she didn't want to dampen anyone's enthusiasm. Not that she approved of murder. Certainly not. However, some degree of anticipation when starting out on a new case was definitely called for.

"Let's hope not," she said cheerfully. "After all, our inspector will be the one who discovers the body. He'll be right there 'on the scene,' so to speak. It wouldn't make sense to bring another inspector in after the trail had gone cold." She hoped the Chief Inspector felt that way.

"Well," Betsy said bluntly. "I don't care which Inspector gets this one, we're going to have to investigate it as well. If anyone saw Smythe goin' in or out of that house, he could be done for. We've got to make sure we find out who the killer is. It wouldn't be fair for Smythe to be gettin' blamed for something he didn't do."

Smythe stared at her incredulously. Betsy sounded as fierce as a lioness defending her cubs. He wasn't sure if he should be insulted or flattered, but he knew it gave him a nice warm glow inside to see how much she cared.

"I told you, lass," he said gently. "No one saw me. The servants was all in the kitchen."

"What about when you jumped out the window?" Betsy argued. "Someone might have seen you then."

"Of course we'll investigate this one," Mrs. Goodge said briskly. "After all, it's our murder. And if Smythe said no one saw him, I expect that he got clean away. Stop all the worrying, Betsy. It'll not do a bit of good."

Betsy opened her mouth to argue, noticed the strange expression in the coachman's gaze and then clamped her mouth shut. "All right," she muttered, looking down at her lap. "I guess Smythe knows what he's about."

Wiggins yawned loudly. "What do you want us to do first?" he asked, turning sleepy eyes to the housekeeper.

"What we always do first," Mrs. Jeffries replied. "We learn everything we can about the victim. Smythe, can you recall anything about him or about the study? Anything which might be important?"

Smythe's face grew thoughtful. "Don't think so. I was in and out pretty quickly. Once I'd seen Barrett with that sword pokin' out of 'is 'eart, I didn't notice much of anythin' else."

"Tell us what you can recall about the dead man," Mrs. Jeffries said softly. She wasn't positive the victim was William Barrett—though it didn't seem likely it could be anyone else.

"He looked to be middle-aged," Smythe said, "and 'is 'air was dark but it was thinnin' on the top. When I looked over that chair, I could see a bald spot as big as one of Mrs. Goodge's scones on 'is head."

"How was he dressed?"

"Like a city gent. Dark suit and vest, a white shirt."

"And the murder weapon?" Mrs. Jeffries pressed. "Are you sure it was a sword and not just some sort of long knife?"

"It were a sword, all right. It had one of them fancy hilts to it," Smythe continued. "Besides, there was an empty scabbard 'angin' on the wall."

"A what?" Wiggins asked.

"A scabbard," Smythe explained. "That's the thing the sword fits into when it's not being used." As the footman continued to stare at him blankly, he sighed. "You know, it's what they hung on to their belts to put the ruddy things in when they was goin' off to war or gettin' their pictures painted."

Wiggins nodded sleepily.

Mrs. Jeffries ran her finger around the rim of her teacup. There was so much more they needed to know. "Anything else?"

"Not really. The room was so dark it was 'ard to see and once I discovered what was sittin' in that chair, all I could think of was gettin' out of there."

Mrs. Jeffries understood. Smythe might appear to be a big, rugged bull of a man; indeed, he'd proved he was perfectly capable of taking care of himself on more than one occasion. But underneath it all, he was really quite sensitive. And finding a dead body would be a shock for anyone. They could wait until later to get more information. She'd stay up and see what the inspector had to tell her. No need to press Smythe further tonight.

"You want me to start with the pubs in the area?" Smythe asked.

"Oh, yes," she answered. He started to get up, but she waved him back into his chair. "But not tonight. It's too dangerous."

Smythe raised an eyebrow and sat back down. "Dangerous? Mrs. Jeffries, I've gone out hundreds of nights to the pub."

Betsy snorted derisively.

"If you go out asking questions tonight, the very evening Barrett was murdered, you could be asking for trouble," she explained. "Betsy's concern is valid. Someone may have seen you climbing out Barrett's window. If you were seen, and then a few hours later, you're identified as someone who went round to local pubs asking all sorts of questions about the dead man, well . . ."

"I get yer meanin'," he said quickly. He glanced at Betsy. She'd gone pale again. "But I don't think anyone saw me. Do you mean you don't want me askin' questions at all about this case?"

"Of course not," she replied calmly. "But do give me a day or two to determine if the police have a witness to your leaving the Barrett house."

"It won't hurt you to wait till tomorrow," Betsy chimed in.

"All right," he agreed. "If it'll keep you ladies 'appy, I won't set foot out of this 'ouse until I'm told to."

"Good," Betsy gave him a quick smile and turned to the housekeeper. "What do you want me to do?" she asked.

"Talk to the shopkeepers in the area. Find out what you can about Barrett and his household." Mrs. Jeffries turned to Wiggins. His elbows were on the table, his chin propped in his hand. His eyes were closed.

"Has he gone to sleep?" Mrs. Goodge asked. "Hey, boy! Wake up. We've not got all night."

"I'm not asleep," Wiggins mumbled around another yawn. "I'm just restin' me eyes. Besides, I already know what I've got to do. Mrs. Jeffries wants me to make contact with one of the servants in the Barrett house, right?"

"Right," Mrs. Jeffries agreed.

"And I suppose you want me to get me sources talking," Mrs. Goodge said. "Course I'll have to get up extra early and do some baking. People talk so much better when you're filling their bellies."

Mrs. Goodge had a whole network of people from delivery boys to chimney sweeps tramping through her kitchen. She plied them ruthlessly with hot tea, fresh buns and savory rolls. She managed to wring every morsel of gossip there was about anyone in London out of them. Add to that her many years in service and the attendant number of housekeepers, footmen, butlers and maids she knew, and she had a veritable army of informants.

"You're correct as always, Mrs. Goodge," Mrs. Jeffries said.

"What about Luty and Hatchet?" Smythe asked. "Luty'll have a fit if we don't give her something to do. You know 'ow she 'ates bein' kept out of things."

"Luty?" Betsy protested. "What about Hatchet? He's just as bad."

"Never said 'e wasn't," the coachman replied.

"We'll have them both around tomorrow," Mrs. Jeffries said quickly. She didn't want another problem on her hands. On their last murder, the women had been utterly furious at the men. Not that they didn't have good reason, she thought. The men had been unbelievably arrogant, convinced that because they'd been born male they'd been blessed with superior intellect and character. Well, the women had set them straight very quickly. Very quickly indeed.

However, it wouldn't do to revive that silly rivalry. Mrs. Jeffries had a feeling they were all going to have to work together on this case. If, in fact, there was a case. It could well be that Mr. Barrett had been skewered by a member of his own household, someone who had already been overcome with remorse and confessed to the police.

But she didn't think it likely. A sword thrust through the back of a chair didn't smack of a killing done in a fit of rage. More like someone had deliberately tried to sneak up and kill the victim while he was unaware. "If Wiggins will drop a note off to the Crookshank household on his way out tomorrow, we'll all meet back here for the midday meal. We can fill Luty and Hatchet in then."

"Are you goin' to wait up for the inspector?" Betsy asked.

"Indeed I am." Mrs. Jeffries rose to her feet. "But the rest of you should get to bed. You're going to need your rest."

The kitchen of the Barrett household was ablaze with light. The servants were huddled in the butler's pantry, whispering among themselves and waiting their turn to be questioned. The police surgeon and the uniformed officers were upstairs examining the body and searching the study.

Witherspoon nodded at Barnes, and a moment later the constable ushered Hadley into the cozy room. "Do sit down," the inspector said, thinking to put the fellow at ease. He didn't want him to start mumbling to himself again; it was very distracting. "And pour yourself some nice, hot tea."

"Thank you, sir," Hadley replied with a heavy sigh as he sat down and reached for the teapot. "This has all been a terrible shock to us, sir. Absolutely terrible. You can't imagine how awful it's been, sir. Mr. Barrett upstairs dead with a sword poking through him, police everywhere, place colder than a tomb in a January graveyard. Horrible, sir." He stopped talking long enough to take a long, slurping drink of tea.

"Yes, I'm sure you're all most upset." Witherspoon cleared his throat. He always hated this part the most. Getting started. Trying to decide what to ask and what not to ask. He didn't know why it was so difficult, but it jolly well was. "Now, what was the last time you saw your employer?"

"Like I told you sir, it was when he went into his study around five o'clock."

"You didn't see him after that?"

"No, sir. As I told you earlier, Mr. Barrett didn't like being disturbed. He had me bring him some stamps and his stationery, closed the door and told me he'd ring the bell if he needed anything more."

"And you're absolutely certain there were no visitors to the household, no unexpected guests?"

"Absolutely, sir."

"The front door was open all day, is that correct?" Witherspoon prodded.

"Yes, sir."

"Then how can you be sure Mr. Barrett had no visitors?" the inspector asked. "Isn't it possible someone could have come in and gone up to Mr. Barrett's study without being seen by any of the servants?"

"It's possible, sir," Hadley admitted. "Mind you, with the front door being open it was cold. I did spend most of my time downstairs today."

"Where, exactly, were you?"

"In the kitchen," Hadley said. "Most of us was in the kitchen. Like I explained, Mr. Barrett had the doors and windows wide open and the house was cold. The kitchen was the only place where you could get a bit of heat."

The inspector frowned. "The doors and windows were open because Mr. Barrett was having the third floor painted, is that correct?"

"And having the ceilings tinned and some carpentry work done as well." Hadley nodded enthusiastically. "Mr. Barrett was going to work in his study, there was workmen tramping up and down the stairs and getting under our feet, so we left them to it and stayed in the kitchen. All exceptin' Fanny, that is, and she was doin' up the drawing room."

Witherspoon sighed. Anyone could have gotten into the house and up those stairs without being spotted by a servant. No doubt the maid in the drawing room had the doors closed to keep the cold November air out. Drat. This was going to be another difficult case. "Did Mr. Barrett have any enemies?"

Hadley hesitated. "Not that I'm aware of, sir."

"Has anything odd or unusual happened to Mr. Barrett lately?" The inspector pressed.

"What do you mean 'unusual'?"

"Oh, anonymous letters, threats against him, that sort of thing?"

"Not that I know about, sir." Hadley smiled apologetically. "Mr. Barrett wasn't one to talk about his private business."

"Was he well liked by his household?" The inspector remembered that his housekeeper had once remarked that one could gain insight into a person's character by finding out how those dependent on that person felt about him.

"Well liked . . ." Hadley hesitated again. "I shouldn't like to say, sir."

"Come now," Witherspoon persisted. "I'm not asking you to speak ill of the dead. But this is a murder investigation."

"But none of us killed him," Hadley yelped. "None of us would have gone into that study. Not with him telling us he didn't want to be disturbed."

"I'm not accusing any of you of murder. I merely want to know if he was a good employer or a—"

"He was a right old bastard," Hadley finished. Then he glanced at the door as if he was afraid of being overheard. "He didn't pay much, treated us like we was dirt and squabbled with everyone. His neighbours couldn't stand him. He didn't have many friends, and I, for one, won't shed any tears at his funeral."

Taken aback, the inspector stared at the man. Hadley's face was flushed, his hands trembled, and he was gulping air like he'd just run a footrace. Gracious.

"But that don't mean any of us killed him," the butler continued. "We were all in the kitchen until almost eight o'clock."

"The sword . . . er . . . was it Mr. Barrett's?"

Hadley nodded slowly. "Looks like the one he had hanging on the study wall. He pretended like it was a family memento, but he only got the blooming thing last year. Bought it from a family he'd turned out of their home."

That sounded like a good line of inquiry. "What was the name of this family?"

"Bennington, sir. But they didn't do it. After Barrett foreclosed on their home, they emigrated to Canada to live with relatives."

"What did you mean when you said Barrett squabbled with his neighbours?" Witherspoon asked.

"Exactly that." Hadley took another gulp of tea. "Around this garden, he's about as welcome as a case of typhoid fever. Mr. Barrett can be quite rude, abusive even. I'm not accusing any of the neighbours of murder, but he wasn't particularly well liked. He had a nasty row with one of them just this afternoon." Hadley realized what he'd said and flushed guiltily. "I'm sorry, Inspector, I know you asked me if anything unusual happened today, but well . . . it's so undignified. I really hate repeating such a sordid incident. A man like myself, sir, having to take employment with a man like Barrett!" He shook his head in disgust. "It's humiliating, sir. That's what it is. Did you know I once worked for the younger son of Lord Lynfield, sir."

"No, you didn't mention that," Witherspoon replied. "But do please tell me what happened today with Mr. Barrett and his neighbour."

"And I was trained in Lord Lynford's house, sir. Indeed I was!" Hadley exclaimed, waving his arms around for emphasis. "But those days are behind me, sir, I've been reduced to working for someone who gets involved in fisticuffs with his neighbours." He sighed. "Mr. Barrett had a row with Mr. Spears. He lives next door. Spears's dog was found dead in Mr. Barrett's portion of the garden this afternoon. Mr. Spears accused Mr. Barrett of killing the animal. Words were exchanged and they got into a brawl."

Witherspoon stared at the butler. "What time was this?"

"About four-thirty, four forty-five, something like that." Hadley hung his head as though he were personally responsible for his employer's behaviour. "It was shameful, sir. Absolutely shameful."

The inspector tried asking a few more questions, but for some odd reason, Hadley decided he'd said enough. Witherspoon got nothing more out of him. He hoped he'd do better with the parlour maid, Fanny Flannagan.

She was a petite, dark-haired girl of about nineteen or twenty. She was also very pretty; large blue eyes, a small, straight nose and a perfect complexion. Witherspoon smiled kindly at her as she curtsied and motioned her into the chair the butler had just vacated. "Do sit down and have some tea, Miss Flannagan," he offered.

"Thank you, sir." Her voice was low and rather musical.

"Now, I understand you were cleaning the drawing room late this afternoon?"

"Yes, sir," she replied, toying with the rim of her teacup.

"Wasn't that an odd time to be cleaning?" Witherspoon couldn't remember any of his servants cleaning a drawing room at that time of day. Surely those sort of chores were done in the morning hours.

"Usually I did it of a morning, sir," she said slowly. "But I couldn't this morning. So I had to do it before supper, you see."

"Why couldn't you do it this morning?"

"Mr. Barrett was entertaining. He had a guest. I could hardly be in there polishin' and dustin' in front of a lady, could I?"

"A lady," Witherspoon repeated. "Do you happen to know this lady's name?"

"No, sir, I'd never seen her before." She dropped her gaze to her lap and bit her lip.

The maid was clearly nervous. "Is there something you'd like to tell me?" the inspector prompted softly.

"Well, I'm not sure if I should." She looked up at him and her eyes swam with tears. "Oh, sir, I don't like to think ill of the dead and I'm not a bad girl, but I couldn't help overhearin'."

"There, there." He reached over and patted her awkwardly on the shoulder. Egads, what if she started crying? "I'm sure you're not a bad girl at all. And sometimes it is impossible not to overhear. Now, why don't you tell me all about it."

She swiped at her eyes and gave him another dazzling smile. "I'd come up to clean about eleven o'clock, sir. Mr. Barrett didn't say he was havin' a guest, so how was I to know he was in there?"

"No, of course you didn't know," he murmured sympathetically. "What happened?"

"I opened the door and started in. All of a sudden Mr. Barrett's screamin' at me to get out. He were standin' in front of the fireplace. There was a woman standin' there, too, but she had her back to me, so I didn't know who she was. But I think she was cryin'. Her shoulders were shakin' and she was all hunched over like she was tryin' to hold herself together."

"Did you see her face?"

"No, sir."

"Is that all that happened?" he queried. Drat. If only the girl had seen the woman's face.

"Yes, sir."

"Oh, dear, it's a pity you didn't get a good look at the woman."

"Yes, sir, it is."

"Did you see or hear anyone coming or going out the front door when you were cleaning the drawing room this afternoon?"

"I thought I heard one of the workmen going down the stairs at about a quarter to six."

"Wouldn't the workmen have used the back stairs?" Witherspoon asked.

"Not this time, sir." Fanny replied with a grin. "You see, the painters had gotten into a row with the carpenters. They was squabblin' and arguin' and gettin' in each other's way that it like to drove us all mad. Mr. Barrett finally said the painters was to use the front door and the others the back. That's why I didn't think nothing of it when I heard them footsteps in the hall this evenin'." She shrugged. "And I had the door closed to keep out the cold, so I didn't see no one."

"Mrs. Jeffries, you are truly an angel of mercy," the inspector said several hours later. He reached for the glass of sherry she'd placed on the table beside his favorite chair and prepared to unburden himself. His dear housekeeper had waited up for him, providing him with two things he desperately needed: a glass of good Harvey's and a sympathetic ear.

"I take it there really was a body in the study?" she said softly.

"Unfortunately, yes." He paused and took a sip of sherry, "And I don't think it's going to be an easy case, either." Witherspoon sighed and told her everything that had transpired that night. It was so good to be able to talk to someone about these difficult cases.

Mrs. Jeffries nodded and smiled sympathetically as he told her about the corpse with the sword sticking out its chest and how anyone, absolutely anyone, could have done the foul deed. The doors were unlocked most of the afternoon and all the servants except for one were in the kitchen.

"Oh, dear," she said.

"Precisely," he agreed miserably. "I don't know how I'm going to solve this one."

"Perhaps you won't have to, sir," she said. "After all, isn't Inspector Nivens . . . er, chomping at the bit, so to speak?"

"He is, indeed," Witherspoon said gloomily. "But I've a feeling I'm going to get stuck with this one. You know how the chief is, he won't want to bring in Nivens now. Frankly, there's nothing I'd like more than to let

Inspector Nivens have a crack at this one. It's going to be jolly difficult. The killer could have been anyone."

He went on to tell her how the servants didn't like their employer but he didn't seem any worse than many employers in London and how the victim wasn't a particularly popular man with his neighbours. She shuddered when he told her about how Barrett had been accused of killing a neighbour's dog.

"But that's dreadful, sir."

"That it is," he agreed.

"Did the police constables find anything when they searched the house?"

"Nothing out of the ordinary," he replied, taking a sip of his sherry. "And none of the neighbours had seen or heard anything, either. The killer was either extraordinarily clever or lucky."

Mrs. Jeffries sagged against her chair in relief. So far, no one reported seeing Smythe leaping out that window. "I can see why you think it might be difficult," she finally said, "I take it no one confessed?" She held her breath.

He shook his head. "No. Worse luck."

"If his staff didn't like him. . . ." She hesitated, not wanting him to think she was suggesting one of the servants might have killed the man. However, if they didn't like him, they might be feeling guilty and shocked. It would be easy to miss an important clue if that were the case, but the inspector interrupted her.

"Oh, it's not likely to be one of the servants," he said morosely. "All of them were in the kitchen at the time of death."

"Oh, you know what time he was killed?"

"Not precisely. Barrett was last seen alive at five o'clock this afternoon. However, he shouted at the workmen at sometime around a quarter to six, so we know he was alive then."


"I knew I'd get this one," Witherspoon moaned softly to Barnes. He peeked over the railing to make sure Inspector Nivens wasn't lurking about.

"Not to worry, sir," Barnes said. "The coast is clear. Nivens got called out on a house burglary this morning."

"Thank goodness." He started down the stairs. "Not that I'm afraid of facing the fellow, but he does rather make me feel guilty."

Barnes snorted. He didn't think much of Inspector Nivens. None of the uniformed lads did. "It's not your fault you're good at homicides, now, is it? If Inspector Nivens has a problem with your gettin' this case, he'd best take it up with the chief, hadn't he?"

"Well, yes, I suppose you're right." Witherspoon still sounded doubtful. "But we've work to do. Come, Constable, let's find a hansom."

Luty Belle and Hatchet arrived a good half hour before lunch. "I couldn't stop her," Hatchet explained as he handed Mrs. Jeffries their heavy coats. "Once she heard the word 'murder,' she was bound and determined to get here."

"Nell's bells, Hepzibah!" Luty yelped. "You shoulda sent fer us last night. The killer could be halfway to New York by now."

"Only if he sprouted wings and flew," Hatchet said.

"Please sit down. I'll tell you everything we know before the others get back."

By the time Smythe ambled in for his noonday meal, Luty and Hatchet were fully appraised of everything that had transpired the night before. Mrs. Goodge, who'd been setting the table as Mrs. Jeffries talked, had frequently added her opinion as well.

Betsy and Wiggins showed up next, and by the time the cook had the vegetables and meat on the table, they were all seated and eager to begin.

"Hear you had yerself a mighty fine adventure last night," Luty said to Smythe.

"More of a trial than an adventure," Smythe replied with a cocky grin. "I was pleased to find out from Mrs. Jeffries this mornin' that none of the neighbours had seen me leapin' out of Barrett's window." His grin faded. "But I did find out a bit more about that argument Barrett had with his neighbour yesterday afternoon. There was more to it than what the inspector 'eard."

"Mrs. Jeffries already said he wasn't popular with the neighbours," Betsy pointed out. She was annoyed. She'd spent half the bloomin' morning trampin' up and down the high street in that area and hadn't learned a bloomin' thing. Now that she knew Smythe wasn't goin' to be carted off by the police for breakin' into a dead man's house, she didn't mind tweakin' his nose a bit. Kept him from getting such a big head.

"My ears work, lass. But bein' unpopular ain't the same thing as havin' someone threaten to kill ya."

"Someone threatened to kill 'im!" Wiggins exclaimed.

"Man named Adrian Spears, Bachelor, lives in the house next door to Barrett's." Smythe spread a thick slab of butter on his bread.

"Mrs. Jeffries already told us all this," Betsy pointed out.

"I know, lass. But I'm repeatin' it just so Luty and Hatchet will know everythin'. Anyways, as I was sayin' before I was interrupted." Betsy snorted delicately but the coachman ignored her and went right on. "Seems Barrett didn't like Spears's dog. Barrett was always chasin' it off and throwin' stones at it. Claimed the animal dug up his plants. Yesterday Spears couldn't find the dog at all. He and his servants went outside and they searched the garden. They found the animal outside Barrett's house in some bushes. His head had been bashed in with a hammer. Spears went crazy. He screamed for Barrett to come out and face him like a man. Well, of course, with Barrett's doors and windows wide open, the whole ruddy household come out to see what the ruckus was. When Barrett showed up, Spears went for him. He would have ripped his throat out right there if it hadn't a been for the servants steppin' in and breakin' them apart. But Spears was heard to threaten Barrett, said if 'e found out for sure that Barrett had killed the dog, 'e'd wring his neck."

"That awful man!" Betsy exclaimed.

"Who?" Smythe asked curiously. "Barrett or Spears?"

"Barrett, of course. Anyone who'd take a hammer to an innocent dog deserves what he gets."

"But we don't know that Barrett killed the animal," Smythe pointed out reasonably. "It could have been someone else."

"That's very odd," Mrs. Jeffries said.

"What is?" demanded Mrs. Goodge.

"When Barrett's butler told the inspector what had happened, he said nothing about Spears issuing a death threat. His account of the whole incident was far more casual that what Smythe has just told us."

"Maybe the butler didn't hear the death threat," Hatchet suggested. "Or perhaps he was in such a state of shock, he forgot to mention it. What's the man's name?"

"Hadley," Mrs. Jeffries answered. "Reginald Hadley. Do you know him?"

"No." Hatchet frowned slightly. "I don't think so, but perhaps I'll ask about and see what I can learn about him."

Smythe leaned forward. "That's not all I found out. Seems that Barrett and Spears 'ave been squabblin' for months. The two men don't like each other. Course, from what I 'eard, not many round that neighbourhood much liked Barrett."

Mrs. Jeffries looked thoughtful. "Any idea what they'd been quarreling about?"

"Didn't have time to get many details," Smythe admitted. "But I'll keep at it."

"Excellent, Smythe." She looked at Betsy.

"I didn't learn a bloomin' thing," the girl admitted honestly. She fiddled with the skirt of her blue broadcloth dress. "None of the shopkeepers knew anything and all the shops were so busy this morning, I didn't really get much of a chance to talk to many of the assistants."

"Not to worry," the housekeeper said smoothly, "It's early days yet."

"Don't feel bad, Betsy," Wiggins said. "I didn't find out anything, either. No one from the Barrett 'ouse so much as stuck their nose outside today." He glanced at Mrs. Jeffries. "Do you want me to keep at it?"

"Of course, Wiggins." She decided that both the maid and the footman could use some encouragement. "Both you and Betsy must keep at it. You're both far too clever and far too valuable to us to stop now."

"I found out something," Mrs. Goodge announced. She waited till she had everyone's attention. "It seems Mr. Barrett isn't much of a gentleman."

"Course 'e's not," Wiggins interrupted. "Gents don't go about bashin' dogs on the 'ead." He reached down and stroked Fred, a mongrel who'd been adopted into the Witherspoon household some months earlier. Fred's tail thumped against the floor.

"We don't know for sure that Barrett did bash the dog," Smythe argued. "Accordin' to what I 'eard, he denied he'd touched the animal."

"We're getting off the point," Mrs. Jeffries said calmly. "I believe Mrs. Goodge was about to tell us something."

Mrs. Goodge's eyes narrowed ominously, "*If* everyone's finished, I'll continue. Now, as I was sayin'. I found out that Barrett is no gentleman." She paused and waited till there was utter silence. Even Fred had stopped banging his tail against the floor. Then she said, "He did the worst thing a man could do to a woman."

"Murdered her?" Luty asked.

"Ravished her?" Betsy guessed.

Mrs. Goodge shook her head at both these suggestions. She smiled triumphantly. "He left her at the altar."

"Nell's Bells!" Luty cried. "Is that all? Gettin' left at the altar ain't the *worst* that can happen to a body. Why, I can tell ya dozens of worst things than that; gettin' scalped, gettin' shanghaied, gettin' stuck in a blizzard and freezin'—"

"I think we get the point, madam," Hatchet interrupted smoothly.

"I think being left at the altar in front of a church full of people is quite enough," Mrs. Goodge snapped. "Imagine the pain, the humiliation, the disgrace . . ."

"Disgrace," Luty snorted, "Why should *she* be disgraced? He's the one who acted like a no-good skunk-bellied polecat."

"I suppose being jilted in such a public manner could be a motive for murder," Mrs. Jeffries mused.

"Murder! Humph!" Luty shouted. "If'n that woman stuck a sword through the varmint's heart, it weren't murder. It was justice."

# CHAPTER 4

Inspector Witherspoon wished that Adrian Spears would stop pacing. But he could hardly say so. After all, it was the man's home. "Now, Mr. Spears," he began for the third time, "we're questioning everyone who lives on these Gardens."

Spears stopped and stared at him. He was a short, middle-aged man with thick black hair liberally sprinkled with gray, dark brown eyes and a large misshapen nose that looked as though it had been broken a time or two. "I don't expect you'll find out very much. People have a natural reticence about speaking ill of the dead. Especially as we're talking about a murder here. But rest assured, Inspector, regardless of what others say, I wasn't the only one of his neighbours who loathed Barrett."

"We're aware of the fact that most of Mr. Barrett's neighbours didn't care for him," the inspector replied. "His own staff admitted that much. But—"

"Neighbours!" Spears exclaimed. "His neighbours were the least of his problems. The man was being sued by practically everyone who'd ever done business with him. If I were you, I'd stop wasting my time questioning us about our petty squabbles and get on to the people who had real motives for wanting him dead."

"And who would that be?" Barnes asked softly.

"Thornton Astley for one," Spears replied, pacing again. "He's filed a lawsuit. Barrett cheated him in a business deal. He actually stole money."

"Why would this Mr. Astley kill him if he was getting ready to take him to court?" the inspector asked.

Spears lip curled. "To save himself the cost of a solicitor. No doubt once he heard how much it would cost him to take Barrett to court, he decided to take matters into his own hands." He clamped his mouth shut, closed his eyes and sighed. "Forgive me, Inspector. I didn't mean that. Thornton Astley is an honourable man, I know him socially. He wouldn't murder someone, no matter how much he deserved it."

Witherspoon started in surprise. Deserved it? He didn't think anyone *deserved* to be murdered, and he certainly was rather shocked to hear a seemingly respectable man say such a thing. "Could you tell us about your dispute with Mr. Barrett?"

"Which one?" Spears asked. "Barrett's been a thorn in my side from the day he moved into the Gardens. He's been a thorn in everyone's side."

Witherspoon made a mental note to come back to that issue. But for right now he was most interested in another incident. "I'm referring to the death of your dog," he said.

"You mean his murder," Spears said softly, his voice suddenly shaky. He blinked rapidly to hold back tears. "Poor King, he never had a chance. Barrett slaughtered my dog, Inspector, and for that act alone, I'm glad the bastard's dead. Anyone capable of killing a helpless animal deserves to die."

Witherspoon didn't approve of killing dogs. He could certainly understand Mr. Spears's sentiments, but goodness, he hoped the man would bring himself under control. It would be very difficult to question a man who was blubbering, very difficult, indeed. "Er . . . why did Barrett kill your dog?"

Spears turned his back and stared at the brass candlestick on the carved mantel. He took a long, deep breath before answering. "He never liked King," he said softly. "Barrett had the gardener plant bulbs over in the beds outside his house. He accused King of digging them up. Claimed the dog barked at all hours and was generally a nuisance. But it wasn't true. King was well trained." He whirled around and gestured with his hands. "Oh, occasionally he barked—what dog doesn't? But he didn't go near Barrett's wretched plants."

"Were the flower beds dug up?" Witherspoon was sure that was completely irrelevant, but he was curious and he wanted to keep Spears talking.

"Of course not," Spears gestured impatiently. "Oh, there were a few spots here and there where the dirt had been disturbed. But that doesn't mean it was King that had done it. The garden is full of cats and dogs."

"But apparently, Mr. Barrett was convinced your King had done the digging?" the inspector prompted. "Why? Why single out your animal for that kind of revenge."

"He's hated me for a long time. He was always looking for an excuse to be unpleasant."

"And why was that, sir?" Barnes asked, looking up from his notebook.

"Because I bought this house right from under his nose," Spears said with a note of triumph in his voice. "Barrett had offered on it, but his offer came in after mine did and I was willing to pay more to get it. Barrett was furious. Threatened to sue the estate agents and myself. Naturally, he'd not a leg to stand on. He ended up buying the house next door to me, but, of course, he never forgave me for getting this one."

Spears paused and gazed round the drawing room, an expression of intense pride on his face. Witherspoon could well understand why the man was proud.

Dark, rich wood panelling accented the lower half of the walls. The upper half was painted a deep forest green. Paintings of the English countryside and several well-done portraits softened the masculine decor. Unlike many drawing rooms, this one wasn't overly furnished. A settee, several comfortable chairs and a table or two, and that was it. A carved marble mantel and a polished hardwood floor gave the exquisitely furnished room an air of wealth and dignity. An air that was distinctly missing in the Barrett house.

"Barrett," Spears continued after he'd finished his slow perusal of the room, "wasn't one to forgive and forget. After he moved in here, he was less than neighbourly. I did my best to be civil, of course. We were frequently at the same social gatherings."

"These social acquaintances you had in common?" Witherspoon queried, somewhat hesitantly. He was guessing on this point, but sometimes he'd found a guess could pay off tremendous dividends. "That's somewhat confusing. If, as you say, Barrett was habitually unpleasant . . ."

"He was never overt when he was a guest in someone else's home," Spears replied. "I tell you, the man was an utter hypocrite. He had no compunction about stabbing you in the back one minute and then acting as though you were a long-lost friend the next. It was appalling. But what was even worse was how successful it was. Take the Astleys for instance. Here they were suing Barrett, yet he fully intended to show up at their dinner party last night."

"Why did the Astleys invite him?" Witherspoon asked.

"They invited him some time ago. Maud Astley had planned this dinner for months. Naturally, when they brought suit against him, they expected he'd send his regrets. But the man actually had the gall to send Maud a message last week telling her he was looking forward to seeing her." He shook his head in disgust.

"I see," the inspector said slowly.

Barnes cleared his throat. "You were going to tell us about yesterday afternoon," he said to Spears. "About your dog, sir."

Anguish flared briefly in the man's eyes and he quickly turned away. Witherspoon threw Barnes an appreciative nod. Sometimes he quite forgot where he was when he was questioning people.

"Yesterday afternoon I noticed King was missing." Spears spoke so softly both the policemen had to lean toward him to hear. "I was worried."

"Were you worried for any particular reason?" the inspector asked. "Or merely because Barrett had been so generally unpleasant?"

"I had a reason. Barrett had thrown stones at the poor dog only the day before. One of them had hit him quite hard in his forepaw, and I was concerned about him being outside and unprotected." He smiled sadly. "King was such a sweet-natured animal that he wouldn't think to run if Barrett came out and began abusing him. In any case, no one in the household had seen the animal, so I called out the servants and we started to search for him out in the gardens." His voice dropped to a whisper. "You know what I found. King was lying in the foliage behind Barrett's house. His head had been bashed in with a hammer."

"I thought you said there were flower beds behind Mr. Barrett's house?" the inspector asked, puzzled.

"There are both. Each house has two planting beds bisected by a small path that leads to the communal garden. Most of the owners have generally agreed to plant the same sorts of things, give the gardens an air of continuity, or refinement. But not Barrett. He hadn't been here more than two weeks before he had the gardeners putting bushes and shrubs in one of his beds and those blasted bulbs in the other. That's one of the things the other neighbours didn't like about him. He didn't give a fig for what the rest of us wanted. Those were his wretched beds and by God, he'd put what he liked in them whether it made the garden look ridiculous or not." Spears made a derisive sound. "Believe me, Inspector. It did make the gardens look ridiculous too. Not that Barrett had the good taste to notice. He was actually proud of what he'd done, was showing those silly beds off to one of his acquaintances the day before yesterday. That's when he threw the rocks at poor King. And all the dog wanted to do was be friendly. I tell you, Barrett was a dreadful man. Positively dreadful."

"How unfortunate," the inspector murmured. He thought it an odd way to behave. But he hardly saw a quarrel over flower beds as a motive for murder.

"What time did you go lookin' for your dog, sir?" Barnes asked.

"Late in the afternoon, about four-thirty or five o'clock. I don't remember exactly. But it was getting quite dark."

"And you immediately went to Barrett's house?"

"No," Spears admitted. "I was so enraged I stood there and bellowed for the blackguard to come out and face me. The bastard had the sheer effrontery to demand we get off his beds!"

"Was he angry?"

"He was always angry," Spears said with relish. "But this time I was enraged. When I yanked the bushes back and showed him poor King's body, he acted as though it were my fault. Completely denied he'd had anything to do with the dog's death. I knew he was lying, of course. We quarreled."

"We understand you did more than quarrel," Witherspoon said bluntly. "According to witnesses, you attacked Mr. Barrett."

"I did," Spears confessed. "And I'm not the least bit sorry."

Witherspoon sighed silently. This case was getting more ridiculous by the minute. Not that the death of a beloved pet was absurd, he could understand that. He'd be most upset if someone harmed his beloved Fred. What truly amazed him was the way two seemingly adult men had behaved over the entire episode. "Had anyone seen Mr. Barrett in the garden? Did you have any witnesses that Barrett had actually been the one to kill King?"

"Barrett claimed he hadn't been out there all day." Spears laughed derisively. "But what else could he say? He didn't want to admit to being such a savage in front of everyone. Ye Gods, Inspector, there were dozens of people watching us. My servants, his servants, some neighbours, even the workmen who were redoing his house came out to watch."

"Did you threaten to kill him, sir?" Witherspoon asked. As a motive, vengeance over a murdered pet might seem farfetched to most people. But as a policeman, the inspector knew that even wealthy intelligent men like Adrian Spears were capable of committing heinous crimes if sufficiently provoked. And Spears certainly must have been provoked, But angry enough to murder? To take a human life?

"I didn't mean it, of course," he muttered. "But yes, I did threaten him. Pembroke, my butler, had the good sense to intervene before things got too heated." He smiled sadly. "Pembroke's been with me a long time and he knew how much King meant to me."

"I see. Was that the last time you saw Mr. Barrett?" Witherspoon asked.

"Yes, thank God. At least I was spared the sight of the man over the dinner table."

"Where were you between six and seven yesterday afternoon?"

Spears looked surprised by the question. "I went for a walk. For God's sake, man, I'd just found my dog with his head bashed in. . . . I needed to get it out of my system. So I went out to be on my own for a while and came home about six-twenty or so. I was due at the Astley house at seven."

"Where did you walk?" the inspector pressed.

Spears hesitated before answering. "I'm not really sure. . . . I was most upset, Inspector. As well as I can remember, I walked 'round the gardens to Kildare Terrace and out onto Talbot Road."

"Did anyone see you?"

"Of course not. It was quite dark by that time. I walked for about an hour, came home, poured myself a good-sized whiskey and got ready to go to the Astleys'. The last time I saw William Barrett, he was alive and well."

"Oh, no, what am I going to do?" Mrs. Goodge wailed. She shook her head as she stared at the telegram in her hand. "I can't leave now! We're on a murder."

"But you must go," Mrs. Jeffries insisted. "You'll never forgive yourself if your aunt . . . uh, passes on and you didn't go to see her."

"Bloomin' Ada!" Mrs. Goodge cried, for once so upset she didn't care if she used strong language. "Why now? Aunt Elberta's never had a sick day in her life."

"Well," Mrs. Jeffries said soothingly, "she is getting along in years. And it has been dreadfully cold lately. It's no wonder the poor old dear has pneumonia."

"I've got to go, don't I?" Mrs. Goodge shook her head sadly and tucked the telegram into the pocket of her apron. "She's got to be eighty-five if she's a day. What do you think the inspector'll say when he gets back and finds me gone? Do you think he'll mind?"

"Of course he won't mind," Mrs. Jeffries assured her. "Inspector Witherspoon would be the first to tell you you must go. Why, your dear aunt may be failing—he'd never forgive himself if he kept you from her sickbed."

"Do you think I can get a train today?" Mrs. Goodge asked, looking anxiously at the clock. "It's already gone two."

"You go get packed," Mrs. Jeffries told her firmly. "I'll check my timetable and see when the next train for Devonshire leaves."

"But who's going to get the goods on Barrett?" Mrs. Goodge wailed. She looked at the tray of fragrant brown buns cooling on the kitchen table, her expression mournful. "Who's going to question my sources? I've got half of London due in here this afternoon and tomorrow."

"Now, now. Don't worry," Mrs. Jeffries said as she gently shoved the cook toward the stairs. "I'll take care of your sources. Go get packed. I'm fairly certain there's a late afternoon train today. But you must hurry, you don't want to miss it."

Muttering mutinously about crotchety old ladies taking it into their heads to get ill at the worst times, Mrs. Goodge trudged off to her room.

Mrs. Jeffries thought it amusing that Mrs. Goodge wasn't in the least concerned about who was going to cook for them.

Betsy smiled at the young man walking beside her. He was no more than sixteen, red-haired, with a pale complexion sprinkled with freckles and spots. Underneath his overcoat he wore a footman's uniform.

"I 'eard there was murder in that 'ouse," she said, nodding towards the Barrett home with her chin. "Cor, it fair gives me a queer feelin' it does, just walkin' by the place."

She deliberately mangled her speech, and she was smiling so hard her cheeks hurt. But she couldn't afford to miss this chance. The shop assistant at the fishmonger's had pointed the young man out. He worked at the

Spears house. When Betsy saw the way he stared at her, she'd tossed her curls and given him her boldest smile. Let him think she was loose and had no morals; she didn't care. The footman worked next door to Barrett's. Not as good as actually talking to someone from the victim's house, but close.

"Don't worry, miss," he said, puffing put his chest. "I'll walk you to the end of the street. No one'll bother ya if you're with me."

"Do you work 'round 'ere, then?" she asked, flashing him another smile.

"Right next door to where the murder happened," he said.

"Oh, you must be ever so brave," she replied. "Why, I couldn't sleep knowin' there'd been murder done so close." It never hurt to butter them up a bit, Betsy thought. She'd noticed that men would believe the most outrageous flattery.

"Don't bother me none," he said, slowing his footsteps as they neared the house.

"But what if it's one of them maniacs?" she persisted.

"Nah, it were someone who hated Mr. Barrett," the footman said easily. "I don't expect they'll come back and kill anyone else."

"Whyever not?"

"It was Barrett they was after. Mind you, I'm not surprised. If anyone was askin' to get done in, it was 'im. My own master had a row with him yesterday, not that Mr. Spears would ever do murder, but it just goes to show what kind of man this Barrett was. A real brute if you ask me."

As Betsy already knew about Spears's altercation with Barrett, she didn't need to hear about that. She wanted to go back to Upper Edmonton Gardens with something new. "Did this Mr. Barrett have a lot of enemies?"

"Just about everyone who knew him." He jerked his chin toward the late unlamented Mr. Barrett's house. "My guv hated him. Course I don't much blame him. He killed Mr. Spears's dog. Nice dog it was too, real friendly old feller. Course that's put everyone in an uproar."

"Well, an animal gettin' killed is pretty awful," she said quickly, "but—"

"Oh," he continued blithely, "it weren't just King gettin' done in that's got everyone all het up. Janie, that's one of the maids, is scared she's goin' to lose her position and Matilda's shakin' in her shoes as well. Course I told 'em, if they keeps quiet, no one will know that Janie left the door open. That's how King got out, ya see."

She didn't care how the dog had gotten out. She wanted more information. "Did—"

He continued on as if she hadn't spoken. Betsy wondered if he was deaf. "And now Matilda, that's one of the upstairs maids, is wonderin' if she'll be sacked 'cause she didn't tell Mr. Spears that it were Janie that left the door open in the first place."

"Did you hear anything about the murder?" she asked, interrupting him and knowing it was rude. But they were almost at the end of the road and she was desperate.

"Huh?" The boy stared at her in such shocked surprise that she thought she might have made a big mistake.

She gave him a big smile. "I mean, I hope you don't mind my askin', but someone like you, you seem so smart an' all. I thought you might have found out somethin' even the police don't know."

"Well . . ." He blushed to the roots of his hair. "I've always prided myself on knowing what's what, if you get my meanin'."

"I do." She couldn't believe it. He believed every word she said.

"Well, I don't rightly know much about the actual killin'," he said. "But I do know that he was havin' some kind of a row with a woman the night before he died. Don't likely think a woman could have killed him, but that just goes to show that he weren't really a gentleman."

"What woman?" Betsy asked softly. She had to be careful here. She had him talking; she didn't want to make a mistake.

"Don't know what her name was," the lad replied. "But she and Barrett were havin' a fierce row the night before last. I heard them arguin' when I took out the ashes to the dustbin."

"Maybe he was just havin' a row with 'is missus," she suggested.

"Barrett weren't married."

She sniffed. "Well, you're right, then. No gentlemen has a row out in public."

"They wasn't in public," he said, laughing. "That's why I thought it was so strange. They was in the gardens and it had gone on eight o'clock. But there they was, standin' behind some bushes hissin' at each other like a couple of cats."

"Did ya 'ear what they was on about?"

"Nah, but I could tell they was squabblin'. He weren't out there with the lady to steal a kiss or anythin' like that."

"Wonder who the woman is?" she mused. "Course we'll never know. With this Mr. Barrett bein' dead, it would take someone really clever to find out who he'd been squabblin' with." She glanced up at him through her lashes to see if he'd taken the bait. By the thoughtful expression on his face, she thought he had.

"I reckon someone could find out," he said slowly. "But why are you so interested?"

She shrugged. "Everyone's interested in murder. That's why they put it in the newspapers. I'm just curious, that's all."

They'd come to the end of the Kildare Terrace. Betsy stared out at Talbot Road. She could feel his gaze on her and she shifted uncomfortably. He was a nice lad and she was taking shameless advantage of him to get information.

"Uh, do you work 'round here?" he asked hesitantly.

"Not far," she replied.

He looked around suddenly. "I'd best be gettin' back. They only sent me out to get a newspaper."

"Oh." She contrived to look crestfallen. "It was ever so nice of you to walk me this far. I don't usually get lost." She had given him a silly tale of getting lost trying to find a shortcut while out on an errand for her mistress. "But I must say, havin' you with me made me feel ever so much safer. Thank you."

"Uh, look, if'n I could be so bold—" He paused and took a deep breath.

"Yes," she prompted. Betsy knew she'd hate herself later. The lad obviously was taken with her. She was far too old for him and she wasn't interested in him. But this was murder, so she wasn't above flirting a bit to get the information she needed.

He opened his mouth to speak just as a four-wheeler clattered past, one of its wheels creaking so loudly she didn't hear a word the lad said.

"Uh, if'n I can be so bold," he repeated, blushing furiously. "I'd like to see ya again."

"I'd like that," she replied, ignoring the nasty voice of her conscience. "You seem like a nice chap. Tell you what, I'll be along here tomorrow about this time. Maybe you can slip out and we can have another walk."

"Tomorrow?" He looked puzzled. "But I thought you said you only come this way 'cause you was lost?"

She thought fast. "I am lost." She laughed coquettishly. "But I go out every afternoon to get my mistress her chocolates. She likes them fresh. I'll make certain I get lost this way tomorrow."

A slow, pleased smile crept over his face. Betsy couldn't believe it. Men would believe any old load of rubbish you told them, as long as it was *them* you was butterin' up! She was torn between wanting to box his ears for believing such a silly tale and thanking her lucky stars he was so gullible.

"Well, in that case, I reckon I can find an excuse to get out. By the way, my name's Noah. Noah Parnell."

"I'll see ya tomorrow, then, Noah." She started across the street, then stopped and looked back at him. "Oh, and I do say, I think it's ever so clever of you to know so much about that murder."

"I'll tell you more tomorrow," he promised.

Betsy dashed across the road and started down the other side.

"Hey!" he yelled. "What's yer name?"


Thornton Astley was a man of about fifty, still youthful looking, though there was plenty of grey streaked through his dark auburn hair. Clean-shaven, his eyes were a clear, cool grey. His face was relatively unlined, though there was the hint of sagging flesh beneath his chin.

His wife, seated next to him on the overstuffed burgundy settee, was stunningly beautiful and a good thirty years younger than her husband. Small, blond-haired and blue-eyed, Maud Astley reminded the inspector of one of those lovely china dolls he'd seen in the window of a shop on Regent Street.

A third person, a thin, rather attractive young man with a full mustache, dark brown hair and deep set hazel eyes sat a respectful distance away from the Astleys. He was Mr. Astley's private secretary, Neville Sharpe.

"I don't think we can tell you anything about this unfortunate business," Thornton Astley said. "We haven't seen Barrett for some time."

"I believe he was due to have dinner with you last evening?" Witherspoon replied.

"He never arrived," Mrs. Astley said coolly. "We held dinner as long as we could, but finally Cook was getting most upset, so we went in."

"Didn't you wonder why Mr. Barrett hadn't come?" the inspector asked. Surely, he thought, they'd be somewhat curious when an expected guest failed to turn up.

Astley shrugged. "Not really. Barrett wasn't exactly what one would call a gentleman."

"Then why did you invite him to dine at your home?"

The Astleys exchanged a quick, furtive glance.

"Barrett was a business acquaintance," Astley said. "We'd extended the invitation some time ago. He might not have been a gentleman, but I am."

"When did you decide to sue Mr. Barrett?" Witherspoon watched him closely, but Astley's expression didn't change. The inspector realized that the man was prepared for the question. Drat. He'd so hoped to take him by surprise. Sometimes one could learn so much by a person's reaction to an unexpected question.

"So you know about that." Astley replied. "I'm not surprised. I've made no secret of my opinion of the man. Naturally, as I was suing the bounder, I'd hoped he'd have the decency to stay away from my home. But he actually had the gall to send my wife a note saying he was looking forward to seeing her. Unbelievable, really. But that was the kind of man he was. As to when I decided to sue him, it was some weeks ago." He turned to his secretary. "Do you recall exactly when, Sharpe?"

"You contacted your solicitor two weeks ago," he answered. "Sometime around the fourth or the fifth."

"That's right," Astley agreed. "However, Inspector, you should also know, I had decided to drop the lawsuit. Frankly, it would have cost me a great deal more than I could ever hope to recover from Barrett."

"That's true, Inspector," Mrs. Astley added.

Witherspoon was really puzzled now. "Precisely what was it Barrett had done to you?" he asked.

"Stolen a great deal of money." Astley grimaced. "And it was my own fault. You see, there'd been rumours about the man for ages. But I ignored them. Didn't place any credence in them at all."

"You're too hard on yourself, dear," Mrs. Astley interrupted. "You couldn't be expected to take gossip and innuendo seriously."

"Yes, but I should have been more careful," he replied. "I needed a partner for one of my business ventures. A building company. I've a number of business ventures and frequently take in partners because I can't run them all."

"And Barrett ran this building company?" the inspector prompted.

"Oh, yes. We weren't making huge profits, but I thought nothing of it—it was a new concern and growing. Then my secretary"—he glanced at the young man sitting behind him—"brought some invoices to my attention. Invoices the company had paid. He told me I ought to investigate them. I did so. Barrett had been paying false invoices to accounts that did not exist. Further investigation revealed he'd been doing this virtually since we went into business together."

"So you were going to take him to court?" Barnes asked softly.

"Yes, more fool I." He shook his head in disgust. "I knew there was talk about Barrett, I'd heard the rumours. But I was in a bind, Barrett had ready cash to go into the business, and I thought he had the ability to run the company. It was a rather good opportunity and I didn't want to let it slip away. So instead of investigating him as I should have, I blindly plunged ahead."

The inspector nodded sympathetically. "What kind of rumours, sir?"

"Let me see, well"—he frowned slightly—"supposedly he'd left some poor woman standing at the altar."

"Really, Thornton," Maud Astley said quietly. "I don't think that's the kind of rumour the inspector is interested in."

"But it shows the man's character, Maud," he argued. "Shows what he was capable of doing. And then there was that awful business with that poor chap who hanged himself. Of course, that was fifteen years ago. Now, what was the man's name. Blumm, Borden . . ."

"Blunt, sir," Neville Sharp said. "Thomas Blunt."

"Oh, yes." Astley nodded. "And there are all sorts of rumours about Washburn."

The inspector was thoroughly confused but determined not to show it. "Washburn?"

Astley smiled tightly. "His current business partner. One of the reasons I went into business with Barrett was that he was already overseeing what I thought was another thriving business. Washburn and Tate. They're also builders, but they do commercial property outside of London, so there wouldn't be any conflict of interest or competition between the two firms. Then, of course, I heard about Owen Washburn."

"What about him?" Witherspoon hoped Barnes was taking excellent notes. This was getting most confusing.

Astley hesitated briefly. "Some say that Barrett blackmailed the man to do business with him."

"Really, Thornton!" Maud looked embarrassed. "You must be careful what you say."

"Why? One can't libel the dead, and if Barrett weren't dead, these men wouldn't be here."

"I mean you mustn't say anything about Mr. Washburn," she corrected. "That family has coped with enough disgrace."

"Disgrace?" Witherspoon queried.

"I really mustn't say more," Mrs. Astley said, her porcelain cheeks flaming. "It would be most unkind."

The inspector smiled sympathetically. "I appreciate your position, Mrs. Astley," he said softly. "But this is a murder investigation."

She looked at her husband, who nodded, encouraging her to go on. "Very well, then. It was Mr. Washburn's sister that Mr. Barrett left standing at the altar. It was so humiliating for the poor woman. He'd not even the decency to come to the church himself. He sent a cabbie in with a note. Poor Miss Washburn fainted—and in front of the bishop too!"

"How dreadful!" Witherspoon exclaimed. Gracious, sometimes it was so very difficult to have much sympathy with the victim. William Barrett sounded like a most disagreeable person. Imagine leaving a poor woman standing at the altar in front of all her relations, friends and acquaintances.

"It was," she agreed. "Most dreadful. No one could quite understand why Mr. Washburn continued to do business with Barrett after that. But if the rumours we've heard are correct, I don't really think he had all that much choice."

"Of course he did," Thornton Astley corrected. "He should have refused to have anything more to do with the blighter. I know I certainly did when I caught him cheating me. I immediately took action."

"How did you do that, sir?" Witherspoon asked curiously.

Astley blinked. It was Neville Sharpe who answered. "Mr. Astley instructed his solicitors to dissolve the partnership."

"Yes, but precisely how does one do that?" the inspector persisted. He hadn't the faintest idea how one dissolved a partnership, especially as there seemed to be money involved.

"My solicitors drew up papers formally dissolving it," Astley replied stiffly. "They also put my half of the company on the block."

"Does that mean that Mr. Barrett bought you out?" Barnes asked.

Astley's eyes grew cold. "He would have, eventually."

Witherspoon leaned forward. "If you weren't going to sue the man, how could you have persuaded him to buy you out?"

"Barrett didn't know I was dropping the suit," Astley explained. "He was quite upset about it as well. I suspect that's why he was planning on coming to dine with us. No doubt he wanted to find out just where he stood. Believe me, Inspector, I wasn't going to let him off the hook until I got his agreement to buy me out."

"I see," the inspector said, though he wasn't sure he did. "Mr. Astley, where were you yesterday afternoon between six and seven o'clock?"

Astley's jaw dropped.

"Really, Inspector," Sharpe said angrily. "I hope you're not implying that Mr. Astley—"

"I'm implying nothing," Witherspoon replied. Gracious, this was so tedious. How did people think homicides got solved if the police didn't ask simple questions?

Astley clamped his mouth shut. "I was working at my office in the city."

"Did anyone see you there?"

"No, the staff had gone home. I worked here for most of the afternoon and didn't get to the office until about half past five. I stayed for about a half an hour and then came home to get ready for dinner."

"Was Mr. Sharpe with you?"

"No."

"I went to the dentist," the secretary hastily explained. "Mr. Astley kindly gave me some free time so I could take care of a tooth that had been bothering me."

"How long have you worked for Mr. Astley?"

Sharpe smiled slightly. "Six months. I had a position in Birmingham before I came here."

"I assure you," Astley snapped, "my secretary barely knew William Barrett. His private business isn't any of Scotland Yard's concern."

"Nevertheless," Sharpe said quickly, "I'll be happy to tell you the name of my dentist. It's Pellman. He's got offices on the Richmond Road."

"Thank you, Mr. Sharpe." Witherspoon had the feeling there was something he was forgetting to ask. But he couldn't, for the life of him, think of what it was. "Mrs. Astley, did the other guests at your dinner party know William Barrett?"

"What has that got to do with anything?" Astley asked harshly.

"I'm merely wondering if the other guests were concerned when Mr. Barrett failed to arrive?" He knew he'd asked what seemed like a pointless question, but as Mrs. Jeffries frequently said, sometimes it was those kinds of questions that gave you the right answers.

Maud Astley shrugged helplessly. "I don't know how to reply, Inspector. No one was in the least concerned when he didn't arrive. Why should they be? None of them were overly fond of the man, and I know for a fact that Minerva Kenny absolutely loathed him."

# CHAPTER 5

———◆◇◆———

Smythe glanced over his shoulder, hoping that no one he knew would happen to come into the bank. "If you don't mind, Mr. Pike"—he turned his attention back to the white-haired banker—"I'm in a bit of a 'urry 'ere. Could ya get on with it, please."

Mr. Bartholomew Pike narrowed his eyes slightly. He was not of the nervous nature of his predecessor, a man Smythe had easily intimidated into leaving him alone. Mr. Pike was not going to be bullied. They had serious business to discuss here. Money. Decisions had to be made. "This matter is most important, Mr. Smythe," Pike said calmly. "You made enormous profits off the selling of your interests in those American cattle ranches. You must do something with it."

"Can't ya just leave it in my account?" Cor blimey, Smythe thought, wasn't that what bloomin' banks was for, hangin' on to cash? "I don't have time to make any decisions now, I'm in the middle of—" He clamped his mouth shut. He'd almost said he was in the middle of investigatin' a murder. Cor, the old boy would probably 'ave a stroke if he'd let that slip. "Something important."

Pike appeared not to hear him. "I strongly advise you that leaving that amount of money in a general account is most foolish. There are any number of investments you should consider."

"And I told ya, I don't 'ave time," Smythe snapped, losing his patience. The business about his money was becomin' more than an irritation. It was becomin' a ruddy pain in the arse.

It were bad enough he had to hide the fact that he was a wealthy man from everyone he cared about in this world. Now this bloomin' banker was takin' to pesterin' him about every little detail. "I'll 'ave to come round next week and we'll discuss it then."

"You said that last week," Pike reminded him. "Mr. Smythe, we're talking about thirty thousand pounds. By most estimates, that's a small fortune."

"I know how much it is," Smythe said sharply. "Now, if you don't mind, I'll have that cash I asked ya to 'ave ready fer me."

Pike's mouth hardened into a thin, flat line, then he lifted his hand and gestured toward the young bank clerk. Holding a pouch, the clerk scurried forward and handed it to the stiff-necked banker. "Here you are, Mr. Smythe." Pike handed him the pouch. "I'll send you a letter early next week reminding you to come in. We'll make an appointment at your convenience."

Smythe shoved the pouch into his coat pocket. He wasn't sure gettin' letters from banks was a good idea. Then again, people 'ad bank accounts. Even Wiggins 'ad opened a post office account. But Mrs. Jeffries was gettin' suspicious. He could see it in her eyes every time he bought a little gift for one of the household. Not that they knew the gifts come from him. They didn't 'ave a clue and that's just the way he wanted to keep it. But the housekeeper was gettin' close. "That'll be fine, Mr. Pike."

Smythe pondered the problem of his money as he hurried out of the bank. He turned in the direction of the Bishopsgate Underground Station, dodging around a cooper's wagon and a costermonger to cross the street. He knew that one day he'd have to tell them the truth, but not yet. He couldn't stand the thought of them treatin' 'im differently. Of not bein' one of them.

It was all Euphemia's fault, he decided. God rest her soul. He should never 'ave gone along with pretendin' to be 'er ruddy coachman when he came back from Australia . . . but, at the time, it seemed like a grand idea. Then she'd up and died, makin' 'im promise to stay on and keep an eye on her nephew, Inspector Witherspoon. Euphemia had been convinced either a fortune hunter or a confidence man would separate her Witherspoon from his inheritance. He'd stayed on, not just to look out for the inspector but to make sure Wiggins had a place in the household too. By the time he'd realized the inspector was innocent but not stupid, Mrs. Jeffries, Mrs. Goodge and Betsy had come. They was investigatin' murders and lookin' out for each other and actin' like a family of sorts. No, he couldn't stand the idea of givin' all that up. Not yet. Not until he knew for sure there was no hope for him and Betsy havin' a future together.

"Really, madam, you're not being very subtle," Hatchet hissed as soon as he was alone with his employer. "These things call for tact and diplomacy."

"I got plenty of tact," Luty shot back. She glared at her butler. "You're just jealous 'cause I got old Tilbert to spill his guts and you ain't found out nothin' yet."

"I would hardly call one vague reference to the victim, 'spilling his—'" Hatchet broke off as the door opened and an elderly gentleman, a large bound volume tucked under his arm, moved slowly into the room. "Excuse me for taking so long, Luty," he said. "But it took a few moments to remember where I'd put this."

"May I help you with that, sir?" Hatchet asked. Unlike Luty, he wasn't sitting down in front of a tea table but stood stiffly at her back. That was the only way he could get in to hear everything that went on. Generally butlers were banished to the servants' hall during social calls. However, Luty being an eccentric American, insisted on keeping him close. Most of the people she called upon had gotten used to him hanging about.

Old Tilbert gratefully handed the heavy volume to him. "If you'd be so kind as to spread it open on the settee, Luty won't have to move. You'll see it's my clippings." He smiled proudly. "I've been collecting them for years. Now, what was that name again, Luty. Parrett?"

"Barrett," Luty corrected. "William Barrett."

She'd come to see her old friend because he had once been someone important in the City. But that had been years ago. Now he was old, alone and spent most of his time cutting out newspaper articles about anyone and everyone who did business in London. When it came to gossip in the business community or in the City, Tilbert could be counted on to know it all. "Have you ever heard of him?"

"You needn't repeat yourself, Luty," Tilbert said patiently. "I'm not completely senile yet. I remember what you asked. As I told you, the name does sound familiar, Give me a moment or two to think on it. In the meantime, amuse yourself by looking at my clippings. Perhaps you'll find something useful there."

Luty nodded. From behind her, she heard Hatchet stifle a snicker.

Luckily, Tilbert was slightly deaf, so he didn't hear a thing. She leaned forward and began turning the pages.

"Barrett, Barrett, Barrett," Tilbert muttered softly. "Shipping agent, I believe. For one of the South American companies. Or was that another Barrett?"

Luty turned more pages, her eyes skimming stories about share prices, bond slumps, investment opportunities in Malaysian tea plantations and bankruptcies.

"No, no, I believe it was William Barrett," Tilbert said loudly. "That's right. He was in partnership in a shipping firm up in Liverpool a few years back. Yes, yes, now I recall it well. Barrett sold his interest in the agency right before it went under." Tilbert laughed loudly. "How clever I am— 'went under' and it was a shipping agency. Sinking ships."

Luty gave him a weak smile. Nell's Bells, Tilbert was gettin' worse all the time. Course he always did make bad jokes. "That was mightly clever, Tilbert. So you're sayin' William Barrett sold his interest in this agency right afore it went bankrupt?"

"That's right. There was some speculation that Barrett had been stealing money from the firm . . . but no one ever proved anything. He disappeared for a while after that."

"Who else was involved in the bankruptcy?" Luty asked. Maybe someone had skewered Barrett because of old grievances. Wouldn't be the first time someone had bided their time before takin' a little revenge.

Tilbert smiled sadly. "I'm sorry, Luty. I can't remember the names of the people involved, but I do know that there were whispers that Barrett had gotten his own money out and left the other partners to pay the piper so to speak."

"So first he bled the firm dry and then he yanked his own cash out?" Luty asked. Behind her, she could hear Hatchet clearing his throat. She grinned. Having to keep quiet was almost chokin' the man.

Tilbert cocked his head to one side, his wrinkled face tight in concentration. "That's what people said," he replied. "But remember, it was a long time ago." He straightened suddenly. "Chidwick!" he cried.

Luty tossed Hatchet a quick look over her shoulder. "Huh?"

"Lester Chidwick!" he yelled excitedly. "Talking about it has brought it all back. That's the name of one of the partners who went bankrupt . . . and there was someone else—" He broke off, concentrating again. After a few moments he slumped down in the chair. "I can't recall the name. But I think that one of the partners was totally ruined. There was a suicide. That's right. One of them threw himself off a bridge."

"When was this exactly?" she asked sharply.

"Oh, it was years ago." Tilbert waved his hand in the air. "Fifteen at least. Like I said, it happened in Liverpool. There's not much else I can tell you about this Mr. Barrett except that he's involved in a number of ventures. Let me see, he's partner in a building firm or two, and he's got interests in an ironworks and a rubber company." Tilbert shook his head. "He's got his fingers in a lot of pies, if I may use one of your more colorful expressions." He laughed again.

Owen Washburn was short, slender, dark-haired and sported a mustache. He motioned Inspector Witherspoon and Constable Barnes into the two straight-back chairs sitting in front of his desk. "What can I do for you, Inspector?"

"I take it you have heard of the death of your partner, Mr. William Barrett."

"You mean his murder." Washburn smiled faintly. "Of course I've heard, it's been in every newspaper."

Witherspoon nodded. "I understand you did business with Mr. Barrett?"

"Yes. As you mentioned, we were partners."

"How long had you been in business with Mr. Barrett?"

Washburn leaned back in his chair. "About six months. My former partner, James Tate, passed away last year. I didn't have the capital on hand to buy his share of the firm from his widow. Barrett did."

"Did Mr. Barrett take an active hand in running the business?"

"Yes, he did," Washburn replied. "But he had many business interests."

"When was the last time you saw Mr. Barrett?" Witherspoon asked. Drat, he was going to have to be most delicate here. But he was decidedly curious about Washburn. How could he have continued to do business with the man who'd publicly humiliated his own sister?

"The day before yesterday in the afternoon," Washburn answered promptly. "I stopped by Barrett's house to bring him some papers that required his signature."

"While you were at Barrett's that afternoon, did anything unusual happen?" Witherspoon asked.

"Unusual? Not really." Washburn thought about it for a moment. "The house was in a bit of a state. He had workmen on the third floor, and they were making such a racket with their banging and pounding that we went out into the garden to talk."

"Did anything happen while you were out in the garden?"

Washburn looked puzzled for a moment. "Oh, the dog. I see you've heard about that. It was rather disgusting, really. This little black-and-white spaniel came bounding over when we were standing by the terrace. Friendly little thing. Barrett picked up a handful of stones and began heaving them at the poor animal. Revolting, really. The dog wasn't doing anything. But Barrett claimed it was ruining his flower beds." His lip curled in disgust. "But then again, he wasn't a very nice man."

"Mr. Washburn, forgive me for bringing up a painful or embarrassing subject—"

"I know what you're going to ask," Washburn cut him off. "And Mr. Barrett's abominable treatment of my sister has nothing to do with his death. She was home all day yesterday."

"I wasn't accusing her of anything," the inspector said. "I was going to ask you why you continued to do business with Barrett after what he'd done."

"Unfortunately," Washburn replied, "I'd no choice in the matter. When Barrett bought into the firm, he brought a substantial amount of operating capital with him. When Tate died, some of our creditors, fearing that with Tate gone, the business wouldn't be as successful, demanded immediate payment. It put a strain on the company coffers. I needed Barrett's cash to keep the business operating."

"So Mr. Barrett really held the upper hand in the company?" the inspector said speculatively.

Washburn's eyes flashed angrily. "No one held the upper hand," he insisted. "We were partners. Furthermore, I'd managed to raise the money to buy him out. That's why I went to see him a couple of days ago. I took him the necessary documents to start the process. So you see, Inspector, I wasn't planning on continuing the relationship with the man."

"Would you mind telling me your whereabouts yesterday afternoon between six and seven?" The inspector fully expected Washburn to protest. They always did. But surprisingly, the man answered the question without hesitation.

"I was here, working in my study."

"Did anyone see you?"

"Well, it was the servants' afternoon out, but my sister was home."

The inspector drummed his fingers on the armrest. "May we speak to your sister?"

"I'd prefer that you didn't," Washburn protested. "Eliza is very nervous. What with the wedding being cancelled in such a shocking manner and Barrett's murder, she's been dreadfully upset."

"Why?" Witherspoon asked quickly. "Did she still have feelings of affection for him?"

"Certainly not!" Washburn snapped. "But she was engaged to him. For God's sake, they were supposed to marry only last month. Barrett might have behaved disgracefully, but my sister isn't an unfeeling monster. She certainly didn't hate him enough to want to see him brutally murdered."

"Mr. Washburn," Witherspoon said gently, "I fully appreciate how upset Miss Washburn must be. But as you said, Barrett was brutally murdered. I really must speak with your sister. Rest assured, I will be as discreet and delicate as possible."

Washburn glowered at the two policemen for a few moments then nodded curtly, stalked over to the bellpull hanging next to the door and gave it a hard yank.

A few moments later a maid hurried in, her white cap bobbing and her apron fluttering. "Yes, sir. You rang?"

"Could you ask Miss Eliza to join us," Washburn instructed. "And bring us some tea, please."

As soon as the maid left, Washburn resumed his seat.

"You've known Mr. Barrett for six months, is that correct?" Witherspoon asked. He couldn't think of anything else to ask, and sometimes it had proved helpful to get as much background information as possible.

"No, I said I'd been in business with him for six months," Washburn corrected. "I actually met him a little over a year ago."

"And where did you meet?"

"At the Astleys'. Mrs. Astley is a good friend of my sister's." Washburn closed his eyes for a brief moment. "Thornton Astley had just gone into business with him. Barrett seemed eminently respectable and appeared to have excellent prospects, so I had no objection to his courtship of my sister. We got to know him." He smiled bitterly. "I introduced him to my sister, and I was the one who suggested he contact James Tate's widow to buy into the company. God, I was a fool. The man brought us nothing but grief."

Witherspoon shot a quick look at the closed study door. There was one thing he wanted to ask before Miss Washburn arrived. "Did Barrett give you any reason for what he did to your sister?"

Washburn also glanced at the door. "He told me he realized he didn't love her."

"Did he tell Miss Washburn the same thing?"

"Oh, no, the note he sent her merely said she wouldn't make a suitable wife and that if they married it would be a grave mistake." Washburn slammed his hand against the top of the desk. "The bastard, I'm glad he's dead."

Mrs. Jeffries was exhausted. She'd coped with half a dozen people trooping into the kitchen looking for a nice natter with Mrs. Goodge, helped get the cook bundled off to Paddington Station, and she still had to do something about getting a meal ready.

She jumped as she heard footsteps coming down the hall. Lady Cannonberry's head popped round the corner. "Hello, Hepzibah, I do hope I'm not intruding. May I come in?"

"Of course, Ruth." Mrs. Jeffries started to get up, but her guest waved her back in the chair.

"I just thought I'd come round and give you a report," Ruth said, dropping gracefully into the chair next to her.

"A report?" Alarmed, Mrs. Jeffries stared at her. Goodness, did every living soul in London yearn to be a detective?

"About Barrett's murder. I've found out ever so much." Ruth gave her a cheerful smile. "First of all, Minerva was at the Astleys' last night for dinner, and of course, Barrett didn't arrive. Naturally, you know that. He was already dead. But what was interesting was that no one said a word, not one *word* about him! Well, don't you think it strange? I mean if one of my dinner guests didn't appear, I'd certainly comment on the situation."

"I suppose that could be considered unusual." Mrs. Jeffries glanced at the clock. Gracious, it was getting late.

"Exactly my thinking," Ruth said. "From what Minerva told me it sounded as though everyone at the Astleys' was avoiding the subject of Mr. William Barrett. She said it was the most peculiar evening. Everyone was nervous and jittery. Mr. Spears kept dropping his cutlery, people kept having to repeat themselves to Mr. Astley because he didn't appear to be listening to anyone, and Mrs. Astley dropped a glass of red wine all over her good damask tablecloth. Minerva said it was the most uncomfortable dinner party she's ever attended."

"Who all was there?" Mrs. Jeffries asked. She really didn't wish to be rude, but heavens, she had so much to do.

"Adrian Spears—he lives right next door to Barrett," Ruth explained. "And according to Minerva, the two absolutely loathed each other."

Mrs. Jeffries already knew that so she didn't pursue the matter, she just nodded. "Who else?"

"Both the Astleys and Mr. Astley's secretary, Neville Sharpe. Owen Washburn was supposed to come, but he'd sent his regrets. His sister, Eliza, had been invited too, but Minerva says she never goes anywhere these days, so no one expected her to come."

As Mrs. Jeffries already knew about Eliza Washburn, she didn't want to waste any precious time discussing it. "And who else?" she prompted before Ruth could repeat the gossip about Barrett leaving Miss Washburn at the altar.

Ruth paused. "Well, Minerva was there and some elderly gentleman who was visiting from Australia. I thought it might put your mind to rest to know that Minerva has an alibi."

"An alibi?"

"She was shopping." Ruth beamed proudly. "She was shopping all afternoon, and then she stopped for tea at Lyons. She didn't get home till almost seven. Her maid was most put out. She had to rush to get her ready for the dinner party. Naturally I didn't come right out and ask Minerva where she'd been. I was very subtle."

"I'm sure you were," Mrs. Jeffries said. "Wasn't she in the least curious as to how you'd managed to get the china bird from a dead man?"

"Not really." Ruth shrugged. "I merely told her a friend of mine had helped."

Mrs. Jeffries closed her eyes as a sudden realization hit her. They'd made a dreadful mistake. She should never have let Lady Cannonberry give that wretched china knickknack back to Minerva Kenny. Not until after this case was solved. "Oh, dear," she murmured.

"What is it?"

"We've done something very foolish and it's all my fault."

Alarmed, Ruth stared at her. "Your fault? What are you talking about?"

"I should have told you not to give the bird back to Miss Kenny."

"But whyever not?"

"Because the police are bound to talk to her. If she tells them anything about Barrett having that knickknack in his possession on the day he was killed, we're all in a great deal of trouble."

"Is that what's worrying you?" Ruth laughed softly. "Minerva won't say a word, I promise you. She'd rather die than have people find out about her uh . . . problem. Take my word for it, she'll not mention the bird at all."

"But what if someone else does?"

"Who else could possibly know about it?" Ruth said calmly. "Other than Minerva, the only person who knew she'd stolen it was William Barrett and he's dead."

Mrs. Jeffries sincerely hoped no one else knew about it. She knew Smythe hadn't killed Barrett, but he was in the house only moments after the murder had been committed. And he was there to steal. It might be in a good cause, but she didn't think the authorities would see it that way. "Do you mind if I have a chat with Miss Kenny?"

"Not at all," Ruth replied. "She's expecting you to call 'round. She's ever so grateful for your help. Of course, now she must think of a way to smuggle the bird back into the Astley house."

"I expect she'll come up with something," Mrs. Jeffries said. She glanced at the clock again and realized she'd better get the tea ready. They were all due back in less than half an hour, and after that, she'd have to cook some kind of supper.

Lady Cannonberry, correctly interpreting the housekeeper's expression, got up. "I'll run along now, Hepzibah. But do keep me informed as to your progress. I'll keep my ears open as well. One never knows when a clue will pop up."

"Thank you, Ruth." Mrs. Jeffries smiled weakly. "You've been a great help." She waited until her guest had disappeared and then she leapt into action. Domestic chores occupied her for the next half hour. She couldn't help thinking, as she sliced the bread, that if women didn't have to stop three or four times a day and feed a household, they could get ever so much more done.

Inspector Witherspoon was surprised by Eliza Washburn's appearance. She was quite lovely. Small and dark-haired, with the clearest blue eyes he'd ever seen. He didn't know why he was so taken aback by her appearance. Possibly because the mental image of a jilted woman was so at odds with the elegantly gowned and graceful lady sitting on the settee and pouring tea.

"Miss Washburn," he began, "er, I'd like to ask you a few questions."

"So I assumed, Inspector. Tea?" She arched one perfectly formed eyebrow and handed him his cup when he nodded an affirmative. "You'd like to speak to me about William's murder, correct?"

"That's correct," Witherspoon agreed. Perhaps this wouldn't be so difficult after all. She hadn't blushed or become hysterical at the mention of the man's name. That was certainly a good beginning.

"There's not really much I can tell you," she continued as she handed another cup to Constable Barnes. "I've had no contact with William Barrett since he broke off our engagement."

"When was that, exactly, miss?" Barnes asked.

"Last month." She cocked her head to one side and smiled. "I suppose you've heard the story, William Barrett left me at the altar. He humiliated me in front of everyone. Frankly, I'm not in the least bit upset that someone killed him."

"Eliza!" Owen Washburn gasped. "You really mustn't say things like that."

"Why not?" She shrugged. "It's perfectly true. The man was a cad, a bounder and a cheat. Eventually it had to catch up with him."

Witherspoon was rather surprised; she looked like such a gentle, delicate woman. Furthermore, she wasn't at all like the upset, nervous creature her brother had described. "Would you mind telling me where you were yesterday afternoon?" he asked.

"I was here."

"Alone."

"No. Owen was here as well. He was working in his study and I was taking a nap."

"I understand your servants were gone?" Witherspoon pressed. It never hurt to make doubly sure of the facts.

"It was their day out," Eliza said. "But Cook was here all afternoon."

"I didn't know that!" Owen exclaimed. "I thought she'd gone out as well."

Eliza Washburn smiled at her brother. "She wasn't feeling well, Owen. I think she may have that wretched influenza that's been going about. She spent the afternoon resting in her room."

"And where exactly is her room in the house?" the inspector asked. It would be so much simpler if the cook could verify that both the Washburns were safely at home at the time of the murder.

"On the third floor," Owen said. "She shares the box room with the maid."

"I'd like to speak to your cook," Witherspoon said. He put his teacup on the table next to him and rose to his feet.

"I'll get her," Owen said, starting to get up.

"That won't be necessary," the inspector said hastily, "If you'd be so kind as to point us in the direction of the kitchen, we'll have a quick word with her." The last thing the inspector wanted was one of his suspects hovering over the domestic who might be providing the alibis. Not that Washburn was yet a serious suspect. Unfortunately, Witherspoon thought, as yet he had no real suspects. Merely a number of people who seemed to loathe the victim.

"Very well." Washburn shrugged. "The kitchen's downstairs."

"Oh, do go with them, Owen," Eliza chided. "Mrs. Gantry will be frightened to death if two policemen come stumbling unannounced into her kitchen."

Before the inspector or Barnes could protest, Owen Washburn was leading them down into the kitchen.

"Mrs. Gantry," he said as they entered the room. "These men would like to ask you some questions. They're from Scotland Yard. This is Inspector Witherspoon and Constable Barnes."

"Coppers are they?" Mrs. Gantry, a tall, grey-haired woman wearing a cook's apron, wiped the flour off her hands. "Now, what do you want with the likes of me?"

"We'd merely like to ask you some questions." Witherspoon's stomach grumbled and his taste buds tingled. He and Barnes had had only time for a quick bite at lunchtime, and the tangy smell of simmering meat coming from the oven reminded him he was hungry.

"I expect you'd like to speak with Mrs. Gantry alone," Washburn said, excusing himself. "Have her bring you upstairs when you've finished."

Witherspoon smiled and nodded. Then he turned to the cook. "Were you here all afternoon yesterday?"

"Oh, yes." Mrs. Gantry went back to kneading the slab of dough on the table in front of her. "It were my day out, but I was feelin' poorly, so I stayed in and had a nice sleep."

"And how are you feeling today?" the inspector asked politely. He'd found that getting people to talk about themselves often proved most helpful.

"Much better." She slapped the dough one last time, picked it up and flopped it into a waiting bowl. "Miss Washburn insisted I have a nice glass of sherry yesterday afternoon. Right decent of her, I thought. Put me right out, it did. Just what I needed too, a good sleep. I got up this morning feelin' right as rain."

"Can you confirm that Mr. and Miss Washburn were in the house yesterday afternoon?" Witherspoon asked hopefully.

"Miss Washburn went to take her rest right after she give me the sherry, and Mr. Washburn was workin' in his study," Mrs. Gantry said easily. "And they was both still here when I woke up."

"What time was that?" Witherspoon spoke loudly; his stomach was starting to make embarrassing noises.

"About half past six. Dulcie, that's the maid, woke me when she come in."

Witherspoon nodded. "What time did you go to sleep?"

"About half past two. Went right out, I did, and slept like the dead till Dulcie come in."

"What do you mean, Mrs. Goodge is gone!" Wiggins wailed. "Who's goin' to cook?"

"Isn't that just like a man," Betsy snapped. "Always thinkin' of their stomachs. What about poor Mrs. Goodge's aunt? It's not like the poor woman wanted to take sick. Mrs. Goodge had to go to her."

"But who's goin' to feed us?" the footman persisted. "We'll starve to death if she don't come back soon."

"Don't make such a fuss, Wiggins," Mrs. Jeffries said calmly. "I'm sure that in a houseful of adults we'll manage to keep our stomachs full."

"I'll send some vittles over," Luty said quickly. "It'll give Antoine somethin' to do."

Smythe grinned. "I'll do a bit of the cookin'."

"You?" Betsy gasped.

"Why not? I've done it before. Nothing fancy, mind you, but I can do a fry up and cook beefsteak."

"Thank you, Smythe," Mrs. Jeffries said calmly. "As for tonight's meal, I've already taken care of that. Now, does anyone else wish to volunteer to try their hand?"

"I'll have a go at it," Betsy said softly.

"Don't look at me," Wiggins put in, "I've never even boiled an egg." He reached down and patted Fred, who was sleeping by his chair. "And I'm not sure I want to learn how now," he mumbled to the dog.

"Anyway, enough about yer bellies," Luty stated. "With Mrs. Goodge gone we've lost us a good source of gossip. I propose to take on that task myself. Is that all right with everybody?"

Mrs. Jeffries smiled. "That would be wonderful, Luty. Mrs. Goodge's inquiries have been invaluable to us in the past."

"I ain't sayin' I'll get as much as she does," Luty warned, "but I'll do my best. Now, I'd best tell you what I found out today."

"I?" Hatchet said archly. "Don't you mean 'we'?"

Luty waved her hand dismissively. "All right, what 'we' found out today. Not that I heard you askin' any questions, Hatchet." She ignored his snort and continued. "But that's by the by." Luty told them everything she'd learned from her friend Tilbert. "So you see, seems to me this here Barrett feller ain't no more than a cleaned-up scallawag. I think it'd be a good idea if I kept on learning what I could about him."

"Yes, I think you should," Mrs. Jeffries said. She told them about Lady Cannonberry's visit, taking care to give them all the details. Then she turned to Betsy. "Did you learn anything?"

Betsy sighed. "Not much. I had a chat with the footman from the Spears house. He was a right old chatterbox too. Kept goin' on about Janie and Matilda bein' scared of losin' their positions because they'd left the ruddy door open when Spears's dog got out. But I finally managed to get a bit of useful information out of him. He saw Barrett outside in the gardens the night before the murder, and he was havin' a row with some woman. Noah couldn't hear what they was sayin'—"

"Noah?" Smythe interrupted softly.

"Yes, Noah," Betsy said impatiently, annoyed at being interrupted. "It's his name. Anyways, like I was sayin', he couldn't hear what they was sayin' but he could tell they was quarrelling. He said they was hissin' like a couple of cats. And they was tryin' not to be seen—Noah said they was hidin' behind the bushes."

"How very interesting," Mrs. Jeffries said.

"Did this young man see what the woman looked like?" Hatchet asked.

Betsy shook her head. "He didn't say, but he was fairly sure it weren't a neighbour. I'm seein' him again tomorrow and I'll try and find out more then."

"Don't bother," Smythe put in quickly. "If she weren't a neighbour I can probably find out who she was from one of the hansom drivers."

"But you don't know that she come there by hansom," Betsy protested. "Besides, Noah might have more information." She glared at the coachman.

"I'm only tryin' to save you some time and trouble," Smythe said defensively.

"Well, thank you very much, but I'd like to do my own investigatin'."

"Now, Betsy," Mrs. Jeffries interjected. "Smythe was only trying to help. However, I think you're right. Perhaps you should talk with this young man again." She turned to the coachman. "Were you able to learn anything?"

Smythe stopped frowning at the maid. "Not much. But I did find out that there was lots of hansoms comin' and goin' from Kildare Gardens yesterday."

"More than usual?" Mrs. Jeffries asked.

"That's 'ard to say," he admitted, "but the jarvey I talked to said he'd talked to a couple of cabbies that had picked up unexpected fares. It's worth lookin' into. I thought I'd go out tonight and suss out a few pubs in the area, see what I can learn."

"I think that's a very good idea, Smythe," Mrs. Jeffries said. "And do talk to those cabbies. One of them might know something."

"I didn't learn nuthin'," Wiggins complained. "Me and Fred spent the whole afternoon tryin' to find someone from the Barrett 'ouse to talk to. Didn't see hide nor hair of nobody."

"It's early days yet, Wiggins," Mrs. Jeffries said calmly. "And I've another chore for you. I think you need to try and find out if any of the workmen in the Barrett house that day saw or heard anything."

"Won't the police be doin' that?" Wiggins asked. But he looked delighted to be given something to do.

"They probably already have," she explained. "But what a workman will tell a policeman may be quite different from what you could find out. You know what I mean, Wiggins. Get them talking. See if there's some small detail that may be important that perhaps they've forgotten to mention."

"What about Minerva Kenny?" Hatchet asked, his expression thoughtful. "No disrespect meant to Lady Cannonberry, but I do think it would be best if we ascertained that she really was shopping yesterday afternoon."

"Are you thinkin' she might have killed him?" Luty asked.

"I'm thinking that nothing is out of the bounds of possibility," he explained. "Lady Cannonberry has already told us she'd rather die than have anyone find out she . . . uh . . ."

"Steals," Luty supplied,

"Well, yes." Hatchet leaned forward. "And I'm wondering if she might feel compelled to kill to keep her secret."

"It's certainly worth looking into," Mrs. Jeffries agreed. She glanced at the clock. "If there's nothing else, I expect I'd best get some supper started."

"Are you cookin' tonight?" Wiggins asked hopefully.

She nodded slowly. Poor Wiggins, he did so love his food. How unfortunate that she was such a bad cook.

# CHAPTER 6

―――⋘∘⋙―――

"Poor Mrs. Goodge," the inspector said sympathetically. "How very upsetting for her. She must be terribly concerned about her aunt. I don't suppose she's much family left?"

"No, sir, that's why I was sure you'd want her to go." Mrs. Jeffries was stretching the truth a bit. In fact, Mrs. Goodge had relatives (especially cousins) all over London. "I do hope I did the right thing, sir. But there was no way to track you down, so to speak. Furthermore, I don't like to burden you with household decisions when you're in the middle of an investigation. So I took the initiative and sent her off. But really, sir, considering Aunt Elberta's age, I thought it best to get Mrs. Goodge on her way as soon as possible."

"Don't give it another thought, Mrs. Jeffries," Witherspoon said. He reached for the glass of sherry sitting on the table beside his chair. "You were perfectly right to send Mrs. Goodge to her aunt. Family is important, and if the poor woman is dying, well, we'll just have to make do." He paused and a frown creased his forehead. "Perhaps I should call around at one of those employment agencies tomorrow and see if they can send us along a temporary cook?"

"Oh, no, sir," Mrs. Jeffries said hastily. At his look of surprise she forced herself to smile. "That won't be necessary. You're far too busy for that sort of thing. Gracious, you shouldn't have to worry about temporary cooks while you're trying to solve a heinous murder. The staff and I will make do. We've all volunteered to have a hand at the cooking."

"But everyone has enough to do already," he protested. "I won't burden the household with trying to cook as well."

Sometimes, Mrs. Jeffries thought, the inspector's thoughtfulness could be a bit of a nuisance. "Really, sir—"

"No, I insist," he replied.

Truly alarmed, Mrs. Jeffries blurted. "Then let me go around to the agency, sir. You're very busy right now. Your time needn't be taken up with silly details like kitchen help."

She absolutely refused to have a stranger take Mrs. Goodge's place. Gracious, they were in the middle of a murder, it was far too dangerous to have an outsider hanging about the kitchen and listening to their conversations. There were already too many people who were privy to their secret.

"Are you sure you don't mind?" Witherspoon asked. He looked at her over the rim of his spectacles. "It *would* save me some time. I've a full day tomorrow."

"Not at all, sir. Now, I'm all ears. How did your investigation go today?" She took a seat opposite him and gave him a placid smile.

"Not too badly," he admitted cautiously. "There is certainly no shortage of people who hated William Barrett, but so far, I've no evidence that any of them murdered him."

"How dreadful, sir, for someone to be that universally disliked." She clucked sympathetically.

"Yes, it does rather give one pause," Witherspoon said. "I shudder to think what the man's funeral will be like. I don't think there will be anyone in the church except the vicar."

"What about his family, sir?"

"As far as we can tell, Barrett has no family. Ah, well, as the Good Book says, 'As ye reap, so shall ye sow,' or is it the other way around?" He shrugged. "Well, it doesn't matter, you do take my point. Now, as to my day." He then told her about everyone he'd seen and talked with.

Mrs. Jeffries listened carefully. She waited until he was finished before she asked any questions. By the time Betsy stuck her head in the drawing room and announced that dinner was served, Mrs. Jeffries had determined precisely what she needed to do the next day.

"Oh, it's a cold supper," the inspector said as he stared at the block of cheddar cheese, joint of cold beef, pickled onions and fresh bread sitting on the dining table. "How nice."

"You're being very good about it, sir," Mrs. Jeffries said appreciatively. "I know it's not a proper meal. But I'm afraid that by the time I got Mrs. Goodge to Paddington, I didn't have time to do any real cooking."

Although he was dreadfully hungry, Witherspoon didn't wish his housekeeper to feel bad. "This will be fine, Mrs. Jeffries." He sat down, pulled his serviette on his lap and reached for the plate of beef. He stopped and looked up. "Mrs. Jeffries," he said curiously. The beef slipped onto the edge of the plate with a goodly portion of the flesh resting on the white linen tablecloth.

Mrs. Jeffries darted forward, snatched up a nearby serving spoon and rescued the inspector's beef. "Yes, sir."

"Uh, oh, dear, thank you. What are the rest of you eating tonight?"

"A cold supper like yourself, sir," Mrs. Jeffries admitted. She didn't bother to tell him she'd sent out to the baker's for some meat pies and cornish pasties. She didn't want to waste any more time worrying about their stomachs. There were one or two points she wanted to make about the murder. But she must be very careful here. "Sir, you didn't say if you'd spoken to any of the workmen who were at the Barrett house yesterday?" Might as well see if she could wangle a name for Wiggins to pursue.

"The uniformed lads took their statements," Witherspoon replied. "But none of the workmen saw or heard anything on the day of the murder. One of them had lost his hat the day before and another one had found one of his tools missing, but that's about the most interesting thing any of them had to say."

He tried to fork a pickled onion, missed and shot it out of the serving dish. It landed neatly next to his water glass. Mrs. Jeffries scooped it up and plopped it onto his plate. "Why?" He gazed at her curiously. "Do you think I ought to speak to the workmen?"

Mrs. Jeffries smiled brilliantly. "Oh, sir, I'm sure your lads did a wonderful job, it's just that . . . that—" she deliberately broke off.

"What?"

"Well, I don't quite know how to say this."

"Please, just go ahead and say it," Witherspoon prompted. His housekeeper sometimes had the knack of pointing out just the right thing. Putting him on the right track, so to speak. In the past two years, he'd learned a great deal of respect for a woman's intuition.

"It's not that I think the uniformed lads were in any way derelict in their duties, sir," she said slowly, "it's just that you're so very good at asking the right questions."

Witherspoon stared at her for a moment, then said, "What sort of right questions?"

"You know what I mean, sir. You're good at getting people to talk. Don't be so modest, sir. Not with me. We both know that one of your, shall we say secret weapons, is the way you get people to open up to you."

"Do you really think so?" he gazed at her hopefully.

"But of course, sir. You're good with people because you treat them with respect. Whether it's a washerwoman or peer of the realm, it's all the same to you." She shrugged in helpless embarrassment. "Oh, dear, I'm not saying this right. But I think if you'd questioned those workmen, you'd have gotten some very different answers than what the police constables obtained. You'd have asked them questions such as had they *heard* anything unusual on the afternoon of the murder."

Witherspoon's brow furrowed as he pondered her words. For one dreadful moment Mrs. Jeffries thought the jig was up. But then he smiled. "Of course, you're right. I would have asked that question. Naturally, it's important." He couldn't think why it was important, but he didn't let that worry him. These matters had a way of sorting themselves out. As Mrs. Jeffries often told him, his brain was a bit like a sponge. He soaked up all sorts of disparate information, and then, presto, like magic, he came up with the right answer.

Mrs. Jeffries relaxed. The workmen probably hadn't heard anything at all. However, at least now, the inspector would talk to each and every one of them personally. Who knew what tidbit he might pick up and pass on to her?

Smythe hoped a pint would ease the burning sensation in his stomach. He elbowed his way through the crowded pub to the bar. Them cornish pasties and that meat pie felt like they was made of lead and sitting smack in the center of his belly. He ordered a pint of bitter from the barman and turned to gaze around the room.

Smoke from the fire combined with the heavy scent of beer, gin and unwashed bodies and filled the room with an earthy, faintly acrid odor. Along the far wall men and women sat on the long benches, talking and laughing over their drinks. All of the round, rough-hewn tables were occupied, and the crowd at the bar was big enough to crush a lesser man than he.

He eyed the crowd carefully until he spotted a fat, red-headed man wearing a dirty rust-colored porkpie hat, a short checkered waistcoat and a white shirt with a bright red scarf hanging round his neck. The man looked up then and caught Smythe's glance. He raised his glass and Smythe motioned him over.

"Evenin, Smythe," he said, belching slightly.

"Evenin', Blimpey." He nodded toward an empty corner. "Let's move over there."

"Got the ready?" Blimpey asked. He wasn't one to waste time on amenities when there was money to be had.

"Got the information?" Smythe retorted.

"Does a dog 'ave fleas? Course I got the story, it's what you're payin' me for, inn't it?" He wiped his nose with the sleeve of his coat, turned and stalked off toward the corner, leaving Smythe to follow him.

Two day laborers vacated a table as they made their way to the other side of the room. Blimpey sat down, ignoring the high-pitched squeak of protest as his backside made contact with the stool. Smythe cautiously sat down on the other one. He wasn't fat like Blimpey, but he weren't no feather, either, and these stools looked like they'd been here since Cromwell's time.

As soon as they were seated, Blimpey looked pointedly at the front pocket of Smythe's heavy pea coat.

"'Ave I ever cheated you?" Smythe demanded, getting irritated at Blimpey's blatant greed.

"Just bein' careful, mate." Blimpey gave him an ingratiating smile. What few teeth he had left were rotted and yellow stained. "Can't be too careful these days, you know. Times is hard."

"Times is always 'ard," Smythe retorted, "but I ain't cheated you yet and I'm not plannin' to start now. So what did ya find out?"

"Well, they was three hansoms that will be of interest to you Three, I mean, that was for the times ya give me. All of 'em went there between five-thirty and six-thirty on the day in question. Mind you, I 'ad to do a bit o' fast talkin' to get this information . . ."

"Get on with it," Smythe said impatiently. Blimpey wasn't just greedy, he'd talk a tree stump to death if he got half a chance as well. Tonight Smythe wasn't goin' to put up with it. He wanted to get home. His stomach rolled as he caught the scent of a particularly cheap cigar from the group of men at the next table.

"'Ang on a minute," Blimpey said. "No need to rush these things.

The first cabbie let the fare off at the top of Talbot Road, that's right up the end of the terrace from Kildare Gardens."

"Why should that one be of interest? I'm payin' you to find out who went to bleedin' Kildare Gardens." Oh, Lord, Smythe thought, as a wave of nausea hit him, he'd never eat another meat pie again. No matter how hungry he got.

Blimpey smiled craftily. "Because the fare had asked to be taken to Number fifteen Kildare Gardens and then changed her mind."

"It was a woman?"

"Nice-lookin' one too." Blimpey nodded enthusiastically. "Real lady she was, accordin' to the driver."

"Where'd he pick her up at?" Smythe asked.

"Regent Street, and she offered to double his fare if he hurried."

"What did she look like?" Smythe asked. A description would be useful.

"She were young and slender, but he didn't really get a good look at her face. She was wearin' a veil."

"Then 'ow the bloody blue blazes did the driver know she was a good-lookin' woman?" Smythe snapped. That was the trouble with usin' Blimpey Groggins as an informant. He couldn't bloomin' well stop 'imself from addin' to the facts. Man was a natural born storyteller. He swallowed as another wave of nausea swept him.

"'Cause of her voice and her figure," Blimpey said hastily. "Now, you want to hear the rest or not?"

"Go on." Smythe decided he'd better listen to what the old liar said— God knows he was goin' to be payin' for the information whether it was useful or not. "And just stick to what them drivers actually told ya."

"All right, all right, don't get your trousers in a twist," Blimpey took another swig of his beer. "Now, the second one was even stranger. It were another woman. She had the cab take her all the way to Kildare Gardens, got out and paid the bloke, then just as he's gettin' ready to drive off, she jumps back in and demands to be taken to Royal Oak Station." He emptied his glass, looked inquiringly at Smythe, who nodded and then yelled to the barman, "Another one over here, mate!"

"Where'd this one get picked up?" Smythe took a sip of his own beer. A moment later he frowned as the bitter brew started to battle with the undigested meat pie in his stomach.

"Cabbie said he'd picked her up on the Richmond Road—" He broke off to nod his thanks at the serving woman who brought his beer. "But he couldn't say what she looked like. She was wearin' a veiled hat too and a big oversized wool cloak. He couldn't even tell if she were young or old. Woman was bundled up tighter than a spindle o'cotton, the cabbie told me. But I asked him, now"—Blimpey waved a finger at Smythe—"don't want ya thinkin' I wasn't doin' what you're payin' me for. I asked all them questions you give me."

"And the third hansom?" Smythe asked, pushing his unfinished pint away. If he didn't get out into the fresh air, he was going to be sick.

"This one was a man. Toff, dressed nice, top hat and real expensive overcoat. About five-fifteen the cabbie picked him up at the Great Western Terminus and took him directly to number fifteen Kildare Gardens."

"Did the cabbie see if the man went inside?" Smythe asked. He put his hand to his mouth as a soft belch slipped out.

Blimpey grinned again. "He saw him go in, all right. The toff was in such a hurry he hadn't closed the door. So Roland—that's the cabbie—had to climb down and shut it himself. By the time he got back up, he saw the toff walk right inside the house. Figured the fellow musta lived there. I mean, he walked straight in, bold as brass. Mind you, the front door was wide open. But this fellow went in like he owned the place."

Smythe reached inside his pocket and pulled out some notes. He handed them to Blimpey and then added an extra one more than they'd agreed. "What's the name of them drivers and where can I find 'em?"


"Mr. Spears is waiting for you in the drawing room," Pembroke the butler said to Witherspoon and Barnes.

As they followed the butler down the hall, Barnes whispered to the inspector, "That's odd. He made it sound like he knew we was coming here this morning."

"Perhaps Mr. Spears realized we'd be back since he hadn't an alibi for the time of the murder."

Adrian Spears was sitting on the settee waiting for them. "Please do sit down, gentlemen," he said, gesturing toward the chairs opposite him. "I expect you want to ask me more questions."

"Thank you." The inspector desperately wanted a cup of tea. His breakfast was sitting rather heavily on his stomach. Mind you, he really shouldn't complain, Mrs. Jeffries had done quite an admirable job. But he'd no idea that sausages could be so tough. And the eggs. Gracious, fried harder than rocks and swimming in fat. Well, he'd just hope that his dear housekeeper managed to find them a temporary cook as soon as possible. "First of all, Mr. Spears, we'd like to ask you for a few more details about your disagreement with the victim."

"Details?" Spears frowned slightly. "I'm afraid I don't understand?"

"Well," Witherspoon began. He wasn't sure what to ask. But at breakfast Mrs. Jeffries had said something about how convenient it was for the murderer that a neighbour had threatened to murder Barrett. Now how exactly had she put it? He suddenly remembered. "What I mean is, when you accused Barrett of throwing stones at your dog on the day before the murder—"

"I didn't accuse him of throwing stones," Spears interrupted, "I saw the man do it with my own eyes."

"Yes, I'm sure you did," Witherspoon said. "But what I want to know is did you threaten him at that time?"

Spears stared at him incredulously. "Threaten him? You mean physically?"

Witherspoon shook his head. "I mean did you threaten him verbally."

"I'm not sure I ought to answer that," Spears blustered. "Don't I have the right to a solicitor?"

"We're not accusing you of murder, sir," Barnes put in softly. "We merely want to know how many other people might have overheard your altercation with the victim on the day before the murder."

"Oh." He sank back against the seat. "You mean someone may have overheard our argument and then decided as I was conveniently screaming that I would kill the blackguard, that person might decide to do it themselves."

"Er, yes," Witherspoon said. He frowned slightly as a wave of heartburn raced up his chest.

"Well, then." Spears shrugged. "I'll admit it. I did threaten him. I told him if he didn't leave my dog alone, I'd wring his bloody neck. But for goodness' sakes, I didn't mean it literally."

Witherspoon heard footsteps in the hallway. He looked hopefully in that direction praying it was a maid with a tray of tea. It was the butler and he walked straight on past the drawing room. Drat, it was terribly difficult to concentrate when one's innards were on fire.

"Sir?" Barnes prompted softly.

The inspector cleared his throat. "Did anyone hear you threaten Mr. Barrett?" he asked. "I mean, were there other people out in the gardens who could have overheard you?"

"A number of people heard me," Spears admitted. "I was rather embarrassed afterwards, making a spectacle of myself and all. Frankly, I'm not sure who was out there. . . ." He paused, his face a mask of concentration. "Let me see, Owen Washburn, Barrett's partner, heard me. He was with Barrett. The Astleys and Miss Minerva Kenny were having tea with me when the ruckus started. Thornton came outside with me and I'm sure he told Maud all about it. Miss Kenny is a dear lady, but rather inquisitive. I'm sure she got the whole story out of Maud Astley."

Witherspoon momentarily forgot his discomfort. He stared at Adrian Spears. "Mr. Spears. Why didn't you tell us about this when we were here yesterday?"

Spears looked surprised by the question. "You didn't ask. I frequently have people 'round for tea. I saw no need to advise Scotland Yard of my social engagements. Furthermore, I didn't think it important."

"Yes, well, is there anything else you neglected to mention?"

"Now, see here, Inspector." Spears got to his feet. "There's no need to be rude."

"I do beg your pardon, sir." Witherspoon sighed silently. Gracious, people were so very sensitive. "I did not mean to cause offense."

Spears closed his eyes. "None taken, sir. I'm afraid I'm not myself. It isn't very nice losing a beloved pet and becoming a murder suspect all on the same day. What else would you like to know?"

It was Barnes who spoke. "Did Mr. and Mrs. Astley and Miss Kenny know that Barrett had workers comin' and goin' from his house?"

Spears smiled wearily. "Yes. He was always bragging about the improvements he'd made to his home. I know the Astleys were aware of it because Thornton told me he thought Barrett was a fool to have work done this time of year. Takes ages for paint to dry in this damp weather."

"And did the Astleys know that the front and back doors were being kept open?" Witherspoon prodded.

"Possibly." Spears sighed. "It was hard not to see them open. The painters had their equipment and tools littering the front of the Barrett house."

"I see," Witherspoon said slowly. He wasn't sure what to make of this new information. But he wouldn't worry about it now. "Mr. Spears," he said suddenly. "Are you absolutely certain you saw no one who knew you when you went for your walk on the afternoon of the murder?"

Spears shook his head. "Absolutely. A workman coming down to get something saw me leaving my house, Inspector. That's the best I can do."

"And this was at five o'clock?" Barnes asked.

"As near as I can recall, but you must remember, I was very upset. It could have been four forty-five or it could have been five-fifteen. I didn't really look at my watch till I had gone some distance and only then because I knew I had a dinner engagement. Otherwise, I might have walked the streets all night."

"I do wish someone had seen you, sir," Witherspoon said truthfully. "It would make our task so much easier."

"Yes, I'm sure it would." Spears suddenly got up and walked toward the window. He stood for a moment staring out into the street.

Barnes and Witherspoon exchanged a puzzled glance.

"Before you ask me any more questions, Inspector," Spears said softly, hesitantly. "I've something to tell you. Something which may be important."

"Yes, sir, what is it?"

Spears turned and stared at them, his face a mask of anguish and turmoil. "I . . . oh this is so very difficult." He glanced down at the floor and then raised his eyes to meet the inspectors. "I don't believe in telling tales out of school, and I don't for one minute mourn the passing of that odious man, but this is a murder case."

"Yes, sir. It is."

Spears cleared his throat. "I realize I'm a very likely suspect. I did threaten to kill Barrett, but that was in the heat of anger."

Witherspoon didn't point out that shoving a sword through someone generally was considered a pretty angry act. "You've admitted that, sir."

"After I found King's body, I told you I went for a walk," Spears continued. "And that is the truth. But what I didn't tell you was that I saw someone when I was leaving the gardens. Someone who also had a reason to dislike William Barrett."

Witherspoon leaned forward. "Who would that someone be?"

Again, Spears looked at the floor. After a moment he raised his gaze to meet the inspector's. "This is much harder than I thought it would be. Perhaps I ought not to say anything. Perhaps she had a good reason for visiting Barrett that afternoon."

"Please, Mr. Spears," the inspector said patiently, "as you pointed out. This is a murder case. Regardless of how odious a person Mr. Barrett was, no one had the right to take his life. Now, whom did you see?"

"I didn't actually see her go inside the house," Spears hedged. "But the hansom pulled up right outside and I saw her go up the walkway."

Witherspoon straightened. "Her?"

He nodded, his eyes sad and troubled. "Yes, it was a woman. Someone who I know is a dear, kind lady who wouldn't hurt anyone. She's no more capable of murder than I am."

"Who is she?" Witherspoon pressed. "Please, you must tell us."

Spears drew a long, deep breath before he spoke. His voice was barely a whisper. "It was Minerva Kenny."

"Minerva Kenny? But why would she have a reason to dislike William Barrett?"

"I can't tell you why she hated him," Spears replied softly. "Only that I know she did."

"How do you know, sir?" Barnes asked.

Spears shrugged. "Because she told me."

"I told you I'd be here." Betsy smiled at the blushing young man and fought with her conscience. Was leadin' the boy on the right thing to do, even if they was investigating a murder?

"And I told you I'd tell you more about that murder house," Noah said proudly. He fell into step beside her. "But I don't have much time. I only slipped out when the butler turned his back. If he catches me gone, he'll 'ave me 'ead."

Her conscience rose up and almost strangled her. Either that or them awful sausages Mrs. Jeffries had fed them for breakfast. "You'll not lose your position, will you?" she asked in alarm. "I don't want you to get in trouble."

"Nah, old Pembroke's listenin' to them peelers through the keyhole, he'll not notice I'm gone."

"There's police at your house?"

Noah nodded and grinned, "They think Mr. Spears might 'ave done it. But they'd be wrong. Mr. Spears 'ated old Barrett, but he wouldn't hurt nobody. Mind you, he had cause. He and Barrett had been squabblin' for months. But Barrett fought with everyone 'round the gardens. Wasn't no one that liked the man."

Betsy pretended to be shocked. "How awful to be always fightin' with yer neighbours. This Barrett sounds like a right old tartar."

"Yeah, he was," Noah frowned slightly. "Course I don't know if he was as bad as everyone thought he was."

"What do ya mean?"

"Barrett was a funny old bloke. He pretended he hated all the cats and dogs 'round there, specially King. But I don't think 'e did hate 'em and I don't think he killed the dog."

Betsy frowned. "I still don't know what you mean."

"Well," Noah said thoughtfully. "I was out there when Barrett was tossin' them stones at the dog, and I'll admit 'e did it. But funny thing is, it looked to me like he was aimin' to miss him. Truth is, I've seen Barrett out in them gardens with King and when he thought no one was lookin', he'd pet the dog, play with him like. Then someone would come out and he'd shoo the poor old thing off. It were odd, but I think that secretly he were a bit lonely. Does that sound daft?"

"Not to me." Betsy favored him with another brilliant smile. "People are always a lot more, well, peculiar than they seem, if you know what I mean."

"I know just what you mean. Take Mr. Spears for instance, he were daft about that hound of his, treated it like a member of the family. Course, it's no wonder. He doesn't really have any relations. His wife died a few years back and he never had no children. That's why Janie's in such a state."

"Janie's the maid?" Betsy asked as they crossed the road into Kildare Terrace. Betsy tried slowing her steps again, but if she walked much slower, she'd end up tripping over her own feet.

"Yeah and she's still frettin' that Mr. Spears will find out she left the door open and that's how King got out that day. She's been cryin' about it for two days now. Course she's a bit silly, Janie is. She claims she were just lettin' some fresh air into the kitchen, but we all knows she'd seen that painter she's sweet on in the gardens and that's why she went runnin' outside."

Generally, Betsy loved hearing about the romantic adventures of others. But not today. She wanted to get as much information as possible out of Noah. "Sounds to me like you're a right good judge of character, you are."

Noah's cheeks flushed and his chest swelled. "I do me best. I found out about that woman Barrett was havin' a row with the night before he was killed."

"You found out her name?" Betsy was genuinely impressed. She stopped and stared at him, her eyes wide with appreciation. This was better than she'd ever hoped. Smythe would be green with envy, she thought. Then she caught herself; she wasn't doing this to show up the coachman, even though he could irritate the very devil out of her. But sometimes he didn't irritate her, sometimes he made her feel all funny inside. She quickly shoved that silly thought to the back of her mind. "You must be really clever," she said.

"Nah." He blushed bright red and Betsy felt another prick at her conscience. He was only a boy. She had no right to be playin' the poor lad like this, even if they was investigatin' a murder.

"I'm just good at listenin'," he continued. "But I weren't the only one that saw them out there arguin'. Janie was out there too, and she was close enough to recognize the woman's voice." He broke off and glanced around him. "It was the wife of one of Mr. Spears's friends. A woman named Maud Astley."

"Goodness," Betsy gasped. She'd slapped her conscience into silence. "What on earth could a decent woman be doin' out havin' a row at that time of the evening?"

Noah laughed. "Well, I don't know if'n she's decent or not. For that matter, I don't really believe Janie was out for a nip of fresh air. More like a kiss with the painter from next door. But accordin' to what Janie heard, Mrs. Astley and Mr. Barrett was quarrelin' about some letters."

"Me name's Wiggins and this 'ere is Fred," he said to the tall, dark-haired young man.

"Pleased to meet you," the lad replied. He stared at Wiggins and the dog for a minute. "I'd invite ya in, but me mam don't allow animals in the 'ouse."

They were standing on the narrow door stoop of a small grey house in Brixton. The area was poor and working class. The homes were tiny and cramped with most of them broken up into flats housing whole families.

The road was unpaved, and the air smelled of rotting garbage, grease and boiled cabbage.

But Wiggins noticed that this house was neatly painted and the door stoop scrubbed clean. The young man staring at him so curiously wore a clean but frayed white shirt. His hair was dark brown and his hazel eyes deepset in an angular, intelligent face.

Wiggins gave him a grin. "Sorry to be botherin' ya, but my guv sent me over. You was workin' on that Barrett house, weren't you?"

"You a peeler?" he asked angrily. "If you are, you can bleedin' well take yourself off, I already talked to you coppers, and I got nuthin' more to say."

"I ain't no copper." Wiggins hated to lie, but then again, he hated being the only one who wouldn't have a bloomin' thing to report tonight if'n he didn't get this bloke to talk some. "Like I said, my guv sent me over. He saw the job you and your mates did at ole Barrett's 'ouse. He figured that since you ain't workin' there, he could get you to work for 'im."

The young man's face cleared. "Oh, well, that's different, then, inn't it? You'd need to come in and talk to me brother. We works together and he's the oldest." He glanced at Fred, who picked that very moment to cock his head and sit down in a very polite manner. "He's a funny little feller, inn't he? Mum's gone for a while. I reckon you and your dog can come in. Me and Mick could sure do with the work. Me name's David. David Simms."

"Aren't you goin' to finish Barrett's house?" Wiggins asked as he followed the young man inside.

"Can't," David said shortly. "The police won't let us in to finish the job 'cause they was searchin' the place, and besides, who would pay fer it? Hard luck too. We was countin' on the money from the Barrett job to make the rent this week. God knows when them solicitors will ever get around to payin' us what we're owed."

He led the way into a small, rather dark room. Despite the chill in the air, there was no fire in the grate. The windows were covered by thick, brown curtains. The settee was a lumpy mass of grey, and the carpet was thread-bare in spots. But the room was clean with a faint scent of disinfectant soap lingering in the air.

"Wait 'ere," David ordered. "I'll just nip up and get Mick."

Alone, Wiggins stood stock still as the memories came back to him in a silent rush.

Memories of a small room much like this one and a slender, sweet-faced woman with dark brown hair, round cheeks and the prettiest blue eyes in the world. She was kneeling in front of him and wiping the tears from his face with a white handkerchief. He could still see that hankie. Her initial had been embroidered in pink thread in the corner. "Don't worry, lovey," she'd said. "We'll be together soon. It won't be for long. Just until I can find a position where I can have you with me."

He shuddered slightly and blinked hard to fight off the tears that sprang into his eyes. Fred, sensing something wrong, whined softly and licked his hand. Wiggins sniffed and wiped his eyes before the tears could roll any further down his cheeks. His throat hurt as he struggled for control.

This room was so much like the one from his childhood. So much so that standing here, had brought it back to him like it had happened yesterday.

He'd been eight years old when he'd left her. Just a little lad sent off to live with relatives till his mum could find a position. But that day, the day she'd promised it wouldn't be for long and that she'd come get him soon, had been the last time he'd ever seen her.

# CHAPTER 7

Miss Minerva Kenny was a small, thin woman with bright green eyes, dark hair heavily streaked with grey and a fluttering, twittery manner that reminded Witherspoon of a sparrow. As she was dressed in a gown of bronze and brown stripes, the image was further reinforced.

"Do sit down, gentlemen," she invited, gesturing at two stiff-backed chairs. "I suppose I ought to ring for tea," she muttered, more to herself than either of them, "but perhaps this isn't a social call."

"No, ma'am," Witherspoon said hastily. "It isn't. But a cup of tea would be most welcome."

"Of course," she said as she hurried to the door. "I'll just tell the maid."

Witherspoon took the opportunity to look around. The room was small and cluttered. Every available surface was covered with china figurines, delicate crystal, fringed shawls and inlaid boxes. Gracious, there was enough in this room alone to stock a shop, the inspector thought.

Constable Barnes cleared his throat and whipped out his notebook as Miss Kenny returned. "Tea will be ready in a moment," she announced as she sat down on one of the high-backed chairs. She fixed her gaze on the inspector.

"Thank you, ma'am." Witherspoon smiled politely. Miss Kenny continued to stare at him. "Now, we've some questions for you—"

She interrupted. "Is this about Mr. Barrett's death?"

"I'm afraid it is," Witherspoon began. "As you know, he was murdered—"

"I don't know a thing about it," she broke in again. "So as soon as you've had your tea, I expect you'll want to leave."

"Leave? But that's impossible. We really must ask you some questions," the inspector tried again.

"Why? I don't know anything." She smiled blandly.

Witherspoon nodded patiently. "Miss Kenny, you don't know if you know anything."

"Well, if I don't know if I know anything, I don't see how I can tell you about it," she replied reasonably.

"But that's the whole point," he countered. His head was beginning to hurt now and the indigestion was getting worse. "You won't know what you don't know until we ask you some questions."

She cocked her head to one side and crossed her arms over each other. "Inspector, if you don't mind my saying so, you're not making a great deal of sense."

Witherspoon sighed silently. Of course he wasn't making any sense, but neither was she. However, he was far too much of a gentleman to point that out to her.

"Forgive me, ma'am," he said, giving her another patient smile. "But what I meant to say was perhaps you've information that you don't know you have. I understand you were visiting Mr. Spears the day before the murder," he said quickly, trying not to breathe so she wouldn't have a chance to interrupt him. "And I understand you witnessed an incident between Mr. Spears and Mr. Barrett."

"Oh." She sagged against the back of the settee. "I did have tea at the Spears house, that's true, But I can't honestly say I witnessed any incident. Mr. Spears is always a perfect gentleman. He's hardly in the habit of having public quarrels with his neighbours."

Barnes looked up from his notebook. "The inspector didn't say he'd had a public quarrel," he told her softly. "He said he'd had an 'incident.'"

Miss Kenny's hand flew to her mouth. For a moment, she didn't reply, then she caught herself and straightened her spine. "Well, I assumed that's what you meant. How many different kinds of 'incidents' are there?"

Witherspoon sighed inwardly. This was not going to be an easy interview. "Miss Kenny, I believe you know what we're talking about. We shan't leave until you've answered our inquiries."

She gave him a long, calculating look before she answered. "I suppose I might as well tell you, then. I didn't see it myself, of course. I was in the drawing room with Mrs. Astley when it happened. But Maud told me about it."

"What did Mrs. Astley tell you?" Witherspoon prompted. He hoped the maid would hurry up and bring the tea.

"She said that Mr. Spears had caught that awful Mr. Barrett throwing stones at his dog. He and Mr. Astley had gone outside to smoke a cigar. Barrett didn't see them, of course. But when King went into Barrett's flower beds, Barrett started heaving stones at the poor animal." She paused as the maid brought in a tray of tea. They waited patiently while Miss Kenny poured. The inspector noticed her hand was shaking as she handed him his cup.

"I take it Mrs. Astley found out what had happened from her husband?" Witherspoon asked as soon as the maid had left.

"Not really." Miss Kenny gave him a strained smile. "Thornton thinks that's how she knew, but the truth is, she watched the whole thing from the window. As soon as she heard the raised voices, Maud dashed over and opened a window. Pembroke, Adrian's butler, was most put out. Of course, he could hardly order her back to her seat as if she were a schoolgirl, could he?"

"I see." Witherspoon took another gulp of tea. The brew soothed his raw stomach. "Did you get up and go to the window?"

She shook her head. "Oh, no, I stayed right where I was on the settee."

"And could you hear what was going on with the window open?"

"Not really and it was no good asking Maud, either." Her green eyes flashed with remembered irritation. "She kept shushing me every time I opened my mouth."

"When did she tell you what had happened?" Witherspoon was trying to picture the whole thing in his head. It was jolly difficult.

"Right before Adrian and Thornton came back inside. She said that she'd heard Adrian tell Barrett if he ever caught him hurting his dog again, he'd wring his wretched neck."

Witherspoon wanted to be absolutely clear about this. "So Mrs. Astley distinctly mentioned that she'd overheard your host threatening William Barrett, is that correct?"

"Yes."

Barnes and the inspector exchanged glances.

"Miss Kenny," Witherspoon said softly. "Would you mind telling us why you went to William Barrett's house yesterday afternoon?"

· · ·

The heavy footsteps in the hall shook Wiggins out of his reverie. "It's all right, boy," he whispered to Fred, "I'm fine. Just havin' some odd notions, that's all." Fred stared up at him intently out his big brown eyes. For a moment Wiggins was convinced the animal could understand everything. There was such sympathy, such devotion in those eyes that it was almost as if ole' Fred understood exactly how sad he'd been when he'd lost his mother as a little lad.

"This 'ere's me brother, Mick," David said as he and another man walked into the room.

Mick was a bigger, older and harder version of David. Wiggins smiled politely. "I'm Wiggins and this 'ere's Fred."

Mick nodded but said nothing. He crossed his arms over his chest. Wiggins swallowed heavily as he saw the hard muscles bulging beneath the fabric of the thin, blue shirt the man wore. He had hands big enough to crush a man's skull as well, the footman thought.

"My employer sent me 'round."

"And who would that be?" Mick asked.

Wiggins stared at him. He could hardly tell 'im the truth now. He had a feelin' this bloke didn't take kindly to people who worked for Scotland Yard inspectors. "Uh, I work fer an American lady. Name's Luty Belle Crookshank. She seen yer work when she was at the Barrett house and thought you might be willin' to do some paintin' for her. Last bunch she had in made a right old balls up of the walls."

"A woman?" David said suspiciously. "But when you come in 'ere, you referred to your guv as a 'he."

"I take my orders from the butler," Wiggins explained quickly.

Mick's frown turned into a narrow-eyed glare. "I don't think we want to work fer anyone who's a friend of that bastard Barrett."

Wiggins blinked at the man's tone. Fred's ears picked up. "She's not really a friend of Barrett's—"

Mick interrupted him. "She were at his house, weren't she?"

"Only because she had to be there!" Wiggins cried. He desperately tried to think of something to say.

"Look"—Mick stepped closer—"maybe you'd better shove off." He uncrossed his arms.

A low-pitched snarl came out of Fred's throat. Wiggins reached down and patted the dog's head. "It's all right, boy. We's only talkin'."

David came out from behind his brother. "Give the lad a chance," he said to Mick. "We may not be paid for the Barrett job and we need the work."

"We'll not be workin' for the likes of people like Barrett again!" Mick yelled, taking another step closer to Wiggins.

Fred jumped between them, snarling fiercely with his legs spread wide. They stood there for a moment, the dog's ears pinned back, the big man staring at him, and Wiggins wondering if he ought to make a run for it or brazen the situation out.

Then Mick started to laugh. He stepped back, holding his hand out in a placating manner. "It's all right, fella, I'm not going to hurt anyone."

Wiggins exhaled the breath he'd been holding and grabbed the dog. "Down, Fred," he soothed. Fred immediately flopped onto the floor and wagged his tail. He gave them a big dog grin.

"You've got a good dog, there," Mick said brusquely. "See that you treat 'im right."

"I will," Wiggins said quickly, sensing that the man had only backed off because he liked animals and hadn't wanted to have to kick Fred in the head if he attacked. "And my employer ain't no friend of Barrett's," he continued, suddenly inspired. "She were only at his house to threaten to sue him." That didn't seem to be stretchin' the truth too far. Seems like everyone who knew Barrett either wanted to box his ears, take him to court or stick a sword in him.

"That's not surprisin'." Mick jerked his head toward the settee. "Have a seat and we'll talk about this 'ere job."

Wiggins scrambled toward the lumpy couch. Fred was right on his heels. Now that he had the two men talking about Barrett, he didn't want to waste a minute. "Uh, seems like you didn't like Barrett much," he said.

"Like him?" Mick snorted. "The bastard were nothin' but aggravation from the minute we started workin' there." He jerked his chin at David. "I'da walked out the first day, when he started in on Davey here about takin' a tea break, only by that time we'd already bought the bleedin' paint. I knew if we didn't finish the job, we'd not see a bloody bob for our labour."

"Blimey." Wiggin's really was amazed. "Barrett didn't want you takin' a tea break?"

"He didn't want us stoppin' for nuthin'," David put in. "And he expected us to work seven days a week. We soon put a stop to that. Mum won't let us work on the Sabbath. Barrett couldn't make us, neither. By that time we'd put the word out to our mates about how miserable 'e was to work for. Barrett knew he couldn't find anyone else to do the job if he fired us, so 'e had to give us Sunday off. He was in a right hurry to get the work done."

"Wonder why?" Wiggins leaned over and scratched Fred behind the ears.

"He was tryin' to sell the 'ouse," Mick answered. "That's why he had us workin' twelve hours a day and them carpenters up there at the same time. It were bloomin' daft, too. We kept gettin' in each other's way. Finally old Barrett come up with a plan to have the carpenters use the backstairs and us use the front. Worked for a while."

"Like 'ell it did," David muttered. "One of them bloody carpenters knicked me hat and coat."

"They claimed they didn't," Mick said with a shrug. "Coulda been Barrett for all we know."

"Now, what would he want with a workingman's clothes?" David said reasonably. "He was a mean bastard, but I don't think he'd have much use for my old hat and overcoat. But them carpenters, now, they 'ad a reason to pinch me stuff. They was gettin' back at me 'cause they thought I'd taken their bloody hammer."

"Uh, was you there on the day of the murder?" Wiggins asked. He knew all about the petty squabbles people forced to work together could get into, and he didn't want to waste time listenin' to it now.

"Course we was," Mick said shortly. "Not that we seen anything."

"Oh." Wiggins desperately tried to think of something useful to ask.

"Mind you," Mick continued, for he was fond of the sound of his own voice, "I'm not surprised someone shoved a sword into Barrett. He was that kinda feller, if you know what I mean. Had his fingers in a lot of pies, had a lot of people dancing to his tune and bouncing around on his string."

"What do ya mean?"

"I mean, he was a bit like a lad that plays with fire." He dropped his voice to a conspiratorial whisper. "He didn't half care who he made angry. Had some poor woman in tears the day he was killed. I could hear her beggin' and cryin' at him when I went down to get me paint."

"When was this?" David demanded. "You never said nuthin' to me about any woman."

"It slipped me mind until we started talkin'," Mick said. "It were the mornin' of the day he were killed. Barrett had this poor woman in his drawin' room, and he was threatenin' to do somethin' to her. I could hear her beggin' him to keep quiet, askin' him to please let her have it back—"

"'Ave what back?" Wiggins interrupted.

Mick shrugged. "Don't know, couldn't really hear good by that time. The butler was comin' up the stairs and stompin' his feet loud enough to wake the dead."

"Cor blimey," Wiggins said, "I guess Lu—Mrs. Crookshank weren't the only one in town who didn't like him."

Mick threw back his head and laughed. "Not bloody likely, mate. Like I said, he had more enemies than you and I've had hot dinners. You'd think someone who was hated that much would have better sense than to leave a sword hanging on the wall. Whoever killed 'im didn't even have to bring their own weapon."

From the corner of his eye Wiggins saw David staring at him suspiciously. He thought it might be time to change the subject. "Uh, are you interested in another job?"

"This Mrs. . . . Kurshank—"

"Crookshank," Wiggins corrected.

"Is she a decent sort?" David interrupted. "I mean, is she likely to pay us?"

"Course she will," he replied honestly. "And she'll not expect you to work like dogs either. She's a good sort." Wiggins fervently hoped that Luty would have something that needed painting. He'd rather gotten to like these two.

"All right," Mick said. "We're interested. When's the job start?"

"Uh, not for a week or two," Wiggins said quickly. "Mrs. Crookshank only sent me 'round to find out if you was willin' to do it."

"We're willin'." Mick got to his feet. "You just call round and let us know where we need to go."

They walked him and Fred to the door. With each and every step Wiggins felt more and more depressed. These men really needed the work, and here he was raisin' their hopes. Bloomin' Ada, as Smythe would say.

"There's someone to see you, sir," the young constable said as soon as Witherspoon and Barnes got back to the station.

Witherspoon glanced longingly at the stairs leading to the second floor and the canteen. He was dreadfully hungry. "Who is it?" he asked the constable.

"Cabbie, sir. Name of Roland Moodie. He claims he's got information about the Barrett murder."

Witherspoon sighed. "Go on up to the canteen," he said to Barnes. "I'd best see what this chap has to say."

Roland Moodie was sitting in a straight-back chair beside the inspector's desk. He was a round, bald man wearing a houndstooth coat, several layers of scarves and holding a battered bowler hat on his knees. "You the copper that's in charge of that killin' on Kildare Gardens?" he asked as Witherspoon approached.

"Indeed I am, sir." He introduced himself as he sat down behind his desk.

"Name's Roland Moodie," the cabbie said, "and I've got some information that might be useful to you." He put one hand in his pocket and fingered the fistful of pound notes that strange bloke had given him for coming here. Moodie didn't have much use for coppers. Always pushin' you off when you was lookin' for a fare. But the bloke and his lolly had convinced him to come and tell about the fare he'd dropped at Kildare Gardens. "I dropped a fare off in Kildare Gardens on the day of the killin'. Thought you might want to know about it."

"How very good of you to come in!" Witherspoon exclaimed, genuinely pleased. "It does one good to see one's fellow citizens doing their civic duty. You know, you'd be utterly amazed at the number of people who won't come forward with information. It's positively dreadful how people don't like to get involved."

"Uh, yeah." Moodie didn't want to get involved, either. But the big bloke who'd been askin' him all them questions this mornin' had been real insistent. Mind you, he'd paid for Moodie's time. Moodie decided he'd better not say anything about the big feller. Wouldn't want this peeler thinkin' he was in here tellin' tales 'cause someone had greased his palm with silver. Besides, that big feller had paid him extra to keep his mouth shut about their conversation. Seemed like a decent enough bloke, but he was awfully big and, if the truth were known, a little mean-lookin' too. "Well, I likes to do me duty."

"I'm sure you do, sir." Witherspoon paused to think what to ask first. He said the first thing that came into his head. "How did you find out about the murder?"

"It were in all the newspapers," Moodie replied, thinking it was an odd question. "And when I saw the address where it were done, I remembered I'd taken a fare there that very afternoon."

"Was the fare a man or a woman?"

"A man. Real gent he was too."

Witherspoon nodded. "What do you mean, 'a real gent'?"

"You know, a toff," Moodie said impatiently. "Had on a big black top hat, his boots were as shiny as new pennies, and he were wearin' quality clothes. I can tell, ya know. I picks up a lot of gents."

"I see." Witherspoon pursed his lips. "Where did you pick this person up?"

"At the railway terminal."

Witherspoon drummed his fingers on the desk. "Which one? London has a number of railways."

"The Great Western." Moodie might be in here talkin' to the copper, but he hadn't been paid enough to make it easy for 'em. They could bleedin' well work for what he had to say.

"What time was this?" Witherspoon's stomach growled. He swallowed heavily, thinking of the greasy fare in the police canteen. He hoped that Mrs. Jeffries had had some success in finding them a cook. The staff were doing their best, but really, he hadn't slept well last night, and this morning's breakfast had been almost inedible.

Moodie took his time about answering, his beady eyes squinted, and he scratched his nose. "About five-fifteen."

"And where did you take the man?"

"I told ya, to Kildare Gardens."

"Do you remember which number?" Witherspoon asked, trying hard not to sound impatient.

"Course I do," Moodie exclaimed. "Number fifteen. That's the house where the murder happened, isn't it? Why the blazes do ya think I come in 'ere?"

Witherspoon closed his eyes briefly. "Of course. Now, could you describe the man?"

"I told ya, he was a gent wearin' expensive clothes."

"You described his clothes, sir." The inspector wondered if it was him or was this man particularly obtuse. "Now I'd like you to describe the man himself. What color hair did he have?"

"It were like a dark red, but it had a bit of grey in it. Mind you,"

Moodie explained. "I couldn't see how much he had 'cause he was wearin' a top hat. For all I know he might have been bald on top."

Witherspoon straightened. Dark red hair? Auburn perhaps? "Er, how old was this man?"

Moodie shrugged. "Maybe fifty, fifty-five."

"And how tall?"

"About six feet I'd reckon." Moodie rolled his eyes toward the ceiling as if he expected the right answer to be written up there. "Maybe an inch or two shorter."

The inspector forgot about his empty stomach and the police canteen. "Did you see him go into the house?"

Moodie grinned and nodded. "He walked straight in like he owned the place. I figured he lived there, you see. Even though the doors was open like, this gent didn't even bother to bang the brass. Just went on in."

"I see." Witherspoon asked him a few more questions and then wrote down his address. He wanted to be able to get his hands on this man when they went to court.

By the time Mr. Moodie had finished his statement, Barnes was back from the police canteen. He looked at the cabbie curiously, but said nothing until the man had taken his leave.

"Who was that, sir?" Barnes asked. He flicked a bit of breadcrumb off his sleeve. "A witness?"

"A most valuable witness, I think," Witherspoon murmured. "He's a cabbie by the name of Roland Moodie. He took a fare to the Barrett house the afternoon of the murder. It was a man, Barnes. One of our suspects."

"Did the cabbie know his name?" Barnes asked eagerly.

"No. But from the description he gave me, I've no doubt who it was." Witherspoon paused dramatically. "Thornton Astley." He proceeded to tell the constable everything the cabbie had told him.

Barnes scratched his chin, "But why would Astley take a cab to Barrett's house? Especially from the railway station. Why not just walk there?"

"Why, to throw us off the scent," Witherspoon explained. "He couldn't risk being seen walking there. Much better to nip out somewhere, pretend to be going to an office in the City and then grab a hansom back."

"I see what you mean, sir," Barnes replied, but his expression was doubtful. "Then again, we only have Astley's word that he was droppin' the lawsuit. Perhaps he decided that would be a waste of money and wanted to get his own back by killin' Barrett. Wouldn't be the first time murder's been done over money."

"True," the inspector replied. "Of course, we don't know for certain it was Astley in that hansom, but it seems a reasonable assumption. Still, I mustn't jump to conclusions. Astley wasn't the only person to call upon the victim. Remember, Miss Kenny was there too."

Barnes shrugged. "But she claims she wasn't. She claims Mr. Spears is mistaken."

"That's why we've sent some lads round to Kildare Gardens," Witherspoon said patiently. "For goodness' sakes, someone other than Adrian Spears must have seen Miss Kenny. Have you sent the PCs off yet?"

"Not yet, sir. I was going to do it after I had me tea." Barnes belched softly. "Sorry, sir. Bit of chop come back up."

The mention of food had the inspector's mouth watering.

"But I'll do it straight away," Barnes continued. "I'll have them check with the neighbours again and the local tradespeople and cabbies. If either Miss Kenny or Mr. Astley went to the Barrett house, someone is sure to have seen them." He started off and then stopped. "Will we be going back to the Astley house now?"

The inspector thought about it for a moment. He was torn between wanting to get something decent in his stomach and doing his duty. Duty won. "Yes, Barnes, give the PCs their instructions. I'll meet you downstairs and we'll see what Mr. Thornton Astley has to say for himself."

Barnes nodded and started off again. "Oh, forgot to tell you something, sir. Ran into one of the lads in the canteen, and he told me a bit of interestin' information. Seems that Astley's secretary, that Mr. Sharpe, the one who told us he was at the dentist the afternoon of the murder? PC Micklewhite says he weren't."

Witherspoon wondered why that was so interesting. He didn't see that Neville Sharpe had a reason to murder William Barrett. But he didn't wish to sound critical. "Excellent, Barnes. Do pass my compliments on to PC Micklewhite. What made him think to check the secretary's alibi?"

Barnes grinned. "He didn't, sir. But he were the one who took Mr. Sharpe's statement yesterday, and he noticed they went to the same dentist. Micklewhite's mother-in-law had a toothache late yesterday evenin', and he had to take her in. While he was there, he asked the dentist.

The man had never heard of Neville Sharpe, and he insists he wasn't a patient."

"How very odd," Witherspoon said. "I wonder where the man really was? Oh, well, make sure we ask him this afternoon."

Betsy stared at the oven as if it were a snake. She weren't much of a cook and that was a fact. But tonight was her turn and she promised them she'd have a meal ready. She glanced at the clock and saw that it was getting close to teatime. She gave the oven another worried glance. Surely she'd done it right? Before she'd put the joint in, she'd put lots of salt on it, just like Mrs. Goodge always did. Maybe she'd put too much salt on it, she thought. But then again, maybe she hadn't. And what about them roast potatoes? Had she salted them too? She couldn't remember.

Betsy filled the kettle up and put it on to boil next to the big pot of cabbage she'd put on before putting the pork in the oven. Roast pork and potatoes and cabbage. That should make for a good dinner. She stared at the bubbling cabbage, the heavy steam rising off the open pan. Had she salted it? Betsy wasn't sure, but to be on the safe side, she thought, reaching for the salt cellar, maybe she'd add a bit more in.

Smythe leaned past the driver and pointed at the woman going into the Astley house. "Is that her?"

The cabbie's eyes narrowed. "Well, it could be. You've got to remember, I didn't get a good look at her face. She were wearin' a veil."

"But you musta got a glimpse of her hair colour," Smythe pressed. "If it were that colour"—he pointed to the woman walking rapidly down the street—"you'da noticed, right?"

"Maybe . . ." he answered doubtfully. The cabbie frowned slightly as he watched the retreating figure. The woman's hair was a bright blond—even with that big hat on he could tell what colour it was. But he weren't sure she were the woman, and even though this bloke were payin' him to come round here and have a look-see, he didn't care how much money the feller had, he weren't goin' to say something was true unless he knew it fer sure. "I still can't tell," he finally said. "It were an overcast day the afternoon I picked the woman up, and it weren't half decent light, not like today."

Smythe sighed. There was no point in pesterin' the cabbie for an answer. The fellow simply couldn't tell if Maud Astley was the woman he'd picked up or not. "Would you tell me again what the woman was wearin' that afternoon?"

This time the cabbie sighed. "Listen, I ain't got all day."

"I'm payin' ya for yer time," Smythe snapped.

"All right, all right. She had on a dark hat with a big veil. The hat was black, if I remember rightly. She were all wrapped up in a big cloak. It was navy blue. I do remember that."

Smythe turned as he heard the *clip-clop* of another cab pull up behind them. A moment later the door opened and a slender, older lady stepped lightly to the ground, paid off the driver and then walked briskly up the walkway to the Astley home.

"I don't suppose you recognized that woman, did you?" Smythe asked the driver.

"Never seen her before," the cabbie said. "Why?"

"Just hoped she might be familiar to ya."

"Can I go now?"

Smythe reached into his pocket and pulled out the promised money. He handed it to the man and jumped down to the road. "Thanks for yer help," he called as the cabbie released the brake and then snapped the reins.

The man tipped his cap and the team shot forward. Smythe frowned. This case was costin' him a lot of lolly, not that he minded spendin' it. But he was payin' plenty out and not gettin' much in return. Just then another cab came down the square.

Smythe crossed the road so he wouldn't be facing the occupants when they went past. It wouldn't do to become too familiar a face in this neighbourhood, not with the police still hanging about.

He kept his eye on the hansom as he began walking toward Kildare Square. Maybe he'd get on back and have tea with the others. See what they'd found out.

The hansom stopped in front of the Barrett house. Smythe saw the door open and then a uniformed constable stepped into view. As soon as he saw who it was getting out of the cab, he ducked behind a lamppost and turned sideways. A second later the inspector stepped out.

Smythe held his breath and prayed neither man would glance this way. He could never explain why he was hidin' behind a bleedin' lamppost.

But the two policemen went into the Astley house without looking across the road.

"That was a ruddy close call," he muttered to himself as he started moving. There was no point in temptin' fate. If the inspector saw him hanging about, they'd all be in a right old mess.

Mrs. Jeffries dashed into the kitchen, tossing her coat and hat on an empty chair. "Are the others back for tea, Betsy?" she asked.

"They're due in a few minutes," Betsy said. She picked up the tray and carried it to the kitchen table. "Where 'ave you been? A man from the gasworks was here and a fruit seller stopped by. They was both looking for Mrs. Goodge. I reckon she must have put the word out that she was needin' information."

"Yes," Mrs. Jeffries muttered, looking distracted, "I expect she did. Did they tell you anything."

"Not really," Betsy said as she took a cloth off the Madeira cake she'd bought from the bakers. "Just passed on some gossip about Maud Astley. Do you want me to tell you now or should we wait for the others?"

Mrs. Jeffries thought about it for a moment. "We'd best wait."

They heard Wiggins and Fred come in the back door. "Come on, boy. Let's go see what there is for tea. 'Ello, 'ello," he said, hurrying to the table and licking his lips. His face fell when he saw nothing but bread and butter and one ever so tiny Madeira cake. He didn't even like Madeira cake. "Is this all there is?"

"That's plenty," Betsy protested. "I'm cookin' a big meal for tonight. You don't want to be spoilin' your dinner."

"What we havin?" Wiggins asked suspiciously. "I hope it ain't sausages. Them sausages we had for breakfast is still in my stomach."

"It's not sausages." Betsy glared at him and jerked her head toward Mrs. Jeffries, warning Wiggins to watch what he said. "Besides, there was nothing wrong with breakfast."

"Course there wasn't," Smythe agreed as he popped into the room. "If you was a starvin' man stuck in the middle of a ruddy desert," he added under his breath.

"Are we all here?" Mrs. Jeffries pretended not to notice their comments about this morning's meal. Goodness knows, she didn't claim to be much of a cook, and all in all they were being quite good about it. But really, it wasn't as though she'd meant to burn the sausages.

"Are we goin' to wait for Luty Belle and Hatchet?" Betsy asked. She put the big brown teapot on the table next to the bread.

"They said they'd be by this evening after dinner," Mrs. Jeffries said. "By the way, Betsy, something smells good."

Betsy smiled. "It's just a joint of pork and some potatoes," she said. "But I think it'll do nicely for supper." She'd put the cabbage in the cooling pantry. She hoped that letting it sit awhile in it's own juice might make it a bit more appealing. Funny, she'd never have guessed that cabbage went all mushy and green when you cooked it.

"Good," Mrs. Jeffries said. "Let's get right into it, shall we. First of all, something has happened, I went to see Minerva Kenny this afternoon."

"Is she a small, older woman with dark hair gone a bit grey?" Smythe asked, recalling the woman who'd stepped out of the hansom.

"Why, yes. How did you know?"

"I think *I* saw her this afternoon too," he said, reaching for the teapot.

"Really?" Mrs. Jeffries frowned. "Where?"

"Going into the Astley house."

"Oh, dear, I was afraid of that. She wasn't home when I called, and the maid didn't know where she'd gone."

"What are you so worried over?" Betsy asked, not liking the expression on the housekeeper's face. "It's only natural she'd go to see her friends, what with the murder and all. What's so terrible about her goin' to visit with Maud Astley?"

"There's nothin' terrible about it, exceptin' that Mrs. Astley isn't home," Smythe interjected. "She'd just gone out when Miss Kenny showed up."

"Oh, dear," Mrs. Jeffries muttered, "This is disastrous."

"What's a disaster?" Wiggins asked, just to keep up his end of the conversation. He wished Betsy had sliced the bread thicker. These slices was so thin you could read a ruddy newspaper through 'em!

"Because I'm afraid Miss Kenny may have gone there to put that silly china bird back in place," Mrs. Jeffries replied. "And that's the last thing we need. If someone sees her, it will only muddle things."

"Blimey, let's hope not." Smythe shook his head. "If the inspector walks in and catches her takin' that bird out of her pocket and shovin' it on a table, she'll have a lot of explainin' to do."

"The inspector!" Mrs. Jeffries cried.

"'Fraid so. I saw him goin' into the Astley house right behind Miss Kenny."

# CHAPTER 8

⚫━⚫⚫⚫⚫━⚫

"What's so awful about Miss Kenny puttin' the bird back?" Wiggins asked. "She's not likely to get caught, now, is she? I mean, she's been snatchin' things from her friends and returnin' 'em back for a long while now, and she ain't been caught by any of 'em."

They all stared at him.

"You know, Wiggins," Mrs. Jeffries replied thoughtfully. "I do believe you're right. She's apparently rather successful at her, uh . . . activities. As you pointed out, she's done it for years."

"That's right," Betsy agreed. "So what are we worried about? Miss Kenny won't get—"

"Aren't you all forgettin' somethin'?" Smythe interrupted. "Seems to me the old girl's losin' 'er touch. The last time she 'ad sticky fingers, she did get caught! And the man who caught 'er is now dead. Someone shoved a ruddy sword through 'is 'eart."

No one said anything. Wiggins broke the silence with a loud groan. Betsy slumped back in her chair. Even Mrs. Jeffries looked disappointed.

"Then we'd better hope that keeps her wits about her this afternoon," Mrs. Jeffries said softly. "Otherwise, we may all have a lot of explaining to do to the inspector."

"Do you think she's likely to say anything about how she got the bird back?" Betsy asked. She gave the coachman a quick, worried look. "It wouldn't be fair if Smythe got into trouble. We was *all* in on it."

"Sufficient unto the day is the evil thereof," Mrs. Jeffries said.

"What does that mean?" Wiggins asked.

"It means," Smythe replied, "don't go lookin' for trouble."

"Right," the housekeeper nodded. "Furthermore, even if Miss Kenny were to tell the inspector someone had retrieved the bird for her, she couldn't identify Smythe by name. Ruth never told her any of our names."

"But if he finds out it was Lady Cannonberry," Betsy countered, "how do we know she'll not say something? You know the inspector would ask her about it."

Mrs. Jeffries gave them her calmest smile. She was concerned too, but fretting over something that hadn't even happened was a waste of useful energy. Much better to concentrate on finding the real killer. "Let's keep our fingers crossed that Miss Kenny gets in and out of the Astley house without anything untoward happening. Now, we really must get down to business. Who wants to go first?"

"Better let me," Smythe said. "I may need to nip out before supper and talk to a cabbie."

"Very well." Mrs. Jeffries nodded. "Go ahead." She didn't have much of her own to report, and she was hoping that one of them had picked up something useful.

"I found out that there were three hansoms goin' to Number fifteen Kildare Gardens on the afternoon of the murder." He told them everything he'd learned, taking care not to mention Blimpey Groggins and implying that he had spoken to all the cabbies himself. Which, of course, he had, so on this matter at least, his conscience was clear. "So you see," he finished, "that's how come I know that Miss Kenny is at the Astley house."

Betsy eyed him suspiciously. "You mean you talked a cabbie into goin' all the way over to Kildare Gardens and then just sittin' there and waitin' till Maud Astley come out?"

Smythe was ready for that question. "I was headin' over there myself, so I paid the fare."

"Oh, dear, Smythe." Mrs. Jeffries clucked her tongue. "Hansoms are dreadfully expensive. I know how devoted you are to the inspector, but really. No one expects you to spend your hard-earned wages on taking cabs just so you can get them to give you information."

Smythe gave her a gentle smile. "My feet were hurtin', Mrs. J., and I didn't relish fightin' the crowd on the omnibus or the underground. Besides, I've not much else to spend my wages on. Anyway, we now know that at least one of them three went into the Barrett 'ouse. The cabbie was sure the man did. Course, by my way of thinkin', any of the three of 'em coulda gone into the Barrett 'ouse and killed the man."

"How do you figure that?" Betsy asked.

"First of all, the woman that was dropped on Talbot. Road coulda slipped in without bein' seen," Smythe explained. "Seems to me that's why she 'ad the hansom drop her where 'e did; she didn't want no one connectin' her to Barrett's."

"But the second woman went to Royal Oak Station," Mrs. Jeffries pointed out.

"And that's less than a ten-minute walk from Kildare Gardens," the coachman countered. "Maybe that's why she jumped back in the hansom: She'd figured the cabbie would remember takin' her to Barrett's house."

"I wonder who the man was?" Wiggins said thoughtfully. He slipped Fred a bite of cake under the table.

"We'll know by tonight," Smythe said and then wanted to bite his tongue. They were all staring at him again. "I mean, I, uh, convinced the cabbie he really ought to go to the police."

"Very good, Smythe," Mrs. Jeffries said, "And I trust you made sure they wouldn't mention they'd spoken to you?"

"Course." He sank back into his chair.

Mrs. Jeffries glanced around the table. "Who'd like to go next?"

"I will," Wiggins said around a mouthful of bread. He told them about his visit to the Simms house. "They sure hated workin' for Barrett," he concluded. "Do you think they'll ever get paid?"

"I certainly hope so," Mrs. Jeffries replied. "Did they have any idea who the woman was in Barrett's study? The one they heard crying?"

"Neither of them got a look at her," Wiggins answered. "But tomorrow I'm goin' to see the carpenter. Mick thinks one of them might have got a look at her."

"Sounds like this is the same woman that Barrett's maid saw cryin' in his drawin' room," Smythe said.

"Must be. Even a man as miserable as Barrett wouldn'a 'ad two women weepin' on the same day. No one's that mean." Wiggins eyed another piece of cake. He really didn't like it, but he was so hungry he felt like his belly was touchin' his backbone. He started to reach for the cake plate and then snatched his hand back. No, he'd wait till dinner. Betsy was cookin' them a good supper and he didn't want to spoil it.

"Barrett wasn't real good with women, was he?" Betsy said, smiling blandly at the coachman. He grinned back at her. One of them big cocky grins that was so irritatin'. Well, just wait till he heard what she'd found out. That would wipe that silly smirk off his face. "Noah found out the name of the woman Barrett was havin' the row with the night before he died." She looked around the table. "It was Maud Astley."

"Miss Kenny," the inspector said to the woman standing on the chair. "Do you really think it's safe to be standing on that chair?"

Startled, she whirled around, lost her balance and toppled forward. Witherspoon made a lunge for her just as the chair slipped out from under her feet.

"Oww . . ." he moaned as Miss Kenny's weight sent them both tumbling through the air. They hit the carpet with a loud thud.

"Oh, heavens!" Miss Kenny cried. She tried throwing herself to one side and ended up shoving her elbow into the inspector's open mouth.

"Good heavens!" Barnes cried as he scrambled toward the two bodies seemingly locked in mortal combat on the floor.

Witherspoon tried to get a foothold on the floor so he could shove Miss Kenny to one side, but his boot got tangled in the hem of her voluminous skirts. He couldn't ask the constable for help; Miss Kenny's elbow was in his mouth. His arm shot out and smacked hard against Barnes's leg. The constable, who was leaning over trying to get a grip on Miss Kenny's arm, lost his balance and toppled forward, pinning both Miss Kenny and Witherspoon to the ground.

"*Ahh . . .*" the woman screamed as the constable's full weight slammed on top of her.

"Uhhh," Witherspoon moaned as the breath was knocked out of him for the second time.

"I say, what on earth is going on here?" Thornton Astley's scandalized voice thundered into the room.

Barnes finally managed to roll off to one side and scramble to his feet. He managed to get a grip on Miss Kenny's waist. He lifted her off the inspector and set her on her feet.

"Oh, goodness," a breathless Miss Kenny murmured as she adjusted her hat.

"Are you unharmed, Miss Kenny?" The inspector asked as he climbed to his feet.

"I say!" Astley shouted. "Will someone please explain what is going on in here?"

"I'm fine, Inspector," Miss Kenny said, ignoring her outraged host. "You startled me, though."

"My apologies, madam," Witherspoon replied. "But when I saw you on that chair, I was afraid you'd fall and hurt yourself."

"Chair?" Astley yelled. "What chair?"

"Miss Kenny fell off a chair," Witherspoon explained. "Unfortunately, I tried to catch her as she fell and we both tumbled over. Constable Barnes was trying to help us up, but he lost his balance and toppled over as well. That's why we were all on the floor when you came in."

Astley stared at them, his expression incredulous. Finally he walked over and rang the bellpull. The butler, who Witherspoon was sure was eavesdropping outside the door, immediately appeared.

Astley ordered tea. "I think," he said slowly as soon as the butler disappeared, "that we'd better sit down."

Witherspoon turned to Miss Kenny. "Are you sure you're all right?"

"There's no permanent damage, thank you," she replied politely.

"That was a right hard fall you took," Barnes said conversationally. "Would you mind tellin' us what you was doin' on that chair?"

Miss Kenny pretended she hadn't heard the question. "I do believe I'll sit down. I'm a bit shaken."

"Perhaps we'd all better sit down," Astley said loudly.

Witherspoon decided that was a good idea. His tailbone hurt and his knee throbbed rather painfully. He hobbled over to a nice, comfortable-looking wing chair and gingerly sat down. Barnes perched on the edge of the settee. Miss Kenny took the chair on the far side of the settee. It was as far away from them as she could get.

An awkward silence filled the room. Witherspoon cleared his throat. He felt like an absolute fool. Whatever must Astley think of him? But he could hardly have stood and done nothing while an elderly woman took flying leaps off chairs.

Barnes shuffled his feet against the floor and dug in his pocket for his notebook. He didn't start grinning until everyone's attention was diverted by the maid arriving with the tea tray.

Astley handed the tea 'round and then sat back, his expression still puzzled. "Minerva," he said gently. "Would you mind telling *me* what you were doing on a chair in my drawing room."

She stared down at her cup. "I . . . uh . . . wanted to get a closer look at those china birds on that top shelf," she finally said, her voice so soft that the inspector had to lean forward to hear her.

"I see," Astley said. "Well, next time, do say something to me and I'll have one of the servants take care of getting things down for you. You're far too valuable a friend to risk losing by a bad fall off the furniture." He looked at the inspector. "Why have you come here today?"

"I need to ask you some more questions," Witherspoon replied. He wondered if Constable Barnes had seen what he'd seen when they walked into the room. Minerva Kenny wasn't looking at those china birds, she was taking one out of the pocket of her dress and reaching up to the shelf when they had their accident. Why was one of Mr. Astley's birds, in her pocket? But that question could come later, when he questioned Miss Kenny alone.

"I've told you everything I know about Barrett's murder," Astley said.

"Is Maud here?" Minerva Kenny asked timidly.

Astley smiled at her. "No, she's gone out. Shall I tell her you called?"

Minerva nodded and put her teacup back on the tray. "I'm so sorry for the upset," she said as she got to her feet. "Perhaps it would be best if I left. Please tell Maud I called."

"I'll ask her to call 'round and see you." Astley rose as well.

Miss Kenny turned and looked at the two policemen. "Good day, gentlemen," she said.

Astley escorted her to the door, talking to her in low soothing tones.

As soon as they were out of the room, Barnes leaned toward the inspector. "She's lyin'," he whispered. "I distinctly saw her take somethin' out of her pocket when we come into the room. She was puttin' somethin' up on that shelf."

"I quite agree," Witherspoon whispered back. "But I think it best if we ask her about it when she's alone."

"Right, sir." Barnes hastily sat back as they heard Astley's footsteps coming back down the hallway.

"Inspector," Astley said abruptly. "Will you please tell me what is going on?"

"Well, sir, it's as we told you," Witherspoon said. "We came by to ask you a few more questions."

"This has been a most unsettling day." Astley ran a hand through his hair as he sat down.

The inspector studied him carefully. Thornton Astley had dark circles under his eyes and his face was drawn, as though he hadn't been sleeping. "Murder is frequently unsettling. Mr. Astley, we've had a report that you were seen going into Barrett's house on the afternoon of. the murder."

Astley's head jerked up and his mouth opened slightly. "I don't know what you're talking about," he protested. But his voice was thin and hollow, lacking conviction.

"The cabbie who took you to the Barrett house has already given us a statement," Witherspoon said softly. Really, it was almost embarrassing watching people try to lie their way out of a situation. "So please, just tell us the truth. It will be easier on you in the long run."

Astley stared at him a moment and then slumped back against the settee. "I suppose I've known all along you'd find out," he laughed bitterly. "Yes, I did go to the house."

"You went inside as well," the inspector stated.

"I'll admit I went upstairs into the study. But I didn't kill him!" Astley cried. "When I walked into that room, Barrett was already dead."

"What time was this?" Witherspoon pressed.

"About half past five. Maybe as late as a quarter to six, I don't know. I didn't look at my watch."

"Did you see anyone as you were going in or out?" The inspector was confused. Astley sounded as though he were telling the truth, yet one of the workmen had claimed that he'd heard Barrett alive at six o'clock.

"No." Astley shook his head. "I could hear the painters and carpenters up on the third floor. There was a great deal of pounding and shouting."

"You saw no servants?"

"No one," Astley admitted. "Except for the cabbie, of course."

"Are you certain that Barrett was dead?" Barnes asked.

"Yes. There wasn't much light in the room, the fire had burned low and he'd not turned on the gas lamps. But he was dead, all right. I checked for a pulse and there wasn't one." Astley sighed. "Will there be no end to the misery that man has caused? Even dead he finds a way to torment people."

The inspector asked, "Why had you gone to see Mr. Barrett?"

"To tell him I was dropping my lawsuit." Astley explained. "I know it sounds odd. But Maud had been pressing me to let it go. She claimed it would take months to sort out and that with Barrett selling his house and planning to go off somewhere, I'd never see a farthing of the money he stole from me."

"Mrs. Astley had talked you into dropping the lawsuit?" Witherspoon asked. He wanted to make sure he had all the facts right. "Is that correct?"

"I've just told you it is," Astley snapped. "My wife is a very sensible woman. We probably couldn't have won in court. Sharpe, my secretary, had come across some papers that shed a whole new light on the situation. It seems that Barrett might not have been robbing me blind after all. So you see, Inspector, I'd no motive for murdering Barrett."

"Mr. Astley," Barnes asked quietly, "how did Mrs. Astley know that Barrett was selling his house?"

Luty Belle Crookshank poured a cup of Earl Grey and handed it to her guest. She'd much rather have had a good shot of whiskey, but Myrtle was an old fussbudget, and she wanted to get the woman gossipin'. Not that it would be hard, she thought as she watched her neighbour delicately pick out a tea cake. Myrtle was about the biggest talker in London.

"Barrett, did you say?" Myrtle Buxton shook her head. "I've never heard of him."

"Don't you read the papers?" Luty asked. "He got himself skewered with a sword a couple of days back."

"Oh." Myrtle made a face. "*That* Barrett. Well, I've still never heard of him. He was, after all, in trade."

"What's wrong with bein' in trade," Luty snapped. From the corner of her eye, she saw Hatchet frowning at her.

Myrtle laughed. "You Americans are so innocent! There's nothing wrong with it, exactly. It's just that people in trade aren't generally as—"

"I know what you're goin' to say," Luty interrupted her. She knew if she and Myrtle got into this argument, she'd be here all night, and she didn't have time for that. "And I don't agree. So let's just leave it at that. So you're sayin' that you never heard of the feller until you read about him bein' murdered."

Myrtle smiled coyly. "Well, actually, now that you mention it, I do recall one bit of scandal. Did you know he left some poor woman at the altar?"

Hatchet coughed. Luty shot him a quick glare. He was smirking. She knew exactly what he was thinkin'. All she was gettin' today was old gossip.

"I heard he left that Washburn girl at the altar," Luty sniffed. "If it'da been me, I'd a shot the varmit. But I reckon you English don't believe in settlin' scores the way we do back home."

"We're a bit more civilized than that." Myrtle smiled. "Of course, Eliza Washburn was practically ruined. Why, Octavia Haines told me that Miss Washburn was so distraught and nervous after being so publicly humiliated, her own brother took to slipping her sleeping draughts in her sherry."

"Seems to me she wouldn'a been so shaky if she'da taken a shot at the polecat," Luty replied. Honestly, women like Eliza Washburn made her itch to slap 'em 'round the side of the head. Any woman that couldn't stand up for herself and let a no-good bushwacker like Barrett walk all over 'em deserved what they got.

"Don't be absurd, Luty." Myrtle chose a napoleon from the silver tray in front of her. "Eliza Washburn is a lady. Of course, she virtually went into hiding after it happened. Everyone thought she'd gone abroad."

"She ain't," Luty said glumly. Myrtle had been here half an hour now and hadn't told her a blasted useful thing. Hatchet must be delighted. He'd been out this morning doin' his own snooping and had come back lookin' like a fox that had spent the night in the henhouse. And they were due at Upper Edmonton Gardens after dinner. She had to have something good to tell everyone.

"I know that," Myrtle said impatiently. "I said everyone *thought* she'd gone abroad."

Luty stared at her with renewed interest. From behind her, she heard Hatchet come closer to the settee. No doubt the old goat wanted to make sure he didn't miss a word. "What do you mean by that?"

Myrtle gave her one of them superior, real irritatin' smiles. "Because Eliza Washburn was seen a few days ago. Mind you, according to Henrietta Oxton, that's my friend. You may have heard of her, her aunt was a lady-in-waiting to one of the royal princesses, I forget which one." She frowned. "There were rather a lot of them at Buck House before they got married off."

"Go on, Myrtle," Luty urged. Once Myrtle got onto the subject of all her fancy friends with their fancy titles, her mouth never stopped. That was fine with Luty, but she wanted her talkin' about Eliza Washburn or William Barrett, not some weak-chinned aristocrat who wouldn't last a day back home. "What was you sayin' about the Washburn girl?"

"Oh, yes. Well, Henrietta was ever so surprised. She was riding past the Richmond Road, and there was Eliza Washburn, hailing a hansom. Not that I was surprised, mind you. The Washburns are in trade too. What else can one expect."

"When was this?"

"Tuesday," Myrtle said promptly. "I remember because I saw Henrietta on Wednesday morning, and the first thing she said to me was that she'd seen Eliza Washburn the day before."

"Did she say what time?"

"What time?" Myrtle repeated, looking puzzled.

"What time of the day was it when she saw the girl," Luty explained.

"Oh, it was late afternoon. Henrietta was on her way back from having tea with Lady Worthington." Myrtle's eyebrows drew together. "Why on earth do you want to know?"

"Just curious." Luty grinned. The nice thing about Myrtle was that she was such a gossip herself, she expected everyone else to be one too. "You know, I like to get all the facts straight."

"Yes, I know just what you mean." Myrtle laughed. "I always insist on knowing the details myself."

Luty gestured at the silver tray. Antoine had outdone himself. Napoleons, seed cake, delicate French pastries. Thank goodness the man liked to bake. She gestured at a cream puff. "Come on, Myrtle, try one of Antoine's puffs."

"Oh, I really shouldn't," but Myrtle was already reaching her plump hand toward the confectionary.

Luty wasn't certain, but if she remembered rightly, on the afternoon of the murder, Eliza Washburn was supposed to be restin' in her room. Now this was gettin' interestin'.

Neville Sharpe stood rigidly in front of the fireplace. "I don't know what you mean," he said to Witherspoon. "I was at the dentist."

Witherspoon shook his head. "But we know you weren't, Mr. Sharpe. We've checked with the dentist and he's never heard of you."

Sharpe glanced at the door of the drawing room. Thornton Astley had gone back to his study, and there were no servants lurking around. "All right, but please don't say anything to Mr. Astley. I don't want to lose my position."

"We'll not tell your employer any more than absolutely necessary," the inspector assured the young man. "Now, where were you on Tuesday afternoon?"

"I was walking." Sharpe shrugged. "You see, I'd told Mr. Astley that I had to go and see about my tooth. But that wasn't the truth. I've been thinking about changing my life, sir. I may have an opportunity to emigrate, and I had a great deal of thinking to do. I needed to get out of the house. So I asked Mr. Astley for the afternoon off and went for a walk. Generally I work till half past five or six o'clock, but that day, I left at four-thirty."

"Did anyone see you?" Barnes asked. "I mean anyone who knows you."

"No. I'm afraid not."

Witherspoon didn't see much point in questioning the man further. Neville Sharpe had no reason to murder William Barrett. He barely knew the man. "All right, Mr. Sharpe. That's all for now."

"You'll not say anything to Mr. Astley?" Sharpe said anxiously. "I've decided not to leave England, and I really would hate to lose this position. He wouldn't take kindly to the fact that I'd lied to get the afternoon off on Tuesday."

The inspector smiled. "We've no reason to report your activities to Mr. Astley. I understand you found some evidence that purports to show that Mr. Barrett hadn't been stealing from Mr. Astley?"

"You mean taking money out of the business." Sharpe nodded. "Yes, I did."

"Exactly what did you find?"

"Invoices," Sharpe replied. "Invoices that showed the money we thought Barrett had skimmed into his own account had actually been paid for goods and services the company received. Not many of them, mind you. But enough to cast doubt on our assertion that Barrett was using that method to steal from the company."

"And when did you find these invoices?"

"Tuesday morning. I showed them to Mr. Astley right away."

Witherspoon and Barnes left shortly after their interviews. Barnes waited till they were out of the house before asking any questions. "What do you think of Astley's story?"

The inspector sighed. "I don't know what to make of it. He admits he was in the Barrett house."

"But we know that Barrett was alive at six o'clock," Barnes reminded him. "One of the carpenters heard his voice. But Astley claims he was dead by then."

"Yes, it is a puzzle." The inspector didn't know what to think. He was dreadfully hungry, his head hurt and his knee was throbbing. Perhaps he'd wait until after dinner tonight and then sit down and have a good think about the whole matter.

"I say, Mrs. Jeffries, have you had any luck in finding us a temporary cook?" Witherspoon gazed at her hopefully.

"No, sir," Mrs. Jeffries sighed. "I'm afraid not. The agency is doing their very best, but the earliest they think they can find someone is next week."

"Next week!" The inspector cringed. He looked down at his plate. He really did hate to criticize. Betsy had done her best and actually, if you drank a lot of water and ate fast, the meal wasn't too bad. The joint *was* a bit salty of course, and the roast potatoes perhaps just a little hard. Of course, boiled cabbage had never been one of his favourites, so he really couldn't blame Betsy because he didn't enjoy it. "Oh, well, I suppose if that's the best they can do, we'll just have to make do."

"How very understanding you are, sir."

Witherspoon reached for his water and took a huge gulp. "I'm very tired this evening," he said, putting the glass down. "I think I'll go straight up to bed. I didn't sleep well last night at all."

Mrs. Jeffries nodded sympathetically. She felt very badly for lying to the dear man, but it simply couldn't be helped. They couldn't afford to have a strange cook in the house when they were investigating a murder. "I expect it's because you've so much on your mind, sir. This is a dreadful business with the Barrett murder. It's a wonder to me you've been able to sleep at all. But then, sometimes I forget that you're not like the rest of us."

He gazed at her curiously. "Er, in what way?"

"Well, sir. Once you're on the trail, so to speak, that brilliant mind of yours probably works night and day. I shouldn't be surprised if you were working out the solution even while you were sleeping."

Witherspoon smiled modestly. "Really, Mrs. Jeffries, I'm not that different." But it was so very good to hear her say it. Sometimes he felt overwhelmed by his responsibilities. But just when it seemed as though he would never determine what had happened, something came along and the solution popped into his mind like magic.

"You're far too modest, sir." She took a sip of water. "How did you get along today? I bet you found out an enormous amount of information."

"Actually"—he took another drink of water. Gracious, he was thirsty this evening—"I did."

"I was sure you would, sir."

Witherspoon went on to tell her everything he'd learned. He found that talking with Mrs. Jeffries sometimes helped him to think clearly. She had a way of making comments and asking questions that sometimes opened a whole new line of inquiry.

"So I take it you didn't get a chance to talk to any of the workmen that were in the house?" she said when he'd finished.

"Not yet. But I'm doing just that first thing tomorrow morning." He paused and yawned widely. "I say, I really must get to bed."

"Why don't you do that, sir? A good night's rest will do you the world of good."

As soon as the inspector had gone up the stairs, Betsy and Mrs. Jeffries hurriedly cleared up and dashed downstairs. Smythe, Wiggins, Luty Belle and Hatchet were already there.

"I'm sorry about supper," Betsy said as soon as they were seated in the usual spots.

"Don't be apologizin' now, lass," Smythe said kindly, even though his throat was dry as a bone. "You fixed a right good meal." It was one thing to tease the girl about their investigatin', but he wouldn't hurt her feelins about her cookin' for the world. Women could be awful sensitive about things like that. And supper had been truly awful. His back teeth were still sore from chewin' on them roast potatoes. For once, he was glad he had money. If one of his dreams come true and he and Betsy ever did end up man and wife, he'd be able to afford a cook.

"That's nice of you to say, Smythe." Betsy looked down at the table. "But it was terrible. I saw the way you was all drinking water to choke down that salty joint. And roast potatoes is supposed to be soft inside, not hard as marbles."

Wiggins started guiltily and put down his glass of water. "It were fine, Betsy," he lied.

"You did a very nice job." Mrs. Jeffries patted her on the hand. "Goodness knows, it was certainly better than anything I could have cooked."

"Seems to me that none of you can cook worth a hill of beans," Luty put in. "I'll bring something over tomorrow fer yer suppers. We don't want to spend the rest of the evenin' talkin' about yer stomachs, do we?"

Mrs. Jeffries nodded, delighted to be off the subject of food. If Mrs. Goodge didn't get back soon, they were going to starve to death. Even Wiggins, who had a lead-lined belly, hadn't been able to choke down much of Betsy's dinner. "Luty's right. We'd best get on with it," She quickly told them what she'd learned from the inspector over dinner. "So you see, at least one of our suspects admits to being in the house. But he claims that Barrett was already dead when he got there."

"That's odd," Hatchet remarked. "But I expect we'll sort it out eventually, we always do."

"I'll go next," Luty announced. She didn't want her butler stealing her thunder. She told them about her visit with Myrtle. "She said her friend was sure it was Eliza Washburn she saw on the Richmond Road. So she couldn't have been at home restin' if she was out wavin' down hansom cabs."

"Was she dressed in a cloak and veiled hat?" Smythe asked.

Luty shrugged. "Myrtle didn't know. She hadn't asked Henrietta what Eliza Washburn was wearin'."

"Then we don't know if she's the woman who took the cab to Kildare Gardens," Mrs. Jeffries mused.

"But we don't know that she wasn't," Luty insisted. "We do know that she wasn't home restin', though."

Luty didn't have any more to add. She turned, and cocked her head, frowning at Hatchet. "Better let Hatchet go next. I know he found out somethin' today 'cause he was out all mornin' and when he come back he looked like a cat that had just stole the cream."

"I've never resembled a feline in my entire life," Hatchet sniffed. "But as it happens, I did find out something rather important today."

"Well, go on," Luty urged. "Don't keep us waitin'. We've not got all night, and I want to have plenty of time to hear what the others have found out."

"Honestly, madam, you're so impatient." Hatchet stopped and took a deep breath. "As you all know, I've a number of acquaintances throughout our fair city. As it happens, one of them has some very good connections into the Astley household. Well, I've found out that Maud Astley was trying to get her husband to drop the lawsuit against William Barrett because Barrett was blackmailing her."

"Blackmailin' 'er?" Smythe asked. "What for?"

Hatchet coughed. "Well, I'm not sure I should say in front of . . ." He looked at Wiggins and then Betsy.

"Oh, stop bein' such an old woman!" Luty exclaimed. "Betsy's and Wiggins's ears won't fall off if you tell us. They're both grown-ups."

Betsy giggled. Wiggins grinned.

"All right. Barrett was blackmailing Mrs. Astley because he'd found out she was having an illicit relationship with Neville Sharpe, Mr. Astley's secretary. Furthermore, he was in possession of some love letters that Sharpe had written to Mrs. Astley."

"How'd you find out?" Luty demanded. She was fit to be tied. Damn that old straitlaced butler of hers. He had sources all over the city, and all she had was old Tilbert and that gossipin' Myrtle.

"Never mind how I found out," Hatchet replied. "The point is, if it's true—and my source was certain it was—then it appears that both Maud Astley and Neville Sharpe had a reason to murder Barrett."

"And the inspector told me tonight that Sharpe wasn't at the dentist at the time of the murder," Mrs. Jeffries added. "Add to that the fact that Mrs. Astley was out in the garden the night before the murder, arguing with Barrett—"

"But lots of people was squabblin' with Barrett," Smythe cut in. "And you've already told us Mr. Astley admitted to goin' into Barrett's 'ouse. For all we know, he could be the killer."

"For all we know," Betsy said firmly, "half of bloomin' London could have killed him. Seems to me that everyone who knew him wanted him dead."

# CHAPTER 9

Mrs. Jeffries pulled her shawl tighter and sat back in her comfortable armchair. She stared at the dying flames in the fireplace and sighed. This case was so muddled, she was almost beginning to think they'd never make heads nor tails of it. And everyone was trying so very hard too.

She shook herself, refusing to give in to defeat. They'd solve this one, just as they'd helped solve many others. The Barrett murder might be complicated, but someone had walked into that study and rammed a sword into the victim's heart. That someone had to have made a mistake, left some kind of clue.

She frowned slightly. There was something about the murder, something about the way the entire thing must have happened that seemed . . . She tried to think clearly, to grasp the elusive something or other that had been bothering her almost from the first. The murder seemed what? Cold? Calculating? Yes, that's it. That's what had been nagging at the back of her mind. This was no impulsive killing, there was something about it that smacked of deliberation.

A burning coal flared brightly, filling the quiet room, with a crackling hiss. Mrs. Jeffries reached for the glass of water she'd had the foresight to bring with her before retiring and took a sip. Poor Betsy. She smiled. The girl had tried so hard to cook a good meal. But the best one could say was that it had been barely edible. Perhaps, she thought, one of the reasons we're having such a difficult time is because everyone's famished. It was difficult to think properly when one was hungry. But she had to think.

She closed her eyes and forced herself to go over each and every bit of information they'd acquired. First of all, how well did Lady Cannonberry really know Minerva Kenny? Ruth admitted that Minerva would rather die than have anyone suspect she was a thief. Perhaps she'd rather kill than die. Miss Kenny had been at the Barrett house on the afternoon of the murder. And she could have been the woman whom the painters had overheard crying in the drawing room. It was perfectly plausible that Minerva had come to plead with Barrett first, and when she found he couldn't be moved by her distress, she could have come back and killed him. She had the motive. Becoming known as a thief would ruin the woman.

But there were so many other possibilities as well, she admitted silently. Betsy was absolutely correct. It did seem as though half of London wanted Barrett dead.

And no one seemed to be telling the truth. She straightened as she heard the sound of footsteps from down the stairs. Then she heard the door of the water closet open, and she sank back in her chair. Poor Inspector Witherspoon, she thought with a rueful smile. He'd drunk so much water choking down Betsy's meal, he'd probably make several trips to the water closet before the night was out.

Mrs. Jeffries watched the bright embers grow dark. She really ought to get to bed herself, but she wasn't in the least tired. There was so much to sort out. Hatchet's source claimed that Maud Astley was having an affair with Neville Sharpe. Mrs. Astley was overheard arguing with Barrett the night before his murder, and the secretary wasn't at the dentist as he'd claimed. But did that add up to a motive for murder? And why kill Barrett? If Barrett was planning on exposing them, it seemed to Mrs. Jeffries that *if* either of the lovers was capable of murder, they'd have killed Thornton Astley. Then Maud would have been a rich, young widow and could have told Barrett to go to the devil. And, of course, she mustn't forget Adrian Spears or the Washburns.

She took another sip of water. Spears was a lonely bachelor, devoted to his dog. Barrett killed the dog. Mrs. Jeffries knew that that particular piece of brutality could have pushed Spears over the edge. And who better to know that the front and back door was wide open and that workmen were banging around on the third floor? Who better to know exactly when the servants would all be in the kitchen having their meal leaving Barrett alone in his study? Who better to know that even if Barrett cried out in alarm, the sound of hammering and sawing would cover his cries for help? Adrian Spears was in a perfect position to know all of this.

Furthermore, he didn't have an alibi. The inspector had told her that none of the PCs had found anyone who'd seen Spears on his walk.

She yawned. The Washburns weren't in the clear, either. Luty's friend insisted that Eliza Washburn was out hailing a cab on the Richmond Road the afternoon of the killing. She'd claimed she was home asleep. The Richmond Road wasn't far from Kildare Gardens. "Hell hath no fury like a woman scorned"—the quote popped into her mind as she stared at the dying fire. No, Miss Washburn couldn't be counted out of the running. For that matter, neither could her brother. If she wasn't at home that afternoon, then she could hardly be an alibi for her brother.

She got up and stretched, thinking about the three hansom cabs. Minerva Kenny was in one, Thornton Astley was in another, but they didn't know for sure who was in the third. All they knew was that it was a woman. But which one? Maud Astley or Eliza Washburn? More important, was one of them the killer?

The smell of sizzling beef greeted Mrs. Jeffries when she came down to the kitchen the next morning. Startled, she stopped in her tracks and gaped. Smythe, a long fork in one hand and mug of tea in the other, was standing in front of the stove.

"Mornin', Mrs. J.," he called.

"Whatever are you doing?" She moved closer and peeked around his broad shoulders.

"Cookin' beefsteaks," he replied, "Thought I'd do us a fry-up for breakfast. I've got eggs to go with this lot."

"Wherever did you get beefsteaks? I know we'd none in the cooling pantry, and the butcher isn't due to deliver till this afternoon."

"Popped out myself early this mornin'," he replied, flipping a long, thin strip of beef.

"Smythe . . ." Mrs. Jeffries clucked her tongue. "You mustn't spend your own money on household food." She started back toward the door. "Let me go up and get the money you spent."

"No need for that," he said, expertly turning the last few strips. "It didn't cost all that much, and I don't mind doin' my bit to fill our stomachs."

She started to protest and then thought better of it. She was fairly certain Smythe had no shortage of coins, and he seemed to have a great need to give to them. But that was another matter for another time. One of these days me two of them would sit down and have a nice little chat. Perhaps they'd discuss all the mysterious presents that turned up for each and every one of them from time to time. Or perhaps they'd discuss those letters he kept getting from his bank. But all in good time. Right now they had to catch a murderer.

"Something smells good," Betsy said. She stopped short at the sight of the big, brawny coachman cooking their breakfast. "Are you cookin', then?" she asked incredulously. She dashed over and peered into the frying pan. "And it looks good."

"It will be good." He gave her a quick grin and then reached for a large brown egg. "Watch this." He broke the egg in one hand as he cracked it into another frying pan.

Betsy laughed. "You didn't even break the yolk."

"Don't be too impressed, lass," Smythe replied, reaching for another egg. "You've just about seen it all."

Betsy gazed at him speculatively. "Where'd you learn to do this?"

Mrs. Jeffries paused as she reached for the rose-and-white bone china teapot.

"Oh, picked it up 'ere and there." Smythe shrugged. "Lived for me own a while in Australia. Got hungry for somethin' besides salted beef and beer, so I learned to do fry-ups and all."

"Even a fry-up is better than I can do," Betsy admitted honestly.

"There's more to life than cookin'," he said. "You're good at other things."

"Right, like cleanin' the stairs or polishin' floors." She sounded morose. "Never met a man yet that wanted a clean house over a good meal."

Mrs. Jeffries watched this exchange with interest. Finally the two of them were actually getting around to talking about something important to both of them. She put the teapot down softly so as to not break the mood.

"Since when 'ave you been carin' about what men wants? You thinkin' of gettin' married?" he queried, his voice so low Mrs. Jeffries could barely hear him. She cocked her head to one side as she reached for a teacup.

"Well," Betsy said slowly, "Every girl wants to get married some day. Mind you, I'm in no hurry—and that's a good thing too, considerin' the way I cook."

"Now, don't be worryin' about yer cookin', lass," Smythe said eagerly.

"There's plenty of men about that can afford to hire you someone like Mrs. Goodge."

"Cor blimey, what's that wonderful smell!" Wiggins yelled as he burst into the kitchen. Fred trotted right at his heels. They both rushed over to Smythe.

Betsy, a blush on her cheeks, quickly turned away and began pulling plates out of the cupboard.

Mrs. Jeffries sighed and finished making the inspector's tray. "I'll take the tray up now," she called to Smythe. "Then I'll pop right back for the inspector's breakfast."

The inspector was sitting at the dining table. There were dark circles under his eyes, his face looked haggard, and his hair was mussed. "I'll just have a nice hot cup of tea this morning," he said to Mrs. Jeffries.

"Oh, but, sir"—she put his cup in front of him—"Smythe's doing a really nice breakfast."

"Smythe!" Witherspoon said, his voice horrified.

"Yes, sir—" she began, but he interrupted her.

"Oh, don't bother to bring me any," he said, grabbing his cup and taking a huge gulp. "I've so much to do today I shan't have time for breakfast. No, indeed."

"But, sir—" she tried again.

"I really must be going!" Witherspoon stood up and took another quick gulp. "I'm sure Smythe will do an excellent breakfast, but I must be off." If the truth were known, it would take a whole regiment of the Queen's Guards to force him to eat anything *any* of them prepared. "I've got to talk to Barrett's banker and his solicitor, and then I must speak to the carpenters and the painters." He edged toward the door. "After that there's Miss Kenny and Mr. Spears to be interviewed again."

He broke into a trot, snatched up his coat and hat as he flew past the coatrack and charged for the front door.

"But, sir!" she yelled. "I'm sure it will be good this time."

Witherspoon flung the front door open. "My compliments to Smythe. I'm certain his culinary skills are excellent." He shuddered. "I'll pop back this afternoon for tea and you can tell me all about it."

"Don't forget Luty's bringing dinner tonight," she called out as he ran down the stairs. "It's a nice Mexican recipe."

But her dear inspector had disappeared.

• • •

Mrs. Jeffries washed the last of the dishes and put them in the wooden rack to drain. She'd dry them later if she had time. Everyone was in a much better frame of mind this morning. It showed what a good meal could do for one's disposition. Smythe's breakfast had been very good. Very good, indeed.

Now everyone was out gathering clues and digging up information. Smythe had gone off on some mysterious errand he refused to discuss with them. Betsy had gone over to the Washburn house to see what she could learn about Eliza Washburn's movements on the day of the murder, and Wiggins had gone back to Kildare Gardens.

She'd no idea what Luty and Hatchet were up to. But she had every confidence in their ability to turn up something interesting. Mrs. Jeffries took off her apron. As she didn't have to worry about what they were going to eat for supper tonight, she was going out to do some snooping of her own. It hadn't really been quite fair, this case. She'd spent far too much time inside instead of out and about as she usually did when they were on the hunt.

"Hello, hello," Ruth's voice called from the back door.

Mrs. Jeffries sighed. Much as she liked Lady Cannonberry, she really didn't have time this morning to chat. "Hello, Ruth," she replied.

"I do hope I'm not interrupting," Ruth said as she sailed into the kitchen. "But I've found out something and I thought you ought to hear it straight away."

"Well, I was just on my way out," Mrs. Jeffries explained.

"This won't take long." She headed for the kitchen table, her dark pink skirts rustling as she sat down. "And it is important." Her blue eyes sparkled and her cheeks were flushed with excitement.

Mrs. Jeffries stifled a groan. Lady Cannonberry had no doubt been out snooping again. Now what was it! The dear woman tried so very hard, but really, she'd turned up absolutely nothing of any use. Not that any of them would ever bring that fact to her notice, of course. But Mrs. Jeffries was worried that her friend would get so carried away she'd give them all away. Indiscreet questions were sometimes noticed. "I'm sure it is. Now, tell me what you've learned."

"First of all, I must say I think the inspector has been far too harsh to Minerva." Ruth paused. "Not that I'm accusing him of brutality."

"Brutality? The inspector?"

"I didn't mean that, exactly." Ruth frowned slightly. "It's just that Minerva's in an awful state. She's sure Inspector Witherspoon is getting ready to arrest her. Can't we do something about that?"

"Ruth," Mrs. Jeffries said gently. "I know you're concerned with your friend, but this is a murder investigation. Inspector Witherspoon is only doing his duty."

"Yes, of course he is and I'm sure he was a perfect gentleman towards Minerva." She shook her head ruefully. "But she's a bundle of nerves. Especially since the inspector almost caught her putting that wretched china bird back yesterday."

"We heard about that." Mrs. Jeffries glanced at the clock and drummed her fingers impatiently on the tabletop. "But even if he did see her putting it back, it doesn't necessarily follow that he's going to arrest her for murder."

"Of course, you're right. In any case, Minerva's been nervous for days now," Ruth said thoughtfully.

"Unfortunately her habit of . . . er . . . 'borrowing' things seems to be having a rather horrid effect on the poor woman," Mrs. Jeffries replied. "Perhaps it's all to the good, though. Barrett's catching her may help her to overcome this odd compulsion of hers."

"I certainly hope so." Ruth pursed her lips. "Mind you, I'm not altogether sure she can help herself. Do you know, she told me she was so angry that Barrett was screaming at her that day she stole some of his papers. Served him right, if you ask me—he actually struck her!"

Mrs. Jeffries stared at her, her mouth slightly agape. "Day? What day are you talking about?"

Ruth blinked. "Why, the day of the murder, of course."

"The day of the murder!" Mrs. Jeffries gasped. "You mean she told you she was there?" Gracious, sometimes dealing with Lady Cannonberry would try the patience of a saint. She should have given them this information immediately.

"Oh, yes, late yesterday afternoon after the inspector told her she'd been seen going into the Barrett house, she broke down and admitted to me she was there," Ruth explained. "But she didn't kill him. She only went there to plead with him to give her the bird back. She was most upset, but he didn't care. He actually took it out of his desk and began taunting her, called her a sticky-fingered thief and other horrible names.

Some of them were so awful Minerva couldn't bring herself to repeat them to me."

"How dreadful for her. Do please go on," Mrs. Jeffries urged.

"Well, Minerva got so angry at Barrett, she tried to snatch the bird away, and in the process she knocked some papers off his desk." Ruth snorted. "But he, being no gentleman, got furious. He slapped her hand and called her a clumsy cow. Can you believe it? That dreadful man. It's no wonder someone murdered him."

"And then what happened?" Mrs. Jeffries prompted.

"Then one of the workmen accidentally banged into the door with a length of wood and that set Barrett off again." Ruth leaned forward. "He got up and flung open the door to scream at the workman and Minerva was so angry, she picked up some of the papers she'd knocked on the floor and stuffed them into her pocket. Then she left."

"Why didn't she take the bird?" Mrs. Jeffries asked curiously.

"He had it in his hand."

"Oh, I see. What kind of papers were they?"

"Nothing very interesting," Ruth replied. "Just some letters to a bank."

"Did Minerva open the letters?"

"Of course not." Ruth sounded genuinely shocked by such a question. "Minerva would never open someone else's letters."

"What time was she there?" Mrs. Jeffries asked.

"She wasn't quite sure," Ruth replied. "As I said, she was in a state. But she thinks it was sometime close to five o'clock."

Witherspoon hid a yawn behind his hand. He was dreadfully tired. He'd gotten no sleep at all last night. All those trips to the water closet. Well, tonight he could look forward to a good dinner. Luty Belle Crookshank's cook was one of the best in London. Thank goodness Mrs. Crookshank had taken pity on their plight. It was really a shame Mrs. Jeffries was having such difficulties finding a cook.

"This is Ted Metcalf and Eric Honts." Barnes nodded at the two men he'd brought to the inspector's desk.

"Do sit down," Witherspoon indicated the chair by his desk. "Constable, if you'd be so good as to pull up another chair."

As soon as the two carpenters were seated, Witherspoon said, "I'm sorry to bring you down here. I realize you've already made statements, but I've a few more questions to ask."

"It's all right," Metcalf, a tall, morose-looking man with thin brown hair and a pockmarked face, replied. "We weren't out on a job today. But I don't know what else we can tell you. We didn't see nothin' when old Barrett got himself murdered."

Honts snorted. "Didn't see nuthin' and don't know nuthin', so I don't know why you've made us waste our time comin' down 'ere."

The inspector looked at Honts. He was a short, blond wiry man with deepset hazel eyes and a ruddy complexion. "Both of you were working on the third floor that afternoon, is that correct?"

"Right," Metcalf replied. "The painters were up there too, gettin' in our way and makin' a nuisance of themselves."

"Wasn't it odd that Mr. Barrett had carpenters and painters working at the same time?"

Honts answered this time. "'E was in a 'urry. 'E was wantin' to sell the 'ouse. It were right stupid, though. Barrett didn't want to give us time to do a job properly. We'd just get a room finished and 'e'd 'ave them ruddy painters in doin' it up. You couldn't go back and try and do any finishin' work, Barrett wouldn' stand fer it."

Witherspoon, aside from being dreadfully hungry and tired, was also confused. "What makes you think that Barrett was in a hurry to sell the house?" The inspector didn't think that could possibly be true. He'd spoken with Barrett's solicitor this morning, and the man had categorically denied any knowledge that William Barrett was moving house. Yet the painters had told the inspector the same story.

"We overheard him tellin' that Mr. Washburn he was sellin'," Metcalf said. "And I know it were true 'cause he told Miss Washburn the same thing that very mornin'."

"Miss Washburn?" Witherspoon gasped. "Are you sure?"

"Sure I'm sure. She come that mornin'."

"How did you know who she was?" Witherspoon pressed.

"Barrett called 'er by name, now, didn't 'e," Metcalf said, his tone was exasperated as though he were explaining something to a dull-witted child. "I was standin' right at the top of the stairs when she come waltzing in the front door. 'E asked her what she were doin' there and she says, 'Is it true? Are you selling your house and leaving?' About then he caught sight of me, and he hustled her into the drawin' room."

"Gracious, why didn't you tell the police constables this?" Witherspoon asked.

"They didn't ask." Metcalf shrugged. "Besides, this were hours afore Barrett was killed."

"Did you hear anything else?"

"No, I went back upstairs to work."

"Tell 'im about what we overheard when he was talkin' to Mr. Washburn," Honts urged.

"You were eavesdropping on Mr. Barrett and Mr. Washburn?"

"Eavesdroppin'!" Metcalf laughed. "We didn't have to do that. Washburn and Barrett was yellin' at the top of their lungs about it. A deaf man could of heard them two goin' at it."

"When did this argument take place?"

Metcalf rubbed his chin. "Let's see now, I reckon it were a few days afore Barrett was killed."

"Nan," Honts corrected. "It were at least a week earlier. I remember because we was workin' on that south wall when it happened, and we finished that job at least ten days ago."

"I do wish you'd mentioned these facts when the police constable took your statements," Witherspoon remarked worriedly. This information was undoubtably important. Not that he could see why just at the moment, but it would come to him. He hoped.

"No one asked us," Metcalf said.

"All the peelers asked was what was we doin' at the time of the murder," Honts put in. "None of 'em asked us anything else."

Witherspoon nodded slowly. Mrs. Jeffries had indeed been correct; it was a good idea that he spoke to the workmen himself instead of relying on the PCs' statements, "Is there anything else you can think of that might be important?"

Metcalf and Honts exchanged puzzled glances, as though they weren't used to being asked their opinions.

"Well, let's see," Metcalf muttered. "You know about the ruckus over Mr. Spears's dog? The stones and all?"

"That was the day before the murder," Honts corrected. "I remember 'cause it was the same day that painter pinched me hammer and then 'ad the gall to accuse me of stealin' his ruddy hat and coat."

"That's what I'm sayin', you bloody fool. You gone deaf or somethin'?" Metcalf glared at his friend. "I'm talkin' about the day before when Mr. Washburn was there and he and Mr. Barrett threw stones at Mr. Spears's dog."

"I know what you're talkin' about," Honts shot back, "and I'm only tryin' to 'elp keep things straight."

"You're just confusin' everythin'! If you'd keep quiet and let me finish—"

Witherspoon closed his eyes. He dearly would love a cup of tea. The two carpenters were now engaged in a heated debate on what had happened when.

"You've gone daft, man!" Metcalf yelled. "I know when things happened, and your hammer went missin' the day before the murder."

"I'm daft?" Honts cried. "You've not got enough sense to come in out of the rain . . . and I know bloody good and well when my tool got pinched."

"Gentlemen, please!" Witherspoon shouted. They both fell silent. "Now, let's start over, shall we?"

"Is the inspector home yet?" Betsy asked as she put the finishing touches on the table.

"He's having a glass of sherry in the drawing room," Mrs. Jeffries replied. "The poor man is so worn out, I probably won't get much out of him until breakfast. He was too tired to talk, but I did learn a few things. Barrett was going to sell his house, and Owen Washburn and his sister knew about it. Eliza Washburn is the mysterious woman he was quarreling with in his drawing room."

"Eliza Washburn! She were the one? That's a surprise. I wonder what she wanted?"

"I don't know," Mrs. Jeffries admitted. "I'll see how much more information I can get out of the inspector after he's had a good night's sleep."

They heard voices and footsteps at the back door.

"Yoo-hoo, we're here!" Luty Belle yelled.

A moment later Luty, dressed in a bright blue aqua gown, a gigantic hat festooned with plumes and lace and a matching parasol, came into view. Hatchet was right behind her. He was carrying a huge black kettle.

"Good evening," Hatchet said.

"We've brought supper," Luty informed them gaily. "And wait till you taste it. I made it myself. Just put the pot down on the center of the table," she told Hatchet. "We can dish it up right out of the kettle. No need to be fancy."

"This is so kind of you, Luty," Mrs. Jeffries said. Like everyone else at the table, her eyes were on the food.

Hatchet lifted the lid. Everyone leaned closer to get a better look. The kitchen was filled with strange and exotic smells. Inside the kettle, chunks of meat swam in a bright red sauce. "I had to use my special spices," Luty informed them. "Lucky I went back home this past summer. I brung back a whole load of dried chili peppers. They keep real well."

"Except for those few spots you had to cut out," Hatchet said. His face was straight, but his eyes were twinkling. "I can't wait till our friends taste this dish, madam. I'm sure they'll devour every single morsel." He gave them all a wide grin. "Madam spent all afternoon working on this dish. Do enjoy it."

Wiggins's mouth gaped open, "Cor, look at that, it's red."

"It's a special recipe of mine," Luty said proudly. "Learned it from my neighbour back in Colorado. Rosa Herrera was one good cook. Mind you, Antoine's nose is out of joint, he don't like me shooin' him out of the kitchen. But I wanted to cook this myself."

"I'll just take a plate up to the inspector," Mrs. Jeffries said as she reached for a dinner plate. "The rest of you go on ahead and eat. We've much to talk about tonight."

Mrs. Jeffries left them dishing up Luty's feast and hurried up the stairs with the inspector's dinner on a tray. He met her in the hallway. "Is that my supper?" he asked hopefully.

"Yes, sir, Luty cooked it this afternoon and brought it right over." She hurried into the dining room, the inspector right behind her.

"I say." Witherspoon sniffed as Mrs. Jeffries removed the silver cover on the plate. "That does smell unusual, rather nice, actually."

"It's a Mexican dish," Mrs. Jeffries replied. "And I'm sure it's very good. Admittedly, it does look strange to us, but that's only because we're not used to exotic food."

"Well, it smells delicious." Witherspoon lifted his fork and poked at a piece of beefsteak. "Is Mrs. Crookshank still here?"

"She's dining with the staff."

The inspector took a huge bite. He was so hungry.

"If you don't mind, sir . . . as Mrs. Crookshank so kindly brought our dinner—" She broke off in alarm. "Gracious, sir. Whatever is the matter?"

Witherspoon's eyes bulged, his cheeks ballooned out, and his face was as red as the sauce on his plate. "Mouth burning—water!" He lunged for his water glass.

"Oh, dear." Mrs. Jeffries closed her eyes briefly.

He gulped half a glass of water and choked. Mrs. Jeffries pounded him on the back.

He caught his breath and sighed. "How much longer do you think Mrs. Goodge will be gone?"

A few minutes later Mrs. Jeffries made her way back to the kitchen. Poor man. He really was in a quandary. He didn't wish to hurt Luty's feelings, but obviously that dish she'd brought was hot enough to blister his tongue. She'd left him scraping the sauce off the meat and gulping water between bites.

When she came into the kitchen, she noticed Hatchet grinning like a playful puppy as he watched the others struggle to eat without actually putting any food in their mouths.

Wiggins was gulping water, Smythe was trying to chew and hold his breath at the same time, and Betsy's cheeks were flaming. Luty, on the other hand, was eating heartily.

"Do sit down and have some," Hatchet said, giving Mrs. Jeffries an evil grin.

"Thank you, I'm sure it's excellent." Actually, she rather liked spicy food. Her late husband had been great friends with an Indian gentleman, and they'd often eaten at his table. She took a liberal portion of the stew.

"How'd ya like it?" Luty asked, beaming at everyone.

"It's very nice," Betsy muttered. She used the edge of her fork to cut her meat chunks into sections small enough to feed a mouse. "But I'm really not all that hungry tonight."

"Go on, eat up. Young woman's got to keep her strength up." Luty chuckled. "Especially when we're tryin' to solve a murder. What about you, Smythe? How's it taste?"

"Uh . . ." Smythe gave her a weak smile. "Real good, Luty, ain't had a dish like this in years." Not since he'd been forced to eat fried lizards out on the Australian bush. But that had only been disgustin', it hadn't made his mouth feel like he was chewin' on hot coals.

Luty glanced at Wiggins. He was still gulping water. "Guess it's a bit hot fer ya, huh?"

"A little," Wiggins rasped.

Mrs. Jeffries took a small bite. Her tongue smarted slightly, but the flavour was really quite good. She chewed delicately. "Now," she said, "let's talk as we eat." That would give the others an excuse to slow down and, if they were very lucky, would distract Luty from noticing the real effect her food was having on everyone.

Betsy dropped her fork. "I'll go first."

"All right." Mrs. Jeffries nodded. "What did you find out today?"

"Uh, well . . . uh . . ." She deliberately stumbled over her words. No point in telling her news too quickly. She'd have to eat more of this god-awful stew if she did. "It's not much, really. But I talked to a greengrocer's boy over near where the Washburns live."

"And?" Mrs. Jeffries prompted.

Betsy shrugged slightly. "He didn't say much exceptin' that he had a delivery to make to the Washburn house. But when he knocked on the back door, no one answered."

"And what did you conclude?" Mrs. Jeffries wondered if she was going to have to drag information out of all of them. Gracious, they'd be here all night.

"I thought that maybe that meant that no one was home."

"I'm not so sure," Mrs. Jeffries said thoughtfully. "If you'll recall, Lady Cannonberry told us that there were rumours that Owen Washburn had been giving his sister sleeping draughts for her nerves. Maybe she was asleep? The servants were out and the cook was napping as well. Perhaps no one heard the lad knock."

"But what about Owen Washburn?" Betsy persisted. "He was supposed to be workin' in his study. And what about Eliza bein' seen hailing that hansom on the Richmond Road?"

Mrs. Jeffries didn't know what to think. "There is that. You do have a point. I think perhaps you ought to see what else you can find out about how the Washburns spent that afternoon." She turned to Luty. "Is your friend absolutely certain it was Eliza Washburn she saw that day?"

Luty nodded. "That's what she said. But I found out somethin' real interestin' about Mr. Owen Washburn. My friend Tilbert come by this afternoon when I was cookin'."

"When?" Hatchet scowled. "You never said a word to me."

"I don't tell you every little thing, now, do I?" Luty snapped. "Anyways, as I was sayin', Tilbert come by and he give me an earful."

"What did he say?" Mrs. Jeffries asked.

"Seems Owen Washburn wasn't just partnerin' with William Barrett. The truth is, Barrett was bankrollin' the whole kit and kaboodle. Paid the suppliers, paid the workers and the drivers and kept the creditors off Washburn's back."

"So now that Barrett's dead, what happens?" Mrs. Jeffries asked.

"Probably means that Washburn is straight out of luck," Luty replied. "With Barrett gone, the estate will probably cut off the money."

"Who does get his money?" Wiggins asked. At this point he didn't really care. But askin' questions was a good excuse not to keep stuffing his mouth with food that was so hot it was growing blisters on his tonsils.

"The inspector said the bulk of the estate goes to some cousin that lives abroad," Mrs. Jeffries replied. That was one of the more interesting things she'd learned while the inspector sipped his sherry. "The rest of the estate goes to charity."

"Charity!" Betsy cried. "That don't sound like William Barrett."

"One must do something with one's money." Mrs. Jeffries shrugged. "Perhaps that was his way of trying to make up for all the grief he'd caused during his life."

"So if the money gets cut off . . ." Smythe mused.

"But we don't know for certain that it does," Luty interrupted. "Lots of businesses have survivorship clauses in their company contracts. That would mean that Washburn would still be entitled to whatever operating money Barrett had originally put into the business."

"But if they didn't have such an agreement," Mrs. Jeffries said, "that means that even though Washburn and his sister might have hated Barrett, they would have no reason to kill him. Barrett was more useful to them alive than dead."

# CHAPTER 10

Witherspoon didn't know how much more of this he could stand. He felt worse this morning than he had yesterday. He clutched his stomach as he trudged down the stairs to the dining room and tried not to think about food. He wasn't sure his digestive system would ever recover, but he was sure the roof of his mouth was still raw. Gracious, did people actually enjoy such spicy food? He couldn't believe it. Though it had been kind of Mrs. Crookshank to provide them with a meal, he hoped she wouldn't do it again.

He stopped by the dining room door, steeled himself and went inside.

"Good morning, sir," Mrs. Jeffries said cheerfully. "I hope you slept well."

"Actually, I didn't," he admitted honestly, his gaze fixed on the table. He smiled in relief at what he saw. Lovely brown toast, coddled eggs and three rashers of bacon that looked absolutely perfect. "Goodness, *that* certainly looks good. Who did the honours this morning?" He hoped it hadn't been his housekeeper or Betsy.

"Smythe did," Mrs. Jeffries replied. "He spent some time in Australia living on his own, you know. He's quite a deft hand at cooking. Inspector, do you know that Luty told us the oddest thing last night."

Witherspoon yanked out his chair, sat down and dug right into his meal. "What?" he mumbled around a mouthful of egg. He closed his eyes in pleasure as the first bite slipped down his throat. It was wonderful, delicious. Not overcooked, oversalted or overspiced. Thank God.

"You know how she admires you, sir." Mrs. Jeffries raised her voice. The inspector was eating so intently she wanted to make sure he could hear her. "She follows all your cases. Well, naturally we mentioned this current case and do you know, she'd actually heard of William Barrett." She paused to see if he would react. But he didn't, he merely bobbed his head and spooned another bite of egg into his mouth.

"Of course," she continued, "we didn't say a word about the investigation itself, but as we chatted, it came out that a friend of Luty's knew quite a bit about Barrett's business dealings. This friend, I believe he's retired from the City, told Luty that Barrett wasn't just Owen Washburn's partner, he was actually providing the cash to keep the company going."

"How very interesting," Witherspoon replied. "Except for one thing: Washburn claims he was going to buy Barrett out."

"Do you think it's possible Washburn is lying?"

He took a sip of tea. "It's possible. Perhaps I should look into it further."

Relieved, for that's precisely what she wanted him to do, Mrs. Jeffries poured herself a cup of tea from the pot and sat down in her usual place. She had many items she needed to cover, and she had to be very careful of what she said. Oh, yes, indeed, she must take care, but by the time he was through with breakfast, she'd make sure he had a flea in his ear about a number of things in this case. Inspector Witherspoon was going to have a very busy day. Last night's meeting had turned up several intriguing possibilities.

Smythe walked toward his bank, frowning irritably with every step. That bloomin' Pike, 'avin' the nerve to keep pesterin' a body with them stupid letters! Another one had arrived with the first morning post, and luckily, he'd been in the hall when it had dropped through the letter box. He was goin' to have a few words to say to that ruddy banker when he saw him. Bloomin' Ada, he'd told the man he'd come in next week. That shoulda been good enough. But no, the silly old git had written him two letters remindin' him. Well, he'd soon put a stop to it. He wasn't goin' to let money run his life, and he wasn't goin' to let some banker do it either.

He reached the front door of the bank and pushed it open. Across the lobby Pike was sitting at his desk. As though he had a sixth sense, he looked up at that precise moment. Smythe paused in the open door and glared at him. The banker gave him a thin smile in return.

"Out of my bloody way!" an angry shout came from the street behind him. Smythe turned his head to see what was goin' on. A four-wheeler, with a driver screaming his head off, was caught behind a slow-moving dray. Smythe grinned as the driver of the dray wagon made a rude gesture at the driver of the wheeler. "I said to get that bloody thing outa the way!" the wheeler screeched at the top of his lungs. "Or I'll move it for ya."

"You and what army?" the dray shouted back. Sounded like a right old tussle was startin'.

Smythe's smile faded as he saw a familiar figure walking on the other side of the dray. His eyes narrowed. Now, what was he doin' here? He watched the man hurry toward the end of the street and then turn the corner.

Smythe hesitated only a moment, shoved out the doorway and let it bang shut behind him. He leapt down the stone stairs and almost collided with a woman. "Sorry, ma'am," he mumbled, trying to dodge around her wide girth.

"I should hope so," she snapped.

"Mr. Smythe, Mr. Smythe!" Pike shouted from the door. "Aren't you coming in?"

"Later!" he yelled as he ran toward the corner where Owen Washburn had disappeared. He could still hear the banker blustering as he rounded the corner. Washburn was just disappearing into a bank.

It was a bigger, fancier bank than the one Smythe used. His footsteps pounded on the marble floors as he crossed the wide foyer. Several clerks looked up and he slowed down.

At the far window Owen Washburn was talking with an older man. Smythe reckoned he must be the manager. He was as tight-lipped and disapprovin' lookin' as old Pike was.

"May I help you?" a young clerk asked, leaning out of his cage.

"Uh, I'm thinkin' about openin' an account here," Smythe replied quickly. He didn't want some clerk tossin' him out before he could see what Washburn was up to.

The clerk sniffed. "A deposit account?" His tone implied he didn't believe Smythe even knew what a deposit account was, let alone have the money to open one.

Smythe nodded. "Right." Out of the corner of his eyes, he saw Washburn and the bank manager chattin' away like they was mates.

"There are some forms you'll need to fill out," the clerk said, looking down his nose. "Will you need help?"

"Why should I need any bloody 'elp?"

"I meant do you need assistance reading them?"

Smythe yanked a pouch of money and a roll of notes out of his pocket. The coins jingled as he slapped it right under the clerk's nose. "I can read and write, ya silly git. Now get me the forms."

The clerk at the next window snickered as the first clerk turned a bright red. "Yes, sir."

Smythe turned his attention back to Washburn while the clerk fumbled with some papers on the other side of his cage.

The bank manager had disappeared. Washburn was just sitting there, but his spine was as rigid as a post, and even from this distance, Smythe could see the way he was fidgetin' with his hands.

"Here you are, sir." The clerk shoved some papers toward Smythe. "And please accept my apologies, I didn't mean to imply—"

"I know exactly what you meant me to think," he snapped, incensed on behalf of working people everywhere. Just because you weren't dressed in a ruddy gent's suit, people thought they could treat you like dirt. "I'll take 'em over there to fill out." Smythe jerked his head toward the other side of the bank. There was a long wooden waist-high partition separating the public from the employees. It was a much better spot to watch Washburn. "Don't like people lookin' over my shoulder."

"Bring them back here when you're through, sir," the clerk said nervously.

Smythe walked across to the partition, put the forms on the top and pretended to read them. From this vantage point, even with his head down he could see what was happening. Washburn and the manager was no more than fifteen feet away from him. He cocked his ear to one side, hoping to hear a snatch of their conversation.

The bank manager reappeared and handed a thick, flat canvas bag to Washburn. They talked a few seconds longer, but Smythe couldn't hear what they was sayin'. Finally Washburn took the bag and left. Smythe waited a few seconds and then followed him out. He left the papers sitting on the partition.

"Sir, Mrs. Astley is here to see you," Barnes said to Witherspoon. "She's just outside. Should I bring her in now?"

The inspector looked up from the statements he was going over for the tenth time. "Mrs. Astley? Here?"

"Right, sir." Barnes shrugged. "She won't tell me what she wants. Insists on seein' you."

"Bring her right in, Constable." Witherspoon hastily began trying to tidy his desk. "And pull up another chair for yourself."

Maud Astley, followed by Constable Barnes, marched down the aisle to Witherspoon's desk. "Good morning, Inspector," she said politely. "I'd like to speak with you, please."

"Please have a seat, Mrs. Astley." He gestured at the chair beside his desk. "What is it you'd like to speak to me about?" he asked as soon as she was comfortable.

She fumbled with the handle of her umbrella. "I'm not quite sure how to begin," she said, her voice low and hesitant. "My coming here seems so disloyal."

"I take it what you have to say has something to do with Barrett's murder?"

She nodded and gazed down at the floor. "This is so difficult. But I really felt I had to come. My conscience simply wouldn't let me keep silent."

"Please, Mrs. Astley." Witherspoon didn't wish to press the woman, but he had so much to do today. Ever since breakfast he'd had so many new ideas about the case, and he wanted to get on with his inquiries before he forgot them all. "Just tell me what you think I ought to know."

Mrs. Astley took a deep breath, lifted her lovely chin and looked him squarely in the eye, "It's about Minerva Kenny. She's a very dear lady and a very good friend, but I happen to know she went to see William Barrett on the day he died."

"We're aware of that," the inspector replied. "May I ask how you found out?"

She looked surprised by his statement, but she caught herself quickly. "I found out from Adrian Spears. He came to see me yesterday after you'd spoken with him. He mentioned he'd seen her going into Barrett's home."

"I see." Witherspoon frowned slightly. "But if you knew Mr. Spears had already given us this information, why did you bother to come in?"

"Because there's something else you should know." She bit her lip. "It's about Minerva, Miss Kenny."

"What about her?"

"She had a good reason to dislike William Barrett. Actually, I think she hated him."

"Mr. Spears told us that as well," the inspector said. "But he declined to tell us what that reason might be. Will you tell me?" He was fairly certain she would; otherwise, she wouldn't have bothered to come all the way down here.

"She hated him because he'd found out that she . . . she . . . takes things. Knowing Barrett, he was probably threatening to expose her. Minerva would be ruined socially."

Witherspoon gaped at her. "Takes things? What kind of things?"

"Oh"—she shook her head—"I'm not explaining this right. We've all known about Minerva, at least the women have, for some time. Females tend to be a bit more observant than men in these kinds of circumstances. In any case, Minerva has a . . . problem. Actually, it's more like an affliction. She'll go into someone's home and see some trinket or knickknack she likes, and she'll put it in her pocket and take it home. But she always puts them back. As I said, several of her friends have known about her little habit. We've just looked the other way because it seemed such a harmless, childish thing to do." Mrs. Astley sighed. "But perhaps we should have said something to her, made her realize what she was doing. Maybe William Barrett would still be alive if all Minerva's friends hadn't looked the other way."

"Are you suggesting that Miss Kenny murdered William Barrett?" Witherspoon asked. His expression was grave and his voice somber. This was a most serious charge. He didn't like to think a gentle lady could be capable of murder, but he'd learned that the mildest of countenances could hide the most diabolical of hearts.

"I don't know what to think," Mrs. Astley murmured. "But I know that Barrett had found out Minerva was pinching things."

"How do you know?" Before he accused anyone of anything, the inspector was determined to have all his facts right.

"Because he told me himself. He told me he'd caught her in the act." Her cheeks flushed with embarrassment. "Minerva had tried to put back the bird she'd taken from our drawing room last week. Barrett caught her. I think he was tormenting her in some way. She's been dreadfully upset and very nervous ever since. When we were having tea at Mr. Spears's house, I tried asking her what was wrong, but she pretended everything was fine. Minerva tends to live in a dream world. It's as though as long as she pretends everything is all right, then it is."

"Why did Mr. Barrett choose to confide in you?" Barnes asked quietly.

"He didn't choose to confide in me," Mrs. Astley declared. "We were having a dreadful argument, and during the course of that argument, he lost his temper and it slipped out."

"You were arguing about Miss Kenny?"

"Yes," Mrs. Astley replied firmly. "I suspected that Barrett was the reason for Minerva's nerves, so I confronted him."

"When did this argument take place?"

"The night before he was killed. I ran into him out in the gardens."

Drat, thought the inspector, that was one of the inquiries he was going to make today. Well, he wasn't going to inquire specifically about Mrs. Astley, but he had been planning on going back to Kildare Gardens and asking the servants if they'd seen or heard anything about Mr. Barrett in the weeks or days preceding the murder. That idea had occurred to him while he was chatting with his housekeeper this morning. "And that's when he admitted he'd found out about Miss Kenny's . . . uh . . . activities."

"He admitted that he was tormenting her, Inspector." Mrs. Astley's pink lips curled in disgust. "Our exchange became quite heated. Mr. Barrett hated women. He was delighted that he'd found something out about Minerva that could put her in his power. I told him I didn't care about a silly piece of china, but he said what I thought didn't matter. He said that when he got through, there wouldn't be a decent house in London that would accept Minerva socially."

"Do you think that Miss Kenny killed him?" The inspector watched Mrs. Astley carefully. After all, as Barrett was dead, they had no one to corroborate her statement. For all he knew, she could be making the whole episode up.

"I don't know what to think." She clasped her hands together. "Minerva is a dear woman, a delightful person. I don't like to think she's capable of such a brutal crime. But she was there and she did have a reason for wanting him dead. He was going to ruin her. I don't think she could have stood that. Her social standing is very important to her."

"Why, Inspector," Mrs. Jeffries said, "I didn't expect you home for lunch."

"I hadn't planned on coming home," he said, "but as I was in the neighbourhood, I thought I'd pop in for a cup of tea." He was dreadfully tired, he really wanted to take a bit of a rest, and he could hardly do that at the police canteen. Besides, their food was almost as dreadful as what he'd been eating here.

Mrs. Jeffries forced herself to smile. Oh, bother, she thought. How much worse could today get? There wasn't a thing to eat, Lady Cannonberry would probably pop in any minute with those apple fritters she'd promised, and she'd run smack into the inspector. "It's quite a lovely day, sir," she said enthusiastically. "Why don't you have a seat outside in the garden and I'll bring you out a pot of tea. Are you sure that'll be enough? Would you like some bread and butter?" She prayed he'd decline; they had exactly two slices of bread left.

Witherspoon smiled gratefully. A pot of tea and a short snooze in the sun—what could be better? "That's quite a good idea. It is unseasonably warm today, and I might as well take advantage of it. Just tea will be fine, Mrs. Jeffries. I've been having a slight problem with my stomach, so I don't really want anything to eat." He started down the hallway and suddenly stopped. "By the way, I don't suppose the agency's had any luck finding us a cook?"

"I'm afraid not, sir."

He sighed softly. "Right. Well, I expect they're doing their best. Oh, yes, before I forget, Constable Barnes is calling in for me at one-thirty. Do give me a shout when he comes."

"Yes, sir." Mrs. Jeffries hurriedly brewed a pot of tea. She prayed that if Lady Cannonberry took it into her head to bring those fritters over now, she'd be very careful what she said in front of the inspector.

Ten minutes later Mrs. Jeffries picked up the loaded tray and walked out into the November sunshine. Balancing herself carefully, she shouldered the back door open and stepped outside. She gasped in shock at what she saw.

Inspector Witherspoon was bent forward, his chest and head flat on the table, eyes closed and arms splayed out to the sides.

"Inspector!" she cried in alarm as she charged toward him. "Inspector Witherspoon."

"Hmmm . . . Whatdidya . . ." He opened his eyes, saw his housekeeper running at him with a loaded tea tray and shot straight up in the chair. "Good gracious, what is it, Mrs. Jeffries?"

"What is it?" she repeated breathlessly. "I thought you were dead. You were lying on the table."

"Oh . . . oh . . . I'm dreadfully sorry," he said, giving her an embarrassed smile. "I was so tired, I merely thought I'd rest my eyes for a few moments. I must have dozed off, Gracious, how silly of me. I didn't mean to frighten you."

"That's quite all right, sir." She took a deep breath and set the tray down. "I shouldn't have reacted as I did."

"It's all right, Mrs. Jeffries." He yawned. "I haven't been sleeping well and none of us have been eating—" He broke off as he realized what he'd almost said.

"Go ahead and say it, sir," she said. "None of us has been eating very well these days. It does take a toll on one's nerves."

"Breakfast was very good," he pointed out, not wanting her to feel bad about the situation. "So much so that I was actually able to get a lot of work done this morning. We've had a bit of luck in the case today. We found a neighbour who remembers seeing Minerva Kenny go into the Barrett house on the day of the murder."

"Really? Were they absolutely sure it was Miss Kenny going in?" she asked curiously.

"Oh, yes. They were sure it was her," the inspector replied. "And that's not the only corroboration we've had that she was there. Maud Astley came by and told me the reason Miss Kenny hated William Barrett. It's quite sad, really, the poor woman has a habit of—"

"Hello," Lady Cannonberry's cheerful voice rang out. "I do hope I'm not interrupting."

"Not at all, dear lady." Witherspoon gallantly rose to his feet. "I was just going to have some tea. Do join me."

Lady Cannonberry was holding a small cloth-covered basket in one hand. "Thank you, I'd be delighted." She handed the basket to the housekeeper. "Mrs. Jeffries told me about your cook being gone, so I made some apple fritters and brought them over. Perhaps you'd like some with your tea, Gerald."

"I'll just go get another cup and some plates," Mrs. Jeffries said. She wondered how much Ruth had heard. The interruption couldn't have come at a worse time.

"Thank you, Mrs. Jeffries, that would be lovely." He turned to Lady Cannonberry. "Apple fritters? I'm not sure what those are."

She pulled the cloth back, and the tangy sweet smell of apples mingled with the crisp air. Dozens of dark brown, rather lumpy round objects lay nestled in the basket. "It's an apple batter that's been deep fried," she explained, holding the basket out to Witherspoon. "Do try one. I made them myself. A friend sent me the recipe from America."

Witherspoon reached for one of the brown lumps; he hoped they tasted as good as they smelled. He took a big bite and almost choked as sticky raw batter filled his mouth.

"How are they?" Lady Cannonberry asked eagerly.

"Mmmm," he mumbled. Gracious, did no one in London know how to cook?

"I'm so glad you like them." She smiled proudly. "I wasn't sure how long to fry them, and I wasn't sure if the grease had gotten hot enough."

Loathe to hurt her feelings, he managed to swallow what he had in his mouth. "They're lovely," he stated, reaching for his teacup.

"Oh, Gerald, thank you, I wasn't sure they'd come out right at all. Cook was no help. I think she was quite put out that I was in the kitchen. But I did want to make these for you. Poor Mrs. Jeffries, she and the others seem to be trying so very hard. And cooking and baking is such hard work too."

"Yes," he agreed hastily, "They've been trying very hard."

"Aren't you going to eat the rest of it?" she asked, frowning at the half-eaten fritter in his hand.

"Oh, yes, yes, of course." Luckily, Mrs. Jeffries came back with the plates and serviettes.

"Here you are, sir," she said, "but I'm afraid you won't have time to enjoy your fritters. Constable Barnes has just arrived. You're wanted back at the station."

Witherspoon shot up from the chair. "Then I must be off."

"But, Gerald, you didn't get to drink your tea," Lady Cannonberry protested. "And you didn't get to finish your fritter. Why don't you take it with you?"

"That's quite all right, I mustn't keep my superiors waiting." He started for the back door. "I'm sure Mrs. Jeffries will save me some of those lovely fritters for after my supper tonight." The thought of eating another supper at Upper Edmonton Gardens made him stop in his tracks. "Lady Cannonberry, would you do me the honour of accompanying me to dinner tonight? As you so kindly brought me those delightful, er . . . fritters, I would love to show my appreciation by taking you to Simpson's."

Lady Cannonberry stared at him and then broke into a broad smile. "I'd be delighted, Gerald."

"Excellent. I'll call 'round for you at half past seven."

"I didn't learn a thing!" Luty exclaimed as she popped down next to Betsy. They were gathered 'round the table at Upper Edmonton Gardens. Supper, such as it was, was over.

"Don't feel bad," Wiggins mumbled. "I didn't learn nuthin', either. I spent the whole bloomin' day watchin' the Washburn 'ouse, and the only thing that happened was Miss Washburn throwin' somethin' into the dustbin."

Mrs. Jeffries glanced around the table. Everyone's spirits were low. It was this case. It simply didn't make sense. She knew there was something she was missing, something small and important and right under her nose. But for the life of her, she couldn't think what it was. "Well, the inspector came home for tea today, and he told me that Maud Astley had let the cat out of the bag about Minerva Kenny. The police now know she takes things."

"How'd Maud Astley find out?" Luty demanded.

"I don't know. And I won't get a chance to ask the inspector until either later tonight or tomorrow. He came home so late he only had time to dress before he took Lady Cannonberry to supper."

"It's lookin' bad for Miss Kenny, isn't it?" Wiggins said.

Mrs. Jeffries wasn't sure. "It could be," she said cautiously. "Unfortunately, not only did Maud Astley tell the police about her problem, but one of the neighbours saw her going into Barrett's house that afternoon."

"Do you think he's going to arrest her?" Hatchet asked.

"I don't know. The inspector is always very, very careful before he makes an arrest." Mrs. Jeffries was at a loss, Half of London may have hated William Barrett, but half of London hadn't been seen going into his house right before the murder.

"What about Thornton Astley?" Betsy asked. "He were there too."

"That's precisely why Mrs. Astley decided to betray her friend," Mrs. Jeffries replied. "No doubt Adrian Spears had told Mrs. Astley about seeing Miss Kenny that afternoon. As Thornton Astley was also seen going inside, I'm quite sure Maud Astley decided to throw the poor woman to the wolves in order to take suspicion off her husband."

"So she provided the motive," Smythe muttered. "Clever. That's the one thing the police didn't have. As far as they knew, Minerva Kenny might not have liked Barrett, but she had no reason to want him dead."

"I'm surprised she bothered," Betsy said. She pursed her lips. "After all, Maud Astley was carryin' on with that secretary."

"That's over," Hatchet added. "Neville Sharpe gave notice. He's leaving Astley's employ and striking out for parts unknown."

"How'd you find that out?" Luty demanded.

Hatchet smiled serenely. "I have my sources, madam, and though it pains me to say this, I did promise they'd remain anonymous."

Mrs. Jeffries said, "Has anyone else learned anything today?" Her own investigations had been fruitless.

"I talked to the Spears's maid, Janie." Betsy said. "But she didn't know anything. She's right depressed, though, because the workers from Barrett's house are gone. She was sweet on one of the painters, and she's still feelin' real bad about the dog."

"Why's she feelin' bad?" Wiggins asked. "It weren't her fault that Barrett took a hammer and bashed the poor thing's head in."

"'Cause she's the one that let him out in the first place. She left the door open when she run outside that day," Betsy explained. "She thought she saw David Simms out in the garden, and so she dashed out to have a word with him. But when she got out there, he'd disappeared."

Hammer. Dog. Something tweaked the back of Mrs. Jeffries mind. She went still, trying to snatch the elusive idea and force it to stay long enough for her to examine it.

"Well, I didn't do any better than the rest of ya," Smythe admitted. "But I did see Owen Washburn today at the bank—" He stopped as he realized what he'd said. "I mean, I followed him to the bank. But he didn't do nothing but pick up a bag."

"Where did he go after that?" Mrs. Jeffries asked. The idea was coming closer. She hadn't gotten her hands on it yet, but it was almost there, she could feel it.

"Went to his company offices, stayed there a few minutes and then went on 'ome," the coachman replied. "I stayed a bit and watched, but 'e never come out again. I waited till it started to get dark."

"Gets dark so early these days," Betsy complained. "I just hate it."

"Too bad that the inspector didn't get a chance to find out if there was a survivorship agreement between Barrett and Washburn," Luty said thoughtfully.

"There wasn't," Hatchet said softly.

"Now how in the dickens do you know that?" Luty glared at her butler. This was too much. Did the old goat have a crystal ball!

"As I said before, madam, I have my sources." Hatchet couldn't suppress a smile. "But in the interests of fair play, I'll tell you how I know. I found out from Barrett's butler."

"How does Barrett's butler know?" Mrs. Jeffries asked quickly. Luty looked as though she wanted to strangle her butler.

"It's simple," Hatchet explained. "Hadley overheard Barrett and Washburn arguing over that issue. Barrett refused to put that clause in the contract. Washburn maintained that as he'd already had one partner die which had caused great financial hardship on the company, he thought it a good idea. He was willing to sign a survivorship clause, but Barrett wasn't."

"How long ago did this argument take place?" Smythe asked.

"As well as Hadley could recall, he thinks it was about a week or ten days ago." Hatchet leaned back in his chair. "I gather it was quite a shouting match."

"The killer could be anybody," Betsy said glumly. "I don't think we're any closer to solvin' this one than we ever was. Nothin' makes sense, everyone who knew the victim hated him, and half of London was in or out of his house that afternoon."

"Yeah, anyone coulda stuck that sword in 'im," Wiggins agreed.

"No, they couldn't," Mrs. Jeffries said firmly. "This case is not impossible. This was no impulsive murder; it was well planned and well executed."

"Who did it, then? Do ya have an idea?" Luty asked.

"Yes," Mrs. Jeffries replied, "I've a very good idea. As a matter of fact, there's only one person who could have killed Barrett. One person who had the motive, the means and the opportunity."

"Who?" they all demanded at once.

But she shook her head. "Before I tell you the name, there's something that Wiggins and Smythe need to do."

"Just tell us what it is," Smythe said.

"I want you to go to the Washburns and search through the dustbin. If my theory is correct, you'll find a workingman's hat."

"You want us to go now?" Wiggins yelped. "At this time o' night?"

"Come on, lad, I'll be with ya." The coachman was already getting to his feet. "I reckon we should be back in less than an hour."

"We'll be waiting right here," Mrs. Jeffries assured them.

"I hate it when they go out at night," Betsy said as soon as Smythe was safely out of earshot. "It's always a bit of a worry."

"Don't worry," Mrs. Jeffries said reassuringly. "Smythe can take care of himself, and for that matter, Wiggins has a good head on his shoulders. They'll be fine. Now, who's for more tea? We've got some of Lady Cannonberry's apple fritters to go with it."

"Be quiet," Smythe hissed. "You're makin' enough noise to wake the dead." He eased around the hedge with Wiggins right on his heels. "Where's the bin?"

"It's right over there." Wiggins pointed at the side of the house. "I were standin' beside the 'edge, that's how come I saw her tossin' somethin' in it."

"Stay 'ere," Smythe ordered. "And if anyone come out, you take off runnin', you 'ear?"

"All right. But you be careful now. I'll stay 'ere and keep watch."

Smythe eased his way across the small lawn to the front of the house. Ducking down, he scurried along the paved walkway, keeping his head low so that anyone inside the front room wouldn't see him. He couldn't hear any voices, but that didn't mean the room was empty. As he reached the edge of the brick building, he stretched up and peeked in the corner of the window. The lamps were brightly lit, and there was a fire in the grate, but the room was empty.

Easing around the side of the building, he ducked to avoid another window, slowed his steps and tiptoed to the bin.

The bin was metal and dented on one side. There was no cover on it. Smythe looked up to make sure there were no faces at the window of the house next door. All they had to do was glance out and he'd be done for. But he saw no one."

He struck a match and held it over the bin. Inside, there were some tins, a half empty bottle of Sainsbury's Lavender Water, old newspapers and sticking out from beneath the side of one of the newspapers, a dark patch of something. Smythe stuck his hand inside and pulled out a flat wool workingman's cap. He shook his head, grinned and shoved the cap in his pocket. That Mrs. Jeffries, she didn't half surprise him sometimes. Now how the bloody blue blazes did she know this cap was going to be right where she said it was?

"You'll have to take it back." Mrs. Jeffries instructed them after they'd all examined the cap.

"What—tonight?" Wiggins couldn't believe his ears. "But it's freezin' outside and I'm dead tired."

"We can take it back," Luty volunteered.

"No, that's all right," Smythe said quickly. "I don't mind goin', and the lad can stay here. It won't take two of us."

"I'm afraid it must go back," Mrs. Jeffries said apologetically. "It'll only be useful as evidence if the inspector finds it in the Washburn dustbin."

"Was it Eliza Washburn that killed him?" Luty asked hopefully.

"Oh, no, Luty." Mrs. Jeffries shook her head. "It wasn't Eliza Washburn. It was her brother, Owen. But we're going to have a very difficult time getting the inspector to arrest the right person without exposing our part in the case. Very difficult indeed."

# CHAPTER 11

Mrs. Jeffries was suddenly very unsure. What if she were wrong? There could be another reason that cap was in the Washburn dustbin. No, she shook herself slightly, there couldn't. Given everything they'd learned, there was only one possible conclusion.

"Luty, do you think I can borrow Antoine tomorrow morning?" Mrs. Jeffries asked. "It's imperative we keep Inspector Witherspoon here as long as possible in the morning."

Luty, who was putting on her coat, gave her a curious stare. "Sure. I don't reckon Antoine will mind."

Mrs. Jeffries nodded her thanks and turned to Smythe. "How long do you think it will take you to get that cap back to the Washburns?"

"I should be there and back in less than an 'our."

"Owen Washburn," Hatchet murmured. "Whyever do you think he killed Barrett?"

"I'll tell you everything tomorrow," Mrs. Jeffries promised. "It will take far too long to make sense of it tonight, and I've got to go out."

"Go out!" Betsy and Smythe cried at the same time.

"Yes, yes." She brushed their concern aside. "I know what you're going to say, but I must speak with Lady Cannonberry before she retires for the night."

"Why don't I have Hatchet stay and go with ya?" Luty suggested.

"I'll do it," Wiggins said. "Hatchet's got to see you get home safely."

Luty patted her fur muff. "Long as I got my peacemaker, here"—she patted the muff again—"I don't much worry about bein' bothered none."

There was a collective groan. Luty carried a Colt .45 in her muff. They were all sure that one day she'd accidentally shoot herself, or even worse, one of them.

"Really, madam," Hatchet said frostily. "This is not the American West. There is absolutely no need to carry a firearm in a civilized city like London."

"Wiggins can escort me to Lady Cannonberry's," Mrs. Jeffries said quickly. "Tomorrow, however, I may need your help. Do you think you can stay when you bring Antoine over?"

"Wild horses wouldn't get me outa here," Luty said. "You know I like to be in on things at the end. If the inspector arrests Washburn, I want to be right here where I can git all the juicy details. What time do ya want us here?"

"Early, by seven if possible," Mrs. Jeffries filled them in on a few more details, and then they left. Smythe left right behind them. Betsy turned to Mrs. Jeffries and asked, "Do you want me to go with you to Lady Cannonberry's?"

"No, you'll need to stay here in case the inspector needs something. He would get very suspicious if no one in the household were here."

Wiggins and Mrs. Jeffries hid in the shadows outside of Lady Cannonberry's big three-story house at the end of Upper Edmonton Gardens. Flattened against the side passageway leading to her back door, they had a good view of the street.

Mrs. Jeffries pulled her cloak tighter. The rustle of the fabric sounded unusually loud in the quiet night. Wiggins, who was sulking because she'd made him leave Fred at home, was hunched forward, his arms folded over his chest as he tried to stay warm.

"'Ow much longer, do ya reckon?" he asked, blowing on his stiff fingers.

"Not too much, I hope." Her feet were freezing.

They heard a hansom turn the corner. A moment later the hansom pulled up and Inspector Witherspoon emerged. A second after, Lady Cannonberry came out. Witherspoon took her arm and escorted her out of the range of their vision, up the steps and to the front door.

"Now," Mrs. Jeffries said to Wiggins. They both scampered quietly down the passageway to the gate leading to the communal garden.

Inside the gardens, Wiggins picked up a handful of small stones. They waited for what seemed an eternity and finally, a light on the second floor appeared. Mrs. Jeffries nodded at the footman. He tossed the first pebble toward the window. It bounced against the glass with a gentle *ping*.

They waited. Nothing happened.

"'Cor blimey, do you think she's in there?"

"Try again."

Wiggins threw a second and then a third. Suddenly Ruth Cannonberry appeared at the window. Mrs. Jeffries waved her arms, hoping that in the faint moonlight the woman would recognize her.

Ruth stared at her for a moment and then threw open the window. "Hepzibah! What is it? Is everything all right?"

"Everything's fine," Mrs. Jeffries whispered loudly, "but do please come down, we must talk to you."

It was several moments before they saw the small back door opening. Ruth stepped outside, leaving the door open a crack. "Goodness, you gave me such a start. What is it?"

"I know who the murderer is," Mrs. Jeffries began, "but the only way to catch him without revealing our involvement in this case is for you to convince Minerva Kenny to bring that letter she took from Barrett's office to Inspector Witherspoon."

"Who is it?" Ruth asked eagerly.

"Owen Washburn, but it's going to be very difficult to prove."

"I'm not sure that Minerva will do it," Ruth murmured.

"She must," Mrs. Jeffries said bluntly. "If she doesn't, the inspector will arrest her for Barrett's murder. She's got to bring him that letter, and she must do it as early tomorrow morning as possible."

"I'll pop 'round and talk to her right after breakfast."

"That'll be too late," Mrs. Jeffries said. "You must talk to her at the crack of dawn. She must get that letter to Inspector Witherspoon before he finishes breakfast."

Betsy was anxiously pacing the kitchen when they got back. "What took you so long? The inspector's gone to bed."

"Good." Mrs. Jeffries took off her cloak and laid it on the chair. "Wiggins, why don't you go on up to bed. Betsy and I will wait up for Smythe."

The footman looked doubtful. But blimey, he was cold and tired.

There was no sense in all of 'em losin' sleep tonight. "All right, but you come wake me if'n Smythe don't get back soon."

As soon as he went upstairs, Mrs. Jeffries put on the kettle. She knew that Betsy wasn't going to budge from this kitchen until the coachman was safely home. They might as well have a cup of tea while they waited.

Five minutes later they were at the kitchen table, a mug of tea in front of them. Betsy kept glancing at the clock. Mrs. Jeffries smiled to herself. The girl's feelings for the coachman were as plain as the nose on her face, and his feelings were equally obvious.

"Do you think he'll be all right?" Betsy asked anxiously. "I mean, he knows how to take care of himself, so I don't think anything will happen to him."

"He can take excellent care of himself."

But Betsy was trying to convince herself, not the housekeeper. "For all his cock-o'-the-walk-ways, he's a sensible man. He'll not be takin' any silly chances when he puts that cap back."

"I'm sure he won't."

"But then again, it's a cold, dark night out there and anythin' can 'appen." She bit her lip and looked at the clock again.

She was dropping her h's. Mrs. Jeffries knew that was a bad sign. Betsy was really worried about Smythe. The kind of fear that a woman felt when the man she really cared about was doing something that could get him in a great deal of trouble.

"Don't fret, he'll be fine," she said firmly. "Now, don't you want to know how I figured it out?" That should keep the girl's mind occupied.

Betsy didn't even hear her. "Course Smythe is clever, and even if he were to get caught, which I'm sure won't 'appen, 'e'll talk his way past it."

Mrs. Jeffries gave up and sipped her tea. For the next hour Betsy watched the clock and paced the floor. Finally, when even the housekeeper began to be concerned, they heard the back door open.

"What took you so bloomin' long?" Betsy snapped the moment Smythe appeared.

"Easy, lass," he said quietly, "I had to do a bit a snoopin'."

"What happened?" Mrs. Jeffries asked.

Smythe sat down across from her and poured himself a cup of tea. "I put the cap back, all right, but we've got us a problem. One of the reasons I'm so late was 'cause I peeked in the windows, wanted to see what was goin' on."

"You peeked in the windows!" Betsy hissed. "What for? We've been walkin' the floor, worried sick that somethin' 'appened to you, and you was out playin' about watchin' the Washburns through the windows. . . ."

"Yeah," he gazed at her speculatively. "I was and it's a good thing too." He drug his eyes away from Betsy and looked at Mrs. Jeffries. "As soon as I drink this tea, I think I should go back and keep an eye on the Washburn house."

"Why?" Mrs. Jeffries knew something was terribly wrong.

"'Cause Owen Washburn and his sister is packin' up. I watched 'em loadin' up their trunks through one of the windows. They're fixin' to leave town."

Antoine, arrogant, French and decidedly put out, arrived with Luty and Hatchet very early the next morning. Mrs. Jeffries quietly filled them in on the latest development while the cook clattered around the kitchen making as much noise as possible to show his displeasure.

"Is Smythe keepin' an eye on the Washburns?" Luty asked.

"He's been there all night," Betsy replied. She stared curiously at the black-haired Gallic cook. "Is your cook upset?" she whispered.

"Oh, no," Luty replied. "He always acts like that."

Mrs. Jeffries gave them their instructions. Then she and Betsy hurried upstairs to the dining room.

Witherspoon came down right on time. "I say, something smells delicious." He sniffed appreciatively.

"It's poached eggs Florentine." Mrs. Jeffries lifted the lid of the serving dish. "Luty sent her cook over to prepare you a very special breakfast."

"Gracious." Witherspoon grinned widely as he sat down. "How very kind of her."

"She thought you needed a good meal," Mrs. Jeffries said as she edged out of the dining room and into the hall. She left him happily eating away at his eggs.

While Betsy ferried the various courses from the kitchen to the dining room, the housekeeper hovered by the front door. But Minerva Kenny didn't come.

Mrs. Jeffries went back to check on the inspector. He'd just finished a kipper and was pushing his plate to one side. "I do believe I'm finished. . . ."

"But Antoine made some croissants," Mrs. Jeffries protested.

"I don't think I could eat another bite," Witherspoon protested. "Though it has been thoroughly delightful."

There was a knock at the front door. "I'll get it!" Mrs. Jeffries flew down the hallway, praying it was Minerva Kenny. She flung open the door.

Her prayers were answered. A middle-aged woman wearing a heavy cloak and a scowl stood on the door step. "My name is Minerva Kenny. May I speak to Inspector Witherspoon, please."

"Certainly, do come in, please." Mrs. Jeffries escorted her into the dining room.

"Goodness," Witherspoon said in surprise, "whatever are you doing here?"

"I've come to give you something," Minerva thrust a letter at him. "I took this letter from William Barrett's study the day he was killed, but I didn't kill him. I thought it might be important. Now that I've given it to you, I'll go."

With that, she turned on her heel and stomped out.

"Miss Kenny." Witherspoon leapt to his feet and started after her.

"I should let her leave," Mrs. Jeffries said. "After all, you do know where to find her if you need to. Why don't you read the letter, sir?"

"Do you think I ought to?"

"It's evidence, isn't it?"

"Yes, of course it is." He tore open the envelope, pulled out the letter and read it. "Gracious," he murmured a few moments later, "I'm not sure what to make of this. But I think it might be very important." He looked up at his housekeeper. "It's a letter from Barrett to his bank instructing the bank to immediately cease any and all payments to Owen Washburn or any other representatives of Washburn and Tate."

Mrs. Jeffries relaxed. She hadn't been wrong. The letter said precisely what she was sure it would say. "You mean he was cutting off the money, sir?" She didn't have time to play about. She wanted to make sure the inspector got the point as quickly as possible.

Witherspoon frowned. He looked most confused, "It certainly sounds like it. I believe that as soon as Barnes gets here, we'll nip over to the Washburn house and see what he has to say about this."

But that wasn't good enough. Mrs. Jeffries took a deep breath and started talking. By her estimation, she had about five minutes to drop hints and get the inspector thinking along the lines she needed.

• • •

"Clever of you to think of that, sir," Barnes said admiringly as they got out of the hansom in front of the Washburn house.

Witherspoon smiled modestly. "Not really. It's merely a matter of using one's reasoning powers. But it did occur to me that the murder had been meticulously planned. I had to ask myself who had the means of doing such planning"—he started up the walkway—"and the only possible answer was Mr. Washburn. He was the one who was there the day that Barrett was throwing those stones at the dog, you see."

Barnes wasn't sure he did, but he nodded anyway. They'd reached the front door. Witherspoon banged the brass knocker.

They waited. And waited.

He banged the knocker again. Suddenly the door was flung open. Owen Washburn stared out at them. "What do you want?" he asked rudely. His hair was mussed and his shirt wrinkled.

"May we come in?" Witherspoon asked politely.

"Do you have a warrant?"

"No," Witherspoon said softly. "But I can get one within the hour."

Washburn gazed at him for a long moment and then threw open the door. The two policemen stepped inside.

Valises, carpetbags and suitcases were stacked in the hallway. Witherspoon glanced at Barnes.

"Planning on going somewhere?" Witherspoon asked softly. Washburn ignored the question and stalked into the drawing room. His sister was piling books into a trunk.

Eliza Washburn gasped and dropped the book she'd been holding. "What are you doing here?" she cried.

"I'm afraid you'll have to postpone your trip," Witherspoon said gently. "We've some very important matters to clear up."

"You can't stop us from leaving," Washburn snapped.

Silently Witherspoon handed the letter to him. "Would you like to explain this, Mr. Washburn?"

His fingers trembled when he saw the address on the front. He tore it out of the envelope and read it quickly. "This proves nothing," he said to Witherspoon when he'd finished. "I told you, Barrett and I were thinking of dissolving our partnership. I was going to buy him out."

"But you couldn't buy him out, sir," Witherspoon replied. "You've no money. We know your creditors were pressing you, and with Barrett's withdrawal of funds from your company, you were ruined."

"That's ridiculous."

"I'm afraid it isn't." Witherspoon turned to Eliza Washburn. "Mr. Barrett ended his engagement to you because of your financial position—isn't that correct?"

"Certainly not," she protested.

"Mr. Washburn," Barnes said, "I'm going to call the police constables in, sir. We're goin' to search your house."

"And what precisely do you hope to find?" Washburn sneered.

Witherspoon smiled sadly. "A workingman's coat and cap, sir. But even if we don't find them, we've enough evidence to place you under arrest."

"I saw 'em find David Sims's cap," Smythe said, "and Eliza Washburn kicked up an awful fuss when they took her brother away."

"All right." Luty slapped her hands against the table. "Are you gonna tell us now?" she asked the housekeeper.

"Of course, I was merely waiting for Smythe to return." Mrs. Jeffries took a dainty sip of tea. "You see, I'd realized that the murder was well planned. Therefore, there was only one person who fit all the facts."

"What facts?" Wiggins asked. "Seems to me all we 'ad was a dead body with a sword stickin' out of 'is chest and 'alf a London wantin' the bloke dead."

"It might have appeared that way, Wiggins," Mrs. Jeffries explained, "but the truth was quite different. Once I found out that Barrett was planning on selling his house and, as far as we know, wasn't planning on buying another one here in London, I concluded that he was leaving the city. I started thinking that for most of the suspects in our little drama, Barrett leaving would be precisely what they wanted. Miss Kenny would have liked him out of the way, Maud Astley and Neville Sharpe would certainly liked to have seen the back of the man, and Adrian Spears would be positively delighted to find that Barrett wasn't going to be his neighbour. The same applies to Thornton Astley, especially as he knew that taking Barrett to court would be a waste of time. There was only one person who would be damaged if Barrett left. That was the man who depended on him for money. Once I realized that, the rest fell into place."

"I still don't see how," Hatchet grumbled.

"Don't you?" She smiled, "As I said, the killing was planned down to the last detail. There was only one person who could have planned it and that was Owen Washburn. I think he decided that Barrett had to die quite some time ago. I suspect that Barrett ended his engagement to Eliza Washburn last month because he'd found out how close to bankruptcy the Washburns were. I think Washburn realized he had a golden opportunity to kill the man and get away with it on the day he and Barrett were outside and Barrett threw stones at Spears's dog. With Spears shouting at the top of his lungs that he would kill Barrett if he touched the dog again, Spears became a very convenient suspect."

"You mean that Washburn killed the dog?" Betsy said.

"That's right," Mrs. Jeffries said. "That's how I knew he committed the murder. He stole the carpenter's hammer for that very purpose. He knew the front and back doors of the Barrett house were open because of the painting. Washburn stole David Simms's cap and coat, and the hammer, the day *before* the murder. And he did it deliberately to lure everyone out in the gardens, giving him a chance to slip inside the Barrett house without being seen. Washburn was the only one who could have taken them. The other suspects weren't in Barrett's house that day. On the day of the murder, he slipped into the garden, waited till the poor dog came outside and killed it," she closed her eyes briefly, thinking of that poor, defenseless animal being brutally used to set up a murder. "Washburn knew perfectly well that Spears would come looking for the animal. With all the doors and windows open, he was fairly certain there would be a huge ruckus."

"That's why Janie, the Spears's maid, thought she saw David out in the garden!" Betsy cried. "She caught a glimpse of Washburn wearin' David's cap."

"Correct, that's why Washburn pinched the hat in the first place. He wanted a disguise of sorts." Mrs. Jeffries took another sip of tea. "With the dog dead, I suspect he hid somewhere, waited until everyone from the Barrett household was outside watching the commotion and then slipped inside and hid in one of the rooms on the second floor. A few moments later Minerva Kenny came in through the front door, confronted Barrett and took the letter."

"Do you think that Washburn knew that Barrett had written that letter?" Smythe asked, remembering he'd seen Washburn at the bank.

"I think he hoped he hadn't," Mrs. Jeffries mused. "I suspect that's why he went to the bank yesterday, he wanted to make sure Barrett's funds were still available to him. But I do think he knew the inevitable was coming. The day before the murder, Washburn told the police he'd come by with some papers for Barrett to sign. That wasn't true. I suspect he came because Barrett wanted the meeting. He probably told him he was instructing his bank to stop the funds. That's why Washburn had to kill him and had to do it quickly."

"Git on with yer story," Luty demanded.

"Oh, sorry. As I was saying, Minerva Kenny arrived, and Washburn had to stay hidden until she left. That's where he made his biggest mistake. A mistake we should have seen right away, but didn't."

"What was that?" Betsy asked.

"The room was dark," Mrs. Jeffries replied. "That's what should have been obvious from the first. Both Smythe and the inspector said that none of the lamps had been lit. If Barrett had been alive at six o'clock, he wouldn't have been sitting there in the dark."

"But Barrett was alive at six," Hatchet countered. "He shouted at one of the workmen as they were leaving."

"Washburn yelled at the workman," Mrs. Jeffries corrected. "Barrett had probably been dead since right after Minerva Kenny left. I'm fairly certain that as soon as Miss Kenny left, Washburn slipped into Barrett's study, grabbed the sword and shoved it through the chair. It happened so quickly, Barrett didn't even have a chance to cry out. After that, Washburn had to wait in the study until it was safe to leave. He knew the servants went down for their meal at six o'clock, the same time the workmen left. So he sat there in the dark, waiting. A few minutes after six, he slipped out the front door. Just to be on the safe side, he wore David Simms's coat and cap, in case someone saw him leaving."

"Who was the woman in his drawing room, the one the workmen heard crying?" Betsy asked. "I mean, we know it was Maud Astley who was in the garden the night before, havin' a row with Barrett, but who was the other one?"

"Eliza Washburn," Mrs. Jeffries said. "And it was Eliza Washburn who came back that afternoon in one of the hansoms too. But for some reason or other, she lost her nerve and didn't go into the house."

"Why did she come to see Barrett?" Wiggins asked. "Seems to me 'e'd be the last man she'd want to talk to. 'E did leave 'er at the altar."

"Probably she came to plead with Barrett on behalf of her brother."
Mrs. Jeffries shrugged. "I'm only guessing, but I suspect she knew how
desperate her brother was. No doubt he'd told her that Barrett was planning on cutting off the money. Without the funds, the Washburns were
ruined."

"It didn't do no good, though." Betsy shook her head.

"Why'd she bother? Barrett had already proved he was a heartless
beast."

"Desperate people will do desperate things," Mrs. Jeffries said sadly.
"Perhaps she felt he still had some vestige of feelings for her."

From upstairs, they heard the sound of the front door opening.

"The inspector's back," Mrs. Jeffries got to her feet. "I'll see what I
can find out from him."

Witherspoon sipped at his sherry. "He won't confess, you know. And even
with the cap and coat, we're going to have a very difficult time proving he
did it."

Mrs. Jeffries smiled. They'd been talking for over an hour, and she was
satisfied that the inspector now thought *he* had come up with the sequence
of events leading to Washburn's arrest. She'd been worried all day.

There had been so little time this morning when she started dropping
hints and talking fast. But perhaps she was underestimating him? Perhaps
he would have come up with the solution on his own. She liked to think
so. "But you do have some evidence that isn't circumstantial, sir. The coat
and cap *were* found in Washburn's house."

"Yes, stupid of the man not to get rid of them, but there you have it."
Witherspoon sighed. "Even the cleverest of people will often make a fatal
mistake."

"You also have the letter that Barrett wrote to the bank," she added.
"And the testimony of some of the residents from Kildare Gardens. The
episode with the dog being killed and the theft of the hammer used to kill
the poor animal is evidence that Washburn planned the whole thing. Add
to that Washburn's precarious financial position, and you can show motive. Once a jury hears all that, I'm sure that justice will be done."

"One does hope so, but the case is still very circumstantial, Mrs. Jeffries," Witherspoon replied. "But that's up to some QC to worry about,
not me. I've done my duty. I know we arrested the right person."

"Indeed you have, sir." She took a sip of her own sherry.

"But there is one thing still puzzling me."

"What's that, sir?" She held her breath, hoping that if he asked an awkward question, she'd be able to come up with an answer.

"Who was it that brought that note about Barrett's body being in the study?" He drummed his fingers on the arm of his chair, "I've thought and thought about it. For the life of me, I can't come up with a single idea of who it could have been."

"Perhaps it was one of Barrett's servants, sir. You know how some people will do anything to avoid being involved with the police," she spoke quickly. "Or perhaps it was one of the workmen?"

"Oh, well." He waved his hand dismissively. "I suppose it's one of those little mysteries that we'll never solve. But what's life without an occasional mystery?"

"Quite, sir."

"Er, Mrs. Jeffries?"

She braced herself for another awkward question.

"What are we having for dinner tonight?"


The next morning everyone gathered 'round the kitchen table to discuss the aftermath of the investigation. Luty and Hatchet, with two baskets of goodies in tow, compliments of Antoine, had arrived right after breakfast.

"Figured you could still use some decent vittles," Luty explained as Hatchet placed the baskets on the table. "I've brought some smoked ham, sliced beef, some of Antoine's fancy croissants . . . Oh, I forget what else he tucked in there, but there's plenty here to hold you for a day or two."

"Perhaps by the time your provisions run low, Mrs. Goodge will be back," Hatchet added.

"If you run out before"—Luty popped down beside Betsy—"just give me a holler and we'll bring some more."

"That's very generous of you, Luty." Mrs. Jeffries wasn't about to look a gift horse in the mouth. Whatever was in that basket was certain to be much tastier than what they could cook.

"Madam is a very generous soul." Hatchet arched one eyebrow as he looked at his employer. "Sometimes perhaps too generous."

"Oh, git off yer high horse, Hatchet." Luty shook her finger at him. "Who was it that come draggin' Jon in when he didn't have a place to stay?"

Jon was a young lad from one of their previous cases. He was now a permanent resident of the Crookshank household. Hatchet personally supervised his lessons and vetted his tutors.

"I most certainly did not drag anybody in," Hatchet argued. "At the time, I merely suggested you take the boy into training as a footman. You're the one who insisted on educating him. However, that is a far cry from what you're doing now."

"Exactly what is it she's doing?" Betsy asked.

"What's she doing!" Hatchet snorted. "She's actually thinking of giving that murderer's sister money so she can start over somewhere else."

"You're stakin' Eliza Washburn?" Smythe asked incredulously. "But why?"

"'Cause she got left at the altar, she don't have enough gumption to show her face in London, and what the blazes else do I have to spend my money on?" Luty glared at all of them. "Now, I don't want to hear another word on the subject. That poor woman's had some rough times, and she's gonna have to watch her brother hang. Least I can do is help her to start over somewhere else."

No one had the nerve to say a word. Even Hatchet kept silent.

"Actually, Luty," Mrs. Jeffries said softly, "I think what you're doing is wonderful. If there were more people like you in the world, it would be a much better place for all of us."

Luty's cheeks turned red. "Thank you, Hepzibah."

"Hello, hello," Ruth Cannonberry called. "Can I come in?"

"Please do," Mrs. Jeffries invited.

They all greeted the new arrival. For the next half hour they talked of the murder. Ruth kept clucking her tongue and shaking her head as she learned all the details of the crime and its solution.

"Well," she finally said, "it's a good thing all of us were available to help solve this awful crime. Otherwise, poor dear Minerva would probably be under arrest."

Everyone looked at one another, not sure of what to say. Mrs. Jeffries smiled broadly. "That's quite true, Ruth. But you do understand that we never, ever let on to the Inspector that he had help?"

"Of course I understand." Ruth laughed. "When we were having dinner at Simpson's, I was as quiet as a mouse."

Luty's eyes narrowed speculatively. "You and the inspector seem to be gettin' on real good."

"Indeed we are," Ruth agreed, blushing like a schoolgirl, "He's such a wonderful companion. We're going train spotting next Sunday. Isn't that exciting?"

It sounded about as interestin' as watchin' grass grow, but Luty didn't want to offend her. "Train spottin'," she repeated, "that sounds real nice."

"By the way, Minerva said to thank you for all your help," Ruth continued. "She's ever so grateful for everything you did. Now, don't worry, she hasn't a clue that we were investigating the murder as well. As I said, on that subject my lips are sealed. She's getting Mr. Spears a puppy. Isn't that nice?"

They all agreed that it was. The conversation continued, with everyone asking, talking and making comments. Everyone, that is, except Wiggins.

He couldn't get the Simms brothers out of his mind. Maybe it was because they lived in the same kind of house that he used to live in before his mother died of typhoid, or maybe it was because he knew what it was to be desperate for work. In any case, he owed it to them to ask.

Wiggins cleared his throat. "Uh, Luty, do you happen to have any paintin' that needs doin'?"

"Paintin'?"

"Yeah, them painters that was workin' on the Barrett 'ouse could sure use the work."

"Let's see," Luty muttered thoughtfully. "I just had the front hall redone last year, so it don't need doin'. But Jon's gettin' mighty tired of lookin' at that pink-and-yellow wallpaper in his room, so I reckon that could use a coat of paint. You have them boys come 'round and see me this afternoon. I'll find 'em something to paint. It'll be longer than a January frost before them estate lawyers ever pay 'em what they're owed for that job they did at Barrett's place."

"Thanks ever so much." Wiggins shoved back his chair and stood up. "They'll be so glad for the work. I'll just nip over and tell 'em, all right?"

"That'll be fine, Wiggins," Mrs. Jeffries said.

"Come on, boy," Wiggins called to Fred as he dashed out of the kitchen. "Let's go."

"That's most generous of you, Luty," Ruth Cannonberry said as soon as they'd gone. "Perhaps after they finish at your house, you can send them over to see me."

Soon after that the impromptu meeting broke up. Luty and Hatchet departed for home, Lady Cannonberry went off to her women's suffrage meeting, and Mrs. Jeffries went upstairs to clean the drawing room.

Betsy started clearing up the tea things. Smythe watched her for a moment, thinking of what Mrs. Jeffries had let slip early this morning. The lass had been worried about him when he'd gone out the other night, and that must mean she cared. But what if she only cared about him as a friend?

"Do you want the last of this tea?" Betsy asked, holding the pot up.

"No," he swallowed heavily. "But I'd like to ask ya somethin'."

"What?" She took the pot to the sink.

"Would ya like to go out with me this afternoon? I thought it would be nice if we went for a walk."

Mrs. Goodge arrived home at teatime the next day. She bustled into the kitchen and dropped her carpetbag on the floor.

"Thank goodness you're back!" Wiggins cried. "We've about starved to death since you've been gone."

"How is your aunt?" Mrs. Jeffries asked.

"She's fine," the cook replied. "It weren't pneumonia, it was only a bit of bronchitis. She was well on the mend when I left."

Smythe grinned, "We sure are glad to see you. If it 'adn't been for Antoine, we really woulda starved to death."

"Is that all you can think of! Your stomachs?" Mrs. Goodge demanded as she took her usual seat. "We've got to get crackin'. I rushed back as soon as I could. You'd best bring me up to date on the investigation, then I've got to get some bakin' done so I can feed my sources—"

"Mrs. Goodge," Mrs. Jeffries gently cut her off. "I'm afraid you're a little late."

"Late? What do you mean?"

"We've already solved the murder."

The cook's cry of outrage could be heard all the way across the street.

# MRS. JEFFRIES AND THE MISSING ALIBI

# CHAPTER 1

———◦•◦———

"Poor bloke," muttered George Halisham, the night watchman. "Twenty-five years married and still waitin' for his old mum to leave off and give up." He snorted as his eyes strained in the feeble light to struggle through the article in *The Times*. He weren't much of a reader, but with there being nothing else to do on these long evenings exceptin' to make his rounds every hour or so, readin' a newspaper was better than sitting here watchin' the wind tinkle the windows on the front of the building. Not that he liked *The Times* all that much, but it was the only one he'd been able to dig out of the rubbish bin when he'd come on duty this evening.

"Not that the old girl'll give up, not bloomin' likely," he said, laughing at his own wit. "Queen Victoria won't give up the throne till she's planted six feet under." He caught himself and glanced down the hallway. There were still lights on in some of the offices. He'd best watch his tongue. People thought you was strange if they come out and caught you talkin' to yourself. He sighed and went back to struggling through the article about the silver wedding anniversary of the prince and princess of Wales. It was either read that or all that rubbish about the death of the German emperor. He didn't much care for the Germans.

A blast of cold March wind slipped in through the crack under the double front doors, fluttering the single light on the far wall and sending chills up George's spine. He glanced up, and through the glass he could see the thick damp yellow fog drifting across the deserted, wet street. Nasty night out, he thought, not fit for man or beast. He went back to his paper, turned the page, and then looked up again. Someone was banging on the front door. Blast.

George put the paper down and sidled out from behind his cozy nest behind the high wooden counter. Peering through the window, he squinted trying to decide if he recognized the man standing on the door stoop. But what with the city being too cheap to keep the one gas lamp outside the building working proper, all he could see was a figure of medium height wearing a bowler hat.

"What be your business?" George called through the glass. He'd been told never to open the doors after business hours. Not since them break-ins last month.

"Open up," the man yelled. "I'm from Scotland Yard."

"What?" The wind blew so loudly he could barely hear the fellow.

"Scotland Yard. The police," the man repeated.

George didn't hesitate. He took out his big brass key ring, unlocked the door and flung it open. "Sorry, sir," he ushered the man inside. "Didn't mean to keep you waitin'. But I'm not to open the doors after business hours. We've had a few break-ins in the past months. Is that what you're here about?"

"That's quite all right," the man said. He wore a large dark overcoat, spectacles, and had a mustache. "No, I'm not here about your break-ins. That's a different department altogether. Is Mr. Hornsley still on the premises?"

George strained to hear the policeman's voice, who was standing quite a distance away and had his head down, almost like he was talking to the floor instead of to George. "There's still a light on in his office," he replied, "and I ain't seen him leave yet. So I reckon he's still hard at it. Works hard, Mr. Hornsley does, sometimes he don't leave until close to midnight."

"Which is his office?" The policeman stepped toward the dimly lit hallway.

"It's the last door at the end of the hall. Come on, I'll show you."

"That won't be necessary. I'm sure I can find my own way."

"No, I've got to announce you. It's the rules, you see."

"Thank you. I'm Inspector Witherspoon from Scotland Yard."

"This way, sir," George shuffled off down the hall. He was dying to know why the inspector was here, but he didn't quite have the nerve to ask. Maybe if he did a bit of chattin'. "Miserable night, isn't it, sir?"

"Quite."

"First the fog," George slowed his steps, "and now all this wind and rain. Not fit for man or beast."

"No, it isn't."

"Must be hard on you fellows, the police, I mean. Goin' out at all hours of the day and night," George continued gamely. Ruddy hell, if that fellow kept his chin any lower, he was going to trip over it.

"Quite."

George almost gave up. This copper obviously weren't much of a talker. "Odd you comin' 'round at this time of night, sir. Most of the offices close at half past. Course we do get a lot of clerks and such that have to work late. Makes it hard on me, but most everyone is usually gone by now. Exceptin', of course, Mr. Hornsley."

By this time they'd arrived at the door of the offices of Hornsley, Frampton, and Whitelaw, Insurance Brokers. George knew his curiosity wasn't goin' to be satisfied. He'd never get a word out of Mr. Hornsley, either. Hornsley didn't bother speakin' to the likes of George Halisham. "I'd better announce you, sir. Like I said, people is a bit nervous cause of them break-ins."

"As you wish."

"Mr. Hornsley," George banged on the door. "You've a visitor, Mr. Hornsley."

They waited a moment but heard nothing.

The policeman shouldered the watchman aside, "Mr. Hornsley," he yelled, loud enough to make George wince. "I'm Inspector Gerald Witherspoon from Scotland Yard. I must speak with you."

George glanced quickly at the fanlights above the other office doors. He hoped this screamin' policeman didn't disturb anyone else who was working late.

From inside they heard a muffled shout. "Just a moment."

"Scotland Yard," Witherspoon yelled back. "Inspector Witherspoon. Do please open up."

Cor, George thought, glancing anxiously at the fanlights over the other doors again, the bloke's screamin' loud enough to wake the dead. If the other tenants were disturbed, he'd hear about it tomorrow, that was for sure. No matter what happened in the evenings, he always got the blame.

The door opened and a middle-aged man with thinning dark hair glared out at them. "What's this all about?"

"Sorry to disturb you, sir," the policeman said apologetically. "But I must speak with you. It's rather urgent. You could say it was a matter of life or death."

Hornsley opened the door wider and motioned the policeman inside. "Come in then, though I do hope you'll be brief. I'm very busy."

George waited till the door closed behind the two men, debated about the wisdom of trying to eavesdrop, realized it was time to do his rounds, so he grudgingly left.

"Now what's going on?" Hornsley asked, turning and walking toward a patch of light spilling out of an open doorway at the far side of the room.

"This won't take long, sir," the inspector said. Except for the light from Hornsley's office, the place was in darkness. But even in the dimness, he could see four clerks' desks clustered in the center of the room. As one would expect, there were bookcases and file cabinets as well, but they were nothing more than dark shapes against the walls. High-backed straight chairs were strewn willy-nilly between the desks and the walls. The floor was of plain hard wood and he suspected the walls were painted an ugly pale green. Typical London office, he thought. No comfort for the clerks except a meager pay packet at the end of the week. All in all, it looked a miserable place to work. "But we've reason to believe your life is in danger."

"You're joking!" Hornsley turned and stared at him, his eyes widening in surprise.

"We don't jest about murder," Witherspoon replied. He put his hand in his pocket. It was a special pocket, designed to hold a much larger object than usual. His fingers curled around the hard leather at the top. "Perhaps we should go into your office and sit down."

"Yes, yes, of course." Hornsley swiveled about on his heel.

The inspector pulled his hand out of his pocket, tightening his fingers around the end of the instrument he withdrew. He paused a moment, making sure that Hornsley's back was to him. Taking a deep breath, he lunged forward just as he lifted his arm and slammed the heavy object hard against Hornsley's skull.

"Ommm . . ." Hornsley slumped to his knees and fell forward onto his hands, stunned.

From out of his other pocket, the man behind him pulled out a tie.

Before Hornsley could come to his senses the inspector stepped beside him, slipped the tie around his neck, crossed the ends and yanked with all his might.

It was over in moments.

The killer knelt beside him, rolled the body over and checked for signs of life. He smiled, satisfied when he realized that Hornsley was dead.

From inside his coat pocket, he pulled out a piece of paper and a straight pin. He pinned the paper to Hornsley's chest.

Standing up, he listened for a moment. Then he walked to the door of the outer office, cracked it open and peeked out. The night watchman was still gone.

Walking softly he hurried to the front door, checked behind him to make sure that no one was there, and then stepped out into the dark and fog.

Smythe, the coachman for Inspector Gerald Witherspoon, eyed his quarry warily. Betsy, the maid, had her back turned to him and for that he was grateful. He was as nervous as a kitten in a pen full of bulldogs. He took a deep breath and gathered his courage. "Uh, Betsy," he cleared his throat.

She whirled around, her hand still on the bag of flour she'd just put on the cooling pantry shelf. "What? Is tea ready?"

"No, no," he replied. "I was, uh, wonderin' if you liked the Zoological Gardens?"

"The one in Regent's Park?" She smiled. "Who doesn't? They've just added another cat, somethin' called an Eyra. I was plannin' on going to have a look at it sometime soon. Do you want to come with me?"

Smythe stared at her incredulously. Here he'd been screwin' up his courage for the past week to work up the nerve to ask her to go out with him and she done stole his thunder. He wasn't sure if he should be narked or happy. But as he was half-barmy over the lass, he decided not to look a gift horse in the mouth. "That's what I was fixin' to ask you," he said, grinning. "What say we go next Wednesday?"

"Let's see if we can ask Mrs. Jeffries for Monday instead." Betsy shook her head, sending a blond tendril slipping off her topknot. "It's half price on Mondays, only six pence instead of a whole shilling."

Smythe opened his mouth to argue, to tell her that the cost of admission was the least of his worries, but then he clamped his lips together. No sense in lettin' on about how much money he had. It were a big enough trial to him without Betsy gettin' wind of the fact that he didn't need to be as careful with coin as the rest of the staff.

"Tea's ready," he heard Mrs. Goodge yell from the kitchen.

Betsy, the hem of her blue broadcloth dress swishing prettily, hurried past him and into the kitchen. He shook his head once, called himself a silly git for bein' so bloomin' pleased about their outing, and followed her.

Mrs. Jeffries, the housekeeper, was just sitting down at the head of the table. She looked up, a kind smile on her lips, as the two of them came into the room. Her hair was a deep, rich auburn, prettily streaked with gray at the temples and worn in a loose knot on the top of her head. She had dark brown eyes, a round cheerful face that belied a razor-sharp intelligence, and a short and rather plump stature. Nevertheless, she had the presence of a commanding general when the need arose and when she presided over the evening tea table.

THUMP . . .

Mrs. Goodge, the heavyset grey-haired cook, glared in the direction of the staircase. "When is that boy goin' to learn how to use those crutches properly?"

THUMP . . .

Betsy giggled, her blue eyes twinkling mischievously. "He's not got the hang of it yet," she said, reaching for a toasted tea cake. "And from the sound of it, I don't think our ears are goin' to get much of a rest for some time to come."

"It's not poor Wiggins's fault he broke his ankle," Smythe said loyally. He was a big, muscular man, with dark hair and harsh features that were softened by a cocky grin and a cheerful disposition.

THUMP . . .

Mrs. Goodge snorted. "Then whose fault is it? He had no business trying to ride one of them contraptions."

"But Mrs. Goodge," Mrs. Jeffries interjected. "Lots of people learn to ride bicycles. It's quite a useful mode of transportation."

"Wiggins weren't no more interested in transport than he is of learnin' to read Latin standin' on his head," the cook declared. "He were just showin' off to that girl."

"Well," Mrs. Jeffries said soothingly. "I expect he's going to be more careful in the future." She peered at the cook curiously. Mrs. Goodge had been in a rather irritable state for some time now. "Is your rheumatism bothering you?" she asked softly.

THUMP . . . THUMP . . . THUMP . . . "Bloomin' Ada," Wiggins screeched in alarm. It sounded like he was bouncing down the last three stairs.

Smythe leapt to his feet. "You all right, lad?"

"Fine," Wiggins yelled back. They heard the bang of his crutches as he started down the hall toward the kitchen. "Just slipped a bit."

"My rheumatism's fine," Mrs. Goodge said flatly.

"Then is something else bothering you?" Mrs. Jeffries pressed.

She hesitated a moment. "I'm bored. We've not had us a decent murder in weeks. What's wrong with this city?"

"Mrs. Goodge!" Mrs. Jeffries pretended to be shocked. But only because she thought she ought to for appearance's sake. Her conscience insisted she remind the staff that homicide was a terrible and foul crime. They really mustn't wish it upon anyone.

"Oh," said Mrs. Goodge, waving a plump white hand dismissively. "I didn't mean that the way it sounded. But you know what I'm tryin' to say. Life is so much more interesting when we're on a case. I missed the last one, so for me, it's been such a long time."

"I know what you mean," Betsy commiserated with her. "It is right boring when we don't have us a good murder to sink our teeth into."

"If you ask me," Wiggins propped his crutches against his chair and flopped awkwardly into his seat. "I think the inspector's doin' just fine as he is. Do him good to have a rest."

"Where is the inspector this evening?" Smythe put in. "He weren't upstairs in the study when I was up there filling the lamps."

"He went for a walk," Mrs. Jeffries replied.

"The inspector's out on a night like this?" Betsy exclaimed. "But it's right miserable outside." She shivered and ran her hands lightly up and down her crossed arms. "Maybe he's as bored as we are."

"Now we've no reason to be complaining," Mrs. Jeffries said quickly. She wanted to head off another discussion about the lack of murders. "We've had more than our fair share of investigations."

And they had. Inspector Gerald Witherspoon had a phenomenal success as a homicide detective—due, in a large part, to their very secret efforts on his behalf. Not that the dear man had any idea that he was helped by his household staff. Oh no, that would never do. They worked hard, each and every one, to make sure Inspector Witherspoon was completely in the dark about their activities. Of course as a consequence of their actions, they were all now thoroughly bored with the normal household routine. Honestly, Mrs. Jeffries sighed inwardly, she didn't want to have to lecture them. But really, they'd done nothing but moan for days about the lack of murders. Even their dear friends Luty Belle Crookshank and her butler Hatchet had been complaining about it when they'd come round for lunch today.

"Fair share," Mrs. Goodge snorted. "I haven't had my fair share."

"But that's not our fault," Wiggins said doggedly. He was an earnest, kindhearted lad with brown hair and round apple cheeks. "It was your relation that took sick."

Mrs. Goodge had been called away to nurse a sick aunt when they had their last investigation. And she hadn't let any of them forget the fact that she'd missed one.

"We must be patient," Mrs. Jeffries replied, reaching for the big brown teapot. "I'm sure something will happen soon. Evil sometimes takes a nap, but it never completely disappears."


"I say, Mrs. Jeffries." Inspector Witherspoon peered over the rim of his spectacles. His eyes were a clear blue-gray, his face all angles and bone, his hair dark brown and thinning. "This is a jolly good breakfast. I've not had coddled eggs for ages."

"Mrs. Goodge thought you deserved something special today, sir," Mrs. Jeffries replied. Actually, the cook was still in a testy mood and taking it out on anyone who happened to step into her kitchen. Wiggins was her usual victim, because he, unlike the rest of them, didn't have the good sense to stay out of Mrs. Goodge's way. The only reason the inspector got coddled eggs was because Mrs. Jeffries had cooked them when Mrs. Goodge had gone into the wet larder looking for something to cook for supper.

There was a loud banging on the front door. Mrs. Jeffries put down the toast rack. "Are you expecting someone?" she asked Witherspoon.

"Not this morning," he replied.

Mrs. Jeffries hurried out of the dining room. She flung open the door and found a uniformed policeman standing on the stoop.

"Why, Constable Barnes," she said, smiling at the gray-haired craggy-faced man. "What on earth are you doing here?"

"Good morning, Mrs. Jeffries." Barnes gave her a weak smile. "Sorry to be callin' so early, but I've got to speak with the inspector. It's rather urgent."

Urgent? Mrs. Jeffries glanced at Barnes carefully as she opened the door wider and stepped back. The constable's mouth was bracketed with deep lines and there was an anxious, worried look to his eyes. Something was wrong—very wrong, indeed. "Inspector Witherspoon's having breakfast. Why don't you join him?"

Barnes took off down the hall. Mrs. Jeffries was right on his heels.

"Good morning, Constable," Witherspoon smiled broadly. "I didn't expect to see you this early. I thought we were meeting at the station."

"There's been a change in plans, sir." Barnes took his helmet off and then stared at the teapot. "May I have a cuppa, sir?"

"Of course. Mrs. Jeffries, do be kind enough to bring the constable a cup." But she was already snatching one from the supply she kept in the sideboard. She watched Barnes out of the corner of her eye as she poured his tea. He was pale, as though he'd had a great shock. Her first instinct was correct. Something was wrong.

"Now," Witherspoon said as soon as the constable sat down with his tea. "What's all this about, then?"

"There's been a murder, sir." Barnes looked down at the tablecloth.

Mrs. Jeffries brightened. Perhaps she'd been mistaken. Perhaps Barnes's demeanor was only because this murder was particularly loathesome. But her spirits sank almost immediately. Barnes hadn't even raised his head to look the inspector in the eye. She poured herself a cup of tea.

"Is that so?" Witherspoon sounded confused, as though he too could sense there was something wrong with the constable.

Barnes cleared his throat. "Well, sir, the chief inspector wants you to report to the Yard right away."

"Constable Barnes." The inspector flung his napkin on the table. "I'm getting the sense that there's something you're not telling me. Is something wrong?"

Barnes nodded. "A businessman named Peter Hornsley was murdered last night in his offices on Lambeth Street. That's one of the tiny little streets over in the City, sir. He was strangled."

"There's nothing particularly odd about that," Witherspoon replied slowly. "People do get murdered, even people in the City. Am I being given the case?"

"No, sir, Inspector Nivens is gettin' it." Barnes's shoulders slumped.

"Then why do I need to go and see the chief inspector?"

Mrs. Jeffries wondered the same thing.

"Because, sir," Barnes blurted, "the last person to see Hornsley alive was a policeman. And he called himself Gerald Witherspoon."

The instant the door closed behind the two men, Mrs. Jeffries flew down the stairs. Betsy looked up from the basket of linens she was folding as the housekeeper rushed into the kitchen.

"There's been a murder," Mrs. Jeffries cried.

Mrs. Goodge shoved the sack of sugar she'd just opened to one side. "It's about time."

"Quickly," Mrs. Jeffries said to the maid. "Where is Wiggins?"

"He's upstairs in his room," she replied, kicking the basket of linens out of her way. "We gave him the brass to polish."

Mrs. Jeffries nodded. With a sprained ankle, the footman wouldn't be much use to them on this case. "Betsy, you must get over to Howard's and get Smythe."

"Should we send for Luty Belle and Hatchet?" Mrs. Goodge asked. "Luty gets put out if she isn't in right from the start."

"Yes, we should. We're going to need all the help we can get on this case."

"Should I go, then," Betsy called over her shoulder as she hurried to the coat tree. "I can pop round there as soon as I've seen Smythe."

"No," the housekeeper shook her head. "We need everyone back here as soon as possible. You get on to Howard's. I'll get one of the street boys to run a message over. Get some tea ready, Mrs. Goodge, we'll have a meeting as soon as everyone is here."

An hour later, Luty Belle Crookshank, accompanied by Hatchet, arrived at Upper Edmonton Gardens. The elderly white-haired American woman was grinning from ear to ear as she hurried into the kitchen. Even Hatchet, her stiff-necked and very formal butler, had the ghost of a smile on his stern face.

"Good morning, everyone," Luty cried. "Looks like we've finally got us a murder."

"Really, madam," Hatchet said primly as he pulled out a chair for his employer, "it's rather unseemly to sound so happy about it. Do keep in mind that some poor soul has been foully deprived of existence."

"Don't take that holier-than-thou tone with me," Luty snapped, "I heard you chucklin' to yourself when you was gettin' your hat. You've been grinnin' like a grizzly with his paw in a honeypot all the way over here."

"I'm happy about it and I don't mind sayin' so," Mrs. Goodge said. She put a tea tray on the table. "I've felt cheated ever since I missed that last one."

Mrs. Jeffries decided it was pointless to say anything about their attitude. She could hardly blame them for their enthusiasm. After all, it was only natural that people would enjoy what they were naturally good at. And the truth was, they were all born snoops. Even Mrs. Goodge, who rarely left the kitchen, contributed as much as the rest of them. Mind you, the cook did have the most incredible network of sources. Tradesmen, workers, street hawkers, and, even on occasion, some of her old friends. And she pumped them all ruthlessly in her search for clues.

"What's this all about, then?" Luty asked.

"Perhaps we should wait until Betsy and Smythe get back," Mrs. Jeffries said.

"It wouldn't be fair to start without 'em," Wiggins agreed.

They heard the back door open and a moment later, Betsy, her nose in the air, hurried into the kitchen. Smythe was right behind her. "Sorry it took so long," she said, as she took her seat. She shot the coachman a glare. "But Smythe was *busy*, so it took me a while to get his attention."

To Mrs. Jeffries's amazement, the big burly coachman flushed. "If you'da let me know you was standin' there . . ."

"I yelled at you three times," Betsy snapped.

"I didn't 'ear ya, now, did I?"

"Please." Mrs. Jeffries had no idea what was wrong with these two. But the maid was obviously annoyed and Smythe appeared to be irritated and embarrassed. Well, whatever was wrong would just have to wait. They had a murder to solve. "Do sit down and let's get started."

"Who's the victim?" Hatchet asked.

"A man named Peter Hornsley. He was strangled."

"Where?" Mrs. Goodge asked.

"At his office on Lambeth Street. He was a businessman of some kind." Mrs. Jeffries had a bad feeling about this case. A sense of foreboding that she'd never had before. She wanted them out and investigating. "But we've got a problem. Constable Barnes came by this morning to get the inspector."

"So we know for sure he's gettin' the case?" Smythe said hopefully.

"No, he's not getting this one. Inspector Nivens is getting it."

There was a collective groan. None of them liked Nivens.

"Barnes came by because the chief inspector wanted to see Inspector Witherspoon right away," Mrs. Jeffries continued. "It seems that the last person to see the victim alive was a policeman. And he called himself Gerald Witherspoon."

"He never!" Betsy's jaw dropped. "But our inspector weren't out last night."

"He went for a walk," Mrs. Jeffries pointed out. "But as we don't know what time the murder occurred, we've no idea if our inspector was home or not."

Smythe cocked his head to one side and regarded the housekeeper quizzically. "Exactly what are you sayin'?"

"I'm not sure," Mrs. Jeffries replied thoughtfully. "But I have a feeling . . ." She shook herself. No point in getting everyone else all worked up.

Luty's dark eyes narrowed. "What kinda feelin'?"

Mrs. Jeffries forced herself to smile cheerfully. "Don't pay any attention to me. I just think we ought to get started on this case right away. With Nivens in charge, we'll have to work doubly hard to get any information."

Wiggins scratched his chin. "Why didn't our inspector get the case? He's the one that's best at solvin' murders."

"Because he's a suspect," Hatchet said quietly.

"Suspect!" Mrs. Goodge yelped. "But that's the silliest thing I ever heard. Inspector Witherspoon catches killers, he doesn't do it."

Hatchet looked over at Mrs. Jeffries. She was rather relieved to see that she wasn't the only one to see the significance of the situation. "We all know our inspector is innocent," she said reassuringly. "But someone obviously used his name. Let's not jump to any conclusions until we have more facts."

"What information do we have so far?" Smythe asked.

"Just what I've told you," Mrs. Jeffries said. "It's not much, but it's a start, Smythe, can you snoop around on Lambeth Street and see what you can find out?"

"Right." He rose to his feet. "I'll get over there now." He cast a quick, exasperated glance at the maid but she ignored him.

"Betsy," Mrs. Jeffries continued. "I want you to find out where the victim lived and then get to that neighborhood and start asking questions."

Betsy nodded.

"How about us?" Luty asked.

"Find out anything and everything you can about Peter Hornsley. Use your contacts in the City."

Mrs. Goodge got up. "I'd best get some fresh buns and biscuits made," she murmured. "I've got some tradesmen comin' through today and the fishmonger's lad is due to make a delivery. I might as well get me sources workin'."

"What do you want me and Fred to do?" Wiggins asked eagerly. Fred, as soon as he heard his name mentioned, raised his head. His brown and black furry tail thumped on the stone floor. His expression was uncannily like the footman's. Both of them looked hopeful.

And both of them were going to be disappointed.

"There isn't anything you can do," Mrs. Jeffries said softly. "You can hardly go dashing out and about all over London on crutches."

"What are you goin' to be doin'?" Wiggins asked Mrs. Jeffries. "Maybe Fred and I can give ya a hand?"


Chief Inspector Cecil J. Curling was at a loss. He didn't for a moment believe that Inspector Gerald Witherspoon had anything to do with the murder of one Mr. Peter Hornsley. But the situation was decidedly awkward. "Inspector Witherspoon," he began, "exactly where were you again last night?"

"Just as I said, sir," Witherspoon replied. "I went out for a long walk."

"I see. Precisely where did you walk?"

The inspector was beginning to feel most uncomfortable. It sounded almost as if Chief Inspector Curling didn't believe him. "I went down Upper Edmonton Gardens to Holland Road, then decided to take a turn around Holland Park."

"And how long did you walk?"

Witherspoon shrugged. "About an hour, I expect. Gracious, sir, you don't believe I had anything to do with this poor Mr. Hornsley's murder, do you?"

"No, no," Curling assured him. But like all good policemen, he was privately reserving judgment. It was difficult to cast Gerald Witherspoon in the role of murderer. But in his twenty years with the police, he'd seen stranger things. "But you do understand why we must ask you to account for your whereabouts."

"Of course, sir."

"And you also understand why this homicide won't be assigned to you," Curling continued.

"Yes, sir." Witherspoon wished his superior would get on with it. He didn't much like answering all these questions, though he could well understand the need for them. For the first time, he understood why people resented being interviewed by the police. It was a most unpleasant feeling. Most unpleasant, indeed.

"And you're absolutely certain you've never heard of the victim, Peter Hornsley?"

"Absolutely, sir. I don't know the man."

Curling nodded. "Very well, Witherspoon, you may go."

The inspector hesitated. "Excuse me, sir. Is Inspector Nivens being given the case?"

"Yes." Curling sighed. He could hardly expect Witherspoon to understand the complexities of office politics or the need to placate those who had friends in high places, those persons like Inspector Nivens. Gerald Witherspoon, for all his brilliance as a homicide detective, was rather innocent of such matters.

Until Witherspoon had begun solving murders two years ago, he'd spent most of his career as a clerk in the Records room. Why, rumor had it that he'd never even made an arrest before solving those horrible Kensington High Street murders. "We're hoping he'll be able to crack this case soon." Privately, Curling thought that the odds of Nivens actually solving this murder were about as good as the prince of Wales sprouting wings and flying to the moon. But, of course, he couldn't express that sentiment. Blast office politics and blast that little weasel Nivens as well.

"Yes, sir, I'm sure Nivens will do an excellent job."

Curling cleared his throat. "The sooner the better, that's what I say. After all," he gave Witherspoon a strained smile, "the killer did use your name to get into the victim's office. We can't have that, now, can we?"

"No, sir," Witherspoon replied glumly. "We certainly can't."

# CHAPTER 2

Mrs. Jeffries unrolled the hall rug she'd just brushed and flattened it against the polished floor with the sole of her shoe. She'd spent the morning thinking about what to do and had come to exactly one conclusion: Until she had more information, she couldn't do anything.

Except for Wiggins and Mrs. Goodge, everyone else was out "on the hunt"—and none of them were expected back for the noon meal. She flung open the front door, intending to give the stoop a good sweep. But she stopped, her broom held up in midair, as she spotted the inspector walking slowly down the road toward the house.

She jumped back inside and ran toward the kitchen, pausing only long enough to toss the broom in the small cupboard under the stairs.

"If you don't get out of my way, I'm goin' to wring your neck," she heard Mrs. Goodge shout.

"I was only tryin' to help," Wiggins protested.

Mrs. Jeffries dashed into the kitchen. The cook was glaring at the footman, who was standing hunched over a flattened mound of dough.

Wiggins looked at the housekeeper. "I were just tryin' to give 'er a 'and," he said defensively. "Thought I'd punch the dough a time or two, save her the trouble."

"It weren't ready to be punched, you half-wit," Mrs. Goodge yelped. "And now you've ruined my dough. What am I goin' to do? I've got half my sources due to come through here today! Now, thanks to your 'help,' I'll not have a thing to give them. Unless I give them plenty of tea and some decent bread and buns, they don't hang about long enough for me to learn anything."

"Send Wiggins down to the baker's to buy some buns," Mrs. Jeffries said quickly. "He should be able to manage that, even on crutches."

"The baker's!" The cook was outraged. "I can't feed my sources that rubbish! I've got standards to maintain."

"Well, we'll have to worry about that later." Mrs. Jeffries hurried over to the tea kettle and snatched it up. "The inspector's coming down the road. We must get him a lunch tray ready. Is there any of that beef joint left from last night?"

"Don't worry, I'll get the inspector something." Mrs. Goodge gave Wiggins one more frown and stalked toward the hallway and the cooling larder. "Have it ready in two shakes of a lamb's tail."

Mrs. Jeffries gave the footman a sympathetic smile, put the kettle on to boil, and went upstairs. She met the inspector in the front hall.

"We didn't expect you home for lunch, sir," she said. "But Mrs. Goodge will have a tray ready in a few moments. Would you like some tea first?"

"I didn't expect to come home, either," Witherspoon replied. His shoulders were slumped and his mouth was set in a flat, glum line. "I think I'd like a sherry."

She hid her surprise. "Go on into the dining room, sir. I'll bring you one right in."

Witherspoon was staring vacantly into space when she came in a few moments later. He gave her a weak smile as she handed him a small glass filled with dark amber liquid. "Gracious, I don't know what you must think, me having a drink in the middle of the day."

"I think you've had a shock, sir," she said sympathetically.

"I certainly have." He took a sip. "It's not everyday that one is questioned about one's whereabouts. I daresay, I can quite understand why some of the people I've had to question quite object to the process."

Her mouth opened in shock. "You were questioned, sir?"

"Yes. It seems the killer used my name. Oh, you already knew that, didn't you?" He looked quite dazed. "Fellow gained entrance not only to the building but to the victim's office by saying he was Inspector Gerald Witherspoon. Oh dear, I'm doing it again. You already knew that too, didn't you? You were in the dining room when Constable Barnes told me this morning."

"I didn't know all of it, sir," she said gently. Poor Inspector Witherspoon, he looked dreadfully confused by everything. "My goodness, sir, how awful this must be for you."

"It gets worse, Mrs. Jeffries," Witherspoon said morosely. "The killer didn't just use my name. He also looked like me, too."

"He looked like you?"

"Yes, the description the night watchman gave when he was questioned fits me perfectly." The inspector drained the last of his drink in one long gulp. "For a moment when I was in the chief inspector's office, I rather had the feeling they thought I might be involved."

"That's ridiculous, sir." Mrs. Jeffries was genuinely alarmed. "Why, you don't even know the victim."

"No, of course not. Never heard of the man until Constable Barnes mentioned him this morning."

She breathed a sigh of relief. She wasn't sure how she would have felt if it had turned out that the inspector did know the victim personally. Not that she would ever believe Gerald Witherspoon capable of murder. But she was very glad the late Peter Hornsley was a complete stranger.

"How was he killed?" She already knew he was strangled, but she wanted the details.

"Strangled." The inspector shook himself again, as though to clear his head of cobwebs. "Coshed on the head first and then strangled with a tie. Oddest thing, Barnes told me he had a note pinned to his chest."

"Was the note pinned there by the killer?"

"We're fairly certain it must have been. Most people don't walk about with a piece of notepaper pinned to their chests."

"What did it say?"

"Nothing that made any sense. It was just letters. V-E-N-I. It could be anything. A name, a place—who knows? Fact is, I won't ever find out. This is Inspector Nivens's case."

She pursed her lips and looked away so that Witherspoon wouldn't see her expression. Nivens was not only stupid, he was arrogant, suspicious, and petty. Furthermore, Mrs. Jeffries was fairly certain Nivens was on to them. Or, at the very least, suspected that Witherspoon had help with his investigations when he was on a case. Nivens had hinted on more than one occasion that he knew *she* was up to something. They'd have to be doubly careful now.

"But Inspector Nivens has never handled a homicide."

"Everyone has to start somewhere, Mrs. Jeffries. I'm sure Inspector Nivens will do a fine job. No doubt he'll have the miscreant in hand very quickly."

Not without a lot of help, Mrs. Jeffries thought. Help that Nivens wouldn't want and would insist he didn't need. "Oh, sir, I'm so sorry. It must have been dreadful for you, being interviewed by your colleagues. What are they going to have you do?"

"I'm going to be working on a robbery case," he shrugged. "I'll get Nivens's case and he'll take this case."

Mrs. Jeffries was truly alarmed. Inspector Witherspoon had never handled a robbery case. Gracious, they didn't have time to work on two cases simultaneously. But perhaps she was being unfair. There was no reason to believe that her employer would need assistance solving a simple robbery. "What kind of a robbery is it, sir?"

"Jewelry," he replied. "There's a ring of thieves robbing homes over near Regent's Park. You know the sort of thing I mean. They get in quickly while the house is empty, steal whatever jewels they can find lying about the place, and then get out," he explained, trying to make his voice more enthusiastic than he actually felt. The truth was, he didn't know the first thing about catching thieves.

"That should be an interesting change for you, sir," she murmured.

"Yes, they assigned me one of Nivens's best constables to assist me."

"What about Constable Barnes?"

"Oh, they're having him assist Nivens." Witherspoon's brows came together over his spectacles. "But I must say, I do envy Nivens. This case does appear to be most interesting, most interesting, indeed."

"What were you able to find out, sir?" she asked cautiously.

"Officially, nothing. Unofficially, Barnes told me the victim, Peter Hornsley, was one of four partners of the Hornsley, Frampton, and Whitelaw, Insurance Brokers. They're one of the most successful firms in the City. Supposedly they've made pots of money since they started up."

"And when did they start up, as you call it?"

"Oh, the firm's been around for ages," Witherspoon replied. "Three of the four partners went to school together. After they left Oxford, they pooled their resources and opened the company. So I don't think one can look in that direction for the killer."

"What do you mean, sir?"

"I mean that the men have known each other for ages. They're good friends, so I hardly expect one of the remaining two partners is the killer."

Mrs. Jeffries rather thought you could look in any direction for a killer. In her experience, it was often people who'd known you longest and best who wished you dead. But she certainly wasn't going to contradict the inspector in his current depressed mood. "You said there were four partners," she prompted.

"Oh yes, the fourth one recently bought into the business. Some foreign fellow, I believe." He frowned. "Can't remember what Barnes said his name was, but he couldn't be a suspect. He hadn't even met Hornsley. The negotiations were handled by a solicitor."

"How very interesting, sir. I must say, I'm most impressed. But, of course, I shouldn't be. Trust you to find out so much about the case in such a short time."

A genuine smile flitted across his face. "Thank you, Mrs. Jeffries. You're most kind. Naturally, one would be interested in the case. Not that I'm trying to interfere in Inspector Nivens's patch. Oh, no, I'd never do that. But one can't help picking up bits and pieces, can one?"

"Of course not, sir. Did you pick up any other 'bits and pieces,' while you were chatting with Constable Barnes?"

"Not really, just the first names of the partners. There was Hornsley, of course, and Grady Whitelaw and George Frampton. They were the three original partners." He brightened suddenly. "Why, I've just remembered. The fourth partner is named Justin Vincent. Yes, that's right, that's what Barnes said. Vincent is some sort of entrepreneur. Seems to make his living buying into thriving businesses."

"Did Mr. Hornsley have any relations?"

"Oh, yes, he's a married man. I'm not sure if he has any children. Barnes didn't say. Other than that, I know nothing else."

"Too bad Constable Barnes didn't tell you what sort of paper the note was written on or what sort of ink was used."

"I suppose Barnes didn't think it mattered," Witherspoon sighed, his sudden buoyancy gone as quickly as it had come. The truth was, though he complained about getting stuck with all the homicides, he really quite enjoyed solving them. Made him feel useful, as though he were truly serving justice. Drat it all, it felt rather miserable not to be investigating this one, he thought.

Even worse, he almost felt as though he were considered a suspect.


"It weren't my fault, I tell you," George Halisham moaned. He pounded a fist against the top of the table making his pint of ale shake precariously.

He grabbed at it before it spilled over the top of the glass. "How were I to know the bloke weren't really no copper?"

"Corse it weren't yer fault," Smythe agreed. "Coulda 'appened to anyone." They were seated at a table in the public bar of the Duck and Dog, a pub on the Commercial Docks. Finding the night watchman hadn't been easy; he'd had to cross more than a few palms with silver. But once he'd made Mr. Halisham's acquaintance, he'd had no trouble gettin' the bloke to talk.

"That's what I tried to tell 'em," Halisham replied forcefully. "But them toffs never listen to a workin' man. On me all the time, they is. 'Do this, do that, make sure you keep the front door locked, don't be takin' the newspapers out of the rubbish bins.' I tell you, it goes on and on. And now I think I'm goin' to get the sack. Just because Hornsley was done in by some crazy copper."

"Bloomin' Ada." Smythe shook his head sympathetically. "It ain't fair. But tell me, do you know for sure it were a copper?"

"Nah, it coulda been anybody. But the fellow said he was police, so I let him in. Weren't nuthin' else I could do, now, was there? Besides, with them break-ins we 'ad last month, I thought he were there 'cause of that."

"You mean the buildin's been robbed?"

Halisham shook his head. "Nah, just someone breaking in and larkin' about in the offices. Stealin' pens and inkwells and stuff like that. I don't see why they made such a fuss about it. It's not like whoever done it took anything worth takin', if you get my meanin'. It were a nuisance, nothin' else." Halisham broke off and laughed. "Corse it's nuisance that's done me some good. Them break-ins is why they hired me."

Smythe didn't see that a few inkpots and some pens being stolen had anything to do with Hornsley's murder, but you never knew. "What'd the copper look like?" He took a sip from his tankard of bitter.

"He were a medium-sized like fellow, 'ad on a dark bowler hat and a big overcoat, wore spectacles and 'ad a mustache."

"What'd his face look like?"

Halisham shrugged. "Truth is, except for the spectacles and the mustache, I didn't see it all that close. It's right dark in the building that time of night. Mr. Beersch only likes me to keep one light burnin'."

"How can you be a proper night watchman if they don't let you 'ave decent light?" Smythe said.

"Usually it don't matter," Halisham belched softly. "Most of the offices is empty by the time it gets dark. You don't have a lot of people goin' in and out."

"So it were odd, this Hornsley fellow bein' there?"

"Nah," Halisham said slowly. "Hornsley stayed late lots of times, more than anyone else in the buildin'. That night there were a couple of other firms that had staff workin'. Matter of fact, most of the ground floor offices 'ad someone in 'em."

"So this copper just up and walked into Hornsley's office and done 'im in?"

"I showed 'im in, of course," Halisham corrected. "Walked 'im down the hallway and announced him properly. Not that I needed to, mind you. But rules is rules. Besides, the fellow had a voice loud enough to raise the roof on a cathedral. I'm sure everyone there 'eard 'im shoutin' that he was from the police and 'ad something urgent to tell Mr. Hornsley." Halisham laughed. "Funny that, when he first got there, the bloke spoke so softly I had to strain to 'ear 'im, yet when we got to Hornsley's bleedin' door, he shouted loud enough for the whole street to 'ear 'im."

"Did you see anyone else that night?" Smythe asked.

"No, just the copper."

"Did you see 'im leave, I mean, were he covered in blood and did 'e 'ave a wild murderous look in 'is eyes?"

"I only saw the back of him, he were scarpering out the front door when I got back from checking the rear was locked up proper," Halisham replied. "Fellow were gone by the time I got back to me post. And now Mr. Beersch is talkin' about sackin' me just 'cause I were doin' my job. How was I to know the bloke was murderin' someone? It's not like the copper told me what he was up to, now, was it?"

Smythe clucked his tongue in sympathy. He wasn't just trying to get the man to keep talking, either. He was genuinely concerned about George Halisham losing his position. Life was hard for the poor. Smythe knew that for a fact. He'd been poor most of his own life. Not that he had to worry about that now, but there had been plenty of times when he was younger, before he went out to Australia, that he'd spent more than one night sleeping in the open because he didn't have a roof over his head.

"Corse it ain't your fault, this guv of yours sounds like he's a right old—"

"Right old bastard, that's what 'e is," Halisham finished. "And if I lose me position, I don't know what I'll do. It's not like there's many jobs about, you know."

"Yeah, I know." There never seemed to be enough jobs for everyone. Smythe asked a few more questions, but Halisham could tell him nothing else. He downed the rest of his bitter and tossed some coins on the counter.

"Plannin' on leavin'?" Halisham asked mournfully. His new friend had been most generous with the drinks and he was a sympathetic sort of fellow too, despite his big, rough looks.

"Gotta get back to the stables," Smythe said. "Look, I work over at Howard's. If ya do lose your position, come by and see me. I may be able to 'elp ya out."

"Don't know much about 'orses," Halisham said thoughtfully. "But I'm a fast learner."

Smythe reached into his coat pocket and pulled out a guinea. "'Ere, just in case you get tossed out today, maybe this'll 'elp pay the rent," he handed the coin to the rather astonished-looking Halisham.

George stared at the coin like he was afraid it would disappear, then he looked up at Smythe. "That's right decent of ya. Thanks. If the worst happens, at least this'll keep the landlord from tossin' us into the streets."

"Us workin' men gots to stick together," Smythe said. He nodded to the barman and left.

Outside, he made his way past the stairs of the Dog and Duck, cut through warehouse yards, and skirted wharves until he came to Grove Street. The day had turned dark and cloudy; the dampness from the river seeping deep into his bones. Smythe knew he had no reason to be depressed, but blimey, he was. This morning hadn't gone at all well. Not with Betsy showin' up just as Abigail was throwin' her ruddy arms around his neck to thank him for loanin' her a few bob.

Bloomin' Ada, what rotten luck. Just as he and Betsy was gettin' on so well, too. Wouldn't you know she'd show up at Howard's just at the wrong moment. He'd glanced up to see Betsy standing by the horse stalls with her eyes narrowed and her mouth flattened in a straight line. But what was a bloke supposed to do? Toss Abby into a mound of hay just because she were givin' him a grateful hug?

Frustrated, he kicked an empty coal sack that was lying in the road in front of him. The sack skittered and landed with a thump against the stairs of the Methodist Chapel, earning Smythe a disapproving frown from the well-dressed man coming down those very stairs.

Smythe glared right back. He was in no mood to apologize to a bloomin' Methodist for kickin' a bit of rubbish off the road. His foul mood was all Betsy's fault. The little minx had refused to let him explain that he was just helpin' out an old friend. Corse, he thought, as he dodged round a timber wagon loaded with planks of wood, maybe it was just as well he hadn't explained. Betsy might start wonderin' where he'd got the money to loan Abby in the first place. And he weren't quite ready to tell the lass the truth about his finances. Not yet, anyway. Not till he was sure she cared for him. He had a feelin' Betsy would get right annoyed at the fact that he'd been deceiving all of them from the beginnin'. But what in blazes could he have done? he asked himself peevishly. Euphemia, God rest her soul, had made him promise to stay on and keep an eye on her nephew, Gerald Witherspoon, after she'd left the inspector a moderate fortune and the big house on Upper Edmonton Gardens. Then they'd all come and they'd started investigatin' murders and gettin' to know each other and he hadn't wanted to leave. He hadn't wanted to tell them the truth, either. He was too afraid it would change everything.

He stomped round the corner and stopped in front of the Duke of York Pub. Smythe decided to take a hansom home. Blast a Spaniard, anyway. It weren't his fault he had more money than he knew what to do with.


"Do come in, Inspector Nivens," Mrs. Jeffries said politely. "Inspector Witherspoon is in the drawing room."

"Good day, Mrs. Jeffries," Nivens replied. His dark blond hair was slicked back, his chest puffed out, and his usually pale, pasty cheeks were flushed with pride.

She forced herself to smile. "It's this way, sir."

"Good afternoon, Nivens," Witherspoon said, as the housekeeper ushered him into the drawing room. "How very good of you to come by. I was going to contact you. I've been given your robbery, it seems."

"Good day, Witherspoon." Nivens sat down on the settee without being asked. Mrs. Jeffries had no excuse to hover; it was too early for tea and she wasn't going to offer it in any case. She nodded to the two men and went out into the hall. Making sure her footsteps were good and loud, she walked quickly down the hallway to the head of the stairs. She stomped down into the kitchen, nodded at Mrs. Goodge, who was serving tea and buns (bakery buns, at that) to a costermonger, and then turned around and went right back up the way she'd come. She took care to be quiet. She crept down the hall and stationed herself to one side of the open double doors leading to the drawing room.

"According to the chief inspector," Nivens said, "you were out walking last night when the murder occurred."

Nivens sounded as pompous as a bishop, Mrs. Jeffries thought. She didn't much like the tone of voice he was using.

"I was," Witherspoon agreed. "Walked for miles. Good for the health, you know."

"Did you know Peter Hornsley?" Nivens continued.

"As I told the chief, I'd never heard of the man until Constable Barnes told me about the murder this morning."

"You're absolutely certain of that?"

Mrs. Jeffries drew in a deep breath. Just who did Nivens think he was talking with—a common criminal?

"Of course I'm certain," Witherspoon replied.

"Do you have any idea why someone would use your name?"

Mrs. Jeffries thought that was an amazingly stupid question. Someone used the inspector's name because it was familiar, since it was in the papers so often, generally after he'd concluded a successful homicide investigation.

"I've no idea." Witherspoon coughed. "Don't you have any suspects yet?"

"Of course we've suspects," Nivens snapped. "But I must ask you these questions."

"Why? I didn't kill the man. Are you sure you've other suspects? I'd be quite happy to help you out in any way I can."

"I don't need your help, Inspector," Nivens replied frostily. "I'll have you know we've already interviewed the victim's brother, Mr. Nyles Hornsley. He's not got much of an alibi and he didn't get along with his brother all that well. Furthermore, there's some evidence the victim and his wife weren't happily married, if you get my meaning. So you can see, I've no shortage of suspects and I certainly don't need any help."

"I didn't mean to insult you," Witherspoon said apologetically. "There's no shame in asking for help, you know. I expect I'll have dozens of questions for you about this robbery I've been given. I've never done a robbery before. By the way, why was Mr. Nyles Hornsley estranged from his brother?"

"Witherspoon, I don't think you ought to be asking the questions here."

Mrs. Jeffries's blood boiled. She could feel the heat of anger all the way up to the roots of her hair.

"Yes, yes, of course. It's none of my affair," Witherspoon replied. "Mind you, if you're having difficulties finding out the cause of estrangement, I've always found that asking the . . ."

"I'm not having difficulties," Nivens shouted. Mrs. Jeffries grinned, "Nyles Hornsley hated his brother because of a woman named Madeline Wynn."

"There, there, Inspector," Witherspoon soothed. "Don't upset yourself. Your face is turning a dreadful shade of red. I don't think that can be good for you."

"Inspector Witherspoon," Nivens said slowly. (Mrs. Jeffries thought it sounded as though his teeth were clenched.) "I think perhaps I'd better be going now. You've obviously nothing further to tell me."

"Oh dear, I was hoping you could give me a few details about this robbery."

"Constable Markham is fully informed about the robberies," Nivens snapped. "He'll give you all the details tomorrow. Good day, sir." He stalked for the door.

Mrs. Jeffries scurried down the hall and whirled around; she pretended to have just come up the back stairs, "Leaving so soon, Inspector?" she called. "Do let me see you to the door."

"That won't be necessary, Mrs. Jeffries," he said coldly. "I can find my own way. Witherspoon's house isn't that big."


At teatime, everyone, including Luty Belle and Hatchet, assembled around the kitchen table.

"Inspector Witherspoon is upstairs having a lie down," Mrs. Jeffries announced. "So we'd best be careful. We don't want him coming down and accidentally overhearing us."

"I'll keep a look out," Wiggins volunteered. "Fred's gone up with him and I can 'ear 'im comin' a mile away."

"The inspector wouldn't hear nothing important from me," Mrs. Goodge snapped. "I didn't learn hardly anything. Not with someone hangin' about the kitchen and interfering every time one of my sources showed up."

"I was only tryin' to 'elp," Wiggins yelped. "And that's all the thanks I get?"

Mrs. Jeffries inwardly sighed. The cook was notoriously protective of her "sources"; she didn't want anyone else going near them. For that matter, the rest of them were the same way. But she had to do something. Poor Wiggins mustn't be made to feel left out just because he had a broken ankle. On the other hand, she didn't want him possibly ruining a valuable line of inquiry.

"Wiggins," Mrs. Jeffries said gently, "perhaps it would be best if you stayed out of the kitchen."

Wiggins's face fell and she felt like a worm. "Maybe tomorrow," she said quickly, racking her brain to think of something he could do, "you might go out in the gardens and see to it that Fred has some decent exercise."

"You mean keep out of everyone's way," Wiggins said pathetically.

"That's not what I meant at all," Mrs. Jeffries lied. That's precisely what she wanted him to do, because she couldn't for the life of her think of what he could do to help.

"It's all right, Mrs. Jeffries," Wiggins sniffed. "Fred and I'll go out tomorrow and amuse ourselves. Don't worry about us. We'll be fine."

Luty chuckled. "You ought to be on the stage, boy," she said kindly. "Don't fret so. I'll send Essie around tomorrow with a stack of books for you to read. That ought to keep you busy."

Wiggins grinned. "Thanks. I love to read and I've already gone through most of what we 'ave 'ere."

"Now that that's settled," Luty said, "can we get back to business? Hatchet and I had a bit of luck."

"Hold on a minute," Mrs. Goodge interrupted. "I didn't say I hadn't learned anything today." She shot the footman another frown. "Even with him under my feet I did find out a tidbit or two. Seems this Mr. Hornsley was a bit of a womanizer."

Betsy snorted faintly and glanced at the coachman. "Aren't they all?" she muttered.

Smythe's eyes narrowed.

Blast, Mrs. Jeffries thought, seeing the quick look the maid and coachman exchanged, now they're at it, too. But she didn't have time to worry about that now. The inspector might take it into his head to come down to the kitchen any moment now. It was most inconvenient having him home.

"What do you mean?" she asked the cook. "What kind of womanizer?"

"Well, the usual," Mrs. Goodge blushed slightly. "He was supposedly involved with some woman he kept in a flat in Chelsea. But I couldn't find out her name."

"Is he still involved with her?" Mrs. Jeffries asked.

"No. Supposedly she give him the heave-ho a while back," the cook admitted.

"Can I talk now?" Luty asked archly.

"Oh, sorry," Mrs. Goodge smiled at the American. "Go on."

"Yes, Luty, do go on," urged Mrs. Jeffries.

"Well, Hatchet and I found out that Hornsley's pretty much hated by other insurance brokers."

"Pardon me, madam," Hatchet corrected. "But don't you think that 'hated' is too strong a word? What Mr. Andover said was that Hornsley wasn't well liked."

Luty frowned at her butler. "What he said was that Damon Hilliard had thrown a punch at the man just last week. If that ain't hatred, Hatchet, I don't know what is!"

"Who's Damon Hilliard?" Smythe asked.

"One of Hornsley's business competitors," explained Hatchet. "And Mr. Andover didn't say Hornsley had 'thrown a punch at the man,' he said they'd almost come to fisticuffs."

"Almost come to fisticuffs ain't nuthin' more than a swing that misses," Luty stated. "But let's not argue about it anymore. Andover said that Hornsley's firm was accused of unethical business practices, and this Hilliard fellow claimed Hornsley and his partners were deliberately tryin' to run him out of business."

"By doin' what?"

"The usual—undercuttin' prices, stealin' clients, bribin' clerks for inside information on other firms," Luty replied.

"Did he say anything else?" Mrs. Jeffries asked.

"Not really," she admitted. "But I think that's quite a good start. Nell's bells, this case ain't even twenty-four hours old and we've already got a good suspect."

"Actually, we've got several," Mrs. Jeffries stated. She told them everything she'd picked up from the inspector and, more important, from the eavesdropping she'd done on Nivens. "So you see, we have plenty of suspects about. Hilliard, the partners, the victim's wife and brother, and some woman named Madeline Wynn. I think we're off to an excellent start."

"I didn't learn anything at all," Betsy said. "The shopkeepers in the area didn't know Peter Hornsley from Adam."

"Not to worry, Betsy," Mrs. Jeffries said. "You'll have better luck tomorrow."

"Yeah, you'll probably find out all sorts of interestin' bits and pieces tomorrow," Smythe added.

Betsy didn't even look in the coachman's direction.

"Did you have any success?" Mrs. Jeffries asked the coachman.

"Huh?" He drew his gaze away from Betsy's direction and cleared his throat. "Not much. I mean, I didn't learn much more than we already knew. I tracked the night watchman down and took him to a pub down at the docks."

Betsy mumbled something under her breath.

Smythe frowned at her but kept on talking. "Poor bloke is scared he's goin' to lose his position. Seems they're gettin' at 'im for lettin' the killer inside the building."

"But how was he to know?" Wiggins asked. "The killer claimed to be Inspector Witherspoon."

Smythe gave the footman a cynical smile. "The fact the poor fellow was only doin' his job won't matter. They can sack who they like. If they want someone to blame, they always pick on the poor bloke at the bottom of the heap."

"Is this Mr. Halisham certain that no one else came into the building other than the man calling himself Inspector Witherspoon?" Mrs. Jeffries asked.

"Positive," Smythe stated. "Halisham come back from checking the back door just in time to see the false Witherspoon lettin' 'imself out the front door. He shouted 'good night' at 'im, but the man was out the door by then and didn't answer. Halisham went right up to double-check that the front door lock had clicked into place. No one else came in."

"Did Halisham give you a description of the man calling himself Inspector Witherspoon?" Luty asked eagerly. "I mean, what did this feller look like?"

"Accordin' to what Halisham saw, he fits our inspector right down to 'is bowler 'at and 'is spectacles. Mind you, Halisham did say there were only one light. He didn't really get a good look at the man's face. Corse, he never thought the man weren't really with Scotland Yard, not with 'im bellowin' out who he was and who he wanted to see all the way down the 'all to Hornsley's office. Halisham told me 'e were worried someone would stick their 'ead out just to see what were goin' on. There was others workin' late that night." He went on to give them the rest of the details he'd learned from the watchman.

When he finished, Hatchet leaned forward on his elbows. "Did anyone else go out?"

"Only the few people that was workin' on the ground floor," Smythe said. "There was a clerk working in the architect's office and he left at seven o'clock. The estate agent, he was workin' late, too; he left at around half-past seven."

"What time was the body found?" Mrs. Goodge asked.

"Round ten last night," Smythe explained.

"By whom?" Wiggins asked.

"Halisham. When it got late and Hornsley hadn't come out of his office, Halisham got curious," Smythe explained. "He knocked on the door and the ruddy thing swung open. He said it were a bit dark, the only light was from one of the inner offices, but he said he could see Hornsley there layin' on the floor. He thought the man had had a fit or something. But when he got close, he could tell the man was dead. So he ran for the copper on the corner."

"Was anything missing?" Betsy finally asked. "I mean, could it have been a robbery?"

"Halisham overheard one of the other partners, fellow named Frampton, talkin' to the police this morning. Accordin' to Frampton, nothing was missin'." Smythe tried a smile. Betsy stared at him stone-faced. "Anyways," he continued, "the firm didn't keep cash or valuables on the premises."

"Excellent, Smythe," Mrs. Jeffries said kindly. She felt rather sorry for the poor man. Obviously Betsy was furious at him and, just as obviously, he hadn't a clue what to do about it. She asked if anyone else had anything to report, but no one did.

"Before we continue," Mrs. Jeffries said, "a*word of warning. Inspector Nivens is handling this case and he'll be on the lookout for any of us sneaking about and asking questions. We must be very, very careful. Is that understood?"

"Course it is." Luty thumped her cane on the floor, "We all knows this Nivens is a sneaky little varmint, so I reckon we'll all keep our eyes open."

"For once, madam," Hatchet said, "I agree with you."

For the next ten minutes they discussed what to do next. As soon as everyone had their assignments, Luty and Hatchet took their leave. Mrs. Jeffries, Mrs. Goodge, and Betsy tidied up the kitchen and Smythe took Fred, who'd sneaked downstairs as soon as the inspector had gone to sleep, out for a walk.

Smythe thought his luck had changed when he came back into the kitchen and saw Betsy putting the last of the china in the cupboard. There was no sign of the cook or the housekeeper and Wiggins had hobbled up to his room earlier. Smythe cleared his throat. He saw Betsy's back stiffen but she didn't turn around and acknowledge his presence, "Uh, Betsy, could I have a word, please?"

"What about?"

"About this morning at the stables," he said. Blast! Who'd have thought his past would surface now to come back and haunt him. "I'd like to explain somethin' to you."

"You've nothing to explain," she said. She turned to face him, her chin was raised and her blue eyes glinted with anger. "It's nothing to me what you do or who you spend your time with. If you want to be givin' women money . . ."

Blast and damn, he thought. She'd seen him giving Abigail a wad of pound notes.

"It's none of my business."

"True," he said bluntly. Frankly, it weren't none of her concern. Exceptin' that he cared about her, cared more than he'd ever thought it possible to care about anyone. "But yer my friend and I won't 'ave you thinkin' badly of me. I was givin' that woman money 'cause she's an old friend of mine and she's a bit down on her luck, that's all."

Betsy stared at him poker-faced. He was sure she didn't believe a word he'd said.

# CHAPTER 3

"Haven't you finished yet?" Mrs. Goodge pointed to Smythe's plate. "You've been playing with that sausage for the past ten minutes. And you, Wiggins, are you goin' to eat that egg or not?"

"What's the ruddy 'urry?" Smythe replied. He wasn't in the best of moods himself. Betsy was still acting like she had a poker up her spine and he hadn't slept all that well for worrying about it. "We only just set down a few minutes ago."

Mrs. Jeffries glanced at the clock. It had barely gone half-past seven. "We've plenty of time to enjoy our breakfast, Mrs. Goodge," she said. "It's still very early. The inspector won't be wanting his breakfast for another half hour."

Betsy reached for another piece of toast. "You've been rushin' us ever since we come down," she complained. "What's got into you this morning? Your rheumatism actin' up again?"

The cook put her hands on her ample hips and frowned. "There's nothing wrong exceptin' that I need to get this kitchen cleared. I've got my cousin Hilda's boy comin' by early and I want to have plenty of time to talk to the lad. He works as footman for a family that lives round the corner from Peter Hornsley."

"What time is he due?" Mrs. Jeffries asked patiently.

"Half-past eight," she replied, hurrying over to the oven and opening the door. "But I want to get some things done before he gets here. He's not the only one coming by today."

"I suppose all of us have a lot to do today," Mrs. Jeffries said as she reached for the marmalade.

"I don't," Wiggins complained. "Me and Fred 'as got nuthin' to do but 'ang about 'ere polishin' the ruddy silver."

"Not to worry, lad," Smythe said kindly. "The rest will do you good. But mind you stay out of Mrs. Goodge's way."

"Luty said she was sendin' Essie over with some books for you to read," Betsy added. "That ought to help keep you occupied."

"Yeah, but Essie'll 'ang about for ages," Wiggins groaned. "I'll never get rid of 'er."

"The lass likes ya," Smythe teased.

Wiggins blushed. Essie was a girl that Luty had taken in after she'd lost her position as a maid. They'd met the girl when they were investigating one of their first cases. Oddly enough, Hatchet had taken the girl under his wing, taught her to read, and there was now talk of sending her off to school somewhere. But that didn't make her any prettier, Wiggins thought peevishly. Truth to tell, she was homely. He winced guiltily, wondering if the others could see what he was thinking. He really should be ashamed of himself; Essie was a right nice girl. And smart, too, despite the fact that she had teeth that stuck out funny.

"As we're all getting a fairly early start today," Mrs. Jeffries said, "why don't we meet back here at noon?"

Betsy frowned. "I don't know. I'm not sure that'll give me enough time. I wanted to talk to the shopkeepers 'round the Hornsley neighborhood and then I wanted to have a go at making contact with someone from the household."

"After I do the pubs," Smythe added, "I wanted to talk to the cabbies in the area. You never know what you might stumble across if you get lucky. I'd not like to have to 'urry back just when I've got someone talkin'."

Mrs. Jeffries gazed at them thoughtfully. She was really quite proud. They did take their detecting very seriously. "You're right. I suppose it's not a good idea to meet here so early. Why don't we meet for an early tea before supper?"

"That would be easier on me," the cook said quickly. "That way I wouldn't have to worry about fixing a noon meal."

"What are you goin' to be doin' today?" Wiggins asked Mrs. Jeffries. "Maybe I could 'elp you?"

"I'm sorry, Wiggins," the housekeeper smiled sympathetically, "But I'm meeting Dr. Bosworth."

"Oh, no," Betsy cried. "You're not!"

Surprised, Mrs. Jeffries stared at the maid. "Why shouldn't I see Dr. Bosworth? With any luck, he'll have done the postmortem on Hornsley. He might have some valuable information to tell us."

"But you said we had to be careful," Betsy argued. "What if Dr. Bosworth mentions you were snoopin' about?"

"The lass 'as got a point," Smythe interjected. "We've got to be right cautious on this case. It's not even the inspector's."

Mrs. Jeffries frowned thoughtfully. They did have a point. "But I've used . . ." She broke off, appalled at herself for saying such a thing. "I mean," she amended, "we've had help from Dr. Bosworth several times before. I'm sure he's absolutely trustworthy. Besides, I'll make sure and tell him to keep my inquiries confidential."

"Hello, hello," the voice of Lady Cannonberry came from the back hallway. "Anyone home?"

"We're in here," Mrs. Jeffries called.

"Oh, dear," said Ruth Cannonberry, an attractive middle-aged woman, who blushed to the roots of her blond hair when she saw she'd interrupted their breakfast. "I'm so sorry. I shouldn't have barged in as I did."

"Rest assured," Mrs. Jeffries said politely, "you're most welcome at any time. May we offer you some breakfast?"

"I've eaten, thank you." Ruth took a seat beside Wiggins. She reached down and patted Fred on the head. "But I could do with a cup of tea."

"I'll get the cup," Betsy said, getting up and going to the cupboard.

"I've missed seeing any of you about the gardens the last day or two. Thank you, Betsy," she said as the maid set the cup in front of her. "So naturally I thought you must be investigating this dreadful murder."

"What murder?" Mrs. Jeffries tried to keep her tone as neutral as possible. Blast. How on earth had she found out?

"Why, the one Wiggins told me about yesterday afternoon." Ruth smiled at the footman. Wiggins's round cheeks turned red and he slumped down in his seat as all eyes turned on him.

"Oh, that murder," Mrs. Goodge muttered. She shot the footman a glare that would have singed the blackening off an oven.

"I must say I think it's dreadfully unfair of Scotland Yard to suspect Inspector Witherspoon," Ruth continued.

"I suppose Wiggins told you that, too," Betsy said.

"Inspector Witherspoon is not a suspect," Mrs. Jeffries said firmly.

"But because the murderer used his name to get into the victim's office, naturally, he can't investigate the case."

"Does that mean you're not investigating it?" Ruth asked.

"Well," Mrs. Jeffries would have straight out lied to her guest, but she was fairly sure she'd get caught. All anyone had to do was watch the household and they could see if they were on a case or not. "Actually, we are investigating this one."

"Oh, goody," Ruth clapped her hands together. "I'm so very glad. I was terrified you were going to pass this one up. Now, what can I do to help?"

Constable Barnes felt like a traitor. But duty was duty and he'd been temporarily assigned to assist Inspector Nivens. Translated, that meant the brass was afraid of a right old muck up and they wanted him on the scene to keep Nivens from doing too much damage.

"Do stand still, Constable," Nivens snapped. "We're here to ask questions, not to memorize the paintings on Mrs. Hornsley's wall."

"Sorry, sir," Barnes apologized. He drew his gaze away from the pretty oil of a pastoral English meadow. What was he supposed to look at, he wondered, the furniture?

He glanced about the drawing room. There was a marble fireplace on one side, two wide double windows on the wall facing the garden, a thick red and gold fleur-de-lis patterned carpet, and a number of balloon-backed chairs and settees. It was a nice room, elegant and beautifully but unimaginatively decorated. There was cream-colored paint on the walls and bronze velvet drapes framing the windows, fringed shawls on the tables, and several nice pieces of china and silver knicknacks scattered about, but blimey, there wasn't much to keep a man's mind occupied.

Finished with his examination of the Hornsley drawing room, Barnes gave Nivens a quick frown. Not stare at paintings? Wasn't that what they was there for? To be looked at? Nivens was a ruddy fool.

Nivens straightened as they heard footsteps coming down the hall. A tall, slender middle-aged woman with dark brown hair and blue eyes swept into the room. She was dressed in heavy black mourning clothes that rustled softly as she came toward the two policemen.

Her face was pale, and her lips were bloodless, as though she'd recently been ill. She'd once been a handsome woman, but now there were deeply bracketed age lines etched around her eyes and mouth.

"Mrs. Hornsley," Nivens stepped forward and gave a slight bow. "Do forgive us for intruding at a time like this, but, unfortunately, there are some questions that must be asked."

"And you are?" Glynis Hornsley stared at him blankly.

"Inspector Nigel Nivens," he clicked his heels together. "Scotland Yard. We're here to ask you a few questions about your late husband."

Barnes frowned. Inspector Witherspoon didn't do them poncy little bows or that silly heel clickin'. Who did Nivens think he was—one of the Kaiser's generals?

Glynis Hornsley nodded. "Yes, I thought you might be coming round. I just didn't expect it so soon. Peter isn't even buried yet."

"We have to do the postmortem on your husband," Barnes said gently. "That delays things a bit."

Nivens frowned irritably at the constable. Then he looked pointedly at the settee, but as Mrs. Hornsley was still standing, he could hardly sit down himself. Barnes stifled a grin.

"Mrs. Hornsley," Nivens began, "what time was your husband due to come home last night?"

"I don't know," she replied, "He'd been very busy lately and had been working later and later hours."

"So he didn't tell you what time to expect him?"

"No, he merely asked for the cook to keep something hot for his dinner and that he'd be home sometime in the evening."

"I see," Nivens said.

Barnes couldn't figure out what Nivens had seen; all they'd learned was that the man was a hard worker and had been puttin' in a lot of long hours at his office. But as they'd already learned that same information from one of Hornsley's partners, he didn't see why Nivens was wasting time covering the same ground.

"Were you here all evening?" Nivens asked.

Good, thought Barnes, now he's starting to ask some decent questions.

"Yes, I was. I rarely go out in the evenings." She shrugged. "Peter isn't very sociable. I've learned to entertain myself, Inspector. I read a great deal."

"Did your husband have any enemies?" Nivens asked.

"Of course he did," Mrs. Hornsley said. "He wasn't a particularly agreeable man. There were people in London that loathed him."

"Who?"

"I can't give you names," she said tartly. "Peter didn't confide his business troubles to me. But I know that some of his competitors hated him."

"Enough to murder him?" Nivens prodded.

Barnes felt like shaking the man. For God's sake, there were a dozen or more things he should be askin'. What was wrong with the man? Why wasn't he askin' if someone could confirm her whereabouts last night? Why wasn't he asking *who* was goin' to benefit from Hornsley's death? They already knew that Hornsley's competitors hated him. They'd gotten that information this morning from his nervous Nellie of a partner, Grady Whitelaw.

"I don't know about that." Glynis Hornsley shrugged. "I'm sorry, I know I'm not being very helpful, but this has been a dreadful shock to me."

"Yes, we can appreciate that," Nivens said. "Had your husband received any threats to his life?"

"No, not that I know of."

"Are you sure, Mrs. Hornsley?" Nivens pressed. "Perhaps a staff person he'd sacked, a business rival he'd angered? Anything like that."

"Inspector, he's received nothing that I know about in the way of threats," she said tersely. "As for former staff members, Peter frequently sacked people. He rather enjoyed doing it. But none of them ever threatened him. My husband," her mouth curled in a sneer as she spoke, "always took great pains to bully those who weren't able or likely to fight back. He was quite good at picking his victims, you see. He's been doing it all his life."

"So you've no idea who would have wanted to harm your husband?" Nivens didn't react at all to the woman's tone or words. Barnes wondered if they had even registered on the man.

"All I can think is that it's probably some business rival," she answered.

Ask her about the note, Barnes silently screamed at Nivens. Ask her about the writing on the ruddy note. Ask her if she's any idea what VENI might mean.

"Yes, that's our view as well," Nivens agreed. "Well, we shan't bother you further." He bowed again. "My deepest condolences for your loss."

Barnes could have spit. How the bloomin' blue blazes could Nivens have formed any kind of an opinion? He'd not asked enough questions to know anything, let alone that Hornsley was killed by a business rival.

There were plenty of businessmen in the City, and as far as Barnes knew, most of them didn't get rid of their competition by chokin' them to death. Furthermore, all you had to do was spend two minutes with the grieving widow and it was as plain as the nose on your face that she hated her husband and wasn't terribly sorry he was dead.

"Is this the street, then?" Smythe asked.

"Hornsley's house is the last one at the end," Betsy replied. She pointed down the row of large Georgian homes on the quiet street. "But I think I'll nip back up the High Street and see what I can get out of the shop-keepers."

"No hansoms that I can see," Smythe muttered. The neighborhood was quiet, elegant, and without the clamor of street traffic. "So maybe I'll try that pub we passed on the corner. Uh, Betsy, what time you figurin' on goin' back?"

"I don't know," she replied, looking everywhere but directly at him. "When I get finished, I suppose."

Smythe felt like he was talking to a stranger. All the way over here, Betsy had been so polite you'd have thought he was the ruddy prince of Wales. What did the girl want? He'd told her the truth, told her that Abigail was just an old friend. But she was actin' like she'd caught him kissin' a floozie under the stairs. Women! Who could understand 'em?

He gathered his courage and made one more stab at it. "Do you want me to 'ang about until you get through?" he asked, trying hard to keep his tone casual and matter-of-fact.

Betsy lifted her chin slightly. "I can find my own way home. You don't have to wait for me. I wouldn't want to put you to any trouble, not on my account."

"I know I don't 'ave to do it," he shot back, starting to get really narked by her attitude. "But I thought it would be polite to offer seein' as 'ow we're both 'ere."

"Don't bother." She shrugged.

"All right, then," he snapped. "I'll be off to the pubs. See you this evenin'."

"Fine." She retorted, giving him a quick look. "I wouldn't want to drag you away from the pubs. Maybe your 'old friend' will show up."

With that, she turned and marched down the street, leaving Smythe to glare helplessly at her back.

Constable Barnes's mood didn't improve when he accompanied Inspector Nivens back to the offices of Hornsley, Frampton, and Whitelaw. He'd not sat down all morning, his feet hurt, he wanted a cup of tea, and though he'd been taught to respect his superiors, he couldn't stick Nivens.

The man had finished questioning Mrs. Hornsley and then hadn't even asked to speak to the servants. How would they ever find out anything about Glynis Hornsley!

She claimed she'd been home during the time of the murder, but ruddy hell, Nivens hadn't even had the brains to confirm that with the house-keeper. But when Barnes had gently suggested they question the staff to learn more about Mrs. Hornsley, Nivens had sneered at him. Told him that they already knew the killer was a man, and did Constable Barnes think that Mrs. Hornsley had put on a false mustache and gone out to strangle her husband?

Stupid fool. Nivens had been a copper long enough to know the basics. Hadn't the man ever heard of murder for hire?

Inspector Witherspoon wouldn't have made a mistake like that! He'd have questioned everyone.

It was that kind of attention to detail that made Witherspoon the genius he was at solving crimes. One little word spoken by a housemaid, one clue discovered by an unexpected question, and Bob's your uncle. Inspector Witherspoon would find that last piece of the puzzle and before you could snap your fingers, the killer would be facing a judge and jury.

Barnes glanced at Nivens, who was pacing importantly up and down the room of the outer office, his chest puffed out and his hands thrust into his pockets. The constable snorted softly. Silly git. At the rate they were going, Barnes would be ready to retire before they found this killer.

The door to one of the inner offices opened and a clerk stepped out. "Mr. Frampton will see you now," he said to Nivens.

Nivens and Barnes followed the clerk into the office. George Frampton, a middle-aged portly man with close-cropped blond hair, muttonchop whiskers, and spectacles, rose from behind a desk.

"I'm sorry to keep you waiting, Inspector," he said. "Please sit down." He gestured toward the one chair in front of the desk.

"Thank you." Nivens sat. "We're here to ask you a few questions about Peter Hornsley's death. We spoke with Mr. Whitelaw earlier today."

"Have you made any progress in finding the murderer?" Frampton asked. He drummed his fingers on the top of an open ledger, "I must admit, the whole thing has affected me terribly. Dreadful business, absolutely dreadful."

"Murder always is," Nivens replied. "Mr. Frampton, Mrs. Hornsley seems to think the killer was probably a business rival of Hornsley's."

Frampton's eyebrows rose. "Really?"

"You don't think that's possible?"

"I suppose it's possible," Frampton said slowly. He picked up a pen and began twitching it from side to side. "But I don't believe our firm has any more enemies than any other business. That's hardly an acceptable way of dealing with one's competitors."

At least this one wasn't a complete idiot, Barnes thought.

"But then again," Frampton continued, "one never knows."

"Can you think of anyone who would have wanted Mr. Hornsley dead?"

Frampton shrugged. "No."

Barnes cleared his throat. "Excuse me, sir," he said to Nivens. "But I think I ought to question the clerks, with Mr. Frampton's permission, of course."

Nivens gave him a cold, fishlike stare, but as the constable was only doing his proper job, he couldn't find any grounds for refusing the request. "All right, Barnes," he looked at Frampton. The man nodded. "But mind you don't upset the routine," Nivens warned as Barnes escaped for the door.

Upset the routine, Barnes snorted again. There'd been a bloomin' murder committed, wasn't that enough to upset the routine! He wondered how Nivens had ever made it into the detective ranks.

The clerk who'd shown them into the office was sitting at the desk closest to Frampton's door. "Excuse me," Barnes said, "but I'd like to ask you a few questions. What's your name?"

"Hammer, sir. Jonathan Hammer." He pushed a stack of papers to one side. "But I don't know what I can tell you. I'd already gone home when Mr. Hornsley was killed."

"How long have you worked here?" Barnes asked.

"Five years, sir."

"And on the day of the murder, what time did you leave?" Barnes noticed the other two clerks had given up all pretense of working and were openly eavesdropping.

"I left at half-past five, sir," Hammer said. "With all the others. The only person left in the office was Mr. Hornsley."

"Why was Mr. Hornsley working late?"

Hammer shrugged. "I'm not sure, sir. I expect it had something to do with work. But he weren't one to explain his actions to a clerk."

Barnes nodded. "Do you know if Mr. Hornsley had any enemies?" Ye Gods, he thought, as soon as the sentence had left his mouth. Now he was doing it. Of course Hornsley had enemies, someone had strangled him.

"Well," Hammer glanced at Frampton's door. "Some of our competitors didn't like him all that much."

"Tell him about Hilliard," another clerk hissed. "Tell him what happened last week."

"Hilliard," Barnes prompted. "Who's he?"

"He owns a rival firm," Hammer explained, his voice rising in excitement. "And he come here last week and accused Mr. Hornsley of trying to run him out of business. Claimed Mr. Hornsley had bribed one of his clerks for information and undercut his rate."

"Had Mr. Hornsley done that?"

Hammer glanced uneasily toward Frampton's closed door. "I don't rightly know. But I think it's likely."

"Is that all?" Barnes prompted.

"Tell him about the set-to here in the office," the other clerk encouraged. "Go on, tell him."

Barnes waited. Hammer gave the closed door another worried glance and then leaned toward the constable. "Mr. Hilliard come in here last week. He and Mr. Frampton went into Mr. Hornsley's office. They started out all nice and polite, at least from what we could hear. But before long, Mr. Hilliard was screamin' like a madman and threatening all sorts of things."

"What exactly did he threaten?" Barnes asked. He hoped that Nivens was getting this same information out of Frampton, but he doubted it.

"He was goin' to call his solicitors and sue, then he was goin' to tell everyone what a blackguard Mr. Hornsley was, finally," the clerk's voice dropped, "as he was leaving, he yelled that Mr. Hornsley had better watch his back."

Mrs. Jeffries took a seat at the table and looked around the crowded tea room. There was no one she recognized and more important, no one who would know who she was. She smiled at the waiter and ordered tea for two. A moment later, the door opened and in stepped Dr. Bosworth, an attractive young man of about thirty, with dark red hair and a fair complexion.

He spotted her quickly and threaded his way to her table. "Good day, Mrs. Jeffries," he said, giving her a smile.

"Good day, Dr. Bosworth." She gestured at a chair, "Won't you sit down? I've taken the liberty of ordering tea."

"Thank you," he sat down, "I haven't much time but as your note said it was a matter of some urgency, I decided to see you."

"I think you know why I asked you to come," she said. She'd decided not to beat about the bush. Dr. Bosworth had helped them with several other cases and his opinions had proved invaluable.

"Indeed I do," he replied. He broke off as the waiter brought them tea and cakes. Mrs. Jeffries poured. "You want to ask me what I know about the Hornsley murder."

"Right. I was hoping you might have done the postmortem," She picked up her own cup and took a sip.

"No such luck," Dr. Bosworth sighed. "Potter did that one."

"Oh dear," Mrs. Jeffries was disappointed. Dr. Potter was a plodding, unimaginative, and rather stupid man who could barely distinguish a bullet hole from a stab wound. "How unfortunate."

"How tactful you are," Bosworth laughed. "Don't worry, Mrs. Jeffries. As soon as I heard the circumstances of the killing, I nipped over to the morgue and had a look-see for myself."

She brightened immediately. "And what did you conclude?"

"Actually," Bosworth said slowly, "I concluded the same thing that Potter had. The victim was struck on the back of the head and then strangled with a house tie."

"A house tie?"

"Yes." Bosworth reached for a fairy cake. "Knowing how very interested you are in getting all the details straight, when I got a good look at the actual murder weapon, I realized it was a school tie. Then I got curious so I made a few discreet inquiries on my own. Voilà, it wasn't just a school tie, but a house tie."

"Bravo, sir," Mrs. Jeffries beamed approvingly. "We'll make a detective out of you yet."

He laughed again. "I daresay, it was probably because of my acquaintance with you that got me started in this whole business. I am, after all, just a doctor. But I must admit, your little adventures and my small part in them does seem to have had some influence on me. Anyway, as I was saying, I made some inquiries when I saw the murder weapon. Curious object for a killer to use."

"What did you find out?" she asked eagerly.

"The tie is from a public school near Oxford," he explained. "One of those especially hideous places where we send our male children to be systematically tortured between the ages of seven and eighteen."

Surprised at the vehemence in his voice, she stared at him. "Why, Dr. Bosworth, am I to take that to mean that you don't approve of our education system?"

"I think it's barbaric," he said with feeling. "Stupid, ridiculous, and utterly absurd. Having been a victim of a particularly loathsome school myself, I know what I'm talking about." Shaking his head in disgust, he leaned back in his chair. "If I ever have children, I'll never send them away to school. I'll keep them at home and let them go to a good day school, like the Americans do. You know I spent quite a bit of time in America?"

She did know. It was because of his time in San Francisco and the proliferation of violent deaths in that city that had given them a valuable clue in the first case he'd helped them on. "Yes, I remember you mentioned that."

"I know everyone likes to think the Americans are uneducated barbarians, but it's not true. The Americans don't send their children off to school to be tortured the way we do in this country. Not that they're perfect, of course, but they aren't quite the country bumpkins we like to think they are. And I didn't notice that their young men were any stupider for having been deprived of the fagging system. As far as I could tell, they were perfectly able to read and write and think."

"I'm quite sure you're right."

"But that's beside the point." He waved a hand dismissively. "As I was saying, the tie is from a public school. Packards."

"Do you know what house?" she asked hopefully.

"It took a bit of doing, but I managed," he grinned. "It's from Langley House."

"Goodness, Doctor, you are resourceful."

"Thank you." He reached for a cake. "I do try."

"Was there anything else you learned about the victim that might be important?"

Bosworth chewed thoughtfully. "There are virtually no signs of a struggle. Once the poor fellow was coshed, the killer had a clear field. Hornsley didn't struggle with his murderer. There are no bruises on the hands, and the ligature around the neck is absolutely straight."

"I suppose then that the killer probably thought he'd killed Hornsley with the blow to his head and when he realized he hadn't, he must have used the tie at that point," she mused. Her expression was thoughtful. "Apparently our killer is a very careful man. He brought along a second weapon in case the first didn't work."

"I suspect the murderer didn't plan on the blow doing anything except what it actually did," Bosworth replied. "The blow wasn't hard enough to kill, only to stun."

"Then why not just strangle the victim in the first place?" Mrs. Jeffries queried.

"Because Hornsley was a good-sized man," Bosworth explained. "Unless the murderer were very lucky, very tall, or very strong, he had to stun him with something. Even with a tie choking your windpipe, a man could still defend himself. Besides," he waved a hand in the air. "Head wounds bleed something awful. That's fairly common knowledge. If he'd kept bashing the man's head in, the killer would have been covered with blood."

"Yes," she agreed, "Apparently our killer thought it out most carefully."

"And you must admit, an old tie is a perfectly marvelous way to kill someone," Bosworth continued. "It's one of those things that no one even misses from a household. Why, I've no idea where my old school ties have gone. Into the rubbish bin, I hope."

She smiled. "I'm sorry. It sounds as though your school days were terrible."

"They were hideous," he agreed. "Do you know, I still loathe one of the boys who used to bully me. I ran into the chap a while back, he'd grown into a rabbity sort of fellow. Came up and tried to shake my hand. I could barely bring myself to be polite to the man."

"Sometimes the things of childhood are the most difficult to let go of," she suggested gently. "I suppose it's because as children we have so little power or control over our lives."

"You're helpless when you're a child," Bosworth said slowly, his expression troubled. "I was quite ashamed of my reaction to Pomfret. I'm sure he'd no idea why I was so rude. But I couldn't help myself." He suddenly straightened and smiled ruefully. "But I survived. It's a wretched system, though. Can't think why we still have it."

"I rather agree with you," Mrs. Jeffries said. "Do you have any idea what the killer used to strike the blow?"

Bosworth dropped his gaze and stared at the half-eaten cake on his plate. "I'm not really sure," he mumbled. "I mean, it's almost impossible to tell . . ."

She knew he was hiding something. Dr. Bosworth was very intelligent, very observant, and not in the least afraid of educated guesses.

"But surely you've some idea," she pressed. "The wound must have been a certain size, a certain shape, a . . ."

He sighed. "Mrs. Jeffries, you know that many physicians don't believe you can tell much by examining wounds."

"I also know that you're not one of them," she argued. "You identified the kind of weapon that was used to kill that American last year merely by examining the bullet wound."

"Yes, but that was just a guess and my statement wouldn't have stood up in a court of law."

"Nevertheless, you were right," she said firmly. "So please, tell me what you *think* could have been used."

He hesitated for a moment, then came to a decision. Squaring his shoulders he looked her straight in the eye. "The blow didn't actually crack the victim's skull, but it was hard enough to leave a strong indention."

"And that means you know the general shape of the object that made the wound," she said. "Correct?"

"Yes, that's correct. But remember, there are a variety of objects of the same shape and size and weight that could cause the kind of indention that I observed."

Mrs. Jeffries thought he was hedging. "I understand that. As you said, Doctor, you're not in the witness box. All I want is an educated guess."

"The wound was rounded and approximately two and a half inches in diameter."

She waited.

He took a deep breath. "It could well have been done by a police truncheon. As a matter of fact, I borrowed one from one of the constables and placed it against the victim's skull. It was a perfect fit."

# CHAPTER 4

Barnes couldn't believe they were back at Peter Hornsley's home. Why on earth hadn't Nivens had the sense to find out where Nyles Hornsley lived before rushing them both all over London and wasting time. He shot his superior an irritable glance.

Nivens was staring at a pair of silver candlesticks on the top of the marble mantle. "They're worth a bob of two," Nivens muttered. He glanced around the room, his gaze stopping at the windows. "And those locks wouldn't keep a professional out for more than ten seconds. The Hornsleys are lucky they haven't been robbed. There's plenty in here that's worth taking."

Barnes remembered that Nivens was considered somewhat of an expert on robbery. Too bad the man didn't know the first thing about homicide.

"Inspector Nivens?"

Both policemen turned toward the door. A young man of medium height and with a slight build stepped into the room. He wore a black suit and white shirt. His sandy-colored hair was parted on the side and his pale face was clean shaven. He stared at them out of wary hazel eyes.

"I'm Nyles Hornsley," he said. "I take it you're here to talk to me about my brother's murder."

"Yes, sir," Nivens replied, "we are."

"I'm surprised you didn't speak to me earlier," Hornsley said. He walked over to the settee, gestured for the policemen to sit down in the chairs opposite, and then sat down. "I was upstairs waiting for you when you were questioning Glynis."

Nivens cast Barnes a quick look and cleared his throat. "We had another matter to attend to," he explained. "A rather urgent matter as it turned out."

What a ruddy liar, Barnes thought contemptuously. Nivens would have done better to explain nothing. It was bad form to start off an interview with a suspect by explaining your actions.

Hornsley continued to stare. "Have you made any progress on catching Peter's killer?"

"We're working on it, sir." Nivens gave him a weak smile. "Now, if you don't mind, sir, I'd like to ask you a few questions."

"That's why I'm here."

"Do you know if your brother had any enemies?"

Barnes gritted his teeth. They already knew that Peter Hornsley had lots of enemies. Nivens was going 'round in blooming circles. Why didn't he ask him something useful?

"My brother was a successful businessman," Hornsley said slowly. "There were a number of his competitors who disliked him."

"Had he ever been threatened?" Nivens asked.

Barnes shifted impatiently, earning him a disapproving frown from his superior.

"Not that I'm aware of," Hornsley replied. "But Peter rarely confided in me. We weren't close. Peter is, was, a lot older than I am. He was almost grown when I was born."

Barnes couldn't stand it anymore. "What about Damon Hilliard? Hadn't he threatened your brother?" He ignored the frown Nivens cast his way.

Hornsley looked amused. "Oh, I'd hardly call that a threat. Hilliard was just upset. Peter had undercut the poor fellow so badly he couldn't possibly compete. But Peter and his partners were always doing that sort of thing."

"What sort of thing?" Barnes pressed. The side of his face burned where Nivens was glaring at him, but the constable didn't much care. Nivens wasn't the only copper at the Yard who had a friend or two in high places. If they were going to catch this killer, someone had to start asking decent questions.

"Bribery. Peter's favorite trick was to find a clerk in a competing firm's office, give him a few bob to find out what the firm was quoting, and then undercut it by at least ten percent."

"But how could your brother stay in business if he was quoting such low insurance rates?" Barnes asked. He wasn't just curious, he really wanted to know. Supposedly the firm made pots of money, but he didn't see how that could be possible if they were always quoting below-cost rates.

"Volume," Nyles Hornsley smiled slyly. "They did an enormous amount of business. They were going to expand, you know." Hornsley waved a hand as though the matter were of no importance. "But, as I said, Peter and his partners did that all the time. They've been doing it for years. I hardly think his competitors would wait till now to kill him. It would have been much more useful if they'd murdered him a year ago."

"And why is that, sir?" Barnes asked.

"Excuse me, Constable," Nivens snapped. "But I'm asking the questions here."

"Sorry, sir," Barnes said, but he continued to stare at Hornsley, silently trying to get him to answer. He was disappointed.

Nivens cleared his throat in that irritating way he had. "Now, Mr. Hornsley, did your brother do anything out of the ordinary on the day he was killed?"

"Not that I'm aware of."

"Did he give any indication of being frightened?"

Hornsley laughed. "No. My brother had far too high an opinion of himself to act like the rest of us mere mortals. Even if he'd had a dozen notes threatening him, he wouldn't have given any outward sign. He was simply too arrogant."

Ask Nyles Hornsley where he was the night of the murder, Barnes silently screamed. He had an awful feeling that Nivens was going to stop asking questions. Ask him if he knows anything about the note. Ask him about Madeline Wynn. Ask him what VENI might mean.

"Well." Nivens rose to his feet. "I do thank you for your help, Mr. Hornsley. If we've any news, we'll be in touch."

Barnes silently groaned. Silly git. At this rate, they were never going to catch the killer. The thought made him furious. The constable realized that the two and a half years he'd spent working with Witherspoon had changed him. His sense of justice was outraged. A murderer was going to go free because of an incompetent police inspector with more friends in high places than sense.

Barnes simply couldn't stand it. "Excuse me, Mr. Hornsley, but would you mind telling us where you were last night?"

"I don't mind in the least," he smiled. "I was at the Alexandra Hotel. My fiancée and I were having dinner with some friends."

"And what time did you arrive at the Alexandra?" Barnes prodded.

"Let me see," Hornsley replied thoughtfully. "I went round to Madeline's about half-past six. We had a glass of sherry with her aunt and then took a hansom to the Alexandra. I'd say we arrived there at seven-fifteen or seven-thirty."

"And the names of the friends you dined with?" Barnes could sense that Nivens was furious, but he didn't care.

"Mr. and Mrs. Arthur Stanley." Hornsley smiled widely. "We were with them until ten o'clock. You can verify it, if you like. The Stanleys live at number twelve Lanham Street, That's in Mayfair."

"Thank you, sir," Barnes said formally. "We will be in touch with them." He would have loved to ask Hornsley more questions, but he was afraid that Nivens would interrupt. Well, there was more than one way to skin a cat. He'd find out what he needed to know without Nigel Nivens around to muck things up!

As soon as they were outside, Nivens turned to Barnes. "In the future," he said coldly, "I'll thank you not to interfere."

"Sorry, sir." Barnes tried to look contrite. "But I was only doing what I always do."

Nivens's eyes narrowed suspiciously. "What do you mean?"

"I mean, sir, that when I'm with Inspector Witherspoon, I'm expected to toss in a few questions. For effect, sir. That's what Inspector Witherspoon says. Claims it gets people talking more, tellin' a bit more than they really wanted to, if you know what I mean. Interestin' method, isn't it?" Barnes smiled blandly.

Nivens pursed his thin lips as though he were seriously thinking about the constable's words. Finally, he said, "That's all well and good, Constable. But I'm not Inspector Witherspoon . . ."

That's a fact, Barnes thought.

". . . and my methods are very, very different." Nivens started down the stone stairs toward the street. "And henceforth, I'll expect you to keep your mouth shut and take notes. Is that clear?"

"Very, sir."

• • •

Mrs. Jeffries was deep in thought as she walked down Adam Street. Dr. Bosworth's information was most helpful. Obviously, the killer had thought everything out in advance. But she already knew that. Equally obvious was the fact that he'd brought two weapons along. One to stun and one to kill. But why a police truncheon? The killer was masquerading as Inspector Witherspoon, a detective. But Witherspoon didn't even carry one. She wondered where the inspector's truncheon was? Hopefully, it was somewhere in his room at Upper Edmonton Gardens.

Mrs. Jeffries was so lost in thought she didn't notice the two men coming down the stairs just a few feet in front of her. When the sound of a familiar voice finally penetrated her musing, she came to an abrupt halt.

"Good day, Inspector Nivens, Constable Barnes." She forced herself to smile calmly. Oh dear, what on earth was she going to say to them? She glanced quickly up and down the elegant row of houses desperately hoping to see a fishmonger's or a greengrocer's on one of the corners. But there was nothing save more homes. Drat.

"Mrs. Jeffries," Nivens eyed her suspiciously. "What are you doing here?"

Barnes gazed at her impassively, but she could see the curiosity in his eyes.

"Actually," she smiled again, "I was looking for you."

Nivens blinked in surprise. "Really, Why?"

She hesitated. "It's rather presumptuous of me," she began, thinking fast, "but the household is very worried."

"Worried about what?" Nivens asked, his fish-eyed gaze never leaving her face.

"About the inspector," she replied. "We're concerned because, well, we were wondering if . . . oh dear, this is most improper, but you see, we're so very worried."

Nivens waved his hand impatiently. "Yes, you've already said that. Now what is it, Mrs. Jeffries? I've not got all day. We've a murderer to catch."

Barnes grinned.

Mrs. Jeffries took a deep breath. "We're wondering if Scotland Yard really thinks Inspector Witherspoon has anything to do with this awful murder."

Nivens's mouth dropped open.

Mrs. Jeffries wondered if it was because of her audacity or because he was just inherently too arrogant and stupid to comprehend that servants would actually be devoted enough to an employer to care.

"Well, really, I don't think that is any of your household's concern," Nivens sputtered.

"But it is our concern," she countered, looking him straight in the eye. This was no time to be timid. Nivens was a bit of a bully, and if he sensed you were the least bit frightened or intimidated, he'd be on you like a starving rat. "We're all very devoted to the inspector. Furthermore, we know good and well he's nothing to do with this murder. If you don't feel like addressing our concerns, sir, that's quite all right. I'm sure Chief Inspector Curling wouldn't mind speaking with me. He's such a very nice man."

They stared at one another for a good minute. Nivens was weighing the consequences of her running and having a chat with his superior and she was holding her breath, hoping her bluff would work.

Nivens dropped his gaze first. "Of course Witherspoon isn't considered a serious suspect. I'm amazed you'd actually be concerned about such a thing."

Graciously, she smiled. "As I said, we're very devoted to the inspector."

"Then perhaps you'd best convince him to tell us the truth," Nivens said. He smiled coldly when he saw her start with surprise.

"The truth? About what?"

"About where he was and what he was doing the evening of March ninth. The night of the murder."

As it was only a few days ago, Mrs. Jeffries rather thought that Nivens was being pedantic. "He was taking a walk," she said quickly. "He's already told you that."

"He might well have been walking." Nivens Shrugged. "But he wasn't walking where he said he was. He was nowhere near Holland Park between half-past six and eight o'clock that night."

"How can you possibly be sure of that?"

"But I am sure," Nivens said flatly. "You see, we've had a rash of purse snatchings in that area. So we had constables on all the pathways leading into and out of the park. Inspector Witherspoon is well known." His voice dripped sarcasm. "After all, he is considered Scotland Yard's most successful homicide detective. God knows he gets his name in the newspapers often enough. Both his name and his face are familiar to most of the lads."

She swallowed uneasily. "Are you saying that none of those constables saw him that night?"

"That's right," Nivens replied casually. "Not one of them. And believe me, if he'd been there, someone would have seen him. Furthermore, they'd have remembered him. As I said, he's quite famous."

"But Inspector Witherspoon had no reason to murder Peter Hornsley," she pointed out.

"True." Nivens picked a piece of lint off his sleeve. "But motive is one of the last things we look for in a case of this sort."

Mrs. Jeffries wasn't sure, but she thought she heard Barnes snort. Nivens must have thought so too. He gave the constable a sharp look.

"I'm sure there's been some kind of mistake about this," Mrs. Jeffries murmured. She looked at the constable. He nodded his head slightly in agreement. "If Inspector Witherspoon said he was walking in Holland Park that night, then I'm sure that's precisely where he was."

"Hmm. Yes, well, I do hope there's some reasonable explanation," Nivens replied.

"Perhaps he got confused as to where he actually did walk," Mrs. Jeffries suggested. "After all, it was quite dark and foggy that night. The inspector goes out walking quite often. He could easily have gotten confused. He might well have been walking in Holland Park the night before the murder and somewhere else the night of the murder."

"Really, Mrs. Jeffries"—Nivens's lip curled in a sneer—"Inspector Witherspoon isn't a fool. He knows perfectly well how important an alibi is in a murder investigation. It's not likely he'd get mixed up about something like that. We are talking about an incident from three days back, not three weeks."

"I know there's some explanation for it," she insisted. No matter what she said, she was sure Nivens wasn't going to believe her.

"Let's hope so. But please, do tell the rest of the household that your dear Inspector Witherspoon isn't seriously a suspect." He gave her another cold smile. "Not yet, anyway."

Mrs. Goodge was in the kitchen when Mrs. Jeffries returned. The cook gave her a short greeting and then went back to cutting up the meat for her stew.

Mrs. Jeffries wasn't in the chattiest of moods herself. When she'd returned home, she'd found the inspector sitting in the drawing room, with an open book on his lap. She'd asked him why he wasn't out investigating the robbery; he'd told her that there was no need. Last night, one of the uniformed lads had interrupted a break-in at a home in Carlton Square. The robbers had confessed to the other burglaries as well. So now the inspector was taking a few days' rest. In other words, he was going to be under their feet.

"Did the inspector tell you his robbery was solved?" Mrs. Jeffries said to the cook.

"He told me." Mrs. Goodge didn't look up from her task. "Do you want a cup of tea now, or will you wait till the others get here?"

"I'll wait." She sighed silently. Unfortunately, she'd also asked the inspector about his walk on the night of the murder. Naturally, she'd been most discreet about her inquiry. He insisted he'd been walking in Holland Park, but he hadn't been able to look her in the eyes while saying so.

She knew, then, that he was lying.

"I believe I will have that cup of tea, after all," Mrs. Jeffries murmured. Why wouldn't he tell her where he'd been? It wasn't like Inspector Witherspoon to deceive. It simply wasn't in the man's character, yet he was lying through his teeth on this matter.

"Suit yourself."

"Can I make you one?" she asked Mrs. Goodge.

The cook shook her head. Mrs. Jeffries put the kettle on and then pulled her favorite cup out of the cupboard.

Oh dear, this case was most worrying, she thought. Most worrying indeed. She forced her imagination to stay in check. There was absolutely no reason why Gerald Witherspoon, highly respected police detective with Scotland Yard, would take it into his head to murder a perfectly innocent stranger.

But was Peter Hornsley a stranger? The uneasy idea crept into her mind before she could stop it. How much did she really know about her employer? How much did any of them really know about each other?

The kettle whistled, interrupting her train of thought. "Are you sure you wouldn't like a cup?" she said, glancing over at the cook. She noticed the cook's shoulders were slumped and her face was set in a worried frown.

"Is there anything the matter, Mrs. Goodge?" she asked. "You seem awfully quiet this afternoon."

"Oh, I wouldn't say anything was exactly wrong," said Mrs. Goodge as she put her knife down and wiped her hands on a towel. "I believe I will have that tea," she sighed. "Maybe talking about it will help me to come to a decision."

Mrs. Jeffries poured them both a cup and they took their usual spots at the table. "Why don't you tell me what's upsetting you?"

"Nothing's really upsettin' me," the cook said slowly. "Actually, one part of me is quite pleased. It's just now I'm in a muddle and I don't know what to do."

"Why, Mrs. Goodge, you're never in a muddle," Mrs. Jeffries said earnestly.

"This time I am." She toyed with the handle of her cup. "You see, I've had a letter from one of my old employers. He wants me to come back and work for him. It's Lord Gurney."

Mrs. Jeffries stared at her. She knew how much the cook enjoyed status. And cooking for a lord of the realm would have far more cachet than cooking for a Scotland Yard detective, even a wealthy, famous one like Inspector Witherspoon. "And what have you decided to do?"

"That's just it," Mrs. Goodge cried. "I don't know what to do. I like it here. I like helping to solve murders and having all of you round and about the kitchen. It's a far different thing working for a lord. There I'd be head cook with scullery and serving girls under me. I'd get my tea brought up to my room each mornin' and not have to do any of the peeling or chopping of the vegetables. There's a strict way of doin' things in Lord Gurney's house. I can tell you that."

"I see," Mrs. Jeffries murmured. "Well, why don't you have a good think about it before you make up your mind?"

Mrs. Goodge nodded. "Right strange, isn't it? How something from the past you think is over and done with can come creeping up on you like a thief in the night. When I left Lord Gurney's employment, I never thought I'd set foot in that house again. Yet here he is, a few years later, writing me letters asking me to come back."

"Yoo-hoo," came Luty Belle Crookshank's voice from the backdoor.

"Really, madam, that's hardly a proper way to announce our presence," Hatchet chided his employer.

"What'd you want me to do," Luty snapped, "blast a trumpet like we was the heavenly hosts?"

"Hello, Luty, Hatchet," Mrs. Jeffries said quickly as the two of them came into the kitchen. "Do sit down. We'll have some tea ready shortly."

Mrs. Goodge got up. "I'll put it on."

"Good," Luty nodded. "I'm as dry as a river gully in a California desert."

They heard the sound of thumping coming from the back stairs and a moment later, Wiggins, with Fred at his heels, hobbled to the table. "I've 'ad a borin' day," he announced. "My eyes is crossed from readin' and polishin' and me ears are ringin' from listening to Essie go on about the rights of the workers."

Luty cackled. "That Essie's a right talker, isn't she?"

Hatchet harrumphed softly. "Should we wait for the others?" he asked.

Mrs. Jeffries shook her head. "No, we'd best get on with it. The inspector is upstairs, reading. He's rather upset. He told me not to worry about getting his dinner; he said he wasn't hungry. Poor man, this case is weighing heavily on his mind. So let's get started while we've got the chance. We can fill Betsy and Smythe in after our own meal this evening."

Darkness had come, even though it was only a little past five. Mrs. Goodge, uncharacteristically silent, poured tea and handed round slices of cake.

"Who would like to go first?" Mrs. Jeffries queried.

"Why don't we start?" Luty said. "I think Hatchet's got somethin' to say."

"That I do, madam." The butler cleared his throat. "As you know, I've a number of sources I can draw upon when the circumstances call for it."

"Yes, yes, we all know about that," Luty said impatiently. "You've told us often enough. Just go ahead and tell us what you've found out."

"Don't rush me, madam," Hatchet replied irritably. "I want to make sure I tell this calmly and clearly. A muddled set of facts is worse than no facts at all. Anyway, as I was saying, I prevailed upon one of my sources to inquire as to the whereabouts of the various members of Peter Hornsley's household at the time of the murder."

"You mean you bribed a butler or a housemaid to spill the beans," Luty said.

Outraged, Hatchet glared at her. "I most certainly did not."

"Don't be such a stuffed shirt," Luty shot back. "There ain't nothin' wrong with crossin' someone's palm with silver if they can tell ya what ya need to know. Anyways, get on with it. We haven't got all day."

Mrs. Jeffries would have intervened to smooth things out, but these two enjoyed sparring with one another even more than they enjoyed investigating murders.

"As I was saying," Hatchet continued. "My sources told me something very interesting. At the time of the murder, Mrs. Hornsley was not at home. Nor was she having tea with Mrs. Frampton, which was where she'd told her husband she was going late that afternoon. As a matter of fact, she didn't get home till past eight that night. So you see, she doesn't have an alibi."

"Does she have a motive?" Mrs. Jeffries asked.

Luty cackled. "Course she had a motive, I found that out. I had a long chat with my friend Myrtle while Hatchet was out today. Accordin' to Myrtle, Glynis Hornsley was this close"—she held up her thumb and finger, leaving a tiny space between them—"to getting a divorce from Peter Hornsley. She hated his guts."

"A divorce!" Mrs. Goodge said incredulously. "But that's . . . that's . . . unheard of. Only actresses and opera singers get divorced."

"That's not true," Wiggins put in. "There was over seven thousand divorces done last year, and they couldn't have all been opera singers."

They all turned and stared at the footman.

"How on earth do you know that?" Mrs. Jeffries asked curiously.

Wiggins shrugged. "I read about it somewheres. But I know it's true."

Mrs. Jeffries had no doubt about that. Wiggins might be a bit of a daydreamer, but he was certainly no liar. "How very interesting," she smiled at him. "And how very clever of you to remember it."

"I don't believe it," Mrs. Goodge said.

"But it's true," Wiggins exclaimed, "Just because I can't remember where I read it don't mean I'm makin' it up."

"I don't mean that." The cook waved her hand. "I mean I can't believe a respectable woman like Glynis Hornsley would even think about getting a divorce. Why, she'd be ruined. Absolutely ruined. No decent people would have anything to do with her."

"But that's what Myrtle claims," Luty argued. "And believe me, Myrtle don't get her gossip wrong."

"Did she say why Mrs. Hornsley was considering divorce?" Mrs. Jeffries asked.

Luty shrugged. "All she said was that the marriage hadn't been happy in years. Glynis didn't much like her husband. Maybe she wanted to get shut of the fellow so she could have a bit of peace and quiet. Myrtle says he was a right domineerin' sort, always onto his wife about something. Then there was the woman he kept, but accordin' to Myrtle, Mrs. Hornsley didn't much care about that." She laughed. "Seems the marriage really started to go sour when Hornsley's mistress left him and he started comin' home more often."

"That lets her out as a suspect, then," Wiggins said firmly. "Why would she bother to kill 'im if she was fixin' to get herself divorced?"

"Not necessarily," Hatchet shook his head. "As Mrs. Goodge pointed out, if she divorced him, she'd be risking social ruin."

"But we know it was a man that killed Hornsley," Luty said.

"Not necessarily," Mrs. Jeffries said. "We know that a man claiming to be Inspector Witherspoon was one of the last people to be seen with Hornsley. That doesn't mean he killed him."

"But it had to be him," Mrs. Goodge pointed out. "There was a night watchman on duty. No one else came into the building."

Mrs. Jeffries frowned. "Yes, I suppose that's true. But Glynis Hornsley could have easily have hired someone to murder her husband. So I don't think we ought yet to write her off as a suspect. Did you learn anything else?"

"No," Luty admitted. "That's all I got."

"Me too," Hatchet said. "But we'll keep working."

Mrs. Jeffries told them about her meeting with Dr. Bosworth, and then went on to explain the disastrous run-in with Inspector Nivens. She then took a deep breath and told them about Inspector Witherspoon's insistence that he was walking in Holland Park the night of the murder.

When she was through she glanced around the table. Luty was fingering the mink muff on her lap, Hatchet's eyebrows were drawn together in a worried frown, Mrs. Goodge was chewing on her lower lip, and Wiggins was studying the top of the table as if he could read the secrets of the ancients in its old wood.

"Well, say something," she cried. "Surely you've some idea why Inspector Witherspoon missed being seen by the constables in the park."

Wiggins looked up, his cheeks flushed a fiery red. "I don't see how he rightly could," he said softly. "I mean, if the police were there, and we've no reason to think Nivens would lie about that, then they should a seen 'im."

"I think it's apparent that Inspector Witherspoon wasn't walking in Holland Park that night," Hatchet said carefully. "Perhaps he was confused. I mean, perhaps he'd been in the park the night before and got his evenings mixed up."

"I already asked him about that," Mrs. Jeffries sighed. She didn't like the tone of this conversation, but she couldn't run away from the truth because it was uncomfortable. "He insists he was there."

"Do you think Inspector Witherspoon could kill someone?" Luty asked bluntly.

"Of course not," Mrs. Jeffries replied. "Besides, even if he could, why murder a complete stranger?"

"If he was a stranger," Wiggins muttered.

"What do you mean by that?" Mrs. Jeffries demanded.

"I mean . . ." Wiggins hesitated. "How much do we know about the inspector? Before a couple of years ago, we'd never laid eyes on each other. For all we know, Peter Hornsley weren't no stranger to our inspector."

"Bloomin' fog," Betsy glared at the pearly mist as she hurried down the road, "I'll never find a hansom in this soup," she muttered. Not that she could normally afford hansoms, but it was already dark and she was in a rush to get home. She had so much to tell everyone. Mind you, she thought as she quickened her pace, her heels clicking smartly against the wet stone pavement, it was clever of me to remember to take those coins out of my drawer. At least if I can find a hansom, I can afford the fare. She frowned and her footsteps slowed as she remembered how surprised she'd been when she'd opened the top drawer of her bureau to grab her money. There was more money in the drawer than there should have been.

Betsy shook her head. She was getting as forgetful as Mrs. Goodge. She must have put more in there than she'd thought. She always kept a few shillings and pence out of her quarterly pay, and this time she'd obviously kept more than she normally did. That had to be the answer. It wasn't likely there was anyone else dropping money in the drawer. But it is puzzlin', she thought. And it's not the first time things like that have happened around the house. Wiggins findin' some brand-new expensive writin' paper in his drawer, Mrs. Goodge's rheumatism bottle always gettin' replaced before she finished it, Mrs. Jeffries finding the new Whitman poems in her bookcase. Why, the only one who hadn't had a nice surprise was Smythe. From behind her, someone grabbed her elbow and spun her around.

Betsy screamed. Her eyes widened as she found herself looking straight into a face she hoped she'd never see again. "You!"

"Hello, Betsy," Raymond Skegit smiled broadly, revealing a set of perfect white teeth. "It's been a long time."

"Not long enough," Betsy jerked her arm away and stepped back. Despite her bravado, she was scared. "I'd hoped never to see you again."

He was a tall, thin man in his late twenties, clean shaven and dark haired. A handsome bloke, the kind that turned women's heads and made men stare at him with envy.

"You don't mean that, girl," he said, still smiling, but the look in his eyes sent a chill up Betsy's spine, "You're lucky I'm not one to take offense. Otherwise, my feelin's would get hurt. You don't want to hurt my feelin's, Betsy. Not again."

She stepped back farther, hating herself for retreating but unwilling to stay close enough for him to get his hands on her—again. She glanced up the road. Not a copper in sight. Blast. Where were they when you needed one? Well, if she had to, she'd scream her head off.

"I couldn't care less about your bleedin' feelin's," she retorted, hating the way her voice trembled and the way her speech had slipped into pure cockney. "Now, if you'll get out of my way, I'll be off," she forced herself to speak properly. "I'm in a hurry."

Raymond laughed. "That's no way to treat an old friend." He came closer, his mouth curling in an ugly way. "And we are old friends, Betsy. Even if you'd like to pretend you've never laid eyes on me before."

"We was never friends," she snapped. She'd have to make a run for it. "The likes of you don't have 'friends,' Raymond. No decent person would have anything to do with someone like you."

"Yeah, but you did, didn't ya? You come to me that night and asked me to take ya on." He gave up all pretense at smiling, his expression now hard and menacing. "Then, before we could do any business together, ya took off. I didn't like that, Betsy. I didn't like it at all. It weren't right." He grabbed her arm. "And I think you'd best come with me. You've got to make amends."

"Let go of me," Betsy tried to jerk her arm free, but his grip was too tight. He started dragging her down the street. In the fog ahead, she could make out a waiting carriage. "Let go of me, ya bastard," she yelled. "Or I'll scream me 'ead off."

"You there," Smythe's bellow came from directly behind them. "Take yer bloody 'ands off 'er."

Raymond stopped. Betsy yanked her arm free and turned in the direction of the coachman's voice. She ran for him like the devil himself was on her heels.

Smythe charged out of the fog. His big hands came out and he grabbed Betsy as she came hurtling toward him. He pushed her behind him. "Stay there," he ordered. "I'll take care of this bastard."

Raymond, who'd for a brief instant considered trying to reclaim his prize, took one look at the huge, brutal-looking man who'd emerged from the fog and changed his mind. Before the enraged man could reach him, he turned and ran for the carriage.

Smythe started after him, but Betsy grabbed his arm. "Let him go," she cried.

"But he's gettin' away," Smythe yelled, torn between wanting to get his hands on that bastard and wanting to stay to make sure she was all right.

"I don't care. Just let him go," she pleaded.

By this time, Skegit's carriage had taken off at a fast clip. Smythe put his hands on his hips and turned to Betsy. "Who the blazes was that?" he demanded. "And why was he trying to drag you off?"

# CHAPTER 5

George Frampton elbowed his way through the crowded saloon bar of the Black Horse Pub. Usually he would have gone into one of the private sections of the pub, but tonight he wanted to be around people. He was nervous.

Reaching the counter, he slapped his money on the polished wood. "Whiskey," he said to the publican. "And make it quick."

Frampton let himself relax a bit as the barman got his order. God, he needed a drink. Needed it more than any other night he'd stopped in here on his way home. He drew a deep breath into his lungs, enjoying the acrid smell of cigar smoke and the scent of bitter and mild ale. The noise level was deafening. Frampton took great comfort in being in the midst of the crowded room. Not that he was seriously worried about being murdered, no, of course not.

"Thanks," he said as the publican put his drink down. He took a long swig of the good Irish whiskey, enjoying the burning sensation as it rolled down his throat and hit his belly. It wasn't that he was frightened, he told himself. But it made sense to be a bit cautious. There was a killer out there.

The police didn't seem to have any idea about who'd murdered Peter. Frampton frowned, thinking about the interview he'd had this morning with that police inspector. The man didn't seem to be too bright. He didn't ask very many questions. Frampton wasn't sure that they would ever find the murderer.

Peter had a lot of enemies. Far more than he'd let on to the police this morning, that was for sure. Frampton sighed, wishing he could feel some real grief for his partner's death. But the truth was, he didn't feel much of anything. He should have. He really should have felt something. He and Peter had gone to school together, known each other for years. But it wasn't as if Peter had been a nice person, he thought defensively. Or even a decent one. He'd always been a mean, arrogant man. Bullying those who were weaker and bluffing those that got in his way. But still, Frampton wished he could feel something other than this emptiness.

The door of the pub opened, letting in a blast of cold, damp air. Frampton felt the wind against the back of his neck, but he didn't turn to see who had just walked in. He finished his drink.

Slapping the glass on the counter, he'd opened his mouth to shout at the barman for another one when a man appeared at his elbow. The fellow was wearing a large dark overcoat, bowler hat, and spectacles. He had a mustache.

"Mr. Frampton?" he queried politely.

"Yes," he replied cautiously. "Who are you?"

"Inspector Gerald Witherspoon, Scotland Yard." The man said firmly. He smiled thinly as Frampton started in surprise. "Don't be alarmed, sir. I assure you, I'm not a murderer, despite having had someone use my name in such a vile manner."

Frampton relaxed slightly. "Well, all right, I suppose . . ."

"Don't worry, Mr. Frampton," Inspector Witherspoon said heartily. "Scotland Yard would hardly let me walk about free if they really suspected I had anything to do with your partner's death."

"What about that other fellow I talked to this morning? Chap named Nivens," Frampton asked. "Why isn't he here?"

"Inspector Nivens is no longer on this case," Witherspoon shrugged. "It happens that way sometimes. Chief Inspector Curling didn't feel enough progress was being made so he called me in." He smiled modestly. "I'm rather well known for solving difficult homicides, if I do say so myself."

"Yes, well, I hope so," Frampton said. "That other fellow didn't even ask me many questions."

"That's why I'm here. That, of course, and some other matters that are urgent."

Frampton straightened up. "Urgent? What's this about then?"

Witherspoon glanced around the crowded room. "Are you ready to leave, sir? There is something I need to speak to you about and I'd rather not do so in here."

"I've finished." Frampton decided he'd have another drink at home. "I only live across the park. If you like, we can talk there."

"That would be excellent, sir." Witherspoon smiled gratefully.

Nodding to the barman, who'd been listening with avid interest to their conversation, Frampton and Witherspoon left the pub.

Outside, the fog had gotten heavier. They crossed Knightsbridge, dodging hansoms and drays. Witherspoon took the lead, walking briskly toward the entrance to Hyde Park that lay just across the next road. Frampton slowed his steps. He looked to his left and saw a vicar going up the walkway into Holy Trinity Church. "Uh, excuse me, Inspector?"

Witherspoon turned. "Yes?"

"Perhaps we ought to go round the other way. I'm not certain it's safe for us to go into the park."

"That won't be necessary, sir," Witherspoon said cheerfully. "You're quite safe. It's important that you don't vary your routine. You take this shortcut through the park every evening, don't you?"

"Yes." Frampton looked at him warily. "But how do you know that?"

"We know a lot more than you think, sir. Do please come on, you'll be safe with me. Furthermore, there are a number of other policemen in the area."

Frampton looked around him. Except for the passing carriages and cabs, there wasn't anyone about. "I don't see anyone."

The policeman smiled. "That's the whole point, sir. We've been following you since you left your office, sir," he explained. "There's half a dozen policemen watching us right now. You're not supposed to see them."

"Why have you been following me?" Frampton asked. His voice was slightly irritated, as though he'd only just thought of what else being watched by the police could mean.

"To insure your safety, sir," the policeman said as he started into Hyde Park. He walked swiftly, and his silhouette was soon disappearing through the thick yellow fog.

Frampton hurried after him. "My safety? But why?"

Witherspoon slowed his steps so that his companion could catch up with him. He glanced back the way they'd just come. The fog had closed up behind them, making it impossible to see the busy road or the park entrance.

"Have you gone deaf?" Frampton sputtered. "Answer my question. Why is Scotland Yard concerned about my safety?"

"I can hear you perfectly, sir," Witherspoon smiled coldly. "We've had word that the killer is going after you next."

Frampton's heart leapt into his throat. He looked wildly about him, hoping he'd see a whole platoon of police constables. He saw nothing but the vague shapes of trees and shrubs. "My God, and you've let me walk into this deserted park? Good God, man, the killer could be anywhere."

Frampton turned to go back the way they'd just come. He hadn't taken two steps when he felt a blinding pain in his head, He dropped to his knees, but before he could do more than moan, he was grabbed under the arms, pulled off the path and dragged behind a mound of shrubbery. He couldn't speak, he couldn't cry out in alarm. All he could do was gasp for air like some great stranded fish.

Then he felt something round his neck. A few moments later, he couldn't even gasp. George Frampton was dead.

The killer pushed Frampton's body onto the ground and rolled him onto his back. He stood up and looked around. There was no one about in the park. Quickly, he reached into his pocket for an envelope and a piece of paper, then he knelt by his victim. He slipped the envelope into the dead man's inside coat pocket. He stared at the paper for a moment, unable to see what was written there because of the darkness; he smiled, anyway. He knew what it said. Carefully, he pinned the note to the man's chest.

Standing up, he again checked the area for people, but it was still deserted, The damp, unfriendly night and the heavy fog were now his allies.

He bent down and grasped the dead man's arms. Grunting slightly, he pulled the body to the edge of the shrubbery and made sure the legs were sticking out far enough to be seen by anyone passing by.

He wanted this body to be discovered.

"'Ave you gone deaf, Betsy?" Smythe demanded in a harsh whisper, "Who the devil was that bloke?"

Betsy leaned back against the back of the hansom. She wished Smythe wouldn't keep on at her. The sound of the horses' hooves was loud on the wet street, but not loud enough to keep her from hearing the coachman's angry questions. Questions he'd been asking since he'd hustled her into this hansom a few minutes after chasing Raymond off, "I told ya, he was nobody."

"But he knew your name," Smythe persisted. "I heard him use your name so you must 'ave known the blighter."

Betsy closed her eyes. She felt lower than a snake. Smythe had rescued her, so he deserved some answers. But how could she tell him? How could she tell anyone about Raymond Skegit? If she did, she'd have to tell about herself. And she'd die before she'd ever let Smythe know about that.

She bit her lip. "He was just someone I used to know, that's all."

Smythe glared at her. He'd been scared out of his wits when he'd come round that corner and seen the fellow draggin' Betsy off. He thanked his lucky stars he hadn't let his pride stop him from keeping an eye on the lass, despite her insistence that she could take care of herself. "Why was he tryin' to drag you off? And don't try tellin' me he weren't, I've got eyes in me 'ead. I saw he 'ad you by the arm and you was fightin' him."

Betsy sighed. She knew Smythe wouldn't let up. She decided that half a lie was better than being badgered all evening. "He's just a bloke I used to know, that's all. His name is Raymond. He'd had a bit too much to drink and he was trying to make me go to a pub with him. He wasn't going to hurt me." That was a lie. She had no doubt at all that if she'd fallen into Raymond's hands, he would have hurt her.

Smythe stared at her, his expression openly skeptical.

Betsy turned her head and stared out the narrow window. She wasn't that good an actress, God, she was shakin' like a leaf just thinking about Raymond Skegit. Smythe had eyes in his head and he was a smart man, good at putting two and two together and coming up with four. He could see that she was terrified, He could also probably see that she was lying her head off, too.

"Where do ya know 'im from?" he persisted.

"Where do you think?" she shot back. "The East End. We grew up in the same area."

"What's 'is name again?" Smythe asked. He had his own way of gettin' information. Blast a Spaniard—how could he protect the lass if she wouldn't tell him the truth?

Betsy considered lying again, but then decided against it. She'd already said the name once. He'd know if she gave him a different one now.

He'd know for sure she was hidin' something. "Raymond Skegit," she mumbled.

"Where's 'e live?"

"How should I know?" Betsy snapped. "This is the first I've seen him in years."

He started to ask more questions and then clamped his mouth shut. In the dull glow of the lamplight, he could see she was deathly pale, and despite the bravado of her words, her eyes betrayed her. She was still terrified.

"Easy lass," he murmured, he reached across and patted her shoulder. "I'm only trying to 'elp. We don't want you havin' another set-to with this fellow, do we?"

Betsy gave him a weak smile. "Just let it be, Smythe. All right? I'm not likely to run into him again."

"Well, then," he lied, "if that's what you want, I'll let it alone."

He'd get word to Blimpey Groggins tomorrow. With enough money, Blimpey could find out anything. "How are ya feelin'? He didn't hurt you, did 'e? Let's see that arm, he was hangin' onto you pretty tight. Are there any bruises?" He reached for Betsy's hand, intending to take her arm and have a good look at it.

But Betsy's fingers clamped tightly around his. Surprised, he glanced up at her. She kept her eyes closed as she leaned her head against the seat. "My arm's fine," she said softly. "He didn't hurt me. Besides, you couldn't see bruises, my sleeves are too long."

Uncertain of what to do, Smythe started to pull away, to give her some breathin' room. But her fingers tightened around his. She held onto his hand all the way home.

Betsy and Smythe joined the others at the table. Before coming into the house, Betsy had made Smythe promise he wouldn't tell anyone what had happened.

Mrs. Jeffries watched the two of them as they took their seats. She knew something was wrong. Betsy was as white as a sheet and Smythe, despite his polite words of greeting, looked as if he wanted to take the room apart with his bare hands. "I'm glad you made it back before the meeting broke up," she said. "We were starting to get worried."

"We're fine," Smythe said shortly.

"That's right," Betsy agreed, "It just took a bit longer to get home than we thought. Have we missed much?"

Mrs. Jeffries told them everything that they'd talked about. "What about you two? Who wants to go first?"

Smythe cleared his throat. "I'll start. I found out more about why Nyles Hornsley hated his brother. Seems Nyles has a sweetheart, a woman named Madeline Wynn. Big brother doesn't approve of her. But accordin' to me source, that's not the only reason there was bad feelin's between the brothers. Peter Hornsley has control of Nyles's money."

"Bet that rankles a bit," Mrs. Goodge interjected. "It's always one or the other. Women or money. Looks like in Hornsley's case, it were both."

"And that's not all," Smythe continued. "Two days ago, Peter give Nyles orders not to see this Madeline Wynn again. Nyles supposedly told him to go to the devil and that he'd see his sweetheart whenever he wanted. The footman I talked to overheard Nyles threatening to kill Peter if Peter didn't let up on the purse strings so that Nyles and Madeline Wynn could get married."

"That certainly sounds like a good reason for hatin' someone enough to kill," Luty put in.

"Does Nyles Hornsley have an alibi?" Hatchet asked.

Smythe shook his head. "I don't know. He weren't at home on the evening of the murder, the footman knew that much. But that doesn't mean Nyles weren't somewhere else."

"Are you going to pursue that line of investigation tomorrow?" Mrs. Jeffries asked.

"If it's all the same to you," Smythe said smoothly. Checking up on Nyles Hornsley's alibi shouldn't take long, he thought. That would leave him plenty of time free to set Blimpey on Skegit's trail.

"I think that's a splendid idea," said Mrs. Jeffries as she pursed her lips. "Oh, this is so wretched," she cried. "If Inspector Witherspoon were on the case, we wouldn't have to be running about trying to see if someone had an alibi in the first place. We could already know! At least with our inspector, we had access to what the suspects have told the police about their whereabouts at the time of the murder."

"Now, now, Hepzibah." Luty patted the housekeeper's hand. "Don't get all het up. We've got to do what we've got to do. The inspector bein' off the case makes it a bit harder, but it ain't impossible."

"I know." She sighed. "It's just that I've got such awful feeling about this case. The whole idea that someone would use the inspector's name and then commit murder . . ."

"I think I've figured out why," Smythe interrupted.

Everyone stared at him.

"Why what?" Wiggins asked.

"Why he used the inspector's name," the coachman explained. "It's dead simple once you think about it. To begin with, the inspector gets his name in the paper every time he solves a murder. If I was a killer lookin' to get into a buildin' and strangle someone, what better name to use?"

"And secondly," Mrs. Jeffries prompted. She too had an idea as to why the killer was using Witherspoon's name, but she wanted to learn whether the coachman had come to the same conclusion she had.

"Well, we don't know much about this Hornsley person, and what little we do know makes me believe that he weren't a very nice man," Smythe said slowly, his idea forming and taking shape as he spoke. "Seems to me he might have been the kinda bloke that was on his guard. Maybe whoever killed him needed to pretend to be a policeman so he could get close enough to kill him, if you get my meanin'."

Mrs. Jeffries nodded thoughtfully. She hadn't thought quite along those lines, but she rather admired Smythe's reasoning. "Yes, I rather think I do. You're saying that the victim had so many enemies he might have been on his guard should a strange man have tried to get into his office after hours. The one person who he would have allowed in and turned his back on with no sense of danger would have had to have been a policeman—right?"

Smythe grinned. "Somethin' like that."


"How long do you think he's been dead?" Inspector Nivens asked the police surgeon.

"I wouldn't care to guess," Dr. Potter snapped. "Not until I've done the postmortem."

Barnes smiled in the darkness. Same old Potter. Still wouldn't tell you the sun had come up unless he'd looked out and seen it for himself. Beside him, he heard Nivens snort in disgust.

"But you must be able to tell us something," Nivens pressed. He shuffled his feet to keep warm.

"The man's dead, strangled by the look of it," Potter said irritably. "That's all I'm going to say at the moment."

"The body's still warm, sir," Barnes said softly. "I'd reckon he couldn't have been killed more than a couple of hours ago."

"And where did you take your medical degree?" Potter asked. He stood up. In the dim light cast by the policeman's lamps, he glared at the constable.

"Beggin' your pardon, sir," Barnes said to the doctor, "but I have seen a few bodies in my time on the force."

Nivens ignored them both. He pulled his pocket watch from his coat and checked the time. "It's almost nine," he mumbled. "Which means death probably occurred around seven."

Potter, incensed that the inspector was actually listening to a uniformed man, glared at both of them and scurried away. "I'll do the postmortem tomorrow," he called. "Until then make no assumptions, Inspector."

Barnes sighed. He watched Nivens bend down and start searching the pockets of the late George Frampton. Bad luck, the poor bloke had got it just like the other one. He even had a note pinned to his chest. Not that it made much sense, but it was a clue all the same.

The note had been printed on the same kind of paper and the word VIDI had been printed on it. Barnes had no idea what it meant. For that matter, neither did Inspector Nivens.

Small clusters of uniformed police were everywhere, keeping the curious away from the body and vainly trying to search the area in the dark and fog. Nivens had sent several lads off to see if they could find any witnesses, but Barnes was willing to bet his next hot dinner that they'd find no one.

This killer was too careful, too cunning. By some means, he lured his victim into a deserted park on a dark and foggy night, insuring that no one else would be larking about and then he'd struck. Stunning first and then dragging the poor bloke behind a bush to finish him off.

Made Barnes half sick, it did. He turned his gaze away from the late George Frampton. What made him even sicker was that whoever had done it was probably going to get away with it. With Nivens investigating the crime, the murderer didn't have to worry about getting caught.

"I've found something," Nivens called. "Barnes, grab that lamp and hold it closer."

Barnes did as he was told. He stepped around the fallen man's legs and held the lamp up. Nivens was holding up a plain white envelope. He opened it and drew out a piece of paper. "I found this in the victim's inside coat pocket," he said. "Hold the lamp closer, I can't quite make this out."

Barnes bent closer, bringing the lamp to within inches of Nivens's skull. He heard the inspector gasp in surprise. "What is it, sir?"

"It's a note," Nivens said, his voice rising excitedly. "And it says, '*If you want to know who murdered your partner, be at the Black Horse tonight at six o'clock.*'"

"Is it signed, sir?" Barnes had a sinking feeling in the pit of his stomach and it had nothing to do with the fact that he'd not had dinner.

Nivens laughed nastily. "It's signed alright, Constable. By none other than Gerald Witherspoon!"

Mrs. Jeffries poured the inspector a cup of tea and placed it next to his plate of bacon and eggs. "How was your walk last night, sir?" she asked. She took her own tea and sat down.

"My what?" Witherspoon said, looking puzzled.

"Your walk, sir," she repeated.

"Oh yes, well, I had a jolly good walk. Went quite a long ways."

"You were gone a time, sir," she replied. "We were beginning to get worried. You didn't get in till quite late."

"Hardly late, Mrs. Jeffries," he chided. "I was home by nine."

"You looked quite winded when you came in," she persisted. "I do hope you're not overdoing things. Moderate exercise is all well and good, sir. But too much can't be good for you." She didn't think he'd been out walking, but one could hardly accuse one's employer of lying.

"I think it did me the world of good," he replied. "As I said, I walked a long way. Felt wonderful when I got home. I slept like a baby."

Betsy stuck her head in the dining room. "Constable Barnes is here to see the inspector," she announced. "Should I show him in?"

"Oh, yes," Witherspoon replied eagerly. "Mrs. Jeffries, pour another cup."

Barnes appeared a few moments later, smiled at the housemaid and nodded at Mrs. Jeffries. "Mornin', ma'am. Sir."

"Do sit down and have some tea," said Witherspoon as he gestured to the chair on his left.

"Thank you, sir," Barnes replied. His words were polite enough, but Mrs. Jeffries could tell by his expression and the way he carried himself that something was terribly wrong.

"What brings you here so early this morning?" Witherspoon asked cheerfully. "Not that I'm not delighted to see you, of course."

"I'm afraid I've got some bad news," Barnes interrupted.

Witherspoon and Mrs. Jeffries stared at him.

"George Frampton was found murdered in Hyde Park last night," the constable blurted.

"Was he killed the same way as the other victim?" Witherspoon asked.

Barnes nodded. "Coshed on the head and strangled. There was a note pinned to his chest too, just like Hornsley. Course it didn't make any sense."

"What did it say?" the inspector prodded.

"It didn't say anything," Barnes replied. "Just had VIDI printed on it. Doesn't mean anything. Doesn't make any sense at all."

Mrs. Jeffries simply could not stop herself. "What was he strangled with?"

Barnes looked over and stared at her for a long moment. Finally, he said, "A school tie."

"Just like Mr. Hornsley," she murmured.

"Any idea when he was killed?" Witherspoon asked urgently. He knew this wasn't his case, but dash it all, he couldn't stop himself from asking questions.

Barnes laughed. "Potter was the police surgeon on duty last night," he said, "so he wouldn't tell us anything. But we had a bit of luck. The body was discovered fairly soon after the murder."

"Who discovered it?" Oh well, Mrs. Jeffries thought, in for a penny, in for a pound. The constable didn't seem to mind her asking questions.

"A policeman."

"That's a bit of luck," Witherspoon exclaimed.

"Not really, sir," Barnes said quickly. "He was out lookin' for Frampton when he found the body."

Witherspoon was puzzled. "I don't understand."

"When Mr. Frampton didn't get home by seven last night, Mrs. Frampton sent one of her footmen to the Yard with a message. We started lookin' right away," Barnes explained. "That's how I happened to be there. The message from Mrs. Frampton come in just before I was fixin' to go home. So we started searching and a young constable found his body in the park just before nine o'clock."

"I say, that was jolly clever of you to search the park." Witherspoon beamed at the constable. "Whose idea was that—yours?"

Barnes shook his head. "We weren't bein' clever, sir. Mrs. Frampton told us where to look. She told the constable we sent round to take her statement that her husband usually cut through the park on his way home from work. He had a routine, he did. Frampton would stop off at the Black Horse for a drink, cut through the park to give himself a bit of exercise, and be home for dinner at seven."

Mrs. Jeffries's mind worked furiously. "I take it that Mr. Frampton hadn't varied his routine because of his partner's murder."

Barnes shrugged. "We're not sure . . ."

"Then he must not have felt he was in any danger," Mrs. Jeffries continued, unaware of the uncomfortable expression on the constable's face. "Therefore, we can conclude that Frampton felt that Hornsley's murder had nothing to do with him."

"I don't think I quite follow you," Witherspoon said.

"But, sir," Mrs. Jeffries said earnestly, "I'm merely using the kind of reasoning you always use when you're on a case."

"Oh, yes," the inspector smiled. "Do go on. I'm, er, curious to see how you've applied my methods."

"Frampton wasn't a fool," she continued. "If Hornsley was murdered because of something that had gone on with his business, then Frampton would have felt himself in danger as well and taken precautions. Apparently, he took no precautions at all. He obviously felt safe enough to walk through a deserted park on a dark, foggy night. I mean, no one in their right minds would go into Hyde Park if they thought there was someone trying to kill them."

"I'm not so sure about that," Barnes said softly. But they didn't seem to hear him.

"I don't know, Mrs. Jeffries," Witherspoon put in, "People occasionally do very foolish things. Frampton's going into the park could just as easily mean he was one of those stubborn fellows who won't change their routine for anyone, certainly not for a murderer."

"Er, Inspector," Barnes said softly. "Frampton was scared. We already know that."

"He was?" Witherspoon said in surprise.

"Yes, sir," Barnes cleared his throat. "His clerk told us that Frampton was real nervous. You see, sir, he didn't go into that park alone."

Mrs. Jeffries felt a cold, hard hand clutch her heart. "Who did he go in with?"

Barnes fiddled with the handle of his teacup; he couldn't meet her gaze. "He went in with a fellow he'd met in the Black Horse. The publican overheard them talking."

Even the inspector knew something was wrong. "And did the publican happen to get this man's name?"

Barnes finally looked up. "Yes, sir. The man introduced himself as Gerald Witherspoon."

For a moment none of them said a word.

"Oh, dear," Witherspoon broke the awkward silence. "This is most odd. I was nowhere near Hyde Park or the Black Horse Pub last night. Did the publican say what the fellow looked like?"

"He had spectacles . . ."

"Oh dear," the inspector murmured.

"A bowler hat."

"Just like mine, I suppose."

"And a great big heavy overcoat," finished Barnes.

"I've got a great big heavy overcoat, too," Witherspoon said morosely.

"And that's not the worst of it, sir," Barnes said.

"You mean there's more!" The inspector couldn't make heads or tails of this. How much worse could it get?

"They found another note on Frampton's body. It was in an envelope in his top pocket. It said, '*If you want to know who killed your partner, meet me at the Black Horse Pub at six o'clock.*'"

"Was the note signed?" Mrs. Jeffries asked. She already knew it was and by whom.

Barnes nodded sadly. "It was signed Gerald Witherspoon."

"That is nonsense," Witherspoon burst out. "Utter nonsense. I would never do such a silly, melodramatic thing as that. That's ridiculous. If I wanted to meet someone I'd go round to his home or ask him to come to the Yard. I certainly wouldn't send silly little schoolboy notes to lure the victim into a deserted park!"

"Of course you wouldn't, sir," Barnes said soothingly. "Everyone knows you wouldn't do such a silly thing."

"But I have a feeling that there are some who do think I'm quite capable of such stupidity."

Barnes shook his head. "No one seriously considers you a suspect, sir. If that's what you're thinkin'. Even Nivens knows you've no reason to want to kill either Hornsley or Frampton."

Reason or not, Mrs. Jeffries knew that things were getting very bad for their inspector. Very bad, indeed. "Reasons for murder can be manufactured," she said softly. "Just as easily as a mysterious note found in a dead man's pocket."

"What?" Witherspoon looked at her curiously. The expression on his face indicated that he hoped he hadn't understood her clearly.

"Someone," she said bluntly, "is trying their hardest to make sure Inspector Witherspoon is arrested for these crimes. That person will, no doubt, manufacture a suitable motive at the appropriate time. A motive, I feel, that even someone as abysmally stupid as Inspector Nivens can't fail to see."

"Why, Mrs. Jeffries," said Witherspoon, deeply shocked. "Who would do such a wicked thing? And why to me?"

"There's lots that would do it," Barnes answered. "And especially to you. You're a good man, Inspector, but there's plenty of criminals that you've sent to prison. This could be someone's idea of the perfect revenge."

"But Inspector Nivens wouldn't arrest me," Witherspoon protested. "Surely he'd see that I was being made to look like the killer?"

"Nivens would arrest you in two shakes of dog's tail," Barnes interrupted. "He'll be here this mornin' to see if you have an alibi for last night between the hours of six and seven-thirty. But that's fine, once Nivens knows you were here at home and that your staff can confirm . . ." but he broke off when he saw their expressions change.

"I'm afraid I wasn't here at that time," the inspector admitted. "I was . . . uh . . . out walking. I didn't get home till almost nine."

"You were out takin' a ruddy walk!" Barnes stared at him incredulously. "Did anyone see you? Did you stop anywhere, have a drink or bite to eat? Did you run into any of the lads? For God's sake, man, where did you go?"

"That's just it, I didn't go anywhere. I just walked. No one saw me." Witherspoon slumped in his chair. "I'm afraid I just wandered around. To be perfectly truthful, I've been a bit upset about that first murder. You'd be upset too if someone used your name to kill a man. So I wasn't paying attention to where I was going. I was just walking and thinking."

"But did you stop anywhere?" Barnes asked hopefully. "Anywhere at all?"

"No. I wasn't hungry and I didn't stop for a drink, either. Nor did I run into any uniformed lads. I'm sorry. I saw no one."

Barnes closed his eyes. For a long moment he couldn't find his voice. Finally, he said, "Oh Lord, sir, let's hope Mrs. Jeffries is wrong."

"I'm praying I'm wrong," Mrs. Jeffries interjected, But neither Barnes nor the inspector appeared to hear her.

"Let's hope that this killer isn't deliberately trying to get you arrested for these murders," the constable continued sadly. "'Cause if he is, you're done for."

"No, he isn't," Mrs. Jeffries announced calmly.

Both of the men stared at her. She smiled serenely. She was going to take a big gamble here—there was no choice.

If she didn't act, if she didn't take this step, there was a good chance that Inspector Gerald Witherspoon would be arrested for murder. She could feel it in her bones. Mrs. Jeffries had learned to trust her instincts, and right now they were screaming at her that Inspector Witherspoon was in peril. If not his life, then at least his reputation was at stake.

No matter what the risk, she couldn't allow him to be arrested for a crime she knew he didn't commit. If Inspector Witherspoon couldn't see the danger he was in, she had to do it for him.

"What do you mean?" Barnes asked. "I don't see that there's much we can do. Not with that nitwit Nivens investigatin' this case." He laughed bitterly. "Take my word for it, he'll never catch the real killer."

"Of course he won't," Mrs. Jeffries said calmly. "But we will."

# CHAPTER 6

"Have you taken leave of your senses?" Mrs. Goodge asked incredulously. She stared at the housekeeper over the rim of her spectacles.

"Cor blimey, Mrs. J.," Smythe added. "I don't like the sound of this."

"Hell's bells, Hepzibah," Luty snapped, "I thought the whole idea was to keep our activities *secret* from the inspector."

Wiggins gaped at her in shock. Betsy groaned. Hatchet's mouth was pursed in a disapproving frown, and even Fred seemed to be looking at her as though she'd just lost her mind.

Mrs. Jeffries held up her hand. "If you'll all give me a moment to explain," she began for the third time, "I think you'll see that I had no choice whatsoever in the matter. I had to do something."

"No choice," Betsy bleated. "What does that mean?"

Mrs. Jeffries tried again. "It means that we've got to do this case differently. Now, if you'll all calm down and let me tell you what happened, I think you'll find there is absolutely no reason to panic. The inspector has no idea we've been helping him on all his previous cases, he only thinks we're going to help on this one."

They started talking again.

Hatchet banged his fist on the table. "I think we owe Mrs. Jeffries the courtesy of listening to what she has to say," he said loudly.

Everyone fell silent, even Luty, who contented herself with giving him a quick frown. Hatchet smiled slightly, reminding Mrs. Jeffries of a schoolmaster who'd settled down a roomful of boisterous children. "Now, madam"— he nodded at her—"do continue. I assure you'll we'll not interrupt you again."

"Thank you, Hatchet," she replied. She took a deep breath. The truth was, she wasn't sure if she was doing the right thing, but she still didn't see that she'd had any choice in the matter, "First of all, do keep in mind that the inspector has no idea we've helped him in the past."

"Then why is 'e lettin' us investigate this one?" Smythe asked.

"Because he has no choice," Mrs. Jeffries said quickly. She told them about everything she'd learned from Constable Barnes, taking care not to leave out any of the details. When she got to the part about the note with Witherspoon's signature being found in the dead man's pocket, there were gasps of shock and surprise around the table.

"So you see," she finished, when they'd all quieted down again. "I had to do something. We can't let our inspector get arrested for murder."

"Do you think there's a chance that's going to happen?" Betsy asked anxiously.

"Not if we're as clever as I think we are," Mrs. Jeffries replied. "But we need to know what the police know. For that we need Constable Barnes. We can't keep muddling about in the dark, so to speak. Inspector Witherspoon's reputation and possibly even his liberty are at grave risk. There's a chance we'll miss something important if we try and do this one completely on our own."

Smythe shook his head in disgust. "Nivens has always looked down 'is nose at Inspector Witherspoon, but I can't believe he'd arrest 'im for murder."

"Nivens is desperate to solve this case," Mrs. Jeffries pointed out. "And this killer is very, very clever. The real danger isn't our inspector getting arrested on such flimsy evidence. It's giving the killer a chance to plant the kind of evidence that will force Nivens to arrest Inspector Witherspoon."

"You're assuming the killer is deliberately making it look as if Witherspoon is guilty?" Hatchet said slowly, his face creased in a thoughtful frown.

"We'd be fools to assume otherwise," Mrs. Jeffries replied. "The killer used Witherspoon's name twice to gain access to his victims. What's worse, he's actually planted evidence on George Frampton that points blame directly at our inspector."

Smythe leaned forward, resting his elbows on the table. "Then that means it's got to be someone who's got it in for Inspector Witherspoon," he said.

"I think that's a fairly sale assumption."

"Could it be someone he's arrested in the past?" Luty queried.

"I'm not sure," Mrs. Jeffries hesitated. "Before he started solving homicides, he spent most of his career with the police in the records room. Yet"—she paused and thought for a moment, then she shook her head—"I can't think of anyone he's arrested for murder who's at liberty now."

"Most of 'em are either 'anged or doin' time," Smythe mused. "So maybe it's someone's relation? You know, I mean it could be a brother or a cousin or even a friend of someone the inspector arrested."

"Well, whoever it is," Mrs. Jeffries said, "is keen and very daring. We've no time to lose."

Betsy's brows drew together in a puzzled frown. "There's somethin' I don't understand. Are we goin' under the assumption that it's the inspector the killer is really after? I mean, gettin' him arrested for murder and ruining his career? Or is the killer really wantin' the victims dead and out of his way?"

Mrs. Jeffries had pondered that question too. "Unfortunately, I don't have an answer for you. At this point, we simply don't know," she said, shrugging her shoulders helplessly. "But there are two people dead. I don't think the killer picked them arbitrarily. Let's assume that for reasons that aren't clear yet, the murderer also wants certain other people, mainly those he's already murdered, out of the way."

"Killing two birds with one stone, so to speak," Wiggins smiled at his own wit.

"That's an excellent way of putting it," Mrs. Jeffries said to the footman; she was delighted to see that he wasn't sulking anymore.

"What do we do now?" Betsy asked. "Continue as we are? Or should one of us hang about here and keep an eye on the inspector?"

Mrs. Jeffries thought for a moment. "There's no need to do that. I don't think Inspector Witherspoon is in any immediate danger. But, I do think we ought to shift the focus of this investigation."

"Shift it how?" Mrs. Goodge asked.

"I'm not exactly sure. It's more complex than we first thought," she replied slowly. She was thinking aloud, hoping that something she said would spark some ideas in the others. "Perhaps we ought to spend more time concentrating on the firm of Hornsley, Frampton, and Whitelaw? Oh dear, I'm not explaining this very well, but since Frampton was the second person killed, I suspect that the murders have more to do with the victims' business lives than with their personal lives."

"So what do ya want us to do?" Smythe asked.

"Well, I'd like you to learn what you can about Grady Whitelaw," she said. "He's the last of the partners left."

The coachman nodded. "Alright, I'll get onto 'im today."

"What about me?" Betsy asked.

"You take Justin Vincent, the silent partner," Mrs. Jeffries instructed. "Find out what you can about him."

"I take it you want Madam and me to continue using our sources in the City to learn what we can about the firm," Hatchet said.

"That's right," Mrs. Jeffries replied. "But don't ignore your gossip sources either," she said, smiling at Luty. "Your friend Myrtle seems a very fountain of information."

Luty chuckled. "Oh, don't worry, Hepzibah, I won't be forgettin' Myrtle. She knows more about the people with money in this city than the Queen's tax boys."

"What about me?" Mrs. Goodge asked. "My sources won't know much about the goings on of the firm, so what am I supposed to do?"

"What you always do," Mrs. Jeffries said firmly. She wasn't going to have the cook feeling left out and unimportant. "Even a business firm has a past. I've every confidence you can find out a great deal of useful information. Besides, we're not going to totally ignore the victims' personal lives, so find out what more you can about that, too."

"I guess Fred and me won't have nuthin' to do again," Wiggins complained. He shot his bandaged ankle a fierce glare. "'Ow long is this ruddy thing goin' to take before it 'eals?"

Mrs. Jeffries gazed at him sympathetically. In truth, she still couldn't think of a thing that poor Wiggins could do. "I know it's difficult," she began, "but there's really nothing you can do right now. You must give yourself time to heal. It would be far too dangerous for you to try and go out and about in your condition. We can't have you hurting yourself."

"Don't worry, lad," Smythe said kindly, "that ankle won't take forever to 'eal. You'll be out and about on the next case."

"If there is a next case," Wiggins muttered.

"Remember everyone," Mrs. Jeffries said, "Constable Barnes is coming by tonight after supper to give us a progress report. So let's all try to have something to contribute."

Hatchet cleared his throat. "Does the inspector know that Madam and I are helping?"

"No," Mrs. Jeffries replied, "he doesn't. I thought it best not to mention your participation."

"Then perhaps Madam and I ought to drop by after you've had your meeting with Constable Barnes," Hatchet suggested.

"That's a good idea," she said, relieved that neither Luty nor her butler had taken offense. "Shall we say half past nine?"

"I've no idea why anyone would want to kill George or Peter," Grady Whitelaw said to the two policemen. "No idea at all."

Whitelaw was a thin, nervous man with receding brown hair, bushy eyebrows, and crooked nose. Though it was only nine in the morning, his pristine white shirt was rumpled, his expensive black coat was wrinkled and creased, and his tie askew.

Barnes thought Whitelaw was the most fidgety creature he'd ever seen. They'd only been in the room two minutes and the man hadn't been still a moment. His hands fluttered, his shoulders jerked spasmodically, and he'd jumped up from his chair at least twice. Barnes cast a quick look at the other man in Whitelaw's office—Justin Vincent, the silent partner.

Vincent was about the same age as Whitelaw, but that was the only thing they had in common. His hair was light brown and his face clean shaven. He sat in the chair to one side of Whitelaw's desk, his brown eyes reflecting confidence and good humor. He was tall, dressed in a dark brown suit with fawn-colored gloves, and, most of all, calm.

"Of course Peter was a blighter," Whitelaw rattled on, fluttering his hands like he was batting at flies. "Always has been, even when we were in school. Made the younger boys miserable."

Barnes saw Vincent wince. He didn't much blame the man. If Whitelaw didn't pause to take a breath, he was going to work himself into a fit. It was bloomin' embarrassin' to watch.

"But George was a decent sort," Whitelaw cried. He ran a hand through his hair, causing it to stand straight up. "Why would anyone want to kill George?"

"That's what we're going to find out," Inspector Nivens replied.

"Yes, but *when* are you going to find out?"

Nivens ignored that question. "Do you know if either man had received any threatening letters?"

Barnes stifled a sigh. Nivens was at it again. Why didn't the man ask something useful? Why didn't he ask them about their alibis? Why didn't he ask them about the notes pinned to the dead men's coats? Bloody fool.

"Threatening letters?" Whitelaw repeated. His pale face creased in thought as he contemplated it. "I don't think so. Neither of them ever mentioned it if they did."

"Do you know of anyone who'd want to ruin your firm?" Nivens asked.

"Of course not," Whitelaw exclaimed.

"But I understand some of your competitors don't like the way you conduct business," Nivens said.

"*Most* of our competitors don't like the way we do business." Whitelaw shrugged, but it wasn't a simple movement. His whole body shook as his head bobbed and his shoulders shot up so high that Barnes was amazed that he stayed in his chair.

"But that's hardly a reason for murder," Whitelaw's voice cracked. "We've been doing business this way for years."

"What about Damon Hilliard?" Nivens pressed. "Does he like the way you operate?"

"Hilliard's complained about our tactics for years," Whitelaw replied. "We don't pay much attention to him."

"Wasn't he in here a few days ago, the day that Peter Hornsley was murdered?" Nivens said. "And didn't he threaten him?"

"Oh, no."

"No?" Nivens repeated in surprise. "But we've had it on good authority . . ."

"Hilliard threatened Peter a few days before Peter was killed," Whitelaw corrected. "But we didn't take it seriously. It wasn't the first time it had happened. He's a bad temper, but I don't think he's a murderer."

Nivens opened his mouth but before he could get a word out, Vincent interrupted. "Excuse me, Inspector, but do the police seriously think these murders were done by someone with a grudge against the firm?"

"We think it's possible, sir," Nivens replied.

"How long have you been associated with the company?" Barnes asked Vincent. He didn't much care whether or not Nivens liked his asking questions. He wasn't going to stand by and let a killer walk free because of his superior's incompetence.

"I bought into the firm several months ago." Vincent smiled.

"Had you known either of the victims previous to your buying in, sir?" Barnes pressed.

"Oh no," Vincent laughed easily. "I haven't been in England long enough to know many people. I only came over from America a few months ago."

"And how did you happen to invest money in Hornsley, Frampton, and Whitelaw?"

"I can answer that," Whitelaw interrupted. "I ran into Justin at my club. We were introduced by a mutual acquaintance. He was looking to invest some capital, and I thought, why not us? We're a safe investment."

"So you bought in as a silent partner?" Barnes probed.

Beside him, Nivens cleared his throat. "That'll be all, Constable. I don't think Mr. Vincent's business dealings have any connection to this matter."

"As you wish, sir." He forced himself to smile. "But I do believe we've forgotten to ask these gentlemen where they were last night between six and half past seven."

Nivens's eyes widened at the constable's audacity. But for form's sake, he couldn't make an issue out of the statement. "Gentlemen," he said, "if you'd be so kind as to answer the constable's inquiry."

"I was at my fiancée's home," Whitelaw replied.

"What time did you arrive there, sir?" Barnes asked quickly.

"About eight-fifteen, I think."

"So you left your office quite late?"

"Oh no, I left at my usual time," Whitelaw explained. "Half past five. George was still here when I went. I popped my head into his office to say good night," he sniffed.

"And it took you three hours to get to your fiancée's?" Barnes asked incredulously. "Where does she live?"

Whitelaw wiped his eyes. "She lives near Regent's Park, but I went home first and changed clothes. Then I got a hansom, but there was a dreadful amount of traffic. It took ages to get to her home. She was most annoyed with me for being late."

Barnes turned to Vincent. "And you, sir, where were you last night?"

"I'm afraid I've no alibi, either," Vincent said. "My servants were home but I was shut in my study working. I didn't see anyone after, oh . . ." he paused for a moment. "I guess it must have been half-past six."

"Didn't you eat an evening meal?" Nivens asked.

"I'm afraid I've taken on a number of habits from my adopted country," he said, smiling broadly. "Americans tend to eat earlier than we do. I had my meal at six."

"I don't see why you're asking us all these questions," Whitelaw suddenly cried.

"It's our duty to ask you these questions," Nivens said pompously. "A murder has been committed."

Whitelaw's eyes narrowed angrily. "I'm aware there's been a murder. Two of them, in fact. But instead of wasting time badgering me, you'd do better asking those that are going to benefit from my friend's death where they were last night."

"Whom do you mean, sir?" Barnes queried softly.

"Ask Stuart Frampton where he was last night when his father was being murdered," said Whitelaw, his head bobbing wildly in excitement, his face flushed a bright red. "After all, now that George is gone, Stuart gets it all."


"Is that where you work, then?" Betsy asked the young woman she'd been walking with. They were in front of a lovely redbrick house in Mayfair.

"This is the place. Lovely i'n' it?" Martha Dowling said eagerly, obviously taking pride in working in so grand a house. She was a tall, big-boned girl in her early twenties with light brown hair tucked neatly under a maid's cap. Her face was round and her complexion almost perfect. Betsy thought she had the loveliest hazel eyes. "I've been there for three months now," she continued. "I used to work for a solicitor and his family over on Bulstrode Street, but I come here when me mum saw an advert in the newspaper. It's much better here. Mr. Vincent don't work his servants like they was dogs."

"And he lets you out every now and again," Betsy said, giving the girl a cheerful smile. "That's always nice, too."

"Well, there's always errands that need doin' and such like that," Martha agreed. "Mr. Vincent doesn't have a butler, just a housekeeper. She's not one for running about and such. Like this morning, for instance, Mrs.

Tottle didn't want to have to take Mr. Vincent's boots to the shoemaker, so she let me do it. I like gettin' out."

Betsy nodded. "I suppose Mr. Vincent has lived here a long time," she mused. Martha didn't seem to be in a hurry to get inside and start scrubbing floors, not that Betsy could blame the girl. Housework was about the most boring thing a body could do.

Martha shook her head and leaned against the wrought-iron fence in front of the house. "Mr. Vincent only come here a few months back. He's from America, you know. He once worked in a traveling show. Can you imagine that?"

"But this house is so big," Betsy said, feigning amazement. "I thought he must be someone from one of them old rich families. You know, the kind that are always braggin' and sayin' things like their ancestors come over with the conqueror."

Martha laughed. "Mr. Vincent's not at all like that. Not that he's isn't rich as sin, he is. But he's only lived here a few months."

"You mean he's a foreigner!"

"He's as English as the Queen," Martha replied. "Went to school in Abingdon. But he's lived in America for years. Somewhere out in California . . ." She broke off, her eyes taking on a dreamy glazed expression. "I've always wanted to go to California. Mr. Vincent says the sun settin' in the Pacific Ocean is one of the most beautiful sights in the world. He's fixin' to go back soon. I wish he'd take me with 'im."

"You like 'im then?"

Martha gave her a sharp look. "I like workin' for him. He's not so fussy as some are, if you get my meaning."

"Pays well and keeps his hands to himself," Betsy stated.

Martha grinned knowingly. "That's right. I'd rather work for the likes of him than for some I've known."

Betsy knew she had to find out where Justin Vincent was on the evening of the murders. She hoped the man wasn't the killer. Vincent sounded much nicer than most of the employers in London. But justice was justice. Because a man treated his servants well didn't mean he wasn't capable of coshing someone over the head and strangling the life out of them.

But Betsy had to go carefully. Martha seemed a right chatty, trusting sort of girl, but she wasn't stupid. Betsy didn't want to ask too much. "Is he married?"

"No." Martha sighed. "And it's a right shame, too. He's such a nice

man and not bad lookin' for his age. I think he had his heart broken when
he was a lad, if you know what I mean."

"Really?"

"Oh, yes," Martha continued. "Sometimes I see him sittin' in his big
wingbacked chair in front of the fireplace. He'll have the saddest expression on his face. And one time, I was bringing some fresh towels into his
bedroom, and I saw him bent over this old carpetbag he keeps under
his bed and you'll never guess what he was holdin'."

"What?"

"A lock of a woman's hair." Martha's hazel eyes widened dramatically.
"I think it must have belonged to his sweetheart." She sighed again. "It's
so sad. He could do with a bit of softness in his life. Oh well, maybe he's
got someone waitin' for him in California."

"Doesn't he ever go out?"

"Not much." Martha made a face. "If I had his money, I'd be out every
night. But all he ever does is shut himself up in the study after supper and
work."

"I suppose he makes you all bring him tea and coffee while he's
workin' them late hours," Betsy said disgustedly, as though she was very
familiar with inconsiderate employers.

"Nah," said Martha, pushing away from the fence and straighten-
ing her spine. "He doesn't like to be bothered after supper. He doesn't
even have a servant to help him get ready for bed. Like I said, he's a good
master."

Betsy felt like pulling her hair out. Martha was giving her lots of information, but she couldn't for the life of her think of a way to find out if
Vincent had been out on the night of the murders. Out of the corner of
her eye, she saw a tall, white-haired man getting out of a carriage in the
street ahead of her. It gave her an idea.

"Is Mr. Vincent a tall, dark-haired gentleman?" she asked Martha. "I
was up on the High Street last night, and I saw a man like that having an
argument with a cabbie." She forced herself to laugh. "I thought they was
goin' to come to blows."

"I don't think so," Martha said slowly, her face creased in thought.
"Mr. Vincent's got light brown hair and he's not all that tall. More medium height like. But he's not the sort to be gettin' into fights. What time
was it?"

"Around seven o'clock," Betsy replied. "I was on my way home. My employer insists we've got to be in by nine even on our day out."

"Then it couldn't have been Mr. Vincent," Martha said firmly. "He was shut in his study from half-past six on. He's done that every night for the past couple of weeks."

That's all Betsy needed to know. She smiled at Martha, chatted a few minutes more and told her new friend she had to go. Martha gave her a friendly wave and went into the house.

Betsy's shoulders slumped as she went back up to the main road. It was bloomin' hard to concentrate. Even when she'd been talking with Martha and tryin' her very best to keep her mind on this case, she'd not been able to stop thinking about Raymond Skegit. Why did he have to show up now?

She rounded the corner and almost bumped into an elegantly dressed woman. Betsy gave her an apologetic smile and dodged round her ample bulk. Blast a Spaniard, as Smythe would say, she didn't want the likes of Raymond hanging about and ruining her life. The truth was, she was scared of Raymond. There'd been stories about him, ugly stories.

But there was nothing she could do but be on her guard. Make sure she didn't put herself in a situation where Raymond could get his dirty hands on her again. She'd have to be careful. Betsy stepped off the curb into the street. Immediately, the air was filled with the squeal of brakes and the sound of horses' hooves.

"Hey, girl," an angry cooper's driver screamed, "watch where yer goin'."

She leapt back out of harm's way and waited for the dray to pass. Blast, blast, blast, she cursed silently to herself. This was awful. She was so rattled she'd be lucky to get home without being killed. And to make matters worse, she'd been so upset yesterday evening, she hadn't even told the others what she'd learned.

And what was she goin' to do about Smythe? She looked around her quickly just to make sure he wasn't hangin' about. Not that she'd mind him hangin' about. He'd come in right handy when Raymond was tryin' to drag her off yesterday, but she didn't want him spyin' on her all the time. She sighed and crossed the road. What was she goin' to do? What if Smythe found out? Oh Lord, why did this have to happen now, just when she and the coachman were really gettin' to know each other.

She liked Smythe. Really liked him. Recently, she'd had hopes that maybe, if she was real lucky like, the two of them could have something more than just a friendship. But if he found out about her past, he'd want nothing to do with her. Smythe was a good man, but he was still a man. Blast a Spaniard! It just wasn't fair.

"I'm sorry to have to bother you at a time like this," Nivens said softly. He gave Rosalind Frampton a sympathetic smile. "But we really must ask you a few questions."

Rosalind Frampton was dark-haired, dainty, and very beautiful. She was also a great deal younger than her late husband.

She smiled weakly at Nivens and fiddled with the black bombazine fabric of her mourning skirt. "I understand. Poor George was murdered . . ." Her voice broke and she looked away.

Barnes shuffled his feet. Bloomin' awkward this was, a weeping widow and dozens of questions that needed answering. Thank God Inspector Witherspoon was willing to snoop about some on this case. Barnes smiled slightly, thinking of Witherspoon's housekeeper and her daring offer to have the inspector's servants take a hand in as well. It couldn't hurt, Barnes thought, shooting Nivens a disgusted glance. He just wanted this case solved so he could go back to working with Inspector Witherspoon. He knew how to treat his constable properly.

"Would you tell us the sequence of events that led you to send for the police last night?" Nivens asked.

Rosalind Frampton looked confused. "Sequence of events," she repeated. "You mean, why did I send the footman to Scotland Yard when George didn't come home last night?"

"That's correct."

"Because he didn't come home," she explained. "George is always home by seven o'clock. You can set the clock by his coming in the front door. When it had gone seven fifteen, I knew something was wrong."

"You were alarmed?"

"I was terrified," she said, looking at Nivens as though he were thick as two short planks. "There had been another murder, if you'll remember. Peter Hornsley isn't even buried yet. Of course I was worried. So I sent Chandler, that's the footman, out with a message for the police. A few hours later, they came and told me George was dead."

"I see." Nivens bobbed his head. "Did your husband have any enemies?"

Barnes gritted his teeth. Not that again.

"Enemies?" Rosalind repeated the word like she'd never heard it before. "I don't know what you mean."

"He means," said a voice from the door, "did someone hate him enough to want to kill him."

Barnes turned and saw a dark-haired youth who looked to be in his early twenties leaning against the frame of the double doors. The young man smiled slightly when he saw he had the attention of everyone in the room.

"I'm Stuart Frampton," he announced. "George Frampton's son." He cast a quick cold look at his stepmother. "You really should have let me know the police were here."

"Why?" the look she gave him was equally cold. "They didn't ask to speak to you."

"Mr. Frampton," Nivens interrupted. "Do you know if your father was in fear of his life?"

Stuart shrugged and ambled to the settee. He perched on the arm. "He was frightened. But I don't think that's particularly odd. He had good reason to be. After all, his partner had just been murdered. He didn't have much faith in you lot, either. Said you hadn't a prayer in catching this killer."

Nivens's expression hardened. "Mr. Frampton, where were you last night between the hours of six and seven?"

"Oh," Stuart smiled cheerfully. "Am I a suspect then?"

"Just answer the question, sir."

"Did you ask my stepmother where she was?"

"I was right here," Rosalind Frampton exclaimed. "Every servant in the household can vouch for me."

"They'd say anything you want them to." Stuart glared at her. "They'll do anything to keep their positions. And even if you were here, did you tell the police where you were on the night Peter was killed?"

She gasped, outraged. "I was visiting friends that night," she sputtered. "And they can vouch for my whereabouts . . ."

"Oh, yes," he smiled slyly, "your friends. Father wouldn't have them in the house, would he." He turned to the policemen. "My stepmother used to be an actress. She's got the oddest assortment of 'friends.' Some of them quite dangerous looking. Why, I expect there's one or two that would cut your throat for half a bob."

"That's despicable," Rosalind cried angrily. "I'm not the one who benefits by George's death. You are."

"With him dead you've got the house and an allowance and that which you wanted most, your freedom," Stuart yelled.

"You cur," Rosalind half rose from the settee. "If you're trying to imply I had anything to do with these murders . . ."

"I'm not implying anything . . ."

"Mr. Frampton," Nivens cut in. "Would you please answer the question?"

Barnes looked at his superior incredulously. For God's sake, both of them had lost their tempers and were losing control of their tongues! And Nivens had been stupid enough to interrupt. Why hadn't he kept his mouth shut? They might have learned all kinds of useful information if Nivens had let them keep on goin' at each other.

"Oh, very well," said Stuart, folding his arms over his chest. "If you must know, I was at Balour's. There was a reception and concert."

Damn, thought Barnes, half of London was at Balour's last night. "Did anyone see you, sir?" he asked quickly. He didn't much care that Nivens had told him to keep his mouth shut. Inspector Witherspoon's reputation, if not his life, was at stake.

"I'm sure dozens of people saw me."

"Do you happen to know their names?" Nivens asked. He contented himself with giving Barnes a cold stare. The constable ignored it.

"If you're asking did I see anyone I know"—Stuart made a helpless gesture with his hands—"then the answer is 'no,' I didn't."

"You were there on your own, sir?" Barnes continued. "Isn't that a bit odd?"

"Not at all," Stuart replied. "I was supposed to go with some friends, the Cullens. But at the last moment, they had to cancel. You can verify that with them."

Barnes nodded slowly. "Where do the Cullens live?"

Stuart frowned. "Let's see, it's number ten Dowager Court or is it . . ."

"It's number twelve," Rosalind Frampton interjected. "And you didn't say anything to me or your father about going with the Cullens."

"I didn't consider it any of your business," Stuart shot back.

"What time did you leave?" Nivens pressed.

Barnes noticed that Rosalind Frampton had relaxed back against the settee. The ghost of a smile hovered on her mouth. She seemed to be enjoying listening to her stepson being questioned.

"It was early," Stuart replied. "Frankly, the whole thing was a bit of a bore. The music wasn't very good, the food was mediocre, and the company was hardly stimulating. I suppose I actually left at about eight o'clock."

Nivens stroked his chin; he appeared deep in thought. Finally, he asked, "Did you come straight home?"

"No," Rosalind interrupted, "he didn't." She paused and gave her stepson a malicious smile. "Stuart didn't get in until almost ten o'clock. Not more than half an hour before the police came to tell me they'd found George's body."

# CHAPTER 7

Blimpey Groggins raised his glass to his lips, took a long swallow of bitter, and then sighed in satisfaction. "Nothin' like a good drink at the end of the day to chase a man's troubles away, eh, Smythe?" He was a fat red-haired man wearing a dirty, rust-colored pork pie hat, a misshapen checkered coat spotted with grease stains, and a pristine white shirt.

Smythe stared at him for a moment, wondering how someone as filthy as Blimpey always managed to keep his shirt looking clean. The man surely enjoyed his drink too, judging by the expression on Blimpey's face. Smythe wished it were that simple for him. If pale ale or bitter was all it took to rid himself of his worries, he'd have been in the pub all day. But he wasn't much of a drinker, and he didn't think there was enough alcohol in all of England to keep him from frettin' over Betsy. "That's what some say. Look, 'ave you found out . . ."

"Now, don't be in such a 'urry, lad. I only just got 'ere. Give me a minute to enjoy me drink before you start jumpin' down me throat with questions." Blimpey wiped his mouth with the cuff of his soiled sleeve.

Smythe forced himself to be patient. It didn't do any good to try and hurry Blimpey. For all the man's irritatin' ways, there was none better than Groggins at snoopin' about and learnin' what a body needed to know. "You got my note, then," Smythe said casually as though the matter was of no importance.

"I'm 'ere, ain't I?" Blimpey grinned. "Mind you, almost didn't come when I found out what pub it was you wanted to meet in," he said, glancing scornfully around his surroundings.

The pub was a new one called the Brighton. There was heavy oak panelling along the walls, ornate etched glass in the windows, padded seats on the benches in the private bar, and, most bizarre of all, potted plants along the bar. Blimpey wrinkled his nose. "Don't much 'old with these new ways of doin' things. What's wrong with nice plain walls and good hardwood floors, that's what I want to know."

"I wanted to meet you 'ere because it was the closest pub to where I was goin' to be," Smythe explained. "Besides, why do you care? The bitter here is just as good as any you'd get somewhere else." He really was starting to run out of patience. "Now, 'ave you found out anything or not?"

Blimpey sighed and put his glass down. "Don't get your trousers in a pinch," he mumbled. "I've learned plenty."

"Well," Smythe demanded, "get on with it."

"First of all, it weren't easy trackin' the likes of Raymond Skegit." Blimpey's cheerful countenance vanished. He looked at his companion speculatively. "What you wantin' to know about someone like Skegit for?"

"Never mind why," Smythe replied impatiently. God, he'd forgotten how hard it was to actually get Blimpey to get to the point. The man did like the sound of his own voice. "Just tell me."

"All right, alright, keep yer shirt on." Blimpey cleared his throat. "Skegit's a bad lot. Runs a string of whores out of the East End. Mind you, 'is girls is better quality than the street whores, right pretty they are and young too." Blimpey took a quick sip of his drink. In the weak gaslight, he didn't notice that his companion had gone pale.

"Not that runnin' whores is what makes him such a bad lot," Blimpey chuckled, "there's plenty that do that. It's a way of life over in the East End. But most of 'em watch out for their girls, keep an eye on 'im and make sure they don't get knocked about by the customers. Old Jebidah Mantell even pays for his girls to go to the country once a year. Can you believe it? But nobody'd accuse Skegit of doin' something that decent. The man is different."

"Different 'ow?" Smythe hoped his voice sounded normal. Truth was, what he'd just heard had fair knocked the wind out of him. Of all the things he imagined, he'd never for a moment thought that Betsy could be a . . . no, he shut off that line of thought. He wasn't passin' judgment till he knew more.

"Got a mean streak, 'e does," Blimpey went on. "A customer cheats one of 'is girls and Skegit'll take it out of the man's hide. But that's not the worst."

Smythe's fingers tightened around his glass. "Go on," he ordered.

Blimpey drew closer and tossed a quick look about him to make sure no one was eavesdropping. "There's been a couple of his girls that 'ave disappeared. You know, gone. And it was always a girl who crossed him."

"Crossed 'im how? You mean like not givin' the bastard their earnin's?"

"Nah," said Blimpey, shaking his head. "Skegit would just beat 'em for that. These was girls that wanted out. One of the girls was named Molly Owens, she were only nineteen but she got tired of the trade, got 'erself a job at the Two Bulls out in Essex. Well, word 'as it that Raymond didn't much care for that. Molly was one of his best earners. Anyway, one night Molly didn't show up for work. No one ever seen 'er again."

"Cor blimey," Smythe exclaimed. "Are you sayin' he killed 'er! Just for wantin' out? Why? There's plenty of girls over in Skegit's part of town he could get to take 'er place."

"He's a mean bastard, that's why." Blimpey took another swallow. "And Skegit don't find it easy to replace girls." He smiled slyly. "Some of 'is customers 'ave, shall we say, rather peculiar tastes. He pays well, but a lot of the girls won't 'ave anything to do with 'im. Not if they 'ave any smarts."

Smythe took a drink. He was shocked all the way to his toes. This monster was someone who knew Betsy. Knew her well enough to try and drag her off.

"I've got to get goin'," Blimpey said. "Got me money?"

Smythe fumbled in his pockets, his shaking fingers grasping a roll of notes. He tossed the money on the counter. "Can you do another job for me?" he asked.

"Corse I can." The sight of all those pound notes had Blimpey's eyes shining. Smythe was a funny bloke. Tough as nails, yet there was something about him that made you think the man had a heart. Like if you was in trouble, bad trouble, you could go to him and he'd give you a hand. Mind you, the fact that the fellow weren't cheap didn't hurt none either. "What do you want?"

Smythe smiled coldly.

Blimpey drew back a little, as the expression on his companion's face sent a chill up his spine. "I mean, what else can I do for you?"

Smythe fingered another wad of notes. "I want you to find out Raymond Skegit's whereabouts."

"You mean, where 'e lives and such?" Blimpey wasn't so sure that was a good idea.

"That's right. Where 'e lives, where 'e drinks, and where 'e 'angs about."

"Smythe," Blimpey said hesitantly. "You don't want to do that. Skegit's a right bad 'un . . ."

"Let me worry about Skegit," Smythe ordered. "You just get me the information. I'll take care of the rest."

"I'm not so sure this is such a good idea," Mrs. Goodge hissed.

The staff was gathered round for their nightly meeting. But what made this one so different was that instead of being cozily ensconsed in the kitchen, they were sitting stiffly around the dining room table.

Constable Barnes and the inspector were there, too.

"I say," the inspector smiled. Really, he was so very touched that his staff was willing to try and help him. Not that he actually thought they could solve this case, but at least he felt less alone. Less like his reputation was going to be torn to shreds with no one to have faith in him. He hadn't been sure he ought to let them get involved. This was police business, after all. But what harm could it do? It wasn't as if they were actually going to find out anything useful. Their hearts were in the right place, and for the world he wouldn't make light of their generous offer. But really, it wasn't as if they were actually going to catch the killer. "It's jolly good of all of you to want to help me."

"But of course we want to help you, sir," Mrs. Jeffries said stoutly. "We know you're innocent."

"Of course you are," Constable Barnes interjected.

"We wouldn't work for somebody who killed people," Mrs. Goodge declared.

"Corse we knows you didn't kill those blokes," Wiggins said around a mouth full of Battenberg cake. Smythe and Betsy shook their heads in agreement.

Mrs. Jeffries glanced at the carriage clock on the sideboard. Delighted as she was to see how the staff had rallied around Inspector Witherspoon, time was getting on. Luty and Hatchet would be here soon.

"Constable Barnes," Mrs. Jeffries said firmly, "how is the official investigation proceeding?"

Barnes smiled cynically. "Let's put it this way, if the likes of Inspector Nivens was all that stood between us and bein' murdered in our beds, then we'd best all say our prayers. The man couldn't find a bun in a bake shop, let alone solve a murder. Take today. Here we was questionin' the other partners, standing right there in the same office with Grady Whitelaw and Justin Vincent and all that Nivens could think to ask was did the victims have any enemies?" He shook his head in disgust. "Of course the men had enemies! They're dead, aren't they?"

"You mean he didn't ask about the notes pinned to the victims' chests?" Mrs. Jeffries asked. Surely Barnes was exaggerating. Surely.

But he wasn't. "Didn't say a thing about them. Every time I tried to get a few words in, askin' something useful like, Nivens would interrupt."

Witherspoon clucked his tongue. "Now, Barnes, we mustn't be too hard on Inspector Nivens. He's never done a murder before. Perhaps he's unsure of himself, lacks confidence, so to speak."

"He's got enough confidence for ten men," Barnes shot back. "What he lacks is thinking ability! He doesn't question any of the servants, he pretends the clerks and the staff at the victims' office are deaf, dumb, and blind, and he's so scared of offendin' someone important, he's going to let a murderer go free." Barnes suddenly realized he was shouting. He looked at the startled faces around the table and blushed. "Pardon me, I didn't mean to yell like that. It's just it makes my blood boil to see him making a right old muddle of this case."

Mrs. Jeffries understood precisely what the constable meant. "What do you think the notes mean?"

Barnes shrugged. "I don't rightly know, I tried asking Hornsley's staff if they had any notions about what V-E-N-I might mean. I asked Frampton's clerks the same thing about V-I-D-I, but no one had any idea."

"Maybe Veni has somethin' to do with Venice," Wiggins suggested. "Maybe that's where the killer first met Mr. Hornsley."

"That's a most interesting thought, Wiggins," said the inspector, beaming at the footman. "Perhaps we should find out if Hornsley ever visited Venice."

"I'll see to it tomorrow," Barnes said. "Wonder what VIDI could mean?"

Mrs. Jeffries suddenly thought of something to keep Wiggins occupied. "Why don't we let Wiggins have a go at figuring that out?" She turned to him and asked, "Do you think you could make your way to Mudies if I put you in a hansom tomorrow?"

"I could do it," Wiggins said excitedly. "But would they let me 'ave a go at their books?" Mudies was a n excellent lending library. But he wasn't sure if they'd even let him in the door, let alone touch their precious books.

"I'll send a note along to Mr. Masters, the director," Mrs. Jeffries said confidently. "I'm sure he won't mind if you do some research on the inspector's behalf."

Wiggins's happy grin faded as he realized the enormity of the task he'd been given. "Uh, Mrs. Jeffries, what am I supposed to find out?"

"Anything you can think of which will give us some clue as to what those notes mean." She smiled confidently. "You're a smart lad. Try the atlas first." She didn't really expect Wiggins to come up with anything, but it would give him something to do and, more important, it would keep him out of Mrs. Goodge's way.

"I say, Barnes," asked Witherspoon, "did you find out anything else?"

Barnes grinned. "Despite Nivens's best efforts to the contrary, we did learn a few interestin' bits."

He told them about the remainder of the interview with Justin Vincent and Grady Whitelaw. "We got the most important information right at the end of the interview." He took a quick sip of tea. "Grady Whitelaw practically accused Stuart Frampton of murderin' his own father. Seems that now that the old man is gone, the boy gets it all."

"Gracious," Witherspoon exclaimed. "Did he really? But what about the Hornsley murder? Why would Stuart Frampton want Peter Hornsley dead?"

"That's what I wondered. But Nivens seemed to think there could be a conspiracy between Nyles Hornsley and Frampton. Each of them had a good reason to want the victims dead. Nyles so that he could marry Madeline Wynn and get his hands on the money Peter controlled, and Stuart for just about the same reason—money."

"Did either Vincent or Whitelaw have alibis for the time of the murder?" Mrs. Jeffries asked. She still thought the murders had something to do with the firm, not with the personal circumstances of the victims.

"For the Frampton killing, Whitelaw claims he was stuck in traffic, which is possible, I suppose. A dray overturned on Oxford Street and things come to a standstill for a long while. But considerin' that Frampton was killed in Hyde Park, the killer could easily have known about the traffic situation and used it to his advantage. The carriages and hansoms was backed up all the way to Hyde Park Corner."

"Has anyone asked his fiancée what time he arrived?" Betsy asked.

Barnes nodded. "I had one of the lads nip over. Miss Rawlings-Rand confirms that Whitelaw arrived at her house a little after eight."

"What about for the Hornsley murder?" Witherspoon asked.

"Whitelaw claims he was home by himself. Said he went straight home at half past five last Friday night. But we can't confirm that alibi. It was the servants' day out."

"What about Vincent?" Smythe said.

"He was at home both nights," Barnes replied. "His servants confirmed it. They've only been with him for a few months, so I don't think any of them would lie on his behalf. Seems that Vincent eats an early meal and then goes into his study to work."

"That's true," Betsy said eagerly. She blushed as everyone looked at her. "I mean, I talked to one of Vincent's maids today and she says that's what he does every night. Eats early and then goes into work."

"How very clever of you, Betsy," said Witherspoon, genuinely impressed. "Gracious, I'd no idea you could be so very resourceful."

"Thank you, sir."

"Perhaps one day we'll have female detectives at Scotland Yard," the inspector chuckled, as though the very idea were so absurd it was amusing.

Mrs. Jeffries shot him a disapproving glance, but he didn't see it. She rather thought women as detectives was an excellent idea. And women doctors, solicitors, bankers, and barristers, too. In short, the world would probably be a much better place if women had equal say in how the world was run. But right now was not the time to have a debate about a woman's place in society. "Did the maid tell you anything else?" she asked Betsy.

"Not much, just that he's a good employer, treats the servants decently, and doesn't work them like dogs." Betsy told them about the rest of her encounter with Justin Vincent's housemaid. She took care to give them all the details, no matter how unimportant they seemed. As Mrs. Jeffries always said, sometimes it was the details that gave you the last little bit needed to solve the case. But as soon as she'd finished, an awkward silence fell. The staff simply wasn't used to discussing their murders with Inspector Witherspoon and Constable Barnes.

The quiet was finally broken by Smythe, who said, "Well, I 'ad a bit of luck today. I tracked down one of Whitelaw's clerks at a pub on Morgan Street." He didn't add that he'd tracked the poor man and crossed his palm with silver to get his information. "Accordin' to 'im, now that the other two partners is dead, Whitelaw gets complete control of the business. Too bad Whitelaw doesn't have any real money, because if he did, he could not only control the firm, he could own it, too."

"He'll have real money soon," Mrs. Goodge interrupted. "Come June, he'll be marrying Fiona Rawlings-Rand."

"Rich is she?" The coachman looked amused.

"As sin. And once she's married to Whitelaw, that'll give him enough money to buy anything he wants."

"I say, Mrs. Goodge," Witherspoon stared at his cook in amazement. Like the rest of the household, he was aware that the cook rarely left her kitchen. "How did you come across that bit of information?"

Mrs. Goodge shrugged modestly. "Oh, it's nothin', really. Just a bit of gossip I picked up." She didn't add that she'd sent word to her cousin's husband's sister who worked in the house down the road from Fiona Rawlings-Rand. There were simply some things she didn't share with anyone.

"So Whitelaw stands to benefit the most from the death of his partners," Constable-Barnes mused. "Not only will he have control of the company, but now he's got the money to buy it as well. And being stuck in traffic isn't much of an alibi, if you ask me."

"But Whitelaw has been friends with the victims since they was in school," Mrs. Goodge protested. Despite her firsthand exposure to the realities of murder, there was still a sentimental streak in her makeup. "I can't believe he'd kill his lifelong friends."

"And why wait till now?" Wiggins added.

"Do you know when he got engaged?" Mrs. Jeffries asked the cook. Unlike Mrs. Goodge, she wasn't in the least sentimental. She'd seen plenty of cases where friends who had known one another all their lives suddenly decided the world would be a better place if one of them weren't in it any longer.

"He got engaged at a party over Christmas," Mrs. Goodge continued eagerly. "But he and Fiona Rawlings-Rand have had an understanding for over a year. They had to wait to announce their engagement until the mourning period for her mother had passed. The poor woman died of consumption year before last."

"So Whitelaw couldn't count on havin' any cash until just a few months ago," Smythe muttered. "Women 'ave been known to change their minds before they get that ring on their fingers."

Betsy snorted delicately. "Men change their minds too, you know."

"I know that, Betsy," Smythe said patiently. "I wasn't castin' stones at females. I was just statin' a fact."

Mrs. Jeffries interrupted. "What are you thinking, Smythe?"

He shrugged his powerful shoulders. "Give Whitelaw a month or so to make 'is plans and a month or so to get his disguise. Seems to me the timing's just right."

Smythe tried not to watch Betsy too closely as they took their seats around the kitchen table. Since he'd come in this evenin', he knew he'd been watchin' her like a fox stalking a nice, plump chicken, but he couldn't help it. Blimpey's information had stunned him.

"Have I got a spot on my face?" Betsy demanded irritably. "You've been starin' at me since you come in this evening."

He grinned sheepishly. "Sorry, didn't mean to. I've got a lot on my mind, that's all."

"Thank goodness that's over," Mrs. Goodge sighed with relish and heaved her ample bulk into her favorite chair. "Right nerve-wrackin', havin' to talk in front of the inspector and Constable Barnes."

"Gives me butterflies in my stomach," Betsy agreed. "Not that the inspector weren't nice about it, but I was scared to death every time one of us opened our mouth."

"Do you think we gave too much away?" Wiggins asked. "I mean, do you think he's goin' to guess this isn't our first investigation?"

That was the question on everyone's mind.

Mrs. Jeffries shrugged slightly. "I don't know. I hope not. But whether we've given the game away or not doesn't matter. We had no choice in the matter."

From the back door they heard a sharp knock and then, a moment later, Luty's voice. "Come on, Hatchet, we ain't got all night. It's gittin' late and I've got to pump that danged banker tomorrow morning."

"Good, Luty and Hatchet are here." Mrs. Goodge poured two cups of tea to have ready.

"Evenin', everyone," Luty cried as she came into the room. She was dressed in a bright red satin dress festooned with ruffles, lace, and sequins. Bright red and black feathers decorated her hat, and she carried a black fur muff tucked under her arm. "Hatchet and I just got back from havin' supper at Lord Amsley's and he knows everything that goes on in the City! I'm burstin' to tell you what I've learned."

"Sit down and have some tea," Mrs. Jeffries smiled. She was glad that neither Luty nor Hatchet had taken offense at being excluded from the meeting with Barnes and Witherspoon, but it had been necessary. It was one thing for Witherspoon to think his staff was devoted enough to try and help him, but Luty and Hatchet were another matter indeed.

"Good evening, everyone," Hatchet said formally as he took his seat. He removed his elegant top hat and placed it carefully on the chair beside him. "I hope everything is in good order."

"We didn't give the game away, if that's what you're worried about," Smythe said. "Leastways, I don't think we did."

Mrs. Goodge poured the tea.

As soon as Luty and Hatchet had a cup in front of them, Mrs. Jeffries said, "Do tell us all your news."

"I don't know if Hatchet has any news," said Luty as she shot her butler a disgusted frown. "He's bein' as tight-lipped as a lawyer at a wake. But I found out plenty." She tossed her muff onto the table.

Everyone jumped back.

"Don't worry," Luty laughed. "It ain't in there. Hatchet made me leave my peacemaker at home tonight."

As Luty's muff generally had in it a loaded Colt .45, the staff had good reason to be cautious when she started tossing it about the room.

"I didn't think it appropriate to take firearms to supper with a distinguished man like Lord Amsley," Hatchet explained. "It simply isn't done. Furthermore, I don't know why Madam persists in carrying that weapon. Perhaps you'll be good enough to help me prevail upon her to lock the wretched thing in a cupboard. London is hardly the Wild West."

"No, it's a lot more dangerous," Luty shot back. She waved her hand impatiently. "Anyways, we ain't got time for this. These folks is waiting to hear what I've found out. You'll never guess who don't have an alibi for the time of either murder." She paused and waited. "Damon Hilliard. We had us a nice little chat with the night porter at his building. Seems Mr. Hilliard told the police he was at his office working on both nights, but the porter told us he'd seen the man sneakin' out the back door."

"The porter also said that Mr. Hilliard often did that," Hatchet put in. "So I'm not certain we ought to put much store by the information."

"Where does Hilliard go?" Betsy asked. "I mean, why sneak about like that?"

Hatchet shrugged. "I don't know, but I have some sources working on the problem."

"You mean you bribed a street lad to follow Hilliard," Luty corrected. "But that's okay, I've crossed a few palms with silver myself to get information I wanted."

"I rarely need to resort to bribery, as you call it," Hatchet sniffed. "Generally, my subtle but clever questioning elicits all the information I need."

Luty snorted.

Ignoring her, Hatchet continued, "Today, for instance. By cleverly questioning some of my sources in the City, I learned a great deal about the firm of Hornsley, Frampton, and Whitelaw."

Mrs. Jeffries nodded in approval. Now they might be getting somewhere. "Go on," she urged.

"Well," he learned forward eagerly. "It seems the firm is one of the most successful privately held companies in the City. In the words of my informant, it's a veritable moneymaker and has been for years."

"If they were makin' so much money," Smythe asked, "why did they let Vincent buy in?"

Hatchet smiled. "They wanted to expand. The plan was to open branch offices in Birmingham and Manchester. Even though the company made plenty of money, that kind of growth is expensive. By letting Vincent in, they acquired the capital they needed without depleting their own cash reserves. Vincent approached them right after Christmas. He'd made investments in a number of other businesses and was looking for more. Hornsley, Frampton, and Whitelaw must have seemed like an excellent opportunity."

"So Vincent approached them?" Mrs. Jeffries queried.

"Actually," Hatchet hesitated, "my source wasn't sure on that point, so I don't know."

"Well, I do," Luty said. "That's what I found out from Lord Amsley. It weren't Vincent that approached the company. It was Hornsley that come to Vincent. Vincent was actually thinking of buying into Hilliard's firm. Hornsley, who it appears bribed one of Hilliard's clerks into feeding him information, found out about Vincent and cornered him one night a while back at his club."

"But why did he invest 'is money there if 'e was fixin' to go with this Hilliard fellow?" Wiggins asked.

"Probably because he got a look at both their books," Luty replied. "Like Hatchet said, Hornsley, Frampton, and Whitelaw was pretty successful. From what Elliot told me . . ."

"Elliot?" Mrs. Goodge interrupted. "Who's he?"

"She means Lord Amsley," Hatchet explained.

"Quit interruptin'," Luty demanded, "or I'll never get this story told. Like I was sayin', Vincent got a look at both companies' books. One firm's loaded with enough money to buy half the Queen's diamonds and the other's just hangin' on. Which would you invest in?"

"Yes, I see," Mrs. Jeffries said. "So, of course, Hilliard has even more reason to hate Hornsley. He deprived him of an investor."

Luty nodded. "Looks like it. Hilliard's got no alibi and lots of reason. Seems to me we should keep an eye on him."

"We will," Mrs. Jeffries agreed. She filed all the information in the back of her mind. It was one more piece of the puzzle, but experience had taught her that trying to put the pieces together too early was pointless. "It's getting late, though, so we'd better tell you what we learned today."

For the next half hour they told Luty and Hatchet every little detail, including the information Barnes had shared with them about the police end of the investigation.

"So what do we do now?" Luty asked. "Seems to me we don't know which rock to look under this time. Could be the killer is someone connected with the victims' personal lives or it could have something to do with the firm itself. That's a lot of territory to cover."

"Oh, I forgot to tell you," Betsy interrupted.

"Forgot what?" Mrs. Jeffries asked.

"Madeline Wynn. I found out something about her yesterday. She had a right screamin' match with Peter Hornsley on the afternoon he died. Her maid told me Hornsley came to her house and upset her something fierce."

"What'd 'e do?" Wiggins asked curiously.

"The maid didn't know. They had the door closed while they was talkin', but all of a sudden she heard Madeline screamin' at Hornsley to get out. Said if he didn't leave them alone, she'd kill him."

Mrs. Goodge frowned at the maid. "How could you forget to tell us something that important?"

Betsy felt her cheeks turning red. Everyone was staring at her. She could see the same question in all their eyes. She could hardly admit that she'd been so upset by seeing Raymond Skegit again that she hadn't been able to remember her own name, let alone properly pay attention to her detecting. "I, uh . . ."

"Don't be so 'ard on the lass," Smythe interrupted. "You can't fault her for not sayin' anything. She were probably a bit rattled after she come across me havin' a bit of a dust-up with a bloke on Bernabe Street." He broke off and grinned. "It's me you ought to be yellin' at. I took exception to the way a fellow was beatin' 'is poor 'orse. Betsy came 'round the corner just as things was gettin' really nasty."

"You got in a fight?" Wiggins exclaimed.

"Not really, but I would 'ave if Betsy 'adn't been there to stop me." He gave her a quick glance. "She stopped me from whalin' the tar out of the bloke. Never could abide a man who mistreated 'orses."

Mrs. Jeffries gazed at the two of them curiously. She suspected they were both lying. Betsy was staring at her lap and Smythe's voice, for all its bravado, sounded as hollow as a tin drum.

But why? What had really happened yesterday afternoon?

"Well, there's no harm done then," she said calmly. "I'm glad Betsy was able to prevent you from harming someone, even a horsebeater. You're right, of course, it's quite understandable that Betsy would be upset by such an incident. We'd all be upset if you were injured while indulging in fisticuffs."

Betsy finally looked up. She smiled gratefully at the coachman and then turned to Mrs. Jeffries. "Should I keep on doggin' Madeline Wynn? I mean, after everything we've learned today, do you think it's worth pursuing?"

"Everything is worth pursuing," Mrs. Jeffries said firmly. "Despite the fact that the evidence seems to be pointing toward the business as being the motive for these murders, we don't really know what the truth is yet. We mustn't let ourselves be sidetracked."

"What do you suggest we do now?" Hatchet asked.

"I think Betsy ought to continue investigating Miss Wynn," she said, turning to the maid. "Find out if she's had any unusual meetings in the last month."

Puzzled, Betsy frowned. "What do you mean?"

"I mean, has Madeline Wynn had any dealings with ruffians or unsavory persons in the last month."

"You think she might 'ave 'ired someone to kill Hornsley?" Smythe said.

"I think it's possible."

"But why would she want to kill Frampton, then?" Wiggins asked. "I could see she and Hornsley didn't get on . . ."

"We don't know that she killed anyone," Mrs. Goodge interrupted. "Mrs. Jeffries is just sayin' we ought to investigate every possibility, that's all." She looked at the housekeeper. "You want me to keep diggin'?"

"If you wouldn't mind," Mrs. Jeffries replied. "We really must have more information. Smythe, would you keep on with Grady Whitelaw? We mustn't lose sight of the fact that, so far, Whitelaw stands to gain the most from the death of his partners."

"What do you want us to do?" Luty asked, gesturing at herself and her butler.

"Unless you've a better idea," Mrs. Jeffries said slowly, "I think you ought to concentrate on Stuart Frampton's alibi and on Damon Hilliard."

"What about Nyles Hornsley?" Hatchet asked. "Shouldn't I try and verify his alibi?"

"If you would, please." She made a face. "I don't like giving Inspector Nivens credit, but his idea of a conspiracy between Frampton and Hornsley to rid themselves of unwanted relatives isn't as farfetched as one would think."

"The thought of Nivens bein' right sticks in my craw," Smythe muttered.

"I expect we'd best get goin',' then," Luty said. She stood up as did Hatchet. "We'll pop in tomorrow evenin' with a full report."

As soon as they'd left, Betsy started to help Mrs. Goodge clear the tea things off the table.

"I'll take care of the clearin' up," Mrs. Jeffries said firmly.

"Are you sure?" Mrs. Goodge asked.

"Positive. I'm not the least tired. My mind is so active I don't think I could sleep yet."

"All right. Good night, then," said Mrs. Goodge, nodding gratefully, and she shuffled off toward the back stairs.

"I'll just lock up," Betsy murmured.

"No, I can do that," Mrs. Jeffries smiled kindly. "You go on up to bed. You look exhausted, Betsy. Go get some rest."

The girl smiled. "Thank you, Mrs. Jeffries. I am tired."

Betsy found Smythe waiting for her on the first floor landing. He was leaning against the staircase, with his arms crossed over his chest.

Suddenly shy, she looked everywhere but at him.

"Betsy," he said softly, "I'd like to talk to ya."

"I'm tired, Smythe." She couldn't face talking to him tonight. "But thanks for what you did for me. Lettin' on that it was your fault I forgot to tell them about Madeline Wynn. That was right decent of you."

He didn't say anything for a moment. Finally, he said, "It's all right, Betsy. I didn't mind. We're friends. There ain't nothin' I wouldn't do for you."

# CHAPTER 8

Mrs. Jeffries gathered the teapot and the cups onto the tray. She carried them over to the sink and laid them on the drain board. They could wait until tomorrow; tonight she didn't want to be distracted by washing them up. She went back to her chair, sat down, and rested her chin in her hands.

This case wasn't going at all well. Even with Constable Barnes feeding them information about the official investigation, she still felt as though they were muddling through in the dark. Like the good constable, she had no faith that Inspector Nivens would catch the real killer.

Think, Hepzibah, she told herself, think. There are bound to be some answers somewhere. But where? What did the notes pinned to the victims mean? Were they nonsense words that had meaning only to the killer? Or were they a genuine clue? What about the weapon? A schoolhouse tie. Did that have any significance? She frowned, suddenly annoyed with herself. Of course, it was so obvious. Why hadn't she suggested it to Constable Barnes? Someone really should find out which school the victims had attended. Then she frowned again, annoyed at herself for grasping at straws. The school the victims had gone to didn't matter. Hornsley and Frampton were middle-aged men; if their killer was someone from their school days, he would hardly have waited thirty years to kill his victims. She sighed. Dr. Bosworth was probably right. The murderer used an old school tie because it was the sort of object that was easily overlooked. Once gone from the old box it was kept in, or the bottom of a broom cupboard, no one even noticed when it was gone.

"Hepzibah." A soft voice whispered her name.

Mrs. Jeffries jumped and whirled around to see Lady Cannonberry standing in the doorway. "Gracious, you gave me a start."

"I'm sorry, I didn't mean to frighten you," Ruth apologized. "I knocked, you see, and then the back door was unlocked, so I thought I'd pop in and see if you were still up. May I come in?"

Mrs. Jeffries summoned a weak smile. She really would have liked to have continued her solitary thinking, but she didn't want to hurt Ruth's feelings. "Of course you can, but I'm afraid I'm the only one still up."

"That's all right," Ruth said, hurrying over to the table and slipping into a chair next to the housekeeper. "I can't stay long. But I did want to give you my report."

"Report? Oh, yes, yes, of course, your report. Please, go right ahead." Mrs. Jeffries was suddenly so tired she almost yawned. And she was irritated, too. If Lady Cannonberry hadn't interrupted her, she was certain she could have put her finger on what it was about this case that she was missing. Still, one couldn't be rude.

"You'll be very pleased with me," Ruth smiled happily. "I've found out quite a bit. Now, don't worry, I was most discreet."

"I'm sure you were."

"But I must say, I'm appalled, Hepzibah, absolutely appalled that some monster is using Gerald's good name to commit these terrible crimes."

"Yes, we feel the same way," Mrs. Jeffries murmured. She hoped Ruth would be brief and to the point.

"Poor Gerald must be at his wit's end," she said, clucking her tongue sympathetically.

Mrs. Jeffries knew she was in for it. Ruth was not going to be brief. She wondered if she dare ask her to leave and come back tomorrow.

"But as I said," Ruth continued without drawing a breath, "I've found out quite a bit. I've been dying to pop over and tell you, but some of my late husband's relatives came by for a visit and I've been entertaining them. Goodness, that can be such a trial. It's not as if they liked me all that much in the first place. I rather get the feeling that my sister-in-law resents the fact that I'm not in mourning anymore. Well, really, it has been three years. How long is one expected to wear black?"

"How very tiresome for you," Mrs. Jeffries muttered. She was barely listening.

"It hasn't been too terribly awful," Ruth shrugged. "As relatives go, they're not too bad. But they do eat up one's time. This is the first chance I've had to slip out and see you." She laughed. "Now, I suppose I ought to get on with my report. Otherwise, we'll be here all night."

Mrs. Jeffries forced another weak smile. She was suddenly dead tired. But it was a good kind of exhaustion, the kind that let her mind wander aimlessly and, in that state, make all sorts of interesting connections. Why was the killer masquerading as Witherspoon? Was he really out to get the inspector arrested for murder? Could it be a vengeful relative from one of their past cases? Or was the answer so much simpler? Could it be, as Smythe suggested, only a way of gaining access to the victims? Or was there another, more complex reason they hadn't even thought of yet?

"A lot of people don't like Marisole Pulman," Ruth chattered, "but I've always been rather fond of her. She knows ever so much about people, too. She knew all about Peter Hornsley."

Peter Hornsley. The name penetrated Mrs. Jeffries's thoughts. She shook herself slightly; she really must listen to what her guest was saying.

"He was a notorious womanizer," Ruth said earnestly. "It's a wonder his poor wife didn't have a nervous fit the way the man carried on."

Mrs. Jeffries sighed inwardly. This was the same old territory. Ruth hadn't discovered anything new. Perhaps it wouldn't be so terribly awful if she didn't listen all that carefully. "How dreadful," she murmured.

"Mind you," Ruth said, "I don't think womanizing is any reason to be murdered. If that were the case, half the married men in London would be in their graves."

"Yes, I expect so," Mrs. Jeffries agreed. Had Stuart Frampton and Nyles Hornsley entered into a conspiracy to rid themselves of unwanted relatives? No, she didn't believe that. In the first place, conspiracies had a way of coming apart, and in the second, why go through such an elaborate charade of pretending to be a Scotland Yard detective? However, she wasn't going to ignore anything.

"And George Frampton was quite stingy," Ruth continued. "His second wife is always complaining about the paltry allowance he gives her, but just between you and me and the lamppost, Rosalind Frampton probably married George for his money. Not that she gets much. According to what I heard, all she's going to end up with is the house and a yearly allowance. Still, it'll probably be more than what she had before. I mean, financially she'll be better off with her husband dead than alive.

Oh dear, that sounded quite crass. I didn't mean it the way it came out . . ."

"Don't worry, Ruth," Mrs. Jeffries said. "I know what you meant. What else have you found out?"

"Well, Grady Whitelaw, the third partner, is coming into packets of money after he marries Fiona Rawlings-Rand," said Ruth, shaking her head. "I don't see why she wants to marry him. He's ages older than she and not precisely what I would call a 'good catch.' But then again, perhaps she really loves him."

Mrs. Jeffries almost groaned. She completely stopped listening. Ruth hadn't learned anything they didn't already know.

"Of course all three of the men went to school together," Ruth continued eagerly, totally oblivious to the fact that her audience had completely tuned her out. "Marisole knew all about that too. Her husband was at the same school."

Mrs. Jeffries made a mental note to drop a few hints to Constable Barnes tomorrow. She was more and more convinced these murders had happened because of the business. After all, they'd found out that Damon Hilliard's alibi was worthless. Surely Hilliard wasn't the only one who hated the firm of Hornsley, Frampton, and Whitelaw. And what about Whitelaw? It seemed to Mrs. Jeffries that the man stood to gain an inordinate amount of money and power with the deaths of his partners. Once he married, he could not only finance any expansion, he could probably afford to buy the late partner's shares from their estates.

"It was one of those awful public schools the British are so proud of," Ruth sneered. "Mind you, they did have to hush up that awful scandal about that boy's hand getting so badly burned. Poor child, Marisole's husband said it ruined the lad's life. The other boys lied, you see, so the Osbornes had to take their son out of school."

Mrs. Jeffries nodded vaguely. Sometimes she forgot that Lady Cannonberry, for all her aristocratic trappings, was really quite a radical. Not that she faulted her for her political opinions, of course. She was in sympathy with many of them herself. "Scandal," she repeated vaguely.

"Oh, it was years ago," Ruth waved a hand dismissively. "And the family left the country after it happened. I believe Marisole said they went to Australia or Canada or . . ." she hesitated, trying to remember. "Some such place like that. Anyway, it doesn't matter now. But I did find out there's some sort of scandal attached to Rosalind Frampton. Should I follow that line of inquiry?"

Mrs. Jeffries suspected she knew precisely what the scandal was, too. And they already knew all about it. Constable Barnes had told them. Rosalind Frampton had been an actress before her marriage. Hardly earthshaking, but right now, Mrs. Jeffries would agree to anything to have a bit of peace and quiet.

"That's a wonderful idea," she said.

"Oh good," Ruth beamed with pleasure. "I do so want to help Gerald. I'm so looking forward to going to Edwina Carrington's April ball with him. I want to make sure he enjoys himself. He's such a very good man. He deserves some pleasure in life."

Her statement made Mrs. Jeffries feel small enough to crawl in a tea tin. She ought to be ashamed of herself. She had no right to patronize Ruth. Lady Cannonberry was just as concerned about Inspector Witherspoon as they were and she was doing her best to help.

"Well." Ruth suddenly stood up. "I believe that's about it, then. Tomorrow I'll get out and about and see what I can learn about Rosalind Frampton. Perhaps I'll pop round tomorrow evening, if that's all right."

"Uh, that'll be fine." Mrs. Jeffries got up as well. "Do come round as soon as you hear anything." Guilt-stricken because she hadn't really heard a word that Ruth had said, she tried to make amends. "And do see what else you can learn. Remember, anything you pick up, no matter how insignificant it seems, could be the clue that solves the case."

Ruth smiled happily, delighted to be of service. "Oh yes, I'll remember and I'll keep my ears open. My husband's relatives are leaving tomorrow. I'll have plenty of time to 'go on the hunt,' as they say."


"I say, Mrs. Jeffries, these eggs are excellent this morning. Mrs. Goodge has really outdone herself." The inspector shoved the last bite of coddled eggs into his mouth and picked up his napkin.

Mrs. Jeffries, who was serving breakfast this morning because Betsy and the others had already gone out, pushed the toast rack closer to his plate. "Yes, she has, sir. Do have more toast. Mrs. Goodge's bread is particularly good today, too."

"Thank you, I believe I will." He reached for what was his third piece.

He cleared his throat. He had something important to tell his house-keeper, something he'd thought about for hours last night. He wanted to say it just right. "I must say," he began, "I'm quite amazed by all of you."

"Amazed, sir?" Mrs. Jeffries said cautiously.

He smeared butter and marmalade on the toasted bread. "I don't suppose 'amazed' is really the right word. I should have said I'm touched by how devoted the staff is to me. Gracious, to think they're actually out there in the City, trying to help me clear my name! It's so very kind of all of you." Drat, he thought, why had his speech sounded so much better in his head than it did when he said it aloud.

"We're not being kind, sir." Mrs. Jeffries relaxed. "We're doing for you only what we are sure you would do for us. You are, after all, both an exceptional employer and an exceptional policeman."

Witherspoon smiled proudly. "Well, er, I'm glad you think so. But there is one thing I must say . . ." He paused and nibbled on his toast.

Mrs. Jeffries waited patiently. She was relieved he wasn't going to go on about how good the staff was at snooping. That was hitting a bit too close to home. She wasn't sure how much longer she could convince him and Barnes that the information the staff picked up was just luck and not experience. "And what's that, sir?" she prompted.

He swallowed and took a deep breath. "Whatever happens, I want the staff to know that I'm proud of them and that I know they've done their best."

She stared at him, not sure she understood exactly what he was trying to tell her.

"But sometimes, despite our best efforts," he continued, "the wrong thing happens and justice is not served. But whatever happens, I'll never forget how my household rallied round me and tried to help."

As she listened to him, that sense of foreboding she'd been plagued with since the start of the case came back to her with a vengeance. Her stomach clenched and a shiver crawled up her spine. She didn't like the tone he used. She didn't like it at all. It was almost as if he was resigned to the worst.

"I assure you, sir, the staff has the utmost confidence in you. The only thing that's going to happen is that we're going to find the real perpetrator of these awful crimes."

He stared at her for a long moment. "Do you really think so?"

There was a note of desperation in his voice. A note that told Mrs.

Jeffries quite clearly that he was dreadfully worried. "Of course I think so, sir. But it would be most helpful if you could remember exactly where you walked on the nights of the murders," she pleaded. "Surely someone must have seen you."

Witherspoon threw his hands up. "But that's just it, I've told Nivens where I was." He looked away, his gaze darting about the dining room as though he'd never seen it before. "But you know, I don't think the chap believes me. As for someone seeing me, well, there's a good explanation for why no one did. Both evenings were wretched. There weren't many people out and about in the wet and the fog."

Mrs. Jeffries knew he was lying, and for the life of her she couldn't understand why. But she knew he wasn't a murderer.

"I'm sure Nivens understands that, sir."

"I don't think so, Mrs. Jeffries," he said, shaking his head. "I have an awful feeling about this case. I'm not ashamed to admit I'm worried. Very worried, indeed."

"That's nonsense, sir," she said bluntly. "You've done nothing wrong. In the end, we'll find the real killer. Now, sir, give me your professional opinion. Why do you think these crimes are being committed?"

He appeared surprised by her sudden change of subject; then he thought about it for a moment and relaxed against the back of his chair. "Well, I've come to the conclusion it has something to do with the firm."

"Yes, I think so too."

"Two partners isn't a coincidence," he continued. "It's the only real connection between the victims. Therefore, I've come to the conclusion it's the firm itself which is under attack."

"But the victims have known each other since their school days," Mrs. Jeffries ventured. She agreed with the inspector, but she didn't want to leave any avenue of inquiry unexplored. "Surely there could be a connection from the past we don't know about."

He waved his hand in the air dismissively. "I don't think so. Among the upper classes in Britain, half of London went to school together. So I don't think we can look for any motives from the past. Besides, the victims may have known each other for years, but I haven't seen any evidence that they were genuinely fond of one another. According to what Barnes said, there was a conspicuous absence of grief about the company when Hornsley died. Goodness, they didn't even shut the place for the man's funeral."

"Whitelaw isn't going to close it for Frampton's funeral either," she murmured. She'd picked up that little tidbit from Barnes last night.

"Ah, yes, Whitelaw," Witherspoon mused. "He does quite well out of his partners' deaths, doesn't he?"

"So it would seem, sir." She was glad the inspector agreed with her assessment of the situation. The murders probably were centered on the company. All the evidence seemed to point that way. But what if they were wrong? What if it were a conspiracy? What if the killings had nothing to do with the people murdered but were actually just arbitrary, and the murderer's true purpose was to ruin Gerald Witherspoon? The thought depressed her. "Perhaps we ought to keep a close eye on Mr. Whitelaw."

"Yes, I certainly hope Barnes is able to do so without Nivens's interference. I should never forgive myself if that man was murdered as well."

"But he may be the killer, sir."

"And he might not be," Witherspoon replied.

Mrs. Jeffries said nothing. She was suddenly terribly unsure of herself. She'd no idea what to do next, where to look for answers, or even what to look for!

Witherspoon reached for the last piece of toast. "Appearances aren't always as they seem, Mrs. Jeffries. Whitelaw may be our most likely suspect, but then again, I don't believe that anyone is guilty until I've found evidence proving beyond a shadow of a doubt that they are."

They discussed the case for another half hour; then the inspector decided to he'd take Fred and go for a walk.

Mrs. Jeffries gathered up the breakfast things on a tray and took them down to the kitchen. Wiggins, his face creased in intense concentration, was sitting at the far end of the breakfast table. There was an open notebook in front of him and he had a pencil in his hand.

Mrs. Goodge was bustling about like a general readying troops for battle. A tray of buns was on the counter, a plate of biscuits next to them, and the kettle was whistling furiously.

"Morning, Mrs. Jeffries," the cook said cheerfully, as she flipped a clean linen over the still warm buns. "Did the inspector enjoy his breakfast?"

"He did indeed," Mrs. Jeffries replied. She put the tray of dishes on the drainboard. "What are you doing, Wiggins?"

"Writin'," he replied. "I thought I'd try me hand at writin' a novel.

Seems to me it's dead easy. All you got to do is make up some tragic tale and put in lots of bits to make people cry their eyes out."

"I think there is more to it than that," Mrs. Jeffries said carefully. She never liked to discourage people.

"Corse there is," Wiggins agreed, "but it's not like I've got anything else to do right now. Mudies don't open till half past nine. Besides, all it takes to write a book is practice."

She started to point out that it probably took more than just practice, but as he was already depressed about having a sprained ankle and doing nothing but going to lending libraries, she decided to say nothing. Besides, one never knew. Wiggins might be a literary genius. "I think writing a novel is a wonderful idea. You scribble away now, and then when we've time, after this case is over, you can read us what you've written."

From behind her she heard Mrs. Goodge snort. But when she turned to look at the cook, she saw nothing but bland innocence on her broad face.

Mrs. Goodge caught her eye. "Mrs. Jeffries," she asked, "would you help me write a letter this afternoon?"

"Certainly," Mrs. Jeffries replied.

"I can 'elp you," Wiggins volunteered.

"No, no," Mrs. Goodge said quickly. "Thanks all the same, Wiggins, but this is a special letter. It's for a lord." She smiled at the housekeeper. "I've decided not to accept Lord Gurney's offer of a position."

"I'm so glad, Mrs. Goodge," Mrs. Jeffries said earnestly. She smiled. "I was so afraid you were going to leave us, and, frankly, it wouldn't be the same here without you."

Pleased, Mrs. Goodge's cheeks turned a bright pink. Behind her spectacles, her eyes misted. "Well, that's what I thought, too. Lord Gurney is in the past. This is my future. Truth is, Mrs. Jeffries, after gettin' used to the way we do things here, I don't think I'd much care to go back to a 'proper' household. Besides, Lord Gurney isn't a police detective. There'd be no murders at his house."

Barnes wasn't sure if he was irritated or amused. Inspector Nivens was actin' like a lovesick cow. He watched Nivens's mouth gape as the lovely young woman came farther into the drawing room.

She was tall, dark-haired, and slender with the most perfect complexion Barnes had ever seen. Her nose was small and straight, her eyes a deep blue, and her mouth was full and beautifully shaped. Cor, she was a looker all right, but that didn't excuse Nivens from actin' like a fool.

"I'm sorry to keep you waiting," Madeline Wynn said coolly, "but I wasn't ready to receive visitors."

"That's quite all right," Nivens said quickly. He took a step toward her and stumbled over a footstool. "Oh dear." He glared at the offending piece of furniture. "How clumsy of me. Now, Miss Wynn, we're sorry to have to intrude upon you, but we've some questions to ask."

"Would you like to sit down?" she inquired politely. She gestured to the worn brown settee by the fireplace. "Would you care for a cup of tea?"

"How very kind of you," Nivens said. "But we mustn't put you to any trouble."

Barnes stifled a sigh. They were at this little house in Notting Hill to question a suspect, not to play silly games. Didn't Nivens realize that? But then again, Barnes thought, Nivens wasn't the brightest chap in the force.

Nivens settled himself on the settee. Madeline Wynn sat down in a balloon-backed chair opposite him. She stared at the policeman patiently, making no attempt to speak, her hands folded demurely in the lap of her light blue day dress.

Nivens cleared his throat. He was staring at the woman like he'd never seen one before. His voice, when he finally spoke, was a rusty croak disturbing the silent room. "Uh, as you've probably guessed, we're here to ask some questions about the recent murders of Peter Hornsley and George Frampton."

"Yes, I'd assumed as much." Her voice was deep and throaty, and very seductive. "But I've no idea why you think I would know anything about it. I barely knew the victims."

"But aren't you engaged to Nyles Hornsley?"

"Yes."

"So, therefore, I assumed you knew the family quite well," Nivens said hesitantly.

"Your assumption was wrong."

Nivens frowned.

Barnes had to turn his face to hide his grin. The girl had good nerves, he'd give her that. She wasn't going to make this easy on Nivens. Good.

"But surely you've met your fiancée's family?"

"Of course," she smiled. "But I'm sure you're also aware of the fact that they weren't too happy Nyles and I were engaged. Especially his brother."

"Mr. Hornsley objected to your impending marriage?" Nivens said.

"Let's not waste one another's time, Inspector," she replied. "Peter Hornsley did everything he could to end my engagement."

"Why?"

"I should think that would be obvious," she said, gesturing around at the small drawing room, her gaze raking over the worn brown velvet curtains at the windows, the old-fashioned and fading furniture, and the tiny fire in the hearth. "I'm not rich."

"You're not rich?" Nivens repeated. "But surely that's no reason to . . ."

Madeline Wynn interrupted. "Peter didn't think I was quite good enough to marry into his family," she said impatiently. "My family is respectable but quite poor by comparison to his. He wanted Nyles to marry well, to increase the family's wealth and position."

Nivens jumped slightly as the front door slammed. Both policemen whirled around just as the drawing room door burst open and Nyles Hornsley charged into the room.

"What's going on here?" he demanded. "Have you been badgering my fiancée?"

"Nyles," Madeline Wynn said softly.

"Mr. Hornsley," said Nivens at the same time. "I'm glad you're here. Miss Wynn was just telling us that your brother didn't approve of your forthcoming marriage."

Nyles Hornsley hurried over to his fiancée and put his arm protectively around her shoulders. He ignored Nivens's statement. "You've no right to badger her," he said angrily, "She's nothing to do with these murders."

"We're only asking questions, Mr. Hornsley," Nivens snapped.

"It's all right, Nyles," Madeline said. "I don't mind talking with the police. I've nothing to hide."

"In that case, Miss Wynn," Nivens said quickly, "would you please tell us if you were acquainted with Mr. George Frampton?"

"I'd met the man once or twice," she replied. "So, yes, I was acquainted with him."

"And you, Mr. Hornsley," Nivens asked, "you knew Mr. Frampton as well?"

"Of course I did. He was Peter's partner. Really, Inspector, you're wasting our time. Neither Madeline nor myself had any reason to murder George Frampton. She barely knew the man."

"Are you both acquainted with Mr. Stuart Frampton?" Nivens pressed.

"What a ridiculous question." Nyles frowned. "Of course I know Stuart, so does Madeline. But what's that got to do with anything?"

Nivens smiled slyly. "Well, sir, perhaps you and Miss Wynn didn't have a reason for murdering George Frampton, but his son certainly did."

"Exactly what are you implying?"

"I'm implying nothing," Nivens said. "I'm merely asking a few questions. Tossing a few ideas about, as they say."

"You're being ridiculous," Nyles said with a sneer. "Stuart didn't murder his father."

"Perhaps he didn't, sir," Nivens shrugged. "He has an alibi for the time of that murder."

"That murder?" Madeline repeated.

"But he doesn't have a particularly good one for the time of your brother's murder," Nivens said.

Barnes cleared his throat, trying vainly to get Nivens's attention. The silly git was going to ruin everything if he kept talking.

"And you, Mr. Hornsley, don't have a very good alibi for the time that George Frampton was killed," Nivens continued.

Barnes shuffled his feet and twitched his shoulders. Nivens ignored him.

Hornsley's brows drew together pensively, as though he couldn't understand what Nivens meant. But Madeline understood.

"You're trying to say that Nyles murdered George Frampton and Stuart murdered Peter Hornsley?" She looked amused by the notion.

"I'm not trying to say anything." Nivens stuck his nose in the air. "But I find it interesting that you should jump so quickly to that conclusion."

Madeline laughed. "In other words, Inspector, we're conspirators."

"You said it, Miss Wynn, not I." Nivens looked inordinately pleased with himself.

Barnes was furious. The fool was telling them the only decent working theory they had. The constable didn't think much of it; in his experience, conspiracies had a way of unraveling. But be that as it may, it was right stupid to let the chief suspects know you had them under your eye.

"Oh, this is absurd," Nyles snapped.

"I think the police must be desperate if they're reduced to that sort of a silly idea," she replied, ignoring her fiancé and glaring disdainfully at Nivens.

"Madeline, let me handle this," Nyles cried, giving her shoulders a tiny shake to get her attention. "You've no idea about these sort of things. So, please, don't say anything else." He turned to Nivens. "Inspector, this is the most ridiculous thing I've ever heard. You've absolutely no evidence of such a conspiracy because my fiancée and I had nothing to do with murdering anyone."

"I've made no accusations," said Nivens, lifting his chin. "As I said a few moments ago, I'm merely tossing a few ideas about."

"Kindly take your absurd ideas and leave," Nyles ordered. He jerked his chin toward the door. "We're not obliged to stand here and take this kind of abuse."

"Would you both care to come to the station and help us with our inquiries?" Nivens asked.

"That will be fine." Nyles's eyes narrowed. "Of course, we will insist that my solicitor be sent for." He was calling the inspector's bluff and they both knew it.

"Actually, I don't think that will be necessary at this time," Nivens said quickly.

Barnes felt like strangling his superior.

"As a matter of fact," Nyles continued, "neither of us will answer any more questions unless we've a solicitor present."

"I see." Nivens looked perplexed. He shot Barnes a quick glance. "In that case, I suppose we'd better leave. But I do warn you, sir"—he turned back to Nyles Hornsley—"this investigation is far from over. If necessary, we'll ask both you and Miss Wynn to accompany us to the station for questioning. You may, of course, have your solicitor present then."

Betsy was depressed. She crossed Ladbroke Grove and started for the Notting Hill High Street. She might as well take an omnibus home. So far today she'd learned nothing. Her feet hurt and she felt like she'd walked halfway round London. So far today she'd been to Whitelaw's, Vincent's, and now Madeline Wynn's. But she might as well have stayed in bed this morning. She hadn't been able to find anyone to talk to except a footman over at the Vincent house.

So she'd come to Notting Hill hoping to learn something from one of

Madeline Wynn's servants. But that hadn't gone right either. She'd hung about in front of Madeline Wynn's house until she'd spotted Constable Barnes and Inspector Nivens coming down the road. Knowing servants as she did, she was sure that no one who worked in that house was coming out anytime soon. Not with the excitement of policemen coming and going.

It was a completely wasted morning. The only thing she'd gotten out of the footman from Vincent's house was that he was a nice master and he liked to wear fancy kid gloves all the time. The Whitelaw house had been shut up tighter than a bank on Sunday, and the police were at Madeline Wynn's. Blast. She hoped the others were doing better than she was.

She dodged around a fruit vendor and kept on walking. Truth was, she felt a bit guilty. She knew she wasn't giving this case her best effort. She could have pumped that footman more, but she hadn't. And she could have hung around a bit longer at the Whitelaw place, but she hadn't. Eventually, the servants would have come out of the Wynn house, but she hadn't bothered to wait.

She was too worried. What on earth was she goin' to tell Smythe? Oh, he'd been real good about not asking her nosy questions. He hadn't poked and pried too hard. But she could see the worry in his eyes every time he looked at her.

She rounded the corner and came to a dead stop. Her heart leapt into her throat and her stomach tightened. Raymond Skegit's carriage was pulling up on the other side of the road. She stared at it for a moment, saw the door opening and a dark-haired man emerging.

From this distance, she couldn't tell if it was Skegit or not. But Betsy was taking no chances. She turned and ran back the way she'd just come.

She darted past a row of shops, dodged the fruit vendor's cart, and leapt into a small, dark passage separating two tall, narrow brick buildings.

From behind her, she thought she heard footsteps, but she didn't look back, she just kept on going.

Her feet pounded against the old cracked walkway, her heart kept time with her feet. God, what was she going to do? Raymond Skegit wasn't someone to mess about with. She'd been lucky three years ago. She couldn't count on being lucky twice. Why had she had the horrible misfortune to run into the bastard again? Why couldn't he have stayed in the East End where he belonged?

She flew out of the passageway and into the road. She tried to dodge around a tall, broad-shouldered man blocking her path, but at the last moment he turned.

Betsy came to a sudden halt as a pair of strong arms reached out and grabbed her around the waist. "What's the 'urry, lass?"

She let out a yelp before she realized who had hold of her. When she saw who it was, she hurled herself into his arms. "Thank God, it's you, Smythe."

# CHAPTER 9

——◆◆◆◆◆——

"What's wrong, Betsy?" Smythe asked anxiously. "You come barrelin' out of there like the devil 'imself was on yer 'eels."

When Betsy realized she was still clinging to his neck, she pulled away, her face turning red.

For a moment they stared at each other. The worried expression on his face sent a shaft of guilt straight through her. What could she tell him? The truth? But she didn't know if he would understand. Betsy wasn't sure whether she was ready to risk him finding out the worst about her.

"Betsy," he prompted, giving her a light shake.

"I had a bit of a scare, that's all," she replied, glancing quickly over her shoulder to make sure those footsteps she'd heard had only been in her imagination.

Smythe followed her gaze. "Was someone chasin' ya, then?" He pulled away from her and started toward the darkened passageway she'd just come out of. "Maybe they'd like to deal with the likes of me instead of a slip of a girl like you."

She grabbed his arm. "No one was following me."

"Then why were you running like that?"

She hesitated, undecided. In a split instant, she decided to tell him the truth—the whole truth. What was the point in trying to hide it? If Smythe didn't know her by now, he never would. His opinion of her mattered, it mattered more than she'd ever thought possible. But she hadn't done anything wrong. If he didn't understand what she'd done and, more important, why she'd done it, he wasn't worth as much to her as she'd hoped.

"I thought I saw Raymond Skegit's carriage," she said, watching his face. "So I nipped down that passageway thinkin' I could get away from him. I'm scared of him, Smythe. Really scared. He's an awful person, not one to forget a wrong done him."

Smythe nodded slowly, taking care to keep his expression blank. "And Skegit thinks you wronged him."

Betsy swallowed the sudden lump in her throat. "That's right. He . . ."

"Don't tell me yet, Betsy," Smythe gestured at the busy street corner just ahead. "Whatever you've got to say to me can wait until we're alone and we can talk properly."

"But . . ."

"Now don't get het up, lass." He took her by the elbow and started for the corner. "I'm not sayin' I don't want to 'ear. I do. But I don't want to 'ave to be askin' you to repeat yerself every other word 'cause the traffic's so loud. What you've got to tell me is important, it's to be treated with respect. We'll talk tonight after the others 'ave gone to bed."

"But . . ."

"Tonight, Betsy," he ordered softly.

"All right," she replied, thinking that maybe he was right. Saying what she had to say was going to be hard enough. She didn't want to have to say it twice. She only hoped her nerve would hold up long enough. "Tonight it is. But where are we goin' now?"

"To get you in a 'ansom."

"A hansom? Have you lost your mind? I can take an omnibus home." She tugged her arm free and came to a dead stop. "I'm not ready to go home yet. It's still early. I haven't found out much today and I want to keep at it."

"Cor blimey, Betsy, you've just had the wind scared out of ya and ya don't want to go 'ome?" Women, he would never understand them. He wanted her back at Upper Edmonton Gardens. He wanted her safe from the likes of Skegit, at least until he took care of the bastard.

"Well, I'm over it," she snapped. "I'll admit I was frightened. But I had sense enough to run. If I keep my eyes open, I can stay out of Skegit's way."

"You should be 'ome," he said stubbornly. Blast a Spaniard, anyway. Why couldn't the lass see he only wanted what was best for her?

She stuck her chin out, a sure sign that she was digging her heels in. "I can't go home, I've found out nothing."

"That doesn't matter."

"It bloomin' well does. I don't want to be sittin' there tonight when all the rest of you are talkin' about everything you've learned and all I've got to report is that Justin Vincent has more gloves than the prince of Wales."

Smythe struggled to keep a grin off his face. "That might be a real valuable clue, Betsy."

"Right." Her voice dripped sarcasm. "Just like the fact that Rosalind Frampton overspends at her dressmaker's and Nyles Hornsley likes to dance is important." She gestured furiously with her hands. "You see, I've found out nothing important. Nothing at all."

He stared at her thoughtfully, the urge to smile completely gone. Betsy's eyes were haunted, desperate looking. He realized doing her fair share to help solve the inspector's cases was very important to her. Smythe understood that. It was important to him, too. Not just because they all admired Inspector Witherspoon, though that was a big part of it. But because of the way it made them feel inside themselves when they'd done a good job. It made them feel like they were more than just servants, more than just the forgotten people at the bottom of the heap. But he didn't want her roaming around the streets of London, even in the daytime. Not alone. Not until he'd taken care of Raymond Skegit. Bloomin' Ada, he couldn't order her back to Upper Edmonton Gardens.

Suddenly, he saw a solution. "I've got an idea," he said, taking her arm again and starting toward the corner.

"What idea?" She stared at him suspiciously. "Where we goin? I've told you, I'm not through for the day."

"We're goin' up to the corner to grab a 'ansom," he replied quickly, as she was trying to jerk her elbow from his grip. "And I don't want you to go home. I want you to come with me over to the City."

"Why?" Her tone was still suspicious, but also interested as well.

"Cabbie," he yelled, dropping her arm and waving a hand at a passing hansom. The cab stopped and he pulled the door open. "Get in," he said. "I'll tell you all about it as we go."

"Do you know how much a cab to the City is goin' to cost?" she hissed, giving the driver a worried glance.

Her words reminded him he had a few shameful secrets of his own. He shrugged and looked over her shoulder, unwilling to meet her eyes. "Don't fret over it, lass," he lied, grabbing her elbow and practically shoving her inside. "I 'ad a good day at the racecourse last week, so we can ride in style today."

"You ought to be savin' your money," she mumbled, but she got in the hansom anyway. Smythe climbed in after her.

"All right," Betsy said as soon as they started off, "tell me about this idea of yours."

"I thought we'd pool our resources," he said casually, thinking as he spoke. "Mrs. Jeffries is convinced the murders had something to do with the firm, right?"

"That's what she said this morning."

"So I was thinkin' why don't you and I go over to Hornsley's office and see if we can 'ave a nice little chat with someone on 'is staff."

"You mean the clerks and such?"

"Not just the clerks," he replied, "but maybe they have a tea lady or charwoman or someone like that."

"I don't know, Smythe." She looked doubtful. "It's the middle of the day. How are we going to get to them? They'll all be working."

"They've got to have a meal break, don't they?"

Betsy wasn't so sure that was true. "I don't know, do they?"

"I've seen the clerks in the pubs and such when I've been 'round that part of town. So I think we ought to give it a try."

"What were you doin' over in the City?" she asked curiously.

He looked out the small, narrow window. "Uh, on the inspector's cases and such. You know, when I'm out and about." He could hardly admit that his odious banker was always pesterin' him about his money.

Betsy seemed to accept that. "All right," she said, giving him a bright smile, "let's have a go at it, then. We'll see what we can find out."

Smythe sighed inwardly in relief. Short of tying the girl to his wrist he couldn't think of a way to keep her safe. But at least the City of London was the last place that Skegit was likely to show up. And if Skegit did appear, Smythe wouldn't be far from Betsy at all.


Luty stopped in front of the house and squinted at the brass number plate. Number twelve . . . or was that an eight instead of a two? Dang it, anyway, she hated gettin' old. She hadn't minded when her feet went a bit arthritic, and she didn't mind all the aches and pains her stomach would give her when she ate that hot, spicy food her fancy French chef hated fixin'. But dang it, she hated losin' her eyesight.

When she was a girl, she could spot an eagle on a tree branch half a mile away. Now she was lucky if she could make out a blasted house number. She started up the stairs. This had better be number twelve or she was goin' to be mighty mad.

She banged the brass door knocker loudly against the painted black door. Even before she'd started tryin' to read them piddly little house numbers, she'd been in a bad mood. Who would have guessed that her friend Myrtle would pick this case to start asking questions about? Dang Myrtle, anyway. Why'd she have to start gettin' curious all of a sudden?

She'd gone to Myrtle's this morning to pump her for some information. But the silly cow had a bad cold and her ears was plugged up. Luty had to repeat everything twice to make herself understood.

And Myrtle was in a bad mood, actin' like a bear with a thorn in its paw. The minute Luty had started askin' questions, Myrtle's little pig eyes had narrowed and she'd asked why Luty only dropped by to ask her questions about people Luty didn't even know? Well, it was danged obvious that Myrtle wasn't goin to be cooperative, not with that cold. So Luty had told her she'd be back when Myrtle wasn't feelin' so poorly, and then she left.

Luty glared at the closed door. What was takin' 'em so long? Irritably, she pounded the knocker again. Course she felt a little bad, since Myrtle was such a lonely soul. That's why she was always gaddin' about so much. And it wouldn't hurt to drop by every now and again just to visit with the woman. Luty promised herself she'd go see Myrtle again as soon as this case was over and she had more free time.

The door flew open and a tall, bald-headed butler, lookin' even stiffer than Hatchet on a bad day, was starin' down his nose at her. "Yes, madam?" he said frostily. "May I help you?"

Luty lifted her chin, raised her sable muff a notch higher and stared him straight in the eye. "I wish to see Mr. Grady Whitelaw."

"Are you an acquaintance of Mr. Whitelaw?"

"I don't reckon that's really any of your business. But I've already been to his office and they told me he'd come home. So, if you don't mind, I'd appreciate you tellin' him I'm here."

"I'm afraid that's not possible." He started to close the door.

Luty wasn't going to be beaten twice in one day. She slammed her hand flat against the door, shoved it as hard as she could and charged past the butler.

"Really, madam . . ." the butler sputtered.

"I'd appreciate it if you'd tell Mr. Whitelaw I'm here," she repeated haughtily. Then she turned her back on him and started down the black-and-white tiled hallway. Most of these fancy houses were all alike; she'd find a place to sit while ol' stiff-neck rustled up Whitelaw. "I'll wait in the drawing room."

"But, madam," the butler yelped. But Luty had made good her escape and was turning in to the double doors leading to the drawing room. He charged after her.

Luty whirled about as she heard the servant's running footsteps. "Are you deaf, man? I said I'd like to speak to Mr. Whitelaw and I ain't goin' to budge from this room till I see him. Now go git him."

"Mr. Whitelaw isn't here," the butler yelled. He was totally frazzled. One simply did not pick up elegantly dressed old ladies and toss them out the front door, no matter how much one was tempted. Besides, this one looked as if she might object to the whole proceedings.

"Well, where in the dickens is he?"

"Paying a mourning visit. A dear friend has just died and he's paying a condolence call on the family." That ought to shame the woman.

"Nell's bells. When's he due back?"

He couldn't believe his ears. This person obviously had no shame. "I really can't say, madam."

"Name's Crookshank. Luty Belle Crookshank. What's yours?"

The question so startled him he answered without thinking. "Payne, madam. Now, I'm afraid I must ask you to . . ."

"Maybe you can help me, Payne," she said. "You see, I left my shawl in a hansom cab night before last. I dropped it on the floor as I was leavin', you see."

"I see . . ." Payne didn't see anything.

"Well, my friend Myrtle told me she happened to see Mr. Whitelaw get in that very hansom right after I got out of it. Now, I've already checked with the driver and he claims there weren't no shawl on the floor when he got back to the depot, so I figure Mr. Whitelaw must have brung it home with him. Can you run upstairs an' git it for me?"

Run upstairs? Payne had never run up the stairs in his life. "Madam, I assure you, Mr. Whitelaw doesn't have your shawl in his possession."

"Now, I ain't accusin' him of stealin' it," Luty said quickly. "And normally I wouldn't make a fuss over a pink lace shawl, but this one was real special. A friend of mine made it for me and she's dead now. So you see, I'd like to have it back. You just go on upstairs and have a peek in Mr. Whitelaw's drawers. I'll bet he was meanin' to try and find the owner."

"I'm sorry, Mrs. . . . er . . ."

"Crookshank."

"Mrs. Crookshank." Payne's head began to pound. "But I believe your friend must have made a mistake . . ."

"Oh no, Myrtle saw Mr. Whitelaw git into that cab. She was waitin' on the door stoop when it dropped me off, and she knows who Mr. Whitelaw is, ya see, and he got in right behind me. The driver says it was his last run of the night, and he ain't got my shawl, so Mr. Whitelaw has to have it."

Payne shook his head. This woman was obviously of unsound mind. Perhaps he ought to be a bit gentler with her. "I'm sorry," he said kindly, "but that's impossible."

"Are you callin' me a liar?" Luty demanded.

"No, madam, but your friend must have made a mistake." His good intentions disappeared.

"Myrtle don't make mistakes like that. Not about my shawl. She knows how important it is to me, so you git yourself up those stairs and see if you can find it."

"I tell you," Payne's voice began to rise, "your shawl isn't here."

"Yes, it is."

They were both shouting now.

"It couldn't be here," Payne yelled.

"How do ya know?" Luty bellowed. "Ya ain't even looked yet."

"I know because Mr. Whitelaw wasn't in a hansom at all. He walked to his destination. He'd forgotten his gloves, you see, and a *gentleman* doesn't call upon his fiancée without gloves, so one of our footmen went after him. But he didn't catch up with him. He lost sight of Mr. Whitelaw at Hyde Park Corner."

Luty smiled in satisfaction. That was precisely what she needed to know.

"Thank you," Constable Barnes said to Betsy. He reached for the cup of tea she'd poured. "I need this. Nivens was even worse today than usual. Drug us all over London and we didn't learn a bloody thing."

They were all gathered round the dining room table. Barnes had popped in for a late tea on his way home.

"I'm sure Inspector Nivens is doing the best he can," Witherspoon said kindly.

"He may be," Barnes shot back irritably. "But he doesn't know how to conduct a proper murder investigation. We learned nothing today. On top of that, Nivens lost his temper when we were questioning Madeline Wynn and Nyles Hornsley. He got so rattled he told them his conspiracy theory. Well, he told 'em enough so that they figured it out."

"Do you believe Inspector Nivens's idea is correct?" Mrs. Jeffries asked.

Barnes sighed. "No. But whether it were a good theory or not, Nivens had no business lettin' on to two of our main suspects that we was thinkin' along those lines. It's not much of an idea, but it's all we've got so far."

"What about the theory that the murders have something to do with the business and not the victims' personal lives?" Witherspoon asked. "Have you found anything new along those lines?"

Again Barnes sighed. "Not a bloomin' thing. I spent a few hours over in the City today, talking to clerks and bankers and the like, but I didn't find out much. The firm isn't highly thought of by its competitors, but it's not much worse than some of the other insurance firms."

"How about Mr. Hilliard?" Betsy asked timidly. "Is he still a suspect?"

"Near as I can tell, everyone's a suspect. I haven't learned anything about Hilliard that would clear him. We know he was lyin' about bein' in his office on the nights of the murders."

Betsy glanced at Smythe, who nodded his head slightly.

"Constable Barnes," she said. "I think you can scratch Damon Hilliard off your list of suspects."

Barnes's eyebrows shot up. "What have you found out?"

"We were over in the City today, seeing what we could find out. I happened to run into the charlady that does Hilliard's office." Betsy hadn't run into the charlady; she'd tracked the woman down like a bloodhound. But Barnes didn't need to know that. "And she told me something right interesting."

"Go on, Betsy," Witherspoon encouraged. Gracious, he'd never thought that the girl was so devoted to him. Imagine, going all the way over to the City. "Tell us what you've heard."

Betsy blushed slightly. This was goin' to be the hard part. "Mrs.

Miller," she began, "that's the charlady, she's quite a chatty kind, you see. She told me that Hilliard slips out of his office two or three times a week. He goes to a . . ." she broke off, searching for the right word.

"He goes to a brothel," Smythe said quietly. He could see that Betsy was having a devil of a time speaking frankly. He wondered if it was because the inspector and Barnes were here. Usually the lass hadn't a bit of trouble speakin' her mind, no matter what the subject. He gave the maid an understanding smile. "Betsy told me about it when we was comin' 'ome tonight."

"Was he at the brothel," Witherspoon felt his own cheeks flaming, "on the nights of the murders?"

Smythe nodded. "Yes. He were there last Friday night when Hornsley was done in and again on Monday night when Frampton got it." He hoped the policemen wouldn't ask him how he'd found out all the details about Hilliard's activities. Not after the row he and Betsy had had about it this afternoon. Blimey, it wasn't like he'd gone into that place for the fun of it! Besides, he'd made sure that Betsy was safely in the hansom while he was inside. Not that she appreciated his gesture. She'd pouted all the way home.

"Well, that lets Hilliard out, then." Barnes took a sip of tea. "But I'll have to confirm his alibi." He smiled apologetically at Smythe. "Not that I'm doubtin' you . . ."

"It's all right," Smythe said quickly. "We understand you can't just take our word for it." He glanced at Betsy. "Go on, tell 'em what else you found out."

"What else?" she repeated in confusion. Then she saw the mischievous twinkle in his eyes. "Oh yes, I found out that Justin Vincent has more gloves than the prince of Wales."

"That's odd," Barnes murmured, "Vincent didn't strike me as a particularly vain man." He wasn't sure exactly what this last piece of information could possibly have to do with the murder, but he didn't want them to feel like he was taking their efforts lightly. The truth was, he was quite impressed by everything they had found out. "But guess you can't really tell much about a person by just lookin' at them. Anyway, did you learn anything else?" he asked the coachman.

"Not much," Smythe shrugged. "Just picked up a bit more gossip about them break-ins the buildin' 'ad the month or so before the first killin'. Seems right strange, but one of the clerks told me the only firm that got broken into was Hornsley, Frampton, and Whitelaw. And the only thing that was done was someone overturned the inkwells onto the desks and broke the pens into bits." He grinned. "He said that Hornsley almost had a conniption fit when he come in and found ink all over his fancy rosewood desk."

"That sounds like a schoolboy prank, not a proper breakin," Mrs. Goodge said derisively.

"I don't think it means anything," Barnes said. "I spoke to the lads that were called there when it happened. According to the report, there wasn't anything stolen. It was more a case of malicious mischief than anything else. But Police Constable Turgen told me that the incident shook the tenants up so badly that they hired that night watchman. Not that it did much good, though. Hornsley was still murdered right under the man's nose. Oh well, perhaps we'll make sense of it yet." He smiled at the others. "But you've done well. Today hasn't been wasted."

"Of course it hasn't, Barnes," Witherspoon said quickly. "All information is useful in some way or other." He beamed at his staff. "I must say, I'm amazed. You've all learned so very much. Why, it's almost as if you've done this before."

"Thank you, sir," Mrs. Jeffries said quickly. She turned to Barnes. "What have you learned today, Constable?"

Barnes told them every little detail about his day with Inspector Nivens. He could barely keep the disgust out of his voice. When he'd finished, he looked around at the circle of disappointed faces. "Not much, is it?"

"A good day's work, sir," Mrs. Goodge said stoutly. Honestly, they ought to make women detectives. They knew how to talk to people. "You've done your best, and that's what counts. I've learned a bit myself today. It's not much, mind you, but like I always say, you never know what's goin' to season the soup until it's done good and proper. So here's my bit. It seems that Grady Whitelaw wasn't at home on the night of Hornsley's murder." She paused, waiting for the effect her words would have on the others. And she wasn't disappointed by their avid attention. "Accordin' to my sources, he wasn't at home alone at all. He was out somewhere's else. I know because my source told me she saw him comin' home last Friday night quite late. She said she saw Whitelaw slippin' in through the side entrance to his own house instead of usin' the front door."

Barnes stared at her incredulously. "Would you mind tellin' me who this source is?"

Mrs. Goodge shifted uneasily. Admitting she'd sent one of the street lads (whom she occasionally fed cakes and buns to) over to snoop about in Whitelaw's neighborhood would never do. She didn't want Barnes or Witherspoon to know about that. Why, they'd figure out in an instant that this wasn't the first time they'd been snoopin' about.

"Well, I found out through a bit of gossip," she hedged. "A friend of mine knows the maid that lives next door to Grady Whitelaw."

"And was it this maid who saw Mr. Whitelaw coming in late on the evening of March ninth?" Witherspoon asked.

"Right," agreed Mrs. Goodge. She looked quickly at Mrs. Jeffries for guidance. The housekeeper nodded almost imperceptibly.

"It was a Friday night, you see," Mrs. Goodge continued, "and her employers was out for the evening. The girl took advantage. She slipped out while they was gone to meet her sweetheart."

"So we could call this girl to give evidence in a trial?" Barnes pressed.

"I suppose so," Mrs. Goodge said slowly. "But I don't think she'd like it much."

"Do you know her name? I'd like to talk with her. This could be important evidence," Barnes said.

Mrs. Goodge thought quickly. "Her name's Margaret Turner. But I don't think you ought to talk to her unless you really have to make an arrest. If her employers found out what she'd done, she'd lose her position."

"Oh dear, we wouldn't want that to happen," Witherspoon agreed. "I say, Barnes, let's not bother the girl unless we find additional evidence that Whitelaw had something to do with the murders. I don't want anyone losing their positions."

Luty and Hatchet arrived as soon as supper was finished. Mrs. Jeffries and the others told them everything they'd heard from Barnes.

"I didn't get to tell the inspector and Constable Barnes what I'd learned today," Wiggins complained as soon as the housekeeper had finished speaking. "And I found out all kinds of things."

"All right, boy," Luty said kindly, "you go ahead and tell us. My news can wait."

"Yes, Wiggins," Mrs. Jeffries added. "It was most unkind of us to ignore you during our meeting with the constable."

Wiggins shifted uncomfortably. He wished he hadn't raised such a fuss. He hadn't learned all that much. "Well," he said slowly, "tomorrow's the Ides of March."

Everyone stared at him. He felt his cheeks burn with embarrassment. "I'm not tellin' this right," he cried. "What I meant to say was that I think them words pinned on the dead men's chest might be Latin."

"Since when do you know Latin?" Mrs. Goodge asked.

"I don't know it," Wiggins said, "but I can read, and today while I was at Mudies I come across this quote. It caught my eye 'cause the letters was just like the ones in the notes." He dug in his pocket and pulled out a piece of string, a sweet covered in lint, and finally a scrap of paper.

"'Ere it is," he said, smoothing the paper out on the table. "Veni, vidi, vici," he read aloud. "VENI was the word written on Hornsley's paper, VIDI was the one written on Frampton's chest, so I figured it had to mean something."

"I came, I saw, I conquered," Hatchet translated. "I do believe he's right. Well done, Wiggins. How fortunate for us that you happened across a volume of Suetonius."

"I came, I saw, I conquered," Luty repeated. "But what's it mean?"

"Obviously, it means something to the killer," Hatchet replied.

"But what that could possibly be is the difficult part," Mrs. Jeffries mused. "How on earth can we determine what it means? A quote, even a famous one, taken out of context is virtually meaningless unless one can determine what it means to the killer."

"You mean this is useless?" Wiggins gestured helplessly at the scrap of paper. "But I spent hours pourin' over them books, and they didn't even have pretty plates or illustrations."

"Of course it isn't useless," Mrs. Jeffries said quickly. "It's merely a matter of us using our eyes, ears, and brains to determine why the killer would put such a thing on his victims' bodies." She knew it wasn't going to be easy. That kind of a quotation could mean just about anything.

"While we're thinkin' about it," Luty said, "can I tell everyone what I found out?" She paused a moment, waiting for their approval and then plunged straight ahead, telling them about her encounter with Grady

Whitelaw's butler. "So I found out exactly what we needed to know. Not only does Whitelaw not have an alibi, but he was seen practically at the scene of the crime only minutes before Frampton was killed."

"I'd say that just about proves 'e's our killer," Smythe said softly. He glanced at the clock and saw that time was getting on. He hoped this meeting wouldn't last all night. He still had to talk to Betsy, and then he had to go out.

"The evidence certainly does seem to be pointing at Whitelaw," Mrs. Jeffries replied. But something was wrong. That little voice in the back of her mind was telling her that something was definitely wrong about this case. Something so obvious that it was almost a case of not being able to see the forest for the trees.

"So what do we do now?" Luty asked.

"I think we should keep on digging," Mrs. Jeffries said.

"Are we goin' to tell the inspector and Constable Barnes about what they've"—she gestured at Luty, Wiggins and Hatchet—"found out?"

"Yes, but that can wait until tomorrow."


Betsy waited until she heard Mrs. Jeffries's door close and then she crept down the stairs and into the kitchen. The big room was in darkness save for a single candle in the center of the table.

"Come on in, lass," Smythe said softly. "I've been waitin' for ya."

She was grateful for the dim light. It would help her, make it easier for her if she couldn't see his face so clearly.

She took the chair opposite him. "I had to wait till I heard Mrs. Jeffries go up," she explained, wanting to put off the truth as long as possible.

"I know," he grinned. "I 'ad to wait till Wiggins fell asleep. He were snorin' like a drunken lord when I left." He stopped and his smile faded. "All right, lass, tell me about you and Skegit. But before ya say anything, I want ya to know I'll not be sittin' in judgment on ya. I've been poor too and I know we all do things we don't like just so's we can survive."

Betsy blinked to hold back the tears that welled in her eyes. "Thank you," she replied formally. "I appreciate your sayin' that." She took a deep breath. "Raymond Skegit is a . . . a . . ."

"I know what 'e is, Betsy."

She nodded. "Anyways, I was livin' over the East End, me and my mum and my two sisters. Mum worked as a barmaid, and my sisters and I did sewin' and piecework. It weren't much of a livin' but it was enough to keep us in a room to ourselves and buy food and tea. We lived like this for a long time, leastways it seemed like a long time. My older sister got married and left," she swallowed heavily, "and my younger sister died of fever. Mum lost her job at the pub because she'd stayed home and nursed my sister instead of goin' to work. Things seemed to get worse after that. Mum couldn't get work, the clothin' factory that give me the piecework shut down, and we was turned out into the street. We stayed in doss houses for the most part, it weren't too bad, 'cause it was summer. But I'd run into Skegit every now and again, and he'd always ask me to come work for him. He was always at me, tellin' me how much money I could make, how much easier life would be if I worked for him. I wouldn't. No matter how poor we was, I wasn't doin' that." She looked down at the table.

"But then Mum got real sick. By this time it was winter and I was scared to death I was goin' to lose her. So I went to Skegit and told him I'd become one of his girls." She laughed bitterly. "Skegit give me five pounds, told me to use it to get Mum some medicine and a decent place to stay. I thought it was a fortune, I went back to the doss house where I'd left her . . ." Her voice broke. "And she was dead."

"It's all right, lass," Smythe started to get up, but she waved him back to his seat.

"No, let me tell you the rest." She swiped at the tears rolling down her cheeks. "Mum was gone and I was on my own. I used the money Skegit had give me to get her buried. It weren't much, but at least she had a coffin. Then I went to Skegit and told him I wasn't goin' to work for him. He started screamin' at me, callin' me names and tellin' me I owed him five pounds. I give him what little I had, but he didn't want the money. He wanted me." She sighed heavily, as though a great weight had been lifted off her shoulders. "I knew I couldn't stay in the East End, not with him after me. So I took off. I lived on the streets for a while, doin' what I could to survive, gettin' day work and things like that. But my luck run out and I got pneumonia. In a way, it turned out to be the best thing that ever happened to me. I collapsed on Inspector Witherspoon's doorstep." She looked up at his face. "You know the rest. I've been here ever since. I never thought I'd lay eyes on Raymond Skegit again."

Smythe got up and came around the table. He put his hand on her shoulder. "Don't worry, Betsy," he promised, his own voice none too steady and he was glad of the dim light. His own eyes were wet from hearing of her pain and suffering. "Nothing's going to happen to you. Raymond Skegit will never bother you again. I'll see to that."

# CHAPTER 10

"I've got to remember to stop in at the post office on my next day out," Betsy said to nobody in particular at breakfast the next morning. "I hope this case is finished by then."

"That's a good idea," Mrs. Jeffries replied absently. She barely heard what anyone said this morning. Her mind was preoccupied trying to sort out all the different pieces of the puzzle.

Somehow, she didn't think Grady Whitelaw was behind the murders. It didn't feel right. She had a sense that she was missing something, something so very apparent that if they weren't right in the middle of things, she'd see it in an instant.

"We can stop in on our way to the Zoological Gardens," Smythe said. "If this ruddy case is done by then."

"I don't think it'll ever be finished," Mrs. Goodge announced glumly. "Unless, of course, we find absolute proof that Grady Whitelaw is the killer, and in my opinion, he jolly well is. He had reason and his alibis are comin' apart faster than a chicken that's been cooked too long."

Surprised, Betsy stared at the coachman. Despite his words the other day, there was one part of her that thought he wouldn't want to have anything to do with her. "You still want me to go with you?" she asked Smythe.

"Why wouldn't 'e want you to go?" Wiggins asked. He thumped his crutch against the floor as he flopped down in his seat. "Everyone likes the Zoological Gardens. I've a mind to go, too. I like lookin' at animals. Right educational, it is, Mind you, it's not as good as havin' a whole day at Mudies Lendin' Library."

Smythe glared at him. He could hardly announce that he wanted time alone with Betsy, that he wanted to court her properly. "Corse I want us to go," he said, turning his attention to the maid. "It'da be a nice day out. I said we would, didn't I?"

"When we goin', then?" Wiggins asked cheerfully.

"You can't go, Wiggins," Betsy said. She grinned at Smythe. "You'd never be able to hobble around the zoo on them crutches."

"Why don't you wait till I'm off the ruddy things?" he asked. "Then we could all go together, make a day of it."

"'Cause they want to go by themselves," Mrs. Goodge interjected. "They'd like to be alone."

Wiggins's jaw dropped open. He stared first at Betsy, who was staring at the toe of her shoe, then at Smythe, who stared right back at him. "Well, I never. So that's the way the wind blows, is it? No one ever tells me what's goin' on round 'ere."

"I don't think Smythe's and Betsy's private business is any of your concern," Mrs. Goodge retorted. "Anyway, we'd best get this murder solved before we make any plans. Come on, everyone, finish your breakfast. I've got some sources comin' in here this morning and I need this kitchen empty."

"But you just said you thought Whitelaw was the killer," Wiggins complained. He hated being rushed through his meal. "So what's the ruddy 'urry?"

"We don't know who the killer is," the cook shot back. "And we don't stop lookin' just because we've got us a good suspect. Isn't that right, Mrs. Jeffries?"

"What? Oh yes," Mrs. Jeffries said hastily. "That's frequently a mistake the police make. They think someone is guilty so they stop investigating."

They did as they were told, Wiggins hobbled out to the street to flag down a hansom, Smythe took off on some mysterious errand of his own after getting Betsy to promise she'd be careful, and Mrs. Jeffries went out into the gardens to have a good, long think.

Naturally, Mrs. Jeffries hadn't been outside more than five minutes before Lady Cannonberry cornered her.

"I saw you from my bedroom window," Ruth said breathlessly, as though she'd dashed out in a hurry, "and I simply had to tell you what I'd found out."

"Do sit down and take a breath," Mrs. Jeffries advised. Oh, well, she thought, it wasn't as though her thinking was doing any good. She still couldn't quite grasp what it was about this case that was eluding her. She patted the wooden bench beside her. "Do sit down."

Ruth shook her head. "I mustn't. I've a thousand things to do today. But I wanted you to know that I'm still working on 'our case.' I had another chat with Marisole yesterday after I spoke to you, and she told me ever so much more."

"How very resourceful of you," Mrs. Jeffries replied.

"Perhaps I will sit down," Ruth murmured. "I don't think the dressmaker will mind if I'm a few minutes late, and Gerald's good name is far more important than a ball gown." She sat down next to the housekeeper. "Well, before I forget, I did find out something about Rosalind Frampton. Not only was she an actress, but she was engaged to another man when she met George Frampton. She broke off the engagement, though, and the poor fellow, it was an actor, I believe, got so annoyed, he publicly made a scene. Called her all sorts of names when she was dining with George Frampton at a restaurant on the Strand. It was quite a scandal. Frampton threaten to sue the man. But he didn't, he got him sacked instead. Disgusting what people with money can do, isn't it? That poor actor had a perfect right to state his piece. Mind you, I don't approve of making scenes. But . . ."

Mrs. Jeffries wanted to avoid another diatribe on the evils of class system. Not that she didn't agree with Lady Cannonberry on that particular issue, she did. But once Ruth got started, she often wandered off the point. And Mrs. Jeffries had an awful feeling they were running out of time. "Did you find out the actor's name?"

"Nicholas Osborne." She frowned. "No, that's wrong. That's the name of the poor child who went to that school in Abingdon with Hornsley and Frampton. Oh, now I remember, the actor's name was Oswald. Morton Oswald. But he left for the continent after Frampton got him sacked. Pity, too. I hear he was quite a good actor. Poor fellow. I don't see what an English actor can do on the continent. Unless, of course, he can act in a foreign language. Do you think there are many actors that speak German or Italian?"

Something rang a bell in the back of Mrs. Jeffries's mind, but it was gone before she could catch it. "I've no idea. What else did you learn?"

"Not much, really. Marisole couldn't get her husband to talk much about Packards. It was quite a horrid school. I don't think he was very happy there."

"Packards?"

"Why, yes, that's where they all went to school. Hornsley, Frampton, and Whitelaw. Marisole's husband too. It's quite a ghastly place."

Packards. Mrs. Jeffries couldn't believe she'd been such a fool. Packards. Abingdon. Notes. Schoolboy pranks. She jumped up. "What day is it?" she cried.

"March fifteenth," Ruth exclaimed, gazing at her curiously. "Why? Have you forgotten an important engagement?"

"I've been such an idiot! How could I not see the pattern?"

Ruth stood up as well, her expression concerned. "Is something wrong?"

"Ruth, can you get over to Marisole's and find out something for me? It's rather urgent. It could be the key to this whole case."

"Of course I can. The dressmaker can wait. What do you want me to find out?"


Luty and Hatchet arrived as soon as they'd received Mrs. Jeffries's urgent summons. But by the time everyone was back, it was getting dark.

"Isn't the inspector back yet?" Mrs. Jeffries asked for the tenth time.

"No, he's still out," Mrs. Goodge replied. "He's gone for another of them walks. Can't think why he can't walk in the daytime like the rest of us. Why does he want to go out on these silly evening jaunts?"

Betsy came rushing into the kitchen. "Is Smythe back yet?" she asked, taking off her bonnet and hurling it toward the coat tree.

"Not yet," Mrs. Jeffries replied. "He's been gone all day. Did you find out anything?"

"You were right," Betsy cried. "I caught the maid just as she was leaving the house. He's packin' for a trip, all right. He's leavin' tonight on the ten o'clock from Paddington."

"And the rest?"

Betsy shook her head. "It's all true."

"What's goin' on here?" Luty demanded.

"Mrs. Jeffries has figured out who the real killer is," Wiggins said excitedly.

"And if we don't move quickly, he's going to kill again tonight." Mrs. Jeffries rushed over to the kitchen window and peeked out again. "Oh, where is Smythe? Where's the inspector?"

Smythe, whistling tunelessly but cheerfully, came through the back door. "Evenin' everyone," he called.

Mrs. Jeffries whirled around. "Smythe, thank goodness you're back. Have you seen the inspector?"

"I just now passed him. He were 'eadin' for the omnibus stop."

"Hurry," she ordered. "Go after him. It's a matter of life and death."

Smythe didn't ask any questions, he turned and ran for the back door.

"Hatchet, is the carriage outside?"

"Course it is," Luty answered. "We didn't fly over here."

"Good. Then can you go and fetch Constable Barnes?" She checked the clock on the mantel and did some quick mental calculations. "He should be about ready to go home now. If you're lucky, you can catch him at the Ladbroke Grove police station. Either there, or at home."

"And what shall I tell him, madam?" Hatchet put his hat back on and was striding toward the door as he spoke. He, too, sensed the urgency of the situation.

"Tell him to come here. Tell him that Inspector Witherspoon thinks he knows who the killer is and that he needs his help to stop another murder from being committed."

Mrs. Jeffries would never forgive herself if they were too late, if another person lost their life because she'd so desperately wanted Inspector Witherspoon to get the credit for this case that she'd waited too long.

"Excuse me, Hepzibah," Luty sputtered, "but would you mind tellin' me what in the dickens is goin' on here?"

"I say, are you certain of this?" Inspector Witherspoon asked Betsy.

"I got it straight from the maid, and she were the one packin' up his clothes."

He nodded slowly. He wasn't sure he quite understood just what was going on, but he thought it better to act than to risk another murder. Mind you, he told himself, if he was wrong, he'd find himself back in the records room instead of out solving homicides. He was rather surprised to find that idea depressing. Gracious, in the past two and a half years there had been times when he'd wanted to go back to his old job. "And you're quite certain of your information?" he asked Mrs. Jeffries.

"Yes, sir."

"Well, then, I guess I'd better get cracking." He started for the back stairs.

Mrs. Jeffries stopped him. "Excuse me, sir," she said, keeping one eye on the clock as she spoke. "But as Luty and Hatchet had dropped by, I took the liberty of asking Hatchet to fetch Constable Barnes. They should be here any minute."

"Excellent, Mrs. Jeffries. Excellent." Witherspoon was no coward, but he wasn't a fool either. If he was going to arrest a murderer, he would like to have Barnes there to assist him. "But I'm wondering if we should send a message to Inspector Nivens . . ."

"No!" shouted Mrs. Jeffries, Betsy, Mrs. Goodge, and even Luty at the same time.

"There isn't time, sir," Mrs. Jeffries said quickly. From outside she heard the sound of a carriage pulling up.

A moment later, Hatchet, followed by a surprised-looking Constable Barnes, came in the back door.

"I'm so glad you're here, Constable," Witherspoon said. "Er, by the way, where is Inspector Nivens?" Really, he must at least try and bring the inspector in on this. It would be most unfair if he didn't.

"Inspector Nivens left the station early today," Barnes replied, looking pleased as punch about the situation. "He was havin' dinner with some politician over in Fulham. Told me not to bother him till morning."

"Sir," Mrs. Jeffries said urgently, "you really must get going."

"Yes, yes, of course. Come along Barnes," Witherspoon started for the door. "I'd like you to accompany me."

"Maybe I ought to come along as well," Smythe suggested, "seein' as 'ow Inspector Nivens isn't 'ere."

Witherspoon paused. He really should stop and bring along some more police constables. But there really wasn't time. And Smythe was a sensible chap. He wouldn't do anything foolish or dangerous. "I think that's a splendid idea. Thank you, Smythe. But mind you, I won't have you put yourself in any danger. You must take care to do as I say at all times."

Confused, Barnes looked from the inspector to the coachman. "Where are we goin', sir?"

Witherspoon popped his bowler on his head. "We're going to catch a killer, Constable Barnes."

• • •

"Are you sure of all this, sir?" Barnes asked as the carriage came to a halt in front of the house. "I mean, it's pure supposition, sir. If we're wrong . . ."

"If we're wrong, I'll end up in the records room and you'll end up walkin' a beat in Shoreditch," said Witherspoon with a shrug. "I quite understand if you'd like to disassociate yourself from my actions. After all, it's not even my case."

"I'm goin' in with you, sir," Barnes said firmly. "I've confidence you know what you're doin'."

"Thank you. I appreciate your faith in me, Barnes." Witherspoon hoped the constable's faith wasn't misplaced. "And do remember, if I'm right, we may very well be saving a man's life."

"I think I'd better come in with ya, too," Smythe said. He was staring at the house. Except for a flare of brightness from the fanlight over the door, the place was in darkness. The hairs on the back of his neck stood straight up, a sure sign that something bad was about to happen. "I don't much like the look of this."

Witherspoon hesitated. It was one thing for he and Barnes to face a murderer, but it was quite another to ask his coachman to risk his life. On the other hand, Smythe had come in quite useful a time or two in the past. "Uh, why don't you come as far as the door? That way, you can be at the ready if someone has to run and get help."

They moved out of the carriage and up the dark walkway. Witherspoon reached the door first. He raised his hand to knock, but the door was unlatched and standing open a couple of inches. He pushed inside, with Constable Barnes right on his heels.

It took a moment for his eyes to adjust to the light. But when they did, he gasped in surprise.

Grady Whitelaw, on his knees in front of the staircase and holding a hand to his head, moaned softly. Blood spurted from between his fingers and a loose tie dangled from around his neck. He pointed toward an open doorway on the other side of the staircase. "He's getting away. Heard you coming and ran."

There was the sound of breaking glass. Barnes and Witherspoon dashed forward and flew into the drawing room in time to see a man wearing a heavy overcoat and a bowler hat climbing out of the window.

"Halt in the name of the law!" Witherspoon cried.

But the man kept right on going.

• • •

"Is 'e goin' to be all right?" Smythe asked anxiously. He'd come running in as soon as he'd heard Witherspoon's yells.

"He's bleedin' badly, but the wound don't look too deep," Barnes replied. "Mr. Whitelaw, are you able to sit up?"

Whitelaw moaned but gamely tried to sit up. "I let him in," he said softly. "I thought it was the police."

"Where are your servants?" Barnes asked.

"Out," Whitelaw mumbled. He slumped down on his elbow. "I gave them the evening off to go to George's wake. I was on my way there myself when the inspector came . . . he said my life was in danger . . ." His eyes closed.

"Is he dead?" Witherspoon asked anxiously.

Barnes felt for a pulse. "He's unconscious, but he needs a doctor."

"Best leave him layin' where 'e is," said Smythe, helping the wounded man back onto the floor. "I'll nip up to the corner. There's a constable on patrol there. We need some 'elp 'ere."

"Hurry, Smythe," Witherspoon urged as the coachman took off at a dead run for the front door. "We've no time to lose. Otherwise the miscreant will get away."

"You mean you know who he is?" Barnes asked.

"Indeed I do," Witherspoon replied. He sincerely hoped that his conclusions, or rather the conclusions he'd come to with the help of the staff, were correct. But even if they were wrong, they'd at least been in time to save Grady Whitelaw's life.

Smythe must have run all the way to the corner and made the constable run too, for they were back in just a few moments. Witherspoon briefly explained what had happened, while Barnes went out and summoned a doctor.

They left Whitelaw with the constable and the doctor. As soon as they were back in the carriage, Barnes asked, "Where to now, sir? The Yard?"

"Oh no, we've got to make an arrest." He stuck his head out the window and yelled at Smythe, "How quickly can you get us to Mayfair?"

Again, they pulled up in front of a darkened house. This time, when Smythe asked if he should come in with the inspector, Witherspoon didn't hesitate. "If you wouldn't mind, Smythe. That would be a great help. But do stay near the front door in case there's trouble. We may need you to dash out again and find some more constables."

They walked up to the front door. Witherspoon banged the knocker and yelled, "Open up in the name of the law!" But he needn't have bothered. Like Whitelaw's house, this door swung open, too.

Taking a deep breath, the inspector pushed his way inside. The lights were dim, but the house wasn't in total darkness. "I say," the inspector called, "is anyone here?"

"There should be servants, sir," Barnes said uneasily. "This is a rich man's house."

"Yes, well, I don't expect there are any servants about the place tonight," said Witherspoon as he started down the hallway, past a staircase and a table with a large potted fern, to what he hoped was a drawing room or study at the far end of the passage. "I expect he's given them the evening off."

"To go to Frampton's wake?" Barnes suggested. He didn't like this, he didn't like it at all. The place was too quiet.

"No. I don't think our killer will be sending any of his servants to pay their respects to either of the victims."

"You're absolutely right, inspector," said a voice quietly from behind them. "It will be a cold day in the pits of Hades before anyone in my employ pays their respects to those animals."

They whirled about. A man wearing a heavy overcoat, bowler hat, and a pair of spectacles stood at the foot of the staircase. He was holding a revolver in his hand.

Witherspoon's heart leapt into his throat. "Now, there's no need for that."

The man looked at the revolver and smiled. "You're right about that too, sir. There isn't." He put the revolver down on the table next to a potted fern. "I'm not going to shoot you. I don't kill innocent people."

Witherspoon was rather stunned. He wasn't quite sure what to do now. So he did precisely what the law required. "Justin Vincent," he said formally, "you're under arrest for the murders of Peter Hornsley and George Frampton."

"Haven't you forgotten about the attempted murder of Grady Whitelaw?" Vincent asked easily. "Or did I hit him hard enough to kill him before you so rudely interrupted me?"

"He's still alive," Barnes said. "But maybe not for long."

Smythe, who'd been watching the whole proceedings with his jaw hanging open, edged toward the front door. Like it or not, he was goin' for help. This was too much for the inspector to handle.

But Vincent saw the coachman move. He snatched up the gun and pointed it right at his chest. "I wouldn't do that if I were you." Smythe stopped.

"I don't want to kill an innocent person," Vincent continued softly. "But I will if I have to."

Witherspoon blanched. He didn't mind if Vincent pointed a gun at him, but he wasn't having the man threaten his coachman. "Now see here," he started for Vincent.

"Don't move another step, Inspector," Vincent said, "or I'll shoot your man right where he stands."

"What do you want?" Witherspoon cried. "You must know you won't get away with this."

"I don't want to get away with it," said Vincent, smiling. "All I want is for all of you to come into the drawing room. I'd like to make a full confession. Your constable there"—he nodded at Barnes—"can write it down for me."

Witherspoon didn't see that he had much choice. "All right, but I must insist you let my coachman go."

Vincent thought about it for a moment. "All right, there's no harm in letting him leave. By the time he gets back with help, it will all be over."

Witherspoon nodded to Smythe.

The coachman hesitated. He didn't like leavin' the inspector with a madman—especially a madman with a gun.

"Go on," Witherspoon urged. "Go and get help."

Smythe had no choice. He turned and hurried out the front door.

As soon as he was gone, Vincent gestured with the gun toward the open door at the end of the hallway. "Let's step into the drawing room, Inspector. We'll be far more comfortable there."

They did as he asked. There was a cheerful fire in the hearth next to the desk. A leather settee and a small table with a red fringed shawl was next to it. There were various other pieces of furniture scattered about the room, but the inspector was too busy staring at the gun in Vincent's possession to admire the decor.

Vincent motioned for Barnes to sit behind the desk. "There's paper and a pen there, Constable," he said conversationally, as though he were inviting Barnes to help himself to tea and cakes. "Make sure you listen carefully and take down everything I say. I want this read at the inquest."

Barnes, his face pale, but his expression determined, did as he was told.

"Mr. Vincent," Witherspoon began. He was the senior policeman here. It was his duty to take charge of the situation. Only how did one take charge when the other fellow had a weapon and you didn't?

"Oh, do sit down, Inspector," said Vincent, waving the gun at the settee. "This is going to take a few moments. You'll be much more comfortable sitting than standing."

Witherspoon sat. "I take it you would like to confess."

Vincent walked over and poured himself a glass of whiskey from the bottle on a teak table by the window. "Would either of you like a drink?"

"No, thank you, I'm on duty," the inspector said.

Barnes shook his head.

"Well, then, I do hope you don't mind if I do." He took a long drink of his whiskey, and grimaced. "In answer to your question, Inspector, yes, I'm going to make a full confession. But I will do it in my own words. I want the whole world to know what kind of men I killed." He filled the glass again. "And I want your word of honor that my statement will be read at the inquest."

"You're hardly in a position to bargain, Mr. Vincent," Witherspoon retorted.

"Oh, but I am." Vincent smiled. "I've got the gun."

"Yes, quite. I do see your point."

"Your word, Inspector," said Vincent, raising the gun and leveling it at Barnes. "I'm an excellent shot, sir. I learned how to use firearms in America. Los Angeles, to be exact."

"You have my word, sir," Witherspoon sputtered, as he watched his constable turn even paler. "But there won't be an inquest, sir. There will be a trial."

"I doubt that, Inspector. But let's not quibble over details. Whether it's a trial or an inquest, I want my statement read. Is that clear?"

"Perfectly."

Satisfied, Vincent nodded. "Take this down, Constable." He took another swig of the whiskey. "I, Justin Vincent, born Nicholas Osborne, freely admit that I murdered Peter Hornsley and George Frampton. I freely admit that I also attempted to murder Grady Whitelaw. I did this while in full possession . . ."

"Would you mind slowin' down a bit, sir?" Barnes interrupted. "I'm not that fast a writer. Now, how do you spell 'possession'?"

"P-o-s—" Witherspoon started to spell the word.

"Oh, for God's sake, just do the best that you can," Vincent cried. "May I continue?"

Barnes nodded.

"I did this while in full possession of my faculties and with malice aforethought." He broke off and grinned. "That's an American legal expression. Do they have it over here as well? I rather like it though, don't you, Inspector? *Malice*. It's such a good word, and so descriptive. It says precisely what I felt."

"You had a grudge against the victims?" Witherspoon asked.

Vincent laughed. "Grudge? That's hardly what I would call it. Those despicable bullies ruined my life. They were responsible for my mother's death and sent me into exile."

"How very unfortunate."

"It was a bit more than 'unfortunate,' Inspector," Vincent said softly. He put the glass down and pulled off the black leather glove on his right hand. He held his hand up. "Do you see this?"

Witherspoon leaned closer, his eyes straining to see in the faint light. A huge dark scar covered the back of the hand, the thumb, and several of the fingers. "That looks like you've been burned, sir."

"Hornsley held my hand in a fire when I was eleven years old. Frampton held me down and Whitelaw kept watch." Still holding the gun, he stared at his own hand. "I was small for my age. They were sixteen. Hornsley was the ringleader. They called themselves the Conquerors. That was the name of their little group at that wretched school my uncle sent me to. It was a horrid place. A place no one should send a child to."

"Why did they do it, sir?" Barnes asked.

"Because I wouldn't allow them to use me," Vincent said bluntly. "I was small for my age, quite pretty, or so I was told. Hornsley thought he could do with me as he liked, but I refused to cooperate. I was small, but more than capable of putting up a good fight. That's when the bullying started. They made my life miserable. Stole my pens, poured ink on my clothing, they did everything possible to make everyone hate me, and, what's worse, they succeeded."

"Didn't anyone notice the burn on your hand?" Witherspoon asked.

"Of course they did." Vincent laughed. "But they lied about that as well, claimed that I'd burned myself by falling into the fire. That's when I told on them, you see. That's when I told the headmaster that Hornsley was a pederast. But the odd thing was, the headmaster didn't want to know. No one wanted to know. Not the teachers or the prefects or the parents. Everyone looked the other way and advised me not to make trouble."

"So you left the school?" guessed Witherspoon. Really, he should think Vincent had been glad to get away from such an awful place.

"Oh no, it wasn't that simple, Inspector. I didn't get a chance to leave. I was expelled for stealing. The Conquerors had the Latin master in their pockets, you see. Hornsley had been indulging in unnatural practices with Hickstrom for years. The old sodomite would do anything Hornsley wanted. He deliberately claimed I'd stolen his watch. So I was the one that was expelled. I was the one sent home in disgrace. I was the one who watched my mother throw herself in the Thames after my uncle threw us out of his house because I'd ruined the family name." He smiled bitterly. "But the Latin master's dead, too. I took care of Hickstrom first. Poor old fellow toppled off a bridge and into an icy river. I stood and watched him drown. Fitting, isn't it?"

Witherspoon was so stunned by this he couldn't think of a thing to say. Vincent, apparently, didn't expect him to say anything.

"I've spent thirty years planning their deaths," Vincent said slowly. He picked up the glass off the table and drained it. "Thirty years, Inspector."

"Why did you use my name?"

"I'm sorry about that," Vincent said. "But you see, I wanted to make sure that you weren't given this case. I'm not a fool. I've followed your cases in the papers. You've solved some very difficult murders. And you've solved them brilliantly. I didn't want the inspector who'd cracked those horrible Kensington High Street murders snooping about on this case, so I used your name. Silly, really. I oughtn't to have done anything."

"Did you plant that note on George Frampton?" the inspector asked. "The one signed with my name."

"Yes," Vincent admitted. "A miscalculation on my part. Obviously, you took exception to my masquerade. I'd been rather hoping you'd be sent off to the country by the powers that be. Besides, as a policeman I could gain access to my victims so very easily. If you say you're from

Scotland Yard, people will unlock their doors and let you right inside."
He sighed. "It's a pity about Whitelaw, I did so want him dead, too."

Vincent suddenly started to sway. "Did you get this all down, Constable?" he demanded.

"Yes, sir, most of it." Barnes looked up from his paper. "Are you all right, sir?"

"I'm fine—" but Vincent didn't complete the sentence. The gun slipped from his hand and he collapsed onto the floor.

Witherspoon rushed over to him. He knelt down beside him. "Mr. Vincent," he said urgently, "we must get you to hospital."

"It's too late," Vincent whispered. He tried to raise his head. "But you'll make sure my statement is read at the inquest?"

"It will be read," said Witherspoon as he tucked his arm under Vincent's head, protecting it from the floor. "I promise you, it will be read."

"Thank you," Vincent rasped. "I'm sorry I used your name, I didn't mean to . . ."

"Please," the inspector begged, "don't try and speak anymore. Help is on the way. We'll get you to hospital."

"Too late . . . poison . . ." With that, he closed his eyes and died.

"Inspector, Inspector Witherspoon," cried out Smythe, his voice frantic, and a rush of footsteps sounded in the hallway.

"In here," Barnes called as he charged out from behind the desk.

Smythe, accompanied by what looked like a battalion of uniformed police, charged into the room. He skidded to a halt at the sight of Justin Vincent lying on the carpet.

"He's dead," the inspector said softly.

"'Ow?"

"He killed himself," said Witherspoon as he gently lowered the dead man to the carpet. He pointed to the bottle on the table. "Barnes, let's take that whiskey bottle into evidence. Mustn't leave something like that about. Someone might accidentally drink from it."

# CHAPTER 11

"How did you figure it out?" Smythe asked. They were all gathered round the table at Upper Edmonton Gardens. Everyone, that is, except Constable Barnes and Inspector Witherspoon. They were still down at the station, explaining everything to a rather pleased Chief Inspector Curling and a furious Inspector Nivens.

"I almost didn't until it was too late," Mrs. Jeffries admitted. "You see, we'd all been looking at this case the wrong way."

"Wrong way?" Luty frowned. "Nell's bells, Hepzibah, I think we did pretty danged good."

"We did do good," Mrs. Jeffries laughed. "What I meant was that we all accepted a certain premise far too early in our investigations."

"You mean that the murders had something to do with the company and not with the victims?" Betsy said.

"That's right. It wasn't until Wiggins mentioned the Ides of March that I understood, and even that didn't do it until Lady Cannonberry mentioned that name again—Nicholas Osborne, also known as Justin Vincent. Why, his very name should have given us a clue."

"Yes, it should have," Hatchet agreed. "It means 'just conqueror' in Latin."

"Well, how in the dickens was we supposed to know that?" exclaimed Luty, who shot her butler a fierce frown.

"Let me start at the beginning," Mrs. Jeffries explained. "You see, from the very first the notes were important, but because they were difficult, because none of us could make any sense of them, we tended to ignore them."

"So did the police," Smythe added.

"True, but we're not the police. We should have seen what they meant."

"But like Luty says, none of us, except Hatchet, knows Latin," protested Betsy.

"I'm not talking about what the notes *said*, I'm talking about the act itself." Mrs. Jeffries threw her hands up. "The killer pinned a note to his victim's chest. What does that remind you of?"

"Pin the tail on the donkey," Wiggins suggested.

"Don't be daft, boy," Mrs. Goodge snapped.

"That's silly," Betsy said.

"He's absolutely right," Mrs. Jeffries interrupted. "That's precisely what it meant. The killer did something a silly schoolboy would have done. And none of us saw it."

Hatchet pursed his lips. "I'm not sure that it would have made any difference if we had realized the significance of the act."

"No, perhaps not," Mrs. Jeffries said. "But it might have made us start thinking along different lines and asking different sorts of questions. Why, from the very beginning, there was an element of childish, schoolboy behavior about this case, but none of us saw it."

"What do you mean?" Wiggins asked. "I don't see nuthin' schoolboyish about killin' someone, and that's when this case started."

Mrs. Jeffries shook her head. "But it wasn't. The case started a month earlier than that. It started with the break-ins at the office building. But none of us even thought to pursue that line of inquiry. Fortunately, Smythe investigated and found that the office of Hornsley, Frampton, and Whitelaw was the only one broken into. As soon as he told us that nothing had been stolen from the office and that, really, the only harm done was a few broken pens and some ink poured on Hornsley's desk, we should have seen the connection. But we didn't. We were already too committed to another, wrong idea about the crime. Let this be a lesson to us. From now on, we form no opinions until we have all the facts."

"I see what you mean," Hatchet said thoughtfully. "The break-in wasn't really a break-in. It was just the sort of thing that silly boys do when they think they can get away with it. Something to torment and inconvenience, but no real harm meant."

"Seems to me there was plenty of harm done," Luty snapped. She was annoyed at Hatchet for seeming to get the point faster than she had. "There were two men murdered."

"But that break-in was almost like Vincent was tryin' to warn his victims," Betsy pointed out.

"I think he was," Mrs. Jeffries stated flatly. "I think he was trying, in his own sick way, to give them fair warning. But they couldn't see it, either."

"I still don't see how you figured it out," Mrs. Goodge complained. "I'm still muddled up about it."

"It was several things, actually. All along I had the sense that there was something right under my nose and I couldn't for the life of me see what it was," Mrs. Jeffries said. "But nothing fell into place until this morning when I was talking to Lady Cannonberry. She mentioned Nicholas Osborne, but, more important, she mentioned that Hornsley, Frampton, and Whitelaw had gone to school in Abingdon. Then I remembered where I'd heard that name before." She smiled at Betsy. "Vincent's maid had told Betsy that Vincent had gone to school there as well. I knew it couldn't be a coincidence. Then I came in here and looked at the calendar. The first murder happened on the ninth, the second on the twelfth, and then I knew. Vincent was going to kill Whitelaw tonight—the Ides of March— March fifteenth. Children are very much taken with ritual; three is almost a magic number to them."

Luty snorted. "Vincent's no child. The man's got to be at least forty."

"But he was acting out a child's fantasy," Mrs. Jeffries pointed out. "At least that's what I thought he was doing. But it all added up. Lady Cannonberry said Osborne's hand was burned. Justin Vincent always wore gloves."

"So that's why you sent me over to his house to see what he was up to," Betsy exclaimed. "You was certain even then what he was up to." She gave Smythe an impudent smile. "Turns out that clue was important, doesn't it?"

Smythe frowned at her. "You left the 'ouse this afternoon?"

"I took a hansom," Betsy protested. "And I was careful. Besides, I did find out that Vincent had let all his servants go and was planning on leaving town tonight."

Mrs. Jeffries glanced from the maid to the coachman. She wondered what was going on. But now wasn't the time to bring up the subject. "That was when I knew for certain," she said.

"Mind you, he did give them all six months' wages," Betsy said. "So he couldn't have been too bad a person."

"Was that all that made it drop into place?" Luty asked. "Just those piddly little clues?"

"No, there were a number of things. First of all, I remembered Constable Barnes telling us that Vincent had never met the other partners. All the negotiations to buy into the firm had been done through solicitors and through Grady Whitelaw. I thought that odd. Surely, if he was spending a great deal of money, Vincent would have wanted to meet with all the principals in the company. Yet he didn't. Why? Because I think he was planning on killing Hornsley and Frampton first, and he didn't want them to recognize him as their new partner. He didn't care if Whitelaw recognized him, he was going to kill him last, so I expect he thought it didn't matter."

"But he was disguisin' himself as the inspector," Betsy protested. She'd rather liked Vincent. "So how could Hornsley and Frampton have recognized him?"

"No disguise is that good, girl," Luty said. "And remember, he had to get close enough to cosh them on the head and strangle them."

"I think you're right," Smythe agreed. "I do think he planned the order of the murders. I read the statement he dictated to Barnes. Hornsley was the one that held his 'and to the fire, Frampton 'eld him down, and Whitelaw kept watch. He killed the ringleader first. Killed the one that had hurt him the worst first."

"Can't say that I much blame 'im," Luty said. "Only I wouldn't have waited thirty years to get even. Imagine doin' that to a little boy."

"But that's no reason for murder," Wiggins protested. "It's one thing to want a bit of revenge, but 'e didn't 'ave to kill 'em."

"I can't imagine carryin' a grudge for that long," Mrs. Goodge said. "You'd think Vincent would have forgotten as he grew up."

"Some people never forget," Betsy said. She shivered and crossed her arms over her chest. Smythe knew she was thinking of her own brush with the past.

He tried to catch her eye, but she was looking away from him, staring at the clock as though she could will time to run backward. But he was being fanciful. Maybe she was just tired.

Inspector Witherspoon arrived home before they finished their meeting. "I say," he said, "I was rather hoping you'd all be up."

"We wanted to hear what happened, sir," Mrs. Jeffries explained. "Luty and Hatchet decided to stay, too."

"I couldn't leave without knowin'," Luty explained hastily. "And

Hatchet here wouldn't sleep a wink all night if he didn't find out how things turned out."

Hatchet contented himself with a quick glare. He didn't wish to spar with his employer in front of the inspector.

Despite his jovial manner, they could all see the evening's events had taken a toll on their inspector. He was quite pale, his hair was sticking up on end, as though he'd been running his hands through it, and his fingers shook as he took the cup of tea Mrs. Jeffries poured for him.

"It was quite dreadful, really," he murmured. "Vincent, or I should say Osborne, is dead. He took poison; it was in a bottle of whiskey. It was quite deliberate, I'm sure. I think he'd planned on killing himself all along."

"What kind did 'e take?" Wiggins asked curiously.

"We're not sure. The police surgeon thinks it might have been some sort of plant poison, but he won't know for certain till he does the post-mortem. It's certainly something we're not familiar with in England. It wasn't arsenic or strychnine—Vincent died far too quickly for either of those. But Dr. Bosworth happened by and he said that there are a variety of poisonous substances derived from plants in America. We're thinking it could be one of those."

"Gracious, sir, how very awful for you," Mrs. Jeffries said.

"Watching a man die is rather terrible, even if he is a murderer." Witherspoon closed his eyes briefly. "I don't think I shall ever forget it."

"What I don't understand is how he committed the murders," Mrs. Goodge said, "He had an alibi for both of them. Was his servants lying about him supposedly bein' at home?"

"No," Witherspoon explained. "They weren't. But you see, he'd given strict instructions not to be disturbed when he was working. That's why he ate his dinner so early. He'd then tell the staff he was working, pop into his study, put on his disguise, slip out through a small door that most of the servants didn't even realize was there, commit the murder, and come back in the same way. It was very clever. Very clever, indeed. But then, it should have been. He'd been planning his crimes for a long time; that much became obvious when we searched his house."

"What did you find?" Hatchet asked.

Witherspoon toyed with his cup. "We found the disguise he wore, of course. He kept that under his bed in a carpet bag. He even had a fake mustache and wig."

"That must have been the one Martha saw him with," Betsy exclaimed. "She thought he had a lock of his sweetheart's hair."

"Well, that was not a lock of anyone's hair, it was a fake mustache from Herringer and Sons, Wigmakers."

"There's something I don't understand," Wiggins said.

"And what's that?" the inspector replied.

"Well, accordin' to what we know, Vincent didn't ask the partners to let 'im buy into the company. The partners come to 'im. If 'e was plannin' on these murders, why'd he want to go into business with 'em?"

"I think I know," Mrs. Jeffries said thoughtfully. "I think he wanted to watch them suffer. I think he wanted to watch Frampton and Whitelaw fall apart, and then he wanted to kill them."

"I agree," Witherspoon said. "He also wanted to be part of it, too. As a partner, he'd be right in the thick of it. As to their coming to him, instead of the other way round, I think he knew exactly how to manipulate them. Vincent had complete dossiers on the three partners. We found them in his desk. He'd hired a firm of private detectives to watch them. He knew all about their business, their private lives, everything. He even had notes regarding their intention to expand the business. So I suspect that approaching their rival, Damon Hilliard, was all part of his plan."

"Where'd he get his money?" Betsy asked.

"He did very well in land speculation in California," Witherspoon replied. "Actually, he'd made a fortune."

"What a waste of a life." Amazed, Betsy shook her head. "He had all that money and all he wanted to do was kill the boys that had bullied him when he was a schoolboy."

"The sins of the past, Betsy," Witherspoon shrugged philosophically.

Smythe didn't want the conversation to continue in that vein. Betsy's past was over and done with, he'd seen to that. "Is Mr. Whitelaw goin' to be all right?" he asked.

"He'll be fine. He's a mild concussion but nothing a few days of rest won't cure." Witherspoon sighed. "Mind you, I think he's quite lucky."

"He is indeed, sir," Mrs. Jeffries said bluntly. "If you hadn't figured out who the real killer was in time, he'd be dead like the others."

Witherspoon smiled sheepishly. "Come now, Mrs. Jeffries, I can hardly take credit for solving this case."

"Oh, but you can, sir," she insisted. "The only thing we'd determined was that there would be another killing tonight. You were the one that concluded who the killer must be and who his intended victim was." This wasn't precisely true, but Mrs. Jeffries didn't want the inspector to realize it.

"If you'll recall, sir," she continued when he opened his mouth to protest, "the only thing I told you when you came in this evening was that the murders had occurred three days apart. After we discussed the matter for a few moments and I told you what Betsy had found out this afternoon, about Vincent getting ready to leave, you figured out the rest." This statement wasn't true either, but she thought it best to convince him that it was. When Smythe had brought the inspector back this evening, she'd carefully fed him the information he needed to come to the right conclusion.

In the past, she'd observed that people would frequently forget the circumstances of an event and then take all the credit once the deed was accomplished. This trait was especially common in men. Even her dear late husband, who'd been a constable with the Yorkshire police, had been prone to this peculiarity of character. But Mrs. Jeffries didn't mind. It didn't really matter whether or not she and the staff got any credit for helping. What was important to all of them was that they could continue to help. Furthermore, if they wanted to keep on detecting without interference, she'd better convince the inspector it was he who'd solved the case, not them.

Witherspoon considered her words. "Why, I do believe you're right, Mrs. Jeffries. Gracious, perhaps I'm a better detective than I'd thought."

At eleven o'clock, Smythe slipped out the back door and into the garden. He paused, giving his eyes time to adjust to the darkness. Directly ahead of him a match struck. Smythe walked toward the sudden flare of light.

Blimpey Groggins, puffing on a cigar, came out from under the huge oak tree. "Evenin', Smythe, you're right on time."

"Is it done?"

"It's done," Blimpey grinned around his cigar. "Funniest job I ever pulled, a right ole lark it was."

"Any trouble gettin' in?"

"Nah, Skegit's locks were so flimsy a three-year-old could skiffle 'em."

"Did you leave the stuff?"

Blimpey chuckled. "Raymond Skegit should be gettin' a visit from Her

Majesty's excise boys in less than an hour. He'll be right startled, Raymond will. Probably spend the next ten years wonderin' 'ow they got on to 'im."

"That'll be our little secret," Smythe said. "You done good, Blimpey. I owe ya for this."

"And you'll pay, me friend, you'll pay." Blimpey laughed again, taken by his own wit. "But even if you couldn't pay, it would do me 'eart good to 'elp put someone like Skegit away. When the customs lads see everythin' we stashed in Raymond's room, they'll put 'im away for ten years. Governments might let you get away with murder. But smugglin', not payin' duty? They'll lock the bloke up and throw away the key."

"Good thing for me that you and your mates cottoned on to Skegit's second business," Smythe said, as he reached into his pocket and drew out a thick wad of notes. "Otherwise, I was gonna 'ave to find another way to take care of Skegit."

"Wouldn't be no loss if he was put six feet under," Blimpey said. "Not many would mourn 'im, and, take me word for it, the peelers wouldn't look too 'ard to find who done it."

Smythe shook his head. He wanted Skegit out of the way so he couldn't harm Betsy, and thanks to Blimpey and his friends, he'd found a way to do it without resorting to violence. "I couldn't do murder," he said quietly, handing the bills to Blimpey. "Not even scum like Skegit. I'm glad the bastard dabbled in smugglin'. Makes it easier to get shut of 'im."

Blimpey clasped the roll of bills to his bosom. He didn't bother to count it. He knew Smythe was as good as his word. "Skegit *dabbled* in smugglin'. 'E'll be right narked when 'e realizes 'e's been set up. 'Ave you thought of that?"

"I'm not afraid of 'im," Smythe replied. "Besides, by the time 'e gets out, 'e'll be an old man. The kind of contraband your lot planted ought to get 'im a good sentence."

"It cost you plenty," Blimpey agreed. He cocked his chin to one side. "If you don't mind me askin', where you gettin' this kind of lolly?"

Smythe did mind him asking, but he didn't want to offend him either. Blimpey was a useful friend to have. "'Ere and there," he replied casually. "I've saved a bit over the years."

"On a coachman's pay?" Blimpey was clearly incredulous.

"I play the ponies, too," Smythe shrugged. "I'm good at it."

Blimpey raised the wad of notes to his mouth and kissed them. "And I'm glad of it, Smythe. You're a regular gent to do business with."

Smythe waited until Blimpey was out of the gardens before going back into the house. He hadn't liked what he'd had to do, but he couldn't think of any other way to handle Skegit. The man was a pimp and probably a murderer. God knew what he would do to Betsy if he ever got his hands on her. Smythe shuddered as he pulled open the back door. He didn't want to think about that. He didn't want to think of her in the clutches of that monster. Even though what he'd done wasn't exactly right, it weren't exactly wrong either. That's what he told himself as he hurried down the hallway and into the kitchen.

He skidded to a halt.

Betsy was sitting at the dining table.

"I was waiting for you," she said calmly. "I saw you slip down the stairs after everyone else had gone up."

"Oh." He ambled to the table, trying to appear as casual as possible. "What was you doin' outside?"

"Gettin' a breath of air," he replied, dropping into the chair next to her.

She stared at him for a moment. "Who was that man you was— were—" she corrected, "talking with?"

Smythe wondered if he could bluff his way out of this. Then he decided against it. Betsy had shared her secrets with him, she deserved to have a few answers. But he couldn't resist teasing her. "Spyin' on me, were ya?" he asked, giving her his cockiest grin.

She didn't crack a smile. "No," she replied solemnly. "I was just curious when I saw you go out. I was goin' to come out myself and then I saw that other man out there."

"Well, if you must know . . ."

"I must."

"It was a fellow named Blimpey Groggins."

"I saw you give him something," she pressed. "What was it?"

"Nothing. Well, I give him a couple of quid 'cause 'e's skint and 'elps me every now and then."

"How much?"

"A couple of pounds is all," he lied. He didn't want her to know how much money he'd really paid Blimpey; otherwise, she'd feel beholden to him for life. "Look, Blimpey give me a 'and with Raymond Skegit . . ."

"Skegit," she cried. "Why are you messin' about with the likes of him?"

"I fixed it so 'e won't ever bother you again, lass," he said softly.

Her eyes widened in alarm. "What have you done, Smythe? Oh God, I don't want someone like him comin' after you," she cried. "I knew I shouldn't have told you the truth. I knew it."

"Now, don't upset yerself," he said, reaching over and patting her shoulder. "I didn't kill the man. All I did was fix it so 'e's . . ." he hesitated, wondering just how much to tell her.

"So he's what?" she demanded.

"So 'e's off the streets and not 'urtin' anyone," he finished. "By this time tomorrow night, Raymond Skegit will be sittin' inside a jail cell and hopin' 'e's got the money to pay a solicitor."

She opened her mouth but he shushed her by gently putting his fingers on her lips. "Don't ask me no more questions, lass. I did it for you and that's all ya need to know."

Stunned, she gazed at him, "I don't know what to say."

"Don't say anythin'," he ordered softly. "Just know that I'll do whatever I 'ave to to keep ya safe."

"You're a good friend, Smythe," she said, her eyes filling with tears. "No, that's not right," she leaned forward, her lips coming close to his. "You're much more than just a friend, Smythe."

"Hey," Wiggins called. His crutches thumped heavily down the stairs. "What's goin' on down 'ere? 'As there been another murder?"

Betsy jumped back and glanced guiltily at the stairs.

Smythe groaned in frustration. If Wiggins hadn't already had a sprained ankle, the coachman would be sorely tempted to hobble him.


Witherspoon reached for the pot of damson preserves Mrs. Jeffries had just put on the dining table. "I really mustn't dawdle over breakfast this morning. I've got to get to the Yard and write up my report."

Betsy stuck her head in the room. "Inspector Nivens is here to see you, sir."

"I'll announce myself," said a familiar voice, interrupting the maid. Nigel Nivens, his expression hard and grim, stepped into the room. "Well, what do you have to say for yourself, Witherspoon?" he demanded.

"Say for myself?"

"About stealing my case."

"Would you care for a cup of tea, Inspector Nivens?" Mrs. Jeffries smiled blandly.

"No, thank you. Well, Witherspoon, I'm waiting."

"I assure you, Inspector," Witherspoon said hastily, "that it was never my intention to 'steal your case,' as you so harshly put it."

"Then why didn't you make sure I made the arrest?" Nivens snapped.

"Constable Barnes said you were dining with a politician and mustn't be disturbed," Witherspoon tried to explain.

But Nivens refused to listen. "You've made me look like a fool, Witherspoon. And I'll not forget it." And with that, he turned on his heel and marched out of the room.

"Get out of my way, woman," they heard him yell. A moment later, the front door slammed.

"Who's he talking to?" Betsy asked curiously, looking at Mrs. Jeffries. "Mrs. Goodge is in the kitchen."

"He was speaking to me," said an unfamiliar, faintly accented voice. A tall, dignified, elegantly dressed gray-haired woman stood in the doorway of the room. "And most rudely, too."

"Madame Ramanova," Witherspoon cried in surprise. "What are you doing here?"

"I came to see why you missed your dancing lesson last night," she explained. "I was most concerned. If you continue to miss lessons you'll never be ready for that ball next month."

"Dancing lessons?" Betsy repeated because she was terribly confused.

"Inspector Witherspoon has been taking lessons from me for the last week. We started last Friday evening. He's doing quite well," she said, nodding approvingly at her blushing pupil. "Why, at his Monday lesson he didn't step on my foot at all."

"You were taking dancing lessons on the nights of the murders?" Mrs. Jeffries couldn't believe her ears. Why hadn't he just told them where he was?

"Well, er, yes," Witherspoon admitted.

"Gracious, sir, why didn't you tell us? What time were you there?"

"Murder?" Madame Ramanova asked. "What murder?"

"From six till almost eight-thirty."

"So you had a bona fide alibi," Mrs. Jeffries exclaimed.

"I was embarrassed," the inspector explained. "I didn't want anyone to know that I didn't know how to dance properly."

"But sir, your life and liberty were at stake."

"Life and liberty," Madame Ramanova repeated. "What are you saying?"

"Oh, I was going to say something," Witherspoon said earnestly. "But only if Nivens arrested me."

"Arrested you!" Madame Ramanova began backing out of the room. "Excuse me, I think perhaps I'd better go."

"I'll see you tomorrow evening then," Witherspoon called.

"I'm sorry, but I'm afraid my class is full," said the dancing teacher as she ran for the front hall.

"But I'm a private pupil."

"I'll send you a refund." The front door slammed.

"But, but . . . oh dear," said Witherspoon as he looked helplessly at Betsy and Mrs. Jeffries. "Did you get the impression Madame Ramanova was rejecting me as a student?"

"Yes, sir, I'm afraid I rather did," Mrs. Jeffries admitted.

Betsy nodded. "I think the words 'murder' and 'arrest' put her right off you."

"But that's not fair. She's my dancing teacher. She must give me lessons. If she doesn't, how will I ever learn to dance in time to take Lady Cannonberry to that April ball?"

# MRS. JEFFRIES STANDS CORRECTED

To Matthew James Arguile
My own special gift from God

# CHAPTER 1

"So you can see, gentlemen," Haydon Dapeers said to the two men standing on the other side of the polished mahogany bar, "I've done myself proud. The Gilded Lily Pub is a showplace. Take a look at the etched-glass windows." He gestured toward the front of the pub. "You won't see the likes of those very often. I hired an artist, mind you, not some glass cutter, to do that work. And what about the partitions—solid wood, they are. Cost me almost as much as those fancy brass gas lamps and fittings. Not that I'm complaining about the expense; you've got to spend money to make money. That's what I always say. And I say it's money well spent. I'll have customers fighting to get in here."

Edward Magil glanced at his companion, Luther Pump. "The pub certainly is beautiful, Mr. Dapeers," Magil agreed, "but we didn't come to inspect your premises. That's hardly our concern. We came to speak with you about that other matter. The one you wrote us about today."

"A matter of some importance," Luther Pump added. He glanced around the rapidly filling public bar. Dapeers might be a bit of a braggart, but the man did have a point. The pub was beautiful. The lingering rays of the June sunshine sparkled through the large windowpanes at the front. Huge lilies, etched within fantastical curved lines, cast intricate patterns against the dark oak floor. Brass lamplights, their bases shaped like lily stems, decorated the richly papered walls. Potted ferns had been placed strategically around the room and the partitions between the public and saloon bars were dark wood panels polished to a high gloss.

"You've picked a bad day, gentlemen." Haydon pursed his thin lips. "I don't really have time to talk with you now. People are starting to come in. It's my birthday and our opening night. I do wish you'd come around earlier this afternoon. I could have spared a few moments for you then."

"A few moments?" Pump raised one dark eyebrow and picked a piece of lint off the cuff of his immaculate black suit. "Mr. Dapeers, may I remind you that you wrote to us."

"Of course I did," Haydon agreed apologetically. "But I didn't expect you to come so quickly."

"Of course we came straightaway," Magil said. "You've made a very serious charge."

"I'll grant that the matter is important." Haydon gave the ever-increasing crowd a worried frown. "But can't it wait until tomorrow?"

Magil's lips pursed in disapproval. "Mr. Dapeers, we're very busy. . . ."

"The bottom tap is stuck, Mr. Dapeers," Molly, the barmaid, yelled from the far end of the bar. "I can't serve beer if this ruddy things goin' to be actin' up all evening."

Haydon Dapeers rolled his eyes. "Just a minute, Molly."

Luther Pump sighed and looked at his companion. "It's no use, Edward. We might as well make an appointment for Mr. Dapeers to come see us tomorrow. One more day isn't going to hurt." He turned back to the publican. "We'll expect you in our offices first thing tomorrow morning. This is a very serious charge you've made. Very serious indeed."

"I appreciate your understanding," Haydon said pompously. "Molly," he called, "get these gentlemen some beer. It's on the house." He nodded to the two men and started toward the other end of the bar, determined to get that stubborn tap to work properly. But his attention was caught by the couple coming in the front door. It was his brother, Tom, and his wife, Joanne.

Haydon smiled maliciously as he watched them take their first look at the Gilded Lily Pub. People always said that Tom Dapeers was a younger version of himself, not that Haydon could see the resemblance. All he saw was a thin little fellow with a long, bony face, mousy-brown hair and pale hazel eyes. Joanne, on the other hand, was a handsome woman. Black-haired, blue-eyed and with an hourglass figure that could turn heads . . . until she opened her mouth. She had the tongue of a shrew, the carriage of a queen and more clothes than the Princess of Wales. Haydon sneered slightly as he took in her attire. The cow was tarted up like she was visiting the palace! Her dark red silk dress was festooned with lace at the throat and wrists, the double skirt was layered in rosettes and she even carried a matching muff and parasol. Ye gods, Haydon thought, it would be a cold day in hell before he'd ever let Moira make a spectacle of herself like that. But tonight he didn't have to bother with insulting his sister-in-law's clothes. All he had to do was stand back and watch her turn green with envy.

"Come in, come in," Haydon called, waving to the newcomers. "I wondered if you two would come and get a gander at the competition." He'd known good and well that wild horses couldn't have kept his sister-in-law away.

"Of course we came, Haydon," Tom Dapeers replied.

Joanne's lips curled slightly. "A bit too much brass for my taste," she said, turning in a slow circle to take in every detail of the room. "But I suppose there's some that will like it. Nice. But it doesn't hold a candle to any of our pubs."

Haydon Dapeers came out from behind the bar and walked over to them, leaving Magil and Pump to enjoy their drink. "I think there's going to be lots that like it, little brother," he said, totally ignoring his sister-in-law. "And what's more, I think they'll like it enough to leave the two of you wondering where all your trade's gone. You won't have to look far, now, will you?"

"Mr. Dapeers," Mick, the barman, called, "the other tap's stuck now. Can you come and give us a hand?"

"In a minute, Mick, in a minute."

"Having trouble, Haydon?" Joanne Dapeers asked. She smiled spitefully.

"Not a bit, just a couple of sticky taps. I'll get them fixed straightaway." Haydon nodded toward the two men in suits at the bar. "Place is filling up nicely; even have a couple of guests from Bestal's Brewery."

"Expect they're wantin' to see if you're wasting their money or not," Joanne replied shortly. "Come on, Tom, let's get a beer before the crowd gets too thick." She tugged her husband's arm and they wandered to the bar.

The Gilded Lily continued to fill up. Within half an hour Haydon's wife, Moira, his other sister-in-law Sarah Hewett and numerous other friends and acquaintances had come by. Haydon was kept busy darting from one group to another, refilling glasses and seeing to his guests' comfort.

He didn't notice a tall young man with light brown hair and deep-set hazel eyes come in. It was only as he was looking around the room, trying to see if the men from Bestals were still there, that he saw him.

Haydon rushed over to the corner where the man and Sarah Hewett were standing close together. "What are you doing here, Taggert?" he demanded, glaring at the young man.

"This is a public house," Sarah said quickly. She was a lovely young woman of twenty-three with dark blond hair, gray eyes and a full sensual mouth. "He's as much right to be here as anyone."

"Let me handle this." Michael Taggert put his hand on Sarah's arm. "I came by for my money," he said to Dapeers. "You still owe me for the windows and the carving on the bar. I want to be paid."

"I'm not givin' you a ruddy farthing till I'm good and ready," Haydon snapped. "And I'll thank you to stay away from Sarah."

"I can see who I like," Sarah hissed.

"Not while you and your brat are living in my house, you can't."

"She'll not be living there much longer," Taggert warned, "and you'd best keep your bloody hands to yourself. If I hear you've tried to touch her again . . ."

"I don't know what you're talking about," Haydon blustered, but he glanced around to see who might be lurking nearby, listening.

"Michael, please," Sarah begged. "Don't start anything tonight. I told you, I'll be all right."

"Good advice." Haydon sneered. "Now get out before I throw you out."

Michael Taggert hesitated. He looked as though he wanted to smash his fist into Haydon's face, but the pleading expression in Sarah's eyes stopped him. "I'll leave. But be warned, Dapeers, you leave Sarah alone. And I want my money. Either you pay me, or I'll have you in court."

"You'll get your ruddy money; now get out of here before I have you thrown out."

"Is something wrong, Haydon?" Moira Dapeers asked softly.

Haydon whirled around at the sound of his wife's voice. "No, my dear, everything's just fine."

Moira Dapeers smiled warmly at Taggert. "How nice to see you again, Mr. Taggert," she said. "I'm so glad you could come by."

"Mr. Taggert was just leaving," Haydon said.

"On the contrary." Michael Taggert smiled slowly. "I'm in no rush. I think I'll stay for a while."

"Haydon," Moira asked, "who is that disreputable-looking person over there? He said he was a friend of yours." She pointed to the bar, where a portly, red-haired man in a dirty porkpie hat and a brown checkered waistcoat was wiping his nose on his sleeve.

Haydon grimaced. "He's not a friend, exactly," he said quickly. "But I better go and have a word with him." Nodding brusquely at his wife, he stalked over to the bar. "What the blazes are you doing here?" he whispered, hoping his wife hadn't taken it into her head to follow him.

"Now, now." Blimpey Groggins finished wiping his nose. "Is that any way to speak to a customer?"

"Customer," Haydon hissed. He glanced behind him and saw that Moira was still talking to Taggert and Sarah. "This is hardly your sort of place, is it?"

"Wouldn't be caught dead 'ere, if you want to know the truth," Blimpey said amiably. "The beer tastes like cat's piss and all these bloody plants makes me nose run."

"There's nothing wrong with my beer," Haydon said defensively. "But leaving that aside, what are you doing here?"

Blimpey put his glass down on the polished bartop. "I think you know the answer to that one, mate. I'm givin' you a report. I took care of that little message you wanted delivered."

"For God's sake, did you have to come by tonight to tell me that?" Haydon interrupted. "You could've come round tomorrow."

"Look, mate. I don't much like threatenin' people. I done what you wanted done so's I could get it outta the way, like. Now just give me me lolly and I'll clear off." Blimpey Groggins didn't much like doing this kind of work. Fact was, he hated it. But he hated going hungry more.

Haydon looked around to see if anyone was looking at them. But no one was paying attention. "What did he say?"

Blimpey shrugged. "What they always say. That 'e' needs more time."

"That's all?"

"'Ey, mate. I didn't stand and chat with the bloke, I just delivered the bleedin' message like you wanted. Now pay me and I'll be on me way."

"I can't pay you right now," Haydon cried. "I've got a roomful of guests."

"You got a cash box full of lolly too," Blimpey pointed out. "And I don't want to 'ave to make another trip round 'ere. I'm a busy man."

"You'll have to come back tomorrow," Haydon insisted. "It's not convenient just now."

Blimpey's eyes narrowed. "Listen, mate, I done me job and I want me money. Now pay up right now or I'll be 'avin' a little chat with that constable up on the corner. Understand?"

Haydon glared at him, but Blimpey didn't so much as blink. "Oh, all right." Again, he looked around to make sure that no one was watching, then he shoved his hands in his pocket and drew out a wad of bills. Handing them to Blimpey, he said, "Here, now clear out."

"Fine by me, mate." Blimpey pocketed the cash. "I don't see why you don't like payin' what you owe. I thought you was rich? You've got two other pubs beside this one and your wife's got money. But, blimey, you're about the stingiest sod I've ever met. Next time you need a body to do your dirty work, call someone else." He shook his head in disgust, turned and walked out.

Haydon closed his eyes for a moment. When he opened them a moment later, his expression hardened as he saw Michael Taggert bending close to Sarah, his lips inches from her ear as he talked to her.

"Mr. Dapeers, we need another keg." Molly's nasal screech reached him over the noise of the crowd.

Haydon sighed. He was the only one with the key to the taproom. "I'll get one, Molly," he called, pulling the key out of his pocket and heading to the small door at the far end of the bar.

As he stepped into the dimly lighted hallway, Haydon thought he heard a muffled shout over the din from the public bar. He stopped, wondering if there had been an accident or a brawl out on the street. Then he told himself to mind his own business, he had troubles of his own. He continued on, past the unused kitchen on one side of the passageway and the entrance to the saloon bar on the other. The door to the box room was open as he passed. Haydon reached over and yanked it shut. At the far end of the hall, he came to the taproom, unlocked it and stepped inside. He struck a match and lit the gas lamp. He'd just started toward the stack of kegs when the light dimmed, sputtered and then failed completely.

"Bloody hell," he muttered, "what's wrong with that ruddy lamp?" He started to turn when he felt a crushing blow to the side of his head.

The blow stunned him so badly, he didn't even feel the knife slide into his back.

• • •

Mrs. Jeffries, housekeeper to Inspector Gerald Witherspoon of Scotland Yard, reached up and tugged at the collar of her brown bombazine dress. Loosening it a bit, she sighed in satisfaction and continued down the back stairs to the kitchen.

The rest of the household, save for the inspector, who was working late this evening, were already sitting around the kitchen table waiting for her. "I'm sorry to be late," she said, "but it took longer at Luty's than I'd planned."

"They left, then?" Smythe, the coachman, asked. He was a big man with dark hair, harsh features and a pair of rich brown eyes that generally sparkled with good humor.

"Oh yes, I saw them off." Mrs. Jeffries pulled out a chair at the head of the table and sat down.

"How long are they going to be gone?" Betsy, the maid, asked. She brushed a stray lock of blond hair off her cheek. She was a pretty young woman of twenty, with bright blue eyes, a slender figure and an inquisitive nature.

"I believe Luty and Hatchet were still having words over that very issue when I left," Mrs. Jeffries replied with a smile. The housekeeper was a handsome middle-aged woman in her fifties, with dark auburn hair streaked with gray at the temples, a plump motherly figure and a pair of smiling brown eyes that masked a keen intelligence.

"Typical," Mrs. Goodge, the cook, snorted. "Them two are the only people I know who'd be arguin' over how long they was goin' to stay on holiday just as they were boardin' the train to go."

"Luty is bound and determined to stay for the entire two weeks," Mrs. Jeffries explained, "while Hatchet wants to come back after only one week."

"That's funny," Wiggins, the baby-faced, round-cheeked footman said. "It's usually Hatchet that likes goin' to places like Lord Lovan's country house. What's got into 'im?"

"He hates Scotland," Mrs. Jeffries replied. "Claims the air makes him dizzy."

"Rubbish." The cook reached for the pitcher of light ale and poured herself a glass. "There must be more to it than that. Hatchet's never been dizzy in his life!"

"He's probably scared he'll miss a murder if 'e's gone too long," Smythe suggested. "It's about time for another one; we 'aven't 'ad us a good one since March."

"I don't want another one yet," Wiggins cried. "It's too bloomin' 'ot to be dashing about all over London lookin' for clues and—"

"You never want us to have one," Betsy said accusingly, glaring at the young footman.

"That's not true," Wiggins said defensively. "I just don't like the idea of some poor person gettin' murdered just so's we won't be bored, that's all."

"Smythe wasn't advocating killing anyone." Mrs. Goodge jumped into the argument too. "He was merely saying that Hatchet's only reason for not wanting to stay too long at Lord Lovan's was because he didn't want to chance missing one."

"Really, Wiggins," Mrs. Jeffries said soothingly, "none of us like murders, but the fact is they do happen. Why, none of us came to work for the inspector with any idea that we'd end up investigating his cases."

She was referring to the fact that Inspector Gerald Witherspoon, formerly a clerk in the records room, was now, thanks considerably to their efforts, Scotland Yard's leading investigator of homicides. The fact that no one, including the inspector, could account for his phenomenal success, was also their doing.

"What's the matter," Betsy asked, "don't you like investigating?"

"'Corse I like it." Wiggins frowned. "It's just that I don't want to 'ave one now, that's all. It's too bloomin' 'ot."

"You just don't want anything comin' up and takin' you away from Maureen," Smythe teased. "Mind you, I don't blame ya, lad, she's a fine-lookin' girl."

"Maureen's got nuthin' to do with it," Wiggins protested, but his round apple cheeks turned bright red and he couldn't quite look the coachman in the eye.

Mrs. Jeffries decided that debating murder and talking about their friends Luty and her butler, Hatchet, were one thing. Teasing poor Wiggins about his romantic endeavors was something else. "Well," she said firmly, "I don't think it's up to any of us when a murder will happen. Generally, those decisions are made by someone else."

"I'd think you'd be chompin' at the bit for another one," Smythe said, taking a long sip of his ale. "You missed the last one."

"He didn't really miss it," Betsy said. "He only had a broken leg."

"That's right," Mrs. Goodge put in, "and he did his fair share even then."

Mrs. Jeffries beamed approvingly as she saw the footman's blush fade and a pleased grin cross his face. The household was learning. A smile and a few words of praise went a long way to taking the sting out of a bit of teasing.

"And a fine job 'e did too," Smythe added.

"Well, I didn't do all that much," Wiggins said modestly. "And it's not that I don't like snoopin' about and askin' questions; me and Fred enjoy gettin' out and helpin'. It's just that sometimes I get this awful feelin' that we're . . ." He paused, his face creased in concentration.

"We're what?" Mrs. Jeffries prompted. She was genuinely curious now. Wiggins was no fool, something was bothering him, something important.

"I don't know how to put it." The footman shook his head. "But sometimes I almost get the feelin' that we're makin' a murder 'appen just so we can 'ave an excuse to get out and 'unt down the killer."

"Don't be daft," Mrs. Goodge scoffed.

"That's silly," Betsy cried.

"Don't be so stupid, lad," Smythe said.

Mrs. Jeffries frowned at them all. "Just a moment now. Don't be too quick to judge Wiggins's words. His concern is important."

"But, Mrs. Jeffries." Betsy pushed her plate of cheese, bread and pickled onion to one side and leaned forward. "None of us would ever wish death on someone else. Wiggins is just bein' fanciful."

"But if it's bothering him, Betsy," the housekeeper replied calmly, "then I think it's important we bring it out in the open and discuss it." She turned her attention to the footman. "Do you really think that simply because we've proved ourselves to be quite good at solving murder that we're actually causing them to happen?"

Wiggins looked down at the floor and stared at the top of Fred, their mongrel dog's head. "Well, if you put it like that, it does sound silly," he admitted.

"And do you think that if we stopped investigating the inspector's cases, that murder would disappear from the city of London?" she continued.

"'Corse not," he said. "It's just that sometimes I get this feelin' . . ."

"Feelin'?" Smythe interjected. "What kind of feelin'?"

Wiggins shrugged helplessly. "I'm not sure. But sometimes I feel right bad inside. 'Ere we are, sitting around bein' bored doin' the household chores and all of us wishin' we 'ad a good excuse to get out and about and do a bit of snoopin'. Then the next thing you know, the inspector's got 'imself a case and we're all 'appy as larks and some poor person's dead. It don't feel right, that's all."

Everyone gazed at him silently. The only sound was the ticking of the clock on the wall and the far-off sound of street traffic coming through the open window of the kitchen.

Finally, Mrs. Jeffries said, "Wiggins, I'm sorry you feel that way. Would you rather stay out of the inspector's cases from now on?"

"No," he cried, his eyes widening in alarm. "I didn't mean that. 'Elpin' solve murders is important work, we've done a lot of good in this city—" He broke off and smiled sheepishly. "Oh, toss me for a game of tin soldiers, I don't know what I'm on about tonight. Just leave it go, will ya? Must be this 'eat that's makin' me rattle on. We're not such a bad lot, even if we do get bored every now and again and want us another murder."

"Good," Mrs. Jeffries said firmly. "I was hoping you'd come to that conclusion. I too think we do some very important work."

The fact that the entire household and their friends Luty Belle Crookshank and her butler, Hatchet, frequently helped solve the inspector's murder cases was an important part of their lives. Not that dear Inspector Witherspoon had any idea he was getting help, of course. That would never do.

Gerald Witherspoon had been a clerk in the records room when he'd inherited this house from his late aunt Euphemia. He'd also inherited a modest fortune. Smythe and Wiggins had come with the house; Mrs. Jeffries, Mrs. Goodge and Betsy were later additions. How fortunate, Mrs. Jeffries thought as she surveyed the faces around the table, that all of them were dedicated to the man and to solving murders.

They were really quite good at it.

Inspector Gerald Witherspoon tried not to look directly at the body sprawled on the floor next to an unopened keg of beer. He didn't much care for corpses. Especially the ones that still had knives sticking out of their backs.

"Doesn't look like he's been dead long, sir," Constable Barnes said. "The body's still warm."

Witherspoon suppressed a shudder.

"Mind you, the heat could account for the body temperature," Barnes said casually, getting to his feet and brushing his hands off. His craggy face creased in worry. "How long ago was he found?"

"Only moments after the murder occurred," Witherspoon murmured. He hoped that Barnes wasn't waiting for him to examine the body; he wasn't sure if he could. He felt rather faint. Must be the heat, he told himself.

"Don't you want to have a look, sir?" Barnes asked, stepping back respectfully.

"Oh no," Witherspoon said quickly. "We'd best wait for the police surgeon. I wouldn't want to destroy any evidence."

As there was nothing but a dead man with a knife stuck between his shoulder blades, the constable didn't see how the inspector having a look at the body would destroy anything. But he wasn't one to question his superior's motives. Barnes reached up and pulled off his helmet; he ran his fingers through his thick, iron-gray hair and sighed. "At least this one didn't lay here all night. In this heat, he'd have been stinkin' to high heaven by tomorrow morning."

Witherspoon's stomach contracted at Constable Barnes's colorful image. He was rather squeamish about such things and it was getting dreadfully difficult to hide the fact that dead bodies and blood and awful things like that made him feel light-headed. It wasn't that he wasn't dedicated to his work, he most certainly was, no one could ever accuse Gerald Witherspoon of neglecting his duty. He just wished that he wasn't expected to stare at the corpses. Gracious, it wasn't as if the knife in the fellow's back was going to tell him anything. "Who discovered the body?"

"The victim's sister-in-law, Joanne Dapeers," Barnes replied, popping his helmet back on his head. "Soon as she saw the body, she started screamin' to high heaven. Luckily, the barman, when he saw what had happened, had the good sense to lock the door and then send for the constable."

"What's the victim's name?"

"Haydon Dapeers. He owned the pub."

"Were there any witnesses?" Witherspoon didn't know why he bothered to ask. He knew there wouldn't be any. There never were witnesses in the cases to which he got assigned. Somehow, that didn't seem to be fair.

"I don't think so, sir," Barnes said.

"But there's a roomful of people out there." Witherspoon gestured toward the public bar with his thumb. "Surely one of them saw something?"

Barnes shook his head. "I don't think so, sir. According to what Constable Maxton said, everyone was outside or at the window, watching a brawl that broke out on the street when the murder must have happened. That's one of the reasons we got here so quickly. Maxton had come down to stop the fisticuffs. Of course, as soon as he'd arrived the brawlers took off. He'd just started back to his post when the barman comes dashing out and says that someone's been murdered."

"Oh dear," Witherspoon muttered. He took one last look at the corpse and sighed. This wasn't going to be an easy case, he could feel it in his bones.

From outside the closed door, he heard the sound of heavy footsteps and then a sharp knock. "That's probably the police surgeon," Witherspoon said.

Barnes opened the door and a young red-haired man wearing a dark suit and carrying a medical bag stepped inside. "Good evening, Inspector Witherspoon," the man said pleasantly.

"Good evening," the inspector replied. He stared at the man in confusion. "Where's Dr. Potter?"

"Gout," the fellow replied. He stepped over and knelt down by the body. "Poor Dr. Potter's got a ripping bad case of it; he'll be flat on his back for weeks."

Witherspoon couldn't believe his luck. Potter wasn't his favorite of police surgeons. "Oh dear, how awful for Potter."

"I expect he'll be fit as a fiddle before too long, Inspector." He popped open his bag and began rummaging around inside. "Now, let's see what we have here."

"Do I know you, sir?" Witherspoon asked. The man looked awfully familiar, but the inspector couldn't quite put his finger on where they'd met.

"We met some time ago at St. Thomas's. The name's Bosworth. Dr. Bosworth."

"This must be most upsetting for you, Mrs. Dapeers," the inspector said kindly, "most upsetting, indeed. I'm so sorry to have to bother you with questions at a time like this, but it's rather important we start looking for whoever did this foul deed immediately."

Moira Dapeers was obviously in shock. A small middle-aged woman, she had brown hair and a thin, rather mournful face. As she sat back against the bright red velvet cushions of the plush seat, her complexion was as white as a ghost. They'd taken her into the privacy of one of the partitioned sections of the public bar, but even a glass of strong Irish whisky hadn't brought the color back to her pale cheeks. "I understand," she said slowly. Her brown eyes were glazed and her lips trembled.

She brushed a lock of hair off her face. "Please, go ahead. I'd like to get this over with so I can go home."

Witherspoon nodded. "When was the last time you saw your husband alive?"

"It must have been around half-past six," she murmured. "Yes, I know it was then, because it was right before the brawl started. Haydon had just gone into the taproom when I heard this awful ruckus from outside."

"And what happened then?"

Moira Dapeers shrugged. "What do you think happened? Everyone went over to the windows to see what was going on in the street."

"Who do you mean by 'everyone'?" Witherspoon asked curiously.

"I mean everyone who was here tonight for Haydon's birthday celebration." Moira's voice trembled as she said her late husband's name. "We had our friends and neighbors round to help us celebrate, you see. It was Haydon's birthday today and we were opening the pub. It was supposed to be a wonderful night, but—" She broke off and began weeping.

Witherspoon looked at Constable Barnes. "I think you'd better arrange for one of the constables to take Mrs. Dapeers home. She's in no condition to make a statement right now."

"Right, sir," Barnes said, turning toward the door that led to the public bar. They'd asked the other guests to wait there under the watchful eyes of several constables.

"I'm all right." Moira hiccuped softly and brushed the tears off her cheeks. "Really, I am."

Witherspoon let his instincts as a gentleman overcome his training as a policeman. "No, ma'am," he said softly, "you're not. We'll have someone take you home so you can get a good night's rest. Tomorrow we'll come round to take your statement."

As soon as Moira Dapeers had been escorted out, Witherspoon spoke to Barnes. "Have the police constables take the statements of everyone who was here tonight. Make sure they get proper names and addresses. Then tell everyone they can go home."

Barnes stared at him in shock. "Go home, sir? Without us talking to them?"

"That's right, Barnes." He sighed. "We can start asking questions in the morning. I don't think our killer is likely to bolt tonight."

"How do you figure that, sir?"

"Because it's obviously one of them and they think they've gotten away with it." Witherspoon couldn't put his finger on how he knew this, but he did know it. For once, he was going to do as his housekeeper, Mrs. Jeffries, advised; he was going to rely on his instincts. "For the moment that's precisely what I want that person to think too. Once everyone's gone, I think I'd better have another word with the police surgeon. He looks like a bright sort of chap."

Dr. Bosworth nodded at the men with the stretcher and stepped away from the body. "Now, what did you want to ask me, Inspector?"

"What can you tell us about the victim?" Witherspoon asked.

"Well, he died instantly," Bosworth said slowly. "The killer was either an expert on human anatomy or very lucky. The blade sliced clean into the heart, killing the victim within seconds. The heart is a pump, you see." Bosworth's voice rose enthusiastically. "Quite a wonder of nature, actually. People don't really appreciate how very efficient and marvelous an organ it is. Of course, once it stops pumping they learn soon enough. I expect the blade of the weapon lopped off the left ventricle when the knife went into the poor man. Mind you, I won't know for certain till I do the postmortem."

Witherspoon's stomach turned over. "Er, are you certain it was the knife that killed him?"

"There was no evidence of prior poisoning nor any evidence of other bodily injuries except for the blow on the head. But that shouldn't have killed him; it wasn't even hard enough to make a dent in the skull," Bosworth replied. "But again, I won't know for sure until after the postmortem. I'll be doing that tonight, so I should have a report ready for you by tomorrow morning."

"Are you thinking something else killed the man?" Barnes asked the inspector.

"It's always possible, Barnes," Witherspoon replied. "Dr. Bosworth, did you . . . er . . . retrieve the weapon?"

"Naturally." Bosworth pulled a long flat object wrapped in brown paper out of his bag and handed it to Barnes. "We can't have some poor soul being carted all over London with a knife sticking out of his back, can we? Here's your evidence, all nice and neatly wrapped for you."

"What kind of knife was it?" Witherspoon asked. He took the proffered object and quickly handed it to the constable. He was embarrassed to remember he'd not taken a proper look at it when he'd first come in tonight. But drat, he really hated examining things sticking out of people's backs.

Bosworth snapped his bag closed. "It looks like a common kitchen knife. Not a new one, mind you. The wood handle was worn quite badly. The blade is ten inches long and quite sharp. My guess is it was sharpened very recently."

"You say the handle was worn?" Witherspoon said hopefully. "Then perhaps someone will be able to identify the weapon."

Bosworth shook his head. "When I said it was worn, I didn't mean it had any distinguishing features, Inspector. I meant that it had been washed many times and a bit of the color had washed out of the wood. It's a common kitchen knife. There's nothing extraordinary about the weapon. You can probably find one in every household in London."

# CHAPTER 2

"Good evening, sir," Mrs. Jeffries said to the inspector as she took his hat. "You're rather late tonight. We were starting to worry."

"I'm afraid my tardiness couldn't be helped, Mrs. Jeffries. I hope the staff didn't wait dinner on me," Witherspoon replied. "I'm really not in the least hungry."

"It's only a cold supper, sir," Mrs. Jeffries said. "Betsy can bring it up on a tray when you're ready for it. Would you like a glass of sherry before you eat?"

"That's an excellent idea." Witherspoon followed his housekeeper into the drawing room and sat down in his favorite chair. "There's been a murder, you see. Poor chap got himself stabbed tonight. That's why I'm so late getting home."

Mrs. Jeffries deliberately kept her face bland as she handed her employer a glass of pale amber sherry. Wiggins's words tweaked her conscience a bit, but the truth was, she was overjoyed. A murder. They had themselves a murder to investigate.

"How very unfortunate," she said, taking a seat opposite the inspector. "Was it a domestic dispute of some kind?"

She sincerely hoped it wasn't. Those kind of murders were never very interesting to snoop about in; they were simply too obvious. It was almost always a drunken husband or a mousy wife who had been pushed just that bit too hard.

"Oh no, not so far as we can tell." Witherspoon took a sip of sherry. "A publican named Haydon Dapeers was killed. The knife went clean through his heart; at least that's what Dr. Bosworth told me. Can you believe it? The poor man got murdered at his own birthday celebration."

"How awful," Mrs. Jeffries replied. She couldn't believe her good luck. Dr. Bosworth was on the scene! The good doctor had given her information on the inspector's cases on more than one occasion in the past. He was intelligent, observant and most important, he could keep his own counsel. She made a mental note to nip out and see Bosworth first thing tomorrow morning. But for now, she wanted as much information as possible. "Were there any witnesses?"

"No, Dapeers had gone back to the taproom when he was killed. No one saw anything. There was some kind of altercation out on the street when the murder happened. Everyone else in the place had dashed over to the windows or gone outside to have a look."

"Were there a lot of people in the pub when the murder took place?" she asked.

"Actually, it was quite crowded. It was the pub's opening night as well as Haydon Dapeers's birthday. Sad really. Here the man was surrounded by friends and relatives and he ends up getting murdered. I don't know, Mrs. Jeffries"—Witherspoon shook his head sadly—"sometimes I wonder what the world is coming to."

"Well, sir," she said calmly, "I don't really think I agree with you. Remember, you do see the results of violence more than most people. But do keep in mind that fifty years ago or so, there wouldn't have been someone like you to even investigate this unfortunate person's death. Scotland Yard and the entire police force didn't even exist. At least now our society tries to make sure that justice is done, and you, sir, do more than anyone I know to ensure that it is." She decided her dear inspector needed a bit of bucking up. Occasionally, he allowed the more sordid aspects of his work to undermine his self-confidence. She was sure that was what the problem was tonight. He was merely feeling as though he wouldn't be up to the task in front of him.

"How good of you to remind me, Mrs. Jeffries." Witherspoon sighed dramatically. "You're right, of course. I daresay the world hasn't really changed."

"Actually, sir, I do believe that because of people like yourself, it's a considerably better world than it used to be." It never hurt to bolster the man's opinion of himself.

"Thank you. I needed to hear those words."

"It's a wonder you got home before midnight," Mrs. Jeffries said brightly. Now that the inspector was over his obligatory maudlin philosophizing, she wanted to get the details of the murder out of him while they were fresh in his mind. "What with all those people to interview."

"Oh, I didn't bother with that," Witherspoon replied airily. "I told Barnes to make sure we had everyone's name and address. I'll start the interviewing tomorrow."

Shocked, Mrs. Jeffries stared at him. "You don't think one of the guests is the killer?"

"I've no idea who the killer is." He shrugged. "But my instinct was to let everyone go home. I thought perhaps it would be best to let the murderer think he'd gotten away with it." He smiled kindly at his housekeeper. "Ever since you told me about listening to my 'inner voice' that time—you must remember, it was when I was having such a difficult time cracking that case. . . ." He paused, his forehead crinkled in concentration as he tried to recall precisely which case it was. "Oh, I don't remember exactly which one it was, but it was last year sometime. I was having a dreadful time, simply dreadful. You advised me to listen to my instincts, to let my 'policeman's voice' guide my actions and thoughts. Of course, you were absolutely right and I cracked that case in no time. I'm going to do the same thing on this one."

Utterly speechless, Mrs. Jeffries gaped at him. Gracious, who would have thought he'd taken her words so seriously? All she'd ever done was to try to make him feel confident about himself. What had she created? "I see. And you thought it best to let all your suspects leave and go home tonight, is that it?"

"Yes." He beamed at her. "That's it precisely. I saw no point in keeping everyone hanging about the Gilded Lily Pub while I asked questions. I've found that murderers are far more likely to make mistakes when they think they have gotten away with it."

Mrs. Jeffries didn't agree. But she could hardly say so. Especially as the inspector seemed to be basing his behavior in this case on advice she'd previously given him. "Exactly where is the Gilded Lily Pub?"

"It's not far from Scotland Yard." Witherspoon drained his glass. "Quite a lovely place, actually. Brass fittings and gilded mirrors, beautiful etched windows and carved panels on the partitions. It's the sort of place where one would feel comfortable taking a lady, if you know what I mean.

Perhaps when Lady Cannonberry returns from the country, we'll try finding an equally refined pub around our own neighborhood here."

"That's a lovely idea. And the Gilded Lily is close to Scotland Yard, you say?"

"Not far at all." He stood up abruptly. "I say, we haven't gotten another letter from Lady Cannonberry, have we?"

"No, sir," Mrs. Jeffries forced herself to say calmly. She knew he missed their neighbor, but right now she didn't want to discuss the inspector's romantic affiliations. She wanted facts about this murder. "What time did the murder occur?"

"I think I'll have that cold supper now," Witherspoon said just as she asked her question. "I'm suddenly famished."


"Is that all you got out of 'im?" Smythe asked incredulously. "Just the name of the pub and the name of the victim?"

Mrs. Jeffries nodded. She felt rather foolish. As soon as the inspector was safely ensconced in the dining room with his supper, she'd called the rest of the household together to tell them the news. But she had so very little to report. "I know it isn't much, but he was in the strangest mood tonight. He wanted to talk about the murder, but he didn't want to say very much."

"You say he had a room full of suspects and he let them all go home without even interviewing them?" Mrs. Goodge asked curiously. "That don't sound right."

"It isn't right," Mrs. Jeffries replied. "For some strange reason, the inspector seems to think it's best to let the killer think he got away with it. He won't start interviewing the people who were in the pub when the murder occurred until tomorrow."

"Did you get us a few of their names?" Betsy asked hopefully.

"I'm afraid not."

"Where's this pub at, then?" Wiggins pressed.

"I'm not really sure," Mrs. Jeffries admitted. "But it's quite near Scotland Yard."

"'Ow about the time of death?" Smythe stared at her hopefully.

"Sometime this evening."

"What kinda knife was it?" Wiggins asked.

"He didn't say."

"Blimey," Smythe exclaimed, "you didn't get much out of 'im, did ya?"

"It's not Mrs. Jeffries's fault if the inspector has suddenly got tongue-tied," Betsy snapped. "So give it a rest." She turned and smiled at the house-keeper. "What do you think has gotten into him? It's not like the inspector to be so cagey. He usually tells you everything."

Mrs. Jeffries was at a loss to explain the inspector's behavior to the others. If she told them he was simply acting on advice she'd given him in the past, she'd feel absolutely idiotic. It would be difficult to make them understand. "He might have just been tired," she ventured.

"Me too." Wiggins yawned widely. "I'm dead on me feet. So what do we do now? It's not like we've got much to start on."

"We've got plenty of information," the housekeeper said firmly. Just because Inspector Witherspoon had developed a bad case of discretion didn't mean they weren't going to get started right away. "We know the name of the victim, the name of the pub, the approximate time of death and we know the killer used a knife."

"I can find out where this 'ere Gilded Lily Pub is," Smythe volunteered. "If it's near Scotland Yard, I can nip out to the stables tomorrow mornin' and talk to one of the cabbies in the area. They know where all the pubs are."

"But this was a new one," Mrs. Jeffries pointed out. "It had only just opened a few hours before the murder."

Smythe waved a hand dismissively. "That don't matter. The cabbies'll know where it is."

"How quickly can you find out?" Betsy asked.

"Be back before breakfast," he replied, giving the maid a cocky grin. "And then we can get crackin'; right, Mrs. Jeffries?"


Smythe was as good as his word. As they sat down to breakfast the next morning, he rushed in through the back door, paused to pat Fred, who was bouncing at his feet, and then announced that the Gilded Lily Pub was on the corner of Minyard Street and Bonham Road. "It's less than 'alf a mile from Scotland Yard," he finished as he pulled out a chair and sat down.

"So where do we start?" Wiggins asked excitedly.

"I think you should get over to the area and start talking to the street boys and costermongers," Mrs. Jeffries said. "See what you can find out about the victim."

"Do you want me to have a go at the shopkeepers in the area?" Betsy asked.

Mrs. Jeffries regarded her thoughtfully. "No, I want you to find out where Haydon lived and then nip round to his home and see if you can make contact with someone from his household. See what you can find out."

"But he was murdered at the pub," Betsy protested.

"Yes, but Dapeers was at a celebration with his friends and relations," Mrs. Jeffries explained. "So we must find out as much as we can about everyone present and see if any of his relatives or acquaintances had a reason to murder him. The best way to do that is to learn what we can about him and his household. As we all know, it's usually those nearest and dearest to us that are the most dangerous."

"What about me?" Mrs. Goodge asked. "I've only got one name to go on, and Dapeers was only a publican. I don't think my sources are goin' to know much about the man."

Mrs. Jeffries understood the cook's dilemma. Mrs. Goodge had a veritable army of tradespeople who trooped through her kitchen. Coster-mongers, delivery boys, rag-and-bones men. She also had a wide network of friends from her many years of cooking for the cream of London society. But unfortunately, in this case, Mrs. Goodge was right. It was highly unlikely that any of her sources would know much about a common pub owner. Or would they? "I'm not so sure about that," Mrs. Jeffries said. "Perhaps you will find out something. You must try."

"I don't know, Mrs. Jeffries," Mrs. Goodge said sadly. "He's only a pub owner. Not that there's anything wrong with that, but it's not like he had half of London snooping about and watching him when he was alive. Probably no one gave a toss about his coming and goings. It's not like he's anybody important now, is it?"

"Would you like to go out and ask a few questions, then?" the house-keeper said.

"Certainly not," Mrs. Goodge retorted, shocked at the very notion of leaving her kitchen. "I'm staying right here. You just be sure that this lot"—she swept her arm around the table—"gets me some names. My sources may not know anything today about that murder, but they're all just as nosy as we are. A few well-chosen words and I'll have 'em out on the streets learning all sorts of interesting bits and pieces."

"That's the spirit, Mrs. Goodge." Smythe reached for his tea. "Luty and Hatchet'll both be right narked. You know how Luty 'ates to miss a murder."

"What about Hatchet?" Betsy added. "He's just as bad."

"I wonder if we shouldn't send them a telegram," Mrs. Jeffries murmured. "We could use their help."

"Of course we must send a telegram," Mrs. Goodge agreed. "If Luty misses another murder, we'll never hear the end of it."

The Dapeers house was much grander than Witherspoon expected. The tall, redbrick structure was located on Percy Street, off the Tottenham Court Road. "I must say, he lives in rather a large house for a publican," Witherspoon muttered. He glanced around the elegant drawing room, his gaze noting the pale rose wallpaper, the heavy green velvet curtains at the windows, the intricate wood carving on the top of the mantelpiece and the opulent furnishings. The green-and-rose-striped settee and the contrasting balloon-backed chairs would be worth more than six months of his salary.

"Well," Barnes said softly, "he does own three pubs. But even so, this is a right posh place."

"I think we're in the wrong business," Witherspoon joked.

"Good morning, gentlemen," Moira Dapeers said as she swept into the room. "I'm so sorry to have kept you waiting. Please sit down, gentlemen." She motioned them toward the settee. "That'll be all, Perkins," she said, dismissing the servant.

Witherspoon and Barnes both sat down. Moira Dapeers, wearing a stiff, black bombazine dress, sank down in a chair opposite them. "The household is in a bit of a state this morning," she said, smiling apologetically. "It's not my habit to keep people waiting. Haydon couldn't stand to be kept waiting."

"We're sorry to intrude upon your grief, madam," Witherspoon said formally, "but we've no choice in the matter. We really must ask you a few questions."

She waved a hand in the air. "Oh, that's all right. Now that I've gotten over the shock of Haydon's death, I'm quite able to talk about it."

The inspector studied her thoughtfully. She did, indeed, appear to have recovered from the shock. Her gaze was honest and direct, her color excellent, and if he wasn't mistaken, she was wearing just the smallest amount of lip rouge. "Could you please tell us everything that happened last night?"

"That shouldn't be too difficult," she said brightly. "As you know, we had the opening of the Gilded Lily scheduled to coincide with Haydon's birthday. That was his idea, naturally. Personally, I thought it a bit common. Rather like asking everyone you know to drop in to wish you many happy returns and then forcing them to hang about and buy their own drinks."

"Was the Gilded Lily your husband's only business?" Constable Barnes asked.

Witherspoon gave him a sharp look, wondering why he asked a question they already knew the answer to.

"Oh no." She laughed. "We own two other pubs. They're doing quite well too. Mind you, neither of them is near as fancy as the Gilded Lily, but they're decent places and they do us well enough. But Haydon wanted to make the new pub absolutely spectacular. He poured ever so much money into it. Brass fittings, velvet benches, etched windows. Oh my, yes, he was determined to make it a showplace."

"Mrs. Dapeers," the inspector said. "About last evening?"

"Oh yes, well, as I was saying, the pub was scheduled to open on Haydon's birthday. He claimed he wanted to make a celebration of it, you see. So he invited some friends and acquaintances to come round. He said he was going to make a bit of a party of the whole thing. But I noticed he didn't give them free beer. Everyone was paying for what they drank."

Witherspoon tried to be patient. He didn't want to have to interrupt a lady, but goodness, how long was she going to harp on her late husband's boorish behavior?

"My sister-in-law and I arrived a little after five o'clock," she continued. "No, that's wrong. We didn't get there until twenty past; it took some time before we were able to get a hansom."

"And who else was there when you arrived?" Witherspoon asked. He'd no idea what he was trying to find out, but he decided to plunge right on in anyway. After all, Mrs. Jeffries was always telling him to trust his "inner voice." Right now that voice was telling him to learn as much as he could and sort it out later. Perhaps he'd oughtn't to be so impatient with the lady. Perhaps if he allowed her to ramble on, she might tell him more than she intended.

"Let me see. . . ." She paused again, her forehead wrinkling in concentration. "There was Molly and Mick, of course. They're our employees. There were one or two other staff members too. Haydon insisted we have a full staff. And I believe he was going to hire another barmaid; I know he was planning on interviewing another one yesterday morning. He was that sure the place would be a success right from opening night and he wanted to make sure we had enough help to take care of our customers."

"Yes, yes," Witherspoon encouraged. "But back to my question." He already had a complete list of who was present when the murder occurred and he wasn't sure why he needed to know who was there before the killing. But something deep inside was telling him it was important information.

Moira cocked her head and stroked her chin as she tried to remember. "The men from Bestal's were there. And Michael Taggert—no," she corrected. "I tell a lie; Michael didn't come in until after we'd been there a few minutes. I remember distinctly watching him come through the front door. I was thinking there'd be a ruckus, you see. Haydon was being very mean about Mr. Taggert. He kept finding excuses not to pay the poor boy. I think he was really just being nasty, though."

"Mr. Taggert and Mr. Dapeers were enemies?" Witherspoon asked eagerly. He couldn't believe it; Mrs. Jeffries was right. His inner voice was working properly.

"Oh no." Moira laughed gaily. "They weren't precisely enemies. But Haydon had hired Mr. Taggert to do the etching on the windows and some intricate wood carving on the back bar. He kept putting off paying him for the work. Mr. Taggert was getting rather insistent, I'm afraid."

"Was there some kind of altercation between Mr. Taggert and your husband last night?" Witherspoon began.

"Oh goodness, yes," Moira replied cheerfully. "I was rather hoping that Mr. Taggert would take a poke at Haydon. I must say, Haydon would have deserved it. But I think Sarah's presence restrained the young man somewhat. That's Sarah Hewett I'm talking about; she's my sister-in-law. She lives here. We took her and her daughter in after my brother died."

Witherspoon glanced at Barnes to see if he was taking notes. The constable was scribbling furiously in his little brown book. Satisfied that

Barnes would remind him to question Sarah Hewett, he turned and gave Mrs. Dapeers an encouraging smile. "Do go on, madam."

"Let's see; aside from the gentlemen from the brewery, Tom and Joanne were there when I came in." She frowned. "No, I tell another lie. They came in right after I did; I remember noticing Joanne's dress as she came into the pub. Though, again, I've no idea why Haydon invited them, he didn't much care for either Tom or his wife."

"But isn't Mr. Tom Dapeers your late husband's brother?" Barnes asked.

"Yes, but they didn't much like one another. They haven't been close for years." She smiled brightly. "In addition, they're rival pub owners. Like us, they own several pubs. I expect Haydon only invited them because he wanted to rub their noses in it a bit."

Perplexed, Witherspoon stared at her. "Rub their noses in it?" he repeated.

"In the fact that he was opening a pub less than a hundred yards away from one of their pubs," she clarified. "Haydon was like that, you see, never content just to do something, he always wanted to outdo his competition. Especially when the competition was his own brother."

"Anyone else, madam?" he asked, shocked to his very core. He wasn't so much surprised at the late Haydon Dapeers's rather dismal character. Witherspoon had observed that people who got themselves murdered frequently had rather awful character flaws. But he was stunned at the widow's casual cheerfulness in recounting her husband's pettiness. Moira Dapeers wasn't just being honest with them, she was positively enjoying herself.

"Well, all the local merchants and shopkeepers were there," she continued. "And the architect who redesigned the inside of the pub. But he didn't stay long. He had no reason to, Haydon had already paid him. I think that's about it—no, wait, I'm forgetting that awful little man at the bar." She pursed her lips in disgust. "There was the most disreputable-looking fellow there when we arrived. Quite dirty, actually. He and Haydon were talking. It surprised me, really. I was sure Haydon was going to toss him out, but he didn't."

"Do you know this man's name?" Witherspoon asked hopefully. None of the statements he'd looked at this morning at the Yard had mentioned a "dirty person."

"I've no idea who he was. But he was gone before Haydon was killed,

I know that. I saw him leave. Rather portly little man, he had red hair and was wearing the filthiest porkpie hat I've ever seen."

"Would you recognize him again if you saw him?" Barnes asked. He glanced at the inspector.

"I expect so," she replied eagerly. "I did get rather a good look at him."

Constable Barnes cleared his throat. "Mrs. Dapeers, you said your husband owned three pubs. Was Mr. Dapeers well liked by his employees?"

"Goodness no." She giggled coquettishly and batted her eyelashes at the astounded-looking constable. "He was an impossible man. Look at the way he treated poor Mr. Taggert! Got the fellow to spend hours on those windows and then wouldn't pay him."

"He refused to pay wages?" Barnes queried.

"He paid eventually," Mrs. Dapeers said. "But never a minute before he had to and he was a real Tartar to work for. Haydon sacked people all the time."

Witherspoon's head was spinning. He'd never met a widow quite like Mrs. Dapeers. He wasn't sure if he was up to any more questions right at the moment. "Mrs. Dapeers," he said politely, "may we have a word with your sister-in-law?"


Dr. Bosworth's dark brown eyes regarded Mrs. Jeffries steadily as they sat across from one another at Lyons Tea Shop in Oxford Circus. "Actually, it was a fairly simple killing," he said. "There's nothing in the least mysterious about the death itself. The poor chap was stabbed from the back. The knife went straight into the heart. He died almost instantly."

Mrs. Jeffries nodded. She'd sent Dr. Bosworth a note early this morning asking him to meet her here. "There was no sign of a struggle or anything like that?"

"No," Bosworth replied slowly. "Not really. He had been hit on the head before he was stabbed, but the postmortem revealed that the blow didn't do any real damage. It only stunned him for a moment or two. I don't think he knew what was happening until it was too late. Whoever killed him crept up from behind, banged him on the head and shoved the knife straight in. The blade pierced the heart; death would have been very swift."

"Were you able to determine what the killer used to hit him with?"

"No," Bosworth admitted honestly. "The wound only barely broke the skin; there wasn't any particular shape to it and no indentation at all on the skull. But I saw nothing lying about the room where the body was found that had blood on it. I know, because I had a good look round when the inspector and the constable stepped out of the room."

"I see." She fingered the white linen serviette in her lap. So far, she hadn't learned anything from the good doctor that she hadn't already heard from the inspector. Drat. "Was there anything special about the knife?" she asked.

"Not that I could see." Bosworth picked up his tea and took a huge gulp. "It appeared to be a standard kitchen knife; the blade was a good ten inches long. It was very sharp."

"I wonder if the murderer brought it with him?" Mrs. Jeffries mused. She made a mental note to try to find out. If the knife was already on the premises, then it could mean that the killer simply acted on the spur of the moment. But if the knife wasn't already in the pub, that meant the killer brought it with him, presumably with the intention of using it.

"Difficult to say." Bosworth yawned. "Oh sorry, but I've been up most of the night doing the postmortem on this one. Actually, as I said, it appears to be a very simple killing. But I will say that whoever murdered Dapeers was very lucky."

"Lucky? How?"

"With his aim. The knife could just as easily have gone into the victim's back and not hit the heart, in which case, the man might not have died so quickly."

She wondered if that was important. "But surely, stabbing someone in the back guarantees certain death."

"Not necessarily," Bosworth said enthusiastically. "When I was in America, I once treated a miner who'd been in a brawl on the Barbary Coast. Fellow had walked about half the night with a knife sticking out of him, didn't bother to come see me till the next morning. He actually survived. The human body is a lot stronger than most people realize."

Mrs. Jeffries knew he wasn't exaggerating. Dr. Bosworth had worked and studied in the United States; specifically, in San Francisco. The knowledge he'd garnered in that turbulent city gave him a depth of experience with violent death that was unsurpassed by any police surgeon in London. As Bosworth had once told her, "There's no shortage of murder and corpses in America."

"Are you saying that the killer might have known precisely where to stab the victim?" she asked eagerly. Finally, she was getting to something important.

He shrugged. "It's certainly possible. There's quite a number of stabbings here in our own fair city that don't result in death. It could well be that the killer knows something about human anatomy. That knife entered the victim's back directly behind the heart. It could have been sheer luck on the killer's part, or he or she could have known exactly what they were doing."

"Gracious, if that were true," she replied, "then the killer would probably be someone who has studied medicine."

Bosworth laughed. "I wouldn't go that far—your killer could just as easily be a butcher or was just plain lucky. But it's something to think about. The knife virtually pierced the heart at the very center. Good aim, I'd say."

Disappointed, Mrs. Jeffries sighed. For once, they had Dr. Bosworth actually doing the postmortem instead of that idiot Dr. Potter, and the cause of death was so clear-cut and simple that it didn't make any difference. For all the good it did them, they might as well have had old Potter bumbling about with the body. "Is there anything else you think might be important?"

Bosworth hesitated and a slow flush crept up his pale cheeks. "Well," he said slowly, "there is something else, but it's most indelicate of me to mention it to a lady."

As his face was now as red as his hair, Mrs. Jeffries knew she was onto something. Eagerly, she leaned forward. "Now don't be silly, Doctor. There isn't much in this world that shocks me. Please, tell me."

He looked about him to ensure the patrons at the nearby tables weren't likely to overhear. "I don't know if this has anything to do with Dapeers's murder, but I did find something else when I was examining the body."

"What was it?"

Bosworth dropped his gaze and stared at his half-full teacup. "When I got inside the fellow, there were certain peculiarities—deterioration of tissue and that sort of thing."

"You mean he was diseased."

"Not just diseased." Bosworth finally looked up. "He was dying."

"Dying? Of what?"

Bosworth blushed again. "It's not very nice."

"No disease that I've ever heard of is 'nice,'" she said, trying hard to keep her impatience in check. "What was it? More important, do you think Dapeers knew he was dying?"

"He knew he had it all right," Bosworth said bluntly. "The disease was advanced enough that he must have known it."

"For goodness' sakes, what was his illness? Tuberculosis?" A pub owner wouldn't want people to know if he had TB, she thought.

"No, that isn't it." Bosworth took another quick glance around the room and then leaned toward Mrs. Jeffries. "Haydon Dapeers had syphilis."

"I'm Sarah Hewett," the lovely young woman announced as she came into the drawing room. "Moira said you wanted to speak to me."

Sarah Hewett hadn't bothered to wear black. Her dress was pale lavender broadcloth, rather worn from one washing too many.

"Yes, I did." The inspector introduced Constable Barnes. "I'm so sorry to intrude, but we must ask you some questions."

"I understand." Sarah sat down in the chair her sister-in-law had just vacated. "I don't think I can be of much help, though. I didn't see anything."

Witherspoon smiled kindly at her. "How long have you lived here?" He thought getting a bit of background information might be helpful.

"Just a few months," Sarah replied. She clamped her hands together in her lap. "I was married to Moira's brother, Charles. He died last year. Haydon and Moira insisted my daughter and I come and live with them."

"How old is your daughter?" Witherspoon didn't think that had anything to do with the murder, but getting this young woman to relax might help her to talk more freely.

Sarah smiled widely. "She's two and a half."

"I understand you were at the Gilded Lily Pub last night when the murder occurred."

She nodded. "As were a number of other people. But as I told you, I didn't see anything. We were all watching the brawl on the street when Haydon went into the taproom. No one even noticed he was missing until Joanne tried to find him to say good night."

"I see." Witherspoon thought hard about what to ask next. "Er, were you standing with Mrs. Dapeers while you were watching the altercation?"

She hesitated briefly. "Well, no. Actually, as soon as I saw all that blood, I went back to the bar to get another glass of ale. It was quite warm, you see. I was thirsty."

"And did the barman serve you?"

"No, he'd come out from behind the bar and gone to stand at the front door." She smiled slightly. "I guess he was curious as to what was going on outside too."

"Did you see anyone going down the hall or into the taproom while you were at the bar?" Witherspoon asked.

"I wasn't paying any attention." She shrugged. "Besides, I didn't go to the bar right away. I went to the front door with everyone else when we heard the shouting start, but I got pushed outside in the crush. As soon as I saw that drayman smash the cabbie's nose and all that blood started running down his face, I couldn't stand it, so I went back inside. But I had to push my way in; it took quite a few minutes."

"Did anyone else come inside with you?" he pressed.

"A couple of other people drifted in, but I don't remember who they were. As I told you, I wasn't paying any attention. It was hot and I was tired. Frankly, Inspector, I wanted nothing more than to find something to drink and go home. I wasn't there to have a good time, I was there because Haydon insisted I come."

"Did you talk to anyone during this time?"

"During what time?" she asked irritably.

"While you were at the bar," he explained patiently. "Did you speak to anyone?"

"No."

"What about Mr. Taggert?"

"He was still outside," she said quickly. "I remember that."

"What makes you so certain?" Witherspoon asked curiously.

She said nothing for a moment and the inspector had the distinct impression she was trying to think of what to say. Finally, she said, "I remember because I had to brush past him as I came back inside. He stepped aside to let me pass."

"I see. Mrs. Hewett, were you present when Mr. Taggert had words with your brother-in-law?"

"I don't know what you mean, Inspector. What kind of 'words'?"

"Specifically, did you hear Mr. Taggert threaten Mr. Dapeers because Mr. Dapeers hadn't paid him for his work?"

"He didn't threaten Haydon," she cried. "At least not with murder."

"So you were present," Witherspoon pressed.

Sarah Hewett looked down at her lap. "All right, I'll admit I was there. But all Michael said was that if Haydon didn't pay him, he'd have him in court. He didn't threaten him with violence."

"Did Mr. Dapeers threaten Mr. Taggert with violence?" Barnes interjected.

"No, he just asked Michael to leave. But Moira came over just then and she likes Michael. Haydon couldn't keep making a fuss in front of her, so Michael stayed."

"And were the two of you together until the fight broke out on the street?" the inspector asked. He found it significant that she referred to him as "Michael" and not "Mr. Taggert."

"Yes," Sarah replied firmly. "That's why I know he couldn't have had anything to do with Haydon's murder. He was with me the whole time until I came back into the pub. And he didn't come in after me, either. I would have noticed him."

Witherspoon studied Sarah Hewett carefully. Her chin was lifted defiantly, her gaze steady and direct. Though he wasn't terribly experienced at matters of the heart, recent events in his own personal life had made him more sensitive to certain situations. This young woman was bound and determined not to say a word to incriminate Michael Taggert. He decided to try a different tactic. "Did your brother-in-law have enemies?"

Surprised by the question, she drew back slightly. "Enemies?" she repeated.

"Yes, people who didn't much like him," the inspector explained.

"I know what the word means, Inspector," Sarah replied. "I was merely surprised at your bluntness. But yes, Haydon did have enemies."

"Who? Can you give us any names?"

"That would take too long, Inspector." She smiled slightly. "But I think I can safely say that just about everyone who knew Haydon disliked him intensely. Apparently, someone disliked him enough to kill him."

# CHAPTER 3

"You can get a decent pint at one of Haydon Dapeers's pubs," said Dick, a street lad who couldn't have been more than sixteen. He nodded knowingly. "Not like the swill they serve at the Black Horse. Stuff's not fit to drink, tastes like cat's piss."

Wiggins nodded in agreement, as though he knew what the boy was talking about, which he didn't. He didn't think Dick knew all that much about it, either. But at least he'd found someone to talk to, someone who'd been hanging about the streets when the murder took place and seemed to know the victim. "So Haydon Dapeers was a nice gent, then?"

"Nice?" The lad snorted in disbelief. "I never said that! He was a right mean ol' bastard. Most folks round these parts couldn't stand him. But he does serve decent ale. I heard his new place is right posh, not like here. Peeked in through the windows last evenin', but I didn't go in or anythin'."

They were sitting in the public bar of the Pale Swan, another pub owned by the late Haydon Dapeers. It was an ordinary public house with white-painted walls, hardwood floors and high-beamed ceilings. Wiggins rather liked it.

"How come people didn't like 'im?" Wiggins asked. He dug in his pocket, pulled out a few coins and nodded to the barman, signaling they'd like another round. Cor, he didn't think Mrs. Jeffries would much like him drinkin' all this beer, not while he was askin' questions. But it was bloomin' 'ot outside and the only way he could get anyone to tell 'im anything was by buyin' 'em a drink.

The barman brought them two more light ales. "Drink up, lads," he said genially, scooping up the coins and moving on down the half-empty bar.

"This is right nice of ya," Dick said, grabbing his glass and taking a huge gulp.

"Got nothin' else to do today. Might as well 'ave a beer or two, seein' as it's so 'ot outside," Wiggins replied. "Now, you were tellin' me about Haydon Dapeers not bein' so popular round 'ere."

"It's no surprise 'e got murdered." Dick glanced quickly around the room. "He 'ad plenty of enemies, that's for sure."

"Who?"

"His own brother, for starters," Dick replied with relish. "I know that for a fact, 'cause Tom Dapeers give me a job moving the empty barrels in the taproom. This was yesterday morning, it was. While I was in there Haydon Dapeers showed up at their pub and they had the most awful dustup."

"They 'ad a fight?"

"Nah." Dick laughed. "Dapeers weren't the type to use his fists. It were an argument. But I 'eard Mr. Tom screamin' at Dapeers that it was all a ruddy lie, and if he tried spreadin' it around, he'd see Dapeers in court."

Wiggins nodded thoughtfully. "What was they on about?"

Dick shrugged. "Don't know. I only heard part of the row. Then Mrs. Tom come in and Haydon left. But I don't reckon it means anything. Mr. Tom and Mr. Haydon didn't act much like brothers, if you know what I mean. They couldn't really stick each other. Mrs. Joanne, she really 'ated Mr. Haydon. Especially when she found out he was goin' to be openin' that fancy pub right up the road from their place. She went on and on about it. Claimed Mr. Haydon were doin' it on purpose just to ruin their trade. Mind you"—Dick took another quick drink and wiped his mouth with the back of his hand—"if you ask me, she was dead right. Mr. Haydon probably was tryin' to ruin their business."

"Guess the brother and his missus didn't get invited to the opening of the Gilded Lily." Wiggins laughed.

"That's the strange part," Dick said eagerly. "They did. I saw 'em walkin' right into the Gilded Lily yesterday evenin'. Mrs. Joanne was all dressed up like she was goin' to the opera or somethin', and Mr. Tom was wearin' a suit and tie."

"It's a wonder Haydon Dapeers didn't toss 'em out."

"That's what I thought," Dick said eagerly. "I was sure I'd see them come right back out again. 'Corse I was curious, so I had a gander through the window, you know, lookin' to see if Dapeers would boot 'em out. Well, I saw him talkin' to them all nice like, as though the argument at the Black Horse had never happened."

"That's right strange," Wiggins said thoughtfully. "Guess they musta made it up."

Dick shrugged again. "Reckon so. Either that, or Mr. Tom and his wife was so eager to see the inside of the place, they were willin' to swallow their pride."

Wiggins belched softly. "Sounds like an awful lot of trouble to go to just to get a look at the place," he mused. "Why didn't they just look in the windows while the pub was bein' fitted out?"

Dick laughed. "Oh, you wouldna seen nothin'. Mr. Haydon kept the windows covered in brown paper the whole time the work was bein' done on it."

Wiggins took another swallow of beer, grimacing as the brew slipped down his throat. He felt awfully dizzy. He glanced down at his feet and thought the floor looked a long ways away. When he looked up again, Dick's twin brother seemed to be sitting right next to Dick. Even worse, the room was starting to spin.

Betsy studied the young man behind the counter of the grocer shop on Tottenham Road. He wasn't very attractive. He looked the sort of man who would be flattered by a little attention. Short and rather portly with a head of frizzy dark hair and skin so pale it reminded her of a fish's belly, he wore thick, wire-rimmed spectacles that couldn't quite hide his bushy eyebrows and a rumpled white shirt beneath his grocer's apron. She ignored the jab at her conscience because she was being so cold-bloodedly deliberate in picking her choice of prey. But there was a murder to solve. "Excuse me, sir." She smiled warmly. "But I was wondering if I might trouble you a moment?"

He blinked at her from behind his spectacles, as though he was surprised she was speaking to him. "Uh, of course, miss. What can I do for you?"

"Do you know where the Dapeers residence might be?"

"We're not allowed to give out that sort of thing about our customers," he said, blushing all the way to the roots of his hair.

"Oh," she sighed dramatically. "That's too bad. My mistress wanted me to take a letter of condolence around to Mrs. Dapeers, but I've lost the address."

"Terrible business, that," the clerk said.

"Yes." She shuddered delicately. "Dreadful, isn't it? Imagine being stabbed in your own pub."

"And on the opening day too!" he agreed, glancing at the back of the shop to see if his employer was lurking about.

She leaned closer across the counter. "It makes a body scared to walk the streets, it does." She sighed again and made her shoulders droop slightly. "And here I've got to try and find that poor woman's address. . . ."

"It's all right, now," the clerk said quickly. "I think I can help you out. The Dapeers house is at number twenty-eight Percy Road. It's just round the corner."

"Thank you, ever so much. You've saved me an awful lot of bother."

He blushed even redder. "Mrs. Dapeers and her sister-in-law come in here every now and again. They're both nice ladies."

"It must be terrible for her, losing her husband like that."

"Yes," he agreed solemnly. "But just between you and me and a tin of sugar, I doubt that there's many who'll shed any tears at his funeral."

Betsy gazed at him appreciatively. "You mean he wasn't well liked?"

"Not by anyone who worked for him. My sister worked for the Dapeers household a few months ago and she finally left."

"Goodness, why? Didn't he pay proper wages?"

"Hamilton," a booming voice from the rear of the shop bellowed. "Are you through serving that young lady?"

"Almost, sir." Hamilton smiled nervously at Betsy. "Will there be anything else, miss?"

Betsy didn't want to get him into trouble. She might not be above a bit of flirting to find out what she needed to know, but she wasn't going to cause someone to lose their position. "Just that tin of cocoa, there," she said.

He smiled gratefully at her as he turned and pulled a tin of Cadbury's off the shelf. "Anything else, miss?" he said loudly enough for his employer to hear.

"No, thank you." Betsy gave him another smile. "And I appreciate all your help," she said, stressing the last word ever so slightly.

Hamilton busied himself with taking her money and casting furtive glances toward the rear of the shop to see if he was still being watched. But the owner of the shop, a tall, thin man with graying hair and a long, taciturn face, kept his eye on the clerk and Betsy.

Blast, she thought as she saw the proprietor start toward the front of the shop, what bad luck. Just when she'd finally made contact with someone who might know something about Dapeers, this old Tartar has to ruin everything! She decided to try one last thing.

"Excuse me," she said softly. Hamilton looked up from wrapping her tin of cocoa in brown paper. Betsy gave him a bold smile. "But I don't suppose you know of any nice pubs round here, do you?" she asked innocently.

Tom Dapeers smiled uncertainly at the two policemen. He didn't much like policemen hanging about his pub, but as these two were investigating old Haydon's murder, he could hardly ask them to leave. "I don't know what we can tell you," he said. "Joanne and I only went round to the place for a few minutes. We didn't see anything."

Inspector Witherspoon sighed silently. No one seemed to have seen anything. He glanced at Constable Barnes, who was staring longingly at a glass of pale ale sitting on the far end of the bar. "Exactly what time did you arrive?"

"It must have been a few minutes before six," Tom replied.

"It were a quarter to," Mrs. Dapeers put in. "I remember because I looked at the time right before we left here."

"And did you speak to Mr. Dapeers once you got to the Gilded Lily?" Witherspoon asked.

"Of course," Tom said. "We were guests. You can't go to a man's place of business and not talk to him."

"Did Mr. Dapeers seem to be in his usual frame of mind?"

Mrs. Dapeers's eyebrows drew together. "What do you mean by that?"

"I mean, did he appear to be upset about anything?" Witherspoon thought it a perfectly reasonable question.

"He was happier than a pig in swill," Mrs. Dapeers shot back. "Nothing Haydon liked more than showing off. And that new pub of his was his pride and joy." She laughed harshly. "He'd invited the whole neighborhood to come see it. Mind you, I don't care how fancy the place is, it don't hold a candle to ours."

Witherspoon thought that remark strange. The Black Horse Pub, while clean and decent enough, was as plain as a pikestaff compared with the Gilded Lily. But he certainly wouldn't be rude enough to contradict a lady. "While you were there, did you see or hear Mr. Dapeers do anything unusual?"

Tom frowned slightly. "Well, not that I can remember."

"Haydon was talking to that dirty little man in the porkpie hat," Joanne interrupted. "Funny-looking fellow, don't you remember him, Tom? He was standing at the far end of the bar. When Haydon first went over to talk to him, I thought he was going to throw him out. But he didn't, he stood there and had quite a chat with the bloke." She grinned maliciously. "And I don't think he liked what the man had to say, either. By the time the fellow left, Haydon's mouth was open so far, I thought he'd trip over his chin."

"You think that this man said something that upset Mr. Dapeers?" Witherspoon pressed.

"I know he did."

"Now, Joanne," her husband protested, "you're just guessing. It could be that Haydon was still upset by that set-to he had with young Taggert."

Witherspoon made a mental note to remind himself to ask a few more questions about the dirty man in the porkpie hat. But that could come later. "Did you see this, er, set-to between Mr. Taggert and the victim?" he asked.

"Only a little of it," Tom began. "Mr. Jenkins, the owner of the butcher shop down the street, waved me over to the bar about the time they was really getting heated with one another, so I only heard the beginning of the row."

"I saw and heard the whole thing, Inspector," his wife said firmly. "Mind you, Haydon and Taggert weren't troublin' to keep their voices down; you could hear them quite clearly, even over all the noise in the pub."

"Taggert's an artist," Tom added. "Haydon hired him to etch all that fancy stuff on the windows in the pub. Nice young fellow, I don't know why he took that job with Haydon in the first place. He studied in Italy, you know. Comes from a good family too. There's money there somewhere, you can always tell, you know."

Barnes cast a quick look at the inspector. "What was the argument about?"

"Haydon hadn't paid the man," Tom explained. "At least the bit I heard was about money. Mind you, I'm not surprised. Haydon had a bit of reputation for not paying people when he owed them."

Joanne snorted. "Don't be daft," she told her husband. "It was more than that. I was standing right behind them and I heard everything. Michael Taggert wasn't just lookin' for his money, he was warning Haydon to leave Sarah alone."

"Joanne!" Tom glared at his wife. "It's not decent to say such things."

"It's the truth." She shrugged, totally unconcerned by her husband's disapproval. "The old goat never could keep his hands to himself."

Witherspoon sincerely hoped he wasn't blushing. Gracious, this case was getting complicated. "Are you saying that Haydon Dapeers was trying to force his attentions on his own sister-in-law?"

Joanne Dapeers stared him directly in the eye, not in the least embarrassed to be speaking bluntly about such a delicate matter. "That's exactly what I'm saying. He was a disgusting man, Haydon was, always after the young women. Only this time Michael wasn't having it."

"I take it Mr. Taggert, er . . ."

"He's in love with Sarah Hewett," Joanne finished. "And I expect now that Haydon's dead, he'll ask her to marry him."

"Mrs. Hewett is a widow, isn't she?" Barnes asked. "So why does Mr. Dapeers's death have any bearing on whether or not she remarries?"

Joanne shrugged. "I don't know. Sarah hated having to live with Haydon and Moira, not that she had anything against Moira. She's a nice enough woman. A bit wrapped up in her charity work and the missionary society, but she was always kind to Sarah. It was Haydon Sarah couldn't stomach. I know for a fact that Michael Taggert's been after Sarah to marry him and I know that Sarah loves Michael too. But for some strange reason, she kept putting him off."

Tom frowned at his wife. "You shouldn't be repeating gossip, Joanne."

"Why not if it's true?" she queried.

Confused, Witherspoon asked, "Excuse me, Mrs. Dapeers. But are you merely repeating what others have told you about Mr. Taggert and Mrs. Hewett's relationship? Or do you have knowledge of your own about the matter?"

"Am I under oath, then?" she asked irritably. "Despite what my husband says, I'm not repeating gossip. I know bloody good and well that Michael Taggert wanted to marry Sarah, because he told me so himself. He also told me that she loved him but she kept putting him off and wouldn't tell him why. He was sure it was because of some nastiness that Haydon was up to. Now, if you don't believe me, you can ask him yourself."

"When did Mr. Taggert tell you all this?" Witherspoon asked.

"Last week," she replied. "He used to come in here after he'd finished working at the Gilded Lily. He's a nice young man and we chatted quite a bit. He told me all about him and Sarah."

"What time is the inspector due home?" Betsy asked as she laid the table for late-afternoon tea.

"I'm not sure," Mrs. Jeffries replied. "You know he keeps such irregular hours when he's on a murder."

"I hope he's not expectin' a big cooked dinner," Mrs. Goodge grumbled. She put a plate of sliced brown bread on the table next to the teapot. "It's too hot to do much cookin' and I've been busy today. I've had to send word to all my sources and I'm not sure it'll do much good."

"Of course it will," Mrs. Jeffries soothed. The cook was obviously still annoyed that their latest victim was only a mere publican. Mrs. Jeffries didn't much blame her. Not that she felt a publican was any less important than a member of the aristocracy, it was just that it was so much easier to find out gossip about the upper classes. They were so much more visible and they had far larger households than the lower classes. For once, she felt very sympathetic to Mrs. Goodge's plight. It was a bit like her own. Mrs. Jeffries hadn't exactly found out much today either. She certainly hoped the rest of them would have something worthwhile to report.

"Has anyone heard from Luty or Hatchet?" Betsy asked. She pulled her chair out and sat down, grateful to be off her feet. Her head was sore from the beer she'd had at the pub and her stomach was upset. But she was delighted with what she'd found out. If she was very clever, she could find out ever so much information when she met with Hamilton tomorrow. His sister had worked for the Dapeerses, she was bound to know something.

"Smythe sent them a telegram early this morning," Mrs. Jeffries replied. "I shouldn't be surprised if they show up tomorrow."

"But they'll have only arrived!" Mrs. Goodge exclaimed. "Surely they'll not turn round and come straight back."

"Would you like to bet on that?" Betsy asked. "I don't think either of them really wanted to go in the first place."

There was a loud noise as the back door slammed shut. Fred, hearing the sound of familiar footsteps, leapt up and took off in a dead run toward the back hall.

"Down, boy," Wiggins cried. "You'll knock me over if you're not careful."

"Wiggins is back," Betsy muttered. She turned and saw the footman stumbling toward the table. The dog was bouncing around his feet and it was all he could do to keep from tripping. "Are you all right?" she asked. The lad was pale as a sheet; he was breathing heavily and he was clutching his stomach.

"What's wrong with you, boy?" Mrs. Goodge asked crossly.

"Oh . . ." He moaned and launched himself toward the kitchen table. "I've got to sit down, I don't feel well."

"Gracious, Wiggins, are you ill?" Mrs. Jeffries asked in alarm.

He landed heavily in his seat. "I'm just a bit off-color," he belched softly. The smell of beer wafted off him.

"Have you been drinking?" Betsy demanded.

He hiccuped. "Well, only a little . . ." He clutched his stomach again and tried to rise to his feet. "If you don't mind, Mrs. Jeffries, I don't think I want any tea."

"You're drunk," Mrs. Goodge snapped.

"And feeling the worse for it," Mrs. Jeffries said kindly.

Wiggins moaned. "It's not my fault. The only way to get people in pubs to talk is to pour beer down their throat."

"I think you'd better go have a lay-down," Mrs. Jeffries said.

"That's a good idea." He belched again, got to his feet and stumbled out of the kitchen.

"Well, I never," Mrs. Goodge exclaimed. "What would the inspector say!"

"I don't really think that's the sort of thing we ought to tell him," Mrs. Jeffries said blandly. "Let the lad sleep it off. We'll talk to him at dinner tonight and see what he's learned."

"So it's just the three of us," Betsy said cheerfully. She too had been in a pub, but unlike Wiggins, she'd been very careful about how much ale she'd poured down her throat. She didn't really like the taste of alcohol all that much. Besides, she was scared of liquor. She'd seen too many gin-soaked women when she was growing up in the East End.

"Perhaps Smythe will be along soon," Mrs. Jeffries said. "I've no idea what he's off doing."

"I've been doin' the same as you lot," Smythe's voice came from the kitchen door. "Investigatin' this murder."

Betsy turned her head sharply. "We didn't hear you come in."

"I came in the front door," he admitted, grinning at the maid and sauntering over to take his seat.

Mrs. Goodge gave him a quick, disapproving glance. Household servants were not supposed to use the front door! But she held her tongue.

Mrs. Jeffries and Mrs. Goodge took their places at the table. "I'm glad you're back, we've quite a bit to talk about."

"Where's Wiggins?" Smythe asked. "Isn't 'e back yet?"

Betsy giggled. "He's upstairs having a sleep. He's been drinking! Claims that's the only way to get people to talk to him."

"Load of rubbish, that is," the cook grumbled. "You don't see me pouring alcohol down people's throats to get them to loosen their tongues."

"You've found something out, then?" Smythe asked innocently. He was fairly certain that Mrs. Goodge hadn't found out a ruddy thing. Otherwise she wouldn't be so bloomin' irritated.

"Have some tea, Smythe," Mrs. Jeffries said briskly. She didn't want them to start bickering with one another. "And I'll tell everyone what I learned from Dr. Bosworth."

She poured the tea, passed the plate of bread and butter and told them about her meeting with Bosworth. "So you see, there really isn't all that much to tell," she concluded a few minutes later. "But according to the doctor, either the killer was lucky or he might have known something about human anatomy."

"I reckon the killer was lucky," Smythe said. "From what I found out today, there weren't no one in that pub that knew a bloomin' thing about anatomy."

"You found out who all was there?" Betsy asked.

Smythe shook his head. "That's what I've spent most of today doin'." He fumbled in his pocket and drew out a crumpled sheet of paper. "Got their names written right here."

"Goodness, Smythe, that was resourceful of you," Mrs. Jeffries said eagerly. "Now we've at least got a complete list of suspects."

Smythe didn't bother to tell them that the list had cost him a pretty penny. "Not quite a complete list, Mrs. Jeffries. I had a word with Mick, the barman who was workin' last night. There were a number of people left in the public bar when Dapeers was killed." He frowned, trying to make out his own writing. "Mick didn't know all their names, but I reckon the killer must 'ave been someone who was known to Dapeers, so I'm 'opin' that the names that's missin' aren't important."

"Hmm," Mrs. Jeffries said doubtfully. "I suppose a partial list is better than none. Who is on it?"

Smythe squinted at the crinkled paper. "There was Mick and Molly, of course, they worked for Dapeers. Tom and Joanne Dapeers, that's Haydon Dapeers's younger brother and his wife. Sarah Hewett, that's Dapeers's sister-in-law, and Moira Dapeers, the victim's wife. Two fellows from Bestal's Brewery, Luther Pump and Edward Magil. John Rowland, he owns the little hotel next door to the pub, he was there. Michael Taggert, he's the artist that did all the fancy etching on the pub windows, and Horace Bell, he owns the livery down the road from the Gilded Lily." Smythe paused for a breath and then continued reading the names.

"There was over twenty people in that pub when the murder took place," Betsy exclaimed when he'd finished. "And no one saw a ruddy thing!"

"But that's just it," Smythe said patiently. "They weren't *in* the pub. They was outside watching a brawl between a cabbie and a drayman. Musta been a good fight too; the copper from the corner had to come down and break it up."

"I wonder if the people in the Gilded Lily were all personal friends of Dapeers," Mrs. Jeffries mused. "Or were they just customers?"

"Both," Smythe answered. "Mick told me that Dapeers had asked most of them to come around seein' as 'ow it was 'is birthday, but a few of the people 'ad come in just to 'ave a look at the place too. Mick told me Dapeers was a bit worried when the crowd started comin' in; there was some trouble with the beer. Seems there wasn't enough on hand, the brewery hadn't delivered enough."

"I'll bet that's why the men from Bestal's were there," Betsy said.

"That certainly sounds logical," Mrs. Jeffries agreed. "Did you learn anything else, Smythe?"

"Not really." The coachman picked up his mug of tea. "'Ow did the rest of you do?"

"I'm meeting a woman who used to work for Dapeers tomorrow," Betsy said proudly. "Hamilton promised he'd bring his sister along to the Six Gates after he got off work. But I didn't find out all that much today. Hamilton couldn't really remember much of what his sister had told him about Dapeers. All he knew was that Dapeers was always onto his wife about her giving her money away to some missionary society."

"You've done better than I have," Mrs. Goodge said morosely. "I didn't learn anything. No one's heard of Haydon Dapeers. I've sent word to every source I've got and there's nothing. Absolutely nothing."

Michael Taggert lived in the ground-floor flat of a small, redbrick house in Chelsea. "I thought you'd be around soon," he said as he opened the door wider and motioned for Inspector Witherspoon and Constable Barnes to step inside.

The room was messy: clothes were strewn on the furniture, a half-finished painting stood on an easel next to the window and the linen on the daybed in the corner was tangled in a heap. "You'll have to forgive the mess, gentlemen," Taggert said, "but I've been working and I haven't had time to tidy up."

"You're an artist, Mr. Taggert?" Witherspoon asked politely.

"Yes," Taggert replied. He shoved a heap of newspapers off the settee. "At least I'm trying to be. Please sit down," he invited. The two policemen sat down.

"I expect you know why we're here," Witherspoon began. Taggert nodded. "So I'll get right to it. You were at the Gilded Lily Pub yesterday evening, is that correct?"

"Yes."

"Were you an invited guest?" Barnes asked.

Taggert grinned. "I'm the last person that Haydon Dapeers would have invited. But I was there anyway."

"Would you tell us why?" Witherspoon asked.

"Two reasons." Taggert held up two fingers. "One, I wanted to see Sarah Hewett, and two, I wanted to collect the money that Haydon owed me."

"Dapeers owed you money?" Witherspoon said. Of course, he already knew this, but he'd found that sometimes pretending that one didn't know something was the very best way of getting an enormous amount of information out of a suspect. And frankly, from what the inspector had heard today, Michael Taggert was the only suspect he had.

"I'd done quite a bit of work for Dapeers," Taggert explained. "He hired me to etch the designs on the glass partitions in the pub and to do the carving on the wood panels behind the bar."

"I thought you were a painter, sir," Barnes said, glancing at the canvas near the window. He couldn't see what was on the thing, only the back of the easel.

"Painting is my main interest," Taggert said, "but I do a few other things as well. I'd done this work for Dapeers, finished it last week, but Dapeers wouldn't pay me."

"Why?"

"How should I know why?" Taggert exclaimed. "He was a tightfisted sod, but I didn't think he'd stoop so low as to not pay what he owed."

"Did you threaten Mr. Dapeers?" Witherspoon asked quietly. Goodness, the man was certainly being honest. He didn't try to hide his true feelings about the victim.

Taggert hesitated. He crossed his arms over his chest and sighed. "Threaten? Yes, you could say that. I told him if he didn't pay what he owed, I'd have him in court."

"Is that when Mr. Dapeers asked you to leave?" Witherspoon asked.

Taggert laughed harshly. "He tried to throw me out when I warned him to keep his hands off Sarah. But just then Mrs. Dapeers came along, so Haydon had to behave himself and pretend that we were just talking."

Surprised by the man's honesty, Witherspoon stared at him. He'd rather expected Taggert to start lying about now. "He was forcing his attentions on this young woman?" he pressed.

"That's a polite way of saying he couldn't keep his bloody hands to himself." Taggert sneered. "Haydon hadn't actually gone so far as rape, but he wouldn't leave Sarah alone and she was trapped in that damned house with him. I was warning him off when Mrs. Dapeers came over."

"Did you threaten him?"

"I didn't have time," Taggert admitted. "Besides, Sarah didn't want me to make a scene. But Dapeers got my point."

"I take it you and Mrs. Hewett are, er, close friends," the inspector said.

Taggert's expression softened. "We're going to be married. I'm coming into an inheritance soon; the minute I get it I'm marrying Sarah and taking her and her daughter away from here."

Drat. The inspector sighed silently. There was something about Taggert that he rather liked. He was obviously very much in love with Sarah Hewett. Witherspoon glanced wistfully around the room, his lips creasing in a smile. He hoped the artist didn't turn out to be a murderer. Why, as a young man, the inspector had once entertained ideas about being an artist himself. Not that he'd been serious, of course. But still, he glanced longingly at the back of the easel, wondering what was on the canvas and whether or not Mr. Taggert would mind him having a quick peek. From behind him, he heard Constable Barnes clear his throat loudly. Witherspoon snapped his head around to Taggert. "Er, how long have you known Mrs. Hewett?" he asked. The question wasn't particularly pertinent to the case, but he might as well ask. One never knew what one could find out by a little digging.

"About three and a half years. Sarah was living with an aunt in Bayswater when we met. We would have married three years ago except that I had a chance to go to Italy to study and Sarah made me take it." He smashed his fist down on the table, rattling some dirty cups and making the two policemen jump. "I would to God I had married her then. Instead, she married Hewett and ended up widowed and having to live with that pig Dapeers. I'll never forgive myself for leaving her; never."

"Now, now, Mr. Taggert. Please calm yourself."

"Calm myself! Do you know what she's had to endure from that man?" he cried. "He never let her forget that she and her daughter were beholden to him. He taunted her with her poverty and watched her every move. She was a prisoner!"

"Why didn't you marry her when you came back from Italy?" Barnes asked softly.

"I couldn't," Taggert replied. "She refused me; she said I'd end up hating her and the child, because if we married, I'd have to give up my work and find employment. But that's not the case now. I've my inheritance."

Witherspoon found this all very fascinating, but it didn't have anything to do with Dapeers's murder. "Mr. Taggert, did you go outside to watch the brawl that broke out on the street?"

"The brawl was starting just as I was leaving," he replied, shaking his head. "I didn't stay around to watch it."

Witherspoon and Barnes exchanged glances.

"You and Mrs. Hewett didn't go outside together?" he persisted.

"No," Taggert said. "I was gone."

The inspector ignored that and pressed ahead with his own questions. "Are you absolutely certain of when you left the pub?"

Puzzled, Taggert glanced from Barnes to Witherspoon. "Yes. Why? Did someone else tell you differently? The fight hadn't started yet; the cabbie was just starting to yell insults when I left."

"Where did you go?"

"I went for a walk." He folded his arms over his chest. "I was really angry, so angry I didn't trust myself to stay in the same room with Dapeers."

"Then how did you find out Dapeers had been murdered?" Witherspoon asked.

"From one of the barmaids at the Black Horse. I'd stopped in there for a drink."

"The Black Horse?" Witherspoon repeated. "Isn't that Tom Dapeers's pub?"

Taggert nodded slowly. "I drop by there every now and again. Tom's a nice man. Not at all like his brother. Hard to believe they come from the same stock."

"Which barmaid?" Barnes pressed.

"I don't know her name," Taggert replied. "She's just started working there. The other girl got sacked a couple of days ago."

"And that's when you found out that Dapeers had been murdered?" Witherspoon asked. He wasn't sure why he wanted to be absolutely clear on this point, but his "inner voice" was warning him it might be important. "When you dropped into the Black Horse?"

"Of course that's when I heard. Everyone was talking about it," Taggert said. "And none of them shedding any tears for him, either. Look, obviously you don't believe me. Did someone tell you I was at the Gilded Lily when the murder happened?"

Witherspoon hesitated briefly. "In a manner of speaking, yes. Someone did."

"Who?" Taggert asked belligerently. "I want to know who said I was there so I can call him a liar to his face."

"I'm afraid it wasn't a him, sir," Witherspoon said softly. "It was a her. It was Sarah Hewett."

• • •

"Would you care for more sherry, sir?" Mrs. Jeffries asked the inspector. Goodness, she thought, he wasn't very talkative this evening. "Dinner won't be ready for a few minutes, so you've plenty of time for another one."

"This one will do me fine, Mrs. Jeffries," the inspector replied, waving his half-full glass in her direction.

"How is the investigation going, sir?" she asked.

"Oh, we're moving right along."

"Did you manage to talk with the other suspects today?"

"Of course." He yawned. "Quite a busy day it was too. By the way, have you had any more letters from Lady Cannonberry?"

Drat, Mrs. Jeffries thought, he was changing the subject again. He'd done that twice since he'd come home. "Only a short note to tell us she was having a nice time. She enjoys the country, even if she isn't overly fond of her late husband's relatives."

Witherspoon frowned. "It's jolly decent of her to go at all. I was rather hoping she might have mentioned when she would be returning to London."

"She didn't say, sir. Did you find out—"

"Isn't it time for dinner yet?" Witherspoon queried. "I'm hungry enough to eat a horse."

Mrs. Jeffries gave up. She'd try again once the man had his stomach full.

# CHAPTER 4

"I'm afraid the inspector wasn't very forthcoming last night," Mrs. Jeffries told the others at breakfast the next morning. "He didn't tell me very much." To be precise, he hadn't really told her anything worthwhile at all.

"'Ow much is 'very much'?" Smythe asked cautiously.

"Well," Mrs. Jeffries said slowly, "I'm afraid he really didn't say anything at all."

"Nothing at all!" Mrs. Goodge exclaimed. "What's gotten into the man?"

Betsy reached for a slice of toast. "I'm not sure what you mean? Are you saying the inspector doesn't know anything or that he deliberately avoided answering your questions?"

"I mean," Mrs. Jeffries said irritably, "that he talked about everything under the sun except this murder case. I tried all my usual methods of questioning him, but he rather neatly sidestepped my queries. He kept asking me all sorts of silly questions about women's clothing."

"Maybe he was just tired," Wiggins suggested softly. He hadn't said more than three words to anyone since he'd come into the kitchen, bleary-eyed and clutching his stomach.

"He wasn't tired," Mrs. Jeffries replied flatly. "He was deliberately avoiding talking about the murder." She'd spent half the night worrying about the inspector's reticence and she'd finally come to the conclusion there was only one thing to do. Confront the man. Find out precisely why he'd closed up tighter than a bank vault.

"Maybe he's onto us," Smythe mused. "Maybe that last case . . ."

Mrs. Jeffries shook her head. "I don't think that's the problem. Last night he was muttering something about listening to his natural instincts, his inner voice—"

"What inner voice?" Mrs. Goodge interrupted. "Is he hearin' things now? My uncle Donald went like that when he was about the inspector's age. It happens sometimes. Out of the clear blue they start hearing things and then they start seeing things. That's when you've really got to keep a sharp eye on them; once they start seeing things that aren't there you've got to lock them up. Causes all sorts of problems."

"I'm hearin' things," Wiggins muttered, frowning as he turned to stare at the hall. "Either that, or Luty Belle and Hatchet's fixin' to come through the back door. I just 'eard a carriage pull up."

Fred, his tail wagging furiously, suddenly jumped up and dashed out of the kitchen. There was a loud pounding on the back door and, a moment later, footsteps in the hall.

"Good morning," Hatchet, Luty Belle Crookshank's dignified butler, called out. "Is anyone here?"

"Good Lord, Hatchet," Luty cried. "You should have waited till someone come to the door to let us in. We can't go bargin' in on folks at this time of the mornin'."

"We're not barging in, madam," Hatchet replied as he came into the kitchen. "They sent us a telegram." He stopped and smiled broadly, sure of his welcome. He was a tall, distinguished, white-haired gentleman wearing an immaculate black suit and carrying a walking stick in one hand while holding on to his old-fashioned top hat with the other. "Hello, everyone, I do hope you don't mind us coming around this early. But I knew you'd be up and eager to get cracking on our case."

"What he means," Luty said, shooting her butler a disgruntled glance, "is that he hoped you'd be up so he wouldn't have to wait another minute to find out about this murder we've got."

Luty Belle Crookshank was a white-haired, rich American. She was small of stature, sharp as a razor and had a penchant for wearing outrageously bright clothes. Today she had donned a brilliant blue day dress with a matching hat, carried a parasol festooned with lacy rosettes and, of course, her white fur muff. Luty never went anywhere without her muff. She carried a Colt .45 in it, despite both Hatchet's and the household of Upper Edmonton Gardens' pleas that it was dangerous. As Luty was fond of telling them, her "Peacemaker" had gotten the inspector out of trouble more than once in the past.

"Goodness," Mrs. Jeffries exclaimed, "how on earth did you get here so fast?"

"Don't ask." Luty rolled her eyes at her butler. "Once Hatchet got that telegram, he had me bundled up, packed and headin' for London faster than an avalanche in the Colorado Rockies. We got out of Lord Lovan's so quickly, I don't think the man will ever speak to me again."

"Nonsense, madam," Hatchet said briskly; he pulled a chair out for his employer. "Lord Lovan won't even notice we're gone. It was a house party, you see," he explained to the others. "Even if he does notice our absence, I don't think he'll take umbrage at our hasty departure."

"Hasty departure," Luty snorted. "You didn't even let me finish my breakfast yesterday morning before you had me on the move." She plopped down in the chair and grinned. "But enough about that. Tell us who's been murdered."

"Pour yourselves some tea first," Mrs. Goodge said briskly. "And I'll get some more bread and butter. If you've been traveling, you'll be hungry."

"I'll get it," Betsy said, rising to her feet.

Mrs. Jeffries waited until the new arrivals had their refreshments before she began telling them about their latest case.

Luty and Hatchet listened carefully. When Mrs. Jeffries had finished, Luty put down her teacup and shook her head. "Not much to go on, is there?"

"Really, madam," Hatchet said quickly. "I think the household has done a rather good job of it so far. But I am confused as to why the inspector is being so closemouthed."

"'E's listenin' to his inner voice," Wiggins said. "Whatever that means."

Mrs. Jeffries didn't really want to take the time to explain what it meant. She felt just a bit foolish. After all, she was the one who'd told the inspector on more than one occasion to listen to his instincts, his inner voice and his guiding force. But goodness, she'd only said those things to keep the inspector's spirits up when he was feeling inadequate to the task at hand. She hadn't meant for him to take her literally. "Let's not worry about the inspector's reticence right now," she said briskly. "We've quite enough information to start with."

"Would you like me to have a word with these here fellows from Bestal's Brewery?" Luty asked. "I know a few people in the business; I reckon I can get something out of them."

"Madam," Hatchet said, "you own rather a lot of shares in some breweries, but I don't think that means you can go waltzing into this Mr. Pump or Mr. Magil's office and demand to know what they were doing at the Gilded Lily Pub."

"Don't be a pumpkinhead, Hatchet," Luty said irritably. "I can be subtle. And I can find out plenty too."

"I think you ought to 'ave a go at it," Smythe said, giving the elderly woman a cheeky grin. "We ain't been 'aving much luck ourselves."

"Thank you," Luty said graciously. "It's nice to know that someone around here thinks I know how to behave myself."

"Mrs. Jeffries," Hatchet said thoughtfully, "what would you like me to do?"

Mrs. Jeffries wasn't sure. "Why don't you see if you can find out anything about Tom and Joanne Dapeers. But it might be difficult for you, they don't have a lot of servants—"

"But they've got a lot of workers," Smythe interrupted. "They do own three pubs. I've only had a chance to work the Black Horse. Hatchet could dig around at the other two and see what he can find out." He looked at the butler. "The Dapeerses own the Horse and Trumpet over on Curzon Street and the White Boar just off Charing Cross Road."

Hatchet smiled gratefully. "Good, I'll go round today and see what I can dig up."

"I thought I'd have a go at finding out a bit more about Sarah Hewett," Betsy said casually. She didn't remind them that she was also planning to meet Hamilton and his sister at a pub later this afternoon. She wasn't sure that anyone, especially Smythe, would approve. He hadn't said a word yesterday when she'd mentioned Hamilton's name, but she'd seen the quick frown that crossed his face. Only a few months ago she wouldn't have cared whether or not something she did annoyed the coachman, but things had changed between the two of them. Betsy didn't want Smythe fretting.

"I think that's an excellent idea," Mrs. Jeffries said. "What are you going to be doing today, Smythe?" she asked, turning to the coachman.

"I thought I'd have another word with Molly and Mick; they was tendin' the bar that night at the Gilded Lily. They must know something. After that, I thought I'd try trackin' down the cabbie and the drayman that 'ad the dustup out in the street."

"Why do you want to talk to them?" Betsy asked curiously. "If they was fightin', neither of them could have seen anything."

"Maybe," Smythe admitted slowly, "and maybe not." He didn't want to tell them what he was really going to be up to today. It was too humiliating. Besides, he couldn't think of anything else to do. Thanks to Inspector Witherspoon shuttin' up tighter than the bloomin' Bank of England on Christmas Day, Smythe didn't have any idea of where this case was goin' or even who the real suspects were. He thought the others felt exactly the same way; they was just runnin' around in circles but they were too proud to admit it.

"That sounds very interesting, Smythe. I'm sure you'll find out all sorts of things." Mrs. Jeffries smiled cheerfully, delighted that the staff wasn't losing its enthusiasm.

Wiggins sighed. "I reckon you want me to 'ead back over to the Gilded Lily and see what I can find out from the locals."

Mrs. Jeffries gazed at the footman sympathetically. "Do you feel up to it?"

He felt like crawling back into bed and pulling the covers over his head, but he'd never admit it in front of the others. "'Corse I do. I wasn't drunk, you know. Just a bit off-color—"

"Drunk!" Luty exclaimed. "Good Lord, Wiggins, have you taken to drinking yer troubles away?"

"It weren't my fault," the footman cried. "The only way I could get anyone to talk to me was to buy 'em beer. Cost me a pretty penny, it did."

"Gracious, Wiggins," Mrs. Jeffries said earnestly. "No one expects you to do that."

He was immediately ashamed of his outburst. He hadn't spent all that much yesterday. "It's all right. I don't mind. Besides, I've got a bit tucked away. It's not like I have all that much to spend me coins on anyway."

"Mind you don't overindulge yourself today," Mrs. Goodge said sharply. "You don't have the constitution for it."

Mrs. Jeffries silently debated whether or not to continue cautioning Wiggins about his money, but one look at his face convinced her that anything else said on the subject would just embarrass the lad. He, like everyone else in the household, was devoted to the inspector. She turned to the cook and asked, "And what will you be doing today?"

"I've got some sources coming by," she replied. "And I ought to pick up something. I put a few more queries out yesterday, so if I'm lucky, I'll hear a tidbit or two. But I must say, it's not easy picking up gossip about a publican."

The inspector stood in the public bar of the Gilded Lily Pub and slowly turned in a circle. The pub was closed, of course, and likely to remain so for some time. Witherspoon thought it rather a shame. The place certainly was lovely.

"What are you doing, sir?" Constable Barnes asked.

"I'm trying to get a feel for the place," Witherspoon replied. Drat, his inner voice seemed to have gone to sleep. It wasn't telling him a thing. "Sometimes, one picks up all sorts of information just by being very observant," he said hastily, when he realized his constable was staring at him. "Er, is the barman here yet?"

"He's in the taproom. Mrs. Dapeers has instructed him to make an accounting of all the stock they have on hand."

"Really?" Witherspoon was surprised. "Is she going to open it up again?"

"I don't think so, sir. I believe she's probably going to sell out to her brother-in-law."

Witherspoon blinked in surprise. "How did you find that out?"

Barnes smiled slowly. "From Mrs. Tom Dapeers. She didn't tell me herself, sir. But I've worked with you long enough to pick up a few of your methods." He chuckled. "Excellent, they are, sir. You could give instruction to some of our other inspectors, that's what I say."

"Thank you, Constable." Witherspoon beamed proudly, though he hadn't a clue as to which of his "methods" the constable was referring to. "That's most kind of you. Do go on, tell me how you found out."

"Well, sir, Tessie Gainway—she's the barmaid at the Black Horse— she cornered me yesterday to tell me that one of the other barmaids, a woman named Ellen Hoxton, hadn't been around the neighborhood in a few days and her friends was gettin' worried."

"You mean someone's gone missing?"

"Oh no, sir." Barnes waved his hand in the air. "After I talked to Tessie for a few minutes, it become obvious the missing woman wasn't really missing at all. She'd been sacked from the Black Horse. She'd probably taken off to another part of London to look for work. It's quite a common occurrence. She wouldn't get another position around here if she'd been sacked, would she? But anyway, the important thing is that while Tessie and I were chattin' she happened to mention she'd overheard Mrs. Tom telling her husband that Moira Dapeers was going to sell out to them."

"Hmmm." Witherspoon still couldn't see which of his methods the constable had used, but he wasn't going to ask. "That's rather important information, Constable. I wonder if it means that Mrs. Tom has already spoken to Mrs. Dapeers about the property?"

"I don't know, sir," Barnes admitted. "But I think it's worth pursuing, don't you?"

"Indeed I do."

"You wanted to see me, Inspector," Mick called from the doorway. He wiped his big hands on the apron tied around his waist and came to stand behind the bar.

Witherspoon walked over to the bar. "Yes. Would you tell us what happened on the night of the murder?"

"What do ya mean?" Mick looked puzzled. "Mr. Dapeers walked into the taproom and someone shoved a knife in his back."

"No, no, that's not what I mean," Witherspoon said patiently. "What I really meant to ask was, could you tell us everything that happened from the time you came on duty until the murder."

Mick shoved a lock of dark hair off his broad forehead. "Well, I come in that mornin' about ten. Mr. Dapeers wanted us 'ere early because there was so much to do to get the place ready. The workmen were finishin' up in the back—"

"Workmen? What workmen?" No one told Witherspoon there had been workmen at the pub that day.

"The carpenters," Mick explained. "They was 'ere to fix that back door. It wouldn't close right. Mr. Dapeers was fit to be tied too. Kept on at 'em about how 'e'd paid a ruddy fortune to the builders and they'd damned well better have that back door fixed properly by openin' time." He broke off and laughed. "'Corse they didn't pay 'im any mind. Just planed off the side of the door and stuck a bolt on the inside. But they had it fixed right by opening. I checked it myself. It locked, all right, but the hole for the bolt was big as yer fist and a two-year-old could probably toggle it open, if you know what I mean."

"And then what happened?" Witherspoon asked. Perhaps he shouldn't have asked Mick to tell him about the entire day. At this rate, he'd be standing here for hours.

"Then I went about my business, cleaning up, getting the bar stocked, you know, things like that."

The inspector nodded. "Was Mr. Dapeers here the entire day?"

"Most of it," Mick replied.

"Did anyone out of the ordinary come by?"

"Nah." Mick paused, his broad face creased in a puzzled frown. "Well, there was something, but it weren't so odd. . . ."

"What was it?"

"Ellen Hoxton, she was the barmaid at the Black Horse, she come round and wanted to see Mr. Dapeers."

"Did she see him?" Barnes asked.

"No, he'd stepped out for a minute, gone over to the bank, I think, so Ellen left Mr. Dapeers a note. I think she give it to Moll'."

"As I said, sir," Barnes said softly, "she was probably asking to see him to see if there was a position open here. Surprising, though. I'd have thought she'd have gone elsewhere in London to look for work."

"I expect she came here because she knew there was bad feeling between the Dapeers brothers," Witherspoon replied. "Possibly she thought that Haydon Dapeers would be sympathetic to someone who'd been sacked by his brother."

"Ellen were sacked by Mrs. Joanne," Mick put in quickly. "She's got a mouth on 'er, does Ellen. Sassed Mrs. Joanne once too often."

Too bad that Haydon Dapeers hadn't sacked the woman, Witherspoon thought. A disgruntled employee was often a good murder suspect. Then he was immediately ashamed of himself for making assumptions that weren't based on fact. Gracious, if every sacked employee in London killed someone, the streets would be littered with corpses. "Is Molly here this morning?"

Mick shook his head. "No. Since the murder, there's been no reason for her to come. There's nothing for her to do."

Witherspoon turned to Barnes. "Could you nip out and have one of the uniformed lads go get Molly. I think it's important that we speak with her." He also made a mental note to talk to Joanne Dapeers again.

"What time did you start letting people in the pub?" he asked Mick as soon as the constable had gone.

Mick scratched his head. "I dunno, I reckon it would have been about five o'clock."

"And how many people came in when you opened the doors?"

"About a dozen," Mick said. "'Corse, most of them was here 'cause they'd been invited special."

"Could you tell me what happened right before Mr. Dapeers was murdered?" Witherspoon asked. He generally encouraged people to ramble on; it was amazing how much information one could pick up that way. But gracious, if Mick didn't get cracking with a few facts, he'd be here all day.

"I thought I was tellin' you," Mick replied.

"Yes, yes, of course you are, please go on."

"Well, let me see. Right before the murder you say." Mick scratched his head again, as though the event had taken place years ago. "Mr. Dapeers was talkin' to that dirty little man at the bar and then Molly told him that we needed another keg of beer. So he yelled back that he'd get it—Mr. Dapeers was the only one with a key to the taproom, you see. Then he walked down the hall and went inside. 'Bout the time he did that, the ruckus started out on the street and we all went over to have us a look. Most of us was still gawkin' at the fight when we heard Mrs. Joanne Dapeers screamin' her head off."

"How much time had passed between Mr. Dapeers going to the taproom and Mrs. Joanne Dapeers finding the body?" Witherspoon asked.

Mick shrugged. "I couldn't say, a few minutes maybe. No more than that. The copper had just got here to break up the fight when Mrs. Joanne found him. And it were a good fight, too. Two or three minutes of insults and shoutin' and then the fisticuffs started."

"The dirty little man that Dapeers had been talking to at the bar," Witherspoon asked. "Was he here during the fight?"

"I dunno. I think he'd left."

"Did you see him leave?"

"Nah." Mick wrinkled his nose. "But I wasn't watchin' the bloke, if you know what I mean."

"Do you know who he was?" the inspector asked.

"No, but I've seen him here before. He come around a couple of times and talked to Mr. Dapeers. They was doin' some kind of business together."

"Really?" Good, the inspector thought. Now they were getting somewhere.

"'Corse they was," Mick said importantly. "He certainly weren't one of Mr. Dapeers's friends."

Smythe shifted his weight on the small, hard bench, trying to get comfortable. But it was a futile task. The Dirty Duck Pub was ancient, creaking and jammed up smack against the Thames. The place was dark, crowded and filled with the scent of unwashed bodies and stale beer. But the place had its advantages. Mainly, that it was Blimpey Groggins's local.

Smythe ignored the bold smile of the young woman at the next table. She was a streetwalker, tired looking, desperate, and probably with just enough money for a cheap gin before the barman tossed her out onto the docks. He felt sorry for women like her; there were plenty of them in this part of London.

He kept his gaze on the door, hoping that Blimpey would show up soon. If he didn't, Smythe's backside might be permanently ruined from this ruddy bench.

He hadn't told the others about Blimpey being in the Gilded Lily Pub on the night of the murder. Mainly because he hadn't known for sure it was Blimpey until just a few hours ago.

The front door opened. Smythe grinned. His prey had arrived. Blimpey strolled to the bar like he owned the place, which Smythe thought wasn't an impossibility, and ordered a beer. Then he turned to survey the room.

His eyes widened as he spotted the coachman. "What you doin' 'ere?" Blimpey asked as he sauntered over to where Smythe sat and plopped down on the opposite bench. "Waitin' to see me?"

"I didn't come 'ere for the beer," Smythe grimaced. "That's for sure. I want to ask you a few questions." He'd used Blimpey Groggins a time or two himself in the past on some of the inspector's other cases. Of course, Blimpey didn't know he was "helping the police with their inquiries," he was just doing what he always did, selling information for money. Luckily, Smythe had plenty of money.

"Questions? Me?" Blimpey chuckled. "Come on, mate. You know I don't do much talkin' unless me palm is crossed with silver."

Smythe stared at him. "You do a job for a fellow named Dapeers?"

Blimpey lifted his hands and rubbed his fingers together. "You're not playin' fair, Smythe. I don't see any lolly on the table."

Smythe sighed, pulled a few coins out of his pocket and slapped them down next to his glass. "There, 'appy now? Answer the question."

Blimpey's eyes shone greedily. "Now, that's more like it, mate. Yeah, I was doin' a job for a fellow named Dapeers." He snorted. "And it looks like I got paid just in time. Bloke got 'imself stabbed the other evening."

"What kind of a job was you doin'?"

"Took a message or two to a bloke for 'im, that's all." Blimpey stared at him cautiously, as though he'd just remembered that someone had been murdered and that Smythe worked for a Scotland Yard police inspector. "I didn't do all that much."

"What's the bloke's name?"

Blimpey hesitated, his gaze on the few coins under Smythe's fingertips. "Why are you so interested?"

"Never mind that. I'm payin' for information, so give it over."

"You're not thinkin' that I 'ad anything to do with killin' Dapeers, are ya?"

"Don't be daft," Smythe said. He'd known Blimpey for years. "You're not exactly as pure as snow, Blimpey, but you're no killer. Come on now, just give me the fellow's name."

Relieved, Blimpey grinned. "Name's McNally, James McNally."

"And what kind of messages was you takin' to this Mr. McNally?"

Blimpey took a long swallow of beer. "He owed Dapeers money. I was puttin' a bit of pressure on 'im, that's all."

"What kinda pressure?" Smythe asked suspiciously.

"I wasn't threatenin' the bloke," Blimpey protested. "I don't do that kinda work. All I did was tell McNally that Haydon Dapeers was gettin' tired of waitin' for his money. That's all."

"Why did McNally owe Dapeers money?"

Blimpey sighed dramatically and jerked his chin at the coins. "Is that all there is?"

"Maybe." Smythe grinned. "Why? You think your information is worth more than this?"

"Could be. Especially as Mr. McNally might be the kind of man who wouldn't want the world to know what he was up to."

Smythe silently debated. Finally, he reached into his pocket and pulled out a small roll of bills. Peeling a fiver off, he put it on the table next to the coins.

Blimpey reached for it; Smythe slapped his hand over the cash. "Not so fast; you 'aven't told me anything useful yet."

Frowning, Blimpey drew back. "All right, all right, you know I'm good for it. Haydon Dapeers was playin' the bookie for this McNally. McNally couldn't cover a couple of big bets, so Dapeers covered 'em for 'im. McNally's been slow payin' Dapeers back, so he sent me round to tell 'im to pay up or 'e'd be sorry."

"'Ow sorry?" Smythe asked. He wasn't surprised. A number of publicans in London did bookmaking on the side. But considerin' how the Gilded Lily looked, he wouldn't have figured Dapeers for one of them.

Blimpey shrugged. "You know I never ask those kinda questions, Smythe. I just took the message along to the fellow's office." He laughed merrily. "Bloke just about 'ad a stroke when the likes of me come through his front door. Couldn't get rid of me fast enough."

"What kind of offices? Where's it at?"

"Solicitor. Office is over on Curzon Street. Nice place, very posh, if you know what I mean."

Smythe picked up his beer and took a quick swallow. "Did he agree to pay Dapeers what he owed?"

"He said he would, but I didn't much believe 'im." Blimpey shook his head. "Bloke was skint. You can always tell. Claimed 'e'd go round that evening and straighten things out with Dapeers."

"Which evening?"

"The night of the murder, of course." Blimpey tapped the side of his now empty glass. "Care for another round?"

Smythe shuddered and pushed his half-full tankard away. "You go ahead."

"Another round over 'ere, guv," Blimpey yelled at the barman. "Anyways, like I was sayin', McNally said he'd go round that night to Dapeers's new pub and pay up. That's what I told Dapeers."

"So Dapeers was expectin' him to come by?"

"I think so. Mind you, we didn't have much time to talk about it. Dapeers went into the taproom and never come out."

"Did you see anything?"

"Nah." He broke off as the barmaid slapped his drink in front of him. "Ta, luv," he said, reaching for his beer. "I wasn't goin' to wait around for

Dapeers. Didn't much like that pub and I'd told him what I'd come to say. I left right after that."

"'Ad the street fight started when you left?"

"I 'eard some shoutin' as I was leavin', but I was in a 'urry so I didn't bother to stop and have a look-see." Blimpey shrugged. In his world, street fights were as common as muck. It would practically take a riot to get him to stop and pay attention. "Besides, I went out the door of the saloon bar. That comes out on Bonham Road; the ruckus was round the corner. Mind you, I was a bit surprised when I left."

"Why?"

"'Cause I saw McNally walking down Bonham Road as I was going out."

Smythe sat up straighter. "McNally was there that night?"

"Well, I don't know if 'e was in the Gilded Lily"— Blimpey wiped his mouth on the greasy cuff of his jacket— "but I saw 'im skitterin' down Bonham Lane and then duckin' into the mews behind the Gilded Lily. Can't think why else some like 'im would be skulkin' about unless'n 'e were plannin' on payin' a visit to Dapeers."

"'Ave you told the police about this?" Smythe asked, and then immediately knew it was a stupid question.

Blimpey threw back his head and laughed. "Cor, guv, remember who you talkin' to! The peelers and I have a mutual understandin'. I don't bother them and they don't bother me."

Smythe studied Blimpey carefully. This was something the inspector should know about. Blast a Spaniard anyway, the only way Blimpey Groggins would ever walk into a police station and loosen his tongue would be if Smythe was holdin' a pistol to his back. Either that, or he'd have to pay the little crook a pretty penny. But maybe there was another way to get the information to the inspector. Smythe thought about it for a split second. "I don't suppose you'd be willin' to tell the peelers about McNally?"

Blimpey's expression sobered. "You suppose right. Look, Smythe, I make me livin' doin' jobs like this. Carryin' messages and findin' out things for people. People who trust me to keep me mouth shut. I go runnin' to the peelers and runnin' my trap about me tryin' to collect for a bookie and my business'll be ruined." He shook his head vehemently. "You're a decent bloke and all that, and if I could do you a favor, I would.

But I ain't goin' to run tattlin' to Scotland Yard about this. I've got me good name to consider, you know."

Smythe stared at him for a long moment The awful part was, he understood Blimpey's problem. Despite what the good, moral, upstanding citizens of London might think about collecting for bookmakers and running petty-ante gambling games, which Blimpey excelled at, people like him didn't have many choices in life. Poor, uneducated and usually hungry, they did what they had to do to survive. "All right Blimpey, you've made your point. Where does this McNally live?"


Betsy's conscience nagged her at her like a sore tooth. But she gamely pushed it aside. It wasn't her fault this poor boy actually thought she was interested in him. So interested, in fact, that he must have spent half the night talking to his sister about the Dapeers household. She'd been surprised when she'd arrived at the pub to find him there alone. But he'd explained that Sadie had come down with a sore throat and couldn't come. Betsy didn't believe that for a moment. She wasn't conceited, but a two-year-old could work out that the poor lad wanted to be alone with her. Now she felt lower than a snake. Once she found out what she needed to know, she had no plans ever to see him again. Stop it, she told herself fiercely. A murder's been committed. She had to do what she had to do. "Oh Hamilton," she gushed. "I think it's ever so clever of you to know so much about the Dapeers household. You must be very observant."

"No." He blushed to the roots of his curly hair. "I'm just a good listener. Most of what I know, my sister Sadie told me. Like I said, Sadie worked there for a few months. But then she got a chance for a better position in a milliner's shop. It paid more and the hours is better, so she left the Dapeers house. She didn't much like workin' there anyway, it weren't at all a nice place."

"Did they do a lot of arguin' and such?" Betsy asked. She leaned closer across the small table.

"Nah," Hamilton replied. "It were mainly just the kind of feelin' you get about a place that she didn't care for. Said that Mr. Dapeers was always watchin' Mrs. Hewett whenever he thought his wife wasn't looking. And poor Mrs. Hewett went around with a long face and lookin' miserable all the time. The only time she ever smiled was when she was with her daughter. She spent the rest of her time hiding from Mr. Dapeers."

"How awful."

"It was. Sadie overheard a dreadful row the night before she left." He glanced at her empty glass.

"Between Mr. Dapeers and Mrs. Hewett?" Betsy pressed.

"Would you like another ale?"

"No, thank you."

Hamilton picked up his beer and swallowed hastily. "It was between Mr. and Mrs. Dapeers. Seems that Mr. Dapeers didn't like his wife givin' so much time and money to Reverend Ballantine."

"Reverend Ballantine? Who is he?"

"He runs some kind of missionary society," Hamilton explained. "And Mr. Dapeers was right angry about Mrs. Dapeers giving him so much money."

Disappointed, Betsy slumped back in her chair. "Oh. Well, I guess there's lots of husbands who wouldn't want their wives giving away the household money."

Hamilton grinned and shook his head. "It weren't the household money she was giving away." He laughed. "Sadie said she heard Mrs. Dapeers shouting that it was her money she was using and she'd give it to whoever she liked."

Betsy brightened. "Mrs. Dapeers had money?"

"Pots of it, accordin' to Sadie," Hamilton said. "Mind you, most of it is tied up in some kind of trust, that's why Mr. Dapeers don't have control of it. They argued about that lots of times. He was always wantin' her to hire a solicitor and take some old relative of hers to court. But she refused to do it."

"So she gives this Reverend Ballantine money and tells her husband to mind his own business," Betsy murmured.

"If you ask me, Mr. Dapeers had a right to be angry," Hamilton said quickly. "It's not right, a wife having her own money."

Betsy's chin jerked up and she opened her mouth to tell him he was a ruddy fool. Women should have their own money! Then she remembered that she needed this young man to keep feeding her information, so she clamped down the angry retort on the tip of her tongue and forced herself to say, "I think you're absolutely right." The words almost choked her; when she got home, she ought to wash her mouth out with soap.

Hamilton beamed at her, then he leaned forward and whispered, "And that's not all Sadie heard, either. She heard Mr. Dapeers going on and on about how Mrs. Dapeers was making a fool of herself over this reverend."

"You don't mean . . ."

"Yes," Hamilton whispered, "I do mean." He glanced around the pub to make sure there were no ladies in earshot who might be offended by his next words. "According to Sadie, Mr. Dapeers accused Mrs. Dapeers of carryin' on with the Reverend Ballantine. What's worse, the man is young enough to be her son."

# CHAPTER 5

Witherspoon was beginning to think his inner voice had gone mute. But no, he mustn't doubt himself. As his housekeeper always said, "You never give yourself enough credit, Inspector." He decided to be patient. Surely, this investigation would start making sense at some point.

He glanced at Barnes. The constable was staring out the window, his gaze fixed on the courtyard below. Barnes sniffed the air appreciatively, apparently enjoying the pervasive scent of beer. They were in the offices of Bestal's Brewery.

"Did the clerk say he was going to go and get Mr. Pump?" Witherspoon inquired. "Seems we've been waiting an awful long time."

Barnes reluctantly turned away from the window. "It's only been a few minutes, sir."

"I'm dreadfully sorry to have kept you waiting," a voice said from the open doorway.

Startled, Witherspoon whirled about and saw a rather plump gentleman with a full black beard advancing toward him.

The man extended his hand as he approached. "I'm Luther Pump," he said politely. "Mr. Magil will be along in a minute. He's out in the yard."

"I'm Inspector Witherspoon from Scotland Yard and this is Constable Barnes," The inspector replied as they shook hands.

"I know who you are. We saw you the other night when we were at the Gilded Lily. Do sit down, gentlemen." Pump waved at a couple of chairs in front of a huge desk. He went round behind the desk and sat down. "I know why you're here, and I must say, I don't think I can be of much help. Mr. Magil and I only met Mr. Dapeers that night. We were dreadfully shocked about what happened, of course. Dreadfully shocked."

"Naturally." Witherspoon smiled politely. "Murder is always very upsetting. Let me assure you, sir, we won't take much of your time. We've only a few routine questions to ask you."

"It may be routine to you, Inspector," Pump said. "But it's rather upsetting for me, I've never been involved in this sort of thing before. But do go on and make your inquiries."

"First of all," the inspector said slowly, "why were you at Mr. Dapeers's pub that evening?"

"He'd invited us to come round," Pump said. He hesitated. "Actually, he hadn't so much invited us as, well, this is most awkward. Perhaps I shouldn't say any more until Mr. Magil gets here. He's better at explaining this sort of thing than I am."

"I'm here now," Edward Magil strode into the room, dusting his hands off as he walked. "Good day, gentlemen," he said, pulling another chair up next to Pump's desk and quickly seating himself. "I'm Edward Magil."

"Yes, we assumed as much," Witherspoon replied. He glanced at Barnes to see if the constable had his notebook out. Barnes was already scribbling in it.

"I've just asked Mr. Pump why you were at the Gilded Lily on the night of the murder," the inspector said. "He seems a bit unsure—"

"We were at the Gilded Lily because Haydon Dapeers had written us a letter."

"A letter?"

"Yes," Magil said firmly. "A letter about a matter of grave concern to us."

Witherspoon straightened his spine. Now they were getting somewhere. Yes, indeed, he would finally start getting some answers. "Grave concern?" he echoed.

"Indeed," Magil replied. "Inspector, how much do you know about the pub business?"

Witherspoon blinked. He knew as much as any policeman about the licensing laws and those sorts of matters. What else was there to know? "Well, I think I'm as well-informed as—"

Magil waved his hand impatiently. "I'm sure you are," he interrupted, "but there are a few facts about our business that the general public doesn't understand. Did you know that breweries loan money to people who want to go into the pub business?"

Witherspoon didn't know that, but he was loath to admit it. "Er—"

"No, of course you don't. But that's what we do, you see. We loan money to people so they can go into the pub business, and in return, they have to sell our goods exclusively. We're quite particular about who we lend our money to, as well. One couldn't just hand out capital to any person who came along and wanted to open a public house, could one?"

"No, I suppose one couldn't," Witherspoon replied politely.

"Bestal's insists upon the very highest standards of integrity and character. Do you understand?"

"I think so." The inspector was dreadfully confused. What did all this have to do with anything? But he schooled himself to be patient.

"It's quite competitive, the beer business," Luther Pump interjected. "Beer consumption has fallen dreadfully in the last ten years. Those awful temperance lobbies have seen to that. Thank God the Conservatives are back in power. It's a wonder the Liberals didn't drive us all to the poorhouse."

"I'm sure the inspector isn't interested in the political aspects of the brewery business, Luther," Magil said irritably.

As Witherspoon didn't have a clue what the Liberals or the Conservatives had to do with pubs and beer, he said nothing.

"But as I was saying," Magil continued, "we loan money to people to finance their pubs and we have very, very strict rules about that."

"And these rules are?"

Magil waved his hand dismissively. "Oh, most of them don't really matter, at least they had nothing to do with our visit to Haydon Dapeers. What is important is that Dapeers had contacted us telling us that he had information of grave concern to us."

Witherspoon sighed silently. His inner voice was silent, his head hurt and the smell of this place was making him ill. "And what would that be, sir?"

Magil leaned forward, his expression as somber as a vicar conducting a funeral. "I trust you keep what I'm going to tell you completely confidential."

"Er, I'm not sure I can give you that assurance, sir. This is a murder investigation, you know. Whatever you say to me can be used in evidence at a trial."

Magil glanced at his colleague.

Pump nodded almost imperceptibly. "We've got to tell them," he said. "It's far better for the inspector to know the truth now than to risk us having to testify to it in open court."

"But—" The inspector tried to tell them that even if they told him now, they might still have to testify in court.

But Magil wasn't listening to him. "You're right, of course," he said to his colleague.

He turned to the two policemen and leaned closer. Dropping his voice to a whisper, he said, "Haydon Dapeers implied the most awful thing. He said he had evidence that one of our pubs was watering down the beer."

Wiggins's feet hurt, his shirt collar was too tight and his stomach still felt queasy. He wished he were home sitting in the cool of the kitchen rather than hanging about on Bonham Road trying to find someone who knew something about the murder.

"You look peaked, boy," a woman's voice said from behind him.

Wiggins whirled around and saw a woman with blue eyes and dark brown hair smiling at him. She was dressed in a pale lavender dress and had a rather tatty white feather in her hair. At first glance he thought she must be in her thirties, but upon closer inspection he realized she was young, probably not more than a few years older than himself. "It's the sun," he murmured, feeling his cheeks starting to flame as he realized exactly what this woman was. "I expect I ought to get inside and sit down."

Her smile turned coy. "I've got a room across the way." She jerked her chin toward a small, run-down-looking house across the road. "If you've a mind to, you can rest a bit there."

Wiggins didn't know what to do. So he did what he always did and opened his mouth without thinking. "Look, I don't 'ave any money. . . ."

She laughed. "I'm not drummin' up trade, boy. Just offerin' you a kindness. You're as white as a sheet and you look like you're about to faint."

"Sorry," he muttered, ashamed of himself and embarrassed to boot.

Just because this woman was probably poor and made her living walking the streets didn't mean she couldn't be kind to a stranger. "But I thought you was . . ."

"I don't work durin' the daytime," the woman replied. "Look, there's a pub over there."

Wiggins groaned.

"Or," she continued cheerfully as she watched him clutch his stomach, "there's a coffeehouse round the corner; we can go there and get us a bite to eat. You look like you could use somethin' on yer stomach. And I do hate to eat alone."

Wiggins smiled sheepishly. In between the rolls of nausea, he was hungry. And thanks to an unknown generous benefactor at Upper Edmonton Gardens, he did have extra money. Because this mysterious person frequently gifted everybody in the household with small, useful presents, he'd been able to save virtually all his wages for the last two quarters. Patting his pocket, he said, "That sounds a right good idea. But please, I'd like to buy you something to eat. You've been so kind."

"That's ever so nice of you." She batted her eyelashes shamelessly and grinned. "The coffeehouse is just around here." Linking her arm in his, she hurried them both toward the corner.

As she hustled him into the coffeehouse and over to a table, Wiggins had a sneaking suspicion a free meal might have been her aim all along. He was wearing a brand-new white shirt and a new pair of shoes. He probably looked like an easy mark; his new clothes alone set him a cut above most of the working people round here. But as he had nothing better to do and he'd never been in a coffeehouse before, he didn't much mind.

"Will a ploughman's do you?" she asked. He nodded. "Two ploughman's over here and a glass of ale," she called to the waiter. "Do you want one?"

As the very thought of beer made his stomach curdle, he shook his head. "No thanks."

"My name's Bronwen Jones," she said chattily, plopping her elbows on the table and grinning at him. "What's yours?"

"I'm Wiggins."

"Wiggins what?" she asked. "Ta," she said to the waiter as he put two plates of bread, pickled onions and cheese on the table in front of them.

Wiggins would die before he told anyone his first name. "Just Wiggins."

"You work round these parts?" Bronwen asked. She stuffed a huge bite of bread in her mouth.

Wiggins hesitated. He could hardly tell her the truth, that he was over here snooping about finding clues to a murder. He decided to do the next best thing. She might be a local, she might know something. "Not really." He gave her another sheepish grin. "I guess you could say I just come over to these parts 'cause I 'eard about that murder. Curious, that's all. Thought I'd 'ave a gander at the pub."

"You mean that publican that got himself stabbed." She snatched up the cheese.

"Right. Fellow named Haydon Dapeers."

Her eyes narrowed dangerously. "I know the bastard's name. And if someone shoved a knife in his back, good for them, I say."

Wiggins couldn't believe his luck. "You knew the man?"

"Everyone round 'ere knows 'im," she snorted, "And most don't like him much. Real pig, he is. Tryin' to run his own brother out of business. Not that Tom's all that much better than Haydon, but at least Tom and Joanne mind their own business and don't go callin' the law on us just for 'angin' about outside the pub to pick up a bit of trade."

"What do you mean," Wiggins asked, "about his brother-in-law?"

She swallowed her cheese. "Just what I said. Tom and Joanne 'ave worked right 'ard to make their pub a success. Not too many pubs on this street, that's why they come 'ere. And what does that bastard do, he opens one up just a few yards up the road from theirs. Done it deliberately, accordin' to my friend Ellen, and she ought to know: she used to work for Tom and Joanne."

"Who's Ellen?" Wiggins was getting confused and he knew he shouldn't because tonight when he met with the others after dinner, he'd have to give them all the facts.

"Ellen Hoxton. She's a friend of mine. Mind you, she doesn't work at the Black Horse anymore. She got sacked for sassin' Joanne. 'Ard one is Joanne. Real 'ard."

"And this Ellen claims that Dapeers deliberately opened his pub to drive his own brother out of business?" Wiggins hoped he sounded like just a nosy parker and not someone who was really trying to pick up information.

"That's what Ellen said. She said she overheard them havin' a right old row about it. Joanne and Tom was both furious." She broke off and nodded at Wiggins's plate. "You goin' to eat that cheese?"

He pushed his plate toward her. She needed this food a lot more than he did. "My stomach's still not right. You have it."

"Ta," she replied, pushing her empty plate to one side and yanking his over to take its place. "Anyways, like I was saying: Ellen overheard this terrible row. Tom and Haydon was goin' at each other like cats and dogs."

"Where could I find this Ellen?"

Bronwen stopped eating and gave him a long, speculative stare. "You're a curious one, aren't you?"

He wondered if he'd overplayed his hand. "Guess I am, at that. Mind you, you're bein' awful polite about it. Most people just tell me I'm nosy as sin."

She laughed. "No harm in that. Especially when it's something as juicy as murder."

"So where's this Ellen at?" he persisted. Bronwen had tucked back into the food with such relish he hoped she hadn't forgotten his question.

"Don't know." She shrugged. "Ain't seen Ellen since she got tossed out of the Black Horse."

"And when was that?"

"A day or two before Haydon got himself stabbed." She frowned slightly. "No, I tell a lie. I did see Ellen after that."

"Where?"

She grew thoughtful and put the last bite of cheese back down on her plate. "That's the funny part," she murmured. "Mind you, I didn't think anything of it at the time. Considerin' that Ellen didn't much like Haydon Dapeers and all."

"Yeah," Wiggins encouraged.

"The last time I saw Ellen, she was in the Gilded Lily Pub and she and Haydon were chattin' like they was old friends."

Mrs. Jeffries carefully looked up and down the street as she crossed the road to the Gilded Lily Pub. Even with her ability to talk her way out of awkward situations, considering the inspector's present state of mind, she didn't want to run into him just now.

She saw no one she recognized, only a police constable keeping watch on the corner. Smiling serenely and keeping her shopping basket tucked over her arm, she sauntered toward her goal. The Gilded Lily was closed, of course. But she slowed her pace and managed to get a good look in the window. Yet there wasn't much to see; the interior was too dark. Continuing on, she came to Bonham Road, turned the corner and tried looking in the window of the saloon bar. Same problem. Not near enough light to make anything out.

A few yards up the road, she spotted the entrance to the mews. Mrs. Jeffries cast a quick glance over her shoulder and headed that way. Within seconds she was standing outside the back door of the pub. Realizing it was probably foolish, she lifted her hand, grasped the knob and turned. To her amazement, the door swung open.

She hesitated, glanced to her left and right to make sure she wouldn't be seen and then slipped inside. Stepping softly, she made her way down the darkened hall. At the first door, she stopped, tried the handle and sighed in disappointment when it wouldn't budge.

But then she heard voices.

They were low-pitched and quiet, barely above a whisper. Mrs. Jeffries tiptoed quietly down the hall, stopping short of the opening that led to the saloon bar. The voices were louder now, but not clear enough for her to hear properly. She dropped to her knees, tucked her shopping basket out of the way, lifted her skirts and crawled closer to the opening leading to the public bar.

"I think we ought to leave London. I'd like to pack up and go and never come back." It was a woman's voice. Mrs. Jeffries desperately wanted to see who was speaking, but she didn't dare raise her head.

"But we haven't done anything," a man replied. "And I'll not have your name tainted with a murder charge. Not after all that you've endured in that house."

"The police were round. They asked me a lot of questions," she said.

"The police are questioning everyone," he said softly.

"But I hated Haydon," she cried. "And I was stupid enough to let that inspector know it."

"Everyone hated Haydon," he exclaimed. "You had nothing to do with his murder, though. So you've nothing to worry about."

"I've everything to worry about," she insisted, her voice catching. "I came back inside the pub that night. I was here when he was being killed.

Someone probably saw me. I was standing right at the bar. Someone will remember, someone will tell the police they saw me go back inside before that stupid fight finished out on the street. They'll blame Haydon's murder on me."

"That's not going to happen," the man said. "I won't let it."

Mrs. Jeffries had to see who was speaking. She risked peeking around the door. In a dark corner of the bar, she could make out the two figures. Even in the dim light, she could see that the woman was young, blond and pretty. The man was dressed in a white shirt and dark trousers, his face half in shadow.

"But you won't be able to do anything about it," the woman said passionately.

"I've got money now," he replied, grasping her by the shoulders. "And if I have to, I'll spend every penny of it to protect you and the child."

Mrs. Jeffries's knees began to tingle. She wasn't as young as she used to be; she eased back, trying to get more comfortable while still keeping her vantage point. Unfortunately, as she moved, her foot connected with her shopping basket. A loud scratching noise cut through the quiet room as the wicker basket skittered backward. Mrs. Jeffries quickly ducked back behind the door. She glanced down the long hallway, wondering if she could make it to the door before she was discovered.

"What's that?" the woman asked.

The man let go of her and leapt to his feet. "Stay here," he ordered. "It may be the police."

Mrs. Jeffries debated about whether to try to make a dash for it. But she hesitated a moment too long.

The man's face appeared from around the doorway. "Who the devil are you?" he demanded.


"What time is Mrs. Jeffries expected back?" Betsy asked excitedly as she hurried into the kitchen. "I've got ever so much to tell everyone."

"She should have been back half an hour ago," Mrs. Goodge replied. She continued to lay out the tea things. "I expect she got held up and will be in at any moment."

"What about Wiggins and Smythe?" Betsy snatched up her apron from the back of the chair, tied it around her waist and picked up the tea tray Mrs. Goodge had sitting on the sideboard.

"They should be back soon too." The cook slapped a plate of buns on the table. "They know we're having a meeting this afternoon."

By the time the two women had finished setting the table, Wiggins and Smythe had both arrived home. But Mrs. Jeffries hadn't.

"How much longer do you think we ought to wait for her?" Betsy asked worriedly as she glanced at the kitchen clock. It wasn't like the housekeeper to be late. Especially for one of their meetings.

"I'm sure she'll be along any minute," Mrs. Goodge said, but she too looked concerned.

"Maybe we should start without 'er," Wiggins ventured. "I'd like to get back out and do a bit more snoopin'."

"We can't start without her," Betsy snapped. "It wouldn't be right."

"Well, I don't think she'd mind all that much," the footman said defensively. "We can always catch her up this evenin' after supper."

Betsy frowned. "I still don't think it's right—"

"I do," Smythe cut in quickly. "Mrs. Jeffries would be the first to tell us to carry on. Just because she's late is no reason for us to mope around 'ere twiddlin' our thumbs, not when we've a killer to catch."

"You're absolutely right, Smythe," Mrs. Jeffries said. They all turned and saw the housekeeper, out of breath and her tidy bonnet askew, rushing toward the table. "I'm so dreadfully sorry to be late, but I'm afraid it was unavoidable,"

"What 'appened?" Smythe asked. "Are you all right?"

"I'm fine." She pulled out her chair at the head of the table and plopped down. "But a cup of tea would do nicely right now. I'm afraid I got caught snooping."

"Got caught," Wiggins cried. "By who? The inspector? Constable Barnes?"

"No, no, it wasn't as bad as all that." She waved her hand in the air. "But it wasn't the most pleasant experience I've ever had either."

"What 'appened?" Smythe asked.

Mrs. Jeffries took the cup of tea that Mrs. Goodge handed to her. "Well, I decided to have a look at the scene of the crime, so to speak—"

"You went round to the Gilded Lily?" Wiggins cried. "But that's daft—"

"Stop interruptin'," Betsy interrupted the footman, "and let Mrs. Jeffries finish."

"Thank you, Betsy." Mrs. Jeffries smiled at the maid. "And while I was there I discovered the back door was unlocked."

Smythe shook his head in disgust. "Ya didn't go in, did ya? Bloomin' Ada, Mrs. J, that *was* a daft thing to do."

"Possibly," she replied calmly, "but sometimes one has to take risks if one is to learn anything. And I do believe I learned rather a lot this afternoon."

"Go on," Mrs. Goodge encouraged, "tell us the rest of it."

"When I got inside, I heard voices coming from the public bar. Naturally, I was curious; the place was supposed to be closed. So I crept up the hall and listened. There were two people in the bar; obviously they were using the Gilded Lily as a meeting place because they assumed it would be safe from prying eyes. Well, unfortunately, I accidentally kicked my shopping basket; they heard the noise and the man came to investigate."

"Who were they?" Betsy asked.

"Michael Taggert and Sarah Hewett," Mrs. Jeffries said thoughtfully. "And once Mr. Taggert got over the shock of finding me, I must say he was quite a gentleman about the whole thing. Of course, I did have a bit of explaining to do."

"What did you tell him?" Mrs. Goodge asked.

"The truth," Mrs. Jeffries replied calmly.

Their was a collective groan from around the table.

"Now, now," Mrs. Jeffries said quickly, "it's not as bad as all that. But I had to tell them something and it's rather difficult to think when one is on one's knees hiding behind a door."

"Exactly what did ya tell 'em?" Smythe asked.

"Just that I was the housekeeper to Inspector Gerald Witherspoon and that I occasionally helped out a bit with his investigations."

"So you didn't mention any of us?" Mrs. Goodge pressed.

Mrs. Jeffries hesitated. She knew what was worrying them. The number of people who knew the household helped the inspector with his murder cases seemed to be growing by leaps and bounds. It was a problem that concerned her as well. But sometimes one didn't have much choice in these matters. "As a matter of fact, I did."

There was another collective groan.

She ignored them and carried on. "The only way I could get Michael Taggert to believe me," she explained, "was to tell him everything. But don't worry, he's an artist."

"What's that got to do with anything?" Wiggins exclaimed.

"I mean, he's got rather a more open mind than most people," she said hurriedly. "And after I told him what we did, he was really quite forthcoming about everything. If you're worried that he or Mrs. Hewett are going to say anything to anyone, don't be. I think the both of them are rather good at keeping secrets."

"Mrs. Jeffries," Smythe said somberly. "We ain't niggled about that. But bloomin' Ada, this is a murder investigation and you was trapped in a deserted pub by two of the suspects. Don't ya see what we're gettin' at? You coulda been killed. Either of them two could have been the murderer and they wouldn'a thought twice about stickin' a knife in your back."

She was suddenly rather ashamed of herself. Here she was thinking they were only concerned about more people learning their secret, while in reality, they'd been worried about her safety. "But that didn't happen," the housekeeper assured him quickly. "And furthermore, I don't think either of them is the killer. As a matter of fact, I'm sure of it."

"Don't be," Smythe retorted. "'Cause I found out today that Michael Taggert didn't leave the Gilded Lily after his set-to with Dapeers. He come back around Bonham Road and slipped into the saloon bar. He was there when Dapeers was murdered."

"And Sarah Hewett's not exactly a grievin' young widow, either," Mrs. Goodge added. "Accordin' to my sources, there was no love lost between her husband and herself."

"And she hated Dapeers," Betsy interjected. "From what I learned today, she had as much reason to kill him as anyone else."

Mrs. Jeffries threw up her hands. "Listen, this isn't doing us a bit of good. Why don't we all calm down, tell one another what we've found out today and then try to sort things out calmly and rationally. Mrs. Goodge, you go first."

The cook looked as though she'd love nothing more than to continue lecturing the housekeeper on the folly of taking silly risks, but as she actually had something to report, she resisted the urge. "All right, then. First of all, like I was sayin', I found out that Sarah Hewett wasn't in love with her late husband."

"That don't make her a killer," Betsy said. "From what I can tell, half the women in London don't much care for their husbands."

"True," Mrs. Goodge replied. "But after her husband died, Sarah was stuck living in the Dapeers household. Seems she and Moira get along all right, but she hated Haydon Dapeers. Rumor has it that he couldn't keep his hands to himself, if you know what I mean. With him dead, Sarah can breathe just a bit easier. And there was somethin' peculiar about the way she up and married Charles Hewett—poor fellow had been in love with her for a long while and she wouldn't give him the time of day. Then all of a sudden she throws herself at him and they elope."

"Why'd she live there if she 'ated Dapeers so much?" Wiggins asked curiously.

"She probably didn't have any choice, her husband probably left her destitute," Betsy guessed.

"No." Mrs. Goodge shook her head. "He left her an annuity, at least that's what my sources told me, but for some reason, she decided to stay at the Dapeers house."

"That still isn't a motive for murder," Betsy complained. She was rather cross that the cook had found out one of the very things she was going to report.

"Did you learn anything else?" Mrs. Jeffries asked.

Mrs. Goodge shook her head. "Not really, except that Haydon Dapeers wasn't a very nice man. Quite a number of people disliked him."

"Includin' his own wife," Betsy interjected.

"Do go on, Betsy," Mrs. Jeffries encouraged.

"Well, I met Hamilton at the pub this afternoon," she began.

Smythe's brows drew together in a quick frown. "You went to a pub with a stranger?"

"Hamilton isn't a stranger. I met him yesterday."

"Where?" Smythe persisted. Bloomin' Ada, did every female in this household take it into their heads to do something daft and dangerous today?

"He's the lad that works in the grocer's around the corner from the Dapeers house," she explained. "His sister used to work for Haydon and Moira Dapeers. That's why I wanted to talk to him."

Smythe still wasn't happy. "Was 'is sister there today?"

"No," Betsy said irritably. "She wasn't. But Hamilton knew plenty about the Dapeers household and he told me everything."

Mrs. Jeffries could see that Smythe didn't like hearing that Betsy had spent part of her day at a pub with a young man. The maid and the coachman were tentatively finding their way into a courtship. "How very clever of you, Betsy," she said quickly.

Betsy smiled broadly and went on to tell them everything else she'd found out. When she was finished, Mrs. Jeffries nodded approvingly and then turned to Smythe. "Did you learn much today?"

Smythe shrugged. "A bit. Seems that Haydon Dapeers was runnin' a gamblin' game on the side. Actin' as bookmaker to a few select customers. The one that I'm most interested in is a solicitor named James McNally." He supplied them with the details he'd picked up from Blimpey Groggins. "I thought I'd see what I could find out about McNally this evening, seems to me 'e's got to be considered a suspect. 'E was there."

"I think that's a splendid idea," Mrs. Jeffries agreed.

"And I thought I'd see what else I could learn about Moira Dapeers and Reverend Ballantine," Betsy put in, not wanting to be outdone by the coachman.

"Excellent, Betsy," Mrs. Jeffries replied. She turned her attention to Wiggins. "And how did you fare today?"

Wiggins squirmed uncomfortably. He wasn't at all certain how to tell them the only person he'd talked with was a . . . he couldn't bring himself to even think of the word commonly used to describe Bronwen's occupation. He'd liked her. She was a nice person, despite what she had to do for a living. "Oh, I did all right."

He decided to just tell them his information without mentioning who he'd acquired it from. "I found out that Tom and Joanne Dapeers really 'ated Haydon. They thought 'e'd opened the Gilded Lily deliberately on the same street that they was on just to run 'em out of business. Haydon Dapeers 'ad tried to do that before, you know. When they opened one of their other pubs, Haydon had up and opened the Pale Swan just up the road from 'em."

"Do you know that for a fact or is your source just guessing?" Mrs. Jeffries asked.

"She seemed to know what she was on about," Wiggins replied. "And what's more, one of the barmaids from the Black Horse, she got sacked for sassin' Mrs. Joanne Dapeers, she was seen 'angin' about the Gilded Lily the day before the murder or maybe it was the mornin' of the murder, Bronwen weren't sure. But she's disappeared."

They all stared at him. He wasn't making a lot of sense. Finally, Mrs. Jeffries said, "I'm afraid I'm not following you. Does this person have anything to do with Dapeers's murder?"

"Who were you talkin' to today?" Smythe asked.

"What's a sacked barmaid from the Black Horse got to do with the murder at the Gilded Lily?" Betsy exclaimed.

"Wiggins, has this heat addled your brain?" Mrs. Goodge charged.

"Wiggins," Mrs. Jeffries said gently. "Why don't you start over. Start at the beginning and tell us everything."

# CHAPTER 6

———◦◇◦———

"It's been a rather tiring day," the inspector said to Mrs. Jeffries as he followed her into the drawing room. "A nice glass of sherry will be just the very thing I need."

"I'll pour you one, sir," she replied, "sit yourself down and get comfortable. You can tell me all about your grueling day." Mrs. Jeffries sincerely hoped the inspector had got over being so tight-lipped about this case. Everyone in the household had learned something today. It was imperative that she get the inspector investigating a few of the clues the staff had turned up. Not that she could actually come right out and *tell* him, of course. But if she could get him talking, she had her ways of getting the information across.

"Oh, I don't think I want to talk about the case," Witherspoon said, waving his hand in the air dismissively. "As you've often told me, Mrs. Jeffries, sometimes it's best just to let all the information one learns stew about in one's mind until it's done."

Mrs. Jeffries almost dropped the decanter of sherry. Goodness, what was she going to do now? Who would have thought the inspector would have taken her casual words of encouragement when he was doubting his abilities as a policeman so very seriously. She could hardly insist he talk about the murder. But if he didn't, how was she going to get him thinking about Moira Dapeers and the Reverend Ballantine, or Ellen Hoxton, the barmaid sacked from the Black Horse, or James McNally? In the future, she vowed as she used her apron to wipe up the drops of sherry she'd spilled on the sideboard, she'd be more careful in what she said to the man. Apparently he took her words far more seriously than expected. But she refused to give up. As Luty Belle sometimes said, there's more than one way to skin a cat.

"I think that's a marvelous idea, sir," she said cheerfully. "When you're home, you ought to be relaxing, not thinking about an insoluble murder."

"Insoluble?" he echoed, his eyebrows raising above his spectacles.

"Oh dear." She handed him a glass of sherry. "Pardon me, sir. I didn't mean to use that word."

"Gracious, I should hope not," he replied. "Why you've told me yourself, no case is insoluble."

"I didn't mean that quite the way it sounded, sir," she said quickly, feeling like a worm at the terrified expression that had flitted across Witherspoon's face. "What I meant to say was that the case was difficult, not insoluble."

"I should hope so, Mrs. Jeffries." He sank back in his seat and reached for his sherry. "I like to believe that justice will always prevail. It may take me a while, but I do think that eventually I'll catch the culprit."

He sounded as though he were trying to convince himself, not her. "Of course you will, sir," she replied.

"I'll admit this case is, as you say, difficult. But gracious, you've told me dozens of times that no crime is impossible to solve."

"I've absolute faith in your abilities, Inspector," she said. "Eventually, you will catch this killer. I've no doubt of it."

Witherspoon said nothing for a moment. He took a sip of sherry and regarded her steadily over the rim of his glass. "You know, I think perhaps I ought to talk about the case. Get the ideas flowing, that sort of thing."

"If you'd like to, sir," she said casually, as though the matter was of no consequence. "I do so enjoy hearing all the fascinating details of your methods. They're so very, very brilliant." She wondered if perhaps she wasn't piling it on a bit thick.

"You're far too kind, Mrs. Jeffries," he said.

"Did you learn anything useful today, sir?" she asked quickly. She felt rather bad. From the expression on the poor man's face, she knew she'd seriously undermined his self-confidence. Drat. But she'd had to do something.

"I'm not sure." Witherspoon frowned. "Sometimes one isn't, you know. Sometimes one doesn't know whether what one has learned has any connection to the crime, or whether one is just chasing one's tail. Take today, for instance. Constable Barnes and I went round and had a chat with the gentlemen from the Bestal's Brewery. They were at the Gilded Lily the night of the murder."

"And were they able to tell you anything useful?" she asked.

Witherspoon's brows drew together as his spectacles slipped down his nose a notch. "Not really." He sighed dramatically. "Neither of them actually knew the victim. They'd only gone to the Gilded Lily in response to a letter that Dapeers had sent them."

"What kind of letter?" she asked curiously.

He smiled faintly. "It seems they were concerned that someone was watering down their beer. Breweries apparently don't like that sort of thing. Gives them a bad name in the business."

Mrs. Jeffries was somewhat disappointed. She'd hoped for something a bit more interesting than this petty nonsense. Watered beer, indeed. "Did they see anything while they were there?" she pressed. She wanted to get as many facts as possible out of Witherspoon. In his current state of mind, he might dry up rather quickly. Besides, there was always the chance that one of these gentlemen might have noticed some little something which could give them the clue they needed.

"No. Like everyone else, when the street ruckus started up, they dashed out to the front to have a look."

"I see," Mrs. Jeffries replied. "Did you talk to any of the other suspects today?"

Witherspoon started to reply when there was a loud banging on the front door. "I wonder who that can be at this time of the evening," he murmured.

Betsy's footsteps sounded in the hall. They heard the front door open and then close. A moment later Betsy came into the drawing room carrying a letter. "This is for you, sir," she said, handing it to him. "Mrs. Philpott just brought it round. It was delivered there by mistake this afternoon."

"Thank you, Betsy." Witherspoon tore the envelope open and yanked out the letter. He flipped to the last page and read the signature.

"It's from Lady Cannonberry," he cried happily.

Betsy and Mrs. Jeffries exchanged glances.

"How very nice, sir," the housekeeper said.

"I'll take it upstairs to read," he announced, leaping to his feet. Clutching the letter to his chest, he hurried out of the room, pausing only long enough to say, "Call me when dinner is served."

"Drat," Mrs. Jeffries murmured as soon as he'd disappeared. "That was most unfortunate timing. I almost had him talking."

"Sorry," Betsy replied. "But I didn't think. When the letter came, I thought it might be something to do with the case."

"It wasn't your fault," Mrs. Jeffries said. "You didn't know who the letter was from or that he'd dash off like a schoolboy to read it in his room."

"Did you get anything out of him?"

"Not very much," Mrs. Jeffries admitted. "But I hope to do better after dinner. There's so much about this case the inspector doesn't know. I must find a way to tell him. I really must. We've made ever so much progress."

"Do you really think so?" Betsy asked doubtfully. "Seems to me we're all just dashin' about findin' things out that don't make any difference."

It seemed that way to Mrs. Jeffries as well, but she wasn't going to admit it to the maid. There was no point in the rest of the household being as depressed about this case as she was. It was important to keep their spirits up. "It may seem that way," she said firmly, "but believe me, every bit of information we gather is useful."

"What did Inspector Witherspoon tell you?"

"He didn't really have time to say much at all. Only that the gentlemen from Bestal's Brewery didn't really know the victim, hadn't seen a thing and are more concerned with someone watering down their beer than they are with a murder."

Despite the fact that she hadn't gotten another word about the case out of Inspector Witherspoon at dinner, Mrs. Jeffries was in quite good spirits the next morning.

She'd done quite a bit of thinking about the case before she went to bed and had decided that it was moving along nicely, even without the inspector's information. So far, there were any number of suspects who could have committed the crime.

She tied an apron around her waist and then put the kettle on to boil. It would be half an hour before the rest of the household roused.

She wanted to have a nice quiet cup of tea and do some more thinking. She brewed herself a pot of tea, took it over to the table and sat down.

First of all, she thought, who had access to the taproom at the time of the murder? That was easy. Virtually everyone in the pub. Anyone could have slipped down that darkened hallway and stuck a knife in Haydon Dapeers's back. She paused, her cup halfway to her lips, as another thought struck her. The knife. Goodness, she was an idiot. She hadn't found out if the knife had been in the pub or if the killer brought it with them. She'd forgotten to follow up that clue and it was vitally important she do so. She made a mental note to pry that information out of the inspector at breakfast even if she had to use a crowbar!

And what of the two lovers she'd interrupted in the pub yesterday? It was obvious they'd decided to meet at the Gilded Lily because they didn't want to be seen. But why not? Sarah Hewett was respectfully widowed and Michael Taggert wasn't engaged or married. Why not meet openly? She wasn't sure she believed the answer that Taggert had given her when she'd asked him. He'd claimed it was because of the murder. That Sarah was scared either she or Michael were going to be accused of the crime. But why were they so frightened? They weren't the only ones who had a reason to hate Haydon Dapeers.

They could have been telling the truth, but Mrs. Jeffries suspected that they were hiding something else. She definitely felt that Sarah Hewett wasn't being honest. She made another mental note to have a go at Mrs. Hewett.

And what about Smythe's information? How far would James McNally go to avoid paying off his gambling debts? Before she could make any judgment about that, she had to find out how much McNally owed. No doubt Smythe would take care of that.

She smiled as she thought of Wiggins's news. It wasn't much. But then again, one never knew. Perhaps Wiggins ought to go round to the Black Horse today and find out a bit more about Ellen Hoxton. Not that Mrs. Jeffries thought there was anything to learn from that quarter. As the barmaid had just been sacked from the Black Horse, she'd probably gone to Haydon Dapeers about another position. But one never knew. It wouldn't do any harm to find out for certain. If, of course, Wiggins could find Ellen Hoxton. If she was out of work, she might be anywhere in London.

Mrs. Jeffries finished her tea. She had a lot to do today. Luty Belle and Hatchet were due round tonight after supper, Betsy was going to be snooping about seeing what she could find out about the Reverend Ballantine and Mrs. Moira Dapeers, Smythe was going to have a go at James McNally and Mrs. Goodge was expecting half a dozen of her sources through the kitchen today. She, of course, was going to tackle the inspector at breakfast and then try to find a way of having a nice, private chat with Sarah Hewett.

Inspector Witherspoon found himself back at the Gilded Lily. He was loath to admit it, but his housekeeper's gentle inquiries at breakfast this morning had got him to thinking. He'd been rather embarrassed to admit there were a number of practical details about the murder that he hadn't attended to.

"You wanted to see me, Inspector," Molly the barmaid said as she bustled into the empty saloon bar.

"Yes, I've a few questions I need to ask."

"I hope it won't take long, sir. Mrs. Dapeers is insistin' we give this place a good clean today." Molly blew a loose strand of hair off her plump cheek. "I've ever so much to do. Them floors in the public bar's got to be cleaned. I've got to do the glass partitions in the saloon bar and that ruddy Mick won't be in anymore as he's gotten himself a position at the White Hart, so it's all fallen to me, you see."

Witherspoon smiled at her sympathetically. Poor woman, she did look as though she worked awfully hard. Her hands were rough and reddened from strong soaps and disinfectants, her apron, though clean, was a dull gray, instead of white, from having been washed so many times, and her face was creased with lines of fatigue. "Do you mean, you do all the cleaning and then were supposed to work in the bar at night?"

"That's right. Mick refused to do anything but serve behind the counter. They had a couple of extra people hired on the day we opened, but they was only casuals, sir. I thought maybe Mr. Dapeers was goin' to hire someone else t'other day, but as he went and got himself killed, I guess nothin'll come of it. 'Corse, now that he's gone, I expect the place will stay closed until Mrs. Haydon sells it to her brother-in-law."

Witherspoon was genuinely sorry for the poor woman. He certainly hoped that Tom and Joanne Dapeers would remedy this dreadful situation when and if they bought the place. "I promise, Molly," he said softly, "my questions will only take a few moments."

"Well, then, what do you want to know?"

"First of all, as you know, Mr. Dapeers was murdered with a common kitchen knife. It had a brown handle and a ten-inch blade. Does that sound like it was a knife used here at the pub?" He wished he'd thought to have Barnes nip round to the Yard and get the knife from the evidence box. It would make identifying it so much easier.

Molly scrunched up her nose in concentration. "I don't rightly know. But it could have been. A brown handle you say?"

"Yes."

She thought for another moment. "I think it could have been one of ours. Hang on a tick, I'll just have a quick look in the kitchen. It's not been properly fitted out yet. Mr. Dapeers didn't want to bother with servin' meals."

"Then why did he have a kitchen in the pub?"

"It were already here when he got the place," she called over her shoulder as she disappeared down the hallway. A few moments later she was back. "There's two knifes in the cutlery drawer," she announced excitedly. "And I know we had at least two in there before."

Witherspoon felt rather foolish. He really should have investigated this question earlier. But he wasn't going to berate himself. Now he knew something very important. Very important, indeed. "Thank you, Molly, you've been most helpful. Now, could you tell me if the back door was locked on the day of the murder."

"Tighter than a bank vault," she replied quickly. "Leastways it was locked early in the afternoon. I know because we had a delivery that day from the brewery and it took me ever so long to get the door open."

"Are you absolutely certain you locked the door when the deliveryman left?"

"I didn't lock the door. Mick did."

"So as far as you know, the door could have been left unlocked?"

She shrugged. "I suppose it could, but it's not likely. Mr. Dapeers was always onto us about keeping the back door locked—" She stopped and frowned. "'Corse, Mick might have forgot. We was busy that afternoon and there was lots of comin' and goin' through the back. Deliveries and such."

Witherspoon sighed silently. Drat. He'd so been hoping that the door had definitely been locked. If the wretched thing had been left unlocked, then anyone could have popped in and murdered Dapeers. Why hadn't he thought to investigate this matter immediately? Again, he caught himself. He really must have a bit more faith in his abilities. Obviously, his policeman's instincts hadn't considered these two matters of immediate importance. All things would come in their own good time.

"Is there anything else?" Molly asked impatiently. "I really must get crackin'. Mrs. Dapeers will be along any minute now and I've got to get them floors polished."

"Mrs. Dapeers is coming here?"

"That's right." Molly edged toward the door. "Reckon she'll be wantin' to check the place is clean as a whistle before she closes it up."


Betsy stared at the small, rather dilapidated redbrick building on the corner of Conner Street. A set of three stone stairs led up to a door with peeling white paint and a cracked fanlight in the transom. She hesitated, wondering if she was at the right place. Just then the front door opened and a young man wearing a rumpled dark suit and spectacles came out.

He started in surprise. "Can I help you, miss?"

Betsy gave him her best smile. "Is this the Reverend Ballantine's Missionary Society?"

"Yes, it is." He smiled shyly. "Would you like to come inside?"

"Yes. I'd like to make a donation, please," she said boldly. She'd decided the best way to get inside the place and have a go at asking a few questions was to offer them a bit of money. Not much, mind you. Just a pound or two. Betsy wasn't by any means rich, but for the past year someone in the household at Upper Edmonton Gardens had been leaving useful and rather expensive little gifts for all of them. Because of that person—and Betsy suspected she knew good and well who it was—she could spare a quid or two in her quest for clues.

"How very kind you are, miss," the young man said.

"I don't have much, you see," she said innocently. "But I've heard about the good work your society does and I'd like to help."

"Do please come in," he invited, turning and opening the door for her. "You must meet the Reverend Ballantine. He'll be ever so grateful for your gift."

Betsy followed him inside. They walked down a short, dingy corridor and into a small room fitted out as an office cum sitting room. There was a huge rolltop desk in one corner and the far wall was fitted with shelves and filled with books. A settee and two chairs separated by a low table stood next to the empty fireplace. The carpet was threadbare, the curtains thin enough to read a newspaper through and the wallpaper stained with water spots.

"Reverend Ballantine," the young man said to a tall man standing in front of the bookshelves. "This young lady would like to make a donation."

The man turned slowly.

Betsy tried not to stare, but it was absolutely impossible. The Reverend Ballantine was the handsomest man she'd ever laid eyes on.

His hair was blond and had a natural wave off his forehead, his cheekbones were high, his mouth beautifully shaped and his nose strong and masculine without being too big.

"That's very kind of you, my dear," the reverend replied, smiling at her out of the bluest eyes she'd ever seen.

His voice was rich, deep and as perfect as the rest of him. But she wasn't one to have her head turned by male beauty, she reminded herself sharply. Well, maybe a bit turned. But not for a moment would she forget why she was here. "I've heard about the good work you do," she began, "and I thought I'd pop round and see if I could help a bit"

"How did you hear of us?" Ballantine came forward and reached for her hand. He pulled her gently toward the settee. "Please, do come over to the settee and sit down."

Betsy noticed that the young man disappeared. She sat down on the settee. Reverend Ballantine sat down next to her.

"Thank you," she said politely, frowning as she realized he was sitting so close he was crowding her into the corner. "But I'm sure you're a busy man and I won't take up too much of your time."

"I've plenty of time, my dear." Reverend Ballantine edged closer, his knee almost brushing hers, "Please, do introduce yourself."

Betsy took a deep breath. She really didn't much like lying to clergymen, even ones that sat too close for comfort. "Amy Lumley."

"And are you from around here, Miss Lumley?" Ballantine asked.

"No. I'm from Blackpool. I'm just down visiting my aunt. A friend of hers is a great believer in your work. She told me all about you." The words came out in a rush. Though she was beginning to think that handsome or not, there was something she didn't quite like about Reverend Ballantine, Betsy simply wasn't used to lying.

"That's most gratifying," Ballantine said. "Will you be staying in London long?"

"Oh no, I'm on a bit of a holiday," Betsy replied. "But I must get back to Blackpool. I've a position there as a housekeeper."

"A housekeeper." He gave her that breathtaking smile again. "Goodness, we could certainly use you here. Reginald and I try to keep the place up, but with only a cleaner coming in once a week, we don't do a very good job. All of our money, you see, goes into the society." He waved his hand around the tatty-looking room. "Unfortunately, doing God's work can often mean living in somewhat tiresome conditions."

She stiffened as his movement had his knee brushing against hers. Betsy tried to edge away from him, but as she was already backed into the corner, there wasn't anyplace for her to go. "I don't have much to give. Just a pound."

"All gifts are welcome," he replied, shifting slightly so that his thigh was almost flush against hers. "The Lord does provide and I really shouldn't complain. We won't be here much longer."

"Really?" Betsy said. She eased away from him. "Why's that?"

"Because God has sent us a miracle. Why, only a few weeks ago I was praying that we might have the funds to continue our work, and lo, it happened." He shifted closer to her.

"A miracle," Betsy repeated. She was starting to panic. He didn't act like any clergyman she'd ever come across before. His thigh was definitely rubbing against her; she could feel it through her skirt and petticoat.

"A miracle." Ballantine leaned closer, his mouth inches from her lips. "Of course, it was really quite dreadful how it happened. One of our staunchest supporters, a fine lady, very charitable; her husband died. I'm afraid he wasn't as giving as his wife. But as the Lord chose to take him, the lady can now give us all the money she wants without fear of recriminations from her spouse. Rather a miracle, isn't it? And now the Lord has sent us another miracle."

"Another miracle?" Betsy repeated.

He reached over and laid his hand on Betsy's. "You."

• • •

Luty Belle Crookshank glared at her butler. "I'da been just fine if you hadn'a interferred."

"Madam," Hatchet said as he took his employer's arm and practically dragged her out of the Fighting Cock Tavern, "you were almost hit over the head with a flying beer mug." He hurried her out into the street.

From inside the Fighting Cock, the argument that had broken out only moments ago was degenerating into a full-blown brawl. Luty glanced longingly at the door her stiff-necked butler had just hustled her out of. She sighed as she heard the familiar sound of chairs being tossed about and glass breaking. "Kinda reminds me of home," she said.

"Really, madam." Hatchet pulled her toward the corner where the carriage was waiting. "I leave you alone for two minutes and then I have to rescue you from a common tavern fight." He clucked his tongue in disgust.

"Rescue me," Luty snapped, outraged at the suggestion. "I'll have you know I'm right good at takin' care of myself. And if you hadn't come back, stickin' yer nose in and draggin' me off, I'da found out what I wanted to know."

"If I hadn't come back," he retorted, opening the door of the carriage and shoving his mistress none too gently inside, "you'd have been hurt or arrested. But I suppose gratitude is too much to expect. By the way, precisely why were you in that disreputable place?"

"'Cause that's where the man I wanted to question went and I couldn't stand outside and shout my questions at him."

"But I thought you were going to talk to the Dapeerses' old house-keeper."

"I did," Luty explained irritably. "But she's half-senile. Her son used to work for Dapeers too, but he spends most of his time drinkin' at the Fighting Cock, so I went after him. I was doin' real good too, pouring beer down his throat like it was water so his tongue was nice and loose. Then them two idiots at the next table started in on each other about politics and things got right heated."

Hatchet banged on the roof of the carriage and the driver pulled away. Really, there were moments when he thought his mistress ought to be kept on a leash. After spending all day yesterday talking to footmen and maids about Haydon Dapeers, they'd found out absolutely nothing. A chance remark from one of his butler friends about the Dapeerses' former house-keeper had led them to this miserable neighborhood south of the Thames. Hatchet had left Luty safely ensconced in old Mrs. Rawdon's parlor and had gone out to buy some pastilles for his sore throat. When he'd returned, Luty was gone. Luckily, he'd spotted the bright yellow feathers on her hat as he'd passed the open door of the Fighting Cock. The truth was, he wasn't in the least surprised to find his employer in the midst of a brawl. It certainly wasn't the first time. "What did you find out?"

"Plenty," Luty replied. "This fellow, Rawdon's his name, told me that Haydon Dapeers was about the meanest snake this side of the English Channel. Do you know he fired Mrs. Rawdon just because his sister-in-law, Sarah Hewett, was movin' into the house. Said she could earn her keep by keepin' his house. And her a young widow with a child."

"Rawdon told you this?"

"Nah, old Mrs. Rawdon told me. She's only partially gone in the mind. The minute I mentioned Dapeers she snapped right to and started talkin' faster than a traveling showman."

"What else did she tell you?" Hatchet asked irritably. He'd found out a thing or two himself, but the fact that he could gloat over it didn't mollify him one bit. His mistress, annoying as she was, could easily have been hurt in that horrible tavern.

Luty grinned wickedly. "Well, seems she was doin' a bit of snoopin' the day that Sarah Hewett and her little girl moved into his house. Actually, she was probably listenin' at the keyhole. Old Dapeers waited until his wife had gone out to some missionary society she belongs to, then he hustled his sister-in-law into his study."

"Well, what did he say?"

Luty sighed. "That's the problem. Mrs. Rawdon is goin' deaf. She couldn't hear all that good. But she did hear Dapeers tell Sarah Hewett that she'd better do what he said or he'd tell everyone. 'Corse, she only heard that part 'cause Dapeers was screamin' at the girl."

Hatchet sniffed. "Is that all?"

"Is that all?" Luty repeated. "Seems to me I found out a sight more than you have."

"I wouldn't say that, madam." Hatchet smiled maliciously. "I haven't been idle since our return from Scotland."

"Why, you old sneak," Luty cried. "You told me yesterday you hadn't learned very much."

"I've reassessed the information I picked up," he informed her grandly. "And in light of what you've just told me, I think it might have some bearing on this case."

"Well," she demanded. "Tell me."

"I think, madam"—he picked a piece of nonexistent lint off the sleeve of his immaculate black coat—"that I ought to wait until we arrive at Upper Edmonton Gardens. You know how I hate repeating myself."

"All right, then," Luty said tartly, "in that case, I'll wait till we're at the inspector's before I tell what else I found out today."

"Found out from who?"

"From that drunk Rawdon," she snapped. "And believe me, it'll put what little piddling things you learned to shame."

"I've never been in a place like this before," the young woman said softly. She glanced around the crowded Lyons Tea Shop and smiled as the waiter pushed a trolley loaded with cakes, pastries, buns and tea to their table. "It's ever so nice of you to do this for me. Me Mam says I oughtn't to talk to strangers, but you're all right. I can tell, you see. You're not at all like some."

Smythe felt lower than a worm. He'd done some things in his life that he wasn't proud of, but this was the first time he'd ever taken advantage of a woman's loneliness for his own purposes. His conscience niggled at him like a bit of meat caught between his teeth. "I'm right pleased to buy you tea," he said softly, and he meant it. She seemed like a nice girl. But she wasn't very pretty. Her hair was frizzy and brown, her complexion bore the marks of a long-ago bout with the pox and her teeth stuck out in front. He'd approached her because he'd seen her coming out of the McNally house. As she wasn't used to men paying attention to her, it had been almost sinful how easy it was to strike up a conversation.

"Thank you." She smiled as the waiter put their tea on the table and then left.

"What's your name?" he asked. "You never did say."

"Velma Prewitt." She blushed slightly and looked down at her lap.

Smythe felt like the worst of blackguards. Her shy smiles and blushes convinced him the poor girl was as innocent as a baby lamb. She'd no idea he had any ulterior motives. Velma was no doubt thinkin' he was really interested in her and all he was doin' was usin' her. He cleared his throat. "My name's Smythe."

She raised her gaze and smiled. "That's a lovely name. Would you like me to pour?" she asked, nodding at the teapot.

"That'd be fine."

"You're a coachman, you said?" she inquired, lifting the heavy china pot and carefully pouring the tea into the waiting cups.

"That's right," he replied. "Work for a Scotland Yard police detective."

"Then we've something in common." She laughed. "We both work for the law. My employer is a barrister. Well, young Mr. McNally is only a solicitor, but his father is a QC."

"That's interestin'." Smythe picked up his cup of tea. He hadn't a clue how to get her talking. But blimey, he didn't want to go home without learnin' a ruddy thing. "So how long have you worked in that 'ousehold?" he asked, saying the first thing that popped into his head. He knew one thing, he had to keep her chattin'. Once he got her rattlin' on a bit, he could lead the conversation around to where he wanted it to go. Namely, James McNally.

"Not long," She helped herself to an iced tea cake. "They're decent people to work for." She hesitated and gave him a timid smile. "Well, not as bad as some places I've worked."

"That's nice," he said. Bloomin' Ada, he must be losin' his touch. He weren't able to think of a ruddy thing to say. Too bad he'd gotten in the habit of buyin' information off people. That was his trouble. He had more money than he knew what to do with, and on the last few cases he'd gotten shiftless and lazy. Now he couldn't think how to bring the subject round to where it needed to be. Blast a Spaniard anyway, this wasn't the first time his money had caused him trouble. He frowned, remembering he had to try to fit in a visit to his ruddy banker today. The silly git kept pesterin' him with letters. His last one had been right nasty. Old Pike virtually threatened to come round to Upper Edmonton Gardens if Smythe didn't stop in to the bank and give them instructions about his latest investment.

"Is everything all right?" Velma asked softly.

Smythe started. "Yeah, why?"

"You were frowning."

"Sorry." He pushed his money problems to the back of his mind. He'd deal with Pike later. He had enough worries trying to get this shy, homely young woman to confide in him and glarin' at the poor girl wasn't helpin' none. He gave her a cocky grin. "I was thinkin' of something else."

"Oh good." She gave him another shy smile. "I thought perhaps something I'd done had made you angry."

"Don't be daft, I'm enjoyin' myself," he lied. "So, I guess your employer must treat you decent, then."

"Oh yes. Mind you, I work hard. But I'm a parlor maid now. I started out in the scullery, but that was ages ago and I've worked my way up."

"That's nice. You must be a real 'ard worker," Smythe said expansively. Perhaps if he flattered her she'd relax a bit and start talkin'. "Startin' in the scullery and workin' your way up to parlor maid takes some doin'."

"I do my best. How does your police inspector treat you?" she asked.

"He's a real gent, 'e is." Smythe helped himself to a bun. "Kind. Decent. Takes good care of 'is 'ousehold."

"So you like him, then?"

"Sure I do," he replied. "Wouldn't stay there if I didn't."

"Don't think I'd like it much," she murmured, dropping her gaze to her lap as though she were frightened by her own boldness.

He stared at her curiously. "'Ow come?"

"Well"—Velma raised her chin and stared him straight in the eye—"I guess you could say it was because I hate coppers."

# CHAPTER 7

"Thank you for coming," Mrs. Jeffries said to Sarah Hewett. As she hadn't given her much choice in the matter, she'd been relieved when she'd spotted the woman and a small child coming into the park. She smiled down at the little girl peeping from behind her mother's skirts. "I take it this is your daughter?"

"This is my Amanda." Sarah smiled and stroked the child's golden curls. Then she looked up, her smile vanishing. "I told Moira, Amanda needed to get out in the air. It's not good for her to be shut up all day in a house of mourning. That was my excuse for getting out, you see."

"Did you need an excuse to leave?" Mrs. Jeffries asked gently.

Sarah laughed harshly. "Not really, I suppose it was just habit. It was a good idea, meeting here in the park." She gently pulled the child out from behind her dress. "Amanda, say hello to Mrs. Jeffries."

Amanda stared at the housekeeper for a moment then grinned. "Hewwo," she lisped.

"Hello, Amanda."

The little girl pointed to the open space in front of the park bench where the two women stood. "Pway," she babbled. "Pway, pway."

"All right, darling," Sarah said, "but stay right here where I can see you."

Amanda skipped off a few feet and plopped down. Immediately, she began picking up twigs and tossing them into the air.

"How old is she?" Mrs. Jeffries asked.

"Two and a half," Sarah said. She sat down on the bench, her attention riveted on her child. "And she's the most precious thing in my life. I'd die if I lost her."

"Is that what Haydon Dapeers was threatening you with?" Mrs. Jeffries asked quietly. "Taking your child from you?"

Sarah turned her head and regarded Mrs. Jeffries speculatively. "The only reason I'm here at all is because Michael insisted that talking to you might be easier than talking with the police. I didn't want to come."

"Mr. Taggert is correct," Mrs. Jeffries replied, returning the young woman's direct gaze with one of her own. "Talking to me will be a lot easier for you than speaking to the police. Providing, of course, that you didn't murder Haydon Dapeers."

Sarah jerked her head around to look at her small daughter. "I didn't kill him. But I'm not sorry that someone else did. You must promise me, Mrs. Jeffries, that what I'm about to tell you will go no further."

"I can't make you that promise—"

"It has nothing to do with Haydon's death," Sarah interrupted quickly. "It's about my daughter."

Surprised, Mrs. Jeffries glanced at the little girl. She was now lying on the soft grass and kicking her feet in the air. "Your daughter?"

"Yes, but I'll not say a word unless you give me your promise."

Mrs. Jeffries hesitated. "All right, providing the information you give me isn't connected to Haydon Dapeers's death, I give you my word it will go no further."

Relieved, Sarah sagged against the back of the park bench. "Good. Michael's sure we can trust you. I hope he's not wrong. But you asked me if Haydon had threatened to take Amanda from me. The answer to that is no. He had no interest in her. All he wanted to do was to ruin her life."

Mrs. Jeffries stared at her. "How could he possibly do that? She's little more than a baby."

Sarah stared blankly into space for a moment, then her gaze focused on the child. "He could have done it easily. All it would have taken was for Haydon to tell the truth about Amanda and her entire life would have been in shreds."

Mrs. Jeffries cast a quick glance at the little girl. There was nothing odd looking about the child at all. In fact, she was exceptionally beautiful. "Your daughter appears perfectly normal to me," she murmured, wondering if the poor thing was deaf or perhaps a bit slow mentally.

"Do you know what it's like to be a foundling?" Sarah's voice dropped to a whisper. "A bastard?"

"No," Mrs. Jeffries said softly, "I don't." Anguish flashed in Sarah's eyes, her cheeks flamed pink and her mouth trembled. "But I imagine you do," she finished.

Sarah's eyes widened in surprise and then she laughed bitterly. "You're very astute, Mrs. Jeffries. I know precisely what it's like. You see, I am one."

"I'm sorry."

"Growing up was awful," Sarah continued. "The whispers behind my back, the fact that other children wouldn't play with me: it was terrible. I would do anything to make sure my child didn't suffer the same fate. You see, when my mother found herself unmarried and pregnant, she had no choice but to throw herself on the mercy of her family. They didn't quite turn her and me out on the streets, but they made both our lives a living hell."

Mrs. Jeffries gazed at her sympathetically. She knew the woman wasn't exaggerating. Intelligent and well-spoken, Sarah Hewett was obviously from a reasonably well-off home. Judging by her accent and carriage, her family apparently had enough income to ensure she was decently educated. Coming from her background, Mrs. Jeffries had no doubt her life had been utterly miserable when she was growing up. If she'd been illegitimate and poor, that would have been different. Not better, perhaps, since living in poverty was certainly miserable enough, but different in the sense that generally the child wasn't shamed constantly by those around them. Mrs. Jeffries had observed that poor people were far more tolerant of those born on the "wrong side of the blanket" than other classes were. Judging from the expression of remembered humiliation and shame she'd seen on Sarah's face, the young woman had probably spent her entire childhood being blamed for something she'd had no control over. "How awful for both of you."

"Haydon found out"—Sarah glanced quickly around to make sure no one else was in earshot—"that Amanda wasn't fathered by my husband. He told me if I didn't behave myself, he'd make sure the entire world knew the truth. I couldn't let that happen. I wasn't going to let it happen, and then he got murdered."

"Most conveniently."

Sarah gave her a sharp look. "I may have hated him, but I didn't kill him. And neither did Michael."

"How did Dapeers find out about Amanda's parentage?" Mrs. Jeffries asked.

"Be careful, darling," Sarah called to the little girl, who was now running around in wide circles, her arms extended like wings. "Haydon was good at finding out secrets." She sighed. "It was one of his few talents. I suppose I ought to start at the beginning."

"That would be most helpful."

"Before Amanda was born, I lived with my aunt. My parents had both died and Aunt Lillian took me in when I was eighteen. She was a great friend of Moira's family. She had this huge house, you see, and when her income was reduced because the shares her husband had invested in lost value, Aunt Lillian began taking in boarders to make ends meet. Oh, she didn't advertise or anything like that, but she rented rooms to young people from good families. One of those young men was Charles Hewett, the man who became my husband." She paused and coughed delicately. "Charles fell in love with me right away. He was a good man, kind, decent. Honorable. But at the time I wasn't interested. I was in love with someone else."

"Michael Taggert?"

She nodded. "Then I got pregnant."

Mrs. Jeffries remembered the protective way Michael Taggert had hovered over Sarah yesterday at the pub, the way he'd looked at her. "And Michael wouldn't marry you?"

"I didn't tell him." She looked down at her hands. "Michael had just gotten a chance to go to Italy to study under a master painter, I couldn't take that away from him. So I said nothing. I was terrified. Charles found me crying one day in the drawing room, he asked me what was wrong and I told him. He offered to marry me to give my child a name. We eloped that night. Amanda was born eight months later. She was born long enough after the wedding to keep most of the gossip quiet and she was quite small when she was born, so both Aunt Lillian and Charles put it around that she'd come early."

"If there wasn't any gossip and both your aunt and your husband claimed the child was early, how did Haydon Dapeers know Amanda wasn't Charles Hewett's daughter?" Mrs. Jeffries queried.

"Unfortunately, Charles kept a diary. I meant to throw it away after he died, but I never got round to it. I don't know how Haydon found it; I kept it locked in my trunk. But he managed to get his filthy hands on it. Charles, of course, had written the truth in the diary."

"Why did it matter to him? Did he try to blackmail you?"

"He couldn't," Sarah said bluntly. "I've little money. Charles didn't leave me well-off. But it mattered to Haydon because it gave him power over me. Haydon liked to control people. He liked moving them about like they were puppets or pieces on a chessboard. He had no real interest in me or my daughter, he just wanted to keep us under his power."

"He didn't try to pressure you into a more, shall we say intimate relationship?" Mrs. Jeffries asked.

Sarah closed her eyes briefly and cringed. "He tried. But I fought him off. After that, I was careful not to be alone in the house with him. Then Michael came back from Italy. Haydon was really a coward. I think he knew that if he tried to touch me again, Michael would hurt him."

Mrs. Jeffries frowned. Something didn't make sense here. "If Haydon was frightened of Michael Taggert, why did he hire him to do the artwork on his new pub?"

"Haydon didn't. Moira did." Sarah smiled faintly. "Moira knew Michael's work from when she used to visit Aunt Lillian. She insisted that if Haydon wanted any money from her, he had to use Michael to etch the windows and do the wood carving. Haydon was livid, but he needed the money, so he did as she asked. But Haydon had his revenge. After he hired Michael, he threw us together and then stood back and watched us suffer."

"How?"

"Haydon knew I'd never tell Michael the truth. I couldn't tell him he had a daughter and that I loved him and I always had."

"Why can't you tell him the truth?" Mrs. Jeffries asked. Surely there was no reason for the two young people not to be together now. Neither of them was married.

"Because Michael would insist on acknowledging Amanda," Sarah whispered miserably. "He'd want to change her name and tell the whole world she was his. I couldn't allow that. I couldn't allow my child to be branded a bastard."

Mrs. Jeffries thought Sarah Hewett was being overly protective. Certainly, in some circles, it would be considered scandalous. But as the child's parents would be married, she would hardly be considered a bastard any longer. However, considering what Sarah herself had gone through as a child, she could understand the woman's anxiety about it, even if she didn't agree. "Is it possible that Haydon might have told Mr. Taggert the truth?"

"No," Sarah cried, "Michael doesn't know."

"Are you absolutely sure?"

Mrs. Jeffries thought about her talk with Sarah Hewett all the way back to Upper Edmonton Gardens. She didn't like to think of either Sarah or Michael as a killer, but both of them did have a motive. With Michael Taggert, it could be as simple as rage. Sarah, an overly protective mother, could have thought murdering Dapeers was the safest way to ensure that he never breathed one word of scandal about her child.

Furthermore, she told herself as she hurried down the back hall and into the kitchen, there were a number of unanswered questions surrounding both of them. But she quickly pushed the problem of Sarah Hewett and Michael Taggert to the back of her mind when she walked into the kitchen.

Inspector Witherspoon, a plate of food in front of him, was sitting at the kitchen table. "Ah, Mrs. Jeffries," he cried happily. "I've been waiting for you. I do need to ask your advice about something rather important."

Mrs. Jeffries smiled brightly. "Do forgive me for not being here, sir, but I had to—"

"Take them bad biscuits back to the grocer's," Mrs. Goodge put in quickly. "I've already told the inspector that."

"Yes," she replied, grateful for the cook's quick thinking, "I've been to the grocer's. Excuse me, sir, but why aren't you eating in the dining room?"

Mrs. Goodge, standing out of the inspector's line of sight, rolled her eyes heavenward.

"Oh"—he waved his fork in the air—"I didn't want to bother Mrs. Goodge with running up and down the steps. As Betsy had to go to the fishmonger's and Wiggins is over at the boot mender's, I thought I'd just have a sit-down here."

"I see." Mrs. Jeffries glanced at the cook, once again, grateful that Mrs. Goodge had covered for them all. "What would you like my advice on?" she asked eagerly. Finally, the man had come to his senses and was going to start talking about this case. It was getting odd, investigating without the inspector's information, a bit like poking about in a dark room. If they weren't careful, she and the rest of the staff were going to start banging into one another.

"Well, it's rather awkward," he replied. He pushed his now empty plate to one side.

Mrs. Jeffries realized he was probably embarrassed because he hadn't confided in her earlier. "Now, now, sir," she said soothingly, taking the seat beside him and giving him her most encouraging smile, "I'm sure you'll find that if you just tell me what it is, you'll find me most sympathetic and helpful."

"Well"—he smiled hesitantly at the cook—"I'm not certain I can really explain what I need. . . ."

"Try, sir," Mrs. Jeffries encouraged. Goodness, he really was embarrassed. But there was no need. She certainly wouldn't gloat or make inappropriate remarks.

He cleared his throat and cast another quick glance at Mrs. Goodge. But she ignored him and stubbornly continued to cut up apples.

"Actually," he said, "it's a rather delicate matter."

"I'm sure it is, sir," Mrs. Jeffries said. "And I assure you, I'm most discreet." She wished he'd get on with it. For goodness' sakes, this wouldn't be the first time he'd discussed his cases with her. Perhaps it was Mrs. Goodge's presence that was inhibiting him.

"All right, then." He took a deep breath. Gracious, this was becoming far more difficult than he'd anticipated when he'd decided to seek his housekeeper's assistance. "You see, it's a bit complicated."

"Most things are complicated, sir," Mrs. Jeffries said magnanimously. "All your cases are very complex. But you always solve them, don't you?"

He stared at her blankly. "Cases? Oh no, Mrs. Jeffries, I'm afraid you don't understand. I don't want to discuss this case with you. As a matter of fact, I'm trying a new method of detecting on this one."

Stunned, she sat bolt upright in her chair. "You don't?"

"Oh no." He smiled happily. "This case is really quite simple, Mrs. Jeffries. As a matter of fact, I'm making a few inquires, and once those are done, I expect to make an arrest quite soon. Yes, indeed, it's really a very simple matter."

Mrs. Jeffries couldn't believe her ears. He was going to be making an arrest soon! But that was impossible. This case wasn't simple. It wasn't simple in the least. They had half a dozen suspects and all of them could easily have committed the crime. But what could she do? A knot of panic twisted her insides. The inspector was going to make a grave mistake, she just knew it. And it would probably ruin his career.

Witherspoon didn't appear to notice his housekeeper had turned pale. "I need your advice on a far different matter," he said blithely. "A most delicate matter; one could even say, a matter of the heart."

As she didn't have a clue what he was talking about, she simply looked at him. He was heading for disaster. She knew it. She could feel it in her bones. Before you could say Bob's-your-uncle, he'd arrest the wrong person and then he'd find himself back in the records room at Scotland Yard.

"Mrs. Jeffries, I do realize this isn't a normal housekeeping duty, but I need your help most desperately." He blushed like a schoolboy. "You see, Lady Cannonberry's letter to me was most . . . affectionate, shall we say. And I need a bit of help in drafting an equally affectionate reply to her."

That evening, as soon as dinner was over, Mrs. Jeffries didn't waste one moment. The moment Luty and Hatchet arrived, she bade them sit down, poured them both a cup of tea and then plunged right in and told them about her strange encounter with Inspector Witherspoon.

The others were as surprised as she had been except for Mrs. Goodge, who'd been in the kitchen when the Inspector had made his shocking announcement.

"You mean he's close to an arrest?" Luty asked in disbelief. "But that's impossible. We ain't told him nuthin'."

"'Ow does 'e know who the killer is when we don't?" Wiggins exclaimed.

"Was 'e 'avin' you on a bit?" Smythe asked incredulously.

"Excuse me, madam," Hatchet said politely. "But are you sure you understood the inspector correctly?"

"He were dead serious," Mrs. Goodge replied angrily, not giving Mrs. Jeffries time to open her mouth. "And if he's not careful, he'll not only ruin his career with the Yard, but he'll muck up our lives good and proper too. Who does he think he is? Makin' an arrest, indeed. He can't possibly know who the killer is."

Mrs. Jeffries felt somewhat as the rest of them did; however, she did feel she owed Inspector Witherspoon's detecting abilities some show of respect. "Well, perhaps we're all being a bit too hasty. Perhaps he knows something about this crime that we don't."

Smythe shook his head. "'E can't. I've spent two days talkin' to people about that killin' and there couldn't be anything 'e knows that we ain't found out. Just take this McNally person; I found out today that 'e was at the Gilded Lily the night of the murder. Maybe 'e weren't inside the pub, but 'e were seen 'angin' about the back door."

"Does the inspector know about McNally?" Hatchet asked.

"'E couldn't," Smythe replied. "Accordin' to what Velma told me, 'e 'asn't been round to ask any questions."

"So he doesn't even know McNally is a suspect," Mrs. Jeffries said thoughtfully. "Yet he feels he's on the verge of an arrest. We can't let it happen. Arresting the wrong person at this point will ruin his career."

"How can we stop it?" Mrs. Goodge cried, "He's not even talking to you? We don't know what he knows, and even worse, he doesn't know what we know! Why I even found out a few bits myself. Mind you, it wasn't easy, seein' as how the victim was only a publican."

Mrs. Jeffries decided that wasting any more time lamenting Inspector Witherspoon's odd behavior would be foolish on their parts. "What were you able to find out, Mrs. Goodge?" she asked the cook.

"Well, it's not very nice, it isn't, but I had a chat with Rupert Simmons, he's my cousin's second husband's nephew and he works at the house right up the road from where the Dapeerses live. Rupert told me that he heard from the upstairs maid at the Dapeers house that Mrs. Dapeers has been carryin' on with some preacher. And what's more, she didn't much care if the whole neighborhood knew about it. She's completely taken leave of her senses over this man. Of course, this Reverend Ballantine is supposed to be as handsome as sin, not that he sounds like much of a man of the cloth to me."

Betsy, who vividly remembered the awkward moments she'd spent that very afternoon at the Reverend Ballantine's Missionary Society, felt a blush creeping up her cheeks and dropped her gaze to her lap. "He *is* handsome."

Smythe gave her a sharp look. "'Ow do you know that?"

"Yes," Mrs. Goodge asked tartly, giving the maid an irritated frown, "how did you find out what he looks like?"

Betsy glanced up and saw that everyone was staring at her. "Because

I saw him, that's how. And Mrs. Dapeers is giving him pots of money now that her husband's dead and can't nag her anymore. The fact is that Reverend Ballantine told me himself that his society was coming into a lot of money. Called it a miracle, he did."

"Did he actually say he was getting money from Moira Dapeers?" Mrs. Jeffries asked.

"He didn't use her name, but from what he told me, I could tell it had to be her."

"He told ya?" Smythe exclaimed. "And when did you meet 'im?"

Betsy glared right back. Just because she and Smythe occasionally "walked out" together didn't mean he could boss her about. "This afternoon. I went round to the missionary society—"

"And this Reverend Ballantine just up and answered all your questions?" Smythe interrupted. He didn't know that he wanted Betsy out and about and talking to strange men. Especially ones that was handsome as sin.

"Of course not," she snapped. "I didn't let on anything about the murder. It just came up in conversation, that's all."

Mrs. Jeffries could tell by the expression on the coachman's face that he was bedeviled by a touch of the green-eyed monster, so she quickly said to the maid, "Were you able to find out anything else?"

"Not really. But Reverend Ballantine did seem to think that he'd had a miracle come his way. I'm certain he was talking about Dapeers's murder. I think Mrs. Dapeers is in love with him, and what's more, he knows it and is usin' it to get what he wants from her." Betsy quickly told them the rest of her tale and why she'd come to the conclusion that Moira Dapeers wasn't precisely a grieving widow. The only part she left out was the embarrassing details, such as how she'd finally had to give the good reverend a sharp kick in the knee and then bolted like a hare to get out of that house!

"You've done well, Betsy." Mrs. Jeffries gave her an approving smile. "It seems quite clear that Moira Dapeers did have a motive for killing her husband, if, indeed, she is in love with this man Ballantine."

"So did Sarah Hewett," Luty put in. "I found out that Haydon Dapeers was tryin' to make her his mistress. He was holdin' something over her head, threatening to tell everyone some dreadful secret of hers if she didn't cooperate with him."

"And how did you find out that bit of gossip?" Hatchet asked irritably.

As it was precisely the gossip he'd heard, he was most annoyed with his employer for stealing his thunder.

Luty smiled smugly. "From Rawdon; you know, he was talkin' real good before that brawl broke out."

"Brawl?" Mrs. Goodge exclaimed. "What brawl?"

Before Luty could explain, Hatchet said, "I had to rescue Madam from a rather unfortunate incident at a pub this afternoon."

"Rescue me!" Luty snorted indignantly. "I'll have you know I was doin' just fine. I can still hold my own, you know. Just 'cause I'm old don't mean I can't skedaddle outta the way when a few fists start flying."

"Oh dear," Mrs. Jeffries murmured. One of her greatest fears of having Luty and Hatchet involved in the inspector's cases was that the elderly woman would get hurt. "You could have been hurt, Luty."

"Fiddlesticks! This ain't the first time I've seen a fight—"

"Speakin' of fights," Wiggins interrupted excitedly. "I talked to a couple of people that were in front of the Gilded Lily the night of the murder; they was actually watching the fight."

"Did any of these people remember who they saw standing outside the pub?" Mrs. Jeffries asked. There was really no point in badgering Luty; she was far too stubborn to listen to any of them. "I mean, could they alibi any of our suspects?"

"What do you mean?" Mrs. Goodge asked.

"She means," Smythe said smoothly, "that if any of the suspects was actually seen watching the fight, then they couldn't 'ave been skulkin' down to the taproom and stickin' a knife in Dapeers."

"Precisely."

"Well"—Wiggins bit his lip—"the men from Bestal's was seen outside. I know that 'cause the bloke I was talkin' to told me he wondered what they was doin' at the Gilded Lily."

"Selling beer," Mrs. Goodge said. "That's why they was there, to sell beer."

"But that's not true," Wiggins insisted. "Harry told me 'e knew for a fact that the Gilded Lily was gettin' their supply from Midlands Ale. That's why he noticed the men from Bestal's; he'd seen them in the Black Horse and he wondered why they'd gone to the Lily."

"Maybe the gentlemen from Bestal's was tryin' to change Dapeers's mind about using Midlands," Betsy suggested.

As Mrs. Jeffries didn't think who Dapeers bought his beer from had anything to do with the murder, she decided to move things along. "The important thing is that we've now eliminated the gentlemen from the brewery. Does anyone else have anything to add?"

"Only that McNally was really desperate," Smythe said quietly. He winced inwardly as he remembered Velma Prewitt. "Accordin' to what I found out, McNally's father was goin' to boot 'im out of the 'ouse if 'e found out about the gamblin'. Seems he'd paid his son's debts one time too often in the past. Velma told me—"

"Velma?" Betsy asked archly. "How come you never seem to talk to cabbies and porters anymore when we're on a case? Now it's always women you're chattin' up."

Smythe, delighted to get a bit of his own back, gave the maid a wicked grin. "Can I 'elp it if the ladies love talkin' to me."

"Hmmph," Betsy snorted delicately. "And I'll bet you love talkin' to them too."

Drat, thought Mrs. Jeffries, now Betsy had a touch of the green-eyed monster too. Really, she wished these two would make up their minds about each other. Normally their bantering didn't bother her, but on this case, she was finding it definitely annoying. "I think I'd better go next," she said firmly. "Unless, of course, you have any more to add, Smythe."

He shook his head.

Hatchet said, "I found out that Haydon Dapeers was in financial straits. According to my sources"—he gave Luty a superior smile— "Dapeers had overextended himself opening the Gilded Lily. His suppliers were threatening him. Furthermore, I heard that the gambling debt that James McNally owed wasn't a paltry amount. It was two thousand pounds. Two thousand pounds Dapeers desperately needed if he was going to make his new pub successful."

"And we know that McNally was there that night," Mrs. Jeffries said. "If only we knew if the back door was locked or not."

"McNally could 'ave used the side entrance, the one off Bonham Road to get in," Smythe suggested.

"And he could have used the back door, or the front door, or climbed in an open window," Mrs. Jeffries said in disgust. "The point is, we're guessing. We're starting to jump to conclusions and we really must stop. What we need are facts."

But facts were difficult to find in this case, she thought irritably. They had far too many suspects, far too many motives and far too little information from the inspector. "We'll just have to keep at it," she said firmly. "And we'd better do it as quickly as possible. I have a terrible feeling that if we don't come up with some decent evidence soon, the inspector is going to make the worst mistake of his life."

Witherspoon grimaced as he took a quick taste of the pale ale. Gracious, the Black Horse looked like a nice pub, but the beer was dreadful. It had no taste at all.

"Stuff tastes awful," Barnes hissed in his ear. "It's a wonder they have any trade." He glanced around the crowded public bar.

"Well, until the Gilded Lily opened up, there wasn't much competition around here. The nearest pub is a quarter of a mile up the road."

"No wonder Tom and Joanne Dapeers was so upset about Haydon Dapeers opening a pub just up the street from 'em," Barnes mumbled. "I'd be worried too."

"You wanted to speak to me, Inspector?" Joanne Dapeers said as she came into the bar.

"Good day, Mrs. Dapeers." Inspector Witherspoon smiled politely. "I realize you're busy, but I've a few more questions to ask."

Joanne shrugged prettily, "All right, though I don't know what else there is to say. I told you everything I know."

"Could you tell me precisely where you were standing when the fight out on the street broke out."

"Where I was standing? Hmm . . . let's see now," she replied thoughtfully. "I was standing by the window, Inspector. Yes, that's it. Most everyone else ran outside when it started, but I had a full glass of ale and I didn't want to spill it, so I went over and stood by the table and watched out the window."

"And do you remember if anyone else stayed inside?" Witherspoon asked.

Her brows drew together as she concentrated. Finally, she said, "I'm sorry, Inspector, I was watching the brawl, I wasn't looking around me to see who was where or what was going on inside the pub. But I do recall one thing."

"And what's that?"

"Well, when everyone came back inside and I went to find Haydon, I remember being relieved to see that Michael Taggert hadn't come back inside with Sarah. She was standing at the bar on her own. I was afraid Michael and Haydon would have another ruckus."

Witherspoon stared at her. "Are you absolutely certain about this?"

"Oh, absolutely," she replied, picking up a clean hand towel from underneath the counter and flinging it open. "Like I said, they'd already had trouble that evening, so I was right relieved to see that he'd taken himself off. Come to think of it, I don't recall seeing Taggert in the bar before the fight started, either."

"But I thought you weren't paying attention," Barnes said.

She shrugged. "I wasn't. But now that you mention it, I do recall having a quick look around to see if he was chattin' up Sarah, and he'd disappeared. This was right after Haydon went to the taproom."

"Mrs. Dapeers, what made you go looking for your brother-in-law?"

"You mean when I found Haydon's body?"

"Yes."

"Well, I've already told the police all this. It's not something I want to think about again."

"I'm sure it was an awful experience for you, Mrs. Dapeers," Witherspoon said sympathetically. "But please, do go over it once again." He really didn't like asking a lady to recount what must have been a dreadful experience, but after thinking about it, he'd decided that he must. Mrs. Dapeers may have seen or heard something important that night without even realizing it.

"Well, there's not much to tell, really," she replied. "People were drifting back in because the constable had broken up the fight outside. I realized it was getting late and that we'd better get back, so I went down the hall to say good night to Haydon. I'd noticed he'd not come out of the taproom. When I got there, he was lying on the floor with a knife in his back. I screamed and people came running in."

"Did you see anyone?"

Joanne shook her head. "No one. Just Haydon lying there."

Tom Dapeers came out of the back and went behind the bar. He put his arm protectively around his wife. "It's not very nice for her to have to talk about it again," he complained.

"I'm sorry, but it was necessary. Thank you for your help, Mrs. Dapeers."

"If you've finished, Inspector, the wife and I have work to do."

"I am finished. I'm sorry to have interrupted your busy day."

Tom nodded and he and Joanne disappeared back into the hall.

"Odd her rememberin' Taggert's movements," Barnes muttered. "And no one else's."

"Yes, but she did have a specific reason for keeping an eye on Taggert," Witherspoon said slowly. "He and Haydon Dapeers had already had one heated exchange. She seems a strong-minded sort of woman, but perhaps even she didn't want to watch another brawl. Especially after that one out in the street."

The inspector absently picked up his tankard and took a sip, grimacing as he swallowed. His head whirled with bits and pieces of information, none of which made sense or pointed him in the direction of the killer. Perhaps he really ought to talk about this case to his housekeeper; perhaps listening to his inner voice wasn't such a good idea after all. . . .

"Give us a tankard, Tom," a man shouted from the other end of the bar. "And while you're at it, see if you can come up with some decent entertainment. We ain't 'ad anything 'appen round 'ere since that fight the other night."

Witherspoon's eyes widened as he turned his head and stared at the burly figure at the far end of the bar. Gracious, he thought, why hadn't he thought of it before? Putting down his drink, he turned and hurriedly went over to the heavyset man in the flat cap and porter's coat. Barnes, taken by surprise, caught up with him a moment later.

"Excuse me, sir," the inspector said politely, "but did you actually see the fight in front of the Gilded Lily?"

The man grinned. "It were a good one too. 'Ad me a front-row seat. Best bit of brawlin' I've seen in a long time."

"And where were you standing while you were watching the brawl?" Witherspoon asked.

"I were standin' across the road from the pub." Then his face creased in a suspicious frown. "What's it to you? Who the bloomin' 'ell are ya, anyway? And why you askin'?"

"I'm Inspector Witherspoon from Scotland Yard and I think, sir, you may be able to help us with our inquiries."

Fifteen minutes later the inspector had finished questioning Tim Magee. He had more information, but for the life of him, he couldn't quite decide what it all meant.

But he now had a few hard facts. The inspector took comfort in that.

Even if nothing quite made sense yet, he was beginning to get the glimmer of an idea about this murder. He nodded to himself. Yes, it might be a very simple case after all. Very simple, indeed.

Constable Barnes tapped him lightly on the shoulder. "Here comes Constable Griffith, sir," he said, pointing to the uniformed officer pushing his way through the crowd.

"Good day, sir, Constable Barnes." Griffith nodded respectfully. His cheeks were flushed and he was out of breath, as though he'd been running. "I've been sent round to collect you, sir," he said to the inspector. He glanced quickly around the pub and saw people openly staring at them. "You'd best come with me, sir." He dropped his voice to a whisper. "There's been another stabbing. Only this time it's a woman."

# CHAPTER 8

———◦◦◦———

Smythe reluctantly pulled another bill out of his pocket and slid it across the table. "You're a bloomin' robber, that's what you are, Blimpey. But you done good, so I expect I oughtn't to complain."

He was disgusted with himself for having to buy information again, but in this case, there really wasn't anything else he could do. They were running out of time. According to Mrs. Jeffries, the inspector could be getting ready to make an arrest. And considerin' the man didn't have a clue about this case, it would lead to disaster.

"Ta, Smythe, you're a gentleman." Blimpey grinned and pocketed the cash. "Must say I was kinda surprised gettin' that message from you today. Didn't think you'd want to keep doin' business with me after the other day. Sorry about that, but like I said, I've got me reputation to think about."

Smythe shrugged. In truth, he'd been right narked at Blimpey, but seein' as the man could find things out quicker than a bank manager could grab your money, he hadn't had much choice. "You're sure you've got yer facts right about Michael Taggert?"

"'Corse I'm sure." Blimpey laughed, but as he was taking a drink at the time, it came out as a wet snort through his nose. Smythe ducked to avoid being sprayed by the worst-tastin' beer in all of London.

"Sorry," Blimpey apologized, and wiped the spray off the tabletop with his shirtsleeve. "Michael Taggert hated Dapeers's guts, and he didn't take that job with Dapeers 'cause he needed the lolly. Taggert come into an inheritance two months ago. He's got more money than you or I, mate, and that's the truth of it."

"Then why work for a man you 'ated?" he mused. Yet he thought he knew the answer to that question already. Especially if Taggert were really in love with Sarah Hewett. Smythe too had more money than he'd ever spend, and he continued to work for the inspector. But he didn't have any choice. If he said anything, if the others at Upper Edmonton Gardens knew about it, things would change. They'd be different; he'd have to leave and that would be more than he could bear. Leaving would mean he wouldn't be out and about solvin' murders, there'd be no more family-like evenins' with the others, and most of all, he wouldn't be able to see Betsy every day. After hearing what Mrs. Jeffries had told them yesterday, he thought he understood why Taggert took the job at the Gilded Lily. It kept him connected to Sarah.

"Don't know, mate," Blimpey replied airily. "If I 'ad Taggert's fortune, I wouldn't be 'angin' about bein' a slave for someone like Dapeers. I'd be livin' it up in fine hotels and drinkin' French wine—"

"From the way you're downin' this swill," Smythe interrupted, nodding at the tankard of beer in front of Blimpey, "you wouldn't know French wine if it come up and bit you on the arse."

Blimpey laughed. "You got me there, mate, but it's the thought that counts. If I had plenty of lolly, I'd call no man master. Seems to me this Taggert's off his 'ead, but what can you expect, 'e's an artist. They're an odd lot. Even stranger, Taggert's kept real quiet about inheriting his money. It took me a good bit of snoopin' about to find it out."

Smythe wondered if Sarah Hewer knew. He had a feeling she didn't. She was in love with Taggert and at the same time she wanted to protect her child from scandal. Seemed to Smythe the best way to do it would have been to marry the child's father. But she hadn't. Why? The more he heard, the more convinced he was that the only one of the two lovers who had a real motive to kill Haydon Dapeers was Sarah, not Michael Taggert. Unless'n Taggert was so enraged by the victim's attempts to seduce his woman that he killed Dapeers in a fit of anger. But the killing hadn't been done in a fit of rage—it was too neat and tidy for that. "I wonder if Sarah Hewett ever come down to the Gilded Lily while it was bein' fitted out?" he murmured. If he was right in his thinkin', then Taggert taking the job with Dapeers would make sense.

"Is she Dapeers's sister-in-law?"

"Yeah, 'ow did you know?"

Blimpey shrugged. "I pick up lots of things, you know that." He took another swig of ale and belched softly. "I don't usually give out for free," he said slowly. "But bein' as yer such a reliable customer, I'll toss you this one on the 'ouse. I already know the answer to that question. Sarah Hewett was at the Gilded Lily a lot when it was bein' kitted out. She come with Moira Dapeers. Seems Haydon insisted the ladies come round every day or so and have tea with him in the afternoon. Used to drive the workmen barmy. And the ladies didn't like it either. The Hewett woman was always complainin' about 'aving to leave her brat with the maid and Mrs. Dapeers was on about 'ow comin' to the bloomin' pub interrupted her afternoon."

Smythe nodded, satisfied that he had his answer. Rich or not, Michael Taggert had worked for Dapeers because it was the only way he could see Sarah Hewett. It made perfect sense to him. If the only way Smythe could see Betsy every day was to hang about workin' for someone, he'd do it. "Why did Dapeers want them there, do ya think?"

Blimpey, who was quite an astute judge of human nature, shrugged. "To torment 'em, probably. Me sources tell me that Taggert were crazy about Sarah Hewett, made sure he was at the pub workin' every afternoon when she come round. Dapeers acted like a right old bastard every chance he got, yellin' at Taggert, tellin' 'im this was wrong an' that needed to be fixed. Sounds to me like Dapeers made the women come in just so's 'e'd 'ave a chance to act like God Almighty and belittle the lot of 'em. And me sources said it was obvious there was no love lost between Dapeers and his wife either. Molly said the woman barely spoke to her 'usband."

"So they all 'ated 'im."

"And any of 'em coulda killed 'im," Blimpey agreed. "But I'd put my money on one of the women. Taggert's rich enough now that if 'e wanted to murder Dapeers, 'e could hire it done."

"James McNally had a motive too," Smythe argued. Maybe he was gettin' sentimental, but he didn't like to think of Michael Taggert as a murderer. Or Sarah either.

"True." Blimpey drained his tankard. "But 'e's not got the guts. Mc-Nally just about pissed 'imself when I told 'im Dapeers wanted his lolly. Can't see a man like that 'avin' the nerve to sneak up on a bloke and stick a knife in 'is back."

James McNally was a nervous, rabbity-looking fellow with a long, bony face, pale skin and a growing bald spot on the back of his head. Betsy stared at the bald spot as she followed him down Meeker Street. She had no idea why she was following McNally, except that she couldn't think of anything else to do and she, like the others in the household, felt she had to do something. The inspector might be getting ready to ruin all their lives.

Betsy couldn't stand the thought that her dear inspector might find himself back in the records room and, even worse, that she and the household wouldn't have any more murders to solve.

McNally turned a corner and disappeared down a passageway between two brick buildings. Betsy hesitated at the entrance. She'd been following him for what seemed hours, and without her even realizing it, she was now on the ruddy docks. What was a respected solicitor doing down here? Betsy had to know. She was sure he was up to no good. But this area of London wasn't very safe. Once she was off the street, she might be fair game for any ruffian that happened to be hanging about.

She narrowed her eyes as she saw McNally was almost through the passage. Blast a Spaniard, she thought, I've got to do something. But the footpath between the buildings was dark and smelled awful. To be honest, she was a bit scared. Then she thought of never working on a case again, of spending the rest of her life changing linens and dusting furniture. Betsy bolted down the passageway.

Despite the summer heat, it was cool inside. She hurried, trying hard to walk softly as she saw her prey turn a corner and disappear from sight. Betsy picked up her skirts and began to run. She couldn't lose him now, not when things were starting to get interesting. She flew out the end and onto an empty wharf overlooking the river. Suddenly she was grabbed around the waist and whirled around. Betsy tried to scream just as James McNally's hand covered her mouth.

"The victim's name is Ellen Hoxton," the uniformed constable said to Witherspoon. "Been in the water a few days; you can tell by the bloat. Lucky for us, her skirt caught on that piling; otherwise she'd have been carried off by the current."

Witherspoon hated looking at bodies. Thank goodness he'd eaten a light breakfast this morning. He didn't quite trust his stomach. He'd seen victims who'd been in the water before, and they weren't a very pretty sight. But duty was duty. He knelt by the body and steeled himself to look at the dead woman. Her skin was blue-tinged and the fish had been at her. Witherspoon swallowed convulsively and glanced around the deserted dock. There was a heap of rubbish on the far side, some of the pilings were rotting, and several of the planks were missing from the deck. The place looked deserted. "Who found her?"

"I did," the constable replied. "I was chasin' a pickpocket out here and spotted her hair floating out from beneath the wharf. Of course the pickpocket got away when I stopped to investigate. When I fished her out, I knew it was murder. You can see she was stabbed right through the back."

Witherspoon took a deep breath and gently turned the body. He grimaced as he saw the wound in her back.

"It took me a few minutes to pull her free of the piling," the constable continued. "That's how come her skirt's torn so badly. When I saw she'd been knifed, I knew it was murder."

"Indeed it is, Constable," Witherspoon murmured. He shook his head sadly, appalled that this poor woman's life had been so cruelly taken from her. "Has the Yard been notified?"

"Yes, sir, they should be here any moment. I expect they'll bring a police surgeon with them."

Witherspoon nodded. "How did you know the victim's name?"

The constable, a gray-haired grizzly veteran of well past fifty, grinned. "Oh, I've known Ellen Hoxton for years. I've arrested her more times than I can count. She's a prostitute when she can't get work as a barmaid."

"I see."

"And I know she got sacked from the Black Horse, because one of her friends was lookin' for her and asked me if I'd seen her in the past couple of days or so," the constable continued. "Thought it odd that I hadn't, sir."

"Why?"

"Because this is Ellen's part of London, sir. No matter how often she gets sacked, she won't leave the area. Considerin' that she were employed at the Black Horse, and bein' as I knew that was connected with that stabbin' at the Gilded Lily, I sent Constable Griffith to find you as soon as I realized she'd been stabbed. I expect that's what killed her, sir. The stabbin', not the water."

"Ah, I see." Witherspoon couldn't bear to look at the poor soul another minute; he certainly couldn't tell by looking at her exactly what had caused her death. He'd leave that to the police surgeon. Not that it really mattered. Drowned or stabbed, someone had murdered her. She hadn't poked a knife in her back and jumped in the Thames on her own. He eased himself away from the dead woman and rose to his feet.

"Do you think this killin' is connected to Haydon Dapeers's murder?" Barnes asked softly. He knelt by the body, turned her over and stared at the spot on her back where the knife had gone in.

Witherspoon averted his eyes. He couldn't think why his constable wanted to examine the corpse, but he had far too much respect for Barnes to try to stop him. "I really don't like to make assumptions," he began slowly.

"But she's been stabbed in the same spot that Dapeers was," Barnes persisted. He jabbed his finger at the blackened round slash. "I don't think that's a coincidence."

Witherspoon forced himself to take a quick look and then fastened his eyes on a boat going up the river. "I don't think it's a coincidence, either," he agreed. An idea began to form in his mind. A simple yet bold idea that might bring this case to a conclusion far faster than he'd imagined.

"Constable," he said to the other policeman, "who else knows you've found this body?"

The gay-haired policeman looked surprised by the question. "Well, Constable Griffith and the Yard, of course. And the police surgeon's been notified and is on his way too. Otherwise I've told no one."

Witherspoon nodded. "Good." This poor woman had had her life taken. It filled him with sadness and despair. But if he was right, if he was really the policeman everyone seemed to think he was, he'd have her killer behind bars very soon. Very soon, indeed. "Have any of the locals been back here to see what's going on?"

"No, this whole end of the docks is deserted," the constable replied. "These buildings and the wharves are schedule to be torn down next month and rebuilt. The East India Company just bought it."

"Excellent." Witherspoon hoped his policeman's instinct wasn't leading him astray. "Please try and make sure that no one, especially the press, knows exactly where her body was found."

Barnes gently rolled the late Ellen Hoxton onto her back. He got to his feet, shaking his head. "But what difference does it make if people know where she was found? Whoever killed her probably thinks she's halfway to Gravesend by now."

"That's precisely my point, Constable," Witherspoon said briskly. "And we want the killer to go right on thinking that."

• • •

James McNally dropped his hand from Betsy's mouth and leapt back. "Oh dear, dear," he wailed in a high-pitched voice. "Why are you following me? What do you want? Please don't scream. Did my father put you up to this?"

Stunned, Betsy stared at him. "Your father?"

"It would be just like him to hire a woman to spy on me," McNally said shrilly. "It wouldn't be the first time. Are you another of those type-writer girls?" He took a step closer to her. "He tried to foist one on me before. The minx showed up bold as brass at my office last week. She was carrying that silly little machine and she told me she'd been hired to do my correspondence. But I took care of her; I wasn't going to have her clattering away on that thing, watching my every move, seeing who came and went in my office and then running and tattling to my father. I poured treacle on the wretched thing."

"You poured treacle on a typewriter girl?" Betsy repeated. She couldn't believe her ears! James McNally was mad. Absolutely, stark raving mad. And she was alone here on a deserted dock with him.

"Not on the girl, on her stupid typewriter," he explained belligerently. "She took herself right off, she did. Ran screaming down the hall and out into the street. She wasn't there to take care of my correspondence."

"How do you know?" Betsy thought perhaps it would be best to keep him talking. At least until someone else came along or she could think of a way to get out of here.

"Because I don't have any correspondence," he said, his eyes gleaming triumphantly. "I haven't had a case in six months. My father's always complaining about that too. It's not my fault I've no clients. It's his. If he'd only leave me alone, I'm sure I could do nicely." He angled toward her. "He hired you, didn't he?"

"No, of course not." Betsy drew back and cast a quick glance around the area. The dock was still empty. There weren't even any boats out on the river. Not that she could swim. "I don't even know who you are."

He glared at her suspiciously. "Then why were you following me? Don't try and deny it. You've been walking behind me for the last twenty minutes."

"I wasn't following you," she insisted. "I was just takin' a walk and minding my own business when you grabbed me." She shot a quick look toward the end of the passageway. No help there.

"In this neighborhood?" He laughed. But the sound was harsh and ugly and made her stomach churn in fear. "I'm not stupid, you know. There's nothing here but a deserted dock. No one in their right mind goes walking in this area, even in broad daylight."

"You did." Betsy edged back a bit. If she had to, she'd make a run for the passageway, He might not catch her before she made it out to the street.

"I've business here," he snapped. "How much is he paying you?"

It didn't take too much thinking to know what he was on about. "He's not payin' me nothin'," she yelled, hoping that by screaming at the man she'd attract some attention. She was getting tired of this and a little angry too. "Now leave off botherin' me and I'll be on my way."

She started to turn and he grabbed her arm. "You're not going anywhere until you admit he's paying you to spy on me."

"Let me go."

"Not until you tell me."

Betsy saw red. It would be a cold day in the pits of Hades before she'd put up with being handled like this. Instinctively, she made a fist of her right hand, using a method she'd been taught by some pretty tough ladies when she was a girl living in the East End. Before McNally realized what she was doing, she drew her right arm all the way back, shot it forward and smacked him right on the jaw.

"Ow . . ." He dropped her arm and leapt backward. He stumbled and fell, landing hard on his backside. "That hurt."

Betsy turned and started to run. She'd almost made it to the passageway when she realized he wasn't coming after her. She threw a quick look over her shoulder and then stopped dead.

James McNally was sitting on the dock, crying his eyes out.


"Are you absolutely certain?" Witherspoon asked. He and Constable Barnes were standing on the door stoop of a run-down lodging house near the East India Docks.

Molly, the barmaid from the Gilded Lily, shook her head. "'Corse I'm sure. I saw her with me own eyes I even told Mick about it. Not that the silly sod was payin' attention; he never paid attention when I said something."

"But Mick told us she left a note for Mr. Dapeers," Witherspoon persisted. He needed to get this right. He needed to make himself perfectly clear so that Molly understood exactly what he was asking.

Molly waved her hands impatiently. "I give Mr. Dapeers the note she left. But she come back later that afternoon."

"But Mick didn't mention that."

"Mick was too busy jawin' with the workman out in the back to notice. But she waltzed in big as you please and went right into the saloon bar with Mr. Dapeers. They talked for a good ten minutes and then she left." Molly looked pointedly at the street. "I've got to be goin', Inspector. I've got to take the rest of them linens from the Lily over to the laundry. Then I've got to get to work."

Witherspoon and Barnes both stepped out of her way as she pushed past them and started down the short path to the street. "You have a new position?" he asked politely.

Molly nodded and continued moving steadily toward the road. "At the White Hart over on Cory Place," she yelled. "It's not much of a pub, but the pay is decent. Better than what Dapeers was payin' me anyway."

"You didn't happen to overhear what they were talking about, did you?" Witherspoon scrambled after the woman. He didn't want to order her to stay put long enough to finish answering his questions. He knew how difficult employment was to come by for women of her age.

Molly stopped, turned and glared at him, offended by his question. "I don't eavesdrop on people."

"I didn't mean to imply you did," he said quickly. "I do apologize. But occasionally, one does overhear things. Why, it happens to me all the time."

She gazed at him suspiciously for a moment and then her expression cleared. "All right, I guess you're only tryin' to do yer job. I didn't hear what they was talkin' about, I was busy gettin' ready for the openin'. But I did see Mr. Dapeers give her a fiver." She started toward the street again.

"A fiver?" Witherspoon rushed after her. "You mean he gave her five pounds?"

She turned onto the road. "That's what a fiver is."

"And you didn't think it important to tell us this before?"

She shrugged and started to cross the road. "I thought he was just buyin' himself a bit o' fun, if you know what I mean. She were known to do that every now and again." Molly laughed at her own wit. "And he did it all the time. Gossip had it that he'd even tried to tumble his sister-in-law."

"Ruddy men, they don't listen to a word you say," Molly grumbled. "I'm not even sure that police inspector knows how to listen properly. But you're not like them, are ya, lad?"

Wiggins smiled at the woman and heaved the heavy wicker basket he'd just taken from her to his other hip. "Well," he replied doubtfully, "I do the best I can. 'Ow far is it to the laundry?"

"Not far." Molly pointed up toward the end of Bonham Road. "It's just round the corner and then a bit. It's right nice of ya to carry that for me. Bloomin' 'eavy, it is."

"Don't like to see a lady such as yerself carryin' such a load," he said gallantly. He'd hung around the neighborhood of the Gilded Lily all morning. When he'd spotted Molly coming out the back door carrying a large basket, he'd leapt at the chance to do his good deed for the day. "What was you sayin' about the coppers?"

"Oh them." She waved her hands in dismissal. "They come around askin' more questions today. It's not like I 'adn't talked to 'em before, you know. Not my fault that no one ever listens."

"I guess they was askin' about, the murder." Wiggins slowed his steps. The basket was heavy, but he didn't want to arrive at the laundry before he found *something* out.

"'Corse they was askin' about the murder," Molly grumbled. "Don't know why they're tryin' so hard to find the killer. Seems to me the guilty one is right under their nose. Not that I blame 'er, mind you. If my old man had brought 'ome what Haydon Dapeers did, I'd probably shoved a knife in his back too."

"You think Mrs. Dapeers is the murderer?" Wiggins asked incredulously.

"'Corse I do." Molly snorted in disgust. "My daughter works as a housemaid for Dapeers. She only started a month ago and she was goin' to try and find something else. But then he up and got himself murdered, so Agatha decided to stay on. She likes Mrs. Dapeers. Agatha's heard plenty in that house. Not that the police have bothered talking to her, oh no, I guess they don't think a servant's got ears. But Agatha told me plenty."

Wiggins decided trying to worm information out of this woman was a waste of time. He could tell by the eager gleam in her eyes that she was dying to tell everything she knew. "What'd she say?"

"Well, I'm not one to be repeatin' gossip," Molly said with relish. "But Agatha overheard the most awful row a few days before Mr. Dapeers was murdered."

"What was it about?"

Molly gazed at him speculatively. "Well, I don't think I ought to say, it's not very nice to talk about. Especially to one so young."

"I'm older than I look." He shifted the heavy basket to his other side. "Besides, it wouldn't be fair to stop now. I'll die of curiosity."

"I know what you mean, lad. I hate it when people do that. Well, as I was sayin', last week Agatha was cleaning out the closet in the bedroom next to Mrs. Dapeers's room. All of a sudden she heard Mrs. Dapeers screamin' at Mr. Dapeers that he was a depraved animal. Well, it frightened Agatha no end, it did. But she was like you, curious. So she leaned her ear against the wall and you'll never guess what she heard."

"What?"

"Mrs. Dapeers had found out that Mr. Dapeers had caught the shanker!" Molly shook her head, her expression disgusted. "If my old man brought somethin' like that home. I'd do 'im in, I would. I expect that's exactly what Mrs. Dapeers did."

Wiggins wasn't sure if he knew what a "shanker" was. But he didn't really want to ask. He decided he'd wait till tonight and ask Smythe. He'd know. And he wouldn't laugh at him for askin', either.

"I hope you all have had better luck than we have," Luty said glumly. She dropped down into an empty chair and stared at the circle of morose faces around the table. "From the looks of it, your luck has been about as bad as ours."

"I take it you didn't find out anything," Mrs. Jeffries stated.

"Not a dag-gone thing," Luty grimaced. "And I spent all day talking to people. No one seen anything, no one knows anything and no one heard anything."

"I told you it was a waste of time buying those street arabs sweets,"

Hatchet said dryly. "They only told you they'd been hanging about the Gilded Lily on the day of the murder because they overheard you questioning that cabbie."

"I know that, Hatchet." Luty glared at her butler. "But them young'uns never get sweets. I didn't hurt us none to buy 'em some. I saw you slippin' that little boy some money when you thought I wasn't lookin', so don't be jawin' at me none."

Hatchet blushed. "Well, the lad did look awfully thin."

"Did anyone learn anything today?" Mrs. Jeffries asked. She hoped someone had something to report. She'd insisted everyone return for tea in the hopes that one of them would find out something the rest of them could use.

Betsy cleared her throat. "Well, I did find out something," she said slowly. She glanced at Smythe. She had to tread carefully here; she had to use just the right words to explain what had happened this afternoon. Not that McNally had really been mad, but if she didn't tell it just so, it would sound that way. In truth, once she'd got McNally to stop crying and talked with him a bit, she'd actually felt sorry for the poor fellow. But if they knew the details about her encounter, if they knew she'd been stupid enough to follow a suspect down a dark passageway and onto a deserted dock, she'd be shut up in this house polishing silver till her hair turned as white as Luty's.

"Good." Mrs. Jeffries smiled eagerly. "I'm glad one of us has had some success."

"I think we can take McNally off our list of suspects." Betsy smiled blandly and reached for the cream pitcher.

Everyone waited for her to continue. Betsy poured the cream in her tea and concentrated on stirring it with her spoon.

"Well, go on," Smythe urged. "Tell us the rest of it."

Betsy couldn't stare at her teacup for the rest of the afternoon, so she looked up. "There isn't anything else."

"Whaddaya mean, there isn't anything else?" Smythe eyed her suspiciously. There was something she weren't tellin' and that was a fact.

"Betsy," Mrs. Jeffries said quickly, "surely you have a reason for telling us McNally shouldn't be a suspect?"

"Of course I do," Betsy agreed. She swallowed nervously and looked around the table. Everyone was staring at her. Mrs. Jeffries looked concerned, Luty and Hatchet gazed at her like she'd been out in the sun too long, Mrs. Goodge was glaring at her as if she hadn't wiped her feet before coming into the kitchen and Smythe frowned fierce enough to strip paint off the walls.

"But it's a bit difficult," she continued. "You'll just have to take my word for it, he couldn't of done it." After talking to McNally, she'd come to the conclusion that the man was too timid to squash a bug, let alone stick a knife in someone's back.

"You did something dangerous, didn't you?" Smythe said softly.

Startled, Betsy jerked in surprise.

His frown, if possible, grew fiercer. "I knew it." If Betsy didn't know him so well, she'd have been afraid. "I knew you'd been out and about doin' somethin' that coulda got you hurt or even killed! I can always tell, you get all quiet and sneaky like."

"I do not," Betsy cried. "It's just that there's no need to be tellin' everyone all the details. McNally's such a nervous old thing he could no more shove a knife in someone's back than he could walk on the Thames."

"Aha, so you admit you've confronted McNally," Smythe yelled.

Mrs. Jeffries decided to intervene. Smythe was overly protective of all the household, but he was ridiculously protective of Betsy. This wasn't the first time they'd come to words about the issue and it wouldn't be the last. But right now this case was such a puzzle she didn't need an outbreak of war between the two of them. "Smythe, please. Calm yourself. I'm sure Betsy knew precisely what she was doing today. Let's not discuss this matter right now. We're already muddled enough about this case; if Betsy is sure one of our suspects can be eliminated, then I suggest we take her word for it."

Smythe looked as though he wanted to argue the point, but he contented himself with giving Betsy one last frown. "All right," he said grudgingly, "I'll put it aside. For now."

"I don't know that eliminating McNally from our list is goin' to help matters none," Luty said bluntly. "Truth is, I'm as confused as a drunken miner on Saturday night. I can't make heads nor tails of this murder and I don't think any of the rest of you can either."

For once, Hatchet didn't argue. "I agree, madam. So far, we've had a man murdered who was hated by his wife, his family, his employees and everyone else who knew him. Everyone had a motive, we have no witnesses, no physical evidence and the inspector isn't talking. I'm afraid I don't have a good feeling about this one. We may not be able to solve it."

Mrs. Jeffries was hard-pressed to disagree with him. She felt the same way. But they mustn't give up. They had to keep trying. "Let's not get discouraged," she said brightly. "I think we're doing quite well. Has anyone else learned anything today?"

"Don't look at me," Mrs. Goodge mumbled. "None of my sources could come up with anything."

"I did," Wiggins said. He wished he'd had time to have a quick word with Smythe, but he'd got home so late he hadn't had a chance.

"Excellent." Mrs. Jeffries nodded for him to continue.

Wiggins took a deep breath. "Mrs. Dapeers knew that her husband had got a nasty disease. She found out last week and screamed her head off."

"Disease?" Mrs. Goodge asked irritably. "What disease?"

"The shanker," Wiggins mumbled in a low voice. He was pretty sure he knew what it was, and he didn't think it was the sort of thing one discussed in front of the ladies.

"The what?" Luty frowned. "I didn't quite catch that."

"Speak up, Wiggins." Betsy leaned toward him. "I couldn't hear you."

"Say it again," the cook demanded.

"Did you say he had the canker?" Hatchet asked. "Do you mean canker sores? Goodness, they're quite painful, but I can't think why they should cause such distress that someone would scream about them. They're only mouth ulcers."

Smythe looked down at the tabletop. He was trying not to grin. He'd heard Wiggins quite clearly.

"I said he caught the shanker," Wiggins muttered again, raising his voice a fraction. Blimey, from the way Smythe was grinnin', he was dead sure that this disease was what he thought it was. Blast. Now he'd have to say it out loud.

"The what?" Mrs. Goodge demanded. "The shank-hill?"

"Wiggins is trying to tell us that Moira Dapeers had obviously found out her husband was infected with syphilis," Mrs. Jeffries said calmly.

# CHAPTER 9

Mrs. Jeffries had done some thinking. She still wasn't certain of very much, but she did know that what she'd learned from the others this afternoon convinced her that this case was far too complex to leave to the inspector. She was determined to feed him some clues and information, whether he wanted it or not.

Consequently, she had his she sherry poured and waiting by his favorite chair when he came in that evening.

"I've taken the liberty of fixing you a sherry," she announced as she took his hat from him. "You've been working so very hard on this case, I thought you might need a few moments to relax before dinner."

"That's most kind of you, Mrs. Jeffries," Witherspoon replied. "But won't Mrs. Goodge have supper cooked?"

"It's been so warm today that Mrs. Goodge thought you'd prefer a cold meal, sir." She started down the hall. "It'll keep until you've had a few moments to yourself."

He followed her into the drawing room, sat down and picked up the glass. The liquid sloshed over the tips of his fingers. "I say, this is a rather full glass you've given me." He laughed. "Are you trying to get me drunk?"

She was trying to loosen his tongue, but she could hardly admit it. "Oh dear, how foolish of me. I must not have been paying attention when I poured it. Sorry about that, sir. So tell me, how was your day?"

Witherspoon took a sip from the overly full glass, taking care not to spill. "Oh, things are progressing nicely. By the way, did you post my letter to Lady Cannonberry?"

"Yes, sir," she replied quickly. She didn't want him to get started about that again. "Wiggins posted it this morning."

"Good, then she ought to get it tomorrow." He frowned suddenly. "You don't think I was too affectionate in my reply to her, do you? I shouldn't like her to think I'm being overly bold."

Mrs. Jeffries forced herself to smile. "You were perfectly correct in your letter, sir. Right on the mark. Now, sir, did you question more—"

"But I wasn't too formal, was I?" he interrupted. "I shouldn't like her to think I'm stuffy. Lady Cannonberry might be the widow of a lord, but you know, she's quite progressive in her thinking. Why, actually, she's a bit more than just progressive. Just between you and me, Mrs. Jeffries, I think she'd like to see some rather radical changes in our whole system. Not that we've discussed it overly much, mind you. But she does occasionally say things which I find quite extraordinary. Quite extraordinary, indeed. Do you know, she told me she thought that women ought to be able to vote and she was positively incensed at all the public funds that were spent celebrating Her Majesty's jubilee year."

"Im sure she was, sir," Mrs. Jeffries replied. She knew all about Lady Cannonberry's radical opinions, and for the most part she agreed with them. But she didn't wish to discuss it right now. She racked her brain, trying to come up with a conversational gambit that would get the inspector talking about this murder. "There were a number of people who felt the funds raised for the jubilee would be better spent elsewhere. Perhaps those people are right, sir."

"Do you really think so?" Witherspoon took another sip.

"Yes, sir, I do," she said firmly. "Just take this dreadful murder you're investigating. It seems to me that if we had a society that paid a bit more attention to the poor and the unfortunate, we probably wouldn't have desperate people running about killing other people."

Witherspoon waved his hand in the air. "I'm afraid I don't agree with you. Though I must admit that your comment does have merit in some cases, I've seen a number of crimes where the culprit was more to be pitied than imprisoned, but I'm afraid you're way off the mark about the murder of Mr. Dapeers."

Now they were getting somewhere. Mrs. Jeffries smiled brightly, pleased that her trick had worked. "How so, sir? I mean, it seems to me the victim might have been murdered because he walked in on someone trying to rob the pub. That person might not have meant to commit murder at all. He could have been a simple robber. Someone who might have been starving or looking for a few shillings to buy medicine for one of his children. It seems to me, sir, that if our society actually provided a bit more for people like that, they wouldn't be driven to commit crimes."

"This wasn't a murder committed by someone desperate for a few pennies to buy a loaf of bread," the inspector said quickly. "Haydon Dapeers was murdered by someone who knew him, someone who had a pressing reason to get him out of the way."

"So you know who the killer is?" she persisted.

"Well, not exactly," he replied. "But I've a good idea. A very good idea, indeed."

"Really, sir? Oh, do tell me!" she cried enthusiastically. "You know what an admirer of your methods I am. Please don't leave me in suspense. I shan't sleep a wink all night if you do." She was laying it on thicker than clotted cream, but she didn't care. At this point she'd try anything.

He smiled widely. Perhaps he should tell her what he had in mind. The plan was really quite sound. Quite reasonable. It might be just the thing to put it into words. Sound it out, so to speak. Besides, it was really too selfish of him to keep the poor woman in the dark. He knew how much his housekeeper admired him. "If everything goes as I plan," he began eagerly, "by tomorrow night, the killer will be safely under lock and key."

Mrs. Jeffries gazed at him incredulously. Had he lost his mind? Making an arrest at this stage would be fatal to the inspector's career. Absolutely fatal. There was too much he didn't know, too many suspects he hadn't even considered and too many motives for Witherspoon to have sorted it out and come up with a plan. Any plan he came up with at this stage would land the inspector back in the records room faster than you could blink your eye. She had to do something. "How very clever of you, sir. Do tell me more."

Witherspoon smiled proudly. By the expression on Mrs. Jeffries's face, he could tell she was quite stunned by his brilliance. "I've a few more details to take care of tomorrow," he continued, "but—" He was interrupted as Fred came bounding into the room.

Wagging his tail furiously, the dog leapt at the inspector, his forepaws landing on Witherspoon's knees. Fred immediately butted his head against the inspector's arm. It was the dog's favorite trick, one that guaranteed him a walk in the park.

"I'm quite pleased to see you too, Fred." Witherspoon patted the animal's head. "Do you want to go for a walk? Yes, of course you do old fellow. We've not been walkies in quite a while."

Though Mrs. Jeffries was fond of Fred, she shot him a fierce glare. "But what about your dinner, sir?" she said as the inspector put his sherry down and got to his feet. "Aren't you hungry?"

"Oh, as you said, it's a cold supper. Come on, boy, let's go get your lead." He started for the door. "Dinner will keep."

"I want you to stick to him like a piece of flypaper today," Mrs. Jeffries told Smythe. They were all seated around the dining table in the kitchen, eating their breakfast. Mrs. Jeffries had made one last stab at getting the inspector to talk last night, but she hadn't been successful. Right after he'd finished his dinner, he'd announced he was dead tired and gone right to bed.

The housekeeper had told the others what little she'd learned of the inspector's plan, and they were agreed they had to find a way to stop him from making the worst mistake of his career.

The coachman shoved his empty plate to one side. "And 'ow exactly am I to do that?" he asked.

"You've got to think of some way, Smythe," Betsy said earnestly. "Mrs. Jeffries said he was getting ready to make an arrest. If he ends up back in the records room, the rest of us'll spend our lives polishing silver and scrubbing floors. There won't be any dashing about looking for clues and following suspects." She broke off as the coachman shot her a quick frown. She and Smythe had already had a rather heated discussion about the matter of following suspects.

"You'd better come up with something quick," the cook added. "The inspector's almost finished his breakfast."

"Bloomin' Ada, what do you want me to do? I can't just trail after the man all day, he'll see me."

"Let's think," Mrs. Jeffries said. But she'd thought about it half the night and hadn't come up with one logical reason for Smythe to go along with Inspector Witherspoon. "Perhaps you could just follow him at a distance."

Smythe shook his head dismissively. "I don't think that'll work I'd 'ave to stay too far behind, otherwise the inspector or Barnes would notice. Barnes is a right smart copper; not much gets past 'im."

"We've got to come up with something," the cook cried passionately. "I refuse to give up investigatin' murders just because Inspector Wither-spoon's got a bee up his bonnet about listening to his 'inner voice.' I won't give it up, do you hear? This is important. For the first time in my life I'm doin' something that matters. Really matters. We all are and we're not goin' to get the wind knocked out of us just because the man's got some idea he can solve this one on his own."

"What do you suggest?" the coachman snapped, goaded into anger because he agreed with everything Mrs. Goodge said and was just as scared as she was that it was all coming to an end. "I can 'ardly make myself invisible."

"There's no call to be rude, Smythe," Betsy said, raising her voice.

"All this arguing isn't solving our problem," Mrs. Jeffries began.

"I've got an idea," Wiggins said softly.

Everyone turned and stared at the lad.

"*You've* got an idea?" Smythe said incredulously.

The footman blushed. Maybe his idea wasn't so good after all. Maybe he should have kept his mouth shut.

"Don't be sarcastic," Mrs. Jeffries said. "Let's hear what Wiggins has to say."

"Seems to me it's right simple," Wiggins said nervously. "Seems to me that all Smythe 'as to do is tell the inspector that Bow and Arrow is lookin' peaked because they ain't been out in the fresh air for a long time. Smythe could offer to drive the inspector to wherever he needs to go today." He waited for the others to tell him his plan was silly.

But no one said a word for a moment. Finally, Smythe said, "Out of the mouths of babes." He grinned broadly. "You've done it, lad, you've come up with the solution. The inspector's daft about them 'orses. 'E loves 'em."

"It *is* a good idea," Mrs. Jeffries said. She smiled at Wiggins and then glanced at the clock. "How fast can you get the carriage here?"

Smythe was already getting to his feet. "Fast enough. I'll pop upstairs and ask the inspector if it's all right."

"Lay it on thick, Smythe," Mrs. Jeffries said as he started for the back-stairs. "You must stay with him today. You're our only hope."

"What do you want the rest of us to do?" Betsy asked as soon as Smythe was gone.

Mrs. Jeffries had thought about at too. She wasn't sure where the inspector was going with this case, but after listening to him last night, she'd come up with one possible scenario. "This morning, I want you to get out and find out as much as you can. I'll leave where you go and what you do up to you. At this point finding out anything might be helpful."

"In other words, you're as muddled as we are about this case, so it doesn't really matter what we do," Betsy said glumly.

"Correct." The housekeeper smiled sadly. For all the thinking she'd done, she really hadn't any idea who the killer was or why the victim had been killed. She didn't think the inspector had any idea either. But she didn't think that would stop him from making an arrest. However, she refused to acknowledge defeat. There was one thing she could do to mitigate what she was sure was going to be a disaster. If they were lucky, she might buy them enough time to solve this case. But right now her first task was to keep the inspector from making a complete fool of himself and losing the precious reputation they'd worked so hard to give him. Tomorrow they could go back to work on catching Haydon Dapeers's killer; today they had to avert a disaster.

"But just because we haven't solved this particular puzzle doesn't mean we won't. Get out there and find out what you can. As I always say, any information is useful. You never know what little bit of gossip you'll pick up that will be the missing piece we need to put it all together." She got to her feet. "I would like all of you back here this afternoon. Wiggins, could you please pop around to Luty's and tell her and Hatchet to be here as well. We don't know what's going to happen tonight and we ought to be here in case we have to do something drastic."

"What are you going to be doin' this mornin'?" Mrs. Goodge asked.

"I'm going to go and see Sarah Hewett," Mrs. Jeffries said. "If my idea works, I'll be bringing her back with me this afternoon. Betsy, I'd like you to take a note around to Michael Taggert's house. Make sure he reads it. If he shows up here before I get back, don't let him leave."

Smythe was just coming out of the dining room when Mrs. Jeffries got upstairs. "'E went for the idea," he whispered, jerking his thumb toward the closed door. "I'll be back in a bit with the carriage. But 'e said something funny, though. 'E said 'e was plannin' on askin' me to 'elp 'im out with something tonight. This plan of 'is, I reckon."

"Excellent, Smythe," Mrs. Jeffries replied. "And whatever he asks you to do, do it."

"You don't need to tell me that, Mrs. J."

"I'm sorry. Of course I don't." She started for the front door. "In any case, stay close to him. We're all depending on you. You may be the only thing standing between Inspector Witherspoon and the records room."

Mrs. Jeffries reached for the brass knocker on the late Haydon Dapeers's front door. She hesitated for a moment, wondering if she was doing the right thing. But there was no other answer. She'd thought and thought about every aspect of this case. If she were wrong, she might be interfering in a private matter which could be disastrous to the people involved. But if she was right, she might be saving Sarah Hewett untold misery and grief. She knocked on the door.

A maid answered. "Can I help you, ma'am?" she inquired politely.

"I'd like to speak with Mrs. Hewett," she replied.

The maid showed her inside and then led her down the hall to the drawing room. "If you'll wait here, ma'am, I'll see if Mrs. Hewett is receiving."

A few moments later Sarah rushed into the room. "What are you doing here?"

"I need to talk to you," Mrs. Jeffries said firmly. "Is there someplace where we can speak in private?" She didn't want Moira Dapeers suddenly popping in on them.

"We can talk here." Sarah frowned in confusion. She gestured at the settee. "Moira's gone to the missionary society."

"Good. Then we won't be interrupted." Mrs. Jeffries sat down.

Sarah sank down next to her. "I really wish you hadn't come here," she began.

Mrs. Jeffries interrupted. "I'm sure you don't," she said bluntly. "But believe it or not, I'm here to help you."

"Help me?" Sarah repeated. "But I don't need help."

"Did you tell the inspector everything you told me about your movements on the night of the murder? Did you tell him you'd gone back into the pub *before* the brawl on the street was over?"

"Well, yes," Sarah said defensively. "I wasn't going to lie to him."

"And you also told him that while you were inside the room was empty and you saw no one?" Mrs. Jeffries pressed.

"I told him that I was there for a few moments on my own and that I hadn't seen anyone go down the hall toward the taproom," Sarah said gravely. "But I also told him that several other people began to drift in while I was still at the bar."

"Did any of those people see you standing at the bar?"

Sarah shrugged helplessly. "I don't know. I wasn't paying attention."

"Do you know any of those people who came in?"

"They were all strangers. That's what I told the inspector. But what's that got to do with anything?" she cried shrilly, her voice rising in panic. "I tell you I was there. I was standing by the bar. Why are you here? Why are you trying to scare me?"

"You need to listen to me very carefully. I'm not here to cause you grief or stir up trouble, but it's imperative that you do precisely as I say."

Sarah's eyes were as wide as saucers. "Why? Why should I do anything you tell me?"

"Because if you don't, you might be arrested for the murder of Haydon Dapeers."

Mrs. Jeffries was still wondering if she was doing the right thing when she arrived home at Upper Edmonton Gardens. She took her hat off and hurried down the stairs to the kitchen. Luty Belle, Hatchet, Betsy, Wiggins and Mrs. Goodge were sitting around the kitchen table, their expressions glum.

"Hello, everyone," Mrs. Jeffries said brightly, determined to lift all of their spirits.

There was a general murmur of greeting, but it was singularly lacking in enthusiasm. Mrs. Jeffries hadn't seen so many long faces at one table since Mrs. Edwina Livingston-Graves, the inspector's dreadful cousin, had visited them last year.

"Sarah Hewett will be here about one o'clock." She took her usual seat and smiled at Betsy. "Did you get the message to Michael Taggert?" she asked.

Betsy nodded. "Yes, I saw his landlady give it to him myself."

"What's this all about, Hepzibah?" Luty asked. "We've been sittin' here like a bunch of sinners waitin' for the angel Gabriel to blow his trumpet for judgment day. Would you mind tellin' us just what in tarnation is goin' on?"

"Yes, madam," Hatchet added. "Not that we object to making ourselves available to the cause of justice, but young Wiggins here"—he smiled at the footman—"was not forthcoming with any details. He merely told us you needed us here 'in case the inspector makes a right old muddle of the murder.'"

Mrs. Jeffries glanced at Mrs. Goodge. "Didn't you tell them the inspector is planning on making an arrest?" she asked.

"They ain't told us nothin'," Luty said, not giving the cook time to answer.

"We weren't sure exactly how to explain, things," Mrs. Goodge said quickly. "So we thought we'd wait until you got back."

"I see." She quickly brought them up to date on the latest developments. "So you see, we've got Smythe carting him about in the carriage today, hoping, of course, that he might be able to do something if the need arises."

"All right," Luty said thoughtfully, "I understand all that. But why is Sarah Hewett and this Taggert fellow coming here this afternoon?"

"Because I'm afraid the inspector is going to arrest Sarah Hewett," she said. "She's the only one of all the suspects that the inspector could think is the killer."

Luty looked confused. "How do you figure that?"

"Because she's the only one who has admitted being in the public bar while the murder was committed instead of being outside watching the street brawl."

"Excuse me, madam," Hatchet said politely. He glanced at Luty. "But do you really think Inspector Witherspoon would arrest someone on that kind of evidence?"

Mrs. Jeffries didn't think so, but she was hard-pressed to come up with any alternative suspects. "I don't know. But if the possibility exists, I think it's important that Sarah tell Michael Taggert the truth about her daughter before it happens."

For a moment no one said a word. Then Betsy said, "I can see how you might think the inspector's going to arrest her: she's admitted to him she was alone in the pub, probably at the same time the murder was bein' committed. But how is her telling Michael Taggert the truth about him bein' Amanda's father going to help any?"

"It won't stop the inspector from arresting her, but at least it will give her the chance to ensure that Amanda is taken care of properly while she's awaiting trial or in prison," Mrs. Jeffries explained.

"Wouldn't Moira Dapeers take care of the child?" Hatchet asked.

"Not necessarily, not when Sarah's motive—the fact that the child was fathered by someone other than Moira's brother—comes out. If the case goes to trial, it will come out."

"We don't even know that the inspector knows anything about that," Luty pointed out.

"We found out, didn't we?" Mrs. Jeffries shot back. She was feeling most put upon. She could tell by their expressions that they all thought she was grasping at straws. The awful thing was, they were right. She'd no idea what the inspector knew, she'd no idea what he was planning on doing or who he was going to arrest tonight. "For all we know, Haydon Dapeers could have told someone else about Sarah's daughter. That person could have mentioned it to the inspector."

"Well," Mrs. Goodge said slowly, "I think you've done the right thing." She got up. "I think I'll fix us all a spot of something to eat. No use sitting around here being miserable. That may happen soon enough if the inspector ruins his career tonight."


Witherspoon stuck his head out of the coach and yelled at his coachman. "I say, Smythe, this is rather the long way around. It'll take us ages to get to the Yard at this rate. The traffic's dreadful."

"I'll see what I can do," Smythe called. He sighed as the inspector ducked back inside the coach. Of course the ruddy traffic was bad; that's why he'd picked comin' down this bloomin' street in the first place. Cor blimey, he thought, he didn't have any idea what to do now. There was no help for it. He'd dawdled all he could, taken the carriage down every crowded street he could find in the hopes of delaying things a bit, but he was at his wits' end. He had to drive the inspector to Scotland Yard. Witherspoon was going ahead with his plan, whatever in blazes it was. But Smythe knew one thing: the inspector's plan involved more than a few coppers. That's why they was goin' to the Yard. Blast a Spaniard anyway, the inspector was fixin' to make a ruddy mess of things tonight and he was goin' to have half of the Metropolitan Police Force there to watch it.

Smythe grimaced at he turned the coach onto Charing Cross. They'd been all over London today. They'd been to the Black Horse, the Gilded Lily, Michael Taggert's lodging house and the Dapeers home. At each stop, Witherspoon and Constable Barnes had gotten out, popped inside, stayed a few minutes and then popped back out again. Smythe had no idea what they were up to, but he didn't like it much.

But he could dawdle no longer; Scotland Yard was just ahead. He slowed the horses and pulled the brake. Witherspoon and Barnes both climbed out as soon as they'd stopped. Smythe stared at them glumly. "Do you want me to wait here for you, sir? Or should I pull the carriage to one of the side streets?"

"You can leave it here, Smythe." Witherspoon beamed at him "I'll send a uniformed man out to keep an eye on it. I need you to come with me."

Smythe tied the reins off and jumped down. "You need me, sir?"

"Well, I might. I've got to run my idea by the chief inspector first, though. But tell me, Smythe, are you any good at playacting?"

Promptly at one o'clock, Sarah and Amanda Hewett arrived at Upper Edmonton Gardens. As instructed, after a brief introduction, the rest of the household, including Luty and Hatchet, took Amanda and went outside to the communal gardens.

"I almost didn't come, Mrs. Jeffries," Sarah admitted. "But then Inspector Witherspoon came around and told Moira and me we had to be at the Gilded Lily tonight."

"Did he give you a mason why?"

Sarah closed her eyes briefly. "He said he had an important piece of evidence he had to ask us about," she replied softly. "And that we had to be there in order to see it."

"What time do you have to be there?"

"Eight o'clock." Her voice dropped to a whisper and tears Welled up in her eyes. "But I think he's going to arrest me. He asked me again about being in the public bar. He wanted to know if I'd remembered the names of anyone else who was inside then."

"And of course you hadn't," Mrs. Jeffries said sympathetically. "Do you feel up to this?"

Sarah nodded mutely. She grasped the back of the chair for support and took several long, deep breaths. "What if he doesn't come?"

"He'll come," Mrs. Jeffries promised. "As a matter of fact, I expect I'd better go upstairs in a moment, to let him in. Pour yourself a cup of tea. I'll send him down as soon as he gets here."

Sarah sat down but didn't make a move toward the waiting in china teacup sitting next to the pot of freshly brewed tea. She stared blankly into space. "I don't know if I can do it."

"Would you rather he find out from someone else?"

"But what if he hates me? What if he despises me for not telling him straight away?" She swiped at an escaping tear. "I don't think I could stand that."

Mrs. Jeffries tried to think of something sympathetic or comforting. She was having second thoughts about everything. Maybe she had jumped the gun, so to speak. Maybe Witherspoon had no intention of arresting Sarah. Maybe she'd interfered in a very private matter and the end result would be disastrous. Maybe, she thought, I'd better get upstairs. Sarah could use a few moments alone.

She was halfway up the stairs when she heard the heavy bang of the brass knocker. Mrs. Jeffries hurried her steps, threw open the door and smiled at Michael Taggert. "Good afternoon," she said pleasantly. "Please come inside."

"Good day," Taggert replied as he stepped through and into the hall. "Your note said it was urgent."

"It's about Mrs. Hewett," Mrs. Jeffries explained.

"Sarah? Sarah's here?"

"She's downstairs in the kitchen waiting for you." Mrs. Jeffries pointed to the backstairs. "Right down there."

Without another word he rushed toward the staircase and hurried down it, his footsteps echoing so fast on the stairs that Mrs. Jeffries hoped he didn't fall flat on his face. Explaining to Inspector Witherspoon how one of his suspects ended up at the bottom of the kitchen stairs with a broken leg wasn't something she really wanted to do.

She debated for a moment, wondering if she should try to eavesdrop on the two young people. This was, after all, a murder investigation. Even though she didn't think either of them was the killer, she wasn't sure. On the other hand, their conversation was personal and private. "Oh bother," she murmured as she headed for the front door. "I refuse to eavesdrop on such a private conversation. If either of them is the killer, I'll eat my hat."

• • •

"Sarah, what are you doing here?" Michael asked. He stood at the door of the kitchen. "I've been out of my mind with worry ever since I got that strange note from Mrs. Jeffries. She said you were in trouble?"

"I might very well be in trouble," Sarah replied. "But before we talk about that, I've got something I must tell you." She got up from her chair but didn't move. She simply stood there. "It's something I should have told you a long time ago, but I didn't have the courage."

Concerned, he went to stand beside her. "I don't understand any of this. But don't worry, my love. Whatever kind of trouble you've got, we'll see it through. I won't let anyone one hurt you."

"Michael, please sit down and listen to what I have to say. There may not be much time." She sat back down and waited until he took the seat next to her. "Before I say anything else, I want you to know how much I love you."

Michael grabbed her hand. "And I love you. Now tell me, what kind of trouble?"

She shook her head vehemently. "Not yet. First there's something you've got to know. Something you must understand. I have to know she'll be safe if the worst happens. I have to know she'll be taken care of by someone who loves her."

Alarmed, Michael grabbed her by the shoulders. "Darling, what are you talking about? What do you mean 'if the worst happens'?"

Sarah swallowed the lump in her throat and then looked him dead in the eyes. "Amanda is your daughter, Michael. Not Charles Hewett's."

"How long they gonna be?" Wiggins complained. "I'm gettin' hungry again."

"Stop your moaning." Mrs. Goodge smiled as she watched Hatchet duck behind a tree, hiding from the laughing Amanda. "Them two aren't talking about the weather, you know."

"Do you think it'll be all right?" Betsy asked anxiously. She glanced at the back door of Upper Edmonton Gardens. "They've been in there a long time."

"I hope so," Mrs. Jeffries replied.

"Caught ya." Luty, holding Amanda's hand, tagged Hatchet as he pretended to run from the little girl. Amanda giggled uproariously.

"Well, I wish they'd 'urry," Wiggins said, frowning at the back door. But his frown vanished suddenly. "Blimey, 'ere they come."

Everyone, except the child, turned and saw Michael and Sarah coming out the back door.

He took Sarah's hand and together they crossed the lawn toward the others.

Amanda, seeing her mother, came running out from behind the tree she'd been hiding behind. She stopped suddenly and stared at the tall man holding her mother's hand.

Luty, Hatchet, Wiggins and Betsy had all come to stand in a group next to Mrs. Jeffries.

Michael Taggert knelt down and looked at the beautiful little girl watching him. Tears filled his eyes.

"I think," the housekeeper said softly, "that we'd better go inside. Mr. Taggert may like some privacy when he meets his daughter."

# CHAPTER 10

—◆◆◆—

"I know that neither of them is the murderer," Mrs. Goodge announced. She sniffed and swiped quickly at her eyes, wiping back the sentimental tears that threatened to roll down her cheeks.

"'Corse neither of 'em is the killer," Luty agreed. "It's got to be one of the others. Why, did you see the way that man looked at his little girl? I tell ya, he had tears in his eyes, he was so happy. A feller like that ain't capable of murder and you only have to look at Sarah to know she couldn't do it."

"But the inspector thinks it might be Sarah," Betsy said worriedly. "What if he arrests her tonight and that poor little baby loses her mama?"

"It'd be a crime, that's what it would be," Wiggins agreed. "Separatin' a mama and her child ought to be against the law."

Mrs. Jeffries glanced toward the back hall and hoped she hadn't made the mistake of her life. They were all sitting at the table in the kitchen, waiting for Sarah, Amanda and Michael to come inside. Everyone had been deeply moved by what they'd just witnessed. Now they were all convinced that Amanda Hewett was a darling little angel, Sarah Hewett was a saint and Michael Taggert a knight in shining armor.

Mrs. Jeffries was at this point fairly certain that at least Sarah was innocent. Getting the woman to come here had been a kind of a test. She'd reasoned that though Sarah was adamant about keeping her daughter's parentage a secret—in fact, that was really her only possible motive for wanting Haydon Dapeers dead—she'd come here anyway. She'd stood in front of a group of strangers and introduced her child to its father. If

Sarah had been truly unbalanced enough to murder to keep the world from knowing Amanda wasn't Charles Hewett's daughter, she would never have done what she did today. Sarah wasn't guilty. Mrs. Jeffries was sure of that. But what about Michael Taggert? He'd had motive enough. He'd watched the woman he loved stay a virtual prisoner in the Dapeers house. Maybe he'd finally had enough.

They heard the back door open. Everyone turned, their attention on the back hall. Sarah Hewett, followed by Michael carrying Amanda, came into the kitchen.

"Do come in and sit down," Mrs. Jeffries said. "We've some tea made. I expect you could both do with a cup."

Sarah smiled shyly and sat down next to Mrs. Goodge. Michael Taggert took the chair next to Wiggins. He settled Amanda on his lap and then said to Mrs. Jeffries, "Tea would be nice, thank you."

"Your little one's almost asleep." Mrs. Goodge nodded at the child, who was dozing against her father's chest. "Should I take her? There's a daybed in my room; it's right down the hall. You can hear her if she wakes up and gets frightened. She can have a bit of lay-down while you two have your tea."

"Uh . . ." Michael, uncertain in his newfound role as parent, looked at Sarah.

"That would be lovely, thank you. It's way past time for her nap." Sarah got up, plucked the sleeping child off his lap and followed the cook out of the kitchen.

"I don't know how to thank you for what you've done," Michael said to Mrs. Jeffries. "Sarah told me it was you who talked her into telling me the truth."

"Don't thank me. I'm sure Sarah would have told you soon in any case. Did she tell you how I convinced her?"

His expression hardened. "She told me that you think she might be in danger of being arrested."

"I'm not certain that's the case." Mrs. Jeffries hesitated; she wasn't sure how much to tell Taggert. He was still a suspect, albeit a weak one. "But the possibility did exist."

"We've got to decide what to do," Michael said. "I'll not have Sarah arrested for a murder she didn't commit."

Mrs. Jeffries decided to be blunt. "You may not be able to stop it.

Furthermore, as I said, we don't know for certain she is going to be arrested. I'm only making an educated guess. I could be completely wrong." She sincerely hoped she was.

"I'll not risk it," he said fiercely. "I'll not risk losing her now and I'll not risk our daughter losing her mother."

Mrs. Jeffries saw the anguish on his face. "Inspector Witherspoon is a good man," she said gently. "He won't pursue a case against someone unless he has evidence."

"But there isn't any evidence against Sarah," Michael cried. "Not any real evidence anyway. She couldn't hurt anyone."

"And what about you, Mr. Taggert?" Mrs. Jeffries regarded him steadily.

"Michael couldn't kill anyone, either," Sarah declared softly. She walked to the table. "Neither of us could."

"And I won't let either of us be arrested for a crime we didn't commit," he said, getting to his feet. "We can leave. We don't have to go to the Gilded Lily tonight. We don't have to sit there like sheep being led to the slaughter."

"No, Michael, we're not going to leave," Sarah replied. She came around the table and stood next to him. "We're going to face this and we're going to see it through. I've faith that justice will prevail. We weren't the only ones that hated Haydon."

He grabbed her by the shoulders and pulled her closer. "But what if you are arrested?"

"Then I'll stand trial," she said simply, her eyes never leaving his face. "And if that happens, you'll take care of our daughter."

They stared at one another for a long moment, oblivious to their audience. Michael closed his eyes briefly, as though he was fighting an inner battle with himself. "All right. But if it happens, I'm going to hire you the best counsel money can buy."

Sarah smiled weakly. "Let's not think about that just yet. Besides, Moira will help me if it comes to it."

"No. I'll pay for it."

"Oh Michael—"

"I've got money, Sarah," Michael interrupted. "Lots of it. I inherited a fortune several months ago. Enough to keep us for the rest of our lives. That's why I suggested you and Amanda come away with me. We could take the night train to the continent, catch a ship at one of the French ports; no one would ever find us."

She lifted her chin stubbornly. "I won't hide. I feel like I've been hiding since the day my daughter was born. No. We stay here, regardless of what happens."

"All right, my love." He pulled her closer. "We won't run, but I will take care of both of you, come what may."

Sarah looked at him curiously. "You never said anything about having money . . . and you took that awful job etching those stupid windows for Haydon. Why?"

"I was going to tell you, honestly I was." He gave an embarrassed laugh. "But I was afraid that if Haydon found out I wasn't flat broke, he'd never pay me. I only took that wretched job at the pub so I could see you. Didn't you realize? Haydon did, that's why he was such a bast—" He broke off and flushed as he realized what he'd almost said. "Forgive me, darling. I'll never use that word in your presence again. But we must marry straightaway. No one is ever going to call our child that foul name."

This was all very touching and Mrs. Jeffries would have loved to have sat there all afternoon. It was better than one of the serialized novels in *The Illustrated London News*, but time was wasting.

"Excuse me." She cleared her throat loudly to get their attention. "But we really must move along here."

Sarah broke away and took her seat at the table. Michael sat down as well. "What do you want us to do?" he asked.

"What time are you due at the Gilded Lily?"

"Eight o'clock," Michael replied. "That inspector of yours came around right after I got your note this morning. He insists I be there to-night."

"Moira and I both have to be there as well," Sarah added.

"What exactly did he say?" She directed her question to Michael.

"He said that he had important information about Haydon's murder, but he couldn't tell me what it was." Michael shrugged. "He said he had to show me."

"That's what Moira said he told her," Sarah said excitedly. "Do you think he's found something? Something which will show up the real killer?"

Mrs. Jeffries didn't think he'd found anything. But she wasn't certain.

That was what was so impossible about this situation, she didn't know a ruddy thing! "I don't know. But whatever he's up to, I think you both must be there."


"I think we can go in now," Constable Barnes whispered to Inspector Witherspoon. "I just saw Tom and Joanne Dapeers go inside and they're the last ones to arrive."

Witherspoon nodded. He and Barnes were standing in a darkened shop window directly across from the Gilded Lily. A full moon had risen, casting a ghostly light over the quiet street. Witherspoon checked his watch, knowing that he had to time everything perfectly. He was so nervous he was afraid he'd get a headache. On top of that, butterflies were dancing in his stomach, perspiration trickled down his back and his heart was beating so loudly he was sure the constable must hear it. "Are both Molly and Mick inside?" he asked for third time.

Barnes, a patient man, nodded. "Yes. Molly grumbled a bit; she didn't want to come back here. Mick's been inside for over an hour now; he was the first one to arrive."

"Good." Witherspoon took a deep, calming breath, closed his eyes and listened for his inner voice. But he heard nothing. Drat, he thought, this is no time to start having doubts. But what if he was wrong? What if he made a complete fool of himself tonight? He gave himself a shake. There was no point in worrying about that now: the die was cast. Everyone was in position. Visions of the records room swam in his head, and for once Witherspoon didn't find the image soothing.

"Er, sir?" Barnes prodded. "Are you all right?"

"Perfectly, Constable. Thank you for inquiring. Right, then, let's get this done with. We've a killer to catch tonight, Barnes. Justice must be served."

The inspector boldly started across Minyard Street with Barnes right on his heels. Their footsteps echoed loudly on the stone pavement. Witherspoon noticed the night had become eerily silent. The foot traffic had disappeared, and except for the clip-clop of the occasional hansom, the street was deserted.

Bright light spilled out the front windows of the pub. Witherspoon grasped the door handle, gave it a turn, steeled himself and the two men stepped inside.

As instructed, Molly and Mick were behind the bar. Mick was polishing glasses with a white tea towel. Molly was standing with her arms folded across her chest and a disgruntled expression on her face.

The inspector glanced quickly around the room. No one looked particularly happy to be there. Moira Dapeers and her sister-in-law were sitting to the left of the bar, talking quietly. Michael Taggert was standing alone in front of the partition leading to the saloon bar. Tom and Joanne Dapeers were sitting at one of the round tables. Tom was drumming his fingers against the wood and Joanne appeared to be glaring at a gas lamp on the far wall. Her head snapped around at the sound of the door banging shut.

"It's about time you got here," she snapped. "We've been waiting for a good half hour."

That was an exaggeration, but Witherspoon was far too polite to contradict a lady. "My apologies, madam. I didn't mean to keep any of you waiting. Unfortunately, I was unavoidably detained at the Yard."

"What's this all about?" Tom Dapeers asked. "We've got a business to run, you know. Can't hang about here all night."

"And I've got a missionary society meeting," Moira Dapeers added. "I don't like to be late. It upsets the reverend dreadfully."

"Anyone want a beer?" Molly interrupted. When no one answered her, she shrugged and helped herself.

Michael Taggert said nothing.

Witherspoon walked into the center of the room. Barnes moved to the far side of the bar and whipped out his notebook.

"First of all, I'd like to thank all of you for coming," he began.

"We didn't have much choice," Molly muttered loudly enough for the whole room to hear.

The inspector ignored her. "I know you've all been dreadfully inconvenienced, but I assure you, your presence tonight is most important. Most important, indeed."


"Wiggins," Hatchet whispered urgently, "will you kindly get your elbow out of my ribs? It's rather painful."

"Sorry," Wiggins hissed. "But it's hard to see through all these ruddy lines on the glass."

"They're called etchings," Hatchet corrected. "And we really must take care not to be seen. Besides, you're supposed to be keeping a lookout. It wouldn't do for a police constable to spot us and ask what we're doing."

"We ain't doin' nothin' but lookin' in the window of a public 'ouse," Wiggins replied. He wondered why he always got stuck doing the borin' bits like keepin' watch.

"A closed public house," Hatchet pointed out. "And we did promise Mrs. Jeffries we'd make sure the inspector didn't see us." As Hatchet and Wiggins had had to argue for a good hour even to get the others to agree that their coming along to the Gilded Lily to keep an eye on things might be a good idea, Hatchet was determined not to get caught in any embarrassing situations. He wouldn't have liked to explain to Inspector Witherspoon what he and Wiggins were doing out here.

"Oh, all right," Wiggins muttered reluctantly. "I'll keep watch." He dragged his gaze away from the window and dutifully glanced up and down the street. "But I don't see why. No one's goin' to be botherin' us; we're just standin' 'ere. There's no one about. Least not any police that I can see."

Hatchet was worried about the police they couldn't see. But he didn't want to excite the lad.

"Any sign of Smythe in there?" Wiggins poked Hatchet in the ribs.

"Ouch. Will you kindly cease and desist prodding at my person whenever you speak to me?" he snapped softly. "I'm going to be covered in bruises by the time I get home."

"Sorry. But I wanted to get yer attention," Wiggins apologized. "Do ya see him?"

"Who?"

"Smythe. Is he in there?"

"No, I don't see him." Hatchet craned his neck over the etching of a lily. "At least if he is, he's well out of sight."

"I don't think he's in there," Wiggins said. He squinted as he saw a figure turn the corner and head down Minyard Street in the direction of the pub. "We'da seen the carriage if he was. What's goin' on in there now?"

"Very little," Hatchet replied. "The inspector is standing in the center of the room, talking. The others are just sitting there, watching him."

"What's he sayin'?" Wiggins asked eagerly, taking his eyes off the approaching figure for just a moment and glancing toward the window. "Anythin' excitin'?"

"I can't hear what he's saying with you chattering in my ear, can I?"

Hatchet cocked his ear toward the glass. He could hear the inspector's voice, but he couldn't quite make out the words.

Wiggins tugged on Hatchet's sleeve again, taking care not to poke his person anywhere. "Uh, Hatchet, I think we'd best get a move on."

"Shh." Hatchet silenced him. "I think I can hear what he's saying."

Wiggins saw that the figure was definitely a man, a man wearing a police helmet. "Uh, Hatchet." He poked him directly in the ribs again. "Get away from that window."

"Will you please be quiet?" the butler snapped. "I'm trying to hear what the inspector's saying . . ."

"Hatchet," Wiggins hissed frantically, "listen to me. There's a copper coming and he's headed right this way."

"As you are all aware, Mr. Haydon Dapeers was recently murdered in this very pub," Witherspoon said. "He walked through that hallway"—he pointed to the hall beyond the bar—"into the taproom at the end and never came back."

"Yes, Inspector," Moira Dapeers said dryly, "we do know that. But what's that got to do with us being here tonight?"

Witherspoon smiled politely. He could feel beads of sweat running down his neck. He hoped they weren't too noticeable. "Actually, madam, it has quite a bit to do with your all being asked to come here tonight. This investigation has been most difficult, most difficult, indeed. The back door of the pub was probably locked that night and there was a street brawl going on just outside on the street. Most of you claim you were outside watching that brawl when Mr. Dapeers was killed. So what I thought I'd have you do—" He broke off as the front door opened and Constable Griffith rushed inside.

"Sorry to interrupt you, sir," Griffith said respectfully. "But we've got a bit of a situation."

Annoyed, the inspector frowned. "I'm rather busy here, Constable," he complained. "Can't it wait?"

Griffith shook his head. "No, sir, it can't. We've had a bit of a break on that stabbin' victim we pulled out of the Thames yesterday."

"Someone's confessed?" Witherspoon asked eagerly.

"No, sir." Griffith grinned. "But we've got us a witness. An eyewitness who saw the whole thing."

"For goodness' sakes, why didn't he come forward before this?" Witherspoon cried impatiently. "That poor woman's been dead for several days."

Griffith shrugged. "He's a petty crook, sir. Doesn't much like the police. He sent us a note, sir. Seems he's had dealings with you before and you're the only one he trusts."

Witherspoon sighed dramatically. "I suppose you want me to go along to the Yard now and take this fellow's statement."

"No, sir," Griffith said quickly. "He won't set foot in a police station. He wants to meet you at the spot where we found the body. He claims that's where the killin' took place. I reckon it's worth our while, sir. He says he saw the whole thing."

"Do you have a name for this person, Constable?"

"No, sir. But he knows you, sir. Wants you to be there at ten o'clock."

"Ten o'clock?" Witherspoon pulled out his watch and checked the time. "Gracious, I can't possibly do that. It's going to take at least that long to finish here and then I wanted to stop and have a bite to eat. I haven't had anything all day and I'm rather hungry."

"We won't have time to finish here, sir," Barnes interjected. "I reckon we'd best just call it a night, sir. I'm not sure this was goin' to work anyway."

"Inspector Witherspoon." Joanne Dapeers rose to her feet. "My husband and I have a business to run. Obviously, you're going to be busy this evening. I've no idea why you dragged us down here and I've no idea what you hoped to accomplish, but if you don't mind, I'd like to leave."

"I would too," Moira Dapeers echoed. "Coming here has been most inconvenient."

"In that case, madam," Witherspoon said, "you can leave. As a matter of fact, you can all go. I'm so sorry to have troubled you. I'll contact everyone tomorrow."

"Now, just a minute," Michael Taggert yelled. "You didn't even tell us what you wanted. Why you had us come here."

"Sorry, Mr. Taggert, I'll explain everything tomorrow." He nodded at Barnes and started for the front door. "Come along, Barnes. If we hurry, we can have a bite to eat before we meet this witness."

"I knew we should have gone with them," Luty Belle cried. "It's almost ten o'clock and they ain't back yet."

"Now, Luty, calm yourself," Mrs. Jeffries said soothingly. "I'm sure Hatchet and Wiggins are just fine."

Betsy snorted. "Of course they're fine, they're out and about and in the thick of it. We're stuck here in this ruddy house." As she'd wanted to go with the men, she was most put out to be sitting in the kitchen of Upper Edmonton Gardens watching the clock.

"I hate waiting," Mrs. Goodge said. "Makes me all nervous like. I wonder what's happening tonight? Do you think the inspector has caught the killer?"

"Perhaps." Mrs. Jeffries didn't think the inspector had caught anything except a bad case of ruining his career, but she didn't want to infect the others with her dismal view of the situation. She sighed inwardly. By tomorrow, it would all be over. The inspector's career would be in shreds and years of boredom loomed in front of her. Witherspoon would be back in the records room and the household would be doing nothing but polishing, cleaning and cooking. There wouldn't be any more interesting murders to solve, no more dashing about London searching for clues and following suspects. No more adventures.

"Buck up, Hepzibah," Luty ordered. "It ain't over yet. The inspector might know exactly what he's doin'. He might surprise us all and actually catch this killer."

Mrs. Jeffries smiled glumly but said nothing. There was no use in trying to keep everyone's spirits up, she wasn't doing a very good job of keeping her own up.

"Without our help?" Betsy laughed harshly. "Not likely. He don't know half of what we know about this case. He doesn't know about McNally, he doesn't know about Moira Dapeers carryin' on with that reverend—"

"And I don't think he knows about Dapeers havin' that disease, either," Mrs. Goodge put in.

"Maybe he knows something we don't know," Luty argued. "Maybe we ain't as smart as we think we are."

"Oh Luty," Mrs. Jeffries said. "We're not saying the inspector isn't intelligent. He is a perfectly capable policeman. We're only saying there's too much about this murder that he doesn't know."

"And I'm sayin' we don't know what he knows!" Luty cried passionately. "Has it occurred to any of you that the inspector may have important clues that we don't? Just because we think we know more than he does don't make it true. He ain't been sittin' around here twiddlin' his thumbs for the past few days. He's been out investigatin'.""

Mrs. Jeffries stared at her for a long moment and then smiled slowly. "You know, Luty, I stand corrected. You're absolutely right. We don't know what he knows. Perhaps Inspector Witherspoon will solve this murder."

"Well," Betsy said, "much as I'd hate to think he could do it without our help, at least if he does catch the killer, it'll keep him out of the records room."

"And it'll keep us doin' our own detecting," Mrs. Goodge added brightly.


The moonlight reflecting off the Thames cast the deserted dock in a faint glow of light. The lone man stood at the end of the pier, staring out onto the river. He hadn't brought a lamp with him; with the full moon overhead, there was no need. He leaned negligently against the old wood of the piling, his eyes straight ahead on the river.

A figure watched him. It stood quietly in the shadowed doorway of the empty warehouse at the other end of the pier. Wearing a long, dark cloak that blended into the darkness, the intruder stepped forward and looked around, making certain there was no one about. But the place was deserted, empty. There wouldn't be any witnesses to this.

Slowly, carefully, the cloaked figure moved away from the safety of the darkness and stepped out onto the pier. One of the wooden planks groaned and the intruder stopped and stared at the man standing at the end.

The man didn't move, didn't turn to look about and see if he was still alone.

The killer smiled and grasped the knife tighter.

This had better be fast and hard. The man looked pretty big. Best to avoid a struggle. The figure started quickly down the dock, stepping softly, wanting the attack to be a surprise. The planks groaned slightly, but the man must have been deep in his thoughts, for he didn't seem to hear.

He didn't turn and look. Stupid fool.

The knife came out from beneath the cloak, its long blade gleaming in the moonlight. Quickly now, before he spots me.

The footsteps began to move faster, faster. A nervous hand raised the knife in the air. One stab right through the back and it would all be over. No one would ever know the truth.

The victim was only a few feet away now, just a few more feet.

Just at that moment the man turned.

"Halt," a voice cried in the night.

There was a shrill blast of a police whistle and the sound of pounding footsteps. The murderer turned to see half a dozen policemen running at full speed down the pier. The figure lunged at the man, the knife slashing through the air.

"Bloody 'ell," the man yelled. He ducked to one side, threw his arm out and grabbed at the cloak.

The killer stumbled and fell, dropping the knife. The man kicked the knife to one side. The figure, on its knees and hampered by the heavy cloak, lunged toward the shiny blade but, before reaching it, was grabbed by the man and held in place.

They struggled silently in the night.

Suddenly they were surrounded by a half-dozen men.

Lamps were lighted and a worried voice cried, "Smythe, Smythe, are you all right? Speak to me, man, speak to me."

"I'm fine, Inspector." Smythe got off the struggling, cloaked body and moved to one side. The figure went perfectly still.

"Thank God," Witherspoon said. "I'd never forgive myself if you were hurt."

"Not to worry, sir," he said, his attention focused on the person who'd just tried to shove a knife in his back. "There's no 'arm done. I 'eard 'im comin' and was ready. I'm just a bit dirty from rollin' on the pier."

Witherspoon stepped toward the huddled, cloaked figure. Barnes was right beside him, holding a lamp up. "Please get up," the inspector ordered.

It didn't move. Witherspoon thought about repeating himself, but then decided he'd look rather foolish talking to a lumpy mass that refused to respond. He was so relieved his plan had worked that he was feeling rather light-headed. Gracious, for a moment back there he'd been frightened his trap was a bit of a wash. In truth, when he'd come up with this plan, he'd been sure it would lure the killer out into the open. But as the minutes had ticked by and no one had come, he'd grown very worried. Very worried, indeed. But then they'd spotted the cloaked figure stealing onto the dock. He'd known then that his trap would work. But he'd had a bad moment or two. Especially when Smythe had persisted in standing there like a sacrificial lamb. Why, it had almost given him heart failure when he'd seen that knife.

"Er, sir," Barnes said gently, "don't you want to see who it is?"

Witherspoon started. "Of course." He leaned over, grasped the hood of the cloak and tossed it back, revealing the face of the killer. They stared at one another for a long moment.

Finally, the inspector said, "Joanne Dapeers, you're under arrest for the murders of Ellen Hoxton and Haydon Dapeers."

# CHAPTER 11

"There was really nothing we could do to salvage the situation," Hatchet explained earnestly. "Once the constable came on the scene, we'd no choice but to leave." He shrugged helplessly. "When the coast was clear again, so to speak, the inspector had gone."

"Well, fiddlesticks," Luty cried in disgust. "So we're no better off than if you two hadn't even a-bothered to go! We still don't know what the inspector's got up to tonight."

"I told you I should have gone with them," Betsy muttered. "I'da kept my eye on the front door instead of scarpering off like some thief in the night."

"It weren't our fault," Wiggins argued. "That police constable come straight for us. We 'ad to leave; you told us to make sure the inspector didn't catch sight of us."

"Couldn't you have just crossed the road and pretended you was out taking an evening constitutional?" Mrs. Goodge suggested sarcastically.

"No, madam," Hatchet replied stiffly. "We couldn't. What young Wiggins has failed to mention, but is quite pertinent to the circumstances, is that the constable coming down Minyard Street wasn't the only constable in the vicinity. There were two constables on patrol on Bonham Road when we dashed around the corner. Furthermore, we both had the distinct impression they were keeping a sharp eye on us. It was impossible to do anything but carry on and get out of there. Mrs. Jeffries had made it quite clear that it would be disastrous if the inspector had any idea we were even in the area."

"You both did very well," Mrs. Jeffries said quickly. "Very well, indeed."

"But they didn't learn nothing!" Mrs. Goodge snapped. "We still don't know what was going on tonight."

"Useless as teats on a bull," Luty murmured.

"I'da done something," Betsy promised. "I wouldn't have come back with nothing."

Mrs. Jeffries frowned at the women. "Really, you're being most unfair. Hatchet and Wiggins did precisely as we asked them to do. It's hardly their fault that they were unable to complete their assignment. Besides, we do know more than we did earlier. Thanks to these two"—she smiled at the men—"we know exactly which group of suspects the inspector thinks are suspects."

"That's right," Wiggins agreed eagerly. "You wouldn'a knowed who was in that pub tonight unless we'd gone there. Now we know it's got to be one of them that the inspector thinks is the killer."

"What about Smythe?" Betsy asked. She hadn't wanted to bring him up, but the truth was she was getting worried. "You said you didn't see him tonight. What's he up to, then?"

Just at that moment Fred leapt up from his perch under Wiggins's chair. He cocked his head for a moment, listening. Then he ran for the back door just as they all heard the sound of the carriage pulling up.

"That must be the inspector," Mrs. Jeffries warned. She glanced at Luty and Hatchet, wondering how she would explain their presence in the kitchen at half-past eleven at night.

Luty grinned mischievously. "Don't worry, Hepzibah, I'll handle the inspector."

A moment later they heard the back door open and close. From the hallway, they heard Witherspoon greet his friend. "Good dog," he said brightly. He continued to talk to the animal as he walked down the hall, not realizing that he had a kitchen full of people listening to his every word. "You waited up for me. What a loyal fellow you are. Come on, now let's go to the kitchen and scrounge up a cup of tea. Maybe if we're very lucky—" He came into the brightly lighted kitchen and blinked. His entire household, as well as Luty Belle Crookshank and her butler, Hatchet, were sitting at the kitchen table drinking tea. "Gracious, this is a surprise."

"Evenin', Inspector," Luty greeted him enthusiastically.

"Good evening, Mrs. Crookshank." He looked at Mrs. Jeffries, wondering what on earth was going on. "It's very nice to see you."

Hatchet bowed formally in the inspector's direction. "Good evening, sir. I trust you're well."

"Quite well, thank you." As the inspector couldn't think of what to do, he sat down at the table.

"I expect you're wondering why we're here," Luty said conversationally.

"Well, er . . . you know it's always delightful to see you," he began.

Luty interrupted him with a laugh. "Oh don't be so modest, Inspector. You know danged good and well why we're here."

"I do?"

"Now don't be so coy." She smiled broadly. "You know what an admirer of yours I am."

Witherspoon flushed in pleasure, "That's most kind of you to say, but really, I'm only a simple public servant."

Luty waved her hand dismissively. "Nonsense. You're the most brilliant detective on either side of the Atlantic and that's a fact. 'Corse, once I wormed it out of Hepzibah that you was fixin' to catch the murderer of that publican tonight, that you had ya a foolproof plan, wild horses couldn'a kept me away." She leaned toward him eagerly. "Now don't be annoyed with the household, Inspector, it ain't their fault me and Hatchet barged in on the off chance we'd get to see ya. It's my fault. They're just bein' polite. And they was all concerned about ya too, wantin' to make sure you was all right. Police work is so dangerous! They all know how brave ya are, how you'll throw yerself into the thick of things without worryin' about yer own hide."

Mrs. Jeffries raised an eyebrow and glanced at Hatchet. He rolled his eyes heavenward. Luty was laying it on thicker than custard, and by the pleased expression on the inspector's face, he believed every word of it.

Witherspoon smiled broadly. "I wouldn't dream of getting angry at my staff. Their devotion to me is most touching."

"Excuse me, sir," Betsy said. "But is Smythe all right?"

"He's just fine. He's taking the carriage to the livery. Smythe was very brave tonight. Very brave, indeed. Actually, it's a bit nice to come home and find everyone waiting for me. So much better than walking into a dark, empty house. I say, are those Mrs. Goodge's wonderful sausage rolls I see?" He pointed to the plate in the center of the table.

"Let me serve you, sir," the cook said quickly, grabbing an empty plate and forking three of the delicacies onto it.

"I'll pour you some tea," Mrs. Jeffries offered.

"Excellent. I'm positively famished." He smiled broadly at Luty. "As Mrs. Crookshank has gone to all the trouble of being here tonight, perhaps I'd better tell you what happened." He stopped and stuffed a bite of the roll in his mouth.

They all waited impatiently. But the air of tension in the kitchen had gone. He didn't act like a man who'd just ruined his career.

"Let me see," Witherspoon mumbled around his second mouthful of food, "where should I begin? Ah, I know. I caught the killer. My plan worked."

Mrs. Jeffries sighed silently in relief. Betsy and Mrs. Goodge exchanged glances, as though they couldn't believe what they'd just heard. Wiggins said nothing; he just stared at the inspector with a look of awe on his face.

"Naturally, you caught him," Luty exclaimed. "Now, tell us all the details."

"It wasn't a him," the inspector replied. "It was a her."

"A her?" Mrs. Jeffries asked. She crossed her fingers in her lap, hoping that it wasn't Sarah Hewett.

Witherspoon nodded and took a quick gulp of tea. "Indeed. Of course, once I realized why Haydon Dapeers had been killed in the first place, it was simple to determine who the killer actually was, you see. Mind you, I didn't understand what the motive was until I spoke to the gentlemen from Bestal's Brewery. Then, of course, everything fell into place."

Mrs. Jeffries didn't quite understand. From the expressions on the faces of the others, she was fairly certain they didn't have a clue about what he was on about either. "I'm afraid I don't understand."

"It's really quite simple," he replied airily. "Of course, I wasn't sure which one of them it was. Then I remembered what she was wearing the night of the murder. Struck me as odd, even then. It was the parasol and the muff, you see. Far too ornate for a quick trip to the pub, wouldn't you say?" He helped himself to another sausage roll. "I've learned to pay attention to what people are wearing when a murder has been committed. That dreadful business at the Jubilee Ball last summer taught me that."

Everyone knew that Witherspoon was referring to a rather difficult case they'd helped solve the previous year, but knowing he was referring to that old murder didn't help. They were still confused, but no one wanted to interrupt him.

Except Luty. "Hold on a minute, Inspector," she demanded. "My old brain don't work as fast as yours. I'm not following you."

"Sorry," he apologized. "I am going a bit fast. Let me start at the beginning."

"We'd be most grateful if you did, sir," Mrs. Jeffries interjected.

"Let me see now, how best to start," he murmured. "I suppose I ought to tell you about my trip to Bestal's the day after the murder. Yes, that's probably what I ought to do."

Mrs. Jeffries thought he ought to tell them who he'd arrested, but before she could make that reasonable suggestion, he was off again.

"It was what Mr. Magil and Mr. Pump told me that put me on the right trail," he continued. "You see, Haydon Dapeers had written them a letter. That's why they'd gone to the Gilded Lily the night of the murder, you see. They wanted him to name names."

"Name names?" Wiggins repeated.

"Right. Dapeers claimed that someone was watering down their beer."

"Watering down their beer?" Wiggins was beginning to sound like a parrot.

"I don't understand," Mrs. Jeffries said; she fought to keep her voice calm.

"Of course you don't," Witherspoon exclaimed. "And neither did I until they explained it. You see, many breweries loan money to publicans to buy pubs. They do that on the condition that the pub will sell their beer exclusively. Haydon Dapeers had written and told them that one of the publicans Bestal's had loaned money to was watering down their beer. Bestal's doesn't like that. None of the breweries do. As a matter of fact, if they catch a publican doing it, they call the loan." He leaned back and smiled. "As soon as I heard that, I was fairly certain who had the strongest reason for wanting Dapeers dead. Of course, proving it was a bit of a challenge. But we came up with something in the end."

"You mean, sir," Mrs. Goodge asked, "the motive for this murder was watered beer?"

He nodded enthusiastically. "Precisely."

They exchanged glances around the table. Mrs. Jeffries couldn't believe it. All their investigating, all their dashing about and talking to everyone under the sun. All of the time and effort and digging up clues and none of them had even come close to the right motive for Haydon Dapeers's death. James McNally and his gambling debt, Moira Dapeers and her love of the Reverend Ballantine, Sarah Hewett and her desperation to keep Haydon quiet about her daughter, none of it had mattered. She felt like an utter failure. By the stunned expressions on the faces of the others, she thought they probably felt the same way.

"Of course, once I realized what the motive was, knowing who killed him was easy," Witherspoon continued. "As I said, it was proving it that was going to be difficult. Then, of course, Ellen Hoxton's body turned up in the Thames and I knew for certain I was on the right track. That's when I set my trap."

"Who's Ellen Hoxton?" Luty demanded.

"She was a barmaid at the Black Horse," the inspector explained. "And she knew that the Black Horse was watering their beer. That's why she was murdered, you see."

Mrs. Jeffries had had enough. Their dear inspector was enjoying himself far too much; if they let him witter on like this, they'd be here until breakfast. "No, sir, we don't see anything. First of all, who did you arrest tonight?"

"Gracious, didn't I mention that?"

"No," they all cried in unison.

He blinked. "Oh, sorry. I meant to tell you. It was Joanne Dapeers. That's who the killer was. She murdered both Ellen Hoxton and Haydon Dapeers. She killed Ellen first, though. She'd sacked Ellen for talking back to her. Ellen, in turn, threatened to tell everyone that Joanne Dapeers was watering the beer at the Black Horse and their other two pubs. Joanne knew that their loans would be called if Bestal's found out what they were up to, so she stabbed Ellen. But she made a mistake: Ellen Hoxton had already told Haydon Dapeers what was going on. He paid her for the information." He shook his head in disgust. "Five pounds—he gave that poor woman five pounds and it cost her her life."

"How dreadful," Mrs. Goodge muttered.

"Go on, sir," Mrs. Jeffries urged, "tell us the rest of it. How did you figure all this out?"

"To be perfectly honest, I didn't understand for a couple of days. I was fairly certain that it was either Tom or Joanne Dapeers who'd done the killings, but it wasn't until I remembered what Joanne was wearing on the night of Haydon's murder that I was sure that she was the actual killer. It could have been either of them, you see. The killer had brought the weapon to the Gilded Lily. Molly, the barmaid, verified that the knives in the kitchen of the Lily were still in the drawer, so I knew that the murderer had to have brought the murder weapon."

"I don't follow you, sir," Mrs. Jeffries said.

"The knife had a ten-inch blade," he explained. "It would be very difficult for a man to carry a knife of that size in his coat or trouser pockets; he'd be in danger of cutting himself quite badly. No one walked in that night with any parcels or packages on their person and the other women all had on light summer frocks and no parasols. Joanne Dapeers had on a brilliant red dress and carried both a parasol and a huge, matching muff. When I remembered that, I knew it had to be her."

"She brought the knife in the muff," Mrs. Jeffries said thoughtfully. She was impressed with the inspector's reasoning. "She'd planned on killing him."

"Precisely." Witherspoon beamed. "She'd already killed once."

"Ellen Hoxton," Betsy said, "to keep her quiet about the watered beer."

"Right." The inspector reached for his tea. "Poor Ellen Hoxton. I think that she was probably foolish enough to tell Joanne what she'd done. From what the barman at the Black Horse told me, Ellen was quite hot-tempered and bold. Joanne knew she had to do something, she knew that Haydon wouldn't hesitate to go straight to the brewery. If that happened, they'd lose the loans on all three of their pubs and they'd be ruined. I think she planned on killing him that night, but when she walked in and saw that Pump and Magil were already there, she decided to do it quickly. Luckily for her, the brawl broke out just as Haydon went into the taproom. She slipped down the hall, coshed him on the head with her parasol to stun him, shoved the knife in his back and screamed her head off for help. Clever, really, and quite daring. She almost got away with it too." He picked up his cup and drained the last of his tea. "I'm quite tired," he announced with a yawn. "If you don't mind, I think I'll go to bed now."

Several of them opened their mouths to protest, but Mrs. Jeffries silenced them with a look. "Of course, sir. You must be dreadfully tired."

Witherspoon rose, said good night and left the kitchen. As soon as he was out of earshot, they all started talking at once.

"He didn't tell us the half of it," Luty complained.

"What was this plan of 'is, then?" Wiggins muttered.

"Why was everyone at the pub tonight?" Hatchet asked.

"What's this about Smythe bein' brave?" Betsy demanded. "Where is he anyway? He should be home by now."

Mrs. Jeffries raised a hand for silence. "We'll find out the rest from Smythe. He should be home anytime now. It's no good badgering the inspector when he's tired; he'll only get us all confused."

But Smythe didn't show up for another half hour. When he walked in, whistling as he came down the back hall, Betsy was pacing the kitchen. Luty was glaring at the clock, Hatchet was drumming his fingers on the tabletop and Mrs. Goodge was clearing the table. Wiggins was asleep.

"Where've you been?" Betsy demanded the moment he stepped into the kitchen.

"Good evenin', all." He gave them a wide grin. "I've been seein' to the 'orses. They 'ad quite a run today, they did."

"And what's this about you bein' so bloomin' brave?" Betsy snapped. "What've you been up to?"

"Do sit down, Smythe," Mrs. Jeffries invited. "The inspector has told us some of what happened, but not all of it."

"But make it quick," Luty ordered. "It's gettin' late." She reached over and poked Wiggins in the ribs. "Wake up if you want to hear what happened."

Wiggins jerked awake and looked around in confusion.

Smythe sat down at the table. "Did he tell you it was Joanne Dapeers?"

"Yes," Mrs. Jeffries said, "and he told us how he'd figured out she was the killer, but he didn't say a word about how he trapped her."

Smythe grinned. "It worked too, I was sure 'e were fixin' to ruin 'is career." He told the others how he'd driven the inspector all over London that day. "We stopped at Bestal's and the inspector was in talkin' to 'em a long time. He told me later he were confirmin' that all three of Tom and Joanne's pubs were bought on loans from the Bestal's and that they still owed a pretty penny for all of 'em. After that, he made me drive him to Scotland Yard. I dawdled all I could, but we finally got there. When we pulled up, the inspector asked me to come inside. Scared the life out of me, it did. Him standin' in front of the chief inspector and talkin' about this daft plan of 'is."

"What plan?" Mrs. Goodge asked querulously. She was tired, sleepy and getting crankier by the minute.

"I'm comin' to that," Smythe said. "It were a good plan, actually. But at the time I thought it was daft. You see, no one knew that Ellen Hoxton's body 'ad been found. The inspector got everyone together at the Lily that night because he was goin' to trick the killer. 'E fixed it so Constable Griffith would pop in and tell the inspector that there was an eyewitness to the Hoxton murder, but it were a petty crook who wouldn't come into a police station to talk and 'e'd only talk to Witherspoon. Griffith was told to make sure he said the inspector was to meet this crook at the spot where Ellen's body was found. She'd been pulled out of the Thames with a stab wound in her back, just like Haydon Dapeers."

"Then why didn't her body float off?" Wiggins asked.

"'Cause her dress got caught on a piling," Smythe replied. "Anyway, the inspector reasoned that only the killer would know where Ellen's murder took place. So he played like 'e was right irritated and told Griffith 'e'd meet this witness. Griffith made a point of sayin' that the man would be waitin' for him at ten o'clock." Smythe laughed. "The inspector did that on purpose too. He wanted to give the murderer a chance to get there first and try to kill the witness. You'da been proud of him, playactin' with the best of 'em."

"And who was this man?" Betsy asked archly. "This witness."

Smythe shifted in his chair and glanced down at the table. "Well, uh, they was goin' to use a police constable, but the chief inspector was afraid that wouldn't look right when the case got to court." He stopped and cleared his throat. "So the inspector asked me to 'ave a go at it."

Betsy's eyes narrowed. "So you was standing there waitin' for this crazy woman to slip up and shove a knife in your back."

"Now, it wasn't like that, lass," he soothed. "There were police all over the dock." Smythe thought it best not to go into any more details about what had really happened on the pier. "They nabbed her before she got close to me."

"So his plan worked," Mrs. Jeffries said thoughtfully.

"Worked all right, they caught her red-handed. Joanne Dapeers killed two people. She's goin' to 'ang."

The next morning, the household waited until after Witherspoon had left for the day before gathering around the kitchen table.

"We've spent most of this bloomin' case around this table," Wiggins complained. "Might as well 'ave not even bothered tryin' to do any investigatin' at all. Fat lot of good it did us."

"Now, Wiggins," Mrs. Jeffries said soothingly. "We did the best we could." She was as disgusted as the rest of them, but she certainly didn't want it to show. They mustn't be petty. Occasionally, the inspector was going to solve a case on his own.

"Wiggins is right," Betsy grumbled. "We shouldn'a bothered. All that running around I did, following that silly McNally, talking my way into that missionary society, going to that stupid pub with Hamilton. None of it had a thing to do with the murder. Not a ruddy thing."

"Think how I feel?" Mrs. Goodge cried. "I had my sources out sussing up nonsense on a dead publican. My reputation's in shreds, it is."

Smythe shrugged. "We was tryin' to 'elp, so we shouldn't feel too bad about it."

"You're only sayin' that because you was in on it at the end," Betsy said accusingly. She was sure there was a lot he wasn't telling them about the previous night's activities.

"This is pointless," Mrs. Jeffries said bluntly. "We're all sitting around here with long faces and grumbling because we're annoyed the inspector solved the crime on his own."

"Maybe we ain't as clever as we thought we were," Wiggins suggested morosely. "We didn't even come close to figurin' out this one."

As Mrs. Jeffries and the others were well aware of that fact, they didn't find the footman's statement particularly helpful. "We would have figured it out eventually."

"Do you really think so?" Wiggins asked, looking hopeful.

"Of course." Mrs. Jeffries forced herself to smile. "There will be other cases."

"I think we've lost our touch," Betsy said. "I don't think we'll ever solve another murder again."

"He'll hog them all," Mrs. Goodge announced darkly. "He's got a taste for it now that's he gotten lucky—"

"Lucky?" Mrs. Jeffries interrupted. "Really, Mrs. Goodge, I'm as upset as you are about our failure on this case, but I hardly think it's fair to say the inspector got 'lucky.' He solved this case with logic and reason."

"And listenin' to his inner voice," Wiggins interjected rudely. "If it 'adn't been for that bloomin' inner voice, we'da 'ad a decent crack at the case."

"Honestly, you're all impossible today." Mrs. Jeffries rose to her feet. "We'll talk about this later, when you've all had a chance to calm down."

She left them to their misery and went upstairs. She was as worried as the rest of them. Despite their grumbling about inner voices and hogging cases, she knew what was really bothering everyone. It bothered her too. They'd been so wrong about this case. So very wrong. None of them had even come close to determining the motive or the killer. As Betsy had said, maybe they'd lost their touch.

Mrs. Jeffries went up to her sitting room and pulled a volume of Mr. Walt Whitman from her shelves. But she couldn't concentrate on the beautiful words; they failed to soothe her as they usually did.

For the next few days everyone in the household walked about with long, glum faces. Even a visit from Luty and Hatchet failed to cheer people up: it was difficult to be cheered by visitors as morose as you were.

Witherspoon, ridiculously happy himself, didn't appear to notice his household's mood. Or so Mrs. Jeffries thought until early one evening.

"Will you join me in a sherry?" he suggested as she took his hat and put it on the rack. "There's something I want to talk with you about."

"Certainly, sir." They went into the drawing room and she poured them both a sherry. Taking a seat opposite him, she folded her hands in her lap. "What is it, sir? Is there something amiss in the household?"

"Oh no, Mrs. Jeffries. As always, it runs perfectly." He smiled warmly. "I have you to thank for that."

"There's no need to thank me, sir. I'm only doing my job."

He looked disappointed at her words and she wished she could take them back. Sometimes she forgot what a sensitive soul he was. "I mean, it's what I've been trained to do, sir," she explained quickly. "What I enjoy doing. Now, sir, what did you need to speak to me about?"

"My last case." He took a sip of sherry and put the glass down on the table next to him. "I didn't really enjoy it much."

Surprised, she stared at him. "Really, sir?"

"I'll admit I was glad my plan worked and that we arrested the killer, but I must say, I was very worried." He clasped his hands in front of him. "If I'd been wrong, the consequences could have been most severe. Most severe, indeed."

"But you weren't wrong, sir," she reminded him.

"But I could have been." He smiled wryly. "It's all very well listening to one's inner voice, Mrs. Jeffries. But it doesn't make for an interesting case. No, from now on I think I'll go back to my old ways. I know how much you and the others like hearing about my investigations. Gracious,

I hadn't realized how dreadfully selfish I'd been till I arrived home that night and found Mrs. Crookshank and Hatchet lying in wait for me. I've been very selfish."

Mrs. Jeffries's spirits soared. Thank goodness he was coming to his senses. "You mean you won't be listening to your inner voice anymore?" she asked.

"Oh, I'll listen to it," he replied. "But I certainly want to discuss my cases with you. You're an excellent sounding board, Mrs. Jeffries."

"That's kind of you, sir."

"I'm not being kind, I'm being truthful." He frowned. "In the end, this case turned out well, but as I said, it could easily have gone the wrong way."

Mrs. Jeffries got to her feet. "I'm glad you feel that way, sir. To be truthful, I did feel a bit left out. You know how much I love hearing about your methods of investigation."

"I promise you," he said earnestly, "the next time you'll hear all about it. I won't be selfish again."

"Thank you." She started for the hall. "If you'll excuse me, I've got to go to the kitchen."

"But you haven't finished your sherry," he called.

"I'll finish it later, sir," she cried gaily. "I've just remembered an urgent matter I must tell the rest of the staff."